*A DARK PLAN IS SET IN MOTION . . .
IN THE EXTRAORDINARY CONCLUSION TO
THE MONUMENTAL* GLOBAL 2000 TRILOGY

*"It takes quite a writer to write a trilogy and Gloria Vitanza
Basile is up to the task."*

—**Critique**

People never popped by the Zeller Château; they were *requested* to come, their presence *demanded* when it served the lord of the manor.

The guests were all introduced by code names: Zulu, Zebra, Starburst . . . Their line of business was revealed at once by the distinct odor they gave off—the distinct odor of espionage. They were spies. Cloak and dagger men, the lot of them. Each was in possession of something valuable—information to buy and sell for the right price.

A wave of a baton moved players across the globe from America to Europe, from the Balkans to Berlin. Amadeo Zeller's men, whoever they were, were tuning up to play Wagner's *Götterdämmerung* . . .

Pinnacle books by Gloria Vitanza Basile

APPASSIONATO
THE HOUSE OF LIONS
THE MANIPULATORS
THE MANIPULATORS, BOOK II:
 BORN TO POWER
THE MANIPULATORS, BOOK III:
 GIANTS IN THE SHADOWS

GLOBAL 2000 TRILOGY

BOOK I: EYE OF THE EAGLE
BOOK II: THE JACKAL HELIX
BOOK III: THE STING OF THE SCORPION

THE STING OF THE SCORPION

GLORIA VITANZA BASILE

PINNACLE BOOKS NEW YORK

This novel is a work of fiction. Names, characters, places, and
incidents are either the product of the author's imagination or are
used fictitiously. Any resemblance to actual events, places or
persons, living or dead, is entirely coincidental.

GLOBAL 2000: BOOK III
THE STING OF THE SCORPION

An original Pinnacle Books edition, published for the first time
anywhere.

First printing/December 1984

ISBN: 0-523-41962-7

Can. ISBN: 0-523-43083-3

Printed in the United States of America

PINNACLE BOOKS, INC.
1430 Broadway
New York, New York 10018

9 8 7 6 5 4 3 2 1

ACKNOWLEDGMENTS

For the implicit trust and patience demonstrated by my publisher, Sondra Ordover, a true lady and gentlewoman—for her impeccable professionalism during the overwhelming transitional period which encompassed the publishing of the ambitious Global 2000 Trilogy: EYE OF THE EAGLE, THE JACKAL HELIX, and THE STING OF THE SCORPION, I wish to express my deep thanks.

For Liza Dawson's immense confidence and infectious enthusiasm and considerable editorial skills in capably and conscientiously bringing to fruition this last manuscript of the series, THE STING OF THE SCORPION, I express my deep and profound gratitude.

And for Joe Curcio's super talent in cover design, my special thanks.

BOOK ONE

CORSICA

"In a definite act of annexation Italian and German troops occupied Corsica. One hundred thousand troops —half the Corsican population—made up the occupying forces."

—Antoine de Saint-Exupéry
November 12, 1942

Prelude

World War II was ubiquitous. At any given time during the conflict dozens of battles were engaged in simultaneously at various places throughout Europe, North Africa, and in the Pacific.

The North African campaign, representing hundreds of battles strewn across the vast deserts of this continent, continued long after the battle of Bir Hakeim had ended in what had prematurely been labeled defeat. General Rommel now swept victoriously back into Tobruk to prepare his encounter with British General George Montgomery at El Alamein, sixty miles west of Alexandria, in a battle that would eclipse any the desert had seen before. At the same time, Major Darius Bonifacio, his commandos, and other shock-troop battalions moved on new orders to Corsica to engage in a clandestine effort with the American OSS and British SIS to oust the Axis soldiers from the island and establish Corsica as a base from which to prepare for the liberation of France.

Six months before the highly clandestine Corsican operation commenced . . .

Chapter One

In the summer of 1943, Switzerland was a spymaster's dream, a neutral oasis in a hostile desert controlled on all its borders by Axis nations. While the rest of the world was at war, in Switzerland a straw scarecrow representing winter was burned at the shores of the Zürichsee; pilgrimages from the Centovalli crossed the Italian frontier to the Shrine of the Madonna de Ré; and summer festivals blossomed into colorful, gay ceremonies. It was perfect! The infiltration of spies from every war-torn nation managed to slip over the border to congregate here, to wheel and deal, to negotiate in human flotsam and billions of dollars.

A young, dark-haired, strikingly handsome man with perceptive hazel eyes, excellent bone structure, and the classic profile of a brooding Napoleon stared out the train window at the changing panorama. He was one of the few men aboard who was dressed in elegant civilian clothing, but a well studied eye would have noticed that everything else about him bore the distinct mark of the military: his posture, gait, slow, deliberate movements. Even the manner in which he smoked a cigarette appeared premeditated, as though he were unused to his surroundings.

And it was true. Out of uniform, Major Victor Zeller felt like Medusa bereft of her snakelike hair. Summoned secretly to Zürich by his ubiquitous father, Amadeo Zeller, Victor felt the role of a civilian was alien to him. Every fiber of his being reacted to sights, sounds, and landscapes militaristically.

This made crossing over into the neutral zone with Italian cover papers difficult for him. *How do you change the thinking of a lifetime? You don't,* he told himself. *Just be thankful that thoughts are not visible.* Despite the advantage of cover, the adroit intelligence officer exercised discretion to avoid possible linkage to his thought-to-be-dead father by avoiding any and all confrontations with the Germans.

At this moment, Victor's brooding thoughts centered on disturbing evidence he'd witnessed on this train ride that indicated the direct countermand of Italian orders at several post commands and border checkpoints.

Everywhere he looked he saw a glut of Gestapo officers. The praetorian SD (SS Security Service) of German Bureau II massed at every checkpoint pricked his curiosity and jolted his adrenaline. He must be careful. An indication of impatience or anything resembling ruffled composure was out of place in his profession.

Victor left the train and was met by his father's chauffeur. Hustled quickly out of the high-domed station into the open air, he boarded his father's limousine. Soon they were speeding northwest through the city, around the Mythen Quai, past the Reitberg Museum, past the exploding celebrations of Zürich. Victor saw little of the quaint beauty, the frolicking people, the brass bands. He kept glancing at his watch.

Another fifteen, twenty minutes or so and they should arrive at their destination. A premapped route was deeply etched in his mind and he looked for familiar landmarks. He must be extremely careful; after all, the chauffeur himself could be the enemy. *The enemy!* He shuddered and reviewed the mental notes he'd made of the blatant disparity between the Axis powers' border forces. Germans outnumbered Italians nearly twenty to one. Why? He pigeonholed the matter as critical for further study on his return to Rome.

Victor's army records—at Il Duce's suggestion, doctored to inflate his nineteen years to twenty-five—had relieved him of the tedious burden of issuing orders to men his senior without incurring acid resentment. Practically born into the fascist youth movement, Victor became, at age four, the "son of the she-wolf" and donned his first black shirt; at age eight he joined the Balilla; at fourteen, the Avanguardisti. Trained to military discipline, he had used toy military machines to acquaint himself with the feel of weaponry. At age sixteen, Victor was indoctrinated in ciphers and codes and transfered to the quasi-intelligence service ruled by the iron fist of Il Duce. SIM (Servizio Informazione Militare) was headed by Count Ciano, who ranted and raved and concluded that war had been declared because fascism was unable to free itself from its own network of deceit, much of this deceit attributable solely to Amadeo Zeller!

However the vicious rumormongers worked their diabolical patchwork designs, they never openly discussed Amadeo Zeller to his son, nor did they let him forget the sins of his father. At times, Victor, a fascist to the core, found it amusing that the counterespionage divisions of military intelligence actually planted false documents on the competition and arrested each other's agents. The complexity of such duplicitous behavior, as bewildering as it was counterproductive, never failed to baffle him.

Until, that is, the Germans came to roost in Rome!

Then, when the fascist insanity began to make sense and Victor found himself able to make order from disorder, it was time for him to reassess his own mental state. Quick to sense a slight or rebuff, he saw how the Germans laughed and made snide remarks at the apparent tumult and frequent blunders of the farcical SIM. The *fascisti* deficiencies were reflected in the cold, contemptuous eyes of the Nazis. In such moments, the repetitious words of Victor's father played monotonously in his mind. *Your godfather, Il Duce, is master of a three-ringed circus! Misericordia!* Were Italy and Germany doomed in a one-sided symbiosis forever?

Victor arrived at the seventeenth century château just as a brilliant flamingo-pink sunset on the Zürichsee fired the cobalt waters into a sea of flames. Turning in his seat, he gazed down at the stupefying view. Sun, sea, pinnacle-shaped tors, all of it infused him with a sense of power. No wonder his father doted on Zürich—a sense of power was half the battle.

Victor's first inkling of the measure of his father's true

wealth came from the heavily guarded baronial splendor of the château. The only thing missing, thought Victor, was a dragon-filled moat with an ethereal mist rising from it.

In the château, as Victor and Amadeo Zeller ambled about like lord and serf, the measure of his father's power was imparted to Victor bit by bit.

The revelations being made intrigued him. Was he being tested for something ominous?

"My son, I beg you to come to terms with yourself, with me. Begin to understand things as they will be, not as they are. Presently I am filtering money into France, to the Resistance fighters of de Gaulle's Free French guerrillas. In addition, I support the anti-Gaullist forces of General Giraud." Amadeo rolled this information off his tongue as though it were the most natural thing in the world to support opposing enemies. Throughout the sumptuous dinner, he expansively showed off his expertise with fine specimens from his wine cellar. He goaded subtly, interjecting political secrets into his conversation to create distortions in Victor's mind, giving rise to guilt and treasonous feelings. *The whisperings in Rome! Was there some degree of merit to them?* His father's hurried exodus. *Had treason to Il Duce been the bottom line after all?* Amadeo's silky voice had an edge to it and cut into Victor's lugubrious thoughts. Why should he feel mournful? Was it because he realized he didn't know his father, had had a false image of him all these years? What a revolting situation! To see his father for the first time through clear-sighted eyes . . .

"Forgive me, Father, you were saying?"

"Pay attention, Victor. You must not permit your mind to stray. It's a sign of weakness. I was saying that I am simultaneously financing the proroyalist forces of Badoglio and Count Ciano. In Yugoslavia I play both sides against the middle—Tito's forces against Mihailovic's. I am uncertain which of the two I shall ultimately choose." Amadeo poured cognac. "And—"

"Father!" Victor protested.

"—and in Germany, my people have let it be known that not even the Nazis will be turned away if they have information to sell. The same holds for the *fascisti*." He winked an opaque eye at his son.

Victor, outraged, threw his *serviette* across the china service.

"Father, you apparently forget I am committed to Il Duce! I am an officer of the Italian Army Intelligence forces, dedicated to use such information in the defense of my nation!"

"*Fool!* I am telling you how it must be—how it will be—and you disdain me!"

Not, How are you, my son? thought Victor. *How is everything at home? I've missed you and want you here at my side. I deplore having left my family behind.* If the thoughts were present in his father's mind, they remained unspoken. Demonstrable love was absent by default. Victor sighed despairingly. It was their first encounter in years. Singularly disturbed by the pure vitriol spilling from Amadeo's lips, he promised himself he would neither argue nor drive a wedge of alienation deeper between them. His father had requested his presence here in the utmost secrecy. He had come to learn why.

Coffee and cognac were served before the inviting fire in the enormous fireplace in Amadeo's study. The high altitude lent a chill to the night. The banking mogul expanded on the architectural changes he contemplated in the near future. "Those domed lead-crystal windows will be replaced by a magnificent stained glass mural, Victor." His attention focused on the diamond-shaped windows thirty feet in height. "Artists are busy at work creating a mural depicting Jacob's Ladder and his encounter with the Angel of God."

Victor, listening but only half hearing the dissertation, was busy sorting out Amadeo's earlier dialogue. *What had really given Il Duce reason to move against Zeller? Had he intrigued against Italy? Against the Duce himself?* The rumors still circulating continuously surfaced to haunt Victor.

And Ciano! Bastardo! *The Duce's son-in-law was conspiring against him.*

Amadeo left his son, then returned fifteen minutes later to announce he'd placed several telephone calls to associates who would be popping by later.

Popping by later? At the Zeller château? That likelihood was as improbable as a rattlesnake mating with an octopus. People never popped by; they were *requested* to come, their presence *demanded* when it served the lord of the manor. It will be interesting to see . . .

The guests were all strangers to Victor, all introduced by code names: Zulu, Zebra, Starburst, Beetle, Locust, Ghost-

Dancer, Friar, Flora, and Fauna. Only one was a woman: Coco.

What a motley collection. Victor knew their line of business at once by the distinct odor they gave off—the distinct odor of espionage. These were spies! Cloak-and-dagger men, the lot of them, including Coco. Each was in possession of something valuable—information to buy and sell for the right price.

As they talked and Victor listened, it became clear to him that his father was conducting a vast clandestine orchestra. A wave of a baton moved players across the globe from America to Europe, from the Balkans to Berlin. Amadeo Zeller's men, whoever they were, were tuning up to play Wagner's *Götterdämmerung*. What temerity!

Outraged, Victor slipped unnoticed from the conference room. Why would his father place him in so compromising a position? He was, after all, an Italian military intelligence officer and Amadeo was actually forcing him to bear witness to the impending treason, the destruction of Il Duce and fascism! Why would Amadeo do this to him? *Why?*

He wandered about the dark recesses of the cold château like a lost pilgrim, feeling the fatigue of his circuitous journey. He was mortified that he had been relegated to the position of nonentity amid these foreign spies. The imperative for his presence here mystified him. He retired early—who'd miss him?—and tossed about during a sleepless night as childhood demons danced through his dreams.

The next evening the Zeller dining salon glittered brightly as a Christmas tree. An exhilarating fire in the hearth spread a warm, inviting glow to the intimate dinner party held in elaborate secrecy with the same strange guests as the previous evening. The festivities commenced promptly at 7:00 P.M. From seemingly nowhere came the chamber music of a remarkably talented quartet. Against the plush background of exquisite hand-woven tapestries, rare art works, and rarer congeniality, Amadeo demonstrated his extraordinary flair for superb wines and gourmet food. He also provided his guests with a coterie of talented young coquettes who enhanced the scene with erotica. Throughout the scintillating soiree, Victor, attired in black tie, was introduced as "my protégé". Not "my son," but "my protégé, presently studying at Harvard in the States."

Victor's glum, unresponsive manner received a constant

prodding. "Tonight, Victor, will be a true revelation. I promise you your naiveté concerning geopolitical affairs shall be erased forever."

Disquieted, Victor evidenced considerable circumspection. He had a deathly fear that one of these nefariously inclined eccentrics would recognize him. Oh, Christ! As if Amadeo were clairvoyant, he leaned toward his son, his dark-lensed glasses impeccably opaque. "You worry for nothing. *Bei Nacht sind alle Katzen grau.* In the night all cats are gray."

"Not white ones, Father," Victor replied, warming a brandy snifter between cupped hands. "Especially not *that* one." He unobtrusively indicated a well-muscled man, approximately his age, a Nordic type with stringy platinum-blond hair.

"You *are* Zeller's son! You zeroed in on the most austere, ominous, and formidable mystery man present. He is, in a sense, persona non grata in his native Austria, but most welcome here for the commodity he sells. For all intents and purposes, he is known as Ghost-Dancer. Even I do not possess a complete dossier on the man. But—" He held up a protesting hand, anticipating Victor's thunderous assault. "I shall have it within a fortnight. In a sense, he is, shall we say, under my protection."

"Ah—another protégé." Victor inhaled the exquisite bouquet of his brandy, wondering if his father caught the irony of his words.

He ambled about, weaving a path through the thoroughly charming den of anacondas, pondering his father's enigmatic words, catching dribs and drabs of venom spouted from the guests' lips. In his peregrination he was committing every face to memory. In one of the alcoves of the room, Victor paused, leaned against a wall, and swirled the brandy around in his snifter. He studied the man called Ghost-Dancer, a man invisibly stamped with the mark of Cain. Victor moved to a better vantage point where he could see the man through a glass showcase filled with gems. Ghost-Dancer was of medium build, slim, athletic looking, with the sunburned complexion of a skier. The body tapered from wide shoulders to rather slim legs. He turned slightly to his left, revealing more of his face. The face was like stone, the features expressionless, especially the empty blue eyes. But the hair wasn't a stringy blond as Victor had earlier surmised. It was curly; quite curly and clipped short. The hard face looked as if it had been cast in marble. It was a face Victor had never seen before. The man wore silver-rimmed spectacles. He seemed far too young to wear glasses perched at the end of his nose like a scholar. Just when Victor asked himself why he should show more interest in this agent provocateur than in any of the others, Ghost-Dancer turned to study the gems in the case. Their eyes met. The blue eyes held on Victor, deep and probing. Ghost-Dancer moved around the case. He spoke in a distinctive German accent.

"I do not believe we have met. I am known as *der Geist-Tänzer.*"

"Yes, our host pointed you out." Victor gathered his wits about him and blurted, "I am Adonis."

"*Jawohl?* Adonis, is it? You must be careful, Adonis. Your precursor was killed by a wild boar. Is that your nemesis?"

"Not if you believe the myth. Remember, Adonis was favored by Aphrodite. The gods let him spend every spring and summer with her."

"Ah, *ja, ja.* Then your nemeses are fall and winter."

Victor hated Ghost-Dancer's smug arrogance. "So tell me, why do they call you Ghost-Dancer? *Der Geist-Tänzer?*" He repeated the words as if they held special fascination for him, his eyes on the tabula rasa face.

"Why do they call me *der Geist-Tänzer?* The answer is simple enough. I disappear long before anyone knows I've been there." Suddenly the musical string ensemble that had been playing Chopin and Mozart metamorphosed into a marimba band. The exciting refrains of a *habanera,* the current Cuban rage, gave life to the small gathering. Before Victor responded to the enigmatic statement made by Ghost-Dancer, he felt a tug at his elbow.

"*Monsieur,* you can dance the *habanera.* You seem the only one present with either the inclination or agility to have learned the new dance craze."

Victor turned to the woman, then back to Ghost-Dancer. He was gone! No trace of him anywhere. Back to the woman, code name Coco. Slim, fragile, with an exquisite manner of delicate finesse, she stood apart from the others like the essence of a Belle of Portugal Rose. Her hair was like black satin, pulled back to a sleek coil at the nape of her neck. Her skin was sun-kissed by a Costa del Sol tan that added lights and luster to her

electric hazel-amber eyes. She was what the Swiss praisingly
referred to as a "chocolate box of beauty." Coco—what an appropriate name.

Victor, intrigued by the woman in the slinky satin gown,
placed his brandy snifter on a nearby table. He bowed with
panache. "You are in good fortune, *mademoiselle*, or is it *madame*? Weeks ago I abandoned the tarantella for the *habanera*.
Permit me." He reached into his jacket pocket, slipped on a
pair of white gloves, and led her to the center of the floor. He
waited for the upbeat before he began the expert Cuban tango.
Coco's gown, cut as low in back as it was in front, drew raves
and stares from the onlookers. The two moved and glided
across the floor like professionals. Her diamond earrings dangled from earlobe to shoulder and whisked about like thousands
of jeweled stars, reflecting the lights, dazzling the onlookers.

The dance, seduction personified, progressed from phase to
phase and evoked hushings and murmurs from the spellbound
audience. Sultry orbital contact and sensuous electricity oozing
from the dancers communicated its seduction to the envious
gathering. Rounds of applause rose and fell in crescendos. Victor's intention was to light up an otherwise drab evening with
her company. Unfortunately, Ghost-Dancer's last words kept
replaying in his mind: *"I disappear long before anyone knows
I've been there."* And if this weren't enough to disturb his con-
centration during the *habanera,* what happened next with Coco
sent shivers along his spine. He had manipulated her body into
a triple twirl, swinging her out and back again with masterful
control. Then, arching her backward, he leaned over her, coming just a hair away from her lips. At this point, the dancers
were supposed to kiss. Victor refrained. After all, he didn't
know her. At precisely this moment, she leaned forward,
uptilted her head, and kissed him. Deeply.

But there was more.

She had placed something in his mouth, a capsule—at least it
felt like a capsule. For a brief, startling moment, Victor was uncertain whether to spit it out, swallow it, or tuck it under his
tongue. Coco smiled. Her eyes signaled danger. As he pulled
her upright and repeated the triple turn, she leaned hard against
him, lips to his ears. *"Cher,* be careful. Read the message I
placed in your mouth."

The music climaxed, ending on a high note. The applause

was thunderous. Coco smiled, accepted the accolades, and left Victor at once, her attention centered on one of the honored guests. "Zulu, how good of you to come."

Victor moved to the bar. He dabbed at the beads of perspiration on his forehead with his handkerchief, removed his gloves, and slipped them into his pocket. He patted his cheeks, wiped his lips, and quicker than the eye could see, slipped the capsule between the linen folds. Drink in hand, he excused himself, climbed the steps to the *galleria*, and entered his suite of rooms, bolting the door behind him. Hastily he opened the handkerchief and removed the metal capsule. Quickly he unrolled the message inside, spread it out on the desk, and read: "You are marked for death. Take all precautions."

Amadeo, summoned to his son's room, listened intently as Victor read the words, then tossed the note and pellet into the fire.

"In *my* house? In the house of your father you receive such a threat? Tell me, who passed it to you? With whom did you speak?" Amadeo thundered about the room, his colorless eyes turned to blue fire points. "I know them all—all of them."

Victor lied. "I found the pellet in my jacket pocket. I came here to read it at once. You know the rest."

"What insanity that anyone dared to violate you on my premises." He paused thoughtfully. "It's a warning. Yes, yes, that's it, a warning. Someone indeed honors me deferentially to issue a warning at all."

"These are your guests, your *associates*, Father. No one knows I am your son. You made a point to avoid that truth. Keep up the charade. Perhaps we shall identify both the messenger and killer. I have my own priorities to consider. About this man you call *Ghost-Dancer*—"

"Not now, Victor. We'll talk later. A very important guest is due to arrive momentarily. You shall find him vital to your existence. My men will protect you. You won't see them, but they'll not let you out of their sights."

"Gun sights, Father?" He laughed brittlely. "Why don't I simplify matters and remain here in my suite of rooms?"

"No. Trust me. Mingle with the others. It's terribly important that—"

"Your—uh—*protégé* be seen in the proper light?"

"In a manner of speaking, yes," Amadeo snapped.

"What sort of dirty business are you hatching? I remain in the dark concerning your altercation with Il Duce."

"You mean he hasn't set the record straight?" Amadeo turned swiftly at the door. "This dirty business can net the Zeller dynasty billions. As for what went on with Il Duce, it's no concern of yours."

"The ledger *is* your Bible, isn't it? Profit-and-loss statements, net worths."

"If you haven't learned by now that money is the bottom line in all existence, you never will. I, for one, prefer to sit at the top and count it. Come along. I don't want to keep the Prince waiting."

Prince Ludwig Maximilian von Falkenburg was a Sudeten German traveling under a Liechtenstein passport—a document that opened world borders to him in a way that a German passport could not. The Prince was suave, silky, a true gentleman, the epitome of Old World grace and gentility. Moreover, he had the distinct advantage of being married to a wealthy Italian lady, royalty no less. Dear Maximilian, an apologist for the Nazis, a charming deprecator of the insane men of the regime, consistently minimized National Socialism's obscenities and explained them away with a dandified wave of his wrist.

Victor, in the posture of observer rather than participant, let his mind work like the recording lens of a camera, committing to memory both the scene and the animated players. He tried to remain as inconspicuous as possible in the reflective glare of the powerful luminaries.

Just as Victor decided he was through for the evening and was about to retire to his quarters, he was jolted out of his senses. Had he heard correctly? His mind replayed the words.

Dear, dear Max, the Prince, was here in Zürich at the behest of his mentor. The sinister Gestapo chieftain, Heinrich Himmler, had proposed a deal to Amadeo Zeller.

Victor edged in closer to the small coterie of men speaking sotto voce. The Prince was speaking casually; all attention was riveted on him. "It's a simple and forthright proposal, *ja?* Himmler is prepared to revolt against Hitler," dear Max said lightly in his unaccented German. "Topple him from power, if you, Herr Zeller, and your high-powered Allied connections will legitimize Himmler's succession to the throne."

Amadeo and Victor locked eyes. In the glance was the slightest hint of Amadeo's earlier promise to strip away Victor's political naiveté. Victor sat on the arm of a nearby chair, slid into it as he stuffed a cigar into his mouth, bit off the end, and rolled it over his lips before lighting it. He listened to the confabulators with every pore in his body. His attention was riveted to dear Max as conditions concerning frontier adjustments were amicably discussed. The chat became tedious, complex, obscured with ambiguities.

There was no question about it; Victor had heard too much already. Feeling a traitor to Il Duce, Victor excused himself. What he dreaded the previous night concerning his father's untenable position with the *fascista* leader was becoming reality. In Victor's young, adventurous years, he had measured life's difficulties, contemplated its risks, but nothing had prepared him for the perils confronting him presently.

Walking along the upper *galleria* to Amadeo's study, Victor experienced strange, conflicting emotions. Questions buzzed around in his head. Why had his father forced him behind the scenes to bear witness to the inexorable wheelings and dealings of international power brokers? To assure him of Mussolini's declining power? To better recognize the erosion of a carefully constructed superstructure of political might?

Victor chain-smoked. He paced the study floor relentlessly. Finally he broke open a bottle of rare Napoleon brandy and guzzled straight from the bottle, unable to assuage the rage he felt at the way his father manipulated him into this unwanted position. Should any of these slick agents provocateurs sell information to the fascists . . . Double agents, despite their expediency and the control apparatus firing them, were untrustworthy. In or out of uniform, he couldn't chance they might recognize him and report to Rome his participation in the scurrilous treacheries that were being incubated this night against the Axis nations.

In particular, Victor could not understand why his father—if he so hated the Hitler regime—hadn't nipped Prince Max's proposal in the bud by insisting he'd never deal with the bloodthirsty monster Himmler, no matter the stakes.

Victor was enlightened by Zulu on the American's departure from the Zeller mansion. He shook Victor's hand warmly and, noting the reserved expression in Victor's dark eyes, smiled be-

nevolently. "You seem disillusioned. You don't learn of such
goings-on at Harvard, do you, lad?" Oh, how Victor wanted to
enlighten *him*. "These are strange times, indeed," Zulu continued. "But anything that would hasten the end of Hitler's
reign is to be encouraged. The OSS and I are in Switzerland to
encourage the destruction of National Socialism. If the Nazis
are willing to assist in their own destruction, who am I to discourage them?" When Zulu asked Victor about several of his
Harvard acquaintances, the Italian Major demurred. "I've im-
bibed too much wine from our host's fine cellars to speak co-
herently. Perhaps we can discuss old acquaintances over
lunch?" Zulu scrutinized Victor intently, then left.

"Father! Why did you do this to me?" Victor demanded
when all the guests had departed. "Why make me an intimate
part of your shady dealings? You realize you've maximized my
personal danger? On my return I am obligated to make a full
and complete report of your underhanded manipulations."

"Blood is thicker than water. Remember that."

Victor turned a mottled purple. "Dammit, Father, I suppose
you also conspire with the communists? The anti-Nazis and
antifascists in Germany and Italy!"

"Of course."

"Stop it!" Victor protested. "Not another word, you hear? I
know now why Il Duce was never able to trust you!"

Amadeo's achromatic eyes narrowed. "Your political glori-
fication of that straw Caesar must cease, Victor!" Rankled,
Amadeo pointed to Victor's gross naiveté. "I sent for you so
you could envision things the way they will be in the near future. The Duce's uncontrolled ambition will be his undoing. I
believed in him once, until he revealed an overabundance of
Achilles heels."

"What is the point of this cloak-and-dagger foreplay? You
are a banker. Why do you sit at the helm of stench-filled politics
with such duplicitous people? Who can be trusted? I'm fed up
with the irrational, outdated politicians, émigrés, and preju-
diced Jews! In my view, peace must be made in Europe, and all
concerned must have a real interest in its preservation!"

"The temptation to lay before you the extent of your political
naiveté, Victor, is overwhelming, but it must wait until you
grasp the full significance of my work and goals." Grasping the

moment, Amadeo launched into the historical odyssey of the Jews. He graphically described the centuries of oppression foisted on them in nearly all nations on earth. He brought Victor up to date on the Palestinian situation in the Ersatz-Israel, giving it World War II prominence. "Don't you see? The British White Papers invalidated the Balfour Declaration and placed severe restrictions on the Jews. For years we've purchased lands in Palestine at *British* prices, on *their* terms. Now suddenly the Jews are barred from further purchase of the lands. Immigration has been severely restricted. I tell you, Victor, our enemies are the British. The British who are in collusion with the Third Reich! Don't you see? Restrictive immigration at a time when it seems the only alternative to the extermination of the Jews by the Nazis?" Zeller's eyes were blazing coals of condemnation.

"What extermination? What the devil is it you're saying? I've heard no such reports. No such documents, secret or otherwise, have crossed my desk in Rome."

"Such blind loyalty is commendable!" Amadeo snapped acerbically. "The truth is that genocide will not happen. *We* will not permit it. *We* have plans."

"Really, Father, you are a maddening enigma to me. What the hell is it you're talking about? Who are the 'we' you prattle on about?"

Without preamble, Amadeo spilled forth, "You're a Jew, Victor. First and foremost, a Jew. Don't ever forget it."

Victor stood, mouth agape, his anger subdued, for as certain as he was that they were both standing here, his father had lost his senses. "How can I be a Jew, Father? I was born a Catholic, was baptized, received my first communion and confirmation as a Catholic. Il Duce is my godfather."

"No! No, no, no! You are a Jew for as long as it suits my purpose. I am building a dynasty—the Zeller dynasty. One day you shall grasp all the reins. Two more years at best. Yes, yes, the war shall end in the spring of 1945, so be circumspect in all you do in the name of fascism."

Amadeo held his crystal wine goblet up to the light, studying its clarity. "The area at the eastern end of the Mediterranean is the womb of the earth. There, in that Edenic setting, God created man, and from it one day will spew vast riches. Whoever owns that land shall rule the earth. If we cannot purchase it, we shall seize it by force.''

Victor, listening, wondered if his father's exile had produced a psychosis. He seemed deluded, maniacal, too off center from world thinking. For God's sake, if persecution and extermination of the Jews ran rampant in Germany, *certainly Rome would know it!*

''That straw Caesar, your godfather, makes bids for Arab support in North Africa. He buys land cheap since Great Britain has succeeded in alienating Middle Eastern factions. The fool! He names himself protector of Islam! Meanwhile, the mufti of Palestine makes his deals directly with the Nazis, as do the warring tribes of Algeria. I tell you, Victor, our voices arise in protest at this cold disregard for the Jews' plight. Genocide is Hitler's answer—his solution is *Endlosung*! While the world involves itself in global strife to determine how to cut up the bigger pie, our forces shall steal silently into the land apportioned unto ourselves and do what the colonials have done for centuries. Go! Fight war for a counterfeit Caesar who permits the Hun to overrun Italy. We, here in Zürich and elsewhere, shall fight for the cause of our people.'' He wagged an admonishing finger at Victor. ''We shall become Britain's most implacable enemy. The world's also, if need be.''

''Yet you engage in subterranean deals with the British agents?''

''I would deal with Satan himself if it promoted my ends.'' Amadeo stared at his son in protracted silence, barely noticing the changes five years had produced in him. Never emotionally demonstrative, Amadeo was the usual arrogant, imperious person he'd been all his life. He hissed, ''Do you know that thousands of Jewish troops placed at Britain's disposal were rejected for military duty?'' When Victor asked why, his father continued to hurl salvos at him. ''You ask *why* Palestinian Jews are not permitted to fight in this war? I'll tell you why!'' he fired with scathing indictment. ''It's part of a pro-Arab policy.''

''Why can't it be for more obvious reasons? Why must you attach subversive intent to it?''

''Because you, Victor, are naive. Or is it stupidity you parade before me? The reason is—pay full attention to my words—because they suspect, and with good reason, that Jews skillfully trained to kill Nazis will in due course use those skills to win Palestinian independence from the British.''

''And that, Father, tells you the history of mankind from its inception!'' Victor countered. ''My God, any man taught to fight will rise against the tyrant! See what's happening to the British in India and South Africa! The French in equatorial Africa! Why must it be a personal vendetta fomented by the Jews?''

Victor balanced his negative reactions to his father with the knowledge that he'd be leaving this nest of subversive vipers soon. He hadn't wanted it to end like this, but he stood face to face with a total stranger. Amadeo's words were incomprehensible to Victor, and his fierce fanaticism and dedication to so murky a cause was baffling to him. For as long as he remembered, nothing in his childhood had remotely suggested the shadow of Judaism clinging to them. Why would his father champion so futile a cause? *Why?* Victor neither loved nor hated his father. He neither liked nor disliked him. The truth was he barely knew the man. Between them was a tempered detachment bordering on tolerance. As a child, he had needed a father's acceptance and guidance, a role model to provide him with a sense of direction. What he got was the absence of love.

Today, knowing his departure was hours away, he made every effort to understand his father's intentions, but the elder Zeller aggravated the situation.

''By the closed-door policies adopted to appease the Arabs, the British have condemned millions of Eastern European Jews to death. Il Duce's insensitivity to our plight forced me to abandon you and the rest of my family. What insufferable atrocities were done our family, Victor, by those vicious propagandists!''

''I neither understand your sudden departure from Rome nor the necessity of Il Duce's personal protection of our family. Mother, Clarisse, and I are Catholic. For the love of—''

''No! You are Jews! Never forget it! My flight from Rome, regarded by my peers as cowardice, took courage. Courage to believe that I must not live in the shadow of my heritage. For as long as it serves me, I am a Jew who raised millions for *fascista* causes. On my word alone, gold poured into Mussolini's war chests. Shall I tell you my reward? *Betrayal!* Yes, Victor, *betrayal!* Il Duce swore in church to be godfather to the flesh of my flesh, yet the day he allied with Hitler he betrayed me and all Jews!'' Zeller thumped his chest with dramatic zeal and supplicated to the Lord God of Abraham. ''I vow as God and you are my witness this day to destroy Germans and all the enemies of the Jews who dare occupy the sacred soil of God's chosen people!''

Was this wildly agitated mass of madness really his father? An unsaid indictment of Amadeo's megalomaniacal rantings lay behind Victor's cool reserve. Truly, his father spoke with the authoritative panache usually attributed to men of unspeakable power. Those achromatic eyes, potent with cynicism, domineering, direct, cruel, and impersonal, were fired with unmistakable loathing. Victor had grown accustomed to this aura of superiority in recent months; it was the same look he saw in the eyes of the Werhmacht high command and freewheeling SS officers in Rome.

Victor left the château knowing less of his father than he had on arrival. His father's last words echoed after him: *''You'll return to me one day soon to applaud my percipience. That is, if you live long enough.''*

Live long enough? Victor understood the words to mean *if* he survived the war. He gave them no further importance. En route to Zürich by auto, he reflected on his father's rantings and ravings, determined once he was back in Rome to study the allegations, particularly as they affected the shape of Middle Eastern politics.

Inside the overcrowded *Bahnhof,* Victor paused at the kiosk to buy cigarettes. He opened the pack, removed a cigarette, and leaning over the open burner, lit it. That move, at precisely the right moment, saved his life.

A nightmare charging through hell exploded in blinding fire. Wild-eyed, unable to focus as panic followed by pain tore through him, igniting a fire in his neck and shoulder, Victor lurched, reeling off balance, steadying himself against a pillar. He'd seen nothing, no one, save for a whirling mass of confusion, shouts, gunshots. His flesh turned to ice, then burned as if singed by flame before he sunk into an abyss. He was dead. He'd been shot, killed, left to be consumed by the maggots of the earth.

Through the void, through ebony tunnels of ambiguous sensation, he tingled slightly, a feeling of levitation preceding the light. The bright light at the end of a murky gray labyrinth was coming closer . . . closer. The words came from a great distance, muted, growing louder but still indiscernible. The faint outline of movement, an indefinable face, wafted in and out of focus. Was it vaguely familiar? No, he was dead. The floating sensation returned. How could he be dead? He wasn't floating at all. He was alive. *Alive!* Locked in a rhythm of jarring discomfort. Sharp body jolts gave rise to nausea. The rhythm! Recognizable rhythm. What the devil! Think! Think, Victor.

A train! He was on a train. He listened—wheels . . . chugging engine . . . swaying, rocking motion. Yes, yes. Feeling left him. He was beyond feeling, but not beyond hearing. The voice was growing distinctive, audible. It came with a sudden rush of unbearable pain as it struck against his eardrums. *Jesus Christ! Don't shout! I can hear!*

Whoever you are . . . I'm alive, but I can't move!

A woman's voice, soft now, purring, comforting. The face coming into view as his focus sharpened was immediately recognizable.

"*Signore,* can you hear me? Try to return to me if it's only for a moment. You must. Listen to me. You must awaken."

It was the woman, code name Coco. The spy he'd met at the château with whom he'd danced a torrid *habanera.*

"My friend, a doctor, removed the bullets lodged in your throat and ear. You are heavily sedated. In your travel case I have placed a syringe filled with morphine, enough to get you to Rome. We are approaching Locarno at Lago Maggiore. *Signore,* understand I can travel no farther with you. You carry Italian papers. My friend and I do not. We have paid the conductor's assistant to see you through safely to Rome. *Auf Wiedersehen.*" A cool slender hand tenderly touched his face, and cupping his chin, Coco planted a kiss on his forehead.

The angel disappeared. Darkness descended. Victor was unable to protest.

"Inside that head of yours, you were doing some crazy tarantella, Victor. The miracle is that you are alive. Had it not been for the skilled services of the surgeon who removed the bullets . . ." The trenchant Dr. Rinaldo Corsi, physician to the Zeller family in Rome, rolled his expressive eyes toward heaven. "A month's recovery, do you hear me? I insist you remain at home—not necessarily in bed, but you must rest and en-gulf yourself in silence. No music and certainly no ballistic in-volvement, *capisce?* Your hearing in one ear may be impaired. In time we'll know for certain. Your voice is another matter. No, no, don't try to talk. Time alone might heal your vocal cords. Pray God you suffer no irrevocable damage. Do not talk. Say nothing at all. Write what must be said, and if later you can speak, whisper at first.'' Dr. Corsi shook his head. ''You be-long in a military facility where specialists with new technolo-gies and miracle drugs can take better care of you. Why not opt for a more optimistic prognosis?'' he pressed.

Victor, unable to move his head, raised a protesting hand, re-sisting the physician's suggestion. Too many questions would be asked, questions he couldn't afford to answer. He signaled to his mother. The *contessa* ushered Dr. Corsi out the door.

''No one will believe that Victor, expert in weaponry, could accidentally shoot himself,'' Marie Clotilde lamented bale-fully.

Dr. Corsi's dubious expression confirmed her suspicions. ''You realize, *contessa,* to inflict such wounds upon his per-son, Victor would have to be left-handed—which he is not—and be imbecile enough to fire at himself twice.''

Marie Clotilde ushered him along the mezzanine to the spiral steps descending to the first floor. She placed a slender finger over the physician's lips. ''I know, Rinaldo. *Prego,* let it be our secret. If Victor chooses to blame himself, there must be a valid reason. *Forse una amore?* Perhaps a love affair?'' she chided, lighting the older man's eyes wistfully. He remembered twenty years ago. . . .

And so did Clotilde, when Rinaldo had saved her life and that of Michael-Miguel Bertelli.

''Pray, *contessa,* that the injuries will heal properly. Pray to all the saints in heaven. *Ciao, cara mia.*''

The flimsy story, contrived in a moment's desperation, became the official story when Victor's infirmity kept him from his mil-itary duties.

A torrid love affair! Nothing elevated Victor in the eyes of the amorous *fascisti* or caused their imaginations to soar more than the thought of an illicit love affair, which with each narra-tion was embellished with even more lurid details.

In the two-month period of his recuperation, the story lost momentum, and by the time Victor returned to the War Ministry office, the incident had been reduced to a casual wink and the all-knowing glance.

Victor had spent his convalescence desperately seeking to counter his father's beliefs and discredit his Middle East obsession. Driven to extend himself beyond the bounds of his office, he embarked on a covert investigation concerning the plight of the Italian Jews. He suspected that senility had set in with his father, or some form of psychosis not yet written up in medical books.

Victor had found nothing!

By mid-July the hearing in one ear was still impaired, but his voice had returned, husky, more resonant than before. He coddled it and seemed less inclined to speak, and when he did, he spoke like a silver-tongued orator; he had a terrific impact on his listeners. He reflected on his near brush with death and the mysterious appearance of Coco and her companion, his benefactor, the man who'd saved his life. He couldn't imagine who wanted him dead. Moreover, the unrelenting question haunted him: Who knew of his presence in Zürich save his father and those motley espionage agents he'd met at the château?

Victor refused to ponder the imponderable. His thoughts concerning Coco refused to abate and drove him straight to the unrewarding files maintained on international espionage agents. After a waste of time and energy, Victor grew more aware of Count Ciano's lament: Italian military intelligence was greatly lacking and needed drastic reform and upgrading to compete with the British and German secret services. The condition was appalling!

At July's end the Italo-German alliance grew shaky. Hitler's rising popularity dimmed the ormolu luster of the Duce's transitory dominion. Marked hostility between the Axis leaders surfaced. The rivalry spurred Victor into even more intense efforts to check out his father's statements regarding the extermination of the Jews. If he didn't dig for the truth now, he might regret it forever.

But instead of finding answers, Victor came away from his research sorely deluded and disenchanted with fascists. The disenchantment mushroomed. No one knew anything. Specialists in the intelligence field stared at him as if he'd lost his mind. Men he'd grown up revering could offer him no balm, no insights. Like the sculptor who smashes his unfinished work, unable to shape it into the vision he perceives, Victor tried to smash his father's words.

But it didn't work.

If it existed at all, *Endlosung,* the final solution to the Jewish problem, was the most highly guarded secret in Germany. No German in the higher echelons of the Wehrmacht hinted at such an atrocity. In Italy, those lending polite ear to Victor's covert inquiries labeled the alleged atrocities pure rot. They assured Victor it was nothing more than subversive propaganda being disseminated by their enemies. Italy was fed lies by communism and other diabolical forces that succeeded in dividing the nation.

The trick, Victor old boy, is which side to believe.

Major Victor Zeller, a well-trained, disciplined intelligence officer, maintained his childhood ties with Il Duce, a man he knew better than his own father. Obligatory social duties performed by his mother at the family *palazzo* continued to ameliorate tensions incurred by his father's exodus from the *fascisti.*

Rome, when it suited her purpose, chose to believe that Minister Zeller was dead, that he'd taken his life to ease tensions in the fascist political arena. The dictator had squelched all rumors tending to besmirch Victor's name at the considerable risk of incurring Nazi wrath. As an innovative, faultless administrator, Victor found himself falling heir to an astonishing edict by Il Duce that placed him dead center in a festering circle of envy, greed, vicious rivalries, and nepotism. Older men, far more experienced and more capable than Victor, were unceremoniously shoved aside while the Duce indulged himself in a choice plum—annexation of Corsica—and placed Victor in charge of the operation.

In early September, Il Duce's bombastic and egomaniacal need to out-Herod Hitler became a fiasco. And he, Victor, had been duped to become part of that fiasco! Hitler's unique manipulation of power, more formidable than Stalin's or Mussolini's combined, stuck in the Italian chieftain's craw. He sent an imperative message to Victor to convene at his office at once.

The Duce stood at the window in that famous power pose, staring in the direction of Corsica. "It is a child awaiting adoption, Victor. And why not take her? We possess the military might." He turned to Victor, gazed at his open-mouthed stupefaction, and said soberly, "Don't you see? Lately, Godson, I distrust Hitler's sources. Ever since the Nazi-Soviet pact of 1939 I've observed his antics with trepidation. Communists are infiltrating Italy. An expedient is needed. *Corsica!* A combination of resources, clever plotting, and cautious selectivity will produce an appropriate rudder to steady that stormy, mutinous island, an island where hatred, violence, and revenge dictate vendetta to its inhabitants. See the miracles I provide to my beloved Italy! If we should be overrun with too many communists, we shall deport them to Corsica."

Before Victor made sense of this line of reasoning, Il Duce pounced upon him with zeal, his eyes sparkling with fire. "And you, Major Victor Zeller, shall head the Corsican invasion. Yes, you! No one is better suited, and your absence from Rome will resolve a sticky, distasteful problem." There, at last it was flushed into the open.

Victor, still galvanized by the Duce's earlier pronouncement, stood perfectly still, waiting for the Damocles sword to descend upon him.

"Since your *late* father—" he winked broadly at Victor, "—saw fit to disseminate his false Jewish persuasions as one would advance a personal vendetta, I find it difficult, if not impossible, to persuade our German allies that you personally are *not* of the Jewish faith. Oh, how I weary of the Nazis in Rome. Their shrewish demands that I address myself to the Jewish problems in ways that suit Hitler's architects of death make me bilious. Lately I trust less and less those advisers hovering over me. What I need in Corsica is a man I can trust."

Victor studied Mussolini's haggard features, detecting a torment in him, an unidentifiable sickness etched deep into every line on his face. He'd seldom seen a sag to the iron jawline that had marked Il Duce as a man of destiny in those halcyon days when Victor's father had reached his political prime, before gloom had descended on the cherry-blossom *palazzo*.

On November 23, 1942, the French police on the island of Corsica could do little but stand by and make pests of themselves while 150,000 Axis troops descended upon Corsica. Victor Zeller arrived as commander of the invasionary forces, as miscast for such a role as Pirandello would be scoring Wagnerian music in political prose. But since it seemed only Victor Zeller's faith in the Duce remained inexorable, he was the logical man to embark upon the Corsican objective. He took up residence in the confiscated Mayor's palace in Bastia and set up military headquarters on the surrounding acreage in warehouses and ancient battlements. Word of the occupation spread through Corsica, into the depths of the forested *maquis* where hundreds upon hundreds of French Resistance fighters were holed up, biding their time before gearing up for an offensive against the invaders.

Much to Victor's astonishment, there was a total absence of debarkation or preparation for battle with a determined enemy on the part of the Corsicans. Instead, there were speeches, bands, parades. Pistols and guns were shot into the air and people sung ''The Marseillaise'' and screamed and danced for joy. Certainly the frolicking was not to greet the invaders! Not one of the Corsicans he met in those first two days was cordial to either Italian or German troops.

Here he was in Corsica, about to write a portion of World War II history. Standing at the window of the plush baronial palace, staring out at the spectral shadows of Blood Island, he wondered if he could pull it off.

What did this false island gaiety herald? That madmen occupied the island? Only God knew for certain, and at this moment Victor doubted if even the Deity knew where He stood in respect to the Corsicans.

Chapter Two

Months before Victor's arrival in Corsica, Chamois Barbone had arrived at Terra Bonifacio with an astounding proposal. "Lease me the citadel and surrounding acreage. Name your price."

The first statement, "Lease me the citadel," intrigued Vivaldi Bonifacio. When had Chamois Barbone ever leased anything? The second statement, "name your price," alerted the landowner. When had Barbone ever paid for anything? It was only proper that Vivaldi refuse him outright.

But Barbone, one shrewd conniver, capitulated. "You force me to reveal the most secret of secret information. I see it can be no other way than straightforward, as it should be between friends. Very well, landowner, I trust you will keep this information to yourself. Shortly, Corsica will be occupied by the Italian and German forces. Recently I joined the Resistance. We need the citadel to perfect our plans. You also shall play an integral part in the scheme of things, landowner."

"No! Absolutely not. *Never!* It is enough for our lands to be occupied by an enemy, but to bring them here to roost on my doorstep to endanger my family? Are you some crazy man?"

Chamois Barbone, refused outright, left the Bonifacio house-hold in a calm mood uncharacteristic of the Corsican.

A month before Victor's arrival on the island, Chamois re-turned to confront Vivaldi once again. This time he unfurled a *coup de théâtre* upon Vivaldi and his closest friend, Matteus, the Moor. With dramatic panache, he brandished an official document, a roster of powerful Allied figureheads involved in some ambiguous invasion operation called "Vesuvius." "See here who heads the list of officers." He shoved the document under Vivaldi's nose. Vivaldi, seated at the desk in his library, set his glasses into place as he wondered how to handle this sticky situation. He blanched at the sight of the name.

"*Major Darius Bonifacio?* But how is this possible?" Stunned, Vivaldi acquiesced and cemented the deal at once.

That's how it began. Vivaldi's in absentia involvement with the Resistance was at best oblique and covert. On this mid-December day he moved cautiously through the *maquis,* stop-ping at the edge of the citadel grounds at an obscure point where he could see and not be seen. Bringing up the rear was the ever-faithful Matteus. Both men observed the flurry of activity be-low them.

The citadel, in the heart of the *maquis,* had long since been the home of the disaffected. But these two men never dreamed that the sprawling forests and ancient battlements would prove ideal for the covert operations concocted by the Resistance to inspire Corsicans to nationalism. For Vivaldi had continued to envision his own personal dream born of massacre, savagery, and the rape and annihilation of a bloodline, a two-decade-old plan of vendetta! Vengeance! He pledged the total destruction of his nemesis, Amadeo Zeller, the man who had robbed him of his birthright.

Now here was an army of men led by his special son, Darius! *Incredible!*

The transformation was indescribable, thought Vivaldi as he observed the hub of activity. Spirited workers had transformed the ancient battlement into modern barracks and training grounds to house the militant horde about to descend upon the island. To Vivaldi's and Matteus's everlasting amazement, the motley brigands and indolent hillsmen led by an inspired Bar-bone had been converted into a slick machine of coordinated action.

Under normal circumstances Vivaldi would have remained inside his comfortable study at Terra Bonifacio while Matteus supervised the final conversion of the premises, but these circumstances, far from ordinary, brought a flurry of excitement to the Spaniard's heart.

Darius was coming home!

He still couldn't believe it. Yet that day when Chamois had shown him the officer roster headed by Darius, Vivaldi had proudly boasted, "Didn't I tell you my son would one day be elevated to a position of great power?" They both recalled that unforgettable day four years ago, high atop Mount Cinto in a shepherd's hut, when Vivaldi had bartered for Darius's life. Now Darius was a major in the British Army! Commander of a major military offensive in whose hands the future of France and Corsica depended. And he was coming home.

"Any day, Matteus. Any hour Darius is expected to arrive."

Vivaldi, reveling in anticipation, glanced about for a response, but Matteus had moved forward in the brush, out of sight. With age, Vivaldi's handsome, youthful face had deepened into craggy lines. His distinguished look was enhanced by his leonine mane of curly brown hair streaked with dignified gray at the temples. His verdant eyes, though, were still sparked by fires of vendetta against Amadeo Zeller; the vivid images of Seville, Córdoba, the Hacienda de la Varga, and his exodus from Spain were etched in his brain forever. He lit a cigarette and sat observing workers in the final stages of construction when a sound in the brush brought sudden movement. Vivaldi whipped out his gun, ready for anything. He relaxed. The Moor was ambling back toward him.

"*Ecco*, Vivaldi. See below us? Lorries, stockpiled with supplies, weapons, ammunition, and more troops! Chamois performs miracles for the Allies. He produces trucks and vehicles stolen from the Germans and Italians!"

Vivaldi panned binoculars into position, fanning the faces of the new arrivals and bringing into focus two American OSS officers in the lead truck bumping along the lower goat track toward the citadel. "Darius?" He half whispered the name.

"Not yet. Soon. Are you certain you will not meet with the American OSS officers? They express a desire to meet the land baron who cooperates with the Allies."

Vivaldi shook his head. "Later perhaps, *after* we taste victory. Matteus, I've considered the matter carefully. No connection must be made between Darius and his family, do you understand?'' He let his haltered binoculars fall to his chest and gazed up at the enormous moon swelling on the horizon. ''If it is known that Darius has family on the island . . . We must not jeopardize either his life or the family's in the planned offensive, or else we supply the enemy with enough ammunition to defeat the operation before it commences.''

''You need to tell me?'' Matteus rebutted quietly. Their eyes locked for a second. ''Pray that no such hint escapes Barbone's lips.''

''It won't. He understands. And if he doesn't and should let the information escape . . .'' He unholstered a heavy, large-caliber pistol, deftly sprung the magazine from its handle, checked the ammo, and shoved it back into place with an ominous metallic click.

There was no reason to comment.

For a few brief moments moonlight broke through the clouds. The fragrant smell of fresh, chicory-laced coffee brewing on small campfires wafted up to them. Matteus slid off the embankment toward camp to fetch mugs of the fresh brew. He too was unable to subdue the wild beating of his heart in anticipation of Darius's arrival.

Four years ago he had tracked the length and breadth of Corsica, searching for Darius. He had returned to Terra Bonifacio with information exonerating Chamois Barbone of responsibility for the lad's disappearance, but he had been haunted by the words of the assailants, who had every intention of kidnapping Robert and Daniel, Vivaldi's other sons, for ransom. Of course Matteus had been driven to unravel the enigma; he hadn't had any choice. And so Matteus had departed for Rome, determined to seek answers from the right quarters.

Now, as he waited in line for coffee, he thought back on that trip to Rome. His covert meeting with Michael-Miguel Bertelli, Darius's real father, had produced nothing but an angry outpouring of the auto tycoon's wrath: *"Darius was your responsibility! How could you permit this to happen to my son? Was he desperate? Unhappy? Did the family or someone provoke him into running away?"*

With such condemnatory wrath hurled upon him, Matteus had employed the only weapons of negotiation available to him'. "Perhaps the foul play originated in Amadeo Zeller's loathsome mind?" Bertelli's shock and anger subsided. He was forced to agree with the hypothesis. He had refused the Moor outright when a meeting between the *contessa* and Matteus was broached. "No. Never! It would kill her to learn Darius is missing."

By the time Matteus boarded the next ship to Corsica and was able to ponder Bertelli's fervent rebuttal, the truth was beginning to form a pattern in his mind. Couched in Bertelli's emotional whiplash of words was a hidden truth, one Matteus was determined to uncover. He had barely unpacked in his quarters at the family estate when he swiftly repacked, embarked on the same path Darius had taken the day he had disappeared.

Matteus had ended up along the Calvi waterfront, turning Bertelli's words over in his mind. *Had Darius been unhappy? Desperate? Had he run away?*

Pausing along the rickety wharf, glancing at the busy harbor scene, he watched the fishing boats as they glided over the waters toward port with their daily catch. Solicitous waterfront whores snaked by him seductively, bartering silently for their wares. Matteus ignored them. His eyes, riveted to the spectral shadow of the mainland in the brilliant sunlight, swept the sea. The fiery blue sky and unbearable heat that day left nothing to the imagination. Heaven and earth, it seemed, were on fire. Then as the sun fell, the answer to Darius's disappearance fell upon Matteus.

Of course. It could have been no other way! Darius's dream, the burning dream, had driven him to the only place in the world he had thirsted for—St. Cyr Military Academy. As Matteus stared at the grimy incoming ferry from Marseilles, at the dirty little weasel of a man hustling passports and fake identity cards to a few down-at-the heels waterfront bums, an idea took shape in his mind. But was it possible?

His heart had whispered the truth. Darius's thirst for St. Cyr had been insatiable though his dreams had been thwarted by his stubborn father. The only logical and acceptable alternative to him was in Marseilles, at the *dépôt* of the Foreign Legion.

"The Legion asks no questions, demands no age verification. Face that possibility, Vivaldi," the Moor had insisted.

Through Chamois Barbone's efforts, a young Corsican was recruited to execute a unique assignment. In exchange for his services and the financial security provided his family, the Corsican youth traveled to Sidi bel Abbes, found Darius, and negotiated further with Vivaldi. For an additional sum to insure his own future, he agreed to join the Legion to keep tabs on Darius. Thereafter, word arrived on a regular basis from Sidi informing Vivaldi of Darius's progress and well-being. The Corsican, a godsend, had kept the bond between Darius and Vivaldi intact.

Now, on the dark, brush-filled hillside, Matteus handed a cup of the steamy brew to Vivaldi. Vivaldi uncorked a flask and poured two fingers of brandy into each cup. They clinked cups and sipped, their eyes observing movement in the encampment below. Matteus glanced at Vivaldi, noting his rising anxiety as he searched the features of each uniformed man, seeking out Darius. The Moor pondered the wisdom, or the lack of it, in keeping the knowledge of Darius's existence hidden from the rest of the family. To this day Dariana and Sophia, Vivaldi's wife and daughter, believed Darius was dead, the victim of foul play by Corsicans bent on vendetta.

Deception and silence had taken its toll on the Bonifacio family.

Somewhere in the neutral zone of Barcelona, Spain, a British transport touched down on a blacked-out, makeshift airstrip. The Mozarabe, met by Italian *partigiani* and French Resistance fighters, were shuttled off in lorries to a hidden cove along the moonless Costa Brava coastline, where they boarded a motorized longboat and were transported to a waiting fishing trawler anchored offshore. Its motors were idling, the skipper anxious to depart as they scrambled aboard.

As the trawler, *Los Poisson Sabre,* fighting strong December winds, weighed anchor and plowed into choppy seas, the men aboard fought to control their anxiety. Most wore American uniforms with the insignia *Bataillon de Choc* (Shock Troops), sewn onto their shoulders so everyone knew who they were. The tools of their trade were never far from their side. They carried British commando knives, plastic explosives, and booby-trap releases. Squads of their British contemporaries had preceded them, but the Mozarabe had refused to depart unless their regiment, under Major Darius Bonifacio's command, remained intact. After the hell of death engulfing them in the North African desert, the sight of glimmering coastal lights

dotting the midnight waters instilled a curious sense of anticipation in the minds of these unique irregular soldiers. Speculation
was rife, for none had been told their destination.

Darius, code-named Djebel for Operation White Coral,
stood amidships, attempting to obliterate recurring thoughts of
his family. He should have let them know he was alive. At least
he owed them that. The complexity of his involvement in OWC
was becoming more bewildering with each knot the trawler
drew closer to Corsica.

For a moment the moon burst through the cloud cover, illuminating the U-boat-infested waters.

"What will we find, Major?" Lucien Pascal handed Darius a
coffee thermos. Darius, tugging on his jacket collar, accepted
the coffee in silence.

The moon was once again obscured by black clouds. Darius
felt no compulsion to talk; the fear of revealing his past was
locked tightly in his heart. *The less any man knew of him . . .*

Ten hours later, the sudden lurching as the trawler decreased
speed and cut its engines forced Darius to glance at his luminous watch dial. *So soon? Is it possible?* Darius pressed the
lever at the side of the timepiece. "Kiss me once and kiss me
twice and kiss me once again . . ." He re-pressed the lever,
abruptly ending the tune, and wiping Valentina's image from
his mind. *Wherever you are, beloved, may God bless you and
keep you well.*

Up ahead, the shadowy outline of Corsica was unmistakable
even in the darkness. He spotted a semaphore, a battery-
operated lantern, signaling from shore. Longboats coming
from shore approached from a secret cove below Porto on Corsica's west coast. Darius inhaled the mellifluous scents of the
maquis rolling out to sea and was struck at once by a thousand
sense memories.

Oh, Christ! He hadn't counted on waves of homesickness engulfing him!

Twenty minutes later the Mozarabe and their gear boarded
the longboat under the cover of rolling fog banks. Behind them
the trawler had started its engines and was disappearing from
sight. Darius ordered the oarsmen to stop rowing. "It's too
dangerous to stop!" came the protests. "We wait!" Darius
commanded harshly.

In the silence as water plopped against the hull of the long-boat, Darius heard the sleek movement of bodies slicing through water. He held the flashlight beam off the stern of the boat. There—swimming toward them. Longinotti and Tamir Mandel were swiftly helped aboard. Tamir nodded to Darius. Darius gave the command. "Row! Row, all of you! Goddammit, I said move!" Darius held the torch to his watch, silently muttering a countdown: "Three . . . two . . . one!"

Behind them the trawler, prepped with plastic explosives, was blown to smithereens! Before departing from Spain, Darius was told by Marie-Pierre Marnay, the Resistance leader who was accompanying them, "The skipper is a German spy! He must not reach shore safely." Darius had understood. He had assigned his best plastics men to the task, and now it was over.

Two hours before dawn, the Mozarabe boarded waiting lorries. No headlights lit their path as trucks traversed precarious, narrow roads through the *maquis*, unseen and unheard right under the eyes and ears of the Axis soldiers manning the watchtowers.

In the lead lorry, a young, scruffy-bearded Arab unrolled a small pack and unfurled a caftan. He donned it, covering his uniform. The Mozarabe did likewise.

Marnay, the French Resistance leader, nudged Darius. "We're no more than a half hour away. These pathetic, cork-screw roads slow us down," he said, his voice squeaky. The apprehensive men in the antiquated lorries gripped anything fastened down to offset the jostling of the bumpy, harrowing ride. Darius's protracted silence as the trucks followed the sweeping curves of the road inland was for different reasons than the silence of his men. Here, the *maquis* was thicker, densely wooded, impossible to traverse for any but a seasoned native.

I played here as a child, finding new hideaways, wading, swimming in the pools of these gorges. Darius tensed. Bouncing along through the rough terrain with its familiar twists and turns as the predawn light filtered through the trees, the knuckles of his fingers grew white on tightly clenched fists.

Oh, Christ! God at His cruelest wouldn't devise so mad a design! He wouldn't!

It couldn't be! No! No! But it was! Terra Bonifacio came into his sights. Tocsins sounded through him. Not once during the briefing had the words "Terra Bonifacio" appeared as the operational base of the war offensive! Darius would later learn that just as the code name Vesuvius had been changed to General Furstenberg's choice, Operation White Coral, so had the operational base been altered from Porto-Vecchio on the east coast to Terra Bonifacio on the west. The hazards and inequities of war!

Darius cursed inwardly at the sight of the straighter, widening road, at the tree-lined clearing. He knew every tree, bush, and jutting palisade in the shifting shadows. Guard dogs, intent on annihilating unwanted trespassers, barked and snarled viciously, snapping at the trundling lorries that swept past the main gate toward the estate's northern perimeters.

There could be no mistake—none at all—as to their destination—the citadel! It was the ancient fortress where he and Sophia had played, dreamed, and planned a future far different from this.

He felt sick! His stomach knotted at the complex embroidery destiny had spun about him.

A beam of lantern light shot out of the darkness, directing the train of lorries to circle around and enter the citadel under the flying bridge. Marnay followed directions, and the trucks behind him parroted his moves.

Darius was home! Yet in the strictest sense, he could not go home. For security reasons, OWC guidelines had clearly defined why his identity in Corsica must remain covert. *What craftily designed deviltry is this?* he wondered. Why must Terra Bonifacio be their operational base? Why not another part of the island? To the north, south—even Fort Bonifacio, for the love of God. Anyplace but the citadel would have narrowed the chances of confrontation with his family. Who had selected the citadel? *Lucifer himself!* he thought balefully.

To be quartered and fortified less than a kilometer away from his family domicile? It was sheer madness. Knowledge of his identity would increase his vulnerability and place his family in dire jeopardy. Bombarded by these explosive thoughts, Darius failed to realize the lorry had stopped abruptly.

Oh, Christ! Where do I go from here?

Dawn lifted. The pervasive scents of chicory-flavored coffee boiling on camp fires had drawn a horde of milling, sleepy-eyed soldiers spilling from the barracks. At the sight of the newcomers, they waved and yelled welcoming cheers. The rising sun poked through the tall pines, splintering light on the faces of the welcoming committee and lighting up one familiar face. Darius's eyes fixed on the man.

The Moor! Matteus's black eyes trained on Darius like gun sights. He stood behind the American OSS officers, observing Darius's solemnity with unreadable expression. Their eyes locked briefly. In that moment, the communicated warning look was enough for Matteus to retreat slightly from the others. He climbed a slight rise, his hands gripping the choke chains on two guard dogs, and turning, he craned his neck to assess the princely, uniformed Major Bonifacio now flushing with pride at the deference paid him by the welcoming Allied and Resistance leaders.

Thrust instantly into a hive of activity as the Mozarabe were welcomed and shown to their quarters, Darius accepted the hot coffee offered him by the citadel incumbents. His eyes were everywhere. Loading doors were opened. Lanterns hung within the confines illuminated the interior stone walls as the Resistance fighters were directed to place strategic crates of supplies in the proper storage niches. Everywhere he saw smiles, dutiful cordiality, and high expectations among the men. A tiff broke out in the ranks of the Mozarabe when helpful soldiers tried to separate them from their zealously guarded professional tools. It was quickly decided by a strong hands-off gesture by the newcomers.

Torn between his desires to rush back into the *maquis* to alert Vivaldi and to remain here to feast his eyes on Darius, Matteus chose to stay. He studied Darius's lean, hard jawline, the strapping physique, the carefully cultivated gaze. It was a compelling look few could resist, Matteus thought, one that conveyed the dynamic intensity of a man in full control of himself and his life. How pleased Don Diego de la Varga would have been to view such a champion! Then the Moor somberly remembered: *No de la Varga blood flowed through Darius's veins!* He studied the British uniform, bush jacket, paratrooper boots. His eyes fixed on the seven flamed grenade insignia superimposed upon the Cross of Lorraine, the only vestige of Darius's Foreign Legion origins. Around his neck hung the seldom-used death's-head amulet, a gift from Matteus. It was an ancient means of self-protection possessing mystical powers. Knowing that he could not approach Darius, Matteus sighed heavily. Turning to leave, he caught sight of Vivaldi parting the thick lower branches of a chestnut tree. The land baron stood concealed, peering at Darius through binoculars.

Vivaldi had caught the circumspect glances between Darius and the Moor. Very good. He knew the reasons for such posturing, approved of Darius's discretion. How easily he spotted Darius among the new arrivals! Standing in a circle of sunlight breaking through overhead trees, Darius's image was overwhelming. Vivaldi lowered the binoculars.

Darius recognized the two American OSS officers. They saluted one another. He shook Brad Lincoln's hand. Going to the front of the queue lines, the Americans grabbed mugs of coffee and swiftly shuttled Darius about the battlement, eager to brief him in a Cook's tour of the grounds.

How could they possibly know of his, Darius's, intimacy with the citadel?

Sipping the thick black coffee, Darius marveled at the incredible changes incorporated in the citadel by Maquis and Allied engineers.

The area encompassed more than a hundred acres and was filled with gunnery ranges, obstacle courses, livable officer and infantry barracks complete with radio transmitters, map rooms, and a mess hall. Compared to their accommodations in North America . . .

Darius's busy eyes were everywhere, trying to detect possible weaknesses in the fortification. Captain Lincoln, standing in proper military stance, was talking rapidly and, as usual, in the difficult-to-follow American idiom. No matter how closely Darius listened, the jargon baffled him.

"You gotta be some lucky bastards, you and your operational groups. You got nature's protection on your arrival. Fog banks, eh? You know what happened to us on arrival? Man, we damn near backtracked it to our ships! We arrived at approximately midnight, see? Corsica—the mountains and the Bay of Ajaccio loomed in our sights. Damned if the whole island wasn't on fire!"

Darius smiled. "Corsican custom. They burn the *maquis* in the dry season."

"That's what a few of our men told us. But they were wrong.

The next day we learned the Germans set fire to the whole countryside just to annoy the stubborn Corsicans.''

Darius cut him a sharp look.

''We learned,'' continued the American, ''that the Germans were deliberately setting fire to Italian gasoline and ammo dumps. Crazy, ain't it? How do you figure it?'' Before Darius could proffer a reasonable guess, Lincoln continued, ''We expected the Germans to bomb us at the docks and wipe us out to the last man. They could have, you know, and why they didn't bothers the hell outa me.''

Darius mulled over the information in noncommittal silence.

''We've had a hell of a time rounding up vehicles. The damned French government refused us any use of motor vehicles. And to top off their stupidity, they won't sell us gas. I hope to Christ you can persuade them. So far, we got a few natives on the take through the black market. I tell you, Major, this ain't my kind of warfare. I swear this secret war has all the earmarks of a carnival.''

''What exactly *is* your kind of warfare, Captain?'' Darius moved along the ramparts, peering at the activity in the compound. ''By the way, when was the operational base plan changed and how the devil did you find this place?'' His French-accented English was concise.

''The plans were changed while you and your men were en route to Corsica. How we found this place is another story in itself. You really want to know?''

If he hadn't wanted to know, he wouldn't have asked. ''Yes,'' he replied politely.

''Then I'll tell you. Actually, it was a stroke of luck—an accidental discovery during aerial recon by a British officer of the Seventh Reconnaissance Group of the Thirteenth Squadron flying his modified P-38. See, the guy was heading out of England over the Channel toward occupied France, and he dropped over the enemy-controlled coastline at thirty-five thousand feet. Damned if the British tracking equipment didn't spot a patrol of FW-190's Nazi fighters in the area. Warnings flashed to the pilot were blotto—radio was on the fritz. Then the fucking FW's tried everything in and out of the book to trap the high-flying recon plane. The British knew what was happening but couldn't get through to their man.''

Darius was having a hard time following.

"Foul weather hampered the recon pilot—loused him up—and he was pursued by enemy planes ducking in and out of cloud cover, trying to lose the fuckin' Jerries all the time. Son of a bitch, I'd have given my balls to see it. You know what that glorious son of a bitch did? That gutsy bastard banked south over Corsica with half-empty gas tanks. He weighed his options: head back to England using every deceptive trick he could muster and deliver an aborted mission, or take the targeted photos he'd set out to make and chance parking the big bird safely back on home plate. Let me tell you, Major, God sat on his shoulders that day. That son of a bitch found a break in the clouds, dropped down, took photos of Axis ammo dumps and weapons depots, *and* for good measure took a few extra shots of what to him looked like damned interesting stuff, then headed the hell back to the lion's lair." Lincoln paused to light a cigarette and drain his coffee dregs.

"His fuel was so fuckin' low that the prop blew thatches off farmers' houses when he finally glided in under RAF squadron escort. Yeah, the son of a bitch made it! He turned over the film for speedy development. Damned if the photos didn't clue us in to formidable arsenals and fortifications we hadn't known about before. They clearly indicated ammo dumps and a spur line being constructed close to Porto-Vecchio. Actually closer to Fort Bonifacio." Lincoln stopped. "Fort Bonifacio? Same name as yours. Any connection?"

Darius shook his head, accepted a cigarette from Lincoln's outstretched pack. Below them he saw lorries disappear inside the fortification walls. Others were covered with camouflage tarps. His wary-eyed Mozarabe were critically observing the operation in silence. It would take awhile for his men to cozy up to civilization. Lincoln's voice returned him to the moment.

"On the west coast, north of Ajaccio, we spotted the bombed-out walls of a fortress. The British brass were furious. They complained bitterly, accusing the pilot of wasting time, manpower, aircraft, and precious fuel to film a previously destroyed target. Then, Major, came the real bombshell! Allied intelligence reported no such bombings on Corsica. *Zap!* New strategy was effected. The OSS was called in with MI-6 to meticulously study the recon photos. I'm talking blowups. We parachuted an agent and some Resistance fighters into the area to examine the destruction. They radioed us their findings.

Voilà! Operation White Coral was transferred from the east coast to this magnificent setting! A perfect operational base. Geographically, the site was perfect for what hatched on our chief's drawing boards. As it turned out, the place was an ancient citadel ruin, inaccessible by land, hard to find by air. You gotta trespass well-guarded private property before gaining access to it. The landlord himself maintains a small army of well-armed men to guard the place. Perfect.''

''You imply the Germans and Italians have made no aerial reconnaissance photographs of this area?'' Darius pursed dubious lips, and Lincoln shot him an appreciative glance.

''Wouldn't matter a tinker's damn if they did. See the tarps down there? Camouflage. At the altitude needed to obtain accurate photos, they'd detect nothing unless their lenses were twice as powerful as British lenses.''

''Ever hear of German precision toolmaking and glass grinding? The finest in the world,'' Darius said. He tossed his coffee dregs onto the ground and hung the empty cup from a notch on his belt. ''The location is excellent,'' he said quietly. ''I know the land well. You made a fine choice.''

Brad Lincoln's brows shot up. He accepted the compliment with a nod of his head. ''You will be careful, Major. The landlord's dogs are vicious. I'm talking killer dogs. Keep a mountain between you. Your eyes mock me. Don't you believe me?''

''I believe you. Who is our Corsican contact?''

''Barbone. Chamois Barbone. His brother's a big gun in Marseilles. Tough, man. Real tough, these Corsicans. Silent, fierce, deadly men. Why the hell do I tell you? You're Corsican, aren't you?''

The American OSS had done its homework. ''Excuse me, Captain, it's time I set my men at ease.'' He turned to leave.

''Uh, Major Bonifacio?''

''Oui, capitaine?''

''For your sake, I hope your family is not hereabouts. It could prove disastrous. Can't jeopardize our joint effort, you know. If the Jerries and Italians get a handle on your identity, if your family presents maximum danger to you or OWC . . . Do I have to spell it out?''

''No, you don't. Corsicans are as tight-lipped about their business—''

"As a virgin's cunt. I know. We've had dealings."

Lincoln's words cut through Darius's memory like an icy sword. Their first encounter in London at Marboro Hall had produced estrangement and inflated his dislike for the American Captain to giant proportions. As for Jim Greer, the other OSS officer in charge, the man appeared too innocuous for his rank and the insignia he wore. Darius sensed a brooding inner ferocity buried deep inside him. Descending the stone steps, Darius paused briefly to observe his men unloading their gear before he sidestepped them and strode to the Moor's side. In private, they embraced warmly, emotionally. Tears spilled from Matteus's eyes. Overwhelmed by the proximity at which he viewed Darius, he again noted the changes that had registered earlier in his brain and began solicitous murmurings. "When will you come home? The family will shed tears of joy."

Darius, patiently explaining, observed the OSS men peering at him from across the compound. Lucien Pascal sprang to life, moving in protectively behind Darius. Matteus, somberly digesting Darius's explanation, suggested he'd been briefed by Vivaldi on the sensitive role he played. *"Va bene,"* Darius said. "Then you know how I must posture myself. Should the Axis high command learn I am Corsican, my family would become vulnerable. They could implement strong measures, imprison you all. I cannot permit that to happen, nor can I permit this operation to be aborted." As Darius spoke, he noted the expressions on the Moor's and Pascal's faces.

Matteus acknowledged Pascal and engaged briefly in Corsican dialect. "You two know one another?" Darius's blazing green eyes widened in astonishment.

"For many years," Pascal said without thinking. Just as quickly he paused, his face flushing a deep terra-cotta red.

"Yet in all this time you told me nothing. Nothing of Corsica?"

"Nor did you, Major."

Darius, aghast, seethed at Pascal. "You might have told me you knew Matteus!"

"So? I also know your father. What do you want from me?"

"Pascal! Not once did you speak of this friendship!"

"I was under orders to merely observe and become your factotum."

"Facto—" he broke off. *"Orders? What orders?"* Darius spun around to face the Moor. "You did this, Matteus?" He studied the solemn look in the Moor's eyes, then exploded at Pascal. "You put up with the hell of Sidi on orders? I pray to Christ that you were paid handsomely for courting death a thousand times over!"

"I was. To be sure, Major, the fee was more than ample."

The smug, playful tone irked Darius. He poured his wrath on Matteus. "You knew my whereabouts all this time?"

"Not at first. Later. When you failed to show up at Bastia—" He filled Darius in on the great lengths Vivaldi went to find him, eliminating the portion dealing with Miguel Bertelli and the *contessa*.

"I see. Does my family consider me to be in swaddling clothes?"

"Not after the glowing letters Pascal sent describing your personal and professional triumphs in North Africa."

"Is nothing sacred to you, Pascal?" he said scathingly. "You told them everything? What if the letters had fallen into enemy hands?"

"Trust me. I was most circumspect. We used your code name: Samson. As in Delilah's Dream."

"I don't find this amusing. I regret you chose to do this, Pascal. Can you be trusted in this operation?" As friendliness dissolved, Darius's stern features studied him in glacial evaluation. "It is entirely possible you could prove to be a security risk. Our confidentiality has never been more seriously ruptured. Dammit, I could have you cashiered! I've spent four years in life-and-death situations with a man I trusted, only to reach this point of serious suspicion."

Pascal refused to be cowed. "Do as your conscience dictates, Major. If my deeds are not testimony to my loyalty and fidelity—" His emperor-sized Corsican ego swelled beyond containment.

"If I hadn't invested so much time in you— You're a specialist in survival, Lucien. You're important to me and our survival here."

Pascal, insufferably smug, cracked his picket-fence grin, his chest expanding a notch or two like a circus strongman breaking chains.

"Wipe that grin off your face!" Darius snapped. "You'll

pay a stiff penance, just as I shall. Not until after Corsica is liberated will you visit your family! *Comprenez-vous*, legionnaire?''

Pascal blanched. Darius painstakingly explained the ramifications. ''It seems, *mon cher ami*, we are both victims in this war.''

Pascal went stomping off in a snit, snorting like an enraged bull at stud denied mating rites. Darius expressed a warning to Matteus.

''Every moment I am here I shall be under surveillance, especially by my peers, the Allies. You must treat me as a stranger. Explain to the family. My heart is anguished, I ache to see Dariana and Sophia.''

The Moor understood. He collected his dogs and backed away as Darius moved forward to examine the newly sequestered military installation. The ghosts of his and Sophia's childish dreams were gone, as were the secret hiding places in which they had dreamed the impossible. In their stead were instruments of destruction, weapons of war.

''Your code name is Djebel, Major. Ours are Cain and Abel,'' said Brad Lincoln during a private conference in the map room. ''It is my duty to describe the clandestine struggle in which we are enmeshed. It must never be forgotten that special operations in the form of Resistance movements are to a large extent nationalistic in nature and need *political* guidance. To deal with the partisans and effectively control a nationalistic movement, firm, tactful staff officers well versed in special operations and the political background of the country are an absolute necessity. That is our primary function, and we are all well trained. Therefore, it is also my duty to inform you that a number of your men are considered undesirables unfit to serve in this Corsican operation.''

Darius was blazing. He tossed his attaché case on the desk and countered heatedly, ''What you're saying is that my men lack the credentials to get their bloody heads shot off. But this is not to be believed!'' He slapped his thighs in vexation. ''You imply the Mozarabe are unfit for OWC?''

''Like it or not, Djebel, you'd best be aware of their criminal pasts,'' Greer said. He tossed a thick file on the desk. ''It's all documented. Your precious Mozarabe are out-and-out criminals. Let Cain give you a rundown.''

"I don't suppose I have a choice," Darius snapped.

Brad Lincoln picked up the file, leafed through it, and selected several dossiers. "Suppose I enlighten you, Djebel. Let me begin:

"Carlos 'Limey' Whitehall. British subject, twenty-eight years old. A small-fry misfit, petty thief, and scam man with a string of prior arrests a mile long. Joined British Army, caught in flagrante delicto by MI-6 in a plot to swindle money. Sold phony military secrets to enemy agents. Held in prison, dishonorably discharged. A plot by German agents to kill Whitehall was foiled when he escaped England. He fled to Marseilles, joined the Foreign Legion. See SAS commando dossier."

Darius smiled tightly. Lincoln continued, "Next:

"Daniel 'Dutch' O'Reilly. Irish subject. Twenty-eight years old. Dublin police records describe him as a hardened IRA terrorist. His family, hard-core Black-and-Tan forces, fought in the Irish rebellion. The death of his father at the hands of the British soured O'Reilly against the Crown. Refused to join the British Army, fled to escape military confinement. Trail picked up in the Foreign Legion at Sidi bel Abbes. Meritorious conduct with special task force earned him entry to SAS commandos."

Darius leaned back in the wooden chair and propped his feet on the desk, eager for Brad Lincoln to continue. "Go on with it."

"Lucien Pascal. French subject. Origin of birth, Corte, Corsica. A hardened criminal and known felon. Six counts of aggravated assault occupied police blotters in Ajaccio. Attempts to verify the felonies failed. No police records exist to prove or disprove previous reports. A known member of an underground criminal network. Participation in tribal vendettas was reported to our investigators by rival families. Joined the Foreign Legion, member of special task force later recommended to train in England with SAS commandos."

Darius, biting back his contempt, lit a cigarette and sipped the coffee brought to them by an aide. Lincoln continued:

"Pasquale Longinotti. Italian subject. Twenty-five years old. Born in Trieste, an avowed antifascist, conscripted into the Italian Army, served with the forces in Spain, deserted a year later, returned to Trieste, went into hiding until an atrocity done to his sister flushed him from obscurity. The girl, victim of gang rape, identified her rapists. Longinotti tracked them down, killing all five. Disappeared shortly after. Family believes he's dead. He turned up in England with Thirteenth Demibrigade, NAIS division. Cross-check SAS commando dossier.

"Just be thankful, Major, I'm not running this down before British MI-6 or there'd be goddamned hell to pay."

"Please continue this—what is it called?—running down."

"Jean-Louis Delon. French citizen. Former physician identified as Edouard La Fitte. Victimized by extortion, he slew the extortionist. Bound over to authorities to await trial, he escaped. Relatives insist he's dead. Letters intercepted to family members by J.-L. Delon bore Sidi bel Abbes postmark. Investigators demanded search of Legion's records."

"Naturally they were denied that privilege," Darius said.

"Naturally. Do let me get on with it, Major.

"Tamir Mandel. Polish subject. Twenty-six years old. The Jew escaped the Warsaw Ghetto when Nazis stormed and bombarded the city. Little is known of Mandel, who with other refugees enlisted in the Legion and later volunteered for guerrilla training in a special task force. He is on the Wehrmacht high command's most-wanted list for a list of crimes perpetrated against them in Poland. Admitted to special forces of Thirteenth Demibrigade, he trained with the British Eighth Army in North Africa. See SAS commando dossier."

Darius bridled impatiently. "Precisely how many more honorable men do you intend to uh—run down?"

"Honorable, is it?" Lincoln turned the page. "Let's see now . . .

"Musaka Mubende. Nigerian native. Twenty-six years old. Mubende escaped a civil uprising, traveled inland through Cameroon, the Congo, into Uganda. Settled at a Catholic mission on Lake Albert. Civil war between Muslims and Christians drove the missionaries into the Sudan and Libya. Mubende was found by the SAS commandos wandering the lower desert, lost, dehydrated, his body testament to the suffering he endured in his desperate odyssey. Milked by barbarous nomadic Bedouins, sexually molested, he was ravaged and left for dead. He was nursed to health, thought to be without vocal apparatus for at least six months. During this mute period, Mubende made himself indispensable to the SAS. He nursed their wounds with professional detachment. Demonstrates percipience, is skilled in weaponry. And . . .''

''And *what?*''

''Both Mandel and Mubende are dyed-in-the-wool Reds. Communists!''

Darius blinked. ''So? The communists are your allies. Allies of France! Of Great Britain!''

''That doesn't mean we don't keep an eagle eye on them.''

''Why are you doing this? What can be achieved by this impertinent belittling of my men except to drive a wedge of hostility between us? Why do you dig so deep inside their pasts to uncover this garbage?''

''It's what's called a psychological profile. Something new and telling. Look, this isn't some cheap cloak-and-dagger trick to nail your men to the cross and render them ineffective in OWC,'' said Greer. ''We aren't some lynching party.''

''Don't make this any more difficult, Djebel,'' said Lincoln.

''*Difficult! Mon Dieu!* How quickly you turn a glorious name with a ring of bravery to it into *merde*! What more do you demand of men who were betrayed, misused, robbed of youth and life? Inoculated with hates and manias never born in their mind, these homeless men were trained and sent forth to kill or be killed. I thank God for every day I spent with the SAS commandos who honored me by affording me the privilege of leading them to hell and back!''

''War, to coin an old war horse's words, is hell, Major.''

''War, *capitaine,* is a commodity born in the minds of greedy politicians who, standing on the threshold of history, envision their own immortality and perpetuate it at the high cost of human lives.''

''Touché, Djebel. Touché. Despite this profound loyalty you demonstrate toward your precious Mozarabe, let me put it to you succinctly. Americans don't take lightly charges of selling corpses, violation of graves, receipt of stolen property.''

''Nor,'' said Greer, ''do they condone unnatural sexual debaucheries, abduction of native children, burglaries, fraud, usury, extortion, or dealing in contrabrand.'' He tossed a yellow sheet of foolscap containing the charges at Darius.

Darius leaned forward, picked it up, scanned the indictments, and tossed it back to Lincoln with an air of impatience. "What exactly do you expect? Abstemious acolytes wearing chastity belts?" He was outraged, beyond conciliation. "Conspicuous by its absence is the word *bravery*! Bravery demonstrated in the line of duty. *And* loyalty! Loyalty to France and Britain under the most atrocious and devilish conditions, severe hardships, dehumanization suffered at the hands of German NCO's who administered brutality under the noses of the disdaining eyes of the French officers!"

Foolscap in hand, Darius paced the earth floor, attacking the allegations against his men one by one. "Shall we begin with the selling of corpses? This amounted to paying desert dwellers to bury the dead bodies strewn about the Legion outposts in the aftermath of tribal skirmishes. Next, the violation of graves. This concerns the reburial of the dead which were dug up and laid bare by desert jackals and hyenas. Concerning unnatural sexual debaucheries," Darius continued scornfully, "I have no quarrel with this allegation. Anything could happen in Sidi's red light district and did. The same could be said of nearly everyone at the post command. Abduction of native children." He shook his head in disbelief at the insanity of refuting such shabby charges. "Often legionnaires hid young native boys from the rampant sodomy and sadistic practices proliferating in Sidi bel Abbes. As for the charges of fraud, usury, and extortion, let me go on record to say these charges are false. Very often the legionnaires hid children from money-hungry parents bent on turning them to the streets, and in the course of this dirty business, the men often tricked offenders by disguising themselves as the police. So much for fraud. Legionnaires gambled frequently. Winners, unable to collect their monies from my men at once, charged them excessive interest rates. And extortion?" Darius slapped the foolscap on the desk. "Cheated by local merchants, the men often threatened violence until the merchants desisted from price gouging. Let's understand this. I do not label my men innocents—never that."

Lincoln held up a restraining hand. "Hold it, Djebel." He pulled at a note in his file. "This communiqué intercepted by ULTRA and those backroom boys at Bletchley Park who succeeded in breaking the German cipher should explain. It's the Hitler commando order."

"I've seen it."

"Then you know," Lincoln began. "You know the order applies to your Mozarabe and all Allied special forces."

"I would be hard put to interpret the order differently."

"What I'm trying to say is Hitler's Wehrmacht intends to destroy all terror and sabotage troops of the British. Your commando forces countered the Germans' nervous strength in North Africa. *Der Führer* is not a forgiving man. He has decided that—"

"Men who do not act like soldiers, but like brigands and bloodthirsty demons, shall be treated as such by German troops and will be ruthlessly eliminated in battle, whether armed or unarmed, in or out of uniform." Darius recited the order by rote. "Those who fall into German hands are to be slaughtered by the first troops who encounter them. Should any escape death and be caught, they will be immediately turned over to the SS."

Lincoln and Greer swallowed their amazement. Greer pompously questioned Darius's source of information.

"No doubt from the same source as yours. We are no strangers to Bletchley or ULTRA."

"You display no concern over the SD and their clever means of interrogation? Or the SS for that matter?"

"Few Frenchmen doubt the effectiveness of the Sicherheitsdienst."

"Then let's lay our cards on the table. Let me tell you the real reason for this seeming inquisition into the backgrounds of your men."

"At last you favor me."

"My orders are to inform you frankly and fully what your men can expect if captured. Your commandos and all operational groups are essentially volunteers, right?" Darius nodded. "Look, Djebel, I understand your emotional commitment to your men. As highly specialized, skillfully trained men in demolitions, special weapons, scouting, wireless, and fieldcraft, we know they passed tough physical requirements and met stiff standards."

"If you knew that, why did you go into all of this?"

"My orders, Djebel, are to pay strict attention to the character of every man involved in OWC at specialist level. The success of White Coral depends not only on the daring and bravado of the operational groups. Civilian and military men alike must be stable and of good judgment. Understand?''

''You must understand that my men, the best-equipped fighting men on the Continent, will *not* tremble in the presence of Hitler's SD or SS. Not even Hitler himself could cow them.''

''It'll be a bit late to make that determination when they face the SS. And only *after* that eventuality would we ever know.''

Darius, rankled by the Americans' arrogant inflexibility, shuffled through the dossiers in his briefcase. ''What would I find if I fine-combed the pasts of *your* valiant men? Of the Resistance fighters?'' He paused, annoyed at his own display of anger. *Keep steady to your course,* he told himself. Then, because he felt the Americans to be naive, he decided to enlighten them.

''France's criminal element forms the spine of the Resistance and Free France's life-support system. Upon such men the life and future of my nation is dependent. Not upon the high and the mighty. Not the nobility or wealthy collaborators who greeted the conquering Nazis with fife and drum, trumpet and song. The *criminal* factions, my American friends, will restore the nation and its people and deliver victory to them. And you dare denigrate the proven courage of my men, who've paid ten times over for any minor infractions or crimes committed in desperation?''

''I'm doing my job under General Donovan's orders, Djebel. You and your men must know in advance that you'll not be protected by the Geneva convention.''

''The Geneva convention?'' Darius blurted. ''I'm concerned with death and destruction, and you give me Geneva convention? I've just come off the desert, where no one plays by the rules and survives! Understanding the Western mind is a feat in itself. I pray that I may comprehend your OSS and its confusing posturings with more facility than I understand your slang.''

''Yeah, yeah. War makes for strange bedfellows. I concur. Since our orders can change moment by moment, sometimes we are unable to define our strategy. Look, I take orders from the top brass too! I'll take your word that the Mozarabe will stand up to the task. Fair enough?'' Brad's attempt to lessen Darius's growing disenchantment with the OSS failed dismally. Until war's end no one could really know his true ally in a dissident-filled France. Vichy France and Free France were one nation under one flag, but they were also split in two, with Vichy marching to the sound of German boots and swastika-waving flags.

The meeting was adjourned, and Darius broodingly returned to his spartan quarters. The room was bare walled and contained a cot, chair, and makeshift desk made of two sawhorses with a thick wooden board atop them. He needed time to himself now. Why had the criminal and psychological profiles been done on the Mozarabe? He'd received none on the Allied officers and Resistance leaders. He didn't understand the implications of charges against his men or why someone had seen fit to dig up the dirt. He had to assume the Vichy government at Sidi had released the information to the Germans, and the Allies had intercepted the information vis-à-vis special couriers or UL-TRA. But for what purpose?

Darius lit a thin Turkish cigar and lay back on the cot, smoking, listening to the muffled sounds of men talking, cleaning their guns. His thoughts veered to Chamois Barbone. The deference he'd shown to Darius bordered on the obscene. That he supported Free France boggled Darius's mind. Why not Vichy? It was in Chamois's present political posturing that Darius found ominous substance for his suspicions. Chamois's present display of homage and allegiance to a cause rather than to himself was disturbing to Darius, a man who prided himself on understanding the ways of the men working with him. He had had no trouble understanding the men in North Africa, but here in Corsica, Darius realized he knew very little of men beyond the desert, out of the grip of immediate warfare. Worse, he understood little of the complex peculiarities of political expedience. The incomprehensibility of the politics of war ate away at his insides like acid. Was his youth the enemy? The culprit that failed to understand the subtleties of political machinations that lay behind the front lines of war? Power didn't rest in the hands of battle commanders. Hadn't he learned that truth in North Africa? The scepter of power, grasped tightly in the hands of cunning politicians thousands of miles away from the battleground blood and gore, was wielded like a cudgel, like a bloodied baton orchestrating scenarios from Dante's *Inferno*.

Those terrible memories of North African deaths burned vividly in Darius's mind, and he had no desire to share them. At least not with the Americans! The desire to talk with his good friends Youseff and General Furstenberg gnawed at him.

Youseff's parting words at Cairo airport replayed in his mind. "You are as different a man today as you were yesterday, and tomorrow will bring forth a still different man. Be willing to accept expedience if it helps you to achieve your goals. You do not belong to the past, Darius. The future is yours. Grow with it. Guard it well."

Darius sighed despairingly. *The present is my reality. How do I concern myself with a future I am incapable of recognizing?*

On his feet, Darius moved to the desk where earlier he'd tossed his briefcase. He pulled out several files and, catching a glimpse of a wine pouch hanging on a wooden peg, smiled. Matteus had thought of everything. He guzzled some wine from the bag, hung it back, and got down to business.

Momentarily on edge, Darius shuffled through his briefcase, searching for a special dossier. Lincoln's pejorative remarks concerning the Mozarabe refused to abate. Dammit! Lincoln had the distinct advantage and satisfaction of knowing nearly all there was to know about Darius and the Mozarabe, which was immensely more than he himself could hope to learn about Cain and Abel on such short notice. But it wouldn't remain one-sided much longer. Didn't he possess the ultimate power to veto the OSS and British MI-6 participation in OWC? As Darius contemplated this, he collected his wits and removed a dossier from his briefcase. He scanned the file, stopping at the name on it:

MAJOR VICTOR ZELLER. ITALIAN MILITARY INTELLIGENCE.

The name revived haunting, unfathomable dreams, persistent dreams of a man he'd never met yet knew intimately—*Amadeo Zeller!*

Outside, the Corsican winds howled fiercely through the trees. Darius, pacing the earthen-floor shelter with long strides, slapped the dossier against his thighs, deep in thought. He peered through the ancient grilled iron windows, tugged his jacket closer to his neck, and stared at the late morning sun splintered through the tall pines.

He focused back on the dossier, opened it, and studied the separate annotated report attached to an ULTRA-intercepted and -decoded message that Major Victor Zeller had recently transmitted to Rome. Darius read:

ALLIED OPERATIONAL GROUPS TO EMBARK ON A SERIES OF GADFLY ATTACKS ON CORSICA. MAJOR AMPHIBIOUS LANDINGS ON ALL COASTS WILL COMPEL US TO GARRISON THE ENTIRE COASTLINE. WILL KEEP YOU ADVISED OF DEVELOPMENTS. WE HAVE A FRIEND IN THEIR MIDST. JAGUAR.

Darius reread the message. So they had a spy in their midst. The disinformation fed to countless operational groups had gotten through to the Italian intelligence chief stationed at Bastia. *Good.* Darius studied the name again. *Zeller . . . Zeller . . . Zeller!* This stranger, Amadeo Zeller, had gnawed at the core of his existence like a pox for as long as he could remember. Now this *Victor Zeller!* He mouthed the name as an Indian meditator mouths mantras. *Victor Zeller . . . Victor Zeller.* Was there a connection?

Dammit! It wasn't enough that he'd fought a war not of his own doing: Was he now forced to plot a vendetta against a man he had never met? Against whom he had no personal grievance, because of the suggestions of hatred instilled in him twenty years ago by Vivaldi? The name Zeller had become his nemesis. An inexplicable loathing coursed through him.

He must know more about Zeller! He must! Surely Cain and Abel had a more comprehensive report on the Italian officer. At this moment, Darius decided to build up some sort of cautious rapport between himself and the Americans. They had access to more information than he did and he must avail himself of it. *Be willing to sup with the devil for the good of the cause, but at all times be circumspect,* he told himself.

He left his room, searched the compound for Dutch O'Reilly. He found him near the fire, drinking coffee with the other Mozarabe. He called Dutch aside, and they moved to the edge of the activity. They spoke quietly. Dutch had proved himself loyal and resourceful, and his dossier proved he'd be the right man to execute a tidy bit of business. As he listened, his freckled features cracked with amusement. He grinned wildly, slapped his thighs. "Gotcha, Major. Consider it done."

An hour later, Darius burned the OSS files on the Mozarabe.

Strangely enough, neither Cain nor Abel ever mentioned the missing dossiers.

Chapter Three

With prospects of another disastrous winter on the Eastern front, the atmosphere of the Wolfsschanze in Berlin was glum. The Führer had issued orders to completely ignore the holiday season. There were to be no Christmas trees, not a single candle in occupied Europe to celebrate the festival of love and peace. The Wehrmacht had suffered 1,686,000 casualties in the past year. What could they celebrate?

In Paris certain German officers ignored the holiday blackout order out of sheer obstinacy. So on New Year's Eve the Presidential Palace was glitteringly lit with *verboten* festivities. The past year, one of grueling fighting on widespread battlefronts, had shaken the foundation of the Third Reich, and in Paris the entire German diplomatic corps gathered to celebrate a New Year that might be their last. A diva sang opera in a small salon. In another, couples danced to melancholy waltzes.

In the main salon, the German Ambassador bowed decorously to the Italian Ambassador. *"Fröhliche Wunsche zum Jahreswechsel,"* he said, and the Italian returned both the bow

54

and good wishes, *"Buon capo d'anno per tutti."* Ambassador von Ruck then apologized, "If Your Excellency will excuse me, I've suddenly acquired a severe headache."

"I too have a headache, my friend. Perhaps from standing too long," Ambassador Artemiso told the portly man in his fifties, dabbing at the beads of sweat on his forehead.

"From listening too much," the German insisted. "Wagner sickens me."

"Herr von Ruck, I hope your country appreciates you. You are the only unpredictable German I have ever met. Save for Major Hesse."

"I'll consider that a compliment, Ambassador. Now, if you'll excuse me, I see someone far more lovely than you across the room. You understand, I'm sure."

The Italian followed the German's line of vision to a well-known but mysterious woman of spectacular beauty seated at a table by herself. Before he could respond, von Ruck was across the room, approaching the glittering butterfly.

"I cannot recall when I've seen a lady as beautiful as you, Madame—uh—"

"Countess. Countess von Schönlar."

"—nor have I seen anyone eat as heartily as you."

The svelte blond handed a servant an empty plate. "A little more of the *boeuf bourguignonne, s'il vous plaît.*"

"No one admires French cuisine more than I, Countess. Still, the prospect of actually dining from a buffet at a diplomatic reception, New Year's or not . . ." He grimaced effectively.

"The number of dinners I eat these days depends upon the diplomatic receptions to which I am fortunate enough to be invited. A collaborator gets few privileges, Ambassador."

"Come, come. A woman as beautiful as you?" He held a champagne bottle in midair. "Champagne, Countess?"

"Yes, yes, thank you. You were saying, *monsieur*?"

"A woman with your poise, background, and nobility should not lack for proper companions. Were you not married to some Austrian count?" She nodded. "Then why did you leave Vienna?"

"Simple logic, Ambassador. Bombs were falling. I felt in the way."

"But why come to Paris? You and your late husband had friends in London according to your—"

"—dossier. Don't hesitate speaking that awful word. I know one exists on me and that I am followed continuously, but I assure you it's always for the wrong reasons. You asked about London. I don't consider being bombed in London any cozier than being bombed in Austria."

"Why didn't you return to Vienna? The Germans are friendly with—"

"I have no courage to live as chattel."

"We would have protected you."

"The way you protect my estates in Austria? Tell me, who has them now?"

"Who has them now?" he pondered. "Field Marshal Himmler, I believe."

"Ahh. At last it's in the open. He is a man in whom I can find no redeeming features. There is another, actually two other German officers for whom I lack feeling. In my world, Ambassador, a woman can usually choose her companions."

Von Ruck, the eternal diplomat, stiffened. *"Bon appétit, Countess."*

"You find my conversation a bit too sticky to remain?" she said, then added with a note of pleading, "Herr von Ruck, do not desert me. I need money."

"These must be strange times for you. Dispossessed. Abandoned. In a strange land without your usual retinue of servants."

"Please don't be diplomatic. You can help me—truly."

"Nothing would please me more, my dear." He sat at her table, displaying prodigious patience.

"I only want back what belongs to me and to my family."

"Unfortunately, *madame,* there is a war."

"After the war, then."

"I can give you every assurance—"

"But in the meantime, I starve. Listen, I can be of great service to you—to Germany. If I prove my worth now, then after the war it will be easier for me, no?"

"Just how will you go about proving your worth to the Third Reich?"

"Provide me with the means to live in style again. I promise it will be worth your while. Do you know what a fount of knowledge a clever hostess can be?''

''Countess, how would you go about proving your worth to us? Surely you do not suggest what popped into my mind.'' He feigned astonishment. ''You want the German government to set you up as a spy?''

''I am suggesting how capable I am of earning my keep.''

''No. It's a sordid, unrewarding business.''

''Sordid perhaps, but not unrewarding.''

''We are speaking of money, correct?''

''Can you think of any other terms as enticing as money?''

''Sorry, it's quite impossible.''

''What else is left for me to do then?'' Tears welled up in her eyes.

''Call on your friends.''

''Friends? Hah! Like rats they have deserted a sinking ship. Frankly, those who want me cannot afford me.''

The tête-à-tête was interrupted by a nattily uniformed German attaché, Fritz Schmidt. ''Herr Ambassador, it's my duty to inform you we are running late.'' He turned and slipped back into the crowd.

''We have seldom spoken, Ambassador,'' the Countess continued. ''We've seen each other a number of times, but you've always kept your distance until tonight. Do you see in me something that might prove valuable to your government?''

Von Ruck, a dignified man in his fifties, feasted on the blond aristocratic beauty with obvious desire. His ice-blue eyes twinkled at her daring. But he was a sensible diplomat who had endured because he played no foolish games and didn't subscribe to the current *coûte que coûte* attitude afflicting most German officers. He sighed in mock despair, clicked his heels, and kissed her outthrust hand. ''If only I were a younger man, my dear. *Au revoir.* Happy New Year.'' He moved to the edge of the throngs of dancing, bejeweled women and ambassadorial diplomats.

The German attaché, Fritz Schmidt, stood nearby, staring at the Countess. She seemed familiar to this ferret. Where had he known her? Catching Schmidt's studied scrutiny and hazy effort at recognition, the fraudulent Countess, Lomay St. Germaine, returned the stare with enough seductive indignation to bring color to his cheeks. ''Do not look at me as if you had any income besides your salary. You cannot afford my price tag," she quipped icily, praying he didn't recognize her.

Schmidt, red-faced and flustered, clicked his heels, saluted, and departed, leaving in his wake a momentarily shaken woman.

Outside in the limousine carrying Ambassador von Ruck to the German Embassy, Fritz Schmidt sat down in the jump chair facing his superior.

"Excellency . . ." Something nagged at him.

"Yes, Schmidt."

"About the Countess—"

"What about her?"

"I have reason to believe she is in dire straits."

"You too, Schmidt? Have you become a fan of hers?"

"*Nein*, Herr Ambassador. It merely occurs to me that she might prove a tremendous asset to the Third Reich."

"No. Dismiss the thought from your mind."

"She has access to many sources who could lead us to the troublemakers here in Paris."

"Definitely not, Schmidt."

"But, Excellency, I have the distinct feeling she is not—"

"Good night, Schmidt! I believe this is your stop."

Schmidt looked out the window into the darkness. "Good night, Excellency." He got out and stood before his flat on the Rue Chombard near German headquarters. As he watched the limousine pull away from the curb, he completed his sentence. "She is not the person she says she is."

Turning into the entrance to his flat, Schmidt stopped, struck by the sound of screeching brakes. He glanced up, saw the Ambassador's limousine shove into reverse and speed back to where he stood in the wash of a dimly lit streetlight. The Ambassador rolled down the rear window. "*Untersturmführer*, I neglected to give you your transfer papers." He thrust a parcel through the open window. "You have been transferred back to the RASCHUPT under the aegis of your former commander at intelligence headquarters. I understand Sturmbannführer Hans Hesse has recuperated brilliantly. Give him my regards. Happy New Year, Schmidt."

"*Danke*, Herr Ambassador. Happy New Year to you also," Schmidt mouthed the words, crestfallen at the news. He dropped his salute as the car pulled forward, speeding off into the night. He stared at the packet in his hands. Drizzle began to come down. Still he stood rigid, motionless.

Hans Hesse! The last man in the world he wanted to serve under was Sturmbannführer Hans Hesse. Immobilized, he felt the former world of terror rain down on him. Memories of Sidi bel Abbes, El Bayadh, and the Arab chieftain Abou Ahkmed Hassan froze him to the spot. Wasn't four years spent in turbulent discomfort with a man he loathed enough punishment? He deserved better than reassignment to the legendary ball-breaking bastard whose frightening sadism had atrophied Schmidt's *joie de vivre.*

Schmidt hadn't sense enough to come in out of the rain this night. He walked zombielike through the wet, deserted streets. He wasn't certain where he was until the headlights of a sedan careening around the corner blinded him. Schmidt retreated behind a hedge at the sight of the swastika emblazoned on the door. The auto stopped before a two-story brick walk-up. A tall, slender German officer got out and helped a stunning woman from the rear seat. They ran together to the shelter of an awning, laughing, seemingly giddy from the effects of champagne.

Fritz froze. He recognized the Countess Von Schönlar.

The driver saluted and drove off, and Schmidt, lingering in the deluge, wiped his eyes, desperate to catch a glimpse of the officer's face. In the dull wash of a door lamp, he saw the amorous couple embrace and kiss lingeringly before entering the building lobby. They disappeared inside. Schmidt hurriedly removed a pen from his pocket and, using the flip side of the packet containing his new orders, scribbled the address and the license plate number of the Mercedes.

"So soon comes a replacement to relieve me on this miserable night?" A gruff voice from behind him muttered, "*Heil Hitler.*"

Schmidt spun around, his face blanching. The *Gestapo!* "*Heil* Hitler. I suppose you wish to see identification? Who is your assignment—the officer or the woman?" Schmidt asked officiously as the agent inspected his identification. He calmed the rising excitement, eyes lit with exultation. Was this his lucky night? If he found some means of elevating himself to a position of trust, he could ignore Hesse's transfer request, couldn't he?

"The officer. SS Adjutant Karl Schroeder," snapped the older agent. "The woman is an Austrian refugee in need of money, Schmidt. Schroeder's pay is not commensurate with the company he keeps, so we watch him most carefully. *Gute Nacht.* Make your report to Colonel Staffenberg. He will arrive at dawn with your replacement. *Heil* Hitler."

The SS lookout was off before Schmidt *Sieg heil*ed back. He quickly took the other man's position inside a darkened domed archway across the street. He was soaking wet, shivering in the cold, but he felt no discomfort, only the joy of success in refusing to cow to Hesse's orders.

Across the street, lights illumined two windows on the second floor. He saw the Countess move to the window, pull down the window shade, and seductively begin to undress. Then the officer appeared in silhouette. He removed his jacket, flung off his tie and shirt, and gathered the woman into his arms. Schmidt felt a hot erection bulging in his trousers. He tugged up the collar of his wet overcoat, blew his hands to warm them, and moved from one foot to the other to comfort the hardening at his groin. He ached for the hot cunt awaiting him at his warm, comfortable flat.

Gottverdammen! What was he thinking? He wasn't dressed for surveillance on so miserable a night. Why in damnation had he overstepped his position? He could be home in his warm, dry, cozy apartment engaged in *der Geschlechtsverkehr* with his Parisian *Fräulein.* He indulged momentarily in fantasies involving the luscious cocotte.

A black sedan wheeled down the street, turned around, and retraced its path, slowing down as it approached Schmidt. A flashlight fanned on him. Schmidt held his hands before his eyes.

"Just checking, Gruber. Wait! You aren't Gruber. Who are you? Come here at once," a faceless voice commanded authoritatively.

Schmidt ventured into the rain at the curb. He saluted. "*Heil* Hitler. Schmidt here. Untersturmführer Schmidt. Gruber was taken off the assignment earlier."

"I see the Countess has company, eh, Schmidt? It's two in the morning. Who is it? Schroeder again? Lucky bastard, eh?" He made an obscene gesture, grinning suggestively. "Always when it's Schroeder, it becomes an overnight affair."

"Overnight?" Schmidt shivered. His feet were numb in the winter frost. "When does my duty finish?"

"At eight in the morning. Just in time for hot coffee, *ja?*"

Schmidt stood watching in dismay as the sedan rolled down the street. The old Hans Hesse assignment looked better with each passing moment. He remembered halfheartedly that he'd failed to check the passenger's I.D. He retreated to the archway and lit a cigarette, envisioning the warmth of a jigger of schnapps. He leaned against the concrete abutment, mourning his current situation. If he hadn't shown his I.D. to Gruber or given his name to the last SS weasel, he'd leave and let the Countess fornicate in peace.

Schmidt, Dummkopf! *When will you learn to mind your own business?*

Inside the Countess's flat, an orchestrated scenario had played out hours ago, one quite different from the one Schmidt had imagined. Lomay St. Germaine had quickly disrobed, donned a pair of dark trousers and a heavy sweater. Pulling off her blond wig, she carefully stashed it in a hat box and buried it under the clutter of a jam-packed closet while her companion, actually a Resistance fighter, removed his Nazi uniform and dressed in dark workman's clothing. Together they left the flat through an escape hatch to the roof, scampered over tiles to an adjoining building, and shinned down a drainpipe, landing just a block away from where Schmidt was indulging in sexual fantasies.

Peering around in the rainy darkness, Lomay unhooked a flashlight from her belt, clicked it on and off three times, waited, then repeated the signal. A dark sedan appeared from darkness, its lights off. It was the same auto that had earlier stopped near Schmidt's surveillance position, and it was conveying the same man that had demanded to see Schmidt's I.D.

Lomay and Gerard boarded. The car lurched away from the curb, its wheels spinning in the slippery wet street now beginning to be covered with an icy veil. The driver maintained a turtle speed until they reached the city limits. They could take no chances. Everything depended on them.

Twenty minutes later, Lomay boarded a mobile radio transmitting truck with her companions. Behind them, the sky burst with brilliant white fire. A series of thunderous explosions followed one after another. A valuable German ammunition dump and costly stores of new weapons were being obliterated by Resistance fighters. The men with her cheered. Lomay activated a button on a radio console. A recording of "The Marseillaise" began to play. She spoke into a microphone, her voice ringing out loud and clear:

"*Mes chers amis,* this is Zahara, the Voice of Freedom reaching you. I come into your homes, your hearts and beg you not to despair. Tonight, less than two minutes ago, we weakened the German defenses. The munitions factory at Porte D'Auteuil was just blown up! *Oui, mes amis, oui!* We approach victory. Soon we shall begin an earth-shattering offensive. Trust in God and in the Resistance!"

Fritz Schmidt rued the moment he decided to play cloak and dagger. It was ten minutes to seven. Another blasted hour before relief would come. His feet were frozen, his testicles had turned to ice, and he thought his blood would never thaw. But all this changed in a matter of moments as he heard the agonizing wail of sirens, the earsplitting whistles, and the slamming of car doors as the Gestapo poured out of cars and descended on the cul-de-sac like swarms of hungry locusts. Chaos erupted before his very eyes. Right here in this quiet neighborhood, where earlier he had opted to chase a beguiling skirt in exchange for possible promotion in rank and sorely needed respect from his peers, Fritz Schmidt's bubble burst. He stood at the center of a death squad of storm troopers, bayonets at the ready and pointed at him.

He was so astonished he couldn't speak. He stood spread-eagled with his hands up against a building. His identification papers, yanked savagely from his pockets, were scrutinized in the early dawn light by a half dozen red-faced, uniformed men. He was handcuffed, shoved into a military car, and driven to Gestapo headquarters. All his papers, including his transfer to the Raschupt, were scrupulously inspected and tested for forgery.

Four hours later, Major Hans Hesse arrived on the scene.

Schmidt, terrified after the harrowing experience, guzzled welcome schnapps from Hesse's flask. His papers and personal effects were returned along with the slow return of his dignity. Hesse drove him home to change into fresh, dry clothing.

An hour later they sat at lunch in a nearby café, discussing the events of the previous night. "*Ja, ja*, Major, perhaps I acted *cafard*. But I tell you she looked familiar to me, so I followed the Countess. I did not expect a holocaust to descend on me." He munched biscuits and gulped hot coffee, peeking periodically at Hesse's useless left hand. He didn't enjoy the other's cross-examination of either his motives or his actions, but Hesse had bailed him out of a tight spot. He tugged at his thick overcoat, still unable to shake the chill from his body. "Thank you, Major, for permitting me to change into dry clothing. The Gestapo would hear nothing of discomfort! You'd think I was one of those lousy Resistance gutter rats, *ja?*"

"Schmidt, tell me more about the woman. You may have stumbled on something important. The Gestapo has kept her under surveillance, this Austrian Countess, for nearly a year. Needless to say, she is not the Countess von Schönlar, nor is she Austrian. I am anxious to hear what made you suspicious of the impostor?"

Schmidt reluctantly imparted portions of the conversation he'd overheard between Ambassador von Ruck and the Countess. "The face was familiar, even the voice. But something disguised the familiar to distort the images in my mind. She requested that the Ambassador help her in her plight—to use her as a spy."

Hesse's blue eyes narrowed to slits. "*Ja*, Schmidt? And the Ambassador's reply?"

"He refused her outright. Later when I suggested that she might be important to the Fatherland, he still refused."

"Imagine," Hesse snapped acerbically, "locked inside your head is perhaps the most important secret in the history of the Third Reich—*and you cannot remember.*" He wouldn't let up on poor Fritz. "Something drew you to the stakeout—what? You must remember, Schmidt. You will remember if I have to wring your odious, incompetent neck!"

Oh, how Schmidt loathed Hans Hesse!

From the narrow corridors of a mind tutored in vassalage, the vesper bells of survival clanged. A sudden eruption of resignation flowed through Schmidt, the need for serf to pay homage to the overlord.

"I'll try, Major. I'll try very hard. It was stupid of me not to pay closer attention to the woman. Why is she so important?

Did you interrogate the officer? He was German. I saw the uniform.''

"Uniform? *Uniform?* Dummkopf! Did you check his credentials?"

"Credentials? Gruber knew him. Ask Gruber. Yes, yes, ask Gruber. He identified the woman's lover as SS Adjutant Karl Schroeder." He lit up, expecting praise for his well-honed memory. Instead, he got insults.

"*Dummkopf!* Schroeder was a fictitious name! Gruber was a fictitious name. I wish you were fictitious, Schmidt! Don't you understand? You were had! You stumbled on an important project and you shamed us all. Instead of honoring the Raschupt, you . . . you . . . Any new untried recruit would have fared better. Think with your head instead of *der Hoden*! Always playing with yourself instead of concentrating on business! You learned nothing in North Africa, *ja?*''

"Who was the woman?" he asked feebly.

"Zahara, *Dummkopf*! The most wanted criminal on the Gestapo's list of enemies of the Third Reich! What in the woman struck a familiar chord, Schmidt?" Hesse asked, his disarming voice tinged with cunning.

Suddenly Schmidt's face lit up like a Christmas tree. "Perhaps I do have something for you, Major." He fished through his jacket pocket for the envelope containing his transfer to the Raschupt and, puffed up with pride, handed it to Hesse without examining it. "There, it's written clearly. I was such a *Dummkopf*. Look, under the Countess's address. The license number of the car in which this fictitious Karl Schroeder arrived at her apartment. Perhaps if we check the number through our bureau . . ." He drained the coffee dregs, placed the cup down, and patted his belly, contented. He studied Hesse's momentary consternation. "Well, what is it, Major?"

Hesse turned the envelope over and over, scanning every inch of it. He opened it, looked inside. "I see nothing! Did you write with invisible ink? See—a few smears here and there, otherwise nothing."

Schmidt tore the envelope from his hands. He stared, dumbstruck. The rain had erased all traces of his scribblings, leaving only a few smudges.

"*Dummkopf!*" Hesse's condemnatory voice seared through him. "You could have memorized it if you hadn't been playing with *der Hoden*!"

Chapter Four

*He whose generals are able and not interfered with by
the sovereigns will be victorious.*

—Sun Tzu

CORSICA, THE CITADEL

At a quarter to midnight, an unmarked British bomber skirted the
cumulonimbus clouds over Porto, descended to six thousand
feet, and picked up the ribbon of lights strategically placed in Les
Calanches. The pilot slowed the aircraft to parachuting speed,
dropped his landing gear and bomb doors. One hundred and fifty
well-seasoned dogs of war, screened, trained, and evaluated by
British MI-6, tumbled into the sky and landed within ten miles of
the citadel grounds. They were met by a cortege of Mozarabe
and driven back to the citadel to meet with the OWC commanders. The Mozarabe stared with provincial candor at these foreigners with strange uniforms and blackened faces entering their
domicile. Most had never seen paratroopers. Imagine jumping
from a plane! Now, that was some brand of courage.

Assigned to barracks, issued camouflaged combat fatigues
and weaponry, the men fell to vigorous commando training under the tough, strict standards of the Mozarabe. Tested, interrogated, pushed beyond human endurance, each man was
advanced in the stages of training according to his physical and
mental capacity. Each man who passed the stringent require-

ments was absorbed directly into the Mozarabe to practice the most lethal warring tactics. Those failing to qualify gravitated to the less strenuous ranks of the Resistance.

Under the very noses of 150,000 Axis troops occupying Corsica, a ground swell of strength was forming into a powerful force to be reckoned with.

With the solidarity and weight of a growing commando battalion behind him, Darius scrupulously studied the island of Corsica until he knew every possible defense. From the Mozarabe's hidden lookout positions, they peered at their enemies, meticulously studying their movements, locating ammo dumps and weapons strongholds, counting lorries transporting field equipment. Nightly, information was relayed to their chiefs at the citadel. The Resistance fighters, dressed as Corsican laborers, infiltrated and robbed enemy strongholds through various bits of chicanery so the thefts sometimes went undetected for as long as two weeks.

As Darius observed the enemy, it occurred to him that the Italians and Germans gave no indication they either knew or suspected the island had been infiltrated by the enemy. This obvious complacency disturbed Darius no end. He knew the Germans too well. Could he think any less of them in Corsica than he had in North Africa? No, but he had no explanation for their passive attitude.

At the citadel he found Cain and Abel griping over the difficulty of obtaining black market gasoline through the Corsicans. "They are totally intractable jackasses!" Lincoln raved. "Don't they understand there's a war going on? Perhaps you, Major Djebel, will do better than me."

"What do you expect after only two weeks?" Darius replied. "Four weeks from now it will be different. These are rough, tough, self-centered, cynical men who make no apologies for themselves. Brother has fought brother in decades of vendetta. Some would sell their neighbors to put food on the table. Their loyalty is to themselves and they trust no one. Justice doesn't exist for the Corsicans; that's why they take to the *maquis* and become criminals. Now here are strangers on their island giving them orders. They take no orders from the government of France. You expect them to grovel at your feet as liberators?

These are xenophobic people, clansmen who perpetuate themselves within the confines of their own people. They don't even trust the French Resistance. My men will requisition whatever you need. Speak with Pascal, the Corsican. Corsicans will at least listen to—if not trust—a Corsican. What is it you need? Ten drums of gasoline?''

Lincoln nodded glumly.

Darius left the map room and returned in ten minutes. "Cain, Abel, come with me."

Outside as the sun set against an amethyst sky, they saw a broken-down, rusted lorry huffing toward them. It sputtered to an exhausted stop before them. When the dust cleared, the two American OSS agents stood in open-mouthed amazement. The flatbed lorry contained sixteen gasoline drums.

"But where? How did you come by these?" Lincoln asked Pascal.

"Where else? We stole them from the Italians, who stole them from the Vichy French, who had confiscated them from the Germans!"

"Corsican justice prevails," Darius laughed.

In his Paris office, *Sturmbannführer* Hans Hesse glimpsed the flashing red light on a panel on his desk. He tuned the radio dial into the proper frequency with his right hand. The useless, lifeless left hand, a gloved prosthesis, lay inert on his lap. Although he had physically recuperated from the El Bayadh atrocity done him by Abou Ahkmed Hassan's forces in the North African campaign, he wallowed always in the emotional anguish caused by his blatant imperfection. The memory of his folly ate at him like an irrevocable penance, a daily reminder that he sought revenge. If it took him the rest of his life, he'd repay those responsible. He was determined to see Hassan burn at the stake, and with him that infuriating Corsican Bonifacio whom he detested with equal vitriol. If Darius hadn't saved Prince Ben-Kassir . . .

Briefly, as he glanced at his watch, his snarl lost its intensity. Three more minutes. He poured himself a stiff bracer of choice French cognac, reflecting on the intelligence reports made available to him during his convalescence. Delilah's Dream, led by that *Gottverdammen* Corsican Darius Bonifacio, had spirited away Prince Ben-Kassir's body from the mass carnage at El Bayadh. If Kassir hadn't interfered, Hassan's savage counterattack would not have occurred. It had been the noble Prince Kassir who had boosted Bonifacio's stellar rise in the ranks!

There—the beginning of the radio interception! A scratchy rendition of "The Marseillaise"! Hesse listened intently, his inert reptilian eyes fixed on some inner vision awakened by the disturbingly familiar voice. His features jerked; sweat beaded his brow. He cocked his head to listen.

"Fellow Frenchmen, this is Zahara, the Voice of Freedom. The mobilization of the French workers for the Nazi labor camps does not abate. We repudiate this press-ganging. For the glory of Free France, the campaign of terror against our enemies will be stepped up. We shall unite in the *maquis*! The Germans have lost Barbarossa! News from the Russian front brings joy to the hearts of Free Frenchmen! Do not despair. We shall once again be free. This is Zahara, your Voice of Freedom. *Vive la France!*"

Hesse snapped off the radio, eyes blazing. Repetitious gibberish! Underground broadcasts! This romanticized nonsense grated on his nerves. The Resistance! Ugh! But what appalled Hesse most of all were the repeated failures of his men and the Gestapo's to locate, hit, and destroy these ghostlike mobile units.

Hesse paced the elegant offices of the Presidential Palace recently appropriated for the Raschupt and Gestapo headquarters. He mentally reviewed the intensive efforts that had been made against their formidable foe, the Resistance. Although clever spies had infiltrated the underground, still the enigmatic Zahara remained elusive, unidentified. For a year, nothing! Not a shred of evidence. Then on New Year's Eve, his adjutant had the damned woman in his sights and let her slip through his fingers. Worse, he could give no description that fit any recognizable image. Yet the feeling persisted. They both knew Zahara! The "Voice of Freedom" was becoming a razor-sharp thorn in Hesse's side!

Zahara's voice nagged at him, haunted his every waking moment. In his mind he connected the voice to the body of a sensuous, highly desirable woman—or was that wishful thinking? Never mind. One day it would all come together, and when it did . . .

For nearly two years, the Germans had treated Paris like a woman of fine breeding, gently, caressingly, until those proliferating underground sewer rats began their pestilent infestation. Soldiers, Wehrmacht officers, and pro-German Frenchmen were threatened and made the victims of disgraceful acts. *Sabotage*, a new word coined when underground moles jammed the wheels of industry with their wooden sabots, spread like wildfire. They jammed the railroad systems, factories, and industrial complexes confiscated by the Germans. Destruction was hurled against the Germans, necessitating reprisals. All at once thousands upon thousands of communists, Jews, and other antagonistic citizens were seized and systematically shot at a ratio of twenty to each German death. The Vichy government began to organize special courts to deal with hostile elements. Still the underground attacks persisted.

Now as if this weren't enough, another contentious enemy must be dealt with—America! The recent American entry into the war had escalated the Resistance's atrocities. Under orders from his superiors to annihilate and lay the Resistance forces to waste, Hesse had dedicated himself toward these ends with fervor. Every day he came closer to solving the mystery of the elusive Zahara! Ever since German intelligence had become aware of the massive offensive operations taking shape, Hesse had burned with the secret dream of capturing the infamous Zahara. Any day he had expected the coveted victory. And that *Dummkopf* Schmidt had had her this far from his grasp! *Son of a bitch!*

In the week's time that had elapsed since the incident, he'd interrogated Ambassador von Ruck and a hundred others. All gave the same description—blond, aristocratic, with Austrian papers. The same description could have fit a thousand émigrés!

There was a knock at the door. It was Adjutant Fritz Schmidt. He entered, stood at attention, not eager to disturb Hesse. Schmidt cleared his throat. "*Sturmbannführer*, Madame Belgique has arrived." Schmidt goose-stepped to the desk, placed a manila folder on it, and stood to one side, braced.

"Did you complete the dossier on her? Who is she, Schmidt?"

"We only know that she works at the Vichy Embassy as a translator."

"Well, send her in. We must not keep our guest waiting."

Schmidt clicked his heels together, nodded deferentially, and exited, returning in a moment with a slim brunette, wearing a well-tailored black suit. Her hair was wrapped in a black turban. Her eyes, a verdant blue, arrested him. As she breezed airily into the room, her perfume assaulted his senses.

"*Heil* Hitler, *madame*. Please be seated."

Schmidt, burning with curiosity, demonstrated noticeable reluctance as he closed the door. He hurried to his desk, set earphones into place over his head, snapped on a wire recorder, and listened, wondering who the devil this mysterious Madame Belgique was and what business brought her to Major Hesse's office.

Inside, Hesse was both overly solicitous and reticent. "Who are you, *madame*? How can I be of service to you? This persistence of yours this past month to meet with me has indeed aroused my curiosity. Please be brief. My time is valuable."

"No more than mine, Major," she replied in polished French. "Is it—uh—safe to speak freely?"

"Here? In the offices of the Reichsführer? You dare such impertinence?"

"One cannot be too careful, *Sturmbannführer*. I am bringing you the opportunity of a lifetime. You can be the envy of the Reichsführer himself, achieve your ambitions to swim about in *der Führer's* inner circle—the high command. But before I state my proposition, I must warn you not to breathe a word of our conversation to anyone. My life depends upon your discretion."

"*Your* life depends on *me* in any case."

"Uh—not exactly. You see, if it becomes necessary, I can claim diplomatic immunity."

"You can also disappear mysteriously at any given moment."

"Ah. We do not understand one another. Since you do not care to hear my proposition—"

"*Madame*, do not misunderstand me. The facts are—and I make no apology for my contention—women fail to comprehend the logistics of military matters. But speak up. I promise to make fair judgment."

"Very well. I put it to you, Major. Periodically, classified British and American documents come into my possession, military documents of the utmost value to Hitler and your government. I am prepared to sell them. My price—twenty-five thousand British pounds sterling.''

Hesse eyed her attentively, then burst into laughter. ''You come here with fancy tales, *madame,* and expect me to believe such rot. Who are you? What is it you want? Truly, you try my patience.''

''I am a spy. What else? I do not misrepresent myself.''

''Ah, then your profession is espionage?''

''Not exactly. However, I have endeavored ambitiously for several years in this regard.''

''To begin with, your fee is outrageous. No spy—no decent spy—is worth twenty-five thousand pounds, not for all the top-secret Allied plans in Europe.''

''I doubt that. However, no spy—*no decent spy*—has ever had in his or her possession what I have to sell you. Most spies are notoriously inept in business affairs. I am neither a sentimental patriot, frustrated liberal, nor the victim of blackmail. I am simply in the business of making money, since I've learned money is the only commodity that speaks a language of its own—power. Are you or are you not interested in what I have, or do you lack sound judgment in these matters? You, I am told, are the only German with whom to negotiate.''

''And you, I take it, consider that I lack sound judgment for refusing to bargain with an unidentified amateur for so-called secret documents for the excessive sums you request.''

''Not *so-called,* Major, but highly classified. These are most secret documents.''

''*Madame,* you continue to try my patience. Since I am besieged with pressing, serious matters, I'll have my adjutant show you to the door.'' He glanced at the name on the papers Schmidt had placed on the desk. ''Uh, it is *Madame* Belgique, *oui?*''

''The name is not important, but since it appears that I shall have to think for us both, I suggest you take the matter up with your superior, General Kaltenbruner. Surely you must get clearance from the RSHA in Berlin, *oui?* I had assumed when we spoke last week—when was it, December 27?—you were amenable to the joint venture.''

''In all fairness, *madame,* you give me little to go on. I must have much, much more information. Nothing you say is clear.

You speak of tangibles, yet I see none before me. What are these documents you boast of? What do they contain?''

''I hadn't thought to bring you samples,'' she replied acidly, her blue eyes sparkling. ''United States participation in the war has brought in fresh ideas, new schematics, and a diplomacy aimed at wooing the Vichy government. You can see the advantages in turning them against the Germans, no?''

''That's the broadest and most unfounded conjecture I've heard.''

''No. Not conjecture. I have compiled the minutes of their secret talks. On *film*, Major. But if not you, perhaps your General Kaltenbruner will find them informative.''

Hesse stiffened imperceptibly. He didn't trust this woman. The feeling persisted and nagged at him. Certainly he couldn't turn her loose to venture into some ambitious Gestapo colonel's office. What would it cost him to engage her in additional dialogue? ''What exactly do you have?''

''The latest timetable on Operation White Coral.''

''Operation White Coral? What the devil is that?''

''Forgive me. You would know it as *'Vesuvius.'* Plans to invade Corsica. The operation, recently renamed to create confusion, is purposely designed to thwart the German offensive. Corsica will serve your enemies as an operational base to prepare for the liberation of France. The plans will tell you when and where the operation will take place, and who's involved.''

''Go on.'' Hesse's eyes strayed to the sealed communiqué on his desk.

''Don't be greedy. You expect too much for twenty-five thousand pounds.''

''Who are you, *madame*? How do you come by this information? I need to see some credentials to assure my superiors you can deliver what you promise. Your papers are French, *ja?* You are a collaborator?''

''Major, neither my identity nor the names by which I procure the classified documents should concern you. Credentials, you say? My credentials shall be the photographs of the documents I sell to you. No more, no less. You think I'd risk losing my life coming here if I couldn't authenticate the documents?'' A lilting, taunting laugh escaped her lips. ''Destiny propels you toward your desire, Major. Don't let her disappear like a specter. Grab her before she eludes you; hold tightly to what she offers you. Now, if you don't mind I need no nosy adjutants listening to our conversation on recording devices. And *don't* have me followed. If you try to learn my identity before I am willing to impart it, you'll never see me again.''

"But I must identify you as someone."

"You'll think of a code name. Germans are thinkers, I'll give you that."

Hesse, now fully intrigued, said, "Let's see . . . Cassandra. No! Pythia. Yes, yes, Pythia. It's perfect."

"Pythia? Very well. Understand you'll get no games or conundrums from me—no cryptic messages, only clear, incontrovertible facts. However you interpret what I provide is your business. My interest is only in the money, *comprenez-vous?*" Pythia rose to leave.

"I shall speak with my superiors in Berlin. Call me in three days—at this time—and you'll have my answer."

"You keep your distance—I'll keep my promise." She nodded to his *Heil* Hitler and left the room.

Schmidt entered on her heels, saluted smartly, and stood at attention.

"Well, Schmidt, you heard. What do you think?"

"No doubt a trained foreign agent. Very special. A most unique career woman."

"French, of course?"

"*Nein.* A British-bred aristocrat, if I ever saw one. Arrogant, cynical, damnably sure of herself."

"British, eh? Not French? Strange, I detected an American accent in her French." He turned his attention to the communique in Schmidt's hand.

"It's sealed, *Kommandant.* The courier delivered it by diplomatic pouch labeled urgent."

"Go, Schmidt. Bring me a comprehensive file on this Madame Belgique immediately. And Schmidt, pray it doesn't take as long as it has to identify Zahara!"

Schmidt, in hasty departure, lurched slightly to the side as if to blunt the acerbic innuendo. Grimacing at the severity of his taunter, he wisely remained mute and closed the door behind him.

Hesse, back at the window overlooking the guards in the courtyard, caught sight of the woman he'd recently christened Pythia boarding a taxi. Instantly two German agents converged past the duty guards and boarded an unmarked auto in hot pursuit. Satisfied, he returned to the desk, poured a glass of Médoc, a very light, dry wine, and sipped it, his eyes scanning the communiqué. *What is it this time? The capture or defeat of Stalingrad?*

Hesse, with other officers in the Wehrmacht high command, had opposed Operation Barbarossa at a time when it seemed the war with Britain was won. Why Hitler had halted the Battle of Britain then massed his entire armor and air strength against Russia, would forever remain an enigma. On Christmas Eve, Tatsinskaya Airfield was taken by the Sixth and Seventh Panzer Divisions amid an orgy of atrocities. In Hesse's mind, this inevitably marked the beginning of the end. Stalingrad was undeniably becoming Germany's Waterloo. And Hitler seemed unable to discern the similarity.

Hesse sipped his wine. He placed a gold swastika paperweight on the communiqué to secure it and with his right hand slit open the waxed seal. It was from SS Colonel Eugen Dollman. *What orders are these?* He read with indignation: "Prepare departure for Corsica in two weeks. Vesuvius scrapped. Operation White Coral functional!"

Corsica? Operation White Coral? Was it possible? He pushed the intercom buzzer, his mouth twisted with scorn. "Schmidt! The minute our men return from tracking the woman, I want a full and complete report!" Before Schmidt had time to *jawohl*, Hesse snapped off the button. On his feet again, he paced furiously, pondering the orders.

Corsica! Ugh! A savage land away from civilized Paris! What madness was this? What exactly did Pythia know that he didn't know, and who was her source? Was her arrival coincidental to the arrival of the Berlin communiqué? *She tried to reach you long ago, Dummkopf! And you, you imbecile, resisted her! You could have had the drop on Berlin!*

Matters of a material nature crept into Hesse's thoughts. He wondered how the hell he would part with his new Paris flat— the costly furbishings, exquisite vintage wines, the gourmet foods. Recently he'd confiscated, in a most covert manner, the entire Rothstein art collection, which was worth a king's ransom. He'd stashed it away in a safe house outside of Compiègne, awaiting war's end. *Gottverdammen!* It was damned inconvenient to leave Paris!

Hesse, back at the window looking down on the beautifully landscaped boulevard, was suddenly jarred to attention by the loud, wailing sounds of approaching sirens. The courtyard filled with German armored cars blocking all the exits and entries of the war offices and palace. Swarms of Gestapo agents poured from their cars, rushed the building and emerged within moments with a manacled intelligence chief, Gruppenführer Maxim Wolfe. The uniformed man was shoved into a car and whisked away, sirens bleating like oxen felled under hammers.

Hesse sprinted to his desk, pushed the intercom key. "Fritz!" he yelled, "*Kommen! Kommen!*"

Schmidt rushed in, eyes flaring. He saluted and clicked his heels. "*Jawohl*, Major." He avoided eye contact.

"Don't play *Dummkopf* with me. What is happening?"

"The *Gruppenführer* has been labeled a traitor. Embezzlement, expropriation of wealth belonging to the Third Reich. The Gestapo planted a spy in his midst. The adjutant—" He stopped.

Schmidt had answered the question Hesse had refrained from asking. He stared hard at the wooden soldier braced before him, fearing the worst. They'd been together at Sidi, through the worst of El Bayadh and North Africa. Schmidt had become his ears and eyes. Still, could he trust the weasel? What of this business about the fake Countess, Zahara? Hesse turned from him. Schmidt was a dolt, but a loyal dolt. Thus far he had no hard facts by which to condemn the man. Yet something about him didn't inspire confidence. He poured a glass of wine, handed it to Schmidt.

"Drink, Schmidt. We have a lot of work ahead of us. First, compile a dossier on Madame Belgique. Let me add that it must be more comprehensive than the flimsy dossier we have on Zahara, *verstehen?* Drink up, drink up, Schmidt. Ah, yes, the woman will call again. She will use the code name 'Pythia.' Put her through to me the instant she calls."

"*Ja, ja,* Major. I heard. The recorder. It is on wire."

"You heard," he mimicked acidly, then speaking less to intimidate, added, "Of course you recorded our conversation. Excellent, Schmidt. Good thinking."

Three days later Pythia called. A meeting was arranged at 3 Rue Royale at Maxim's, the international café. A private dining room awaited Pythia. Hesse was already seated, sipping an aperitif, a frothy concoction of Pernod, crème de menthe, and egg whites. Pythia, dressed in the identical black garb worn at their first rendezvous, sat opposite him at the round table decorated with a bowl of fresh flowers. An open money pouch was clearly displayed at Hesse's elbow. Pythia stared at it calculatingly.

"It's all there? Twenty-five thousand pounds sterling?"

"Count it if you don't trust me. But first, the film."

As soon as I count the money." She sat down, eyes peering about the small salon.

"Is it developed?"

"Yes. I wanted to make certain I delivered what I promised." She deftly counted the bills. Satisfied, she reached into her bag and turned over the packet of developed films. Hesse opened the pack, removed the contents, and sorted through the film, his eyes scanning the printed matter. He read aloud: "Operation White Coral . . . joint Allied venture . . . scope of operation—" He stopped abruptly, eyes sparkling.

"Well, do you find them interesting, Major?"

"Didn't you, Pythia?"

"I assure you my interest was purely to ascertain their validity. I read little beyond the classified-data heading. Do you find them to your satisfaction?"

"My satisfaction has little to do with it. They are meaningful only if they are genuine. And if they are genuine, my government has authorized me to make further arrangements with you. Should certain, uh, other classified documents come your way—"

"Are they willing to pay my price?"

"You ask a lot of money."

"I deliver valuable information that can determine the victors of this war. My dear Major, I loathe haggling. My price is reasonable. You'll pay it. Truth is invaluable. And you'll get it from me."

"Pythia, it is highly irregular to have an agent with so dubious a background working for us. It is essential for us to know more about you." Hesse's deference was calculated. He was waiting for a break, some hesitation, some giveaway word or gesture. But there was nothing.

"*Mein Herr*, Major Hesse, in a game of cat and mouse, the

cat's main objective is to let the mouse believe she'll survive. If that is removed, you frighten the mouse and she becomes of no further use to you. Understand this: it is essential only that you know the goods I deliver are authentic. Nothing more, nothing less. *D'accord?* Also please understand that I do not work for you. I am my own free agent. If you want, I can deliver more film in a week.''

"You may have to deal with another officer. I'm being reassigned."

"No! None other. Only you. Or it ends here and now."

"Very well, in a week. I can't promise my presence beyond that time. If I assure you of another officer's integrity—''

"No, Major! Only you. Understand?"

"No. I do not understand. You want money, we can provide it. Why is it necessary to deal only with me?"

"Because I trust you. No one else. Just you. Major, your integrity and honesty is legend among the French.''

She was perfect! Too perfect. She was the epitome of professionalism. But anxious to peruse and familiarize himself with Operation White Coral, he tucked aside his impressions and suspicions in order to avoid further confrontation. "Very well, a week then. We shall cross one bridge at a time, *madame.*''

An hour after Pythia's departure, Hesse, now feeling more amenable to the Corsican assignment, summoned Schmidt. Pythia's assessment was perceptive; through Operation White Coral he envisioned the fulfillment of his dreams.

"Compile all dossiers on Major Darius Bonifacio, Schmidt," he ordered crisply. "Berlin considers this legionnaire to be a highly supportive factotum of the felon de Gaulle. Do we still maintain contact with Sidi bel Abbes?"

Schmidt nodded dismally. *Bonifacio again?* "I shall do my best, Major."

Hesse grimaced. How he loathed Schmidt, the petty bastard. He'd fix his ass soon enough. Recently Schmidt had got himself a hot little bundle of French cunt to share a homey apartment with him. A frosty, sadistic smile twisted Hesse's lips. "Ah, yes, Schmidt, before you depart, we have a new assignment. Corsica. Prepare for departure in ten days. *Verstehen?* Now bring me what you can on Bonifacio."

Schmidt, at once deflated, prepared to salute. He raised his arm, stopped in midair, lowered it apathetically. Visions of his crumbling love nest wilted his fervor.

"And Schmidt—" Hesse took perverse delight in noting the other's disappointment. No longer would he come to work with so insufferable and satisfied an expression.

"*Jawohl*, Major?" Schmidt, a defeated man, had lost all vestiges of buoyancy.

"Bring also the dossier on Major Victor Zeller. We are now forced to work with our Italian allies after their innumerable fiascos, and we should be prepared for anything. Don't look so disappointed, Schmidt. The whores in Corsica are exceedingly choice. Most are virgins—not like these venereal Parisian streetwalkers."

Schmidt left the room without his usual snappy salute. As he searched through the files, sounds of Hesse's loud guffaws echoed through to the outer office. *Preposterous, insufferable oaf!* Schmidt thought. *One of these days . . . What will I do without Mimi, though, my forlorn little waif who fucks me to paradise and back every day? What?*

Moments later he reentered Hesse's office without knocking or saluting. He placed the requested dossiers on the officer's desk. "The report on the woman Pythia is on top," he muttered, exiting.

Hesse locked the OWC documents in a desk drawer, poured more of the pale amber Medoc wine. He opened the Pythia file. The contents were brief. It resembled the file of most collaborators, relating a dull, uneventful life before it turned to the excitement and dangers of espionage. "Let's see now: *Renée Belgique. French citizen . . . born in Lyons . . . family dispossessed in the war. Good stock, but impoverished. Employed at Vichy Embassy . . . translator to the French Ambassador and President Pétain for the past four years.*" Hesse slapped the file on the desk before him. One thing was certain: this was no ordinary translator! This was a highly calculating entrepreneur who knew the value of money and what it could buy for her.

Hesse picked up the phone. "Put me through to Berlin. General Kaltenbruner. At once, do you hear?"

GESTAPO HEADQUARTERS, BERLIN
ONE WEEK LATER

General Ernst Kaltenbruner, a burly man over six feet tall with
a saber cut across one cadaverous cheek, was impressed with
Major Hesse's account of his encounter with Pythia. "Incredible, Major. Field Marshal Kesselring and I agree that the Operation White Coral plans are too good to be true. We sniff a trap,
the usual, very cleverly executed British trap. The master
stroke of John York's genius. Who better than John York to
suck us into a well-baited trap? No one knows Germany's military machinations better than Bletchley's golden boy. I'd venture to guess he has broken the German cipher—it wouldn't be
impossible for him. What an abomination it was to permit him
to study our secrets."

"At that time we were certain of Great Britain's cooperation.
But I agree. In my professional opinion, White Coral bears the
John York signature. Like fingerprints, his designs cannot deceive. Sir, I've not discussed the Pythia documents with any
Paris official—nor with the Gestapo, the Embassy, or my superiors at Bureau VI. I determined this to be such high-level material that only you should validate its authenticity."

"Twenty documents in all! All of such high-level material
we have no means of verification!" Kaltenbruner was exasperated.

"How, sir, do we act upon things we cannot verify?"

"The answer is we don't!"

"We don't?" Hesse was crestfallen. "So much work, so
much money expended!"

"First, who is this Pythia? What do we know of her? She
could be anyone planted in the Vichy Embassy—even a Resistance fighter acting out a carefully orchestrated role."

"My feeling is that she is desperate for money. Yes, the dangerous games she plays are purely for monetary gain." Hesse
paused, turning something over in his mind. *"Mein General,*
the dossier compiled on Madame Renée Belgique belongs to a
dead woman."

"A dead woman? Explain, *bitte.*"

"A certain Renée Belgique *did* exist, once. Same description, same statistics, but she died four years ago. A physician's
wife—an incurable illness says the reports. She was buried in

the village of Linkebeek near Brussels. The husband was reported dead, but his body does not lie alongside the grave of the dead Renée Belgique. Supposedly he died in the Battle of Antwerp on May eighteenth when our Wehrmacht decimated the British and sent them scurrying north to escape our Luftwaffe and Panzer bombardments.''

Kaltenbruner stroked the saber cut on his cheek thoughtfully. "A cover, Major. Purely and simply, your Pythia is a foreign agent, not some innocent making a formidable sum of money by selling top secrets.'' He poured French cognac from a crystal decanter into two glasses and shoved one toward Hesse.

Hesse, biting his underlip, nodded. "I agree, General. I had to hear it from your lips, but I agree. Still, I feel there is something more to this too-perfect setup.'' He held his cognac up in a toast. They said, "*Heil* Hitler,'' guzzled their drinks, and exchanged broad winks.

"Good. Then we are in accord,'' Kaltenbruner said, heaving his large frame forward in his chair. He flipped an intercom button, snapped a string of orders in German to the voice at the other end. "I want all you can find on Dr. Charles Belgique from Linkebeek, Belgium. Wife, Renée, files, photos, anything you can obtain.''

He snapped off the communication device and stared at Hesse, peering right through him. Hesse hesitated to intrude on his thoughts.

"Excuse me, Herr General. Would the Gestapo keep files on *all* Belgian citizens? Purportedly *dead* citizens? Why?''

"Ah, Major, you disappoint me. You stated that in the French police files, the husband was reported dead, *nein?* That the woman, Madame Belgique, also appeared in those revealing files?''

Hesse, increasingly perplexed, nodded. Had he overlooked something?

"Why would anyone be listed in police files unless they had previous criminal records or engaged in matters considered criminal?''

Hesse felt like an ingenue. His good right hand touched his forehead in a gesture that capitulated respect to his mentor.

"And where exactly do dead men go when they want the world to believe them dead? And why?''

"But both husband and wife—'' Hesse flushed. The obvious

answer brought painful awareness of his ineptness, a blatant faux pas.

Kaltenbruner raised a protesting hand. "I am a very thorough man, Major. I must be. Himmler keeps a close watch on all of us. Therefore, I cannot afford to indulge in whimsy, only in substantiated facts."

Two hours later, after the extensive files had poured into the General's office, Hesse thought an ordinary man might have abandoned the task and advised him to drop the entire Pythia project. Not the tenacious, enduring Kaltenbruner. His tentacles to Rome had verified possible military activity gearing up in Corsica. Italian intelligence provoked Kaltenbruner's interest. So convinced was he that the provocative Pythia was involved in a diabolical plot against Germany, he determined to unearth it.

Luck showered favors upon them. A photo of Dr. Charles Belgique contained in the files sounded tocsins in Hesse's brain. The features were difficult to discern, but the man's posture, the hunched frame of a frail man, agitated Hesse. "General, earlier you said something—what was it?"

"Major, for the past three hours I've spoken a great deal."

"Yes, General, I know. But this was something about dead men. You said, 'Where do dead men go when they want the world to think them dead?' "

"So?"

"I am certain I know this man. But from where?" Something about Belgique was intensely familiar to Hesse. How did he know the man? Where had they met? Under what circumstances? His features blanched. Belgique was a leader in the Resistance! One of the countless men who had come before him and managed to slip through Gestapo security to freedom. "That's it, General. Pythia is using the cover of a dead woman, with credentials born in the minds of the Resistance. Perfect! Only Belgique could have provided the proper statistics! The man Belgique is also using a cover and is active in the French underground." The image in Hesse's brain was clearing. "General, earlier you suggested we possessed no means to authenticate the Pythia documents. My new assignment is Corsica. I shall personally substantiate or disprove the existence of the Operation White Coral. I think it would be in our best interest to hold off alternate plans of action until we know whether or not OWC is authentic.''

"The Italians are already entrenched on the island. Shall we surprise them? The Duce's dreams of empire get him into constant trouble." Kaltenbruner traced the livid scar on his face and stared at Hesse's useless prosthesis.

"Perhaps we kill a few birds with one stone, *ja?* Check the veracity of OWC, requisition sorely needed food stores, recruit more labor for our factories, and . . ."

"And?"

Hesse frowned. "I'll put the ferrets on Pythia. I've two more scheduled rendezvous with her before I depart for Corsica. I shall persuade her to deal with Ambassador von Ruck."

"What do our twenty-five thousand pounds British buy us this time?"

"A document. Operation Torch."

"What's that? What's that?" Kaltenbruner blurted out. "This is a joke, *ja?* Operation Torch commenced execution in November, four days *after* Montgomery defeated Rommel's forces at El Alamein!"

"What of Operation Tiger Tank? We will be provided with revised Allied plans reacting to our own planned offensives," Hesse said testily.

"They know of Tiger Tank?" Kaltenbruner's features turned deep red. *"The Spanish cipher!* Bletchley has broken the Spanish Code! *Gottverdammen.* Never mind! Plans can be changed. Now, Major, there is something. A certain code name has appeared very ambiguously in some of these documents. Most disconcerting, you see. For example, we are convinced—mind you our conversation ends here—that the Allies plan the invasion of Western Europe. The code name for that event we surmise to be 'Operation Husky.' We need to learn the date and place of this operation, understand?"

"A second front!. . ." Hesse whispered low.

"We'll pay Pythia double for the document—triple her price if need be."

"Double, triple? Seventy-five thousand? Herr General, the Führer would dip you in bronze for such information. The sum is enough to whet Pythia's appetite. But sir, would such documents be likely to turn up at the Vichy Embassy?"

"Only if she is a British spy," Kaltenbruner hissed.

"Ah, excellent." They exchanged knowing glances. "What exactly is Operation Husky?"

"That's precisely what we need to know. We think—a supposition, of course—that it may be the invasion of a key island in the Mediterranean to serve as an Allied operational base."

"Sicily." Hesse mouthed the word in astonishment.

"Sicily." Kaltenbruner gestured for caution. "Churchill is sitting on Allied tails to prove his point. The Soviet bear is grumbling, threatening alliances with the Axis if the operation comes off."

"Political seismographs are rumbling, *jawohl?*"

"Jawohl, Major. This is top-level action. Do not slip up. If you pull this one off, consider your dreams a fingertip away."

Hesse stared at his dead hand, swallowed hard, and said nothing.

The following week, at the appointed time at a new rendezvous near the Étoile, a black sedan waited with its lone passenger, Pythia, the mysterious Madame Belgique. She seemed tired, pale, her features drawn and her body tense from waiting.

Twilight in Paris was magnificent, she thought, clutching the costly photographed documents. Man-made lights blinked on like tired eyes, washing the city in a glitter of electric stars. As twilight deepened and Paris came alive, she felt the scene bore the strangeness of the transcendental, as if she didn't belong to the earth, as if none of her recent involvements were real or had ever happened. Her fears gathered momentum, and for one mad moment she asked herself what she was doing here. At this moment she nearly leaped from the sedan, but it was too late. She recognized Major Hesse's private automobile.

"Be calm, *madame,*" her driver cooed reassuringly. "He is alone."

Hesse alighted from his auto, approached hers, and climbed into the rear seat, sitting alongside her. At the same time, the driver got out and closed the door. He lit a cigarette and walked toward the rear of the car, smoking casually, busy eyes picking out Hesse's ferrets in nearby positions.

Inside the shadowy Mercedes, Hesse stared somberly at the figure clutching the shabby portfolio and wearing the familiar black dress and concealing black turban with wispy dark bangs falling to her brow line. A uniform, thought Hesse; nothing about her appearance ever changed.

"Operation Tiger Tank, I presume," he said quietly, focusing on the file in her hand. "It is encouraging to know you keep your promise the way a virgin keeps her virtue."

"The money first," she snapped. He handed her a pouch containing the sum of money negotiated for earlier. She finished counting, stacked it together, and returned it to him. "Like Operation Torch, Tiger Tank has been relegated to history. Really, Major, you do me an injustice. Do you think I'd risk my life and the loss of my best customer by passing dated material to you? You should have acted with dispatch. Tiger Tank ended with you Germans the victors yesterday at Sidi Bou Zid in Algeria. Your Panzer tanks are formidable. Lady Luck was with you. The Americans are novices at war, and I must admit that you German devils are the real virtuosos of war. The surrender took place at Djebel Ksaria. But why do I tell you? You already know, don't you? I can only believe you would buy dated material to test my veracity, *oui?*"

"You are well informed, Pythia."

She reached over and removed the money pouch from his hand. "I'd hate to see twenty-five thousand pounds sacrificed. It's far safer and more prudent to keep my best client content." She handed him another manila envelope. "Operation El Guettar! Since General Rommel's illness forces him out of Algeria, the Americans are throwing their secret weapon against your forces. Exit the Desert Fox—enter the American iron man, blood-and-guts Patton, a general who doesn't take kindly to what happened at Kasserine. *Merci bien,* Major. Shall we say next week? At the park near the Tuileries? No. Make it Notre Dame Cathedral. It's only fitting we conduct our business under the aegis of God. It is an excellent means of sanctifying our negotiations. *Oui?*"

"What will you bring me then? Do we understand one another well enough for me to make a special request?"

Pythia raised a questioning eyebrow.

"What we're after is something called Operation Husky."

"Major, I don't always have the opportunity to search and seize. I take what I find, when I find it. Are you voicing displeasure concerning the documents I have supplied?"

"None at all. I only suggested—"

"I'll do what I can. Operation Husky, you say?" She thought for a moment. "Very well. Now, please excuse me. And, Major, don't have your men follow me. You Germans are simply not cut out for the rigors of cloak and dagger. Yet you persist, and it causes me more effort to find ways to evade them. If members of the Vichy Embassy catch sight of the Gestapo's shadow everywhere I go . . ."

"I understand. In the future we shall exercise discretion. Before I say *bon soir,* Pythia, there is another matter. In addition to Husky, there is rumor of a project called 'Colossus.' It is, as I understand it, an immense contraption, an electronic computer with storage registers. I've heard it's capable of calculating complicated functions involving some one hundred symbols. But I am told that, however great its expectations, it shall not make your functions as a human spy obsolete. Rather it will enhance your talents, although it might relegate them to second fiddle."

"Colossus? I shall do my best. I think you're suffering delusions, but then, nothing in war is surprising. If I'm to furnish—"

"Yes, I know. The price will be triple."

"No, Major. A hundred thousand British pounds will suit me fine."

Hesse blanched. In the semiglow of the car interior, his consternation was not apparent. He climbed out of the sedan. Pythia's driver stubbed out his cigarette on the toe of his boot and scurried back into the driver's seat. He started up the powerful engine and eased the Mercedes forward along the boulevard onto the Place de la Concorde. It had just begun to rain. The light drizzle metamorphosed into angry torrents as it struck the sedan's roof and windshield, making it nearly impossible to see outside. Pythia glanced through the rear window and spouted orders to her driver. "*Dépêchez-vous, s'il vous plaît!* You must hurry, please!"

"*Oui, madame.*"

Gestapo surveillance was heavy. In the next ten minutes, Pythia changed cars twice, then doubled back through the dismal, slippery streets.

She saw Notre Dame Cathedral up ahead, then spotted her original Mercedes. Pythia leaped from the rear seat of the Chenault-Walker, dashed in the downpour to the Mercedes where her original driver was at the helm. The Resistance fighter expertly directed the auto into the sparse flow of traffic, momentarily foiling the Gestapo. They kept up a steady pace to the city's outskirts, then swerved off the main road onto a back country path that was deeply rutted and growing muddier by the moment. Pythia, bounced and jostled unmercifully, peered out the windows but was barely able to discern a thing in the enveloping shadows of fog. She knew that at a secret, blacked-out airstrip nearby, a camouflaged P-38 Lightning should be warming its motors.

It was! *Thank God!* "There it is," she shouted as it taxied into takeoff position. "Please! You must hurry before it takes off without me!"

The driver careened the Mercedes through the open gates of the fenced-in deserted compound, tires skidding in the muddy ruts as it sped along the darkened runway. He floored the accelerator, flashed his headlights on and off three times. There was no response. The plane revved its motor.

"Hurry, *mon Dieu*! I must board this flight! It must not depart without me!"

"Oui, madame!" he replied. "Hold tight!" He swerved the steering wheel sharply and flooring the gas pedal, swung onto the runway, lights on, speeding ahead of the plane. A hundred yards up ahead, he swung the wheel about, skidded on the slippery macadam, and doubled back onto the blacktop, heading directly into the plane's path, flashing headlights on and off. "I shall force them to see us, *madame*! I shall compel them! Ah, bravo! Bravo! They are signaling!" He swung portside to the plane and swerved around the P-38's tail, pulling up alongside the hatch door.

Pythia leaped out of the car, sprinted the short distance to the opening hatch door, and grasping the pilot's arm, swung aboard. The hatch door swung shut and locked, and the pilot slipped into the cockpit and gunned the motors to a deafening roar. The plane taxied forward, gained momentum, and took off, becoming quickly lost in cloud cover.

On the ground, the driver, elated by his expertise in handling the harrowing task, swerved the wheel sharply to the right and sped back along the dark runway, his headlights off. Just as he was driving out the entrance gates, he was suddenly blinded by the glaring beams of six pairs of headlights and a mounted spot-

light on a flatbed lorry. Frightened but quick-witted, he shoved
the gears into reverse but was stopped abruptly by an obstruction at his rear. Two sedans flanking him cut off all exit. He
slammed on his brakes, but not before metal crashed into metal
in a sickening collision. *"Merde!* The Gestapo!" Panic registered in his ashen features as loud machine gun bursts shattered
the night, electrifying the air overhead.

The machine guns from the flatbed lorry spewed white lightning toward the airborne P-38, but it was already too far off.
The guns were impotent as the determined Gestapo closed in on
the nameless driver fighting for the Resistance. *Do it!
You must!* The driver began his silent countdown. Four . . .
three . . .

With guns drawn, six SS agents closed in on him from all
points in the pouring rain. Behind them the Wehrmacht gunners
trained their machine guns on the obstructed Mercedes, awaiting orders. Caught in the deadlock, no avenue of escape open to
him, the driver rolled down the window and shouted, *"Vive la
France!"* and pulled a lever under the dashboard.

B-A-R-O-O-M! B-A-R-O-O-M! A fury of black smoke, blazing white fire, and lightning bursts rocked the earth, hurling
bodies, autos, and guns into the air. There was a succession of
sickening blasts as gasoline tanks burst into fire. Bodies fell
spastically to the ground and became part of the unrecognizable
carnage. In the catenation of explosions spreading fire and destruction from car to car, only the spotlight on the flatbed lorry
illuminating the death arena gave signs of life. What remained
of the SS agents, drivers, and gunners lay strewn about under a
veil of black death, their pained voices supplicating for death.

At the perimeter of the circle of fire, there was movement.
One Gestapo agent, Wilheim Müller, more dead than alive,
forced himself to crawl from the inferno and sea of human or-
dure on all sides of him. He had run several yards before the
razor-sharp pain in his left shoulder assaulted him. Grabbing
for his arm with his right hand, he was unable to find it. There
was nothing! In the ghastly illumination of the reflecting fires,
he stared at his blood-saturated hand, stopping dead in his
tracks.

Disbelief and panic created pressure in his chest. A rash of
pain spasms engulfed him. The remains of his left arm hung
from bloody tendons and torn cartilage from an open hole in his

shoulder. The sight of the appendage dangling at his thighs plunged Müller into shock. He sank to his knees in a whirl-pooling miasma of fear and pitched headlong into an abyss. *Live!* he screamed internally. *Live, if only to avenge this atrocity!* Wilheim Müller knew the identity of Pythia, alias Renée Belgique! He was the only SS agent who knew. Unfortunately, it would be three months before Müller, hovering between life and death, could be interrogated by Major Hans Hesse concerning the disappearance of the spy Pythia. And by then it would be too late.

As the P-38 soared away, Pythia, unaware of her driver's fate or of the hapless SS agents who had trailed her, shuddered, wondering at her sanity in playing so dangerous a role in this volatile war.

Was she mad? Driven by danger? What compelled her toward these ends? What atavistic urgings drove her into participating in games of war?

"We're over the Channel, ma'am, bucking damned bloody head winds!" The pilot spoke for the first time. "No need to worry, ma'am. I'll get you back safely."

Pythia tensed. The voice! His voice sounded familiar. Damn! She needed no one to identify her, not now. She dared not move, kept her eyes straight ahead and was grateful when he seemed to concentrate on something beyond them both.

Listening through radiophones, he recited his navigational bearings: "Roger. . . . I follow. . . . Repeat my instructions. . . . Roger. . . . Over." He glanced at Pythia seated in the dimly lit cockpit. "As I said, ma'am, no need to worry. Two RAF Spitfire escorts are coming in at twelve o'clock. We're safe. It's just a matter of minutes," the flyer finished in a tone designed to reassure her.

In moments the P-38 touched down at a private airstrip not far from London. A signal corpsman wagged him down and off the runway to a perfect three-point landing, and the plane taxied to a stop.

Outside in the murky fog banks, engineers rolled a loading platform to the hatch door. The pilot, U.S. Captain Hartford Lansing, opened the hatch door and saluted Pythia. "That was a brave act you performed there, ma'am. I'm proud to've been able to help."

His mute passenger shot him a startled glance, nodded, and deplaned hastily. She prayed Hart Lansing hadn't recognized her.

Pythia, still shaken by the risky business in Paris and her narrow escape from the Chantilly airstrip, raced down the steps toward two officers standing near the vintage Rolls. She saluted them smartly, entered the rear door of the sedan, and fell back into the cushioned leather seat, heaving a sigh of relief. Her companions joined her, taking the jump seats facing her.

"You made it, thank God," said General Koenig.

In a sudden deft movement, Pythia yanked off her restrictive turban and black wig. She shook loose her fiery amber locks.

"You made it, just as I knew you would, Lieutenant Varga." General Koenig beamed, telegraphing his approval to General Furstenberg and a third man in the sedan introduced to her as "Intrepid." They nodded in acknowledgment. In the dimly lit rear seat of the sedan, Valentina Varga could just make out a fourth man in the shadows. His name was Cain. They nodded to one another.

"We placed our trust in the right person. Only a neophyte spy could have pulled it off!" Koenig hastened to add. "But never again! I haven't slept a wink in two months worrying over you."

"I'm pleased you trusted my ability. Every moment I spent in Paris intensified my trepidation." Valentina turned over the briefcase filled with British pounds to Furstenberg. "Do you really believe I sold the Germans a bill of goods, sir?"

"Not for one moment. I assure you the German mentality is such they'll prepare for both alternate plans, which reduces the risks for our actual plans, precisely what we need for Operation White Coral to be successful. They'll be taken off the real scent."

"You play dangerous games," she muttered, suddenly aware of the grave personal risks she took in the recent deception.

"No one ever said war is child's play, Lieutenant," said Koenig.

"What you succeeded in doing," interrupted General Furstenberg, "is lightening Major Bonifacio's overburdened detail."

Her eyes lit up. "You'll send me to Corsica?"

"No! Absolutely not. There's no way I'll endanger your life again in this dirty business!"

For an instant disappointment registered on her pale features. "Good," she quipped. "In the past weeks I've aged twenty years. Nothing is as devastating to a woman as the onset of so many years at once."

The generals laughed at her remark, so inconsistent with her obviously youthful beauty.

"Considering the life-and-death situations you've endured recently—" Furstenberg paused. "You look positively exhausted. I suggest we delay the debriefing until morning—although I *am* bloody curious to learn how Major Hans Hesse handles his new-found power. And of course, if Major Bonifacio's in depth profile on Hesse was accurate—"

"The assessment was accurate enough." Valentina shuddered in recollection. "Hesse oozes blind ambition; I detected it at once. If he weren't so concentrated on Berlin and his eagerness to join the exclusive coterie of Hitler's inner circle, he might have perceived my game. He believed the obvious because it suited his objectives." She showed enthusiasm briefly, then the lights in her eyes dimmed. "So many lives are being sacrificed."

"Speaking of lives, it's only fair to tell you the fate of your driver." Furstenberg enlightened her, taking care not to paint the images of death too vividly. Valentina listened, moved at the thought that the Resistance fighter had dedicated his life to Free France.

"Did you hear the news, Henri?" General Koenig spoke in rapid French. "Commander John York at Bletchley just broke the German diplomatic cipher. He heads the entire ULTRA project now. With the German Enigma traffic mastered, I'd predict it's only a matter of time before we win this war."

"Enigma . . . ULTRA . . ." Valentina mused in her fatigue, suddenly alert. "It's important we speak." She glanced at Intrepid hesitantly. Furstenberg assured her it was perfectly safe to speak in his presence. "Very well. Major Hesse requested two documents from me. Operation Husky and—"

"Operation Husky?" Intrepid jerked his head about, staring at her. "He asked you about *Husky*?" The accent was British upper class.

"And something about a futuristic machine with incredible capabilities."

"Colossus," Intrepid said flatly, "our newest computer."

"Yes, as a matter of fact. And he gave me the specifics. I've included them in my report." She turned back to Furstenberg, suddenly uncomfortable.

"Good girl. Now if we could only devise a means to wire our special agents so we could record verbal conversation." Furstenberg sighed impatiently. "Cryptanalysis and deception, the main ingredients to see us through this war. Ever since the Americans created Magic in 1938, we've refined the system through application of high mathematics and analysis. Now we can pluck the damned enemy's signals right out of the ionosphere and transmit them to headquarters. But it's nothing compared to what we'll be able to do."

Valentina Varga was sound asleep.

General Furstenberg awakened her when they reached Marboro Hall. He insisted she go right to bed. "Rest. Call me in the morning when you feel up to the debriefing." She nodded, suddenly fatigued beyond endurance. She entered her luxurious quarters in a near somnambulistic state. Exhaustion fell upon her.

She drew a bath and undressed. Yes, yes. Tomorrow after a good night's rest, she'd tell them everything, all they needed to know. But, tonight . . .

She fell asleep in the tub, awakening when the water turned cold. Stepping from the tub, shivering, she wrapped herself in a thick turkish towel and tumbled into bed, determined to fall asleep this night without ghostly worries. She fell into a heavy sleep but was awakened by a violent nightmare.

Two stalking tigers in a blood-soaked arena were surrounded by walls from which flowed gushers of blood. The tigers—Darius and Hans Hesse—were squaring off. Their faces became more defined as explosions burst all around them. Fires spread, all-consuming flames sprang up, encircling the tigers. Overlooking the arena was the condemnatory face of Hartford Lansing. Jolted from the nightmare, Valentina sat up in her bed, her body soaking wet, heart racing, pulse throbbing, and fear coursing through her blood. *It's a nightmare, Val! A bloody nightmare! Get a grip on yourself!*

Oh, Christ! I pray Darius is safe! She poured a stiff bracer of brandy from a decanter on the night table, wiped her tears on the sheets, and downed the contents in a large gulp. She replaced the glass on the tray, slid under the quilted down cover, and felt the brandy blaze a trail inside her. She tried to blink away the recurring image of Hans Hesse, thinking how he hadn't once tried to force his sexual prowess on her. The realization and its significance brought his ambition into clearer focus. The man was a force to be reckoned with. She was frightened for Darius.

Darius. Beloved Darius, where are you? Miss me, please. Miss me with all your heart! In the past two months, she had found the image of Darius slowly slipping away like a faded photograph. What did it mean?

Exhaustion came again. This time gods and goddesses replaced the demons and drew her to lofty places.

Chapter Five

BASTIA, CORSICA
CHRISTMAS EVE DAY, 1942

Nine weeks before Valentina's harrowing escape aboard the P-38 recon plane, Major Victor Zeller stood rigidly before the rotund, pear-shaped Mayor of Bastia, stating his case clearly and in no uncertain terms.

"Mayor Segretti, due to the spurious and intractable nature of you Corsicans, the present situation borders on catastrophe. I implore you for the last time to instill in your people the importance of cooperating with Italian martial-law edicts. Otherwise we shall be compelled to implement severe measures to force them into obedience. Should they fail to understand and abide by the ultimatum issued today, tell them that Corsica shall then be forced to deal directly with the Nazis. The choice is theirs."

Seated in the Mayor's chair in this sumptuous baronial manor, Major Zeller spoke smoothly, although a highly combustible reserve lurked behind his forced calm. The sight of the ruddy-faced collaborating Mayor standing rigidly before him, his piercing black eyes defiant, caused Victor's calm to erupt with demonstrable indignation. He pounded the desk, startling the Mayor out of his feigned composure.

"This very morning—Christmas Eve day, damn it—five hundred Italian troops were slaughtered in the outskirts of Bastia! Slaughtered, Sindaco Segretti! Massacred while on reconnaissance missions into surrounding hills and the *maquis*. Corsican barbarism is intolerable! We are a civilized people, fighting a civilized war with every intention of remaining honorable and civilized. This morning's atrocity against my men is unacceptable. Is this clearly understood, Segretti? Is it?"

The Mayor's purple, mottled face increased Major Zeller's anger. "First, this needless slaughter of Italian soldiers must cease and desist or else retaliation will commence at this ratio: two dead Corsicans for each dead Italian. Should that fail to impress you intractable Corsicans, the number will escalate to ten to one, then to twenty Corsicans for each dead Italian. *Capisce?* By God," he thundered, "we will have total submission or we shall blow Corsica to kingdom come!"

Victor stalked out of the Mayor's office, leaving a sputtering, red-faced Corsican behind him. He descended to the foyer on the magnificent château's marble spiral steps. Moments later he was in his staff car, being driven through the courtyard with proper motorcycle escort, heading due west toward the shoreline. His destination: Ajaccio on the west coast of the island.

Two hours later Victor arrived to chair a disastrous meeting with Ajaccio's local politicians and collaborating officials in the chambers of the fort in the grand Napoleonic city. Major Zeller, standing before a lectern, reiterated his earlier ultimatum to Mayor Segretti at Bastia. Facing the hostile savages disguised in business suits, white shirts, and ties, Victor realized his reputation and ultimatum had preceded him. The stench of their loathing hung cloyingly in the great hall. Victor abruptly and acerbically delivered his speech, unprepared for the pomposity of the ultimatum hurled back at him.

"Major Zeller, let the record show that peaceful relations with Corsicans is wholly unrealistic. We are not an easily conquered people. Study our history and learn the measure of our will to survive and outlive our enemies."

Victor cut him off. "Am I to understand that no amount of kindness, generosity, or easing of restrictions can hope to encourage Corsican cooperation?'' He stared hotly at the sea of officious asses. *Don't they understand, for Christ sake?* "Total war exists between us—is that the way it shall be? Very well, Corsicans, then let the record show that Italy too is not an easily conquered nation. And behind Italy stands the Hun! Ah, is that a glitter of discomfort I detect?'' He smirkingly scanned the faces.

The local Mayor, a facsimile of the official in Bastia, rose to his feet. He had something to say and refused to be silenced.

"Major Zeller, we Corsicans issue ultimatums to *you*. Unless you leave our land within twenty-four hours, hideous death will befall all undesired trespassers.''

"Corsican ultimatum!" Victor's snide laughter filled the hall. "You dare issue threats to me, the conqueror?'' *What ludicrous asses!* Standing at the lectern, peering at the sea of contumacious faces, he spoke softly into the microphone, his ominous voice resounding throughout the auditorium.

"One hundred and fifty thousand fully armed Italian and German troops occupy Corsica—more than your total population—and you *dare* issue ultimatums to me, commander of the occupational forces? Good God! Your lives depend upon our strength!'' He shook his head as a frustrated schoolmaster might at blundering children who err repeatedly.

A seemingly interminable silence was followed by spasmodic coughing, bodies shifting in creaky wooden chairs, and periodic squawks from a faulty public address system. The Italian's stare unnerved the Corsicans, his words chilled their blood, nearly melting their perverse doggedness.

Victor issued a pronouncement. "So be it! Now I shall spell it out for you, chapter and verse. We—you and I—are finished. Corsica is finished. Your irrevocable rupturing of any and all amicable dialogue between us has led me to force you to adhere to strict military dictates!'' Victor reasoned that fear, a far more effective weapon than contempt or hostility, engendered respect. He strode angrily out of the chambers, issued stiff orders to the military personnel of Fort Ajaccio to double, treble if necessary, the watch at all arsenals. He stepped up intelligence surveillance on recon missions, imposed severe food-store restrictions, requisitioned additional wheat stores for the occupational army, and imposed curfews. Before the day was over, he stood before microphones hooked up to speakers throughout the city of Ajaccio so that the citizens would hear his words firsthand.

"*Attenzione . . . attenzione*. Citizens of Corsica. By your refusal to acquiesce to friendly persuasion, you force IMI to relinquish a portion of its command. I shall no longer obstruct Germans from recruiting Corsican labor for German industry —an action I previously and vigorously protested. After the atrocity at Bastia this morning, I wash my hands of you. The Germans will commence press-ganging shortly, and if you look about for a scapegoat to blame, I suggest you examine your reflections in the mirror. You Corsicans insured the intervention of the Hun!"

Finished, Victor Zeller left Fort Ajaccio in a heated rage, flanked on all sides by a military phalanx. Roiling thoughts coursed through his embroiled brain. Ominous forces at work here in Corsica were instilling the citizens with guts and brazen audacity and the daring to dispute his edicts, and risk offending the conqueror. Whoever the rebellious forces were, to Victor it was a foregone conclusion that a formidable supply of weapons and manpower stood behind them. Changes in recent weeks had signaled an obvious reduction in negotiable options available to him. The numerous allegations festering in his intelligence reports were poisoning the propaganda apparatus he had hoped to deploy and use to coerce the Corsicans into quiet, orderly acquiescence. Everything had boomeranged, paralyzing his espionage establishment, ruining his chances of penetrating the highly clandestine activity breeding insurrection on the island. And they *were* out there! Resistance and operational groups were plotting, planning, regrouping their strength, preparing an Axis demise. Reports flying across his desk prophecied gloom. And Major Victor Zeller was damned if he'd let it happen!

But why were his best men being funneled off? Mysteriously disappearing? Men—sleuths—he'd personally trained!

At the core of this corrosive confusion, Victor was certain he sniffed the workings of the ignominious Gestapo and the foreign intelligence officers of the German RSHA, Bureau VI. Resistance forces, damn their insidious hides, gripped the heart of Corsica! They were the stabilizing forces feeding life to the intractable islanders! If the Germans had done their jobs in

France and not sent the Resistance scurrying like moles to the *maquis* . . .

Victor boarded his staff car, furious over the recent developments on the island. The day of confrontation between Italian and German forces was at hand! Who would emerge triumphant? Damn Il Duce for conspiring with Hitler! As the sedan and its motorcycle escorts wheeled grandly through narrow cobbled streets, Victor cursed the day he'd accepted the Corsican assignment. He could have refused Il Duce's command! Dammit, this wasn't his cup of tea. Why hadn't Ciano been chosen? Or Noro or any of a dozen men more experienced in military command? His specialty was as an intelligence officer, not a battalion commander!

He stared at the grim-faced Corsicans whose eyes followed the passing entourage. What an obstinate, duplicitous, hostile people! Uncouth barbarians, the lot of them! *Thieves! Cutthroats! Murderers!* He reviled them. And the Corsicans reviled him in turn.

Victor, bombarded by the sight of the innumerable shrines erected to the memory of his illustrious ancestor Bonaparte, shook his head in wonderment. Napoleon on horseback. Farther along, Bonaparte, the brooding Roman Emperor, gazing across the Bay of Ajaccio, then immortalized in bronze with his brothers. The statues and posturings were endless!

Suddenly it struck Victor: hadn't he more than a militarist's interest in visiting Napoleon's birthplace? Why not now? It might be his last visit to Ajaccio, and the visit would provide a respite at the end of so intolerable a day. Yes, why not? The intrigue of his being an actual blood descendant of Bonaparte's stoked his enthusiasm. He felt duty bound to view the immortal shrine where Letizia had given birth to her famous son.

Victor let a rare smile play at his lips; the gesture would please his mother, the *contessa.*

So at four in the afternoon, Christmas Eve day, he dismissed his men, issuing explicit orders to return to the cathedral for him in one hour. Turning, he entered the brick pathway leading to the historic cathedral where one of the paths would ultimately lead to Napoleon's birthplace. He was met head-on by a rush of holiday worshipers and genuflecting parishioners zealously toting floral offerings to the elaborate Nativity Scene stretched across the altar. Victor stepped aside, positioning himself in the refuge of an alcove behind an enormous Doric column.

So many people! Some crossed themselves with holy water, hurriedly moving through the enormous church to do their Stations of the Cross. A few stood in line, waiting to light candles, drop coins in the poor boxes. Others, staring with ghoulish glances at his uniform, scurried past him and dispersed in their singular pursuits, avoiding him as if he were contaminated.

Victor stepped out from behind the column and looked for the path leading to Napoleon's tomb. He craned his neck above the crowds. He could see little in the dimly lit amphitheater. Despite the distractions on all sides, he waxed nostalgic. Memories of his youth—delightful, happier Christmas holidays—awakened an undercurrent of vulnerability in him. *Christmas! Time to be charitable, Victor!* But the damn-fool Corsicans afforded him no opportunity to demonstrate charitable traits! Fools! Insipid fools—the lot of them! He'd been fair—more than fair. For these people to regard him as a threat was preposterous. Indeed, to regard him as anything but a man dedicated to healing situations was distortion.

It's Christmas, Victor. Forget these people!

His eyes were riveted on the manger scene illuminated by hundreds of flickering candles.

Suddenly his heart skipped a beat. He caught sight of her—a flash of illumination as if a glowing penumbra marked her for him among the crowds. She moved through the cathedral, paused before a statue of the Blessed Virgin cradling the Infant Jesus. She passed Victor, brushing his arm. Believing her to be an image from his dreams, he blinked hard, grew breathless at the sight of her seraphic beauty in the candle glow.

Their eyes locked; hers widened. The sight of his uniform made her frown. Moving swiftly past him, she plunged into the moving lines of people.

Victor, mesmerized, unable to resist her magnetism, felt compelled to follow her. Her enormous dark eyes and pale, satiny skin framed by coal-black hair sent his heart racing. Enchanted with the girl, Victor lost track of time. Napoleon's birthplace toppled from his list of priorities. His temples throbbed, his heart beat erratically and erotically. He felt a kinship with her, as if he'd known her somewhere before. He realized that he could not live without her, that she'd become—

without a word passing between them—an irrevocable part of his life.

She finished with the Stations of the Cross, passed him again, coming within inches of his position before exiting. Impulsively he reached for her, touched her arm. Startled, she drew back.

"Please, *signorina*." He spoke Italian. "You need not be afraid."

Lifting black diamond eyes from the obstructing hand on her arm, she stared at him. Calmly removing his confining grip, she scrutinized him from head to shiny-toed boots, icy aloofness apparent in her features. Victor marveled at the absence of fear. He persisted with restrained ardor. "With your permission, may we speak? It is not my intention to alarm or harm you."

Sophia Bonifacio tensed, one hand fingering a concealed knife in her skirt folds. But her penetrating eyes searching his sensed no danger. She relaxed slightly, remained still as a statue.

Victor, visored cap in one hand, extended the other toward the flower-filled garden patio outside.

"Perhaps in natural surroundings amid flowers and trees, we might speak as human beings?"

"It's best, Major, you do not speak to me at all," she said, a velvet huskiness purring in her throat. Her eyes swept the flower-banked walkway leading to the Bonaparte house. "I am well protected."

"It's good you know that, *signorina*. I am your protection in Corsica. Permit me to introduce myself. Major Victor Zeller at your service. Commander of the occupational forces," he said with aplomb, unprepared for her cold reply.

"The *Major* is known in Corsica by reputation. You misunderstood me, *Major*. By protection I meant to suggest it is unwise for you, a *foreigner*, to speak with a Corsican woman. Our men are fiercely protective of their women. They take unkindly to any infringements."

"You are spoken for, I presume?" His dismay was apparent.

How much easier life would have been if Sophia had said yes that day and ended everything. She didn't, and didn't know what compelled her involvement. "No—I mean, yes." Feeling frustrated, she tried to pass him and leave.

Victor held her arm. "Which is it? Yes or no?" He forced her to look into his dark, smoldering eyes. "You are the most beautiful creature I've ever seen. Permit me to call upon you and your family. I assure you my intentions are honorable. Something deep inside me demands to know you better."

"You must be mad! You expect a welcome mat for you, the enemy?" She cursed in an unintelligible Corsican dialect. "Italians are our enemies. Surely your naiveté is not such you'd expect us to greet you with brass bands and laurel wreaths!"

Victor, holding her arms pinned to her sides, forced her to gaze into his eyes. "You would ostracize me for doing my duty? For imposing certain laws to save—not kill—thousands of men? You impute offenses to me, accuse me of committing treacheries that the Corsicans themselves bring down on their heads. Look at me! I resent your unjust accusations. I said *look at me*! Do I look like your enemy? Do I?" he demanded in a soft, pliant voice, drawing closer to the breathtaking woman. "Italians will never harm Corsicans. We are protectors. Benefactors. Paternalistic to the Corsicans. France treats you as vassals. Not Italy. We speak the same tongue. We are destined to be allies. Look around you. Genoan influences dominate Corsica."

"Spoken directly from a primer!" she snapped acerbically. "Major, your alliance with Germany speaks for itself. I resent your flagrant, patronizing words. Only today your law was mandated. Frenchmen and Corsicans will be uprooted and transported to German labor camps. It is not so? *German labor camps!* Corsicans will never toil for Germany! You and your co-conspirators are liars, cheats, thieves. Yes, yes. You lie to us, steal our food, appropriate our lands, kill our animals under the guise of confiscation to feed *your* soldiers. You leave Corsicans, the natural inheritors of our earth, to starve and grovel before you. You dare suggest we welcome you with open arms? Let *our* houses become *your* houses? *Dio mio!* You are non compos mentis!"

Victor slowly released his grip on her. No mere peasant girl this one. She was educated, articulate, essentially feminine, and his attraction to her grew. Coincidentally, his increasing cynicism and resentment for the contumacious Corsican mentality fueled his anger.

"*Signorina*, from the moment I arrived, I begged you Corsican fools to make peace with Italy. Have you heeded my warnings? No! I am presently a warrior for my nation under military orders to complete imperative tasks. If in the course of my duties it means I must perform as a liar, a cheat, and a thief in your eyes, so be it. Corsica by treaty is at peace with the Axis nations. Do your people comply? Oh, no! You have done nothing but frustrate my efforts toward peaceful coexistence.'' Victor stopped, annoyed furrows creasing his brow. ''Why the hell do I discuss the policies of war with you, a mere slip of a girl?''

She was relentless. ''You Italians are puppets,'' she said. ''Tin soldiers manipulated by that clown Mussolini and the master puppeteer Hitler. See how he permits your vainglorious Il Duce to engage in circus theatrics while the Nazis concentrate on the choicest plum in the game. I spit on you Italians! You lack spine. Ah well, perhaps I should pity your Duce. Word is, his mind deteriorates daily from a virulent social disease.''

''*Signorina!* You go too far!'' His patience evaporated. ''You reject my gesture of friendship, and war on me with unprovoked malice.''

''You wear the uniform of the enemy, so I spit on you. Wear the uniform of a friend and ally and see how quickly I will succor your needs.''

''Ah, I see. How easy then for the wolf in sheep's clothing to take advantage of you, eh? Why do we argue? I barely know you. Besides, what do you know of the rules of war?'' In this instant, her face was bathed in a stream of sunlight filtering through the cascading bougainvillea covering the flagstone path to the cathedral. He noticed the changes in her eyes, an aloof, cautious reserve as she shifted focus to a point behind him. Victor turned slightly. Coming toward them in the shifting shadows was a towering, hulking, amber-skinned man flanked by four burly mountain brutes.

''*Adieu,* Major. I wish you no harm.'' She fled in a twinkling, scurrying past him, intercepting the approaching men. Struck by the absence of fear in her comportment, Victor watched as her outspread arms enveloped the newcomers, directing them back over the walkway. Her clear, authoritative voice echoed back to him. ''It was nothing. The officer merely asked for directions to Napoleon's birthplace.'' The glowering brutes followed submissively—a rarity for Corsicans.

But Victor had sensed more. If the Moor's eyes had contained daggers, Victor would have become a statistic of war. Relieved by their departure, Victor's discomfort centered upon the girl. *Damn!* He hadn't even learned her name! His dream had vanished before his eyes, and he, like a foolishly smitten adolescent, hadn't had the common sense to request her name!

Then something had caught his attention. On the nearby stone bench provided for weary worshipers was a thin book his Corsican angel had placed on it. Quickly he retrieved it, scanned the title: *The Little Prince* by Antoine de Saint-Exupéry. He shuffled the pages and flipped back to the flyleaf. An inscription in French read: ''To Sophia; May the beauty of the Little Prince's soul touch your heart forever. Affectionately, Antoine.''

Saint-Exupéry! The pilot running aerial reconnaissance missions for Free France! For General de Gaulle! According to intelligence reports stacked on Victor's desk, the celebrated author had touched down in Corsica, supplying information to the Resistance. *Che cosa?* What's this? Thoughts of Saint-Exupéry having ties with the girl Sophia created conflicts of interest. Was it possible the girl played a role in the Resistance? And if she did could she lead him to the man he'd hock his soul to capture, a man of profound mystery, a legend, some superman who purportedly headed one of the toughest, most incredible phenomena of World War II? A savage idea born in British minds to be used as a secret weapon to combat Wehrmacht and Italian troops had been remolded by this one man into a far more devastating guerrilla group than ever previously devised in modern warfare!

Victor had yet to determine if this mystery man was real or fictional. Numerous code names had paraded across his desk ad infinitum: Samson, Delilah's Dream, SAS commandos, Mozarabe. If Rome knew of them, they must be obsolete. Before Victor gave credence to the incomparable feats accorded such a superman, he'd have to encounter him in the flesh.

Still aroused by the lingering image of the girl Sophia, Victor Zeller slipped the book into his tunic pocket. *Sophia! Sophia . . . Sophia . . .* He spoke the name several times; it rolled over his tongue like velvet. It felt natural, familiar, as if he'd spoken it hundreds of times in a dream. It seemed to ease the ache, erase the vestiges of the longing deep inside him. Her face loomed before him, luring him, cooing to him as she had in all those inescapable dreams.

He boarded the waiting staff car. The driver moved away from the curb. Motorcycle escorts positioned themselves fore and aft as the entourage moved through Ajaccio's streets, heading north along the west coastline. Thoughts of Sophia would not abate. *Sophia who?* he asked himself. At least he knew her forename. Very good, Victor. How many Sophias could there be in Corsica? How would he learn more about this woman who was occupying his thoughts like an addiction? He knew he must; it was as if his life depended on it.

As the motorcade traveled past Porto, Victor's training forced him to view the matter in proper perspective. He reflected upon the curious composite of mystery and intrigue presented by the girl and her motley, primitive companions. Those bastards would have killed him without provocation. But the girl. She wrapped around his thoughts like striations of silky light embracing his memory, illuminating each of her features; she was indelibly etched in his mind. An erection surged in his loins, demanding, urgent, intractable.

In Calvi he stopped for refreshments, and after making several discreet inquiries, was taken to a bordello where, with his choice of the whores, he selected one who bore only the slightest whisper of resemblance to his dream goddess. Sexual release, a curiously mysterious phenomenon to men in all ages, of all ages, and taken for granted by most as a natural function, fell short of Victor's expectation this day. Impotence was new and frightening to him. Attempts to conjure up Sophia's image as added reinforcement to his tumescence fell flat. His psyche refused any but the genuine article. And to a man who had been on a speaking basis with erotica, his inability to copulate shook him to the core. He paid off the amused woman, boarded his staff car, brooding, certain Sophia had cast a mysterious spell over him. He'd heard tell of the superstitious backwoods rituals performed on this Blood Island, the land of blood feuds, vendetta, and revenge. The absurdity of his thoughts sobered him.

Bastia loomed up ahead. The lights atop the buildings of the capital blinked on, bringing back into perspective his duties, his obligations to Italy, to Il Duce. *Put aside all carnal thoughts, Victor. It isn't your fault—you expected quality mer-*

chandise and refused to bargain for less. Besides, attune your-
self to her words. Remember them. You are the enemy!

He glanced at his watch. Four hours! If he hadn't stopped at
Calvi . . . At least the trip was made without military incident.
No ambushes. No unexpected fusillades. But for how long?
How long before the disgruntled rumbling he'd heard in Ajac-
cio inflamed the entire island?

The moment he entered his baronial offices, Victor reinforced the orders mandated in Ajaccio. He doubled security at
all Italian and German fortifications, alerted all NCO's and junior officers to ferret out all guerrilla and sabotage squads
aimed at their demise. "Capture them alive if you can! I need
them for questioning. Surely among them traitors can be found,
defectors who'll trade vital information for a soft life on the
Italian Riviera, no?" On the other hand, Victor got tough. "If
you cannot capture them and no amount of coercion can buy
them, deploy the lethal squads, demolish Resistance strongholds. In recent days the Italians have been outwitted, out-
foxed, and led to slaughter. Now it's out-and-out war! No holds
barred!"

Major Zeller's orders, issued powerfully and persuasively, had
inspired his men to enthusiastically pick up the gauntlet, to em-
ulate the excitement he generated. They quickly departed, fully
prepared to do his bidding. Week after week they returned from
daily forays into the *maquis,* beaten, dejected, bedraggled, despondent, and less certain of their prowess as well-trained,
highly disciplined soldiers. Worse, their egos were a total
shambles as word of their losses spread to all Axis post commands. Infantry attacks against the odd, indomitable warriors
on the island had left the Axis soldiers impotent, bewildered.
Fusillades of machine gun fire coming from an invisible enemy
hidden behind boulders in the heart of the *maquis* evoked superstitious fright from normally sensible soldiers.

"They are fucking with your minds!" Victor told his subor-
dinates. "They make you believe you see and hear things that
do not exist!" Victor jerked an automatic pistol out of the hands
of a wild-eyed, shock-crazed corporal. "Listen to me. They are
men, like you. They shoot with the same guns you use. You
shoot—they shoot! The trick is to get the drop on them, not the
other way around!"

Victor's soldiers, by now certifiable, would hear none of his logic. They *knew* what their hearts told them, not what some fancy gold-braid officer tried to convince them was truth. "You can be heroes!" Victor urged them to imagine a hero's welcome in Rome, with brass bands, banners, and Il Duce saluting their heroic deeds from the Palazzo Venezia.

"If we follow your dictates, Major, and fight these supermen, we will go home in pine boxes without fanfare. Brass bands will play dirges and our women will wail during obsequies. These fighters, the Mozarabe, are supermen without equal, better equipped than the Germans! Among global battalions of fighting men, the Mozarabe are without peer. Their forces are legion in Corsica. They are everywhere at once!"

Victor shuddered at the implications. Recognition set in. He knew the tactic. His men had been infiltrated. Propaganda machines had skillfully cranked out misinformation designed to strike terror in the hearts of a superstitious people!

Damn their hides!

He hadn't wanted to implicate Rome, but he had no choice. Rome must be told, if for no other reason than to reverse the propaganda machines in their favor.   .

Victor sat in conclave with three men from Rome, conveying his displeasure at Il Duce's failure to properly support the Corsican invasion with propaganda and a needed supply of arms. "I tell you, if proper help fails to arrive, the Corsican operation will become sheer suicide, a worse fiasco than Greece."

The three men seated around Victor's desk ranged in age from midtwenties to early thirties, young by Italian military intelligence standards. These men, hand-selected by Victor to form his own personal quadrumvirate, worked cohesively as a unit, an unbeatable body for developing covert information. These staunch Italian loyalists believed their work benefited the nation. In their hands rested the fate of an entire nation. The dictatorship, at its most vulnerable point in two decades, depended upon such dedicated men. They knew of the most secret assignments, the most clandestine happenings within their nation and in every foreign land where the presence of Italian soldiers was felt and revered. Each was a trained authority in a specialized field, and more important, they were so aware of the psychology of the Italian mentality, they decided which men would engage in the most dangerous of assignments in the name of their Duce. The trio had arrived in Bastia to confer in an emergency session with Victor Zeller. He had just received a message that Major Hans Hesse was on his way to Corsica, and he was trying to figure out why.

The men sipped their wine and were warmed by the roaring fire on the hearth. Before them their briefs were spread out. Victor raised his wineglass in a toast.

"To Corsica—an imperial jest. A royal pain in the ass. Why are we here? Can one of you enlighten me?" He gestured to the thick brief on his desk. "Somewhere, buried in this hazy, unintelligible mélange of ciphers, lies, distortions, and misinformation coming from Rome, I detect an odious shuffling of ambiguities."

"*Sì*. We agree. That's why we are here in response to your request. To have made this trip in these precarious times was insanity," said the slim, dark, curly-haired officer named Miguel Noro as he studied the reports before him. Noro held the rank of captain in the Security branch of the Intelligence Division; he was an expert at decoding ciphers. "What I read here is much of nothing at all. If Rome has something to say, she must clarify. Clarify and confirm. Truly, Victor, I doubt the message was coded in Rome. A damned good facsimile, but not Rome. I'd stake my life on it." He ran nervous fingers through his thick crop of hair.

"*Berlin?*" Victor's brow shot up.

"Il Duce's insatiable need to inflate his ego by amassing global territories plays like a farce, a comedy of errors," said the impeccable Vincente Girro, a specialist in military law who often counseled Mussolini in technical military prerogatives. "The growing rivalry between our Duce and Hitler borders on insanity. Now Rome is hesitant in formulating orders for you here in Corsica."

"Why?" Victor held his wineglass in midair, awaiting the answer.

"*Why?* Because it's a mistake for Italians to be here in the first place," insisted the young, prematurely gray Roberto Donato. "Why does Rome feel obligated to do something equally as ruthless whenever Hitler makes a conquest? Austria and Czechoslovakia fell to Hitler, and immediately in parliament, at a prearranged cue by Count Ciano, several well-drilled deputies rose to their feet, shouting, 'Nice, Corsica, Tunis!' Are we not entrenched here in Corsica beyond our limits?''

"Rome will taste my wrath for such embarrassment if it proves to be a conspiracy to sabotage my efforts," said Victor sternly. "This Major Hans Hesse—"

"An ambitious superman," muttered Girro. "It is all contained in his dossier. We all know it by rote, no?"

"When have dossiers ever depicted the true man?" Victor said scornfully. "Odds against accuracy and truth increase when the profile is done on high-ranking German officers."

"Why would Rome send RSHA to Corsica?" queried Donato.

"Another imperial jest," said Victor. "We need guerrillas, animals capable of fighting in rugged mountain terrain. We need a Pancho Villa, not some prissy-footed, nazified dandy!"

In the ensuing silence Donato sipped his wine, eyeballing Girro and Noro before he put the question to Victor. "Please understand why we came, Victor. Awareness of the situation in Rome escapes you. Between the Germans and Italians is a delicate, tenuous relationship that is shaking the Party. With respect, Il Duce grows irrational. He suffers both physical and intellectual decline. Word is he is growing soft, dependent on flattery and deceit."

"*What?* What are you saying?" Victor leaped in defensively, turning his good ear toward the handsome Italian lawyer, a specialist in international law.

"Only that rumors are flying. Mussolini is becoming a weak, superstitious man, afraid of the evil eye, afraid of being ridiculed."

"It's true, Victor," said Miguel Noro, peering over his glasses. "We understand your devotion to your godfather, but you must understand that he is in his decline."

Victor poured more wine for his friends. "We've all seen the psychological havoc that infects the rank-and-file soldiers when unfounded rumors are absorbed by their impressionable minds. Can you quash them, Vincente?"

The military lawyer shook his head. "Vicious rumors—we called it enemy propaganda—paraded across all our desks in Rome.

"In Bastia it is the same. Rumors of mass surrenders, desertions, appalling disgrace to Italy! Army morale is falling to an all-time low, and now the enemy's trick is to use subtle psychological ploys to feed the superstitious Italian mentality.''

Miguel Noro sounded off. "The *communiste*. It's their work. I tell you one day they'll be a force to be reckoned with.''

Girro sipped his wine, tilted his head, and smacked his lips together like a connoisseur. "This wine is a bit dry for my taste.'' Victor reached for a decanter of robust red. Girro nodded, drained his glass, and filled it with the red wine.

"Let us get down to the matter of Major Hesse, the German RSHA agent,'' said Victor. "The move bodes ill. What effect will a real German presence have upon our men? Already there are dissenters.''

"We must prepare for all eventualities. When is Hesse due to arrive in Bastia?'' asked the military lawyer.

"Victor, forgive me, but I think I know the German mentality. He means to take over your command,'' Donato explained. "It's the way they work. In Rome. In North Africa. Here. It's always the same. Tell me, has the Duce backed you up?'' The query disturbed Victor.

"To answer your first question, Vincente, Hesse is overdue. He was due yesterday. To my knowledge, he is not here yet. As to his intention to take over my command in Corsica, I shall deal with that when and if it happens.''

"Prepare, Major Zeller, prepare for the worst,'' urged Roberto Donato. "I cannot emphasize how badly the Duce deteriorates. We—Miguel, Vincente, and myself—leave for Rome tomorrow. You remain behind to batten down the hatches, *amico*. Take care the German whirlwind doesn't blow you off the island.''

Victor was willing to listen to any amount of verbal dissection as long as it was constructive and sound. For the next half hour he listened intently to his well-meaning colleagues.

"You mustn't be fiercely protective of the Duce, Victor. Look to your own flanks. In the final analysis, we don't believe the Duce will survive. His illness drains him of good sense. You cannot remain a Paraclete for a losing cause, a failing leader.'' Noro's eyes fell to his file. "Italy is lost. The Germans are dealing the cards,'' he added sadly.

"You've all spelled out the reasons why someone must support Il Duce in his decline.''

"Victor, you aren't listening! By June, the government will

fall. Your godfather will be forced out of office. *Prepare! Prepare! Prepare!"* the trio sounded in unison.

Victor stared hard at his companions. Undercurrents of their conversation, the obviously unspoken words, signaled the unthinkable to him. He shook his head as if to deny his raucous thoughts. *Christ, let my suspicions be unfounded!* He sipped his wine, his glance roving from one face to the other, then staring at the dregs in his glass, he spoke up quietly.

"Tell me what I am thinking—and what you are considering—is untrue. Tell me I am wrong. Absolutely wrong in assuming why you've risked your lives to cross the sea to visit with me. It's true that we all accepted lies, lived with those lies. But are they now so unacceptable you are willing to risk your life to bring about changes? It isn't this smoke screen—you didn't come here to discuss the Germans at all. You have hatched dangerous plottings in those genius heads of yours." His voice was deadly.

"Victor," began Girro, "you've been absent from Rome for—"

"Four months! Count them. November, December, January, February. It's not a long time, Girro."

"Four months in war is a lifetime. Much has happened. Discontent is widespread. Military failure after failure breeds anarchy. Antifascism is everywhere. Newspapers are under strict orders to mention nothing of the enormous shortages. The masses grow torpid, cynical, disgusted. They believe fascism belied the true facts. Soldiers openly hurl invective against the government that led them into war so irresponsibly and ill prepared. Inflation spirals out of control! Drastic purges in the Party begin."

"But to plan a coup such as the one infecting your minds?" Victor demanded.

"Il Duce compares himself to Napoleon, and his latest comparison takes on grander aspects—Jesus Christ! Such delusions swell to compensate for his weaknesses and his failures."

"*Basta!* Enough!" Victor turned ashen. "Don't even consider it!"

His stomach churned. The words of his father echoed back like daggers to his heart. *"I am telling you how it will be,"* Amadeo Zeller had said to Victor, *"and you disdain me! Go! Fight a war for that counterfeit Caesar! Straw Caesar! Coun-*

terfeit Caesar.'' It was all coming to pass just as his father had predicted.

"Under all these crushing blows, cracks are beginning to appear inside the fascist ruling class." Donato leaned forward.

"No!" Victor held up a protesting hand. "I'll take no part in this dirty business. Don't involve me in your insanity. Don't say another word. How can I remain steadfast, loyal to my country when you force me to view it as crumbling internally?"

Noro, the cipher specialist, pulled his chair in closer to the desk. "Victor, be circumspect and sagacious. Dissident factions are edging toward the King. There is talk of deals with the Allies. I know. I see the coded messages. The American presidential agent is offering the moon to anyone who cooperates in breaking Hitler's back."

"You are crazy!" Victor exploded. "Il Duce is too firmly entrenched in power." He spoke the words, lifeless words that he hardly believed.

"Don't permit emotions to cloud good sense. Think on it. Rest assured our words will not travel beyond these doors. In Trieste, the *partigiani* are massing for a coup de main."

Victor sank heavily into his chair, maintaining a strained silence as the others fumbled nervously with their briefs and lit cigarettes. "Oh," he sighed despondently, "what an elaborate web we weave when first we conspire to deceive." He added somberly, "I take no part in this mad conspiracy, nor do I wish you good fortune. Consider that this meeting never took place. My lips are sealed. You know my word is my bond. If when it's over and we meet again—"

The others understood his agony.

Noro remained behind after Girro and Donato left. He appealed to Victor as if a blood bond existed between them. You and I must be very careful to tread lightly. We are both in dire straits. The climate in Rome for Jews grows worse."

"But I am not a—"

"I know. I know, Victor. You've never denied it openly because your godfather spared you by making the denial himself. But your father was well known for his—uh—shall we say Jewish persuasion. The Germans have long memories. Before this war ends we shall all deny our faiths. Our good friends and close companions in the Party frequent bistros less and less these days. Who among us believed Il Duce would fall prey to Hitler's persuasive demagoguery?''

Victor pursed his lips stubbornly, maintaining a silence.

''I understand your pain. The Duce was the parental figure in your life since your father's treasonous debacle.''

''Miguel, I do not wish to discuss the past when we are fighting for our lives in the present.''

''We are, all of us,'' Noro said, ''suddenly caught up in talk involving the lives and destinies of millions of people whose future is soon to be reflected in the crematory of German military minds.''

Goddammit! Victor had known it right from the beginning and had refused to believe it was the truth. Arrogant, goose-stepping Nazis pouring into Rome had prognosticated dooms-day for the Jews, just as his father had said they would. The Duce, once the most promising, powerful, and influential voice in Europe, had fallen limp against draconian Nazi methods.

''*Alora,* it is useless to speak to a deaf man,'' Noro continued. ''I made my point. I will take my leave, but as your friend, I beg you, exercise the utmost discretion in dealing with the German, Hans Hesse. Upon my arrival in Rome, I shall send you a very special dossier by diplomatic courier, one that is kept most secret in Bureau VI.''

''It is useless, I take it, to ask how you came by it?''

Noro tilted his head obliquely as if he were chastising a small lad for daring to ask forbidden questions concerning the act of fornication. ''*Ciao,* Vittorio. May we both survive Il Duce's fiascos and life to tell our grandchildren a story beginning, once upon a time . . .''

Two days later Victor received word from Hesse's adjutant; he'd arrive in Bastia by seven P.M. ''Unavoidably detained'' was his excuse.

Victor, standing at the window of his office sipping cognac, peered into the dusk at the Italian soldiers patrolling the sprawling complex. Beyond them, men from the ranks poured jerricans of precious gasoline into the gas tanks of a few Lancia trucks and Fiat two-seaters. Bored, Victor shifted his focus to the imposing fiery-purple twilight. Everything for as far as he could see was in harmonious juxtaposition. Tall, craggy mountain tors and lush green forests bathed in the light of the deepening amethyst sky colored the earth with brilliant hues. He sighed heavily.

Corsica—a stunning landscape but what a mass of contradictions. On the surface, its people with their half-French, half-Genoan songs and dances seemed peaceful, simple, lively, and gay. Serene and easygoing one day, they were raging and chaotic the next. How he loathed this land of megalomaniacal quasi-Emperors!

Back at his desk, Victor sifted through the daily reports. A sheaf of memos, brought in earlier by his aide, lay in a pile. He knew them by rote. "Proliferation of enemies from mainland France! . . . Massive Allied offensive in preparation. . . . Amphibious landings planned by Allied O.G.'s. . . ." etc. etc.

Dozens of reports—none verifiable!

Reports from collaborators: "Do not traverse the *maquis*!" "Civilized soldiers will be killed!" "There is a growing thunder in the *maquis*!" "Listen. Be wary!" . . . They were all alike and began to sound like echoes of words he'd heard from Donato, Noro, and Girro. Of what should he beware? Some supernatural force other than the usual perils of war? Of being a hated enemy in a strange land?

Earlier in the day, he'd made his daily broadcast to the island's inhabitants. "Italy will conquer Corsica and the *maquis* rebels and all those underground sewer rats spreading their disease through mobile radio units under the guise of the Voice of Freedom!"

Victor poured himself some white Bordeaux, leaned back in his cushioned red velour swivel chair, and glanced impatiently at the porcelain and ormolu clock on the terrazzo fireplace mantel. Damn Hesse! He was late again. Amid this perilous and provocative hotbed of revolution where uncertainties constantly thwarted him, must he be forced to put up with the likes of the Germans too?

There was a knock at the door. Victor's adjutant, Giovanni d'Este, entered. The redhaired, comely young man from northern Italy saluted. The urgency in his eyes communicated trouble.

"Che cosa, tenente?" D'Este placed a communiqué on the desk before Victor.

"The message, Maggiore Zeller, is most unpleasant."

Victor read it. "Damn them! Damn these Corsicans! Fifty of our best men killed! When will it stop?" He hurled his wineglass against the fireplace, shattering it to bits. Flying shards ricocheted and bit into him. One lodged over his left eye.

"*Maggiore, maggiore,* you are bleeding," shouted d'Este.

"Pay it no mind, d'Este. I'll take care of it. Leave me."

Catching the blood dripping into his eye, he entered an adjoining alcove to examine the punctures in a mirror over the commode. He carefully removed the glass splinters, cleansed the wound, and applied a blood coagulant. He patched the area and continued to stare at his reflection from various angles. It was not from a narcissistic bent that he periodically engaged in such charades, rather from his desire to still the nightmares born in his mind in the summer of '42 when he visited his father in Zürich.

Actually, they were manageable nightmares, the sort that relax their grip early in the morning and dissolve upon awakening. The nightmares had been fired by his father's haunting words, words that had followed him into Corsica.

"No matter whose blood flows through your body, never forget you are a Jew for as long as it serves my purpose!"

"And you, Father, are a crazy man!" Victor had wanted to retort that day. *Fool!* he said to himself now. *Why did you listen? Why permit the infection to set in?* Gazing at his reflection, he asked himself if it could really be possible. To what ends was his father willing to carry the farce endangering his life? Suddenly the entire German RSHA and Wehrmacht officers had focused on his so-called Jewish heritage! "Beware of the Germans," the Duce had counseled. "Your father, enemy of fascism, is now the archenemy of the Third Reich. He influences the banking communities of the world and changes, chameleonlike, from day to day. Who knows where his loyalties lie? Remember, the Nazis believe whatever best serves their purpose."

And Victor remembered Zürich. Rampant espionage. And Coco, the woman who had saved his life. From whom? *His father?* Oh, Christ! The Duce knew Amadeo Zeller lived! And his father had tried to have him killed—his own son!

Victor savagely hurled a porcelain pitcher at the mirror, fragmenting his image, splintering the glass. A maelstrom of daggerlike shards assaulted him. His hands flew to his face. He leaned over, gripping the blood-splattered tile counter, shaking uncontrollably as if seized by delirium tremens.

Victor stared with bloodless eyes at the glittering slivers of mirrored glass reflecting hundreds of unwanted images from wherever they had fallen. He cursed aloud, unleashing a string of expletives to reflect his rage. With his back to the shattered mirror, eyes clamped shut, he felt his father's words eat at him.

"Il Duce will be crushed! I am telling you what will be! You are a Jew for as long as it suits my purpose!"

And Victor screamed internally, *No! No, no, no, no! Damn you, Father! Damn you for wishing this catastrophe on me!* He opened his eyes and stared at the multiple images dotted with blood staring back at him. As he cleansed his wounds, he was forced to consider Noro, Girro, Donato, and their alarming words. Worse, he was forced to reconsider his father's powerful edicts which, by the Holy Father in heaven, were coming to pass. Had his own father tried to have him killed for the knowledge he'd gleaned in Zürich? *Zürich! Curse the day I went there!*

Noro spoke the truth, thought Victor. The Nazis' disdain, impudence, and unscrupulous brutalities had appalled Victor. Steeling himself against them, determined to make it impossible for them to pierce his armor, Victor had barely tolerated them in Rome. *Oh, you fool! The Germans had barely tolerated you!*

Now, here in Corsica, he was about to tangle horns with the deadliest, most ambitious of all Nazis—Major Hans Hesse. The composite forming in his mind these past several weeks, reinforced by the updated dossier he'd just received from Noro, grew more and more distasteful. Any liaison with this Jew hater would be dangerous.

The bleeding stopped. Victor removed his bloodstained tunic and slapped cologne on his face, wincing at the acute stinging sensation. He agitated the air about him, forcing swifter evaporation, patting the skin lightly until the burning subsided. He brushed back his hair, slipped into a fresh uniform tunic with gleaming brass buttons, and glanced at the wall clock, becoming angry at the time. Seven-thirty!

Hesse, the bastard, was deliberately late. It was a psychological ploy to shatter his composure. The lesson had been taught him by his father. Nothing is more unnerving to an official than to keep him waiting.

Chapter Six

A knock on the door interrupted Victor's reverie. He put himself in order, closed the door to the alcove, and spoke aloud. *"Avanti."*

Major Hans Hesse strutted into the room like a black pestilence. *"Heil Hitler!"* he snapped, saluting. Victor acknowledged the salute with a fascist wave of his hand. Behind the German, Major Zeller's adjutant, wagging a limp wrist, made an exaggerated expression of mock terror and closed the door behind him.

"You are long overdue, Major Hesse." Victor poured brandy into two snifters, handing one to Hesse. Hesse launched into a toast.

"To our victory, Major." They clinked glasses and sipped the contents. Hesse sat down and began to lament with polite disdain the inequities of duty in Paris. "Nothing in that decadent land of French whores and bourgeois dullards progresses as it should. In North Africa, despite Rommel's illness and absence from the front, we are dusting the perimeters of the totally inept Americans, giving them a real taste of German tankfare. It will please you to know that Operation Tiger Tank was successful." His assessing eyes were everywhere. "Very clever of you fascists to annex Corsica, my dear Major Zeller. Let us make a pact, *ja?* Together we shall outwit the underground moles infesting France. We must insure that Corsica doesn't turn into another Greek or Libyan fiasco.''

Victor had disliked Hesse on paper; in person, the German's loathsome, pompous, and aggravating manner was even worse. He trusted neither Hesse nor his office. RSHA, Bureau VI, was anathema to Victor, more despicable than the storm-trooping Gestapo. His bland expression, however, gave Hesse little indication of his inner revulsion.

Hesse removed a manila file from his briefcase, then handed the stamped top-secret, confidential communiqué to Victor. It was from the Rome office! He glanced cursorily at the signature: Oberstgruppenführer von Ludwig, the Nazi whose monocle, small brush mustache, and rigid bearing suggested a caricature of a somber-faced, heel-clicking Prussian general. He was the man who in 1936 had seized eight thousand Jews in Rome, transported them to northern Italy after collecting handsome ransoms from each as assurance he'd save them, then ordered them killed. *Von Ludwig!*

Victor read the orders. The strained cordiality vanished at once. Outraged, he exploded. *"I am to do what?"* He read aloud: "Begin conscription of the Corsicans to Minsk?" Victor stopped. *"Nein, nein,* Major. There is some mistake. My orders are to keep the Corsicans working the farmlands. We need food stores. Ours have dwindled. These people are farmers with no knowledge of machinery. I suggest you obtain your quotas from the cities on the Continent. I prefer to coalesce with the Corsicans.''

"What you *prefer,* Major, is of no concern. These are direct orders from General von Ludwig.''

"Not from Hitler himself?'' Victor remarked snidely.

"It is the same thing. If misfortune should befall our Führer, only General von Ludwig would replace him.''

"Not Göring? Goebbels? Himmler or God himself? What of Kesselring?''

If Hesse heard the remarks, he feigned disinterest. He moved about the office, impressed with the decor. "I expected to find you quartered in a stable or a loft, consorting with pigs and chickens.''

"You'd find that more appropriate, would you? Here in the

birthplace of Napoleon?'' Victor finished off the brandy. ''Corsicans are too noble, too proud to permit us to find anything but princely splendor here, or haven't you heard about Corsicans? They all believe they are descended from Napoleon.'' Victor's dislike of Hesse grew by the moment.

''What do I report to General von Ludwig? You read the documents, Major.''

''The matter demands clearance from Rome.''

''*Dear* Major Zeller, it *was* cleared in Rome. Von Ludwig is Rome these days. Surely you cannot discount the importance of *Abwehr*?''

Sidestepping the issue, Victor replied with polite mockery, ''Il Duce has stepped down from power? When? How?''

Hesse coolly observed Victor's exaggerated astonishment under lidded eyes. Then in a sudden mood reversal, he laughed. ''You are an amusing man, Major Zeller. *Jawohl,* most amusing.''

Victor sobered. ''It was not my intent to amuse you. Nor am I a capricious man. Clearance on *any* order comes only from my immediate superiors.''

''Ah. Apparently I failed to clarify. You are speaking to your immediate superior officer. Why else would I be here except to relieve you of your duties? On orders, Major Zeller. I take over your command in thirty days.'' He opened his briefcase and with his dexterous right hand removed a sheaf of papers and placed them on the desk before Victor.

''Thirty days, eh? You Germans believe in punctuality, *nein*?''

Victor swiftly sorted through the papers, knowing what to look for. *There—the change in command signed by Il Duce. Incredible!* What pressures were brought to bear to shove him against the wall in this dirty business? Victor's features remained impassive.

''An immense Allied offensive—covert, of course—is taking place under your very nose, Major Zeller. You have failed to report it, to IMI in Rome or to General Command Headquarters. Why?''

''I take it you're referring to Operation White Coral?''

''You *know*?'' Hesse's jaw fell slack in astonishment. ''Why wasn't it reported? What are your intentions, your plans to obliterate it?''

"I have none until the facts are in. We *know* the intent. We don't know *when* it is to take place or how many forces will be arrayed against us. Two of our top men have infiltrated the Resistance in the *maquis*."

"You know the location of their secret encampment?"

"It's the most coveted secret since Operation Barbarossa commenced. Few of the Resistance leaders are privy to it. I shan't describe the nature of the local mentality. If you've done your homework, you know the psychology of these islanders. What is it, Major Hesse? You seem disturbed."

"*Ja*, more than you, perhaps. And you have reason to be disturbed. A most special caliber of men makes up the Allied task force and operational groups. Field Marshal Rommel reports them as formidable, the cause of massive damage in North Africa. One man, personally selected by de Gaulle himself, leads the *Bataillon de Choc*—those shock troops called commandos."

"The SAS commandos, Hesse. Two of these men are on the Gestapo's most-wanted list in Paris? What further information can I render you RSHA men?"

"Why haven't you ferreted out their stronghold?"

"I have no reason to believe they are presently based in Corsica."

"Wrong!" Hesse gloated. "We have intercepted radio communications in Marseilles, broken the French cipher. Now we can beam into their frequency with ease. I won't belabor the point until after aerial reconnaissance photos are in. Masterminding the operation is none other than our enemy, General Donovan, a man with unlimited power. Roosevelt sent him as presidential envoy to incite Europeans to rebel against Germany. His office, Major Zeller, has grown into the largest espionage and sabotage bureau in any Anglo-Saxon country including Great Britain. Donovan intends to create for Roosevelt a huge fifth column in Europe and South America. Terrorism, acts of sabotage, revolts, corruption, and bribery are the main ingredients cooked up in the Roosevelt-Donovan soup."

"Not Donovan in person. His well-trained assistants, men trained by British SOE and the office that spawned Intrepid are co-commanding OWC." Victor poured more brandy for them. "British SIS. Secret intelligence."

"Ja, ja," Hesse muttered lamely. "Do you know who heads the commandos?" He picked up the brandy snifter, stared at his useless hand, his voice a hair above a whisper.

The answer to that question was the missing link in Victor's investigation. In two months he'd been unable to identify the purported leader of the SAS commandos; he knew only that they had been renamed the Mozarabe.

"Why don't you tell me something for a change? I'll brief you fully before you take over your duties."

Hesse sipped the brandy, placed the glass on a silver tray. He lifted his dead hand and let it fall with a thud on the desk. Victor's eyes were riveted to the gloved prosthesis. "Because of that man, that thorn in my side, I am left with this useless facsimile of a hand. He is a dead man, Major Zeller. A dead man! I have vowed to kill him. We were together at Sidi bel Abbes when we Germans infiltrated the ranks for the purpose of espionage, part of our impeccable planning and preparation for the North African conquest." Hesse sat down, placed his useless hand into his lap.

"He is unique. I'll give the Corsican that much. Not ten St. Cyr alumni together can equal his military prowess. The man circumvented tradition, transcended the Legion's rules. . . ." Hesse described Darius Bonifacio, painted an in depth profile without ever referring to him by name. He described the abrasive conditions at Sidi and what followed at El Bayadh in the rout forced upon him by Muhammad Abou Ahkmed Hassan. Hesse graphically described Ernst von Luden's fate at El Kalahara, the massive butchery done the German's body. "Von Luden's body was delivered to his encampment the following morning on the rump of a mule. The victim's identification was pinned to the bloody sack, his officer's helmet sat on the mule's head, holes cut out to accommodate its long ears. The officer's boots were strung together over the mule's ass."

"Odd," Victor said quietly. "Our intelligence agents reported the atrocity was performed by the brother of a man whom your German pederast, von Luden, had cruelly sodomized, debauched, and set afire like a human torch."

Hesse cut him a sharp, reproving look, then gazing into space, muttered, "The desert plays strange tricks on a man's mind. Von Luden went *cafard.*"

"What part did you play in so craven and depraved an act,

Major? Please—please take no umbrage at my query. My curiosity is official. You confess you intend to kill the Corsican whom you blame for mutilating your left hand. Hesse, personal issues have no place in offensive or defensive military action.. Were I to report your story in detail—items missing from your dossier—it might disqualify you from taking over my command.''

''My personal decisions take no precedence over Wehrmacht directives.''

Victor laughed uproariously. ''No? But *our* decisions sure as hell influence the Army, don't they?''

''Since you seem bent on scoring points, shall we see how this data dents that Italian composure?'' Hesse slapped a dossier on the desk before Victor. The name Darius Bonifacio stood out in bold print. Hesse poured more brandy and, glass in hand, sauntered about the room examining artifacts as Victor eagerly scanned the contents.

Was this the missing link in Victor's list of assiduously compiled facts? Darius Bonifacio? Victor projected a casual, disinterested attitude as he perused the dossier line for line, rechecking data entries and stumbling over the stunning revelations. Several moments later he made a casual observation. ''He rose from the rank of enlistee to captain in the Legion in less than a year? No previous military training? Intelligence Corps? The North African Intelligence Service, no less? It's not a move made by your average man in the ranks.''

''I don't recall using the word *average* in describing Bonifacio,'' Hesse said. ''General von Ludwig ordered me to Corsica to speed up defenses, reinforce our installations, spruce up our spy network, and prepare to break the enemy's back. If as you say, you have the matter under control, I shall request transfer back to Paris. I prefer it to this uncivilized land any day. Yes, yes, perhaps if I submit my report to Rome—''

''And deliberately defy orders, Major Hesse? Before I have an opportunity to confirm them? *I don't think so,*'' Victor said slowly, drawing out each word with special emphasis.

Hesse braced himself stiffly, hands behind his back. ''Be assured no doubts have emerged as to the locus of your ultimate loyalty. However, since you are disinclined to cooperate with the orders of my superiors, you leave me with no alternative. We Germans cannot repeatedly conjure up miracles to save your *dummer* Italian *Esel! Der Führer* needs no unexpected defeats at so crucial a point in the war. The Americans are making great strides in North Africa. General Rommel was recalled—''

"So far, Major Hesse, the only talent shown by Americans in this war is the proffering of chocolates, chewing gum, and nylon stockings. Very little indeed." His eyes were riveted on the report.

Victor, aware of the frailties of his office, knew intuitively that Hesse was intriguing against him. Italian military intelligence wasn't the sophisticated tool of the Duce's that it should be. Hesse's eyes showed contempt for the ineptness of the Italians.

"It is neither my intention nor desire to be shoved into an adversary position with an ally, Major," Victor said. *"Gute Nacht, Sturmbannführer. Wie sag man auf deutsch—che sarà sarà?"*

"I shudder at the consequences if *che sarà sarà* becomes the war cry of Axis soldiers in the Corsican campaign," Hesse snapped icily, turning to leave. "I am motoring to Ajaccio to inspect all military installations en route. Shall I *need*, uh—special permits bearing *your* signature, Major Zeller?"

Victor ignored the acerbity. "My adjutant will accommodate you with the proper papers." He saluted snappily with a curt dismissal, but inwardly he bridled impatiently.

Hesse, masking his fury with a bland look, *Sieg heil*ed, clicked his heels, and exited with panache.

Outside Fritz Schmidt fell into step alongside Hesse, escorting him to the waiting Mercedes touring car emblazoned with swastikas. Hesse entered the rear door and sank heavily into the deeply cushioned leather seat. Schmidt took his place next to the driver in the front seat.

The driver leisurely maneuvered the powerful machine over the cobbled streets, heading northwest out of Bastia along the shoreline road toward Nebbio. Suddenly the sickening wail of speeding motorcycles and sirens converged upon the sedan from all points. Two lorries filled with armed Italian soldiers crawled toward the Germans. Hesse ordered his driver to stop as an Italian corporal on a morotcycle pulled alongside the car. The Italian saluted smartly.

"Major Zeller's compliments, Major. An escort is mandatory, since you insist upon traversing the *maquis*. We normally stay clear of the area, Major. Corsican brigands, cutthroats, fugitives from the law—believe me, they all lack respect for a uniform—*any* uniform. They'd just as soon stop you, rob and kill you, and leave your carcass to the buzzards. Attacking a task force or convoy takes no more effort on their part than breaking wind."

Major Hesse, infuriated, turned about in his seat and studied the dim, spectral outline of rugged peaks against the diminishing city lights. The briefing he had received on this island and its inhabitants had conveyed the remoteness of a strange, primordial, dangerous, and uncommunicative people. Clannish, medieval at best, most hadn't the slightest knowledge of the twentieth century. He touched his cap to the Italian soldier, tapped his driver's shoulder with his riding crop. "Proceed," he said tersely. "Follow the Corporal."

Looming in the distance, flickering lights marked the approach to the port of Calvi. Hesse turned on a shortwave receiver, adjusting the tuner past the squawks and burping interference.

There . . . that voice again! That infuriating voice!

"Fellow Frenchmen, you are listening to the Voice of Freedom. Zahara greets you. Daily we grow closer to our objective —the liberation of France!"

Hans Hesse cursed aloud, growing furiously hostile. That voice plagued him, nagged at him constantly. *"Driver!"* he screeched in a falsetto. "Locate a bistro that serves fine seafood. Schmidt, when we arrive, send one of the soldiers to Calvi headquarters. Requisition a radio mobile tracking unit at once! I want that *verdammen* Voice of Freedom found, do you understand?"

"Jawohl, mein Sturmbannführer." Schmidt nudged the driver, wary of Hesse's corrosive temper brewing dangerously close to an explosion. The driver pulled off the main road and headed through narrow streets toward the waterfront, followed by the escort cortege. They pulled to a stop before a dingy waterfront bistro.

"Disregard its shabby appearance, Major," the driver blurted. "Cesare's is the best in Calvi. His crustaceans are *köstlich,* very delicious."

Schmidt alighted from the sedan to have a talk with the Italian Corporal. Hesse, using his radio apparatus, called Bastia headquarters. He was politely informed that Major Victor Zeller had left for the evening. Cursing, Hesse snapped off the set, stepped out of the sedan, and entered the bistro. One military escort positioned himself at the entrance, another at the rear exit. The Major, treated deferentially, was seated at a choice table. He ordered a banquet of seafood for himself and Schmidt.

Schmidt entered the quaint, somewhat dilapidated bistro and went directly to Hesse's table with the bad news. "Two hours, Major, is the best headquarters can do. It takes time to rig the lorry with proper transmitting devices."

Bitterly resigned to his fate in this savage land, Hesse relaxed. "Come, Fritz, we eat. I ordered for you. You deserve a moment's relaxation."

They feasted ravenously and were nearly finished with their coffee when Arabic music started up. Hesse's eyes darted about the shadowy room with its departing diners, noting for the first time the Moorish influence of the bistro's shabby decor. Two belly dancers manipulating finger cymbals entered the room from behind torn burlap curtains and moved through the room with undulating movements and rhythmic body gyrations. They were followed by two men pointing lanterns at them in a poor simulation of spotlights.

Cesare, the obsequious proprietor, short, rotund, and jolly faced, came over to the Germans, subtly hinting at the available carnal pleasures, if the officers were so disposed. Hesse glanced past him at the dark-skinned, black-haired dancers.

"Reminds you of Sidi, *ja*, Schmidt?"

Schmidt crunched the last lobster claw, his eyes critically shifting to the dancers in appraisal. "*Ja, mein Sturmbannführer,* but not as filthy."

Hesse's blond hair shone nearly white in the dim lighting. He spoke to Cesare in Italian, asking him to recite the list of available carnal pleasures as he might request a wine list. The portly proprietor had never before been asked such a ludicrous question, and he shrugged negligently, not knowing how to respond. Could the Major be more specific in his preferences? Hesse assured Cesare his tastes leaned toward the exotic in sex. He placed several Deutsche marks and French francs on the table in excess of what the dinner and the women would cost. "Take what you consider a fair price," Hesse encouraged.

Shrewd street savvy dictated the Corsican's next moves. He raised large workman's hands protestingly and feigned offense at the mention of money. "Major, your money pays for nothing at Cesare's establishment. The privilege to serve you and fill your desires is mine."

A testy anxiety hovered over the German. Avoiding the Corsican's eyes, he stuffed the bills in Cesare's vest pocket. "We Germans do not accept gratuities from honest, hardworking men. Let it be known that we pay our way. I leave the choice of wenches to you. One for my adjutant and one for me." Turning to an astonished Schmidt, he said tightly, "Do what you will with her. Be ready to depart precisely at midnight. Now, proprietor, I shall take that one—the black-haired desert flower with the gold *papillons* in her hair." Hesse stopped abruptly. The words stuck in his throat. Images danced past him, sensuous body movements, voluptuous violet eyes outlined in black kohl. *A dancer with golden butterflies tucked into waist-length hair of ebony!* Thunderstorms of golden lights dazzled his senses, bursting through dusty memories! Flashing white teeth! Throbbing, pulsating sexual energy, undulating rhythm! He gasped. The pieces tumbling in his mind collided, forming a composite.

"St. Germaine! Lomay St. Germaine!" A slow intake of breath followed the words, indicating the gravity of his discovery.

Schmidt's head jerked about, neck craned, eyes scanning the dimly lit room. No one here vaguely resembled the queen bee of Fatima's Pleasure Dome. He turned back to Hesse as if the man were *cafard*. "What is it, Major Hesse? I fail to understand. I see no one." The dreadful smile snaking Hesse's lips into a leer brought shudders to Schmidt. How many times had he cringed at the sight of it? He wiped greasy fingers on a *serviette*, eyes skipping over Hesse's face.

"That's why you remain an adjutant, Schmidt. You *don't* see, do you? Look! The *dancer*, The hair, eyes, body, *and* the golden *papillon*! It stirs no memories? Rings no bells? We've won, Fritz! We've won!" he shouted in hushed jubilation. "She is our elusive Voice of Freedom!"

Schmidt jerked his head about so quickly that pain spasms assaulted his neck. He groaned, rubbed the area gingerly, eyes devouring the dancer. *She* is Zahara?'' he asked incredulously, thinking his chief demented.

''*Dummkopf!* Not her! St. Germaine! Our unending nightmare—the Voice of Freedom under our very noses now, here, and we never put it together! The elusive Zahara is St. Germaine from Sidi.''

''St. Germaine? *Zahara?*'' Schmidt turned the stunning idea over in his mind.

''The obvious is seldom considered! Neither contrary to facts nor impervious to reason, the truth nearly immobilized us. *Gottes Wege sind wunderbar!* Strange are the ways of providence, eh, Fritz?''

There was no need to reply to the rhetorical proverb. Schmidt, squirming in his chair, grimly recollected the bad blood between St. Germaine and Hans Hesse. He watched his chief pour more wine, twirl the contents of the glass, inhale its bouquet before sipping it. Exquisite evil lit his battleship-gray eyes to hot coals. Here it comes, thought Fritz, sitting rigidly in his chair.

''Zahara—Voice of Freedom—how do I loathe thee? Shall I count the ways? Zahara, secret weapon of the Resistance—'' His sarcasm was laced with bitter, black memories. He raised his glass in midair. ''I toast to your demise. May it be slow . . . unmerciful.'' He stared hard at Schmidt. Instantly his adjutant poured wine for himself, clinked glasses with his superior, and gulped it desperately, attempting to piece together the puzzle Hesse had solved in a flash of insight. Why couldn't his mind function as rapier sharp as Hesse's? Plagued by his own deficiencies, he measured men by his own frailties and inadequacies. Scrutinizing the changes on Hesse's face, he knew the riddle would be unleashed on him. *Gottverdammen!* Why wasn't his brain as facile a tool?

Hesse considered Fritz Schmidt's unalterably bungling mind. The recent disgrace of the Pythia episode still troubled him. Her mysterious disappearance. Hah! *Das Dungermittel!* It was conspiracy! A clear case of cleverly executed conspiracy designed to compromise RSHA! Pythia was a spy! A cleverly trained British spy. A plant. He'd known it from the start. It was all there, the instabilities of her profiled dossier, the inconsistencies of her past. But in Berlin General Kaltenbruner had ordered, "Play along with Pythia. Let the ferrets dig up all they can on her. Put your best men on the task."

And Hesse had blindly complied. As a result, he'd suffered irreparable damages, inestimable losses. Choice trained agents, SS specialists sprawled about the Chantilly airstrip in unidentifiable bits and pieces, had been his reward, a testament to Pythia's frenzied, audacious departure. Departure? Hah! *Escape* is what it was! She'd been onto him and his men. What a bold front she'd presented! How many times had she, with imposing fortitude, warned him not to put the SS or SD on her trail? Her resolute azure eyes pierced his without the slightest tremor or suggestion of fear. Attracted to her physically, he'd forcibly restrained himself. And what had he left? One man sequestered in a private hospital who was hovering between life and death! *One man!* The only survivor knew all the events leading to Chantilly, all the stops in between, the possible contacts, the identity of her driver, and what actually happened at that remote, deserted, flying strip. And he was unable to talk! Paralyzed, his vocal cords atrophying from the psychological shock of the nightmare and the severe wounds sustained. He was still on the critical list.

"It was a fiasco, Schmidt, hopeless. Fraught with ambiguities. I complied against my better judgment, but at the proper time I shall make my report to the Führer."

"Pythia." Fritz sighed, recognizing the spiel. He knew when to be obsequious. "Let them all beat their political tom-toms, Herr Sturmbannführer. It will be to your drumbeats that the grand and glorious Third Reich will be goose-stepping."

"At times, Schmidt, you are quite brilliant," he responded to the flattery. He shoved the Pythia matter to the back burner as sparks of inspiration motivated him. A major policy shift—highly irregular in concept—wormed its way through his orderly, cleverly diabolical mind. He leaned forward and spoke in a hushed whisper to his adjutant.

Listening intently, Schmidt played devil's advocate.

"You are reversing your subordinate role to Major Victor Zeller *before* the official orders are implemented? Without his approval on so volatile an endeavor?" Schmidt's eyes rolled upward, his mouth formed the proper, unspoken veneration. He added quickly in passable French, *"C'est magnifique, mais ce n'est pas la guerre."*

"Precisely. As long as the plan works, who cares if it's done according to the rules of war? Actually, Schmidt, I have little choice. I stand at the center of a growing pile of manure. Action is needed! *Jawohl?*"

Action is what Hans Hesse got.

A half hour later, he and his entourage arrived at a sequestered cove along the northern shores of Corsica near Île-Rousse east of St. Florent, at a midway point to Bastia. The touring sedan pulled off the main road, took a hidden path toward the sea, and stopped at the sight of another vehicle. Headlights signaled the proper number of blinks. The uniformed Germans stepped from the car and moved stealthily over the underbrush, guns drawn. Behind them the escorts clustered around the sedan, forming a cordon around it, awaiting the return of Hesse and Schmidt. Guns at ready, the twelve German soldiers peered about in the darkness, inhaling the fresh sea aromas and fragrance of the *maquis.*

Hesse and Schmidt boarded a well-camouflaged, hastily requisitioned lorry that operated between Nebbio and Ile-Rousse, one equipped with high-powered radio transmitters and radar disks. At once Hesse was seated alongside the Signal Corps radio operator and cipher specialist. He prepared coded messages for German headquarters in Marseilles. From there, the highly classified data would be trasmitted to Bureau VI, Berlin, RSHA headquarters in Paris and to General Kesselring in Rome. Hesse subdued his ebullience.

Kill three birds with one stone! Perhaps many more, eh?

Finished, each meticulously detailed message was read back to him by a thoroughly confused, dubious radio operator. "It makes no sense, *Sturmbannführer!*"

"*Gut, Rottenführer.* The messages are not supposed to enlighten anyone save the sender and recipient."

"But, Major! I have my orders! I must follow the prescribed cipher."

"It does not follow the usual cipher. This follows JB-1 priority. *Wolfsschanze*—JB-1. Do not argue, Corporal. You will do as you are told. My credentials are impeccable, as Adjutant Schmidt indicated." With an air of long suffering, he nodded to Schmidt.

"*Kommen.*" He stepped from the mobile radio unit into the

darkness of night by the sea. The sounds of seagulls, wild surf crashing along the shore, and muted foghorn signals pierced the night and added to Hesse's exhilaration. He paused a moment, waited, listened to the tap, tap, tap of the wireless dancing a pleasurable staccato. Each sound multiplied his exuberance and his hatred—a profoundly deep, never-to-be-forgotten hatred.

Within the hour Lomay St. Germaine's description and code name—Zahara—would top the Gestapo's most-wanted list. Every Axis *Abwehr* and RSHA headquarters would feel the impact of his discovery! It was his coup! The Führer would be told, apprised of Hans Hesse's personal triumph. He could feel the well-deserved laurel wreath placed on his head as he lit up a cigar.

What a masterstroke! He owed it all to butterflies and a finely honed memory. Golden butterflies shimmering in a nest of hip-length ebony hair. *Too bad, black beauty, you drew the battlelines two years ago, first by rejecting my manhood, second by your affiliation with Prince Youseff Ben-Kassir. I'll see you dead before this war is over!*

The wounds were deep, the scars hardened by now, but he'd never, never forget the affront! Suddenly Hans Hesse cocked his head, angled around, eyes locking briefly with Schmidt's. The adjutant, grimly familiar with that look, flipped his cigarette into the sand, braced at once. "*Ja, mein Herr?* What is it?"

"The Deuxième Bureau, Paris! The list. The *list*, Fritz! The defectors from Vichy. Do you remember them? Think, man, think! Was the code name *Zahara* on it? Even Lomay St. Germaine? Perhaps Papillon?"

Fritz closed his eyes, forming an image of the list, that terrible list that arrived twice monthly, naming Germany's new enemies.

"Think Schmidt!" Hesse commanded as they approached the touring car. One of the waiting soldiers scurried around to the side of the car, opened the rear door, and stood braced at attention. "Remember, God never rewards a lazy thinker or a coward."

"I've got it! *Papillon! Ja! Ja! Papillon!*"

Hesse's eyes widened. He removed his visored hat with his right hand, held it as he ran his fingers through his tingling scalp.

"Of course! Right before our very eyes and we never figured it out! Papillon was her code name with Deuxième for Vichy," He paused. "Her defection . . . let's see . . . shortly after the occupation. Perhaps a year later in 1941. Yes, I can see it. It was 1941."

"And now she works for Prince Ben-Kassir's staunchest ally—the de Gaulle intelligence services—the Resistance!"

"Charles de Gaulle intelligence—"

Schmidt was cut off. Hesse spun around. "Come back to the mobile unit. We have a most interesting message to transmit."

Suddenly the cigar spilled from Hesse's lips. He tensed, braced himself. The earth roared, rumbled underfoot. Earsplitting blasts shattered the still night. Hesse and Schmidt and the others were propelled helplessly into the air, engulfed by seas of blackness. Hesse felt himself tumbling, spiraling through endless tunnels and falling against a hard, solid wall with such impact he thought every bone in his body was broken. Explosions at all sides of him, streaks of unbearable lights zigzagging everywhere, obscured everything. He saw nothing.

Bombs, grenades, and guns held by hidden hands spewed bullets of fire. Flamethrowers torched the perimeter of the mobile unit where cars and motorcycles formed a cordon at the broad center of sand and underbrush near the water's edge, creating a ring of fire around their target, the radio transmitter.

Betrayal! Hesse could vaguely make out Cesare Barbone's face, contorted, twisted into a leer, dimming as the German's focus weakened. Thunderous blasts of plastic explosives split the radio lorry and surrounding vehicles into shards of broken metal and glass, setting fire to the gas tanks. The last thing Hesse saw before pain and shock took its toll and sent him reeling into oblivion was Fritz Schmidt suspended like a flying rag doll over the crushed hood of the touring car remains.

From their cover positions on boulders overlooking the periphery of the devastation, the trained Mozarabe death squad lowered wired earphones to their necks as the detonations subsided. Inhuman sounds shrieked by men whose bodies were on fire continued to pierce the night. The wretched survivors bolted, lurched, stumbled and fell into the sea, howling animal-like screeches. The body fires were quickly extinguished, but the wailings were unquenchable.

The eyes behind the deadly accurate gunsights observed the

mass carnage. The chiefs spoke into walkie-talkies, signaling the accomplished mission. The targets had been destroyed. No one could survive the holocaust. Now they could return, honor intact, the deed done.

Why didn't they cheer? And one particular man deserved praise for his shrewd assessment and rapid decision in contacting the Resistance camps. But even Cesare Barbone's spirit lagged.

Standing behind the death squad, he stared at the violence in silent sobriety. Earlier, he had overheard the stunning revelation spilling from Major Hesse's lips, and the unquestionable identification of Zahara had forced him into action. Instant contact made via a hidden suitcase transmitter to a Resistance camp in the *maquis* south of Calvi had brought his brother, Chamois, and the fighters on the run.

After the brilliant success, he invited the Resistance fighters back to Calvi for drinks on the house. The fighters advanced toward the devastation to measure the extent of their destruction. They stopped abruptly.

The sound of approaching sirens forced them into retreat. They scrambled back to their cover positions; some crouched on boulders, others fell into a holding pattern some two hundred yards from the debacle, guns at ready, grenades palmed, critically and with growing confusion eyeing the approaching vehicles.

German rescue teams! Orderlies, soldiers, many wearing Red Cross arm bands! What the bloody devil was going on?

Chamois Barbone questioned the activity below them near the shore. Axis soldiers? Corsican police out of Bastia arriving on the heels of crack rescue squads? He counted at least fifty Italian and German uniforms forming a cordon around the perimeter of dying fires as broken, near-comatose bodies were fished from the debris of smoke and ashes.

Son of a bitch! Now the injured and near-dead Germans would be rushed to the Maison de Santé in St. Florent to be mended, given new life with which to avenge and destroy enemies of the Third Reich.

Scowling darkly, Chamois Barbone and a dozen *maquis* fighters, positioned crablike on their bellies over a slew of boulders, peered down at the scene. No one was angrier than the weasel-faced Chamois. He reholstered his gun and gazed through high-powered binoculars at the unfolding drama, his features twisted to a mask of discontent. He was seething inwardly. *Goddammit! It takes no brilliant warring genius to locate the missing piece to this puzzling scenario!*

Betrayal, Chamois! Pure and simple betrayal!

By whom? Why? For what purpose besides the obvious one—to save Major Hans Hesse's ass?

The devil is plotting against Corsica!

It was hot. Plagued by a sirocco, sweating from the exhausting heat and nervewracking activity, the men stripped to their waists and spoke in controlled whispers. Such heat could make men crazy, make them see things that didn't exist. There . . . they looked at the sea! A southwesterly wind whipped the waves to frothy heights. *When had Corsican seas in the north been so choppy? An ominous sign?*

Chamois, listening to the voices carried in the night, turned deaf ears to them. He glanced at the luminous dial of his watch, biting his underlip in vexation. What should have ended neatly tied in a victory ribbon was wrapped in betrayal. A vicious beast had been spared, free—if he survived his injuries—to terrorize again.

Once more, he glanced at his watch, measuring time against distance. He had to be certain. *Christ! You are certain! It takes no mathematician to compute facts!*

The way Chamois read the scenario, Cesare's message had arrived at the *maquis* encampment at Muro, south of Calvi, at approximately the same time, give or take a few minutes, as a second message which had reached Bastia summoning assistance to resist the spur-of-the-moment, hatched-up scheme to liquidate the German officers and the mobile unit.

Betrayal? In spades!

Allowing for muck-ups, the death squad had ridden horseback with swift dispatch inland from Muro, over rough mountainous terrain through Belgodere, increasing their forces with additional men and supplies at various other camps en route to Île-Rousse. *Very well,* thought Chamois, rising on his haunches, eyes still on the evacuation below, his mind fixed on the activity that must have ensued in Bastia. Police, Axis soldiers, rescue squads, all leaving the capital city at approximately the same time would lose no more than fifteen or twenty minutes floundering in narrow mountain passes where corkscrew roads inhibit speed.

Ten, fifteen minutes, even a half-hour delay would have brought the enemy to Île-Rousse about when it did. All their actions, including the timing, did not preclude betrayal.

Someone in the Resistance had betrayed the Mozarabe!

"Son of a bitch!" he cursed aloud in his falsetto voice that pitched higher and higher with rising anger. He slid off the rock, growling like an enraged bear, and moved back toward a flatbed truck hidden in the shadows of a dense thicket.

He had important things to do. He signaled his departure to the others, started up the near-paralytic engine, and headed south. As he drove, the word "betrayal" pounded in his mind. Who would dare betray Corsica? Betray Chamois Barbone, for that matter? His eternal memory for slights and betrayals was legend. Still . . . instinct whispered the truth.

Grow up, Chamois! This is war! Not Corsican vendetta! He thought about this crazy war which brought the incursion of strangers to Corsican shores. Could any of them be trusted? Scholars, criminals, doctors, lawyers, dispatchers, trained technicians, defectors from Nazi-controlled nations, even Russians—communists, for Christ's sake! Who the hell knew *any* of these men, all of whom carried special papers! What a racket—these special papers. He whistled under his breath and returned to the infernal itch plaguing him—betrayal! The old island laws and rules were no longer reliable or applicable to this war scenario. The changes were driving him crazy. Once, you could trust a Corsican to be Corsican. One wrong move and a bullet to the head would end all disputes. Now he must abide by the books.

He spat aloud, glowering darkly at the thought of betrayal, a betrayal he was no longer empowered to deal with. "*Fuck around with Chamois Barbone, eh?* You think you can make me cringe? Shut off my instinct by mental castration? Oh, no!" he shouted loudly to an invisible enemy. "I know what I know. I saw what I saw! This head won't stop working because foreigners trespass our lands."

Grimly tugging on his beaked cap, pulling it over his brows, he gunned the motor, drove roughshod over precarious inland trails to avoid German and Italian installations.

He arrived at Terra Bonifacio as dawn peeked over the eastern horizon. He brought the truck to a screeching halt, jumped off the running board, rang the bell, and snarled back at the guard dogs that snapped and barked at him.

Vivaldi Bonifacio settled back in one of the throne chairs in the vendetta room. Chamois Barbone, seated between him and the Moor, sipped his hot, black coffee and warmed his hands on the crockery.

"Relax. Shall we approach this crisis as usual—in calm?"

They had listened as Chamois laid his critical assessment of the dirty business at Île-Rousse before them, heard the facts as the Corsican related them, and agreed with his reasoning.

"I tell you the plot is critical," Chamois insisted, his squeaky voice rising, barely audible. "If betrayal comes in a minor incident, what can we expect when we prepare for the final thrust to expel the enemy? Annihilation? Must we form our own army to protect those sent to protect us?" He repeated the details of the Île-Rousse scenario as he saw it. "We must lay the carefully detailed facts before your son. Only a Corsican will understand the desperation I feel, the helplessness."

Vivaldi, listening intently, began to question him point by point, missing nothing, repeating Chamois's answers to make certain not the slimmest thread of evidence was overlooked. He wrote everything down, calculating with Chamois the distance between the northern seashore cities.

"Ten minutes sooner and the carefully trained Resistance fighters would have been annihilated. Every last one wiped out." Chamois's weasel eyes trailed around the vendetta room, noting the changes since he and his men had inhabited the premises. "Once I was ugly, unreasonable, insufferable, and inconsistent in my thoughts. I am learning, Vivaldi, learning fast. I am no longer the legend I was becoming. The war has interrupted my reign. But I do not complain. I was once crude, coarse, illiterate, and a barbarian. The war has made no angel of me, but it *has* become my teacher. I am learning radio communications, espionage, and a system of lies by the greatest liars in the world—the military. The war has made me realize how small a big shot I am. But I am learning. In the past I never changed my coat for anyone or anything. I am Corsican. I live and I will die loyal to my credo and my credo is to preserve Corsica and our customs. But right now I need to know where we stand. If a traitor lies in our midst, an uncovered conspiracy threatens our very existence."

Matteus had left moments before and now returned with a copper pan of fried eggs, peppers, mushrooms, and sausage. He placed it on a table before the fire. "Eat, Corsican. You've come a long way. You'll think better on a full stomach."

"Eggs?" He stared at the miracle before him. "I am boss of Corsica and am unable to hatch up a single egg on the entire island. How do you prepare such a feast?" he asked as Matteus poured more coffee.

"Partridge eggs. As tasty as hens' eggs, no?"

Chamois shoveled the food into his mouth, eating with gusto. Between mouthfuls he emphasized the imperative. "Summon your son. He must be told. He is at the citadel with the others."

"He is not there."

"Find him."

"He is not in Corsica for the moment."

"Where, then?" He was surprised. No one had reported Darius's absence from the island. "You must know where to reach him."

"Military business is seldom confided to family. He has confidences not meant for our ears."

"A Corsican who fails to confide in his father?" Chamois shook his head in disbelief. "The world changes too quickly. Old ways are dying."

Once again he described the death and fire at Île-Rousse as if repetition would heighten his credibility, instill in his listeners the desperate need of countering the traitor's treachery. He described the surprise attack, the near success of the mission only to see it collapse before their very eyes.

"It is true, I tell you. These spellbound eyes witnessed the act. The enemy was picked up, carried away on stretchers to be saved, patched up like new to once again release their poison upon us."

"There was no counterattack?" Vivaldi asked.

"The Red Cross arm bands. The men were reluctant to hurl grenades at them or shoot."

"I dare not suggest you bore witness to an illusion—"

"No. Do not dare. For two hours I have tried to unravel the identity of the traitor. How did the Germans escape death? I tell you the timing was masterful, the rescue squad saving that German beast Hesse from the fires of hell and damnation was nothing short of miraculous!''

"You know the German, Hesse, personally?" Vivaldi tried to understand the venom spewing from Chamois's lips. "Is he unlike *any* enemy? Do you enjoy a personal vendetta against him? What?''

Chamois removed the gold toothpick from his shirt pocket, picked at his teeth thoughtfully. "Is it possible that you, scholar Bonifacio, have failed to study the dossiers provided by my brother in Marseilles?''

"The *collaborator*?'' The Moor spat bitingly.

"*Collaborator?* Anyone but you would be killed for daring to impute such treachery to my brother, the boss of all bosses. Collaborator, is it?'' Quicker than the eye could see, a hidden knife materialized in the Corsican's hand. He stabbed the table with it, carved a straight line toward Matteus, crossing it with two horizontal slashes. "The double cross—see? My brother plays both sides. One shall emerge the victor. Why should he be any different from the wise bankers, industrialists, the men who are the power behind the Nazi war chests?''

Vivaldi was livid. "Pray for your sake that I understand what you tell me. Your brother plays dangerous games, and you seek a betrayer among *our* people? How do we know he didn't betray us? Could Cesare have telephoned you, boss of all bosses, then in turn alerted Bastia?''

"What are you saying?'' Barbone yanked hard on the knife, palmed it.

"Merely exploring possibilities.''

"Goddammit it! I should kill you for daring to suggest—''

"You yourself suggested he plays both ends against the middle.''

"But to accuse my brother of betraying us! It is unacceptable, Bonifacio! Unacceptable, do you hear me?''

"Because you refuse to believe it or because it could be possible?''

"There can be only one response to such words. Where do you want the bullet?''

"Through *my* body first, Corsican," the Moor said, rising to full height and staring down at the wiry weasel.

"I've always told you, I have no quarrel with you, Moor. But your friend here dares to insult the house of Barbone."

"Chamois," Vivaldi began resolutely, "you are unable to think, act, or feel by degrees. To the very end, life for you shall be all hate, all love, all war, all peace, all loyalty or defiance."

"Is there any other way to be?"

"Logic and moderation are not part of your life. You trust your eyes, ears, your senses instinctively. Your extreme behavior in the past, appalling at times, has abated because France and Germany are at war. I don't ask you what deals you've made and with whom. But should your subterranean schemes result in harm done to my family, namely to my son Darius—"

Chamois, in a riotous outburst, kicked back his chair, stood up, features suffused with rage. About to verbally assault his hosts, he was silenced by Vivaldi's upthrust hand and quiet, coaxing voice. "Would you deny me preamble to explain my meaning? You came here in good faith. In the past, our friendship, testy at times, has weathered enormous difficulties. Now hear me carefully. Until my son returns, you shall confer with the OSS and SOE agents."

Chamois's vociferous protestations rose to a squeaky crescendo, then disintegrated to a muffled whisper. He picked up the chair, repositioned it, sat down, accepted the proffered brandy and cigar, and listened.

"Follow my instructions to the letter, Barbone. We are about to play a game of Corsican roulette with our allies."

Chamois Barbone stared into the wide, questioning lapis eyes of the American Captain Brad Lincoln. They were arresting eyes, steady, apprehensive, like an animal eyeing a mortal enemy. Riveted to the Corsican in like manner were Jim Greer's eyes, somber, testy, unsmiling.

The trio sat uncomfortably in the map room at the citadel, a near-empty bottle of robust wine on the crude desk, tin wine cups placed before each. Partially lit cigars rested in an empty sardine can at the center. The flickering light from a smoky lantern placed on the desk added an eerie effect to the icy formality of the meeting. Chamois, who prided himself on reading men, felt out of place in the presence of these men of the New World. Yet he felt he was performing admirably. There was no point in being evasive with the OSS. They would sense a distortion and, his veracity put to the test, might corrupt the real truth. He could not risk it. Finished with his repartee, he leaned back in the straight-backed chair carved from an orange crate and picked at a troublesome cavity with his gold toothpick.

Brad Lincoln picked up his dead cigar and relit it, puffing fiercely until it was evenly lit. He leaned forward, elbows on his knees, staring at the curling smoke rings rising upward.

"Tell me, Barbone, have you ever participated in a full-scale war? It does things to a man, especially on his home turf."

"*Qu'est-ce que c'est*—turf?"

"Homeland," Greer supplied.

Barbone's weasel head bobbed up and down, toothpick probing the cavity. He spoke in French, with a bit of broken English tossed in for good measure. "*Je comprends.* You listened to my story, yet I detect disbelief. I am not *cafard.* I take no opium to hallucinate or create fantasies. I am not an ignorant man, yet because I do not understand or speak your language with facility, you consider me ignorant. That, *capitaine,* is your problem. Corsica is mine. *Adieu.* This conversation is *finis.* Perhaps the British Major Charles Alexander will be more compatible to my thinking. *Oui?*"

"Don't go away angry, Barbone," Brad said quickly, trying to smooth the Corsican's feathers. "Understand this. Your nation is at war. My nation and its other ally, Great Britain, are doing their damnedest to ferret out which Frenchmen are our allies and which are our enemies. Admit it, Barbone; it presents serious complications the average man on the street is untrained to cope with. *D'accord?* Now, if we admittedly don't know our enemies from our allies, at least give us this much—we're trying our damnedest, *oui?*"

"Facts are facts, Monsieurs Cain and Abel. You can distort them, misinterpret them. You can see and hear only what you wish to see or hear. But I speak the truth. To substantiate what these eyes and ears beheld at Île-Rousse, I documented the time, place, activity from both sides, noting precisely the time the enemy arrived from Bastia. Here, I wrote it all down." Chamois placed the carefully prepared foolscap papers on the desk.

"You insist Major Hesse was prepared to identify Zahara?"

"And relay the information from a high-powered mobile unit with high-voltage transmitters—the best equipment I've seen in

Corsica. The coded messages were in the process of being sent out when death squads arrived on the scene. Listen to me carefully. Djebel knows the brand of treachery residing in the mind of this heartless German RSHA agent. In Paris Hesse has vocalized his intent to capture Zahara on many occasions. Last night, his mind curiously illuminated by a chance circumstance, he figured out her true identity.'' Barbone rolled his eyes, shook a limp wrist, implying the gravity of the matter. "It is best you consult with Djebel. He and Hesse are mortal enemies.''

Barbone slapped his forehead in chastisement. "But why do I tell you old stories? Of course, how stupid of me. Your dossiers must tell you the entire story—no?''

"We do not minimize Zahara's importance to the cause—nor yours, Barbone. You, our hosts in Corsica are the proprietors of the land. We make no claim to them. Once our task to safeguard your nation is completed, we move on with dispatch to our next operation. It's on to Berlin for us to decimate the Nazi machine. We go wherever our services are needed.'' Lincoln sighed. He was exhausted. "We've so much to do. Collectively the Allies are dedicated to insure that World War II doesn't end as World War I did, with greed and vengeance as the motivation of the victors. It would please us greatly if you handled Corsican matters in the usual manner.''

Chamois was stunned. Eyes widening, he asked Brad to repeat his words. Lincoln obliged. "You will voice *no* objection? No matter who is faulted for any atrocity? You will permit us to implement Corsican justice?''

The eagerness in the Corsican's voice, the unusual light in his anthracite eyes, jolted Jim Greer.

"Captain.'' Greer's eyes darted to Brad's and locked, while his voice managed a steadfast monotone. "The matter must be explored under an Allied umbrella of inquiry.'' His eyes signaled trouble to Brad, and he recited by rote, "Illegal acts performed by partisans, once reported, must conform to war regulations, protocol, and the usual mumbo jumbo. Perhaps the combined co-commanders of OWC should carefully review the facts and come to a more positive conclusion concerning possible inside treachery. If not the co-commanders, at least a homogeneous group, a cross section of the Resistance and operational groups, should be appointed to probe the matter.''

Greer's overt nonchalance didn't escape Barbone for a moment. He'd have plenty to discuss with Vivaldi.

"Yes. You're right, Lieutenant. That doesn't mean, Barbone, that you should not fail to identify and report the traitor to us if you ferret him out. *D'accord?*" Brad opened a dusty drawer, removed another bottle of red wine, uncorked it, refilled the cups, and set the bottle down. He held his cup in midair, then stopped in afterthought. "You mentioned Djebel. Where is he, damn it to hell?"

Chamois clinked glasses with them, shrugged, and gulped down the wine, smacking his lips.

"Convey to your men—should they encounter him—urgent military business demands his immediate return to the citadel. You're certain you don't know his whereabouts?"

"You ask such a question of me? Why would Djebel confide in me, a lowly chief in this Corsican affair, and not you, his co-commanders?" He pretended to a vague befuddlement that incited Brad Lincoln's response.

"Deceptions! Betrayals! Spies in our midst after taking optimum precautions? The truth is, Barbone, if deception exists, its locus originates with your people. Speaking of your people, is it necessary to bring these whores in from Marseilles? One in particular disturbs me. Chou-Chou. Yeah, that's her name."

"Marnay's woman." Barbone shrugged. "What can I say?"

Brad, sensing the duplicity in the Corsican, an unwillingness to be straight with him, paced in the limited confines. He pulled up short, eyeballing him. He asked directly, "Are your Corsican comrades secure? Trustworthy?"

"Are yours trustworthy, Monsieurs Cain and Abel?"

Chapter Seven

Malta was a stone fortress carved from rock. In the doorways, streets, and alleyways of Valletta, the litter and rubble of a war-torn nation had been left behind in the wake of Luftwaffe air raids and precision bombings. Although the might and force of German air power had stormed the island, the Maltese, backbone of the British occupation, had prevailed.

Darius rode through the early amethyst twilight in the rear of a dusty sedan, his pale, haggard features evidence of the recent series of catastrophic events he'd survived. He and his somber-eyed, stony-faced companions were jostled through the narrow streets, bounced over pebbled mounds of jagged rocks and stone as the driver negotiated his way through Queen's Square, past the ruins of the Governor's palace.

With a sudden crashing sound, the passengers were flung forward. The car had plunged headlong into an obstruction, a buttress of rocks. As the frustrated driver cursed aloud and shifted into reverse, trying to extricate the auto from the road hazard, a squad of partisans holding guns rushed them. Loud

142

shouts from short, dark-skinned men with angry eyes and gaunt cheeks and dressed in filthy rags surrounded them, demanding credentials. The copiously sweating driver rolled down the window as leering faces eager for blood peered in at the passengers. Papers were brandished, credentials proffered. The resolute leader scrutinized the items and the faces of the passengers and suddenly stood at attention, saluting, his comportment at once deferential. He shouted to his men in Maltese, and instantly they cheered and helped clear the car of any obstruction.

"Look," said Youseff, indicating the marble-based statue of Queen Victoria propped majestically in the center of the square. "That's Victoria, all right. Not a chip, crack, or bullet hole to mar her royal countenance. Here she sits imperiously, as if she were holding court." He glanced solicitously at Darius. "Are you feeling any better?"

Darius, gazing out at the militant partisans, merely nodded.

"What you see, Djebel," said the General in an attempt at bravado, "is the keystone of British defenses. These men, Malta's base crews, destroyed more than three-fourths of Rommel's shipping lines while we held our ground at Bir Hakeim. King George just conferred the George Cross, the highest civilian award, upon the Maltese.

That's Henri Furstenberg, Darius thought. *Never a display of appropriate emotions. He speaks of inconsequential matters in desperate moments to offset the churning fear gnawing at his intestines.*

Darius grew introverted as the sedan circumvented several hazards. The ambushers trailed in the distance. At the outskirts of the city, the driver wheeled easily along a country road. Darius barely listened to the small talk between Youseff and Henri. Brooding thoughts thrummed at his temples, the sensation worse than the pain spasms assaulting his body. Death had stalked them every step of the way from Corsica.

He had felt an exhilarating high on his departure from the island, but it turned quickly into deep depression, his torment absolute.

A highly clandestine meeting was about to take place. A meeting with a mystery man. Here, on a rock-bound island under constant siege! It was madness. Why not in neutral Spain? In Corsica even. *Anyplace but Malta!* Pray the meeting was worth the desperate chances they'd taken. Darius sat stiff and tense, leaning slightly forward in his seat, forced to favor his recent injuries.

The harrowing and dangerous trip, his maiden submarine voyage, had left him shaken and bewildered. Through no choice of his own, it would not be his last submarine jaunt; the return trip to Corsica had yet to be negotiated.

Merde! Nothing in Sidi bel Abbes—no encounter with the deadly Berbers . . . not the awesome Abou Ahkmed Hassan nor the bloody warfare of Bir Hakeim along the Gazala Line or the SAS operations—had terrified Darius as had the utter helplessness of being trapped inside the British submarine as German U-boat wolf packs scavenged about nearby. Overhead, a goddamned German flotilla protecting a precious convoy of war materials had hurled depth charges one after another the moment their radar screens spotted the HMS *Hyperion*. It had been sheer insanity. And sheer insanity, with no available escape corridors, had taken its toll.

Twelve hours ago, Darius had left Corsica under massive cloud over. Fog banks had plunged Corsica's west coast into obscurity. He thought it had been a good sign, but he was wrong. The rubber shore-to-sea skiff hidden in fog pockets had made it to the proper compass bearings when suddenly the surfacing submarine exploded the waters, spewing plumes of seawater every which way, flooding and capsizing the skiff. Drenched to the skin, unable to ascertain the safety or wellbeing of the men transporting him, Darius, yanked aboard the *Hyperion* by harried crewmen, found himself shoved unceremoniously down the conning-tower hatch belowdeck. Overhead hatches clanged shut, secured at once. In moments the British submarine had heaved its prow, crash-dived, and continued on its way, unwittingly trespassing the deadly lairs of the U-boat wolf packs.

Beneath tranquil seas, after donning a fresh change of clothing, Darius rejoined General Henri Furstenberg, his superior officer and Prince Youseff Ben-Kassir, the Algerian Prince and his closest confidant. The trio, trusted figures operating at the highest levels of the Free France government, were forever burrowing deeper into the most sensitive secrets as embittered exiles from the earlier North African Intelligence Service (NAIS). Both Furstenberg and Prince Ben-Kassir had been deeply affected by the mass divisiveness that followed the German occupation of France and had declared their loyalty to General Charles de Gaulle. They now sat in the officers' wardroom, imbibing food and wine.

Suddenly buffeted by a barrage of depth charges, the submarine rocked, swayed precariously, its superstructure shuddering under the impacts.

Madness erupted. Violent explosions dangerously close to the cigar-shaped hull sent food, crockery, crew, and passengers to the deck, their faces devoid of color. Momentarily disorganized, Darius and his friends scrambled to their feet, listening, immobilized, hanging on to anything anchored for dear life.

A-h-u-u-u-g-g-a! A-h-u-u-u-g-g-a! The sickening wail of alarm systems going berserk matched the frenzied actions and stupefied numbness of an uncertain crew.

Oh, God! Crazed men bereft of reason moved zombielike into emergency action. Screaming shouts blistered the ears. Haunted eyes darted frantically in all directions, searching for exits. Some men were knocked senseless by the unceasing impacts of the charges. Controlled panic took over.

It wouldn't stop! Dante's Fifth Circle of Hell couldn't have been as demonically frightening. Buffeted helplessly by the inexorable depth charges, the men collided, pummeled one another, struggled to cling to anything battened down. A sudden, savage rupture in the hull precariously close to the forward torpedo room unleashed a torrent of seawater flooding into the wardroom. Orders were shouted but went unheard in the thunderous roar of the gushing deluge.

The water continued to rise dangerously. Dead rats floated past. Men frantically fought the furious rush of water, securing hatch doors to the forward torpedo control. Responding at the emotional key of the peril facing them, the traumatized passengers, suddenly impotent in an alien situation, were shoved below into drier quarters by the more seasoned crew, and all hatches were secured behind them.

Darius, flung every which way, enveloped by a maze of floating arms, legs, and leering, bloated faces, suddenly experienced sharp stabbing pains that felt as if he'd been run through with a dozen hot pitchforks. Wrenching free of the bodies, he was flung against a wall as another barrage of depth charges hit the *Hyperion*. Darius stared at the low cabin ceiling as if to see the German battle cruisers overhead.

Bastards! What a field day! Marauding wolf packs were out there, their intimidating presence underscored by the perpetual nervewracking sonar blips echoing through the submarine. The assault of depth charges drew closer and closer, sending shock waves through the human convulsion of officers, crew, and passengers. In the unending sea of frenzied faces, the tangle of arms and legs, the whirlwind activity, there was no time for Darius to search for the source of his discomfort.

Too much was happening too fast! Alarms whined sickeningly, then cut off to a muffled silence. Overhead cabin lights dimmed perceptibly. A rough bullhorned voice—decidedly British—crashed through a warped public address system. "Take 'er down three hundred feet! Check the ASDIC! Get our bearings! Be bloody damn quick, mates! Wolf packs are out there waiting to feast on British iron! Stand by. . . . All hands stand by!"

K-a-p-o-w! . . . *K-a-p-o-w!* More depth charges! *W-h-u-r-r-r-u-p! W-h-u-r-r-r-u-u-u-p!* Alarms shrieked, then whined down to a whimper.

"This is the Captain! Cut the bloody engines! Not a sneeze, mates! Not a bleeding whisper! Do you ruddy well read me?" The Captain's voice could cut through steel.

"Djebel! *Djebel!* Where are you?" said the bedeviled Prince, his voice just above a whisper.

"Youseff," cried Henri Furstenberg frantically. "Djebel! *Mon Dieu!* What is happening?"

Voices, hushed yet clear, echoed through the long, narrow corridor of the submarine.

"Switch on the ventilation cartridges! For God's sake, the fans! Engage the damn fans!"

"Deeper . . . deeper. . . . Easy now. Too damned deep. The bolts are bursting, goddammit! Bring 'er up! Bring her up ten meters!"

"Quiet . . . silence. . . . Don't let the wolves hear you pissing!"

"Bloody hell, the pressure's too much. Bring 'er up more!"

Lights dimmed, the men crashed into one another, propelled by the terrific impact. Hams, sausages, and cheeses hanging in the narrow corridors, collided with humans and were tossed in all directions.

"Report all damage!" cried the Captain as water pipes threatened to burst.

"Engine room's leaking water. Stern is leaking water."

"Gaskets! Someone get the bloody gaskets! We need gaskets!"

"Lights out! Get the ruddy damn torches, knotheads!"

More depth charges shook the superstructure, popping bolts, unhinging essential equipment. Crewmen ran to their bunks, strapped themselves in. "Blessed be the Lord my God—"

Those who could bowed their heads in prayer.

"Medic to the wardroom! Medic to the wardroom! Medic! MEDIC!"

"Valve packing! Someone get the valve packing! Get out of my way. I need valve packing. What about the fuel tanks—are they leaking?"

Darius arched his back and braced himself against a battened-down table as sharp pains again coursed through his body, leaving him gasping. He shot Youseff a look of disbelief and pain. His face contorted. His breathing grew labored as he refused to succumb to the agony.

Youseff sprang toward him, his bright eyes demanding an explanation. "Mon Dieu! You're bleeding! What happened?" he hissed.

Breathe deeply, Darius, really deep. Focus on something pleasant. Think of Valentina—of Dover—Alexandria . . . Of love and warmth.

Valentina was locked into the focus of his inner eye until the excruciating pain became unendurable. Reaching behind him with his hand, he touched warm, viscous fluid. Blood! Unmistakable blood! *Damnation!* Not now! Not at this stage of the game! *"Bloody damned nuisance!"*

"*Bloody damned nuisance be damned!* You've been knifed! Deliberately knifed!" General Furstenberg cursed sotto voce, trying not to convey his discovery or alarm to the others in the crew's mess.

A torpedoed submarine was about to claim his life! Laughing at the exquisite absurdities of life, certain neither Youseff nor Henri would understand the irony of the situation, Darius allowed himself to be propelled to a nearby bunk and pushed down firmly on the hard surface.

For several hectic moments, he fell under the fury of Furstenberg's wrath. "Don't move, you bloody fool!" Orders spewed from his lips like loud pistol shots. He tore open Darius's shirt and with his knife sliced open the waist of his blood-saturated trousers, exposing the ugly knife wound. "*Sacre bleu! C'est incroyable!* Did you at least spot your assailant?"

Violated by pain spasms, growing weaker from the steady loss of blood, Darius shook his head. Youseff quickly hunkered down alongside the bunk and peered intently into Darius's eyes. "You must have *some* idea. I cannot believe you could be caught off guard." He cursed in Farsi, his voice a hushed whisper.

A montage of images blipped past Darius's inner eye in his attempt to reconstruct the events of the past few moments.

Darius shook his head. "*Merde!* It happened too fast."

"Be still! Don't move! Don't talk! Don't even try!" shouted the General. "Highness, hold the open flesh together to encourage coagulation."

"Tear the shirt, Henri. Press it into folds. I hold the flesh together, you press the cloth over the wound, then run! Summon a medic! There must be one aboard this sardine can!" He shoved his precious briar pipe stem between Darius's teeth. "Bite down on this. The truth, Djebel," Youseff insisted the moment Furstenberg left in search of the medic. "Tell it to me. It's not possible that you were rendered incapable of detecting an assailant. You must know. A face! An out-of-kilter movement! Something! Think! Who knew you were aboard?" Youseff searched his own memory. "Only you, Henri, and I, and of course our host awaiting us in Malta, who demanded personal audience with the incomparable Djebel. You were expected. Yes, yes. That must be it. A British officer aboard the *Hyperion!*" Youseff pressed the folds of the open wound closer together. "It must have been one of the King's valiant men. His target could have been Henri or me—it would make better sense—but it was you he sliced. No error. The strike was intentional." He rolled his eyes in mute outrage. "Another inch or two higher—"

Darius's breathing leveled off to a steadier rhythm. "I confided in no one. Only those handling my departure—" He stopped.

"Yes, yes. Who?"

"A cigarette, *s'il vous plaît.*"

Youseff stared down at his hands. Dare he let go for an instant? "You there, sailor," he called to a man lying in one of the narrow bunks in the fetid, cramped quarters. "Light a cigarette for me, please."

The apathetic crewman dragged himself off his bunk and complied. Youseff signaled him to place it between Darius's lips. "Thank you, mate."

"Dinna be too worried, sir," he said in a thick Irish brogue. "We've seen the likes o' them wolf packs before. Their bite can get pretty nasty, but the *Hyperion*'ll come through."

Darius dragged on the cigarette, his face grimacing in pain. Faces flashed through this mind. Not British, but familiar faces. The Resistance fighters, three in a rubber skiff, had piloted him from Corsican shores along the surf between Porto and Piana to the spot where the surfacing *Hyperion* broke through water. Darius had seriously erred! Acting under urgent orders, he'd failed to check out his escorts. Worse, in the dark of the night he'd failed to discern the features of those devil pilots! The error might cost him his life!

"*Je regrette,* Youseff. I saw no one." But he had! A face was forming in his mind, vague, indefinable, the features in shadows. Something glittered in the image. Something metallic! *The knife, fool! No!* Not the knife. Something else. Concentrate!

General Furstenberg returned with a nervous, highly agitated medic. Another depth charge, dangerously close to the conning tower, spread pure terror to the Lieutenant's wide, petrified eyes, the crazed eyes of a fanatic—out of touch with reality, shocked, fatigued, a little mad. Darius, catching sight of him, considered taking his chances without medication, without attention.

"*Allez! Allez, docteur!*" Henri urged. "Apply your most proficient expertise to this patient. He must not die. Unless, of course, you desire castration."

"I don't need this harassment," blurted the British lieutenant with a trace of Cockney in his tremulous voice. But he went to work, his expertise surfacing in moments. He shot Darius with morphine, cleansed the wound, his eyes and ears peeled for life-threatening sounds. He tore open sulpha packets, sprinkled the healing powder freely over the wound, extolling the virtues of the miracle drug, then lamented the lack of proper equipment in the cramped confines of the submarine. "It's a bit nasty, sir. Close to kidneys and spinal column. It's best you get this looked at bloody damn quick. Get it stitched together the moment you deboard—if we survive this bloody rout. Anyway, you're damn lucky to be alive."

Suddenly a thought struck Darius. Someone had gone to extreme lengths to exterminate him. Here aboard a submarine. Why not in Corsica? En route from North Africa? Had he suddenly become a liability? To whom and why?

There was movement on all sides of him. Youseff and Henri posted guard around him. Orders shouted through the P.A. system spurred activity among the crewmen. The men, sweating profusely, scurried about, collecting food remains, laundry, debris as if they searched for gold. "The junk will be ejected through the bilge pumps," Henri explained. "Once the debris surfaces, those Nazi wolves will believe they've sunk the HMS *Hyperion.* Bloody clever camouflage, *oui?* They'll be off in a twinkling. Optimistically, we'll surface to periscope depth, recharge the batteries, and . . ."

Darius, euphoric from the morphine, and plied with a tumbler of strong Irish whiskey, barely heard Henri's words. The stench of raw, primitive odors in the suffocatingly hot confines nauseated him. There was no privacy at all. An hour passed, then another. He had tried counting the depth charges in order to document the incident in his war journal. Earlier when pain assaulted him Darius admitted to a preoccupation with possible escape. Finding no options open to him, he experienced panic, an alien sensation that filled him with disquiet. He turned his head aside, eyes lidding heavily.

How long will we last? He glanced at his watch dial, blinked, unable to read it. He scanned the crew's mess full of faces, sweat-drenched officers sharing the tunneled corridors of hell with the crew. Some played cards, some sipped warm German beer, a few meditated.

"Don the Momsen lungs, mates!"

They passed out the breathing apparatus, vests with attached mouthpieces filled with oxygen. Life-saving devices.

Something inside Darius fought the drug. His eyelids were growing heavy, but he forced himself to study the faces, get a fix on one: an anxious, overly concerned face, a casual expression, a nervous tic or a twitch. Perhaps someone was edging in closer . . . closer . . . to try again what he'd failed to achieve with the initial knife thrust. Look for a face feigning total disinterest!

The HMS *Hyperion* was the last place Darius had anticipated personal danger. He detected a primordial fear in the crew's eyes. He didn't fault them. He felt the same.

The thought of drowning made him shudder. In desert or conventional warfare, man could devise a dozen means of escape, or at least could retreat. But submerged in a watertight cylinder? Manned with impotent torpedoes that could blow you to a Poseidon Hades if depth charges hit their mark? . . .

Face it. Chances of survival are zero!

Cabin lights dimmed dangerously close to blackout. Hanging heavy over the crew was the fear of death, the possibility of never seeing loved ones again. Hanging heavy over Darius, Youseff, and the General was the dread of not reaching their destination, where, ironically, they'd participate in a meeting that would probably end up escalating war globally.

Coughing spasms erupted. The men sucked prodigious amounts of air through their mouthpieces. Nervous tics broke out as nerves frayed. Eyes blinked, lips twitched; there was rampant scratching.

Doomsday! The end was near. The men sensed it. They'd either drown or surface in shamed defeat and take their chances with the enemy.

The moment came, and the shock left them numb. As helplessness and despair gripped the Captain and crew, as defeatist thoughts reached their nadir and submission to the enemy was about to be implemented, the *Hyperion* was favored by the great god Neptune. Foraging wolf packs gave up their prey, surfaced, and trailed along at either side of the tanker convoy.

The all-safe signal sounded. The men were incredulous. Manning their stations in perfect synchronization, the British demonstrated the expertise that had earned Britain the label Queen of the Sea.

Engines sputtered to life. The welcome sounds of squawking radio communications, the whirring of bilge pumps, and the throbbing of diesels were like music to the men's ears. The crew went crazy. They joyously shouted the three pip, pip, pips and a hurrah.

As sonar blips resumed in repetitive monotony, Darius, still euphoric, tried to picture the face of his unsuccessful assailant. Once again faces paraded through his mind, a bland mixture of eyes, noses, lips, chins. He blinked hard. Clearly he saw a face, a face without expression, carved from marble. Dangling askew over the nose were round, silver-rimmed glasses. The features grew more definable. *The face . . . glasses . . . a faint scar . . . piercing, blue eyes . . . triumphant expression. The hair . . . the hair, Darius!* He couldn't remember. He moved slightly. The pains were less acute. His flesh was like ice. He called to Youseff. The Algerian Prince responded at once. He bent over the bunk, listened to Darius, eyes widening. Youseff's mottled face, at first engorged with blood, swiftly drained of color as he listened. Then he straightened and sternly issued a dictum: "No! I forbid it. It's pure insanity!"

But it was too late! Youseff beckoned to Henri. "The fool made the ultimate decision without consulting us!" He explained that Darius had quickly drained the thick, viscous contents of a vial before Youseff could get it away from him. He'd observed in panic as Darius, the death's-head amulet in hand, perforated the skin on his left elbow. Youseff didn't explain the vial's contents, but described the venom in the death's-head amulet.

The shock in Henri's eyes drove him into a paroxysm of frenzy. Youseff felt scandalous shame sweeping through him. To perpetrate so dastardly an act on a dear friend . . . He avoided the General's eyes. Duplicitous tricks to achieve emotional effects could not compete with logic. Darius wanted to convince his assailant he had accomplished his objective. How else but to stun the senses. The sudden, unexpected reversal of circumstances to make the loser think he'd won! Clever—but cruel!

On the heels of what the *Hyperion*'s crew labeled a victory against the U-boats, Prince Ben-Kassir unloosed a terrifying primitive howl.

At this point, Furstenberg's body fell into a train of instinctive spasms, alerted to the indescribable horror by the look on Youseff's stricken face. Taking in Darius's gyrating body jerking about spasmodically on the bunk, Furstenberg howled as loudly and unrestrainedly as Youseff had. Deep, grunting animal shrieks lodged in Darius's throat as his body jackknifed rigidly, sending General Furstenberg, a man who'd seen every brand of death, into borderline shock.

Behind him, men drawn by the earsplitting screams piercing through the sounds of diesel turbulence, came lunging through the hatch, then froze at the sight of the pathetic body thrashing about in the throes of certain death.

The scene was spellbinding—ghastly! The crew members were mesmerized by the wretched and alarming vignette.

Was it contagious? A disease that could spread to them? Throbbing with uncertainty and fear, the crew backed away uneasily, terror in their eyes.

Furstenberg, at center stage, would be avenged. "Where is he? Where is the animal who tended the patient? I'll kill him! With my bare hands I'll strangle him!" It was no way for a civilized, well-seasoned former legionnaire to act, but shock and despair were authors to action.

Youseff sprang to restrain him. Henri, like an unchained beast, clawed at him wildly, kicked with fury, lashed out with both fists, knocking the stately Prince off balance, sending him crashing into the metal safety bars of the narrow bunks opposite them.

It was too much for Henri, and Youseff had no time to explain. The unleashing of despair, utter hopelessness, and sadness over the loss of a dear, beloved brother suddenly suffused Henri with the strength of ten mountain lions. Youseff, in desperation, initiated assistance from available crew and officers to subdue him. The medic rushed to the scene. Sighting both Darius in the ghastly grip of death, and the General's Herculean strength, he winced, cowered slightly, hesitant to be tossed into the melee.

"Sedate the General, for God's sake, man! That's an order!"

"Wh-What o-of m-my p-patient?" stammered the Lieutenant. He appealed frantically.

"Lieutenant!" Youseff snapped. "Your patient is dying—there's no hope! Now *dammit*, you'd bloody well take care of the living!"

The Lieutenant frantically filled a syringe with a powerful sedative. Salty sweat rolled off his face, dripped off his brow into his eyes, burning them, obstructing his vision. He shot Henri, withdrew the syringe, his eyes on the blood spurting from between Darius's lips. At once defensive, he shouted, "I swear, sir, nothing I did caused this. It could be any number of things!'' He tossed the syringe into his bag, trembling, eyes furtive.

"Cover his body. We'll take the dead body off the *Hyperion* when we land.'' The three men restraining General Furstenberg laid him on a nearby bunk and strapped the squirming, protesting body to the mattress. "Go, Lieutenant. You did your best. You are not to be faulted.''

"But sir, I did nothing contrary to ordinance manifestos,'' the shattered medic mumbled. His bulging eyes darted wildly about the cramped confines in search of some penance for his participation in this abomination.

Youseff glanced at his watch, impervious to the other's trauma. "Summon your Captain at once.'' The medic scurried off.

A fatigued, bearded man wearing a tattered turtleneck sweater trudged wearily along the narrow corridor. He approached the Prince. They huddled. Youseff explained the need for urgency. "The problem of getting the General and the dead man to shore without causing a fury is paramount.''

Captain Hood, in no mood for political intrigue after the recent battering of his submarine, turned stormy eyes on Darius's motionless body, then moving to the next bunk, observed the near-catatonic General. Turning to the Algerian Prince, he demanded immediate answers. "I don't understand. My report indicated the passenger sustained serious but certainly not *lethal* knife wounds.''

"The patient *will* expire if we don't get him to the British medical facility at Malta the moment we land. Now, sir, I order you under the strictest of security measures to declare him dead. It is essential you proclaim him dead at this end. Radio our escorts to make haste.''

"You ask the impossible. My report—''

"Bend the report!'' Youseff snapped, his voice strident.

"*Bend the report?* You dare challenge my prerogative?''

"*Bend the report!*''

"I daresay, sir, nothing in my orders clearly permits me to bend any report.''

"You dare interfere in SIS matters? General Furstenberg is British Intelligence.''

"*You dare arrogate my duties?* I could bloody well get my

tail whipped from here to Timbuktu." He shook his head. "Not while Captain Hood commands this vessel."

"If you don't do precisely what I order, you'll bloody well reap the devil's harvest. How about plague? Dysentery? I can take the *Hyperion* out of commission for the duration, Captain Hood. It's a simple matter to report the incidence of plague. I promise you political catastrophe if you don't do as I say. The Prime Minister would not be amused if the *Hyperion* were crippled."

"You wouldn't dare."

"Try me! A special commendation from the P.M. and a promotion from Mr. Churchill wouldn't be difficult to swallow, would it?"

The promise was like precious metal, a currency the Captain couldn't afford to pass up. Scowling, his expression dubious, he sorted through his dilemma, his weary features relaxing. Beams of inspiration melted the lines of fatigue. "I say, sir, the trawler *Los Tiburon* is within radio frequency. The skipper is adept at this sort of thing. If our junior officers, chief, and crew know we've established contact with it—if they sight *Los Tiburon*, my position becomes less untenable and my report absolutely credible."

"I don't understand," Youseff said, covering Darius's face. "*Los Tiburon* means a funeral pyre. The skipper's primary function in these waters is to pick up and transfer bodies of dead VIP's for proper burial at home, where medals of honor are posthumously awarded by the military brass."

Youseff shuddered inwardly. It was settled. A deal had been struck.

The HMS *Hyperion* climbed to periscope depth, recharged its engines, and surfaced four hours later at a point slightly north of Marsamxett Bay near Valletta on the Island of Malta. The *Los Tiburon* sliced through the waters to keep its rendezvous with the *Hyperion*.

Darius's canvas-wrapped body, carefully lifted through the conning-tower hatch by crewmembers under the wary eyes of his devoted sentinels, was transferred with equal diligence to the deckhands about *Los Tiburon*, moored momentarily alongside the submarine.

Under cover of night and amid the flurry of activity aboard the *Hyperion*, a British officer slipped unnoticed off the starboard bow and into the water. He dove under *Los Tiburon,* swam its breadth, and emerged at starboard stern. He grasped at dangling mooring lines, tied himself securely and hovered close behind the trawler as it put about, and headed south.

Hidden in the shadows of man-made coves, observing the proper signals from *Los Tiburon,* a motorized launch held in radio abeyance slipped its moorings and swiftly skimmed the waters toward the approaching trawler. Once Youseff, Henri, and Darius were aboard, the sailor gunned his motors, put about, and sliced through indigo waters, heading for the shoreline battlement.

The human barnacle attached to *Los Tiburon*'s mooring lines was helped aboard. The aquatic funeral pyre's skipper put about swiftly and headed north. Inside the confining skipper's quarters, the muscular young man with a bull-like upper torso and the strong legs of a seasoned skier shed his soaked British officer's uniform. He dressed in dry dark trousers, a turtleneck sweater, and rope-soled boots. From an oilskin pouch strapped to his waist, he removed his steel-rimmed glasses, placed them over his nose, and shaking his wet head like a duck out of water, helped himself to a mug of black coffee from the pot perking on the makeshift galley stove. He looked up as the skipper descended the ladder belowdeck. Captain Simón Bolivar Zacharias, the double-dealing, conspiratorial seaman, glanced at his guest expectantly. "*Heil* Hitler! Is the deed finished?"

"*Heil* Hitler. It is done. He is finished."

"Why is it I fail to share your optimism?"

"Why? What's wrong?" asked the German undercover agent and assassin, code named Ghost-Dancer.

"*What's wrong?* I'll tell you what's wrong! Why wasn't I ordered to return the body to Corsica? Why would I deliver it to Malta?" asked Captain Zacharias, the same man who over two decades ago had transported two men from Spain to Ajaccio, Corsica, and had been craftily twisted out of monies he felt were owed him. For two long decades he'd neither forgotten nor forgiven the Spaniard and Moor for shortchanging him. He'd made proper inquiries of friends. He'd been kept apprised of Signor Bonifacio's activities by friends. These same friends had marched reluctantly to war and chosen sides. Imagine his astonishment upon learning that one of the co-commanders of the Corsican offensive was named Bonifacio. The name had burned his memory for twenty years, never to be forgotten. Further checking among his friends had provided the needed information. Contacts were made, communiqués exchanged, vital information leaked, and the talented assassin Ghost-Dancer was contacted to liquidate Major Darius Bonifacio, code name Djebel.

"The target was wasted, I tell you. I can't explain why the body was transported to Malta," Ghost-Dancer snapped impatiently. "I don't appreciate your impugning my professional expertise, nor do I enjoy the imprecations hurled on me."

"I have my reasons for demanding proof. I shall make further inquiries, Herr Ghost-Dancer. If I learn you bungled the job after all the carefully laid groundwork . . ."

"Enough! I did not fail. It was impossible. But if in your deluded fantasy, your conjecture should prove correct, I shall relish completing the job, and this time I promise it shall be done with perfection. Now, enough of your fishwife protestations! Uncover some of that Napoleon brandy you filched from a recent plundering without our permission or knowledge."

Captain Zacharias, at once obsequious, bowed with panache. "Touché." Glowering inwardly, he unlocked a wall cabinet and produced the contraband liquor recently filched in an unsanctioned raid along the North African coastline. He poured it begrudgingly, with a miserliness Ghost-Dancer found amusing. He deliberately picked up the bottle, filled his cup to the brim, and raising it in mock salute before draining it, repeated the word "Touché."

An hour after he arrived at the Valletta medical facility and had his stomach pumped out, Darius recovered from the deathlike rigors gripping him. The insides of his mouth were raw and chewed to shreds, but the ingested antidote had saved him from the lethal paroxysms of strychnine.

The wrath and strenuous protests hurled upon him by the two men standing at either side of the hospital bed were admirably contained. Furious at the insensible lengths to which he'd gone to prove a desperate point, their spiny words, motivated by fear for his life, proved worse than the aftermath of the drastic life-saving devices used to revive him.

"Never commit so foolhardy an act again!" Furstenberg admonished. "You could have died! Worse, I nearly died from shock!"

Youseff's condemnation was the same. "Never do anything so irresponsible again!" The tears welling in his eyes were worth more than a thousand words.

"What matters," Darius said weakly, sitting erect in bed as a nurse taped his torso firmly to prevent the knife wound from re-opening, "what matters is that I've attained my objective by permitting my assailant to believe I am dead."

Here they were at last, thought Darius, squirming uncomfortably. The dusty sedan had driven to the outskirts of Valletta and began its ascent to a remote hilltop villa hidden behind austere stone walls and acres of orange and tangerine groves. Darius's angry thoughts were momentarily suspended as he listened intently to General Furstenberg.

"Our host's identity must remain secret. You will refer to him as Monsieur Creneau, Djebel, no matter who you find waiting for us at the villa. *Comprenez-vous?*"

Astonishment replaced Darius's pain and brooding hostility. Monsieur Craneur Creneau? Darius was speechless. The mystery man in St. Germaine's life!

"You shall be addressed at all times by your code name, Djebel. Since this meeting is off-the-record, neither the British nor the Americans must learn of this rendezvous or they'll attach the wrong meaning to it. You see, they loathe Creneau. FDR and the British Prime Minister—"

Darius interrupted. "I pray it is well worth the grave risks we've taken the past several hours." Traces of sarcasm were evident in his words as he vividly remembered his close brush with death underwater. Christ! He was tired, drained.

"Another thing: it would serve no purpose to—uh—mention your near accident to our host." Youseff was cut off savagely.

"*Accident?*" Darius shouted. "You call attempted assassination a near accident?"

"I shall demand the ship's log the moment we contact London. The name and dossier of every officer and crewman aboard the blasted *Hyperion,*" Furstenberg snarled.

"The attempt on my life connotes far more treachery than it seems. It means someone tried to prevent this meeting with your mystery man, Creneau, from taking place. It is imperative that Creneau is told what happened. The motive behind the act must be examined from all possible angles," Darius muttered through clenched teeth.

"You took incredible risks. I doubt any man would have matched your bravery," said Furstenberg. Earlier when the plot was explained, his outrage had increased. He had accused both the Prince and Darius of total madness. "And you, Djebel, go too far! You're *cafard*. I promise you one thing: when you meet Monsieur Creneau, you'll understand why allies and foes alike might have decided to prevent history from being written this night."

The general proved to be correct. Now two days later, Darius, stunned to the core, forgot the earlier life-and-death traumas. His eyes were riveted on the grand man poised in the keyhole archway of the tessellated foyer of the Moorish villa. Darius was staring into the piercing blue eyes of the President of the French National Committee, General Charles de Gaulle.

The President greeted each man warmly in the French style. "Monsieur Djebel, what an honor to finally meet you. France is both honored and fortunate to claim you as her son."

Darius heard the words, the voice, but he remained wooden and speechless. De Gaulle laughed, embraced him again, then stood away from him, eyeing his discomfort. "Would that my presence alone contained the power of Mesmer. Think of its effects upon the enemies of France." He smiled at the rush of embarrassment creeping into Djebel's features, the momentary awkwardness. "*Mon Dieu!* How swiftly would the war be won." He chuckled as he escorted his guests through the enormous villa to a salon where refreshments awaited his guests. "Imagine, Highness," he said in an aside to Youseff, "immobilizing an army by my presence."

"Meaning no disrespect, Monsieur Creneau, usually it's the other way around. Djebel exudes the powers you've described."

Darius frowned. He loathed praise, couldn't handle it, certainly not in the presence of his prestigious host. Darius's economy of movement and use of a cane did not fail to escape de Gaulle. He kept his counsel, his eyes measuring Darius with every glance.

The relaxed, casual tone of the encounter belied the urgent undercurrent beneath the decorum and political protocol these men employed. Each man, here at great personal risk, was participating in a crucial, crap-shoot agenda. The stakes: existence or death. Existence meant fortunes, comfortable living, high political office, and all the fringe benefits that went with victory. Death meant—well, death was death, oblivion, ashes to ashes, dust to dust.

Pain throbbed at Darius's temples throughout the amenities. He popped some pain pills, hoping he would stay alert throughout the meeting.

"It is to you that my words are directed, Djebel," said de Gaulle over cognac, rare Havanas, and black Turkish coffee. "The corridors of this most secret mission are fraught with danger. What happened aboard the *Hyperion* was unconscionable. I received a near blow-by-blow report. *Merci Dieu!* At least you survived—all of you. Undoubtedly the secrecy of this mission will incite curiosity among your co-commanders in Corsica. No matter what proof is provided you, this tête-à-tête never took place. Grave information—data my organization failed to obtain in time to prepare for the cataclysm—has surfaced. Charges of treason, murder, unresolved allegations against men at the very core of Allied diplomatic and intelligence establishments have been leveled by manipulating, monied men in high places. So at the risk of ruffling a few Allied feathers, especially those of the OSS and SOE cloak-and-dagger men, we shall hone our senses and become circumspect in all of our dealings. You understand why. National insurrection is at stake."

National insurrection? Infighting, the shaking of governmental structures would be next. The General's next words read like a primer in the strategy and tactics of modern warfare.

"Traditional war is over. The infantry, cavalry, artillery will soon be obsolete. This is psychological warfare! Intelligence communities dictate the actions. The ultimately produced strategic stalemate in war has gone by the wayside. Tactical success is now possible due to the technological strides made by the military and those inventive minds responsible for creating speedy communications.

"*Alors,* Djebel, through Magic, ULTRA, and the Enigma machine, and those brilliant cipher-breaking devils, we know your enemy in Corsica. A formidable enemy, certainly no stranger to you. Never underestimate Sturmbannführer Hans Hesse."

"Hesse!" Darius shifted in his seat, wincing as he popped another painkiller and washed it down with a tumbler of water. He glanced at the others. "The man is ubiquitous, I'll give him that much."

"So he survived Hassan's attack on El Bayadh?" Youseff traced the vivid scar at his neck. He had reason never to forget his eternal enemy.

"Oui, he survived. Soon he replaces another man whose presence in Corsica arouses prodigious curiosity in my mind." De Gaulle shuffled through a sheaf of briefing papers on his desk, his eyes skipping rapidly down the pages. "Ah, *bon.* Here, at the bottom of the last page of the White Coral briefing is a name marked by a double dagger."

Each man turned to his copy. The name appearing in that position was Major Victor Zeller.

The name meant nothing to Youseff or Henri Furstenberg, but it shook Darius.

Zeller! The name had haunted him all his life!

The forename was different, but— His thoughts were summarily suspended as de Gaulle continued without losing a beat.

"We learned he is a Jew, a man to be persecuted by the Nazis. Yet his devoted loyalty to Il Duce is unquestionable. Suddenly the Italian Jew is pitted against a staunch anti-Semite." De Gaulle's bushy brows arched imperceptibly. "So confounding a tactic conjures numerous complexities, *n'est-ce pas?* Does it not follow, Djebel, that Zeller, in light of this unusual development, might prove a valuable ally if we can reach him, cultivate and exchange ideas with him? The créme de la créme of this unusually delicious torte rests in the fact that word comes from Zulu, OSS chief in Geneva, that Major Zeller's father is presently negotiating with top-ranking Nazis to overthrow Hitler."

Prince Ben-Kassir, sipping brandy, was caught off guard. Astonished by the implication of the remark, he daintily caught the brandy spurting from his lips with a *serviette.* Eyes widening, he glanced from Henri to de Gaulle. "You can't mean Amadeo Zeller? Banque Suisse Royale or some such firm. Let's see—"

"Omicron. The cartel. *Oui.* You are well informed. A massive, highly deceptive operation is under way. It is essential, Djebel, that you comprehend the subterranean political scenario being enacted between the Nazis and the Italian high command. With this information, you will profit from the divisiveness and paralysis our secret agents and well-paid collaborators have set into motion to frustrate Axis efforts."

Darius, on a separate wavelength, blinked hard. "This Major Zeller's father, uh—Amadeo Zeller, you say? Who is he? Exactly what role does he play in France's survival? Is he a professional spy? What?"

"A banker. More than a banker, a financial titan. Once the right-hand man of Il Duce. See? His knowledge and acumen is invaluable. He has brought together, through highly clandestine dealings involving both MI-6 and the OSS, a vast assortment of, shall we say, *friends* among the enemy. He baits defectors, buys information with large sums of money flung audaciously before their noses. . . ." De Gaulle, caught up in his narrative, failed to notice how attuned Darius was to his description of the former fascist Zeller's career and present espionage involvements. The enormous complexities involving France and its allies were turning into beasts of unexpected contortions that could spell victory or disaster for France. Which would it be? At the moment, none of these distinguished militarists could predict the future.

De Gaulle took the beast in hand. "We agree France's survival must take precedence and guide your actions in White Coral, *n'est-ce pas?*"

Following a bird's-eye view of the giant clandestine operations being planned simultaneous to OWC, Darius brought them back on track. "Isn't Major Hesse's talent wasted on the Corsican operation? And what if this Major Zeller proves an unwilling victim for Hesse's clever duplicity? How do I connect with him without the whole of Corsica hearing of our intentions? I shouldn't wish to jeopardize Zeller until we know his precise sentiments, where his loyalties lie."

"The Italian's loyalty to Mussolini needs no scrutiny—it is absolute. Survival will dictate Major Victor Zeller's action."

Darius's viridian eyes narrowed in thought. He sensed a tinge of evasiveness in the French Commander in Chief. Henri Furstenberg poured more cognac for the conspiratorial coterie. There was a pause as they sipped the distilled brew.

"There is more you aren't telling us," Darius said quietly.

"Much more," de Gaulle sighed. "Hesse's purpose in Corsica is threefold. First, and a cover, I might add, is to recruit labor for deportation to Germany. Second, to test Major Victor Zeller's loyalty to Italy *and* the Third Reich. Third, and most distressing of all, is the objective to which he has dedicated his existence: to locate, identify, and destroy Zahara. And with her, *you,* Djebel. Your real name is known to Hesse. It was somehow leaked by one of your men or someone closely linked to OWC. Perhaps even one of your own Mozarabe? Someone who at great personal risk tried to kill you aboard the HMS *Hyperion.* You see? Already they know or guess how important you are to France, and to me."

The Prince exchanged concerned glances with Darius and Furstenberg. "We wanted this encounter to be shadowed with no ambiguities, Monsieur Creneau," he said, speaking deferentially. "Since in the confusion we failed to identify Djebel's assailant, it—"

De Gaulle waved a silencing hand. "Permit me, Highness, to emphasize my orders to Djebel. First and foremost, you will protect Zahara and yourself. You will permit Hesse no personal victories. He is a dangerously ambitious Nazi who is determined to sit in the Führer's confidence and policymaking circle. You will not permit this master of rodomontade to taste victory in any of his insane obsessions, which could very well prove crippling to us. *D'accord,* Djebel?"

"Oui, monsieur, d'accord," Darius replied.

Understand I am unable to grant you autonomy, full decision-making powers in Corsica. The status quo as agreed upon by the Allied high command must remain intact. The American presidential agent, General Donovan, is running the war in the Mediterranean. Keep that in mind, but work around it. Play *le renard,* the fox, with Cain and Abel, Donovan's men. Bring France success in Corsica, Djebel, and I promise she will be grateful to you in ways you cannot presently perceive."

Youseff smiled, nodding approval. General Furstenberg, an implacable iceberg, listened intently. The implications and complications involved in executing de Gaulle's orders could prove lethal for Darius and for Operation White Coral. He had studied the complex plans, recognized the bottlenecks. And because he'd had a part in training Darius, he waited to hear how the young genius would present his case. Darius leaned forward stiffly, opened his briefcase, and fished out a set of crudely drawn plans. He crossed over to de Gaulle and laid the plans on a coffee table before him. "*Monsieur,* let me speak frankly. Buried in the OWC literature are provocative hints which clearly suggest that our allies are ignorant of our needs. I see cryptic footnotes here and there indicating this should be attended to, that examined. The plan is shadowed by ambiguities which, in my estimation, point to certain unsettling and unexpected interpretations."

"Have you discussed this with Cain and Abel? The British?"

"No, sir. Not yet. First I must be totally convinced that my perceptions are not biased. I have clearly charted our steps up to and including Phase Five. But sir, in all seriousness, a formidable obstacle impedes our chances at victory unless we expedite matters following the pattern I've set forth on this map. As I perceive it, one impediment precludes victory."

"Only one impediment, Djebel?" De Gaulle laughed goodnaturedly. "Only one obstacle precludes victory?"

"Sir, what I refer to is the lack of—"

"Radio communications, *oui?*"

"Precisely," he said abruptly, flushing. "You anticipated my needs, *monsieur.* Here," he indicated on the map, "we need communications depots strung up and down and across Corsica in this manner. Or else the massive operational groups to be unleashed on the island in our final thrust—Phase Seven— will be to no avail." With radio-com we can synchronize all operational-group offensives. The instant relaying of unexpected last-minute changes in plans— I needn't tell you."

De Gaulle held up a restraining hand. He picked up a house phone and speaking a rapid, regional French, said, "Bring the specialist in to me." He replaced the instrument. "Your request was anticipated, Djebel. Here with me in Malta is a most special man, an expert in radio communications, and with him is his squad of trained signal men. They shall accompany you to your point of origin prepared to install undetectable radio and telephone depots at whatever crucial points you deem vital to OWC. Your dilemma is understood. Off the record, you have my permission to do what must be done to insure victory for France. *Alors,* work it as best you can with the OSS and SOE. Remember, Free France is your first priority. And I need not remind you that this meeting, our conversation, never took place."

"You need not remind me, Monsieur Creneau." *War games again!*

"You should know I had rejected you as co-commander of OWC. Your youth precluded such judgment until Zahara, your most persuasive admirer, disposed of my previous misconceptions." De Gaulle stepped forward, somber eyed, and embraced Darius French fashion, stepped back, and saluted him. "Pray God be with us."

The next morning, after a night's needed rest, Darius boarded the surfaced French submarine *Seraph* with the handsome Italian Major Gabriel Morosconi, code name Pluto, and his squad of expert Signal Corpsmen. Youseff and General Furstenberg remained behind in Malta.

Chapter Eight

The return trip to Corsica was uneventful, much calmer than the trip aboard the *Hyperion*. Darius enjoyed the exhilarating and highly informative narrative of the articulate Italian, Pluto.

Darius, still edgy and insecure in Neptune's watery domain, honed his instincts, taking extra precautions to avoid any recurrence of the near-lethal attack aboard the *Hyperion*. Totally engrossed and a bit confounded by Pluto's futuristic forecast of the marvels awaiting man in postwar electronics and communications, he bombarded the Italian with a rash of questions. "What are computers? What purpose do they serve? How can they surpass God-given brainpower? Certainly Einstein's brain cannot be duplicated, nor the minds of the great thinkers in history."

Only recently Pluto had seen plans of Colossus, the British computer, and he confessed that he had been baffled about how computers were elevated from theory into working models. The developments constituted authentic progress, he insisted now, adding, "Djebel, one day soon we shall witness space satellites capable of circling the globe, penetrating various atmospheres, and transmitting instantaneous photographs and messages. It's

all out there in the future, awaiting man's ability to recognize it
and lift the veils of concealment.''

As Pluto spoke and Darius, seated at the table in the officers'
wardroom, listened, the ever-constant ASDIC ping—the same
sonar detection device he'd heard aboard the *Hyperion*—obviously disturbed him. Noting his disquiet, Pluto explained the
technology of submarine safety, and how the ASDIC ping
helped other subs to escape U-boat wolf packs. He described
the transmitter-receiver encased in a metal dome under the submarine's hull that could detect lurking U-boats and their precise
positions.

"You see, Djebel, the transmitter sends out sound impulses
on a selected bearing; the receiver picks up the impulses when
they strike an object and are reflected back.''

"One moment. Explain it again, please,'' Darius insisted.
When Pluto complied, Darius pondered a moment. "Are you
saying it can be manipulated like a giant searchlight?''

"Ah, you understand, eh? *Molto bene.* Now, when the device is connected to a compass, we learn the direction in which
the submarine lies. Listen carefully. The time between the
transmission of the impulse—''

"—and the return of its echo reveals its range.''

"Bravo.''

"Pluto, is this device infallible?'' Suddenly Darius grew
enormously excited.

"*Che cosa?* Ah, I understand. No. The device works only
underwater, *never* on the surface.''

"Too bad,'' said Darius, crestfallen. Then quickly: "Why
not? Why not *above* water? Say, on land, perhaps?''

"Tell me what ideas are forming in your mind. Perhaps I can
accommodate you.''

"This ASDIC you speak of—who invented the device?''

"Allied Submarine Detection Investigation Committee takes
credit.''

"Is it possible for you and me to form AGDIC?''

"*AGDIC?*''

Darius smiled foxily. "Allied *Ground* Detection Investigation—''

Pluto did not smile. He looked thoughtful. "You mean the
detection of *ground* forces? Armor? Tanks? Ahh, I see what
you're thinking. You mean without *aerial* reconnaissance. Let

me consider the ramifications. The sound beam sent by ASDIC is conical in shape. Radar is a revolving disk. . . .''

Once on Corsica, Darius spent every available moment with the brilliant engineer whose name topped the Gestapo's most-wanted list. Darius also discovered that Morosconi had been singularly responsible for setting up Paris underground communications between the French Resistance and Special Forces headquarters, a division of Eisenhower's Supreme Command responsible for controlling clandestine operations and French Resistance movements.

''You've been in Corsica three months. When will you see your family?''

''Matteus, your constant prodding has not changed my situation.''

''At least see your mother.''

''Especially not my mother. *Nor* Sophia. Make them understand,'' Darius snapped impatiently. The early winter chill frosted the air. He tugged up the fur-lined collar of his windbreaker. ''Do they even know I'm alive?''

''We've told them nothing, yet.''

''*We?*'' Darius, supporting his lower back with his hands, turned slightly, cocking his head. ''Who else—'' He stopped, eyes scanning the immediate area. ''My father knows I'm here?'' he asked sotto voce.

''From the first, when Barbone negotiated for the citadel. He flashed papers naming you as Allied co-commander.'' Darius frowned and Matteus continued, ''Daily he observes you from a distance, aware of your need for secrecy. He refuses any encounter with the Allied officers—British, French, and American. Darius, mistakes were made, some irreparable. There was St. Cyr—''

''St. Cyr is a forgotten dream. There is no need for regrets.'' Darius scanned the nearby area with inscrutability. ''If he can observe me undetected, I shudder to think who else—''

''Only a native familiar with the *maquis*. A stranger? Unlikely.''

''How many natives turn collaborator in these precarious times?'' Darius's cynicism lashed at the Moor.

''Is it for this you summoned me?'' he asked quietly.

''No. Forgive my impertinence, Matteus. I am in desperate

need of your talents—what only you can ferret out without bringing undue attention to yourself. Someone—perhaps more than one—threatens me both personally and professionally."

Matteus's black eyes sparkled. "You need only speak the word."

"Here at the citadel, in our midst, is a dangerous enemy—" Darius began. He described briefly the inexplicable, calamitous series of events aboard the *Hyperion*. "A trap must be set. The order, if it didn't originate in Corsica, was put into work here. A three-man escort boarded a rubber skiff with me, three men of the Resistance. My ineptness—I failed to secure that step of the mission—is inexcusable. I need to know the identities of those men, *if* any returned safely to shore."

He described the gigantic disruption at sea, the enormous ocean swell caused by the surfacing submarine. "The powerful thrust of exploding water capsized the skiff. I too was hurled overboard," he added, visualizing the scene again. "Discretion must be exercised. Queries concerning these men and their involvement in this most secret mission must not originate from me. Understand, if the identity of my assailant and his nefarious vanguard remain covert, our planned operation can be doomed. The freedom of France must be spearheaded from Corsica. It can be no other way." Darius winced at a sudden pain.

"The manner in which you move communicates truth to me. Is the wound healing? Pray Allah those jackals will be swallowed whole."

"The wound, the injuries are secondary to my concern. Can you do the job I require and bring no attention to me?"

"I already know the answers you require. What I didn't know was an attempt had been made on your life. You were correct. Your three escorts were men of the Resistance. The essence of the order was secrecy. Neither the OSS nor SOE were to know of your rendezvous."

"The men, Matteus. Who were they?"

"Marnay, Montreaux, and Columbo. Columbo, Barbone's cousin, failed to return that night."

"*Columbo?*" Darius searched his mind, trying to envision the Corsican's face. He shook his head.

"His body washed ashore last evening in the cove of Les

Calanches,'' Matteus said quietly. ''The answers may be complex.''

''So it wasn't Colombo? That leaves two.''

''There was no sign of foul play, yet his death poses an enigma.''

''*What?* For God's sake, tell me. Perhaps I can sort it out.''

''I was there that night, hidden, observing as you boarded the skiff. My eyes trailed your every move through binoculars.''

Matteus, the ever-constant sentinel, still watched over him.

''And I noticed you all wore flotation vests. On Columbo's body, when it washed ashore, there was none.''

''It could have come off. The turbulence, the power of the waves . . .''

''Possibly, but unlikely. Columbo swam like a fish.''

''What explanations do Marnay and Montreaux give?''

''Same as yours. The sudden concussion of exploding water capsized the skiff, plunging them forcefully into the sea. They swam back, fell exhausted on the beach, failing to notice Columbo's absence. Unfortunately, I can confirm their story.''

Darius reflected a moment. ''Who gave the orders? Who prepared the skiff for my departure?''

''What a complex embroidery to unravel. Orders came via diplomatic courier from Marseilles directly to your father. Vivaldi summoned Chamois Barbone, entrusting him to prepare safe escort to the *Hyperion*.''

''We are back at square one,'' Darius said, dismayed.

''You can exonerate Chamois's cousin Columbo. As you said, that leaves two. Marnay and Montreaux.''

''No, Matteus. Three remain. Marnay, Montreaux, *and* Chamois Barbone.''

The Moor's black onyx eyes flared dangerously. ''But no—it cannot be Barbone. He is not, never has been, my favorite among Corsicans, but he wouldn't dare betray you. The guilt must be with Marnay or Montreaux. Neither can be trusted. In both men there is a sickness, an infection, the passion of war and its tenuous promise of rewards to the victors.''

Darius patted the Moor's shoulder affectionately. ''Do what you can. I must leave you.'' He saw Pluto wagging him off the incline. ''If you need me, summon me. But do so with circumspection, only in an emergency and through Pascal.''

Matteus watched as Darius sidestepped the brambled thicket,

angled around a hedge, and slipped off the perchlike embankment, heading toward Pluto. The wiry man was holding blueprints in his hands and excitedly signalling Darius. Binoculars to his eyes, the Moor swung them around cautiously, taking in every inch of the nearby terrain. He stopped, retraced the last arc, and held fast, struck by unnatural movement, shadows of a man emerging slightly from behind cover. The soldier, in an American uniform, was peering at Darius and Pluto through binoculars, unaware of the Moor's scrutiny.

Below them on the citadel grounds, the Italian genius called to Djebel. "Come, *amico,* we have much to coordinate before we begin our island peregrination to set up the radio depots."

Darius caught up with the radio specialist. Together they trampled through iced-over mud puddles in the early morning frost to the open camp fires, drawn by the invigorating scent of freshly brewed coffee. Steamy mugs in hand, they sipped the brew, warming their cold fingers on the crockery.

"Djebel, I commend you on the Mozarabe. Professionals to the core, the lot of them," Pluto commented, his eyes sweeping around the citadel perimeter, where Darius's industrious men were teaching new recruits the art of commando combat. "What is this fraternal cohesiveness I detect that makes them so special? I detect an unusual brand of reality here—the usual theatricality of war is absent, yet—" he thought for a moment, "—aren't we all, in a sense, waiting for the curtain to come up?"

"No," Darius said with finality. "The curtain has already risen. We are waiting for it to fall. *Alora,* let us go inside to the map room to study these plans of yours."

Observing the duo from the secluded knoll, unable to understand the ramifications of Darius's recent absence from Corsica, the obvious injuries done to him, and the arrival of Pluto and his squad of men without explanation either to the OSS or SOE, Jim Greer wished to hell Brad Lincoln would return from Algiers and his meeting with their chief, General Donovan. They had to figure out as soon as possible what was going on between Pluto and Darius.

After observing Jim Greer from a short distance through binoculars, Matteus glanced at his watch, fixing the time. He crept in closer to Greer, stalking him as a hunter stalks his prey. As Darius and Pluto disappeared into the map room, Greer stepped from shadows into light. Matteus quickly retreated behind a tree, holding his breath, immobile.

Greer slid off the embankment and headed for the open camp fires. The Moor raised the binoculars to his eyes, studied the American's face, committing his expression and movements to memory. Even if it meant his own death, he had vowed in constant supplication to Allah that there would be no repeat performances against his beloved Darius.

Inside the map room, Pluto meticulously detailed plans for the communication depots, employing Darius's clever latticework design. While Pluto ascertained the efficacy of his plans, Darius allowed his mind to wander back to his conversation with Matteus.

Marnay, Montreaux, and Columbo! Three faces, less vague now, intruded upon his mind as he reconstructed their departure from the cove before boarding the *Hyperion.* Marnay, weasel faced with penetrating eyes, remained in the foreground; the others receded in his memory. Marnay's noticeable toadying about and catering to the OSS and SOE, while admirable, wasn't authentic. Claude Montreaux, a young, nondescript, highly impressionable lackey to Marnay's bidding barely fit his hawkish appearance. Darius thought of Montreaux as an unpredictable sycophant with a coiled temper that could easily erupt in any number of ways. *Columbo was dead.* Drowned. *Purposely or accidentally?* What of the flotation vest? *Purposely or accidentally removed?* Only Marnay and Montreaux knew for certain. Which of the two was more inclined to tell the truth?

Coping with the inner tension that preceded the involved effort of problem solving, Darius momentarily forced out the images, leaned in toward Pluto and the plans spread out on a table, and pointed out a flaw. "If we eliminated the depot planned originally for Fort Bonifacio at the southern tip of the island, it would better facilitate our plans. If we placed it in the valley of Tizzano near the megalithic dolmens and ran it straight through Sartène to Zonza, we'd be midway between Propriano and Porto-Vecchio. A perfect triangulation. The O.G.'s could move in a northwesterly direction, slicing through the center of Corsica, in constant radio contact, free to swing to the west coast or east coast, wherever surprises were least expected.''

''*Sì*, Djebel. *Perfetto!* Even by rail, whenever possible, we can move each operational group as it is needed.'' Pluto made the required changes on the blueprints as Darius watched.

Besieged by another rash of images, Darius sat down, one elbow on the table, his face cupped in his left hand, a pencil in his right hand, doodling abstractedly. Once again he tuned out Pluto's words. Faces, swimming faces, surfaced from his subconscious, flashed past his inner eyes, narrowing to one, *only* one. Indefinable at first, vaguely discernible . . . clearing . . . fading . . . clearing . . . holding!

''Give me a minute,'' he said, extending a cigarette to Pluto. The Italian accepted it, lit it, and sat back to observe Darius, marked curiosity creeping into his expression. At the end of Darius's pencil, a crude drawing was forming. Fingers hooked into his belt, Pluto raised one booted leg to a chair and stood watching the sketch materialize.

Darius's eyes closed briefly, better to see the hard face taking form on one end of the blueprint paper. Solid, square jawed. Thick brows over piercing blue eyes—young. Wait! Not so young! Early twenties, maybe younger. The hair was short, extremely short. No! There was no hair! *Bald!* Prematurely bald? Something about the eyes—cold, calculating, lethal. The eyes of a killer! The killer aboard the *Hyperion*!

Quickly, before he lost the image, he snatched the sketch crayon from Pluto's hands. Like a man possessed, he began to sketch broadly, giving life to the image imprinted on his mind. *Now at last, something tangible! The head—average. Neck, broad. Shoulders broad also. Uniform—officer's garb, British. The nose, slender. Nostrils, flaring. Ears, square, prominent. A scar. Yes, yes, a scar! Where was it? At the left temple like a crescent moon extending to the eyes. No, no, no! Too prominent. Erase it to a thin line. That's better. The hair. So thin it seemed bald. Bald at so young an age? Yes, only a thin circle of brown hair. Something else—what?*

Darius studied his handiwork, leaning back, away from it, trying to gain a better perspective, squinting, searching his brain, unaware of Pluto's increasing bewilderment at his frantic antics. A sudden curiosity erupted into amazement. Pluto exclaimed jubilantly.

"Djebel! Are you some clairvoyant? This man—this picture is the face of a friend. Yes, yes, it is so. Well, perhaps not perfect."

Pluto removed the crayon from Darius's hand. "It's the nose. Not quite as it should be. Let me see." He broadened the nose, sketching rapidly with more expertise than Darius, then rubbed the crayon, blending the harsh strokes, softening the lines. "The scar is more prominent and twists downward, changing the shape of the eye. And perhaps something else? A mustache." His hand moved swiftly, in sure strokes, and in moments the mustache was in place.

Muttering a string of colorful expletives as exquisite delight crept into his features, he proceeded to sketch in a shock of hair. About to protest, Darius, infected by Pluto's enthusiasm, felt something unusual was taking place. And in a second things fell into place.

"It's him! My British friend with the Austrian accent, Ghost-Dancer! We worked together—" Pluto stopped. "Djebel, from where do you know him?"

"My question to you exactly." Taking the crayon in hand again, he insisted, "My man had no mustache or hair, but I am certain of these." He sketched in a pair of steel-rimmed spectacles resting askew on the nose. For Darius, the sketched face, no longer wafting in and out of focus, had finally taken form. Swimming in the deep recesses of his mind were the screams, alarms, horrifying explosions of depth charges aboard the *Hyperion*. Darius saw himself hurled across the wardroom, his head striking a bilge-pump chassis. Stunned, his vision blurred by the impact, he tried to lift himself off the deck. Then, fire! Searing pain seized him. More depth charges, one after another, created pandemonium. There—the face of his assailant. The hard face in the sketch loomed over him, the steel-rimmed glasses hung askew. How calmly the assailant readjusted the glasses. Then the face receded, disappeared amid the muddled voices, shock, and turmoil. Pluto's voice cut through his memories. Darius blinked.

"But of course, Djebel. Ghost-Dancer wore glasses exactly like these. He is farsighted. The peacock, a master at disguise, has too much ego to be seen wearing them always. Perhaps he shaved his hair after Paris. We worked together in the Paris sewers. Ghost-Dancer." He stared at the sketch. "I assumed he had died. He was part of the Paris underground operation. We wired Gestapo headquarters. The explosions!'' He kissed his fingertips. ''Superb! My finest work. Is he here in the *maquis* with the British?''

''We met en route to Malta,'' Darius said softly.

''He's alive then?'' Pluto shook his head. ''I know little about this man. Only that he—'' He stopped. ''There are men here in the *maquis* who know him well. The Resistance leader Marnay, the Corsican Barbone. Ask them—''

''No! Not yet. Hear me, Pluto. No reference must be made to this man you call Ghost-Dancer—if the man in the sketch is the man I know. Not until I learn more about him. Tell me straight out. Are we together in victory for Free France? I should dislike having you for an enemy.''

Ghost-Dancer, whoever you are, you shan't remain a ghost forever. The pavane has only just begun.

''You need ask?'' Pluto appeared crestfallen. ''I came as highly recommended to you as you to me, by Monsieur Creneau.''

''You were fascist. When the final curtain comes down, where will your loyalties lie, my friend?''

''With God, *amico*. Only with God. *Dio guardi, Dio liberi*.'' He waved Darius's suspicions aside. ''You refuse to let me off easily? Very well, in the beginning we were all *fascisti*. Until we learned how fascism, like a seductive whore, made promises she was unable to keep. Devotion without payment is a tenuous commodity. Through equilibrium, a balance of order is maintained. The toppling of all tyrants begins with the raping of the people. The people are the backbone of any nation. Use them as whores—''

''Cut the bullshit, Pluto. Whores or not, to whom do you owe your allegiance?''

''Djebel, I am a *partigiano*. I owe no allegiance to Il Duce, fascism, Hitler, or the Third Reich. Hear my words and hear them well. In two months, Il Duce falls from grace and power. By midsummer, his government will be in shambles. Rumblings of discontent already echo across the sea. Secret negotiations are under way with powerful allies who hold persuasive cudgels in their fists. Count Ciano and King Umberto confer daily, hatching schemes to rid Italy of the fascist circus ringmaster.''

"Pluto, so my position to you is perfectly clear, I ask a simple question: How do you come by all this information?"

"You overlook the obvious, Djebel. I prognosticate the future." He laughed that Darius was disconcerted. "You still doubt me? Good. At least you are not one to be fooled by jocularity or other clever ruses. Cryptology, line tapping, and eavesdropping are all facile tools I teach to agent provocateurs. Actually, like Napoleon Bonaparte and Alexander, I am passing through another incarnation."

"*Merde.* I should have known." Darius affected a broad grin and loud laughter, but internally he began to worry. The man on Malta had failed to explain how far this wiry, luminous-eyed, spry Italian genius could be trusted. *No dossier existed on Pluto!* Storm clouds arose in Darius's mind. No higher recommendation than the one he received could be sought. Why then was he so uneasy? He blinked aside his thought. "I assume Ghost-Dancer is a code name." It was not a question.

"You'd like me to unveil his true identity? Convincing literature unavailable to me must exist in Malta. Your formidable cohorts must have knowledge of him. Request it! Like yours, Djebel, mine is a code name. And his is Ghost-Dancer. The great man remains Monsieur Creneau. Safer all around."

"Pluto, the most mysterious and unknown planet in the universe," Darius mused. "Are you so mysterious?" He stared at the sketch, their collaborative effort—the face of the killer. *Bastardo!* He muttered internally, directing his wrath at the crayon sketch. It should never have happened. On the desert, it would *never* have happened. He addressed his rancor at the other. "I thought you professional scholars joined in a cause were fraternally bound by some esoteric mumbo jumbo."

"Professional scholars? I mentioned no such ties." Pluto sobered. "The man is but a boy, and because he is young, recklessness and daring abound in him." He lit another cigarette. "It's true, Djebel, old friendships, tested knowledge, loyalties to a cause are requisite in certain involvements. But in times of war, circumstances alter many previous beliefs. Ghost-Dancer and I were joined in co-conspiracies, *Allied* co-conspiracies, a collective process embarked upon for the good of our collective nations. Ghost-Dancer is unique in his field. He simply delivered to me special materials and parts I needed in Paris. How I altered them, reshaped them to fit my purpose and specifications, was *my* responsibility. How he obtained what he brought me was not my concern. Neither the locus of his power nor his other involvements concerned me. That he contributed to my work enabling me to complete my assignment and move on was all I was and am concerned with. However curious he was about me and my origins, *I fed him nothing. Capisci?* Likewise, I am astounded at the ease with which I imparted information to you. It is unusual behavior for me, Djebel, and the similarities between me and that mysterious, unknown planet from which my code name was born are more the rule than the exception.

Darius pressed, ''The name Ghost-Dancer—has it a special significance?''

''I told you, my job is not to probe. I am not cloak and dagger or the SOE. He volunteered no information. And I, like a specter, moved in, did the job, and vanished just as I will do sometime between now and the culmination of OWC. Where I go is—''

''Don't tell me! I don't want that responsibility.''

''Circumspection is admirable. Unfortunately, Djebel, you already know. You *don't* know? You play games with me, eh?''

Darius, lighting a cigarette, shot him a dubious, somewhat confused glance as he blew out the match. ''No games with you, Pluto. Not with a man I respect.''

''For one so young, with influential friends in very high places, your naiveté confounds me. We talked. I mentioned a timetable, why my work in Corsica demands expedience. Already the communist underground moles prepare Italy for postwar politics. Soon I will rendezvous with the Sicilian guerrilla fighter Guilliano, who with his Separatist Army forms the only bulwark against the Reds until after Operation Husky succeeds. They—the Reds—must be stopped. *Caro mio,* if they succeed? . . . You've not seen anything yet. The Nazis by comparison are sleepwalkers compared to those blood-sucking Draculas.''

''We have yet to finish with Germany, and you are embattled with Russian spies? Our allies? Let us first tame this ground swell of Corsican activity.''

Pluto gave Darius a strange, ominous look. ''*Sì.* Corsica

first. After Corsica everything comes together. The blueprints will become clearer."

Darius laughed jocularly. "It is not acceptable to hold one's intellectual inferior up to ridicule, *amico*. It's like laughing at a cripple."

Pluto's head jerked up from the plans. He inched away from Darius, eyes intent at the change in the Mozarabe leader. "I said something to offend you? How? What? I mean no disrespect."

"I know. I know! Sit down, Pluto. Smoke a cigarette with me. Someplace here, in a drawer . . ." He rummaged in a dilapidated drawer of the desk, turned up the wick of two lanterns, fished out a half-filled brandy flask. "We take a moment's repast, *sì?*" He filled two tin cups and gave one to the specialist. Pluto shoved his cap back on his head and unbuttoned his ever-present flak jacket.

"You want information?"

"I want information, *sì*. Begin with Cain and Abel. Where did you meet? And no subterfuge. I saw the looks passing between you on our arrival. I am not Djebel for nothing."

"*Sì,*" Pluto sighed expansively. "Not for nothing. The great man did not tell you his deepest concerns?"

"Suppose you answer my question. I promise not to lead you astray."

"Djebel, let it be understood. I am Sicilian. Sicilians are crafty men; an inborn cynicism and distrust is inherent in our genes. It is not my nature to speak of things that concern me. To do so would hasten my demise on earth. So I listen, hear nothing, go about my business, at times blind and dumb. I try never to flaunt my stupidity or my intelligence in the wrong places. In this war, centuries-old enemies are suddenly allies against a demon incarnate—the Nazi war machine. The enmity between France and Britain is older than time itself. *Never forget it!* Lock your mind around that indisputable fact." Something was bothering Pluto. He leaned in conspiratorially. "Do you understand Sicilian dialect?"

"Try me. If I don't I'll stop you."

Pluto rested an elbow on the desk, pondered silently. He looked up at Darius, and their eyes locked fiercely. "Cain and Abel, along with Marnay and Montreaux, were with the Corps Franc at Aïn Taya on Cape Matifou near Algiers in late December, 1942. As you were preparing to land in Corsica, they were with Captain d'Aminon of the *Chantiers*. Is the date significant?''

Darius lowered his head, eyes scanning the earthen floor as the date rolled about in his head. ''The assassination of Admiral Darlan!''

Pluto, rising, nodded his head and walked to the heavy oak and iron door to peer out at the men busy in the compound. ''Aïn Taya is much like this place. Cain and Abel were sent by the British SOE under the command of a British colonel, code name Maja. All four men spent a week there, acting as instructors in weapons and explosives to the SOE's Corps Franc recruits. Approval came from someone highly placed in the OSS. The Corps Franc—''

''Corps Franc—reservoir for spies, saboteurs, and guerrilla leaders.''

''Precisely. Something curious happened, Djebel.'' Pluto closed the door, slipped the bolt into place, and for added precaution, firmly lodged a wooden chair under the iron lever. ''You can't be too careful. I need no surprises.''

''Maja, the SOE chief, terminated his association with the Corps Franc, leaving Cain, Abel, Marnay, and Montreaux to shoulder the responsibility.''

''On such short notice? Why?'' Before he asked the question, the unpalatable answer struck him. He demanded and received an explanation from Pluto.

''The Corps Franc personnel and its powerful behind-the-scenes leaders were involved in dirty politics. Cain, Abel, Marnay, and Montreaux tutored a squad of Corps Franc in clandestine activities—a plot to kill the inflexible Darlan. He was, of course, Vichy. Exorbitantly detested and feared by the Allies, the man was an inexorable zealot in his fanatical hatred for the British. He refused to bend to to their dictates; he would not yield a hair.''

''So—they exterminated him.''

''With the Corps Franc commander solidly behind the plot. He suffered grand delusions. He would be King of France. His intent was to call upon General de Gaulle and his formidable Intelligence forces to form a government.''

Darius stiffened, rejecting the implications. ''You're insane,'' he said in a hushed voice, unwilling to believe what

Pluto implied. "The great man would *never*— No! I reject the idea! Pluto, you speak of a man to whom we've both sworn allegiance."

"My allegiance is ephemeral. Yours—I hope—is *not* eternal."

Darius poured another brandy, downed it. "Mistakes were made. *Mistakes!* None so far as to be beyond repair. He will explain it properly."

"Ah. The emerald of your conscience has turned to glass, eh? Djebel, I was there. I recorded everything." He tapped his head. "In here are the unlogged meetings, the spoken words. As usual, I remained a shadow in the background, unseen, busily at work with my wires. I heard everything. There were three plots, not one. I tell you, Montreaux, a born assassin, was primed for the assassination. He was attired in ritual black for the act. The others, tactically primed as backups in case the assassination failed, were strategically placed in the elaborate design to prevent failure."

Pluto paused to light a cigarette. Periodically his eyes trailed to the barred windowlike openings along the two stone walls bordering the citadel compound. Any shadow hovering along the opening of the inner wall of the compound would be spotted at once. Only the opening on the southern wall, placed higher due to the rise of terrain, could create a problem, making detection of an eavesdropper difficult. He continued.

"Early on December twenty-fourth, two months ago, the Admiral held a meeting at his office in the Palais d'Été. He left for lunch, returned at approximately three o'clock. Then, *boom, boom, boom!*" Pluto's hand, held like a gun, was pointed at his temple. He barely whispered the sounds. "Three shots were fired, but they were not from the same gun. The black-garbed assassin—the real one—fled. The second man, innocuous but fanatical, a rabble-rouser of the worst sort, primed to be a decoy, was caught by the police."

"A diversion until the real culprit escaped." Darius, marveling at the tactics, was fascinated and fully caught up in the story.

"At least to buy time. The police, believing the real killer was in custody, relaxed the usual precautionary systems. To sum it up, Darlan died at the hospital later that day. Before nightfall, Algeria was in a state of siege. Allied top brass at the front in Tunisia, General Eisenhower and Giraud, Commander of the French forces in northwestern Africa, returned at once to Algiers."

"An investigation took place, yes?"

"Everyone questioned had unshakable alibis. The decoy—the diversion, you called him—was jailed. Later that afternoon, he was court-martialed."

"*Court-martialed?* That same night? Some investigation."

Pluto shrugged indifferently. "Does it matter? Found guilty, he was condemned to death and executed by a firing squad on the morning of December twenty-six. The men central to the plot were already en route to—"

"Corsica," Darius muttered. He paced the narrow confines, noticeably agitated. "The French were involved. Vichy?"

"Both Vichy and Free French."

Darius stopped pacing. His green eyes turned the color of a murky sea. "Both?"

"It cannot be me who strips the curtains of innocence from your eyes. Be faithful, be loyal, be dedicated, but never incautious."

"Don't use the truth carelessly," Darius cautioned, trying to suppress the sickening sensation at the pit of his stomach.

"We are the tight-lipped, driven fanatics who do the dirty work while the generals, politicians, financiers—the chess players—move us, the pieces, into place."

"*Us?*"

"Both you and me. You think I don't weep at the seduction of my nation by those who wheel and deal in the lives of innocent people? The blind, obedient, innocent victims who trust the madmen? Yes, I am a puppet now. I dance to the strings manipulated by men I trust as implicitly as you. But only for now. Until I learn . . . until I become a player at the top, where I too will consider all options before making decisions. In my solitude I paint sanctimonious pictures of myself posturing about in a mine field of power, but when it happens, Djebel, will I hold to my truth? Will I be capable of extraordinary feats or will I too be seduced by power? God! Power is the key to all things!"

Darius, forced to avert his thoughts from what Pluto was spelling out for him, harked back to the assassination. "The gun—the assassin's gun—was it identified?"

"A prototype. Far in advance of its time. A Colt Hammer-Shroud inflicted the coupe de grace. The third bullet was innocuous. Bullets from the Hammer-Shroud killed Darlan with direct hits to the vitals."

"American. OSS," he uttered in hushed tones.

"Touché, Djebel. You *are* knowledgeable. Not general issue. A private collection. It was traced."

Darius arched his brows prodigiously. "Traced? Yes, go on."

"Abel's gun. A collector's item, made especially for him. An efficient, close-quarters defense weapon capable of shooting through a pocket until the cylinder is emptied without danger of mechanical interference."

"Such as the hammer jamming in a pocket lining?"

"Precisely."

"Greer." He tripped the name softly over his tongue.

"His affection for the Hammer-Shroud was such he used it instead of the general issue forty-five. It was reported stolen two days before the assassination."

"Naturally."

"I can offer no more without violating matters I must hold sacrosanct until after the war, Djebel. You are not a foolish man, *amico*. Let no man treat you as such. Demand to know the reasons behind every order."

"And if I know those reasons in advance?"

"Prescience is a highly lauded virtue."

"No, Pluto, not a virtue—a gift. A gift few men possess."

"Then you know who really plotted the assassination?"

"Of course. Specters who do not exist! Papers will miraculously surface declaring the deceased to have acted against the interests of France, and declaring that the assassin, a fanatical zealot, had acted in the best interests of his nation, for the liberation of France."

Pluto tilted the brandy flask against the light, cursed at the scant pittance remaining, and drained the dregs in half apology.

Darius opened a drawer in the desk and with a sly wink brandished another bottle. "Will this numb the bedevilment searing your soul?"

"The words of a poet," said Pluto, snatching the bottle from him. He bit off the cork, filled his cup to the brim, recorked the bottle, and set it down. "You are no naive Corsican, my friend.

I am the knave who plays the fool.'' He raised his cup in toast and gulped the fiery contents.

''I'm the student with much to learn, but I *am* learning.''

Pluto lamented audibly, ''We are both students with much to learn. But I am the fool, the master choreographer, the wire specialist and *I take orders.* At times when drenched in the isolation of black thoughts, I think there's no hope for mankind. Then I meet bright young men like you, filled with innovation, leadership, and an inborn sense of purpose and I am instilled with hope.'' Pluto smiled, sipped his wine.

Phhhhfffft! Darius heard a familiar sound from his past.

Pluto swatted a sharp bite on the right side on his neck. ''Cursed mosquitoes!'' he said, his eyes observing the curious changes in Darius. The Corsican tensed, held his fingers to his lips. Springing lightly to the balls of his feet, he stacked wooden crates under the south window opening, climbed atop them, gun at the ready, peering over the ledge as he articulated loud and clear, ''So, *amico,* the case is closed. There is no official Allied involvement. Darlan's death was solely the work of royalist zealots, eh?''

Too late! What he saw were quivering brambles left in the wake of a human presence. Moments ago someone had stood there eavesdropping.

But wait! Someone was still prowling through the underbrush.

Matteus! There, easing along the *parados* behind the stone fortress wall! Relieved, then annoyed again, he wondered at the lack of vigilance or security! Where in damnation were his men? Pascal, Longinotti, Delon, Tamir Mandel, the others. Had he been so consumed with his own importance of late he'd failed to reinforce his ties with the Mozarabe?

Darius, suddenly caught up in a gurgling of curious sounds, whipped around, eyes zeroing in on Pluto. *What in Satan's damnation?* He leaped off the boxes, sprang to Pluto's side. The Italian had collapsed in his chair. His head sagged to one side. His breathing was labored and loud; it soon grew erratic as if the air supply was being shut off. Pluto clutched at the side of his neck wildly. Darius tore aside the flak jacket, yanked open the shirt, blinked at a minute drop of blood.

Then he saw it! A needlelike tip of steel. Darius sank his teeth around the offensive object, gripped it hard, and yanked, spitting it out on the desk. Without a moment's hesitation, he bit into the bloodied flesh, sucked hard, spit out the contents. He unsheathed his knife, and went to work. "Hang in there, *amico*. The venom must be excised."

Pluto's flaring eyes rolled upward into his head; only the translucent whites were visible.

In moments, Darius was finished. He rinsed his mouth out with brandy and spat it out onto the earthen floor, grimacing at the taste. He ran to the door, opened it, collided with Pascal, who was about to knock.

He removed the tray of hot coffee from Pascal's hands. "Quick, Pascal, summon Delon! It's urgent! Be quick!" Pascal, dazed, left at once, calling through the compound.

Darius was about to ply Pluto with brandy as Delon crashed through the door. "No! Nothing yet!" Taking a swift look at the blood flowing from Pluto's neck and the long, slender needle lying on the bottom of an overturned cup, he whistled low. "The tricks of the desert follow us about like shadows." He moved in quickly, injected Pluto with morphine, cleansed the wound, praising Darius's expertise and quick action. "How long, Djebel? How long do you estimate it was in him before you moved?"

"Perhaps thirty seconds. What is it?"

Delon frowned, his blue eyes reflective. He completed his work in silence, then picked up the poison dart and inspected the tip. "I am uncertain. Summon the black Phoenician."

"Musaka Mubende! You don't think—"

"Nothing. I think nothing. He may hold the key to such poisons."

"Summon the black man at once!" Darius snarled at Pascal. "Nothing must happen to Pluto," he told Delon. "He is vital to our plans."

Outside the map-room door, hands cupped to his lips, Pascal hooted a desert signal that the SAS had learned in North Africa. At once, several former SAS commandos dropped their duties and rushed into the compound arena. Pascal sighted the towering black man.

He waved Mubende forward, discharging the others. "Come, comrade, the chief needs you at once. On the double."

The moment Musaka Mubende stooped his large frame under the entry beam, entered the map room, and saw Pluto turning a mottled purple, his eyes fell on the poisoned dart. He addressed Darius. "What happened, *sahabti*?" The explanation came step by step. His even white teeth flashed a ready smile. "My ancestors would readily embrace you to their black Phoenician souls. You did the correct thing," he said, touching the tip of the dart to his tongue, spitting it out quickly. From his bush jacket, he removed a handkerchief and carefully wiped the tip of his tongue several times, grimacing. "Snake venom. But for your quick thinking, he would be dead. Black mamba, Naja Haje, or speckled band. Any of the three would be lethal. The resulting death is almost always instantaneous. Luckily, our brother Pluto had the good fortune to have an enlightened man in his presence. You sucked out the venom and an army of antibodies rushed in to control its pervasive power. You are most fortunate, Pluto. May you always bask in Allah's protection. It is most important, Djebel Kebir, that you prevent him from moving. Summon up a cot. He should not be moved."

Darius glanced at Delon. The former physician nodded in agreement.

Pluto lay on the cot after the others left. "I don't like to be coddled, Djebel," he insisted weakly. "It's hot, my head aches, and I long for the consolation of coolness, rest, and quiet, but before I succumb, tell me, did you see anyone at the window?"

Darius shook his head. "I saw no one."

There was a knock at the door. Pascal stuck his head into the room. "Two more operational groups landed last night at Ponte d'Orchino."

"Ponte d'Orchino? North of Cargese? Why there?"

Pascal whirled a forefinger at his head. "You ask me? What can I tell you? They missed their mark?"

"*Christ!* Send a squad of escorts. They'll never get past the German arsenal at Piana. Be careful, Pascal. Listen. Later today, at 1400 hours, I want you and the rest of Delilah's Dream to meet here in the map room—only the originals."

"All? And if it is not possible? Some are at Calvi."

"All who are available. Explain that the meeting is critical."

Pascal closed the door firmly. Darius moved in closer, slipped the bolt into place, poured coffee. This time he strategically placed his chair so both windows fell into his line of vision.

"Where were we?" Pluto began, his voice an octave or two lower.

"And so the case was closed."

"Ah, *bene*. Where do we go from here? To string wire. We begin at Tizzano, southwest of Sartene. Among the megalithic dolmens, menhirs, and stone circles created by your ancient Corsican ancestors."

"You know my land exceptionally well, Pluto," he said, still unnerved by the unexpected catastrophe nearly claiming Pluto's life.

"It's my job to know the terrain better than the lines on my hands."

Darius gulped his coffee, poured more. He scanned the room. He had heard the dart distinctly! Had there been more than one?

On his feet, positioning himself under the south-wall window, Darius carefully measured distances and angles, considering the variable lines of the trajectory. Shoving chairs into position as they were before, he motioned Pluto to silence. With a crayon, he marked out a section of the north wall, the part within his line of vision. He began fanning the area with his eyes, palms spread open, lightly feeling those portions of the walls and the door his eyes might miss.

"*Voilà!* I've found it! A second dart imbedded in the door."

"Here," Pluto whispered, "in my belt, a set of tools. Take what you need."

Pliers in hand, Darius dislodged the lethal abomination. He held it up to the light, touched the steel point lightly with his fingertip, and brought it to the tip of his tongue. He grimaced, spat it out. "No doubt the same venom." He wiped it carefully, washed it with hot coffee, and moved in closer to the wide-eyed Pluto.

"The fact is, *amico*, that there are two. Were they meant for you? For me? *Or for both of us?*"

He poured brandy and coffee moved toward Pluto, handed him a cup. "To eliminate one possibility, I'll arrange that you be quartered at the estate of the owners of this land. It's heavily guarded. Until your mission is complete here, I'll take no more chances with your life."

"And if you were the target?"

"Then we'll know for certain."

"And if we were both the madman's target?"

Darius pulled up a chair and sat very close to him. "You're a Sicilian, eh? I once knew a Sicilian. A clever man, sagacious, powerful, yet most subdued." Darius's eyes grew distant.

"Once you become a hammer, strike as hard as you can, then never again fall under your enemy's anvil." The words of the Sicilian Don Ferrugio had been spoken to a child, a child who had grown up the hard way. *"Never open your heart to let another see inside it."* Darius leaned in closer.

"Tell me, Sicilian, how do you put one over on an opponent who knows you're out to put one over on him?"

"Cleverly? You could shoot him."

"Seriously. Show me some of that Sicilian thinking."

"Ah, with adroit cleverness and masterful accomplishment."

"I couldn't have put it better."

"Dig deep into the most intimate of personnel files and obtain psychological profiles of the most secret—"

"Enough!" Darius stopped him. "*Silenzio.* You've said enough." He remembered the conversation with Brad Lincoln—Cain. The psychological profiles done on the Mozarabe!

Pluto, observing the changes on Darius's face, suddenly sobered. Rising unsteadily to his feet, he crept slowly to to the desk and rolled up the blueprints efficiently. "It's best I leave. I must meet with my men, assure them progress is being made or else they become testy. Djebel?" He hesitated, eyes locking with Darius's. "Why would you believe anything I told you? I could be your enemy purposely planted here to prime you with false testimony. A man parachuted into enemy territory throughout the warring zones of Europe. I could be master at double cross—triple-cross tactics. *How would you know?* When a wire man infiltrates, he becomes a master at ciphers. My falsity could be exquisitely, carefully calibrated, congruent with the rhythms and counterpoints of Allied intelligence and counterintelligence."

"You could be all of that and more," Darius replied softly. "Personally I'd consider it an idle flight of speculation. Besides, Pluto, O mysterious and most unknown of all planets, I fear no ordinary man. I fear only the political jackals whose purse strings control the functional paranoids, confidence men, sleight-of-hand artists, and film scenarists who simulate and stimulate plausible deception plots. Their far-reaching tentacles are lethal.''

"Ten years hence, perhaps twenty, even thirty, if we survive this war, we shall meet again and I will submit to you, as I did earlier, that you haven't seen anything yet compared to what will be.''

"On the strength of that prophetic statement, we drink a final toast,'' said Darius, pouring brandy. He sensed the probing look sweeping over him and lifted his eyes questioningly.

"No drink, Djebel. Something better.'' Pluto sat down, grabbed a pencil, and scribbled on a sheet of yellow foolscap for several minutes, transferring gems of wisdom to paper. Finished, he dotted the last sentence with a sharp, punctuated stab. He pushed back his chair, stood up, gathered his materials. "A gift to you, to be read in my absence. Think on it. And if you fail to understand it, we'll talk. *Adieu,* Djebel. Thank you for an enlightening verbal repast.''

Curiosity propelled Darius toward the foolscap filled with neatly written words. It was a recitation from memory. He read:

Do not dismiss the man dealing with clandestine whisperings. How clear and objective are the scholars who study existing social systems and create blueprints for a society to suit our technology? Will they be heard? Many are stifled, silenced to suit those in higher echelons. Be aware of a great void that must be filled with another power. *A third class of individuals* apart from political leaders and scholars must exist as an arm, an extension to be put to the task of thwarting mistakes, diagnosing areas of potential world disequilibrium, and eradicating potential disturbances. This arm, this extension, must be a *body of formidable men* capable of distilling the grape before it turns into vinegar, or put more succinctly, killing any group recognized as a potential danger against a state.

Such a body must of necessity be covert and fully autonomous, given the broadest discretionary powers by the highest human authority. The British SOE (Special Operations Executive) and their American counterpart, OSS, both trained in covert offensives to act ruthlessly and without fear, exemplify organizations that embody our basic needs. Included are objective scientists, men of the widest political, diplomatic, and economic experience. Long-term, complex undertakings are involved, but I propose that from the two groups mentioned, a smaller group be extracted, sober-minded men without personal ambition, men competent to judge the needs of our world society and to take necessary steps to prevent this society from permanent collapse. There can be no room for error. These requirements do not translate into concrete recommendations. If this sounds too provocative, too farfetched, I put it to you, had such a body existed in the early thirties, Nazi mania and its leaders would have instantly been annihilated—Pluto.

Darius reread the paper with total absorption, committing it to memory. Whoever had originally created this manifesto—he was certain it wasn't Pluto—had to be an integral part of whatever he proposed. A chill coursed through Darius. The message was ominous enough, but why did he shudder? Was it because he was unmistakably part of that *third group* so clearly defined in the scenario? Extraordinary! To view the birth of a new global entity of such scope and magnitude and power as the one described, to be part of it, called for introspection, a reassessment of his involvements and the interpersonal relationships he had formed recently, relationships he'd not explored except in a conventional manner. He thought about his relationship with Prince Ben-Kassir, an Oxford and Cambridge graduate with a brilliant geopolitical mind, a high-stakes player in heady political war games with powerful world moguls that guaranteed the unencumbered perpetuation of his faltering dynasty. He thought too of Henri Furstenberg, a young, impressionable expatriate searching desperately for answers to the ominous questions fermenting in him. The differences between the three men were vast, but the fraternal bond between them was impregnable.

Prince Ben-Kassir, General Furstenberg, and Zahara, his beloved Lomay St. Germaine. The trio had recommended him to the great man who sat perched like a siren on the rocks of Malta orchestrating war scenarios. Darius nurtured second thoughts concerning his compliance, his blind obedience to orders from this giant at Malta. Was it all just more of the rotten politics he'd learned at Bir Hakeim from the intractable British?

He didn't know. Darius, aware of the festering political boils popping up like miniature Vesuviuses all around Corsica, needed time to deliberate.

Ghost-Dancer! Who the devil was he? How did he fit into Darius's scheme of things? Couched in the ambiguities of Pluto's words and prophesies were hints of a terrifying, awesome world Darius possessed no desire to contemplate. And the poison dart! Who was responsible?

The next several days of concerted effort forced Darius to focus sharply on matters that would ultimately determine life or death for Corsica and his people. He completed the intricate blueprints with Pluto, plagued by serious questions that pushed him into thought. Nothing tangible, yet a deliberate, perversely obscure release of implications began to prematurely eat at him. He knew he couldn't contemplate these things until his work in Corsica was done. *You must wait, Darius! Things will fall into place one day.*

The days flew past swiftly. Darius arranged for Pluto to be housed with Matteus and escorted to the citadel and back by Pascal, Longinotti, and Tamir Mandel. The finalizing of Pluto's plans, the proper training of men by his squad of specialists, was under way. Everything would be ready within three days, Pluto had promised. Good. It was still sooner than scheduled.

Darius grew keenly observant; his eyes and ears were everywhere at once. He'd given Matteus the poisoned dart. "Find the culprit. You may have lost him the other day, but find him." Matteus understood.

Darius critically studied the newcomers from the mainland, men and women of the Resistance. He wondered at their personal stakes in this war within a war. Men by the hundreds arrived, men who fought secretly, men whose only hope for reparation lay in American victory.

On this day he stood on the citadel ramparts, gazing at the arrival of a new load of Frenchmen. It was shortly after noon, the warm sun overhead shone through enormous pines, heating the men training below in the compound. Sharpened by his constant chats with Pluto, Darius had become distant, more inscrutable, acutely discerning as he studied the characters and idiosyncrasies of the recent arrivals. No different from Sidi recruits, these were hard-core criminals, smugglers, gun runners, narcotic and dope dealers who boasted they knew every escape route devised by man in every corner of the globe.

Christ! The Allies consider them invaluable!

Why do you suddenly sit in judgment? he asked himself. *This same genre of man saved North Africa! What is it with you, suddenly sanctimonious?*

Darius knew the answer. He was haunted by the words he'd learned from Pluto.

> A third class of individuals apart from political leaders and scholars . . . put to the task of thwarting mistakes, diagnosing areas of potential world disequilibrium, eradicating potential disturbances. The SOE . . . OSS . . . embody basic needs. Sober-minded men competent to judge needs of . . .

Words whirled around him. *Compagnia della Garduna! Tenets of an organization so powerful it can crumble governments!*

"Runaways, Djebel." Brad Lincoln moved in silently behind him, staring down at the new arrivals. "Fugitives from every fucking level of society, from its very dregs to the most intellectual college professor." Darius was jarred by Brad's presence.

How do you outfox the enemy who knows you're out to outfox him? Dig deep into the most secret of secret files. Psychological profiles.

"Hard to tell one from the other," Lincoln continued. It's a strange phenomenon. The intellectual exudes a more savage bent than the worst criminal in his midst. Every last one of them prays for Allied victory."

Greer, a step behind Lincoln, popped open the revolving cartridge cylinder of a very special gun. He twirled it absently, chanting: "America the great! America the generous! America the goddamn dream bubble luring people from all corners of the globe to its mysterious Tower of Babel."

Darius glanced at Greer, caught by the sounds of the revolving chamber. *The Hammer-Shroud!* The son of a bitch had the audacity to flaunt it openly! He gave no sign of discontentment.

Greer saw Pluto wagging his arms wildly like a human semaphore.

"I think the Italian wants you, Djebel. When do you leave?

Are the radio-com emplacements agreed upon and set up?'' asked Lincoln.

Days ago, when the plans were nearly final, he had confided the radio-com plan to his Allied co-commanders. He had received praise from his British counterpart, vague, noncommittal nods from the OSS.

Darius coolly studied the gun in Greer's hand.

''Curious weapon, that. May I look at it? Why is it there's no hammer?''

''Handmade special. My design,'' Greer boasted. ''The only one of its kind. Hand-tooled by a Boston craftsman. Quick-draw McGraw, see?'' He demonstrated his dexterity, extolling the merits of its covered hammer.

''Perfect for assassination, *oui*, Abel?'' Darius grinned with bland innocence. Cain and Abel stiffened, their eyes frigid.

''Adieu. Duty calls. If all goes well, Pluto and I return in three days.''

Chapter Nine

It was not three days. It had taken the better part of four days to implement Phase Five of Operation White Coral. After three solid weeks of meticulously planned strategy, the scrupulous selection of all communications depots was coming to fruition: the last of the wiring was in place, signals created a latticework up and down and across the island. Baffled by the intricacies, fascinated by the elaborate designs, Darius admitted to a layman's naiveté.

"Don't be so hard on yourself," Pluto admonished. "Put to me your systems of tactical warfaring offensives and defenses and I'd go *cafard. Pazzu,* in my language. We all have our specialties. Mine is communication. You can't know everything."

"Why not?" Darius replied glumly, urging the mules to gather speed. Both men, shabbily dressed as interior hillsmen, rode in a two-wheeled *carrozza,* a false-bottomed, mule-driven lorry, loaded with firearms, grenades, plastic explosives, and materials vital to Pluto's work. Above the floorboards, the wagon was filled to overflowing with bushel baskets of ripe melons, chestnuts, tangerines, and oranges as camouflage to cover their clandestine meanderings.

One more stop—the last station—and they'd return to Terra Bonifacio and the citadel. Mission accomplished.

Vizzavona, a thickly forested medieval village thirty kilometers north of Ajaccio, was in sight. As far as the eye could see, mountains rose majestically to snow-capped peaks. Profusions of multicolored flowers extended like a patchwork coverlet over the hills and valleys, between rocky, tree-stubbled goat tracks. Myriad early morning shadows cast by the rising sun worked a spidery network through lacy branches of golden chestnuts.

"I've seen nature's wonders and the architectural splendors of Europe, Djebel, but I admit readily to being awestruck by your land. The wisdom of the Corsican, his restraint in not interfering with nature, is admirable. Massive, lush forests—so green, so thick, so stunning."

"For several centuries, *amico,* the natives have lost both the touch and desire to combat nature."

"Odd, Djebel," said Pluto, lighting a cigarette. "You seem less Corsican than Italian, even French." He puffed languidly on the cigarette, arched his back, a soft lament escaping his lips. "Wooden seats on a mule-driven cart! A bit primitive for a young man whose head swims among the clouds with gods and goddesses."

B-o-o-m! B-a-r-o-o-o-m! The unexpected sounds of explosions jarred Pluto. "Quick, Darius, into the forest—there, between those giant trees." His reaction was so immediate that Darius was forced to restrain him.

Darius laughed. "Just the fishermen of the Manganello Valley dynamiting for trout. If the Italians were nosing around, we'd have been signaled by now."

"Signaled? How? By whom?" Pluto's eyes widened.

"Old men, bandits, rough sentinels hidden in the mountains, watching us, immune to our scrutiny, men who might make you feel you'd prefer to meet Italians and Germans."

"Can't the beasts be prodded to move faster?"

"Jackasses, yes, not mules."

Pluto cursed silently. They were running late. This stickler for schedules, even *impossible* schedules, got itchy at muckedup rendezvous. Sensing his discomfort, Darius filled him in on the quaint Corsican folklore. "Vizzavona—" *Boom! Boom!*

"—is the land of legendary bandits, of vendetta, blood revenge." *B-ar-r-o-o-m!*

The unrelenting sounds of dynamiting continued to make Pluto uncomfortable. His eyes were everywhere, ears sharpened, head cocked, listening, gun across his lap at ready. In a quick movement, he tugged on Darius's right arm, pulling back the reins. "*Firma!* Djebel, *stop!*"

Darius reined hard on the protesting mules. "What is it? What the devil is wrong?" His eyes were on the cursing Sicilian.

Pluto was standing on the seat, binoculars to his eyes, cursing colorful Sicilian expletives. "Whore of the devil! Italians! Germans too! Coming at us from the rear!" He swung the glasses around, looked up the steep incline to the top of the mountain—the convent of St. Francis perched atop it like a crown of thorns. "*Misericordia!* Another half hour and . . ."

Screeching motorcycle sirens from the northern approach grew louder. Darius yanked down on Pluto's jacket. "Get down! Remember we are two peasants returning from market at Porto and Piana. Let me do the talking!"

"On the road to the convent! If they believe that, they'll believe I am Pirandello! You're crazy! Oolala! Italian soldiers!"

"First we stop at the convent to donate fruit to the holy Sisters. *Capisce?* I'll invent the rest as we go along. If luck is with us . . ."

It wasn't. Gunshots split the air overhead. They cringed, trying to look like natives demonstrating fear and respect for authority. Sirens wailed to a sickening halt. An impatient car horn was pounded belligerently. Men shouted. Curses were hurled upon the mule driver, his companion, and on the mules themselves. "Get off the road, damn you!"

Darius tried to oblige; the mules resisted. He flung a whip over their heads, letting it sing loud and clear. Nothing. The intractable mules were immovable. Pluto paled, the cigarette between his lips chewed to shreds. Darius leaped from the wagon, raced to the beasts, yanked on their halters. He pleaded, cajoled, threatened.

Nothing.

The cacophony burst upon them; sirens and impatient auto and cycle horns, car doors slamming. Now pebbles crunched under heavy, angry footsteps. Italian curses sliced the air, shouts followed by impotent orders. A young Italian officer approached Darius, his voice strident, features harsh, impatient.

"What the devil is wrong, peasant?" Major Victor Zeller shouted.

Darius saw the spit-polished boots first. Then his eyes trailed upward, inspecting the immaculate uniform. At once, he postured obsequiously, his manner and tone lamenting at the inconvenience brought to the *maggiore* by his stubborn mules. "My humble regrets, *maggiore.*"

Victor's vigilant, testy eyes swept the protesting peasant, his companion, the fruit-laden cart. He could spare little time. Today Major Victor Zeller, on a vital mission, hurriedly snapped orders to his adjutant, Lieutenant Destro. Destro moved swiftly, ordered both men to stand aside, arms upraised, while another soldier searched them. "Your papers, peasants. *Identificazione, capisce?*" He repeated his words in French. The peasants complied.

The mules, coaxed and urged by two soldiers yanking on their harnesses, refused to budge. Victor Zeller moved forward, unholstered his 9 mm Glisenti-Beretta, and before Darius could utter a protest, shot the beasts through the head. "Now get these stubborn sons of bitches off the road!" he shouted to a soldier-filled lorry. The men scrambled off the truck.

Darius scowled blackly at the felled mules. Pluto, aware of the Major's piercing scrutiny, stiffened imperceptibly. *Oh Christ, don't let the Italian scrutinize me too carefully.*

"You realize you are holding up the Italian Army in its official pursuits?"

Darius had been observing their position. To the left, a steep embankment led to the river; to the right, countless paths led deeper into a larch forest and on into mountainous terrain; straight ahead up the hill was their destination, the convent, forty minutes away on foot; behind them was Corte. They'd come too far, done too much to be stopped now. They couldn't afford to bypass St. Francis. It was their last station stop, the pivotal contact point powered by electrical energy harnessed from the streams in countless gorges nearby. At St. Francis, trained specialists who knew the power of the gun were waiting in abeyance.

Darius counted a dozen regular soldiers and six motorcycle escorts. Eighteen trained soldiers against two peasants. Guns

and plastic explosives were secured under the wagon's floorboards. The soldiers were dragging the mules off the narrow
road, dumping them into the crevasse. If they pushed the
wagon down the rocky incline to the river . . . Jesus!

*Playact, Darius! Playact to the hilt. Don't let them dump the
wagon, the explosives! If they detonate, it's curtains for us.*

"What in Satan's damnation have you done? You killed our
mules! It isn't enough you rape our lands, steal our food. Now
you kill our beasts! *Animales! Animales!*" Darius, taking his
cue from performances he'd witnessed of Arab mendicants at
legionnaire outposts, railed on, hurling abusive pejoratives at
the Italians.

The sweat poured off Pluto's face. *Was Djebel crazy? Stop!
You're making things worse!* They'd made no escape prepara-
tions! *Djebel! Stop the tirade!* He was both fascinated and
petrified at the chance Darius took. *Son of a bitch!* In four days
they'd not encountered a single Axis soldier. Most, housed in
Genoan watchtower strongholds all along the Corsican coast-
lines, were concentrated in ancient battlements and fortifications overlooking port cities, seldom in the forbidding interior.
Unless— What the devil brought them to the remote inland hill
villages? *What? Important business—what else! Think! Think.
Oh, Christ! What else? The radio depots!*

Someone had betrayed them! It made perfect sense. The
poison darts at the citadel. Absolutely no activity en route,
then stalked like animals until the final moment! To be caught
redhanded . . . .

The soldiers were nearly finished. And he and Djebel were
impotent! Pluto's stomach turned queasy. Djebel, with the Italian officer less than six feet from him, continued the tirade.
Djebel raged against Italian injustice, against the Italian officer,
against Corsican obstinacy.

"And you!" Djebel cursed, striding before Pluto and thump-
ing his shoulders, shoving him in a spurt of anger off the road,
into the brush, out of the Major's line of vision. Anything to
hide Pluto's affliction, a deformed foot hidden by expensive,
customized boots. Pluto fell backward onto the rough shoulders. He was coughing, spitting dust, his composure shaken by
the unexpected assault. "Fine brother-in-law, wishing those
stubborn mules upon me! A curse on you! A pox on my wife!
On the mother who suckled you at her breasts! Stone weights at

my neck, the lot of you. Get out of my sight, you son of a humpbacked turtle!''

Major Zeller rolled his eyes in a look of long suffering at the roughhousing between the Corsican hillsmen. He moved in to direct the removal of the last mule into the crevasse, then turned his attention to the unhitched wagon. He waved his hands toward the offending vehicle, and just as Darius predicted, a half dozen soldiers shouldered the wooden conveyance, heaved laboriously, pushing it off the road. One of the wheels stuck in a deep rut.

Don't let them contemplate the weight! It's ten times the load of fruit!

The wagon tilted precariously, listing to one side, fruit spilling down the embankment.

Jesus! We're done for. Our work isn't finished, and it's all over!

Explosions split the air.

Darius and Pluto gave a start. The Italians scurried for cover. Gunshots spattered, grenades exploded dangerously close. Darius and Pluto took cover behind a large boulder.

"What the bloody devil?" Pluto hissed, listening, searching for the direction of the attack. Behind them the wagon lay intact, stuck in a rut.

Darius studied the angle, the line of erratic gunfire. It was a strategy of fear, designed to terrify, not injure or kill! *Friends!* The soldiers boarded their motorcycles one after another, gunned the engines, and raced crazily back over the road, lurching from side to side to avoid the gunfire dusting their paths. They moved on in the direction of the shots. In moments they sped back along the dirt road, kicking up aprons of blinding ocher dust. "Major Zeller! Major Zeller! *Banditi!* Hundreds! We are surrounded. Many men on horseback. *Andiamo subito!*

Ricocheting bullets struck rocks and boulders, spiraling off in sickening wails. Several well-placed grenades exploded portions of the countryside. The Italians ran hell's speed back to the lorry for their larger weapons.

Darius, frozen in his tracks, riveted his attention on the Italian officer. *Major Victor Zeller?* The possible defector? The great man at Malta had attested to his vulnerability. But was this the place? The time? And who in hell was it—God bless them—offering gunfire support? Who were the guns on horse-back in the hills? He was totally nonplussed by the Major's next words.

"Ambush, is it? Is that what this is about? Very clever of you Corsicans to stall a mule in the road, making it impassable for us." Heatedly, tight-lipped, teeth clenched, Victor, with no concern for his safety, stomped forward, stopped before Darius, the visor of his officer's cap shadowing the rage contained in his deadly eyes. Grasped tightly in his right hand was a 9 mm Beretta pistol. He wagged it under Darius's nose and jerked his head toward the mute Pluto. "You two set it up, eh? You were the decoys to lure us? Very well. Let me state it clearly once and for all. We want no truck with you unfortunate criminals abandoned by France and sent here to rot in the *maquis* of Corsica. Understand—"

Darius and Pluto stared at him in stupefaction. The Major's sudden strategy reversal under the harrowing circumstances stopped them cold.

"We are here in Corsica on a peaceful mission to save you from Allied treachery. Go back to your people. Explain that we are not butchers. Call upon them to unite with us as our allies. Otherwise I promise that your land shall once again become Blood Island. *Avanti!* Go back to your rescuers, convey my word. Call off the bloodhounds or prepare yourselves for the bloodiest massacre this island in all its accursed history has ever witnessed!"

Pluto, seizing the moment and Darius's arm, dragged him back over the road. "*Grazie, maggiore! Grazie mille!* We go now. As swiftly as our feet can transport us. *Furriamo, maggiore!* We shall convey your message!"

"One false move," Victor shouted, "and you'll never recover the parts of your bodies you force us to spill on these roads. *Machine guns at ready!*" he shouted to his men. "Fire when I give the signal!" Grasped in the fist of his right hand, the Beretta prepared to shoot into the air. To the men sprinting and loping back along the road, he shouted, "*Presto! Fuggi! Fuggi!* Order your men back, order them to desist firing at us! I give you three minutes before my men open fire."

The rapid gunfire diminished as Darius and Pluto, half running, half laughing, out of breath from the rigors of both, faintly heard Victor Zeller's words. Bouncing off the hills came the *Irrenzia,* the shepherd's call. Darius pulled up short, yanked Pluto off the road behind a large boulder. "Time to re-connoiter, *amico.*"

"What in hell transpires, Djebel?"

Both men, squinting against a blinding sun, shaded their eyes and turning slowly, swept the deceptive panorama. Darius detected at once what only a native could. He counted two . . . four . . . eight . . . twelve men, perhaps a half dozen more pouring down the slopes, guns at ready. The sun at its zenith bounced off a glittering silver object, a familiar object suspended from the neck of the leader. *Matteus! Today let Allah be praised!*

Darius, out of breath, lay back against the boulder, shoving his beaked hat off his forehead, a smile playing on his lips.

Observing the two peasants disappear around the bend in the road, Victor Zeller cursed at every thought popping into his mind. He cursed Il Duce, Corsica, the Army, the stinking food, the thousands of German officers prancing about like strutting peacocks, and now the goddamned savages and bandits!

Worse, he had a flat tire! And the testy looks he got from his men . . .

He launched into a fist-waving lecture on courage, fidelity, and common sense. "We are outnumbered. Why fight it? Come on! We've no time to spare. We've an important mission this day! Hurry it up! Change the blasted tire and be done with it!"

Victor snatched the road map from his adjutant. He opened it up, laid it outstretched on the hood of the lorry, tracing with his fingertip their route from Bastia. "What will Major Hesse say, Destro, when he finds us returning with that felon Major Darius Bonifacio? The infamous Djebel? Eh? Let's see . . . Terra Bonifacio is between Porto and Piana—"

Destro saw the triumphant expression change to one of murder; Victor's face had turned a mottled purple. "What in the name of Satan's black balls are we doing so far south? We should have turned off at Corte, fifteen miles back. Dammit, can't you soldiers navigate a flea's flight? If I hadn't used my head, we'd have been buzzard bait by now!"

The tire was changed. Destro opened the door for his major. "Life is very simple, Major. In reality, very simple. A man lives, a man dies. It's the dirty business in between that makes us crazy.''

"I'll buy that, Destro," Victor said, sitting back in the dusty sedan. "My credo is, don't hurt anyone unless they come after you. And when they come after you, nail them first, and permanently."

The motorcycles gunned their engines, sped up ahead as the dusty vintage Mercedes turned around to retrace their path northward. Destro put the candid question to his C.O. "Why did you let the peasants off?"

"Because business at Terra Bonifacio is a far more important priority that will make heroes of us. *Finalmente* the German, Hesse, will be taught a costly lesson, once and for all. Today we capture the enemy! What a glorious enemy he is. You realize what a feather in my cap that prize shall be."

The Italians got under way. Motorcycles burped their sirens, then, blasting them loudly, purposely disrupted the hillsmen, sending their languidly grazing sheep into stiff-legged stampedes. The Italians laughed at the comical scene, at the scattering sheep and fist-shaking hillsmen promising retribution.

Victor lit a cigarette, opened his briefcase, removed the Bonifacio dossier, and sat back, studying it intently. Five minutes into the file thoughts rushed him. He tapped his driver's shoulder.

"You there, Lieutenant, where is my regular driver?"

Destro replied, "Dysentery today. Corporal Laggairone offered his services. He drives very well, *maggiore*, no?"

"I don't question his driving ability, just his navigational talents. Why the hell didn't you know we should have turned off sooner?"

Corporal Laggiarone, a.k.a. Pasquale Longinotti, dressed in an Italian uniform, shrugged helplessly. "I know Italy, *maggiore*, not Corsica. These road maps were designed by Satan himself, I promise you. Deliberately designed to set us off course."

Victor cursed under his breath. Superstitious oafs. What they didn't understand was blamed on the devil, poor chaps. The devil himself was accused of more deviltry the world over than even God could manage.

Victor settled back in his cushioned seat. He thought of the two peasants encountered earlier, wondering at Destro's concern. The tall one with verdant eyes, erect posture, near-military brace to his well-muscled frame had resembled no Corsican he'd met thus far. He glanced at his watch. Already too much time had been spent on those peasants and their damnable dead mules.

He turned back to the file's contents.

Sounds of roaring motorcycles and sirens grew fainter in the distance. Pebbles rolling downhill in miniature slides under the crunch of horses' hooves played like a symphony to Darius's ears. A smile at his lips erupted into ready laughter.

"*Gesù Cristo!* What in the name of the black Lucifer humors you?" Pluto, appalled at the close call, launched into a tirade as he dusted off his boots. "See these damnable boots? The devil's handiwork is what you see! If the Italian's eyes had been sharper . . ." He drew an imaginary line across his neck. "Djebel! *My boots!*" He engaged in self-flagellation. "My carelessness could have cost us our lives. That poison dart must have affected my senses."

"Why do you think I shoved you off the road?" Darius asked, still laughing, but not at Pluto's hand-crafted boots. His smile was for the tall bull of a man approaching him, a man with the skin of muted umber. "How long have you been trailing us, old friend?" He loped forward, embraced the Moor, slapping his shoulders with affection. "Two more minutes and we'd have been done for."

Pluto shook his stiff legs, rubbed his aching backside, and began to laugh as he took quick inventory of the *banditi*. "The Italians are known for exaggerating the truth. They said hundreds."

"Twenty," said Matteus. "You are late. A day late. Why did you detour to get to St. Francis? It wasn't in your plan. We could have missed you." His husky voice contained a modicum of disquiet and concern.

"You are like the avenging angel of God, forever protecting me. This time you'll receive no tongue-lashing from your most grateful disciple." Darius fingered the death's-head amulet around his neck. "If things get worse, there is always this—my trusty companion."

Matteus's men had scurried down the embankment, retrieved the wagon, and gathered the remnants of supplies. A half hour later they approached the St. Francis Convent.

* * *

It was finished. The plotting, planning, strategy, and the actual work itself was complete. Wrapped up in two hours, ready with men in place for the final thrust of OWC!

After four months of furious activity, training men, enduring hardships, death hovering overhead every moment, suddenly Darius became passive. They rode with the wind at their backs, traversing back roads, taking shortcuts through the hills and steep palisades.

Passive? You're tired. Admit it. You need rest. How long is it since you've slept one solid night?

Back at the citadel, Darius glanced at his watch. It was 1500 hours. Three in the afternoon. He sat on his bunk, fatigued, reflecting on his impression of Major Victor Zeller. The thoughts and images faded, were replaced by those of Dariana and Sophia. *Four months in Corsica without seeing them! An abomination, Darius! They don't deserve such treatment!*

He tried to sleep.

He couldn't. His thoughts trailed back to Matteus's words at the St. Francis Convent. The Moor had counseled him, "Within the melting pot of thwarted ambitions and intrigues abounding in Corsica, every corner holds its group of diabolical planners and plotters; every clique hatches up a dozen plots for getting back at its enemies."

"Matteus, what are you trying to tell me?"

Matteus explained. Darius's eyes had conveyed the measure of his shock, his lips the measure of disbelief. "No! Not him! *It cannot be Musaka Mubende!* You've erred, my friend. You must continue to search for the real culprit! I refuse to believe he has betrayed me or us!"

At the citadel, Musaka Mubende was no longer among the solemn-faced Mozarabe. No one could account for his disappearance. Was he dead? Alive? Had he run away fearing exposure for his crime of attempted assassination? The poisoned darts, indigenous to his native land, if anything exonerated him. It was too pat. Too obvious.

"I insist the mystery be solved!" Darius had stormed at the Moor.

"In time. Time will solve all mysteries."

Amid the political blizzards of shifting factions and fickle loyalties spreading across Corsica, word came less than an hour after Darius's arrival. Mubende had fallen under German bullets in a skirmish to the north, near the Calvi underground encampment.

Darius sniffed the fraud. He said nothing, kept his own counsel, and instructed Matteus to find the body. He'd have to see Mubende's dead body to believe it. He was a survivor! Survivors do not fall. Their foundation is far too solid. *Oh, God! Not Mubende!*

Darius's peripatetic mind could usually handle more than a half dozen subjects simultaneously, but this business with Mubende and his earlier encounter with Victor Zeller turned him monomaniacal. He leaped from his bunk, unlocked the wooden drawers of the old desk Matteus had delivered to him for his use at the citadel, and removed the coded dossier on Victor Zeller. He lighted a cigarette, slipped into a thick sweater, and lay back on his bunk. He couldn't sleep, so he would make use of every moment.

Two hours later, after poring over the dossier, one word illuminated his mind—*ambivalence.* If a word could describe Victor Zeller, it was *ambivalent.*

Or was the word *ambiguous*? Perhaps both?

Before Darius could decide and correctly dissect the dossier in a more succinct, perceptive manner, his eyes trailed about the room, stopped abruptly at the open drawer of his desk. He sprang to his feet, approached the drawer! Why hadn't he noticed it before? *Your wits are dulled!* The thin wire he'd strung up, invisible to the naked eye unless you knew it was in place, was missing! He studied the lock, turned the key in it, jiggled it, and removed it. He struck a match, held the flame to the key. Minuscule bits of paraffin, barely discernible, were melting. He blew out the flame. *Damnation!* Someone had taken an impression, made another key!

Darius searched through the drawers—all of them. They appeared in order. Nothing was amiss. But *something* had been touched or removed and replaced. He rushed back to the bunk, closed the Zeller dossier, opened it, closed it again. *Merde!* The transparent seal had been removed and another put in its place. He detected the fine outline of the previous seal. An expert job done by a professional!

It had been done in his absence! What were they after? Darius swung around. His door was bolted. His quarters were next to the map room, a similar layout, smaller, but the windows were identically placed on north and south walls. He peered out the inner window. Outside at least fifty men were huddled in small teams involved in hand-to-hand combat.

Suddenly he remembered. He ran back to the wall near the bunk where an orange crate camouflaged a loose stone. Darius removed it. He kept his Mozarabe dossiers hidden there. He removed the burgeoning files, shuffled through them swiftly. He breathed deeply. *Take your time. Breathe deeply and begin again. It's there! You missed it. Look again!* Composing himself, he shuffled through the Delilah's Dream dossiers. Intact. All of them. Next, the SAS commandos. Slowly, methodically he fished through the tedium of Delilah's Dream, their transfers to SAS, new recruits, all those tried, tested in London and accepted into the ranks. Finished, he searched again.

It wasn't there! The file on Musaka Mubende was missing!

His composure was melting, patience was on the wane. He searched through every desk drawer—everywhere! It was gone! He bridled acrimoniously, muttering every legionnaire curse word and more. Inflicting a sort of judicial torture upon himself for his lack of prudence in not securing the files in his absence, he shoved them back into the wall niche, reset the large stone, covered it with the orange crate. Oddly enough, now when Darius blazed with anger, he appeared most calm.

There was a knock at the door. Darius strode across the earthen floor, flung open the door. Matteus, harbinger of bad tidings, detected the mounting rancor in him. The presence of his trusted friend, it seemed, licensed Darius to convey his fury. ''What is it this time?''

''The black man's body arrived by lorry from Camp Calvi.''

''Did it, now?'' Darius trudged past him, stepped into the bright afternoon sun, and strode belligerently to the arena. Matteus studied Darius inscrutably as he reached into the lorry and lifted the canvas off a dead body. He winced, averted his eyes from the grotesque, unrecognizable mass of blood-encrusted flesh, broken bone fragments, and charred skeletal remains.

''It was described as an accidental danse macabre; he fell under the impact of a practice grenade,'' the Moor said solemnly.

Practice grenade! Darius snapped back the canvas; it crackled like dry kindling. He ordered the men to remove the body from the lorry and place it on the ground to afford him a better view. His shock, impossible to conceal, turned his eyes murky green. Behind him the Resistance fighters, drawn curiously to the activity, came off the field, disrupting practice drills and bivouac.

Pascal, Delon, and Tamir Mandel approached cautiously, their eyes on Darius, noting his drawn features. O'Reilly pulled his visored cap over his eyes to keep out the sun. Whitehall ended his instruction abruptly and came off the *parados,* dismissing his squadron. The sight of the awesome marble mask set on Darius's features signaled trouble. Catholics crossed themselves, pulled off their caps at the sight of the dead body. Others, muttering inconsequential remarks, backed off once they viewed the desecration. *A dead man! So what else was new?* Veterans of hundreds of deaths—what was one more? Who was he? One of them? Who could tell from the hellish abomination lying at their feet.

Aware of the depth of Darius's concern, his Mozarabe nucleus moved in closer, ordering the others back to their assignments. Only the Mozarabe could grieve for a brother, *if* it was Mubende. The others had no compassion for a black man.

Darius, hunkering down on his haunches, jerked back the remaining canvas to reveal the entire body. It was a black man, burned beyond recognition. His bloodless eyes turned thunderous. He pulled himself up to full height. "*Shallehhuh tishlih!* Disrobe him!" Darius shouted in Farsi. "Peel off the remains of his clothing."

If they considered him daft, insensitive, perverse, or possessed with unsavory carnality, the silent men didn't show it. At once obedient, they began to remove the corpse's clothing, bit by tattered bit, peeling it off the skin where an incalculable heat had fused material and skin together.

Darius saw at once precisely what he was looking for. "That's enough," he commanded harshly. He glanced somberly at the Mozarabe, whose unbroken lines of military successes in the past years had taken no deaths, suffered only minimal injuries. Tears welling in his eyes, he gathered his men in a circle. Speaking French, he expressed his deep and profound sorrow for the untimely death of so honorable a man. "Prepare his body, my beloved brothers, for a burial as befits royalty. Cremation. Erect a funeral pyre at once."

An hour later Darius stood before the enormous pit of blazing fire. On a scaffold rested the wrapped, mummylike remains of the dead black man. The Resistance fighters fired the pyre with logs to intensify the heat to the proper degree for cremation. Darius stood at the center of a circle formed by the Mozarabe. An open sheet of paper fluttered in his trembling hands. He spoke aloud in eulogy. "Oh, beloved of brothers, Musaka Mubende, we, your closest kin on earth, men who shared the rigors of the desert of hell and heaven with you, now command your body into the holy fires of heaven . . . into the hands of your ancestors, the black Phoenicians."

A drummer hastily recruited from the rank and file provided a constant dirgelike roll of drums, softly muted in the open air.

Standing on the ramparts, observing the blazing fire of the burning pyre with curious intensity were the OSS agents Cain and Abel, and an SOE agent. The third man, Lieutenant Colonel Ivar Morely, had recently arrived. He stood in stoic silence, smoking a long-stemmed clay pipe. He was tall, lean, swarthy-complected, with short dark hair shot with a shock of white leading back from a widow's peak. He was thirtyish, perennially wore a paratrooper's uniform, and like Pluto, constantly wore his flak jacket. Cain and Abel's British counterpart was code-named Serpent. Any resemblance this trio bore to the Edenic players in Paradise was purely coincidental. Their participation in the war effort bore the stratagems of fanaticism. These were the liars, cheats, frauds, the legitimate criminal minds, hidden behind the shroud of Special Services. They were crafty, devious professionals whose zeal and personal aberrations often interfered with good judgment. Inevitably they got their way. Why not? They held the purse strings to unlimited currency. The Intelligence and Analysis branches intermingled with the real dogs of war. These three men, whatever their qualifications, shared common goals; their immediate objectives were to confuse the facts, distort the evidence, throw pursuers off the track, and do anything, including murder, to reach their overall objectives. Beyond doubt, each was qualified, each extraordinarily dexterous at keeping the French from fully knowing their plans. Until they knew their *real* French allies, the duplicity, distortions, and manipulations would continue.

Brad Lincoln, observing Darius stride off the compound grounds following the Mubende eulogy, found himself curiously affected by the solid relationship developing between

Djebel and his apparent factotum, the Moor Matteus. He kept his thoughts to himself. The expressions among the trio were smug, satisfied, and noncommittal. Only the slightest flicker of worry was seen on Brad's Lincoln face.

Inside his quarters Darius sat heavily in the chair behind his desk. His eyes were stony, lips drawn tightly over his teeth. He opened a fresh brandy bottle, poured two cups to the brim. He handed one to Matteus and gulped his down, letting the fire course through his insides, hoping it would melt the icy hatred forming around his heart. Their eyes locked. Matteus asked the final question.

"How do you wish the ashes to be disposed?"

"In any manner you wish. The ash remains of *that* corpse are not the temple in which the soul of Musaka Mubende resided. That was the body of a stranger."

Matteus collected the ashes of the cremated black man in an olla. He rode to Angel's Point, scattered the ashes to the wind. Darius's words and instructions burned in his mind.

"The *real* Musaka Mubende was castrated by the El-Ghilan, the North African tribal ghouls. Bands of professional raiders and rapists captured him, subjected him to the debaucheries of Satan. Before he was cut loose to die in the Sahara, he was castrated. A man's testicles are considered a delicacy among the Ghouls. We of the SAS found him, nursed him to health. He didn't speak for nearly six months; we surmised his tongue had been cut. It had not. Mubende trusted no one after his personal mutilation. When he decided I was trustworthy, he confided the atrocious black deeds done him. Someone wishes us to believe Musaka Mubende is dead. Perhaps Mubende himself, for whatever purpose. I shall not disappoint the director of this bloody scenario. I shall play out the farce until I learn the truth."

Matteus sighed. How many more atrocities would occur before Darius returned to the Bonifacio hearth?

Later, when it became obvious he must reveal his tracking of the OSS agent Greer, Matteus sensed Darius's glum introversion. "This Cain, Abel, and the man called Serpent, how do you explain them? Their involvement in Corsica?"

Darius shook his head. "They come from a world I don't understand. I've seen glimpses of it in London, during training. It is a world of technology, of cloak and dagger—not battlefield confrontations. Weapons are no longer imprecise. Technological developments, particularly in the fields of metallurgy and chemistry, have changed the course of war. There will come a time when man can wage war from his desk. Push buttons will bomb half the world. But for now, good friend, what matters is the success of OWC. You may tell my father I shall be more amenable to the teachings of my childhood. We shall speak shortly. Now let it be known that we Mozarabe mourn the death of our brother.''

Chapter Ten

While the drummer drummed and the eulogy was spoken and the funeral pyre blazed high at the citadel, the ululating winds whistled sharply through the treacherous corniche leading to Terra Bonifacio. Major Victor Zeller and his squad of soldiers had arrived at their destination and strained up the incline to the high-walled Bonifacio estate. Greeting the men were the intimidating sounds of awesome attack dogs snarling, barking, snapping at the air, as they leaped and fell hard against the reinforced iron fencing. Eyeing the chained buttress, a Gibraltar separating them from the vicious canines, the Italian soldiers displayed a jackass temerity; they jeered, mocked, laughed at the dogs, waving threatening rifles in the air. *Christ! Who needs this low comedy?* thought Victor, alighting from the vehicle.

He felt for the security of his service pistol before pulling the chain that rang a bell on a stone pillar at one side of a thick wood and iron gate. He sensed danger. Peripherally he saw Corsican hillsmen, standing on rocky tors, wolf guns in hand. Beyond the courtyard, he saw one of several doors crack open. A defiant shotgun was shoved through the opening, glittering a steely blue in the shaft of sunlight bouncing off it.

Inside, peering through the opening, the matriarch of Terra Bonifacio tensed at the sight of Italian soldiers on her property. She studied the officer in silent inscrutability, then spoke out clearly. "Who are you? What do you want? Who is responsible for so barbarous an intrusion?"

"Signora Bonifacio? I am Major Victor Zeller. I come in peace. It is not my intention to frighten you, only to speak of matters of dire importance," he announced. "With your permission, may I enter?"

Dariana's heart stopped at the sound of the name: *Zeller!*

Terror pervaded her being. Had she heard correctly? *No! It's preposterous!* She peered harder at the slim, strikingly handsome officer, trying to find someone else in his face. It was difficult at this distance. She held a whistle to her lips, blew an inaudible signal. Instantly the dogs stopped their clamorous din, backed away from the fence, and became docile.

Dariana opened the door wider, gun at ready, stepping hesitantly closer to the intruder. "The name, Major. I didn't catch the name." *God, don't let it be Zeller!* In all her life she'd never supplicated as hard as she did at this moment.

But God wasn't listening; Victor was, and he calmly complied with her request, unaware he was stirring terrifying skeletons in this Corsican's closet. "Major Zeller, at your service. Major Victor Zeller, *signora*," he said, sensing the woman's scrutiny, her sudden paleness.

Dariana unlocked the gate, permitting him entrance to the courtyard. Victor removed his cap, clicked his heels, and bowed. He stood braced.

"We must talk in private. Inside." He spoke in Italian.

The Corsicans with wolf guns backed away. The *signora* permitted the Italian soldier entrance. Ah, perhaps she knew him. At least she would have signaled if he posed danger.

Inside, Dariana led him to the smaller, comfortable salon bordering the terrace. Slowly, Victor glanced about the unusual interior section by section, along one wall, up the next, around the other and back again. He made an overall assessment. The style was unique—every piece of furniture was hand selected, well coordinated in symmetry, style, grace, and taste. Marked affluence throughout. These Bonifacios were obviously not typical Corsicans.

"Please be seated."

"*Signora,* this is not a social visit. I am looking for your son, Major Darius Bonifacio.''

Dariana whirled around in stupefaction, wild-eyed anguish reflected in her dark eyes. Four years kaleidoscoped past her, four years of pain, uncertainty, desperate hope, then resignation. She was trembling. Lines of strain sagged the edges of her mouth.

"Major Bonifacio? *Darius?*" She swallowed hard. "You came for nothing. My son disappeared four years ago. No one has seen him since." *Are his classic features the combined inheritance of Marie Clotilde and that animal Amadeo? Not in the eyes, but the face, bone structure. The strange half smile is Clotilde's. Oh, Christ!*

She collected herself, her resilience. "Indulge me, Major. If he were alive, what business have you with my son?"

"*Official* business, *signora.* He is wanted for questioning. Perhaps if I may address myself to the man of the house?"

"No!" Her swift rebuttal startled him. "What I mean is—uh—my husband is in Ajaccio today. He is expected tomorrow."

"Mama! Who is it?" Sophia descended the stone steps and ambled through the larger salon to the sitting room. Dressed casually in sweater and skirt, she stopped short, eyes riveted on the familiar uniform. "You!" she muttered, flushed with uncertainty, tugging nervously on the sleeves of her sweater.

Assuming for the moment that his eyes played no tricks on him, Victor, equally stunned and uncertain, fell into disarray. A moment later he disguised his rapture to fit the image his uniform projected. "*Signorina,* what a pleasure to see you again." He bowed politely.

"Y-You k-know each other?" The portent of doom to which Dariana had fallen victim signaled increasing dangers. If Vivaldi returned to find Victor Zeller here . . . *He must not!* The thought dominated her actions. Besieged at once on two fronts, Dariana, shaken, was unsure which should be her first priority. What maddeningly enigmatic complications! She waited for Sophia's explanation.

"I told you, Mama, of the encounter at the cathedral in Ajaccio on Christmas Eve." Sophia refreshed her mother's memory.

"*You are the sister of Major Darius Bonifacio?*" The beautiful woman he'd committed to his brain and memory for all time, the woman who had a personally autographed book by a famous Resistance fighter, now turned out to be the sister of his archenemy. What had he stumbled upon—a nest of adders? Enemy spies? "When did you last see your brother, *signorina*?" His tone was officious, condemnatory.

Sophia's eyes darted to her mother. "The Major asked you a question, Sophia. Answer him truthfully."

Perplexed by her mother's compliance, Sophia, at once intractable, turned into a statue, her lips pursed in silence.

"Tell him," Dariana insisted. "He must hear the truth from your lips."

"Darius disappeared four years ago. We were told he was dead. But you called him *major*! Does that mean—" Sophia dared not hope.

"Your brother is alive. He is here in Corsica engineering commando raids against the occupation forces."

Dariana had never erased Darius from her memory, nor had the wounds of his disappearance healed. Even now, after four years, the scars ached painfully . The tragedy had changed her nature; it had made her less bold, less ready to accept challenge. But all that was wiped away in the Italian's purpose for coming to Terra Bonifacio.

"Major," said Dariana, "you are mistaken. If my son were alive, he'd never subject his family to the cruelty of permitting us to believe him dead. If this is some hideous joke you deign to play on us—some trick—"

"I assure you, I play no games. My men must search the premises. I would prefer your husband's presence or perhaps a caretaker to accompany us. Recently, Italian soldiers are accused of molestation and rape done to Corsican women. To avoid possible condemnation—"

"I assure you my son is dead."

"You apparently—perhaps desperately—wish to believe a fanciful tale. I repeat that Major Darius Bonifacio, an enemy to Italy and the Third Reich, is alive. Unless there exists another family of Bonifacios with a son named Darius? Another Terra Bonifacio? Could the land-grant office be in error?"

"Obviously you are better informed than his family, Major. Uh—what was your name again?" Her hand fluttered to her head in a gesture of forgetfulness. She was stalling for time to control her inner torment. If what he said was true—that Darius was alive—dear God, how could she help her beloved son? How?

"Zeller, *signora*. Major Victor Zeller," he repeated, hungry eyes roving toward Sophia. *Don't be obvious. You'll intimidate her.* Sophia, alert to both his lingering glance and Dariana's animation, stood motionless, wondering at the sudden racing of her heart.

"Zeller?" Dariana, barricading her feelings behind the artful guise of congeniality, exclaimed jubilantly, "Victor *Zeller?* Not the *contessa's* son? The son of Marie Clotilde?" She placed the shotgun against a chair and approached him with open arms.

Totally disarmed by her words and manner, Victor stared in open-mouthed stupefaction. "You know my mother? *Incredibile! Non posso credere!*"

Sophia was certain her mother had gone mad.

"But how? Where? When? How long have you known my mother?"

"Long ago, before you were born, I was her tutor and friend." Dariana pulled him to a sofa. "From the moment she arrived from Vienna, we were inseparable. I am Dariana de Rocca Bonifacio." The consummate actress metamorphosed into a woman affecting womanly vanity. She patted her hair into place, smoothed the folds of her dress, at once self-conscious about her appearance. "Please tell me, how is my dear Clotilde? I feel as if I know you intimately. And what of Clarisse, your sister? She must be the same age as Sophia."

Victor answered as best he could. Nonplussed, unable to resist Dariana's warmth and charm, he excused himself, walked to the front door, and ordered his men to wait in the lorry. He reentered the great house, mixed feelings playing havoc in him. His eyes, telltale, strayed continuously toward Sophia. Dariana, observing the interplay between them, dared hope she might find an ally in him.

"Imagine Clotilde's son, here in my house. I shall make coffee for you. Perhaps you prefer tea or wine? You have but to ask. My house is your house, Victor. Forgive me—uh, Major. Sophia, bring the refreshments at once."

Victor's attempts to subdue Dariana's ebullience failed. Sophia left the room, returned moments later with a tray of wine, cookies, and glasses. She placed the tray on the coffee table and observed as her mother poured wine for the enemy. The *enemy*! She could not believe her eyes.

When Dariana's story of her ties with Victor's mother ended, his bewilderment concerning the complex sequence of events abated. He forced himself to the business at hand. "Now, *signora,* more than before I regret broaching the somber business that brought me here. Intelligence reports indicate that your son spearheads antagonistic forces against us. You are certain you know nothing of his whereabouts?" He held up a protesting hand against any feminine guile. "Please listen to me. Reach him if you can, wherever he is. I implore you. I promise to intervene on his behalf, help him, if only out of respect for your friendship with my mother." Victor rose to his feet, tugged at his tunic and rolled his visored cap in his hands.

Dariana died a thousand deaths in that instant. *Merciful Jesus, do you set brother against brother in this hideous war?* Standing here before her was Darius's half brother, threatening to expose the secret she'd fiercely clutched to her bosom since Darius's strange birth. He was saying something to her. What was it?

"*Adieu, signora e signorina.* Perhaps in the near future you will permit me to call upon your house socially?"

"Here in Corsica only my husband is privileged to make social engagements. Please understand and—" She hesitated. "Give my most affectionate regards to your dear mother." Sighing wistfully, she added, "War is a vicious taskmaster to make enemies of such dear friends."

Victor nodded, checking the compelling urge to speak to Sophia. "I'd best leave. I wouldn't want my men to speak frivolously of my visit with you." He donned his officer's cap and walked toward the front door, the women following.

Dariana swung ahead, opened the door, and smiled politely, her heart pounding as he eased past her through the door.

The moment he was out the door, Dariana slammed it shut, bolted it. Sophia fell into her mother's arms. "What on earth possessed you to demonstrate such drama? Is it possible—what he said—that Darius is alive?"

At once Dariana gave way to sentimental tears. Confusion set in. It was too much to assimilate. "D-Darius a-alive? Here?

I don't know . . . Oh, my dearest, after four years—alive? Here?''

She agonized internally. Darius's half brother sought to arrest him! God, what irony. Had Satan himself devised the tortuous libretto? The truth sobered her. She reached out to Sophia, holding her by the shoulders. "Sophia, your father must never learn of Major Zeller's visit here today. It must be *our* secret. Promise you'll never repeat what happened here today.''

"Why, Mama? You make no sense. You dare keep such alarming information from Father? Why is it so important?'' she asked, wondering at her mother's sudden rebelliousness. She backed away as if seeing a stranger.

"Trust me. You must.'' She led Sophia into the kitchen, set a pot of coffee to brew. "Listen carefully, I'll only tell you this once. You've heard me speak of the *contessa*? Yes, yes, that's right. This officer is her son. I wish him no harm.''

"I can understand. But, Mama, he is the enemy. Major Zeller is our *enemy*—make no mistake—especially if he seeks Darius!''

Dariana's finger silenced her daughter's lips. "Never,'' she said hoarsely, "*never* speak the name Zeller in our house! Never, do you hear me? God help me, don't ask why—not now! One day, perhaps—'' She released Sophia and turned to stare out the rear window, fighting off internal demons she dared not describe to Sophia.

Sophia's imagination took wing. Her heart thumped wildly. Was it because of Darius, that he might be alive, or was it because she saw Victor Zeller again? The memory of their initial encounter had occupied her dreams and many waking moments. Now seeing him here in her house— She poured coffee for them, contemplating Dariana's actions. Seeing her mother through new eyes, experiencing a curious respect for the courage displayed before the Italian officer, she brought the cup to her mother in permissive silence. Dariana was entitled to her thoughts, as was Sophia, who harbored profound concern over the duality in her mother's nature, envy for the experiences of her life, and a deepening suspicion that this tower of strength she'd known all her life was crumbling inside.

And all because this Italian Major came seeking Darius! Why must she never speak of the incident to her father? Why not to Matteus? What the devil did it all mean?

Sophia, shaking her befuddled head, ran from the room. She scurried up the stairs to her bedroom, rushed to the balcony. In the distance she saw the Italian utilities winding down along the rugged, steep terrain until they were out of sight. Giving alternate periods of thought to Victor and Darius, she found that Victor dominated her senses and she didn't know or understand why. Inside she lay across her bed, closed her eyes, and relived those moments in the cathedral. If Matteus had known he was the unmentionable Zeller . . . What mystery was bound up in this forbidden name? For the moment, a filial obedience was expected. But in a day or two, Sophia intended to be very firm with her mother. The whole thing was preposterous! *Perhaps it wasn't?* Sophia had always sensed an aura of mystery around her father. He never spoke of his childhood. At times he acted as if he'd been born a grown-up.

Perhaps if she waited, listened, and carefully observed the men in the *maquis,* she'd sniff out the game they played. She resented the restrictions imposed upon her since those men arrived at the citadel. Her friends Arrigo and Columbo had explained these men were Resistance fighters, men of the *maquis.* Was it possible Darius could be with them? Be one of them? She did not know. Perhaps if she rode into the *maquis* to look for Arrigo and Columbo . . .

Victor and his entourage were five miles from Bastia when an afterimage assaulted his senses. A photograph, one among many gracing the baby grand piano in a corner of the sitting room, flashed across his mind: the youthful face with the serene expression of a young religious acolyte. *The eyes; it was the eyes.* Where had he seen the young man before? *Where?* The past twenty miles riding over treacherous terrain had jolted his senses. Dariana's story, the incredible closeness shared between the *signora* and his mother, the *contessa,* had indeed captivated him and held his fancy. And the shock! The presence of the angelic beauty, Sophia, had caused a digression. He had failed to concentrate on duty, purpose, his reason for traversing the dangerous Corsican interior. Now, in his approach to Bastia, the photograph played havoc with his senses. *The eyes!* Oh, Christ, they were the eyes of one of the peasants he'd encountered near Vizzavona! Add a few years, maturity, a change of clothing and *voilà!* It was him! The man he pursued! *The en-*

emy! Damn all the demons in hell! It *was* Major Darius Bonifacio! He'd had him in the palm of his hand and let him escape! *If Hans Hesse ever learns of my folly . . .*

"Destro!" He thumped his adjutant's shoulder. The soldier seated alongside the driver turned around.

"*Sì, maggiore? Che cosa vuole? Parli più forte!*"

"Stop the car. *Dio maledetto!* Climb into the back seat with me."

The order was obeyed. Destro now sat alongside his major, questioning him silently with his eyes.

"You must make certain that none of the men mention this trip to the interior. I want it stricken from the logs, understand? The matter is most secret. The Germans must not learn of our plans."

Destro's eyes widened with interest. "*Sì, maggiore.* I shall silence the men. They hate the Hun. It will remain our secret."

"*Va bene. Grazie.*"

The driver chuckled internally. *It shall not remain my secret.* Longinotto couldn't wait to get to Bastia and disappear into the *maquis.* He had one more job to do at the citadel that would bring laughter to Djebel's lips.

Seated at the massive hand-carved desk in the early evening, Vivaldi Bonifacio reviewed the last-minute data he had received on the Zeller file, unaware that his sidetracked dream of vendetta was again turning into a nightmare.

At the sounds of familiar footsteps padding along the outer corridor, he raised his head. A frown creased his brow at the sight of Matteus's anguished expression. "Tell me straight what bad tidings you bring me? Darius is safe—"

"Sophia is missing."

"*What?* What is this—*missing*?"

"I left her with her grandparents in Ajaccio. 'Come for me in two hours,' she told me. Signor de Rocco left her to supervise some workmen in the pharmacy. He returned in a half hour. Sophia was gone. We've combed the land between Ajaccio and Terra Bonifacio for eight hours. I tell you she has disappeared."

Vivaldi fell back in his chair, disbelieving, as if the wind had been knocked from him. He removed his gold-rimmed glasses, rubbed his eyelids, sighing. He mentioned the unmentionable.

"The *Germans*! They've stolen her from us, press-ganged her into labor. For months, nothing. Now suddenly a mass of incomprehensible activity." He moved to a gun case along one wall, removed two high-powered wolf guns and two smaller handguns. Patiently, he loaded the weapons, handed one of each to Matteus. "Eight hours, you said? By now she could be in Germany. Did you tell my wife?"

"You need more earthquakes to shake this family's foundation?"

"Good. Say nothing. First we collect the facts. Locate Chamois Barbone. His men must comb the island for my daughter. I want her found." He removed a photo of Sophia from a gold frame on his desk. "Show this to the men of the *maquis*—the soldiers at the citadel. If any of them has dared to harm her—"

"It is essential that Darius be told."

"Yes—essential. At once."

"You know the consequences of exposing him?"

"God almighty! What options remain? First Robert and Daniel flee to escape the Germans. Now Sophia! What evils within crush me at every turn? I've marked time, exercised patience, acquired detachment, waiting for the moment when all we've suffered will be avenged. But it never stops. Woes and tribulations continue as if I've been marked by the right hand of God and am only awaiting the treacheries promised in his left. It's driving me insane! Better to have followed the ways of the devil!" Matteus shoved a stiff glass of brandy at him. "Drink!" he ordered, pouring a second for himself. "We both need it this night."

Where in the name of Allah has Sophia gone? People were disappearing from their homes, churches, off the very streets in villages and cities. Had the Germans abducted her just as Vivaldi said? These and many more thoughts flooded Matteus's mind as he galloped his stallion off the lands, heading toward the citadel.

Anything was possible in war. And Sophia? The girl could handle herself, couldn't she? His thoughts focused sharply on Sophia. The rape done her four years ago, never discussed openly by the family, had obsessed her. Victimized by irreconcilable circumstances, gripped by unassuageable melancholia at Darius's disappearance, she had blamed herself and the vio-

lation done her by that trash for Darius's separation from his
family. She had wallowed in misery and despair, believing that
Darius lay dead somewhere because of her. No longer a virgin,
shamed and disgraced, doomed forever to spinsterhood or relegated to the back streets of whoredom in Marseilles, what had
she to live for? Isolation, introversion followed. When her daily
prayers to religious icons failed to ease her pain, her fragile
mental state grew worse.

Time had failed to ameliorate Sophia's grief. Then, one day
a miracle occurred. Six months to the date of Darius's departure
from Terra Bonifacio, Sophia, garbed in riding attire, had sad-
dled a mare and gone riding in the *maquis*. Thereafter she'd ridden in a daily ritual, traversing forbidden areas considered
dangerous since a tough, hardened brand of mainland escapee
or criminal sought refuge in Corsica. The mysterious riding so-
journs stretched from a few hours daily to an entire afternoon.
"Soon it will stop," Dariana had predicted. It did not. And
when it did not, then began the reprimands and questions. Sophia, intractable and mute for three months, broke her silence
one day, lifting the pall of gloom hanging over Dariana but
leaving her with a riddle to ponder. *"No one shall ever accost
me or defile me again and live to boast of it!"* she had announced.

Matteus, a miracle maker in the past, had heard the remark,
pondered the riddle, determined to solve the mystery. Noting
the subtle changes in Sophia, the bold self-determination, overt
defiance explicit in the way she walked and talked, he had followed her daily peregrinations, tracking her one day through
the *maquis* to the citadel ruins. Shielded by thick-trunked pines,
he had borne witness to an alarming scene. Sophia, the star attraction, stood at ease between two brigands. Matteus recognized Arrigo and his ragtag ruffian companion, Columbo.
Arrigo, a comely, well-educated youth, had fallen prey to the
tentacles of vendetta. As eldest son in his family, the task of
seeking Corsican justice by killing the man who'd murdered his
father had fallen upon him. The fugitive, relegated to the legion
of homeless men, had taken refuge in the *maquis*.

Shocked by Sophia's presence with such men, Matteus, gun
at ready, about to interrupt the tableau, stopped abruptly to observe a skillful, astonishing display of knife throwing. Then, as
guns replaced the knives and Sophia demonstrated her skill and

bulls-eye capabilities, his trepidation increased. When the skilled players before him carried their talents over into hand-to-hand combat and offered no advantage to Sophia because she was a woman, Matteus's ambivalence took on fierce proportions. How could he condone her consorting with lunatics? Torn between his duty to stop his foolishness and a provincial curiosity to learn more, he chose to conceal Sophia's activity from Dariana and Vivaldi. Daily he stalked her, observing, assessing the martial skulduggery, wondering where it would lead. Should either of the men dare cross over the invisible line, his gun was always at ready, his attention riveted on Sophia. Her attitude, one of controlled, tigresslike ferocity, never ceased to amaze him.

What in the name of the unholy Moloch is she up to? he continually wondered.

His answer came six months ago. Matteus had heard Columbo put it to her clearly and in no uncertain terms. "Signorina Sophia, your skills are beyond belief. I ask you, in the name of Corsica and France, to join with us, the Resistance, to help us remove the enemy from our lands. We need you. Corsica and France need you. Say the word!"

Matteus, wary eyed and prepared to jump into the fray and cart the foolish girl home, was arrested by the sound of Arrigo's chastising but sensible voice. "Columbo! Are you some crazy fool to promote such trouble for us? It's bad enough we failed to discourage the *signorina* in this crazy business! If her father learns of our part in this conspiracy, we'd become capons—castrated roosters—overnight!"

Digesting the words of the sagacious Arrigo, something far more ominous struck Matteus. The rumors of the impending invasion of Corsica were true!

And it had happened! Axis forces had overrun the island. Europe was in turmoil. The Germans occupied France! That day he first heard word of the impending invasion, Matteus had fled to Terra Bonifacio, eager to impart the frightening news to Vivaldi and discuss implementation of the volatile plans discreetly held in abeyance for two decades. Sophia, that little vixen capable of handling ten men, could fend for herself.

Fool, Matteus! Dazzled by her exceptional martial skills, he had invented a forgery, an exaggerated distortion of her ability to resist danger. *Now see the folly of your thinking! Allah, most merciful of Gods, forgive me!*

Back in the present, Matteus spurred his horse savagely, raced to the citadel. He must find Chamois Barbone and meticulously impart Vivaldi's instructions. Sophia was missing! And he, lacking prudence and wisdom of forethought, had let it happen. Matteus, the enduring, all-knowing sentinel endowed with prescience had made a terrible mistake.

The fierce-eyed, motley men of the *maquis* studied Sophia's likeness. Within the hour Corsicans spread the word of her disappearance. Much must be accomplished in the next twelve hours if they were to find her. Waterfront bistros were scoured, informers questioned, rewards offered.

Vivaldi, in hearing the Moor's secret, sternly repudiated Matteus's insistence on personal responsibility for his failure to intervene and put a stop to Sophia's foolishness. "I cannot fault you for the one injudicious act in your lifetime," an impassioned Vivaldi counseled. But Matteus was not as forgiving a man. Refusing to extricate himself from the guilt he harbored, he joined search parties twenty-four hours a day every day for the next week, finally returning to Terra Bonifacio exhausted from lack of sleep and nourishment.

Vivaldi prepared himself for the worst. He had failed in Seville. In Corsica he had not succeeded in his ultimate goal. He could not fail again, not with Dariana. He must face the awful moment. Dariana must be told the truth. Would love sustain them now?

He found his wife staring solemnly out the rear window of her kitchen, gazing at the sea of her beloved jade green roses. She failed to turn or acknowledge him.

"Dariana, beloved, we must talk. Sophia—"

"What of Sophia?" She came alive, eyes sparkling. "Something's wrong. I see it in your eyes."

"Between us a strong core of truth has always existed."

"What of Sophia?" Her voice grew strident.

"She is— Dariana, she is not with her grandparents in Ajaccio. For a week we have searched. Our friends are still searching, dedicatedly. They will not stop until—"

Dariana moved away from him numbly. She had things to say but knew the dangers in speaking her mind. Death hovered over her house. She'd sensed it, felt it for too long. She skulked about the kitchen and pantry, randomly removed bowls from shelves, flung them on a butcher-block table. With the unbroken cadence of a whirlwind, she began pouring various baking ingredients unmeasured into the bowl. Mixing, shredding the contents with her bare hands, she kneaded the mass into bread dough. She pounded, pummeled, rolled, pounced upon the sticky mass, taking out her frustrations on the hapless dough in a seemingly inexhaustible fashion.

Observing as she enveloped herself in a cocoon of emotional frenzy, Vivaldi approached her, pulled her to him in a gesture of compassion. He held her close. "Cry, beloved," he said tenderly, tears misting his eyes. "Cry, and I too will shed tears of remorse with you." He was totally unprepared for the maelstrom of curses and malediction hurled upon him.

She wrenched herself free of his grip, her features jerking uncontrollably. "Stay away from me, you monster! You drove Darius from us! Your own sons, Robert and Daniel are gone, fighting with the Resistance! And now, *now*, Sophia, my beloved Sophia is gone!" Tears engulfed her, sobs tore from her throat. Vivaldi had never seen her so out of control. "I've had enough," she railed at him. "Enough, you hear? Enough!" Her fists, dotted with clumps of dough, beat on him furiously. "Go away from me!" she managed to say between convulsive sobs. "Go, habitate with those satanic demons with whom you conspire!" she raved, unleashing the wrath and silence of two decades upon Vivaldi.

"Stop it! You don't know what you are saying, woman!"

But she did, and out came the venom she'd tucked away, never knowing how it had multiplied. "Monster! Evil monster!" she screamed hoarsely. "Everything you touch turns vile. You corrupted Darius with your insane philosophies and blood revenge. You drove him from our house!" Sobbing uncontrollably, gasping for air between the heart-wrenching sobs and condemnatory expletives, she finally collapsed against Vivaldi, calling out in a helpless, forlorn voice, "Daniel . . . Robert . . . Sophia . . . and you, my sweet, sweet Darius . . . all gone. You left this poisoned house. How I loved you . . . suckled you . . . raised you all loving you more than life itself. Now you are gone—what will I do? *What will I do?*" Dariana's body slid to the floor in a heap at Vivaldi's feet. She re-

sisted his attempts to lift her again, let her body go limp, as if
the very life had drained from her.

Vivaldi grabbed a towel, poured water into a porcelain bowl,
and rushed back to her side. He wrung out a cloth, applied it to
her forehead, wiped the tears. She recoiled like a frightened animal, resisting him, large eyes widening in terror.

At the sight of her, Vivaldi stopped, his heart breaking. "Is
your hatred of me so all-consuming that it registers in your eyes
like daggers preparing to bleed me? Have I done you so much
wrong?" he asked quietly, urging her with gestures to take a
calmative. She shook her head resolutely, then finally accepted
the proffered spoonful Vivaldi had poured from the bottle.

She stole a few glances at him, aware of the stoic mask he
wore to protect himself from hurt. Locked in her breast was the
knowledge of Darius's presence in Corsica and her secret encounter with Victor Zeller. Dare she tell Vivaldi of the secret
looks that had passed between Sophia and the son of his archenemy, Amadeo Zeller? No. She would die first. "What is happening to us?" she asked, regaining composure. "In God's
name, what is it you want? How did you estrange Darius? Tell
me. I want to understand. Your silence is killing me, Vivaldi.
Talk to me, but I beg you, be through with lying."

Vivaldi sat vacant-eyed on the floor next to her, his thoughts
and perceptions quickened by the reality of her words. "Darius
is a prince. So special—everything I should have been and
wasn't—a true de la Varga."

"Deluded fool. He's a *Bertelli*! The flesh and blood of Marie
Clotilde and Miguel Bertelli!"

"Never! He's my son, a Bonifacio."

"*Bonifacio?*" Dariana, bereft of any generosity of spirit,
dried her tears on her apron. "A Bonifacio? Hah! Even the
name is empty! How pathetically it reeks of ghosts! Specters of
antiquity!"

Vivaldi cut her a sharp, reproving look. "I am a de la Varga,
descendant of royalty, of famous warring generals, landowners, *conquistadores*. The name Bonifacio is merely veneer under which exists a fortune that spans three continents. One day
my sons shall know the extent of that wealth and what Darius
has known since birth."

Dariana stared at him, trying desperately to understand. His
words remained convoluted and stillborn in her brain. Vivaldi

gazed at her, read the intensity of the pain in her breast. He reached for her, held her cold, trembling body in his arms. "How in the name of the bleeding Jesus can I expect you to still love me after my absence of so many years from your bed? How? What have I done, beloved, to make our love crumble?"

Slowly he removed the sticky bread dough from her fingers, washed her hands with the towel. "It's true we are confronted with the tragedy of Sophia's disappearance, but consider some good news."

Her mental landscape allowed for no meanderings into flights of fancy, not now. Victor Zeller's words seemed a thousand light-years away the moment the words spilled from Vivaldi's lips.

"Darius is alive, here in Corsica! He'll be coming home soon."

She stared at him, numb, unable to grasp the moment.

"Darling, did you hear me? He's alive. The entire island is searching for Sophia. But Darius is returning. He'll find her."

I am hearing only what I want to hear—an illusion. She blinked hard.

"Darius has always epitomized you as a tower of strength. You wish him to find you in such disarray?"

Her dark eyes lifted to his. Her voice was hollow, hesitant. "Darius is dead. You told me four years ago."

"No! No! He's alive, I tell you."

"Lies! More lies!"

"There are some things a man cannot tell his wife. You, a Corsican, should know this."

Dariana gave him no quarter. "The past four years, you've forced me to believe he disappeared or was dead. Now suddenly without explanation he's here, alive? You lie, just as the Italian Major lied that day."

"What Italian Major? What are you talking about?"

Dariana panicked. She forced a duplicitous vagueness to surface, made a disorganized gesture, rose unsteadily to her feet.

"Wh-What—Italian? I don't know. I am uncertain of anything. My head is swimming. I need another calmative."

"Here, let me help you."

"Don't touch me!"

Vivaldi sprang back as if contaminated. "This is the thanks I get for imparting truth? Didn't you know I'd never rest until I found Darius? A month to the day after his disappearance, I sent emissaries in search of him. Later when I knew where he was—''

A ferocious tiger spat at him. "You've known for four years and let me believe him to be dead?" she agonized, eyes narrowing, catlike. "I could kill you!"

Vivaldi raised his hand, struck her across the face. "For whatever I am or were, for whatever I must do and shall do to protect my family, I deserve no threats from you. I am your husband. I have loved you, cherished you and the sanctity of our home. I always shall. But never, I repeat, *never* speak thus to me again or I shall banish you from my house forever.''

"So be it!" The tigress traced the sting of his blow with her fingertips. "The lord and master of the manor has spoken," she mocked.

"*Dariana!* Listen to yourself—your words. I told you Darius is coming home. Soon so shall Daniel and Robert. We shall be a family again. I swear to you, I shall find Sophia, forfeit my life for hers, if need be." He reached for Dariana, held her tightly against him. "Let not black deeds of the past mar the present and future. The investment of love in a life we've shared is too precious to abandon. How did I dare tell you of Darius's presence here?" he muttered remorsefully, annoyed at his vulnerability in a moment of passion. "We are enmeshed in troubled times. Our son is involved in high-risk assignments for France. Trust me, Dariana. My mysterious comings and goings were not for naught. I too work with Daniel and Robert with the Resistance. For many months—"

"You couldn't have confided in me? Since when can a Corsican not be trusted to keep silent?"

"The less you know the safer for you and Sophia."

"Not knowing would make us immune to the will of the occupational forces?" she scoffed angrily, grabbing a knife faster than the eye could see and slashing her left wrist before Vivaldi could deter her.

Blood spurted from the open gash. She held it up to him. "See, my husband? Women bleed just as much as men. If captured or tortured by our enemies what difference does knowing or not knowing make? Would they believe us if we said we knew nothing?"

Logic sputtered from her lips as Vivaldi hurriedly tore off her apron and ripped it into shreds, binding her wrist with the length and making a tourniquet above the wound to stop the arterial bleeding.

"You don't understand, do you? If the enemy got hold of you or Sophia, we, Daniel, Robert, Matteus, *and* Darius would be putty in their hands. They could compromise us, force us to do their bidding. Do you understand? For the love of God, woman, you saw what the Germans and Italians did when they sought to imprison Daniel and Robert. Didn't I force you and Sophia to hide so they wouldn't see you? Is your memory so short? Your eyes speak louder than your lips—you do not believe me."

"Too much hatred pours from your heart."

"But not for you or my family! Oh, God. Once I tried to tell you, but you refused to listen. You told me my plans had nothing to do with the man you met, loved, and married. At war's end I shall unmask the treachery done to Francisco de la Varga, to me!" He finished binding her wrist and left the house disconsolate of spirit.

Sunk in the depths of despair, Dariana held aside the lace window curtain with a trembling hand, her eyes fixed on Vivaldi until he disappeared beyond the terraces. Apathetically she let the curtain fall back into place. She wiped her tear-stained face with the back of her hand, ambled aimlessly through the house, finally ascending the stone stairs to her bedroom. She saw her bed in tunnel vision coming closer . . . closer. . . . She fell upon it, exhausted. The room spun about dizzily. She muttered in a stupor. *Stop this foolishness! Darius is coming home. He'll find Sophia . . . Darius here in Corsica.* She tried to lift herself from the bed. *He must be warned. His life is in grave peril!*

She fell under the grip of the sedative. Her dreams were muddled, disconcerting. She slept restlessly, was finally jolted from a dream she couldn't remember. She glanced at the porcelain clock ornamented with pastel angels and cupids. She'd been asleep for three hours.

She moved groggily toward the door. The sounds of barking dogs, ringing doorbells, and honking car horns swirled about her. She rubbed her eyes, caught her reflection in the cheval glass, and paused to examine the image. She listlessly patted stray strands of her hair into place, adjusted the dog whistle around her neck, picked up the wolf gun from its niche on the wall, and like a sleepwalker moving in a dream, descended the stairs to the front door. She peered through the Judas hole. Suddenly her heart pounded. She stared hard at the face of the woman at the gate.

Dariana gasped. She quickly flattened back against the door to catch her breath. The resemblance! The uncanny resemblance stunned her. The woman at the gate was the image of the oil portrait carefully wrapped and stored on the third floor of her house! *Hair the color of fire; eyes of turquoise gems.*

Had the portrait suddenly sprung to life?

Two decades of womanly curiosity and a tinge of vanity made her pause, tweak her cheeks for added color. She pulled down on her wrinkled shift, put herself in order, and opened the door a crack. She shoved the gun muzzle through the door, blew on the high-pitched whistle until the fury of the barking attack dogs abated.

"Who are you? What do you want here?" She spoke in Italian, repeated the words in French.

"Lieutenant Varga here. Official business with Major Bonifacio." Valentina's eyes were riveted to the shaft of blue steel protruding through the opening. "It's urgent, *signora*. May I please enter?"

Stealthily, Dariana emerged from behind the door. She squinted at the bright sunlight, held the wolf gun at an angle, ready if needed. Midway to the gate she stopped abruptly, eyes widening in disbelief. *A woman in uniform?* She glanced uneasily at the driver, gun cocked at once. "You, a woman, wear a French uniform? Why? How did you slip through Italian and German checkpoints?"

"Please? Are you Darius's mother? We have no time to stand here and chance being spotted by patrols. I'll explain inside."

"Inside will be too late."

"I am in the British service with your son Darius. I swear I bring no malediction upon your house. Keep the gun on me, but in heaven's name, *signora,* tell my driver where to hide the lorry."

Dariana, secure with her gun, noted that the woman wasn't armed and instructed the driver, "Through the archway, around the side of the house on to the stables." She unlocked the gate. "Come with me, *soldata*. Into the house. For your sake, pray you play no charades on me."

Together they entered the house.

"Mother!" Dariana heard his voice. Startled, uncertain, she lowered her gun and ran toward the large salon. "Mother, where are you?"

Dariana, excited and still shaken with uncertainty, ran to his arms, unable to believe her eyes or ears. The gun fell to the floor with a loud thud as Darius's strong arms embraced his mother. "Oh, God! It's really you, Darius!" Amid the outpouring of affection and solicitous murmurings, she shed copious tears of joy. She clung to him fiercely, felt him stiffen suddenly, pull away.

Darius's eyes held Valentina in their sights. Thunderous explosions and lightning bolts crashed through the dark recesses of his mind, triggering alarms. He firmly shoved his mother aside. "Val? What the devil are you doing here? From where in the blazing pit of Lucifer did you emerge?" he demanded harshly. Her presence evoked both concern and dread in him.

"Urgent official business, Major, I assure you." She spoke as harshly to him. "May we speak in private, sir?" She glanced past him at the two men entering from the sunlit terrace.

Vivaldi and Matteus blinked, adjusting their focus to the dimly lit interior. The woman in a French uniform startled them. What was this crazy woman doing here in a French uniform in Axis-occupied territory? Suddenly Vivaldi gasped. He stood motionless. The face! The eyes! *Oh, Christ! It cannot be!*

Matteus reacted. Images lurching through a two-decade storehouse of cobwebbed memories stirred powerful forces deep inside him. He agonized, eyes darting to Vivaldi.

Dariana, studying the vignette of controlled emotions, thought, *I am not imagining things. She is the woman in the portrait come alive!*

Valentina, growing uneasy under their probing scrutiny, moved protectively toward Darius. Darius, electrified by their strange behavior, introduced her properly to his family and suggested to Valentina that they step outside to the garden to conduct their business. He ascribed his family's reactions to culture shock, a quaint provincial reaction to the uniform and stunning beauty.

They exited through the French doors and sauntered down the steps, pausing under the shade of a chestnut tree to talk.

Inside, watching them, a flood of beleaguered memories and a rash of denials held Vivaldi mute, frozen to the past. *Blessed Christ!* It was not his imagination! His eyes were playing no tricks! She was the image of *Victoria Valdez!* Vivaldi turned to Dariana, but his wife had turned ashen and scurried quickly toward the butter rooms.

"Forgive me, Val, this isn't my best day. Too much is happening. It's my first visit home since my arrival." He explained his position, the news of Sophia's disappearance, his mother's shock at seeing him after believing him dead for four years. He kept it simple, with no embellishment of facts. "Now tell me how the hell you found me."

Listening intently, her body melting at the touch of his hand on hers, Valentina forced herself back to reality. She glanced about apprehensively, then spoke softly. "I bring you worse news. Your brother Robert is—he's been badly injured in a bloody rout with the Germans. He's—" She hesitated. "He's at St. Florent—the hospital!"

"St. Florent? That's Axis controlled. What in the name of the bleeding Jesus is he doing? Christ, you didn't tell my mother?" He glanced behind at the house, his mother's gaunt, pale face vivid in his mind. "She can't take much more."

"I just arrived. I told her nothing. Please tell me how to help."

"First get rid of that damned uniform! How the bloody hell— Who gave you permission? Dammit, in that uniform you could have been killed! If not by the Germans, then the Corsicans. How did you manage to get through the checkpoints?"

"An angel sat on my shoulders. Chamois Barbone. Does the name ring a bell?"

"Oh, yes, it rings a bell, all right. Too fucking many bells!"

"Why? What's wrong? He's my contact with the Resistance."

Darius wasn't listening. He was assessing her critically. "Those eyes, that hair will be picked out of any crowd. My sister's clothing, a little Corsican ingenuity perhaps. *Damn!* I shouldn't be here. *You* shouldn't be here. Listen. I am called Djebel, got it?"

"Because you resemble a mountain?" she played with him, sobering at once at his scowl as he leaned in conspiratorially.

"I will return with you to St. Florent. Say nothing of Robert to my family. Understand?" She reached up, slid her arms around his neck, and kissed him longingly. She sensed his discomfort. "Not now, Val. My family wouldn't understand this. There'll be plenty of time later, I hope."

Dariana, confused at the rapid order of events, peered at the embracing couple through the kitchen window. She turned, set a pot of coffee to brew. If her thoughts could be properly assembled this day, what would they reveal? The unthinkable? The unbelievable? It was all too complicated to sort out.

In the sitting room, a shaken Vivaldi confronted the Moor. "It cannot be coincidence. Even the name, Valentina Varga, is too close. Think, Matteus, *think* back to that night, the night that haunts us eternally. Were they all dead? Could Victoria Valdez, my betrothed, have lived? Escaped the heinous massacre?" Haunting images raced through his mind.

Seville, Spain! The villa! The massacre! A human abatoir created by Amadeo Zeller! Blood-streaked walls! Screams! Unending nightmares of terror. The foolish dreams and aspirations of immature youth had ended in that nightmare of horror, never to be forgotten.

"Help me clear the cobwebs, dust off my memory!"

The Moor despaired. "Must I replay that night of demoniacal horror over and over? I told you a hundred times, I witnessed the atrocities, fled to the vaults to do Don Diego's bidding. I encountered my beloved brother Pablo. There were shots . . . I buried him. I had neither time nor desire to again witness that tableau of execution. Instinct drove me far from the hacienda at once, to find you."

Vivaldi lit an American cigarette, puffed thoughtfully. "I cannot be evasive with my wife. She would sense it at once. If there is romance between Darius and the girl, he must be told."

"No!" Matteus's words cut like a stiletto. "Why? There is no need. No impediment mars the relationship if they are in love. If the girl is your daughter, as you suspect, there exists no bloodline to Darius. Say nothing, Vivaldi, or you will lose Darius forever."

Their eyes locked, each man relegated to his personal agony.

Time had reduced the scalding torrents and painful images. To unearth the past two decades was insanity. This wasn't the time.

Dariana reentered the sitting room carrying the silver service set, Marie Clotilde's wedding present, as if to remind Vivaldi that Darius was the son of another man. Darius and Valentina entered from the garden. Everyone wore masks, thought Dariana, to force the appearance of normality.

Normality! What, on this day, in this house, could be normal?

The polite amenities were nearly over, the coffee sipped in strained silence, the cookies nibbled scantily. Darius, giving in to an overwhelming urge to leave the uncomfortable social quagmire, asked his mother to find suitable clothing for Valentina. "The Lieutenant risked her life traveling in that uniform. I want her out of jeopardy for the return trip. Perhaps something of Sophia's?"

Dariana nodded dutifully, left the room, her husband's words trailing after her. "You are an American, Lieutenant Varga?" The conversation faded. Dariana, angst coursing through her, gripped the banister and wearily climbed the stairs. Why listen? She *knew* the answer.

In the sitting room, Valentina politely answered all of Vivaldi's queries. "I was born in America. My heritage is Argentine—American and Spanish."

Vivaldi's heart stopped. Blood thrummed at his temples. Cold sweat beaded his forehead. Darius, disquieted, observed the trio, aware that something very strange was occurring.

"Your parents reside in America?" Vivaldi asked.

"Mother only. My father and grandfather died, victims of revolution."

"Your father was Spanish. Your mother, Argentine and American?"

"How did you arrive at that?" Valentina's astonished eyes widened. "Amazing perception, Signor Bonifacio. Most people find it difficult to unravel the complex tapestry of my birth." She smiled dazzlingly.

Oh God! I am not most people! It's possible I am your father!

Darius signaled his annoyance. "Father! Time is precious. It is neither the time nor the place to research the Lieutenant's genesis."

Not imperative, my son? If only you knew how imperative it is!

"I don't mind, Major," she continued. "My grandmother Veronica was in America burying her father. She returned to Buenos Aires, forced to perform similar obsequies for my grandfather, her husband. His remains had been shipped home from Spain. Shortly after, my mother, Victoria Valdez, left a hospital in Seville, returned to Argentina, and was whisked away to Chicago where I was born. I'm uncertain why they left Buenos Aires so swiftly. Badly botched up business interests, I was told. Foreign investors—from Zurich, I believe—put a choke hold on our properties and business interests. My grandfather had dealings with a cartel—" She sipped her coffee. "I have little patience with the past. Litigation has spanned two decades. Both sides are tenacious, intractable. But why do I bore you with my family history? Corsica is so beautiful." Her eyes trailed around the room and locked with Darius's stormy eyes. *What the devil's bothering him now? Would she ever know him?*

"Are those green roses I see?" She stood up and moved toward the terrace. "May I see them, Major?"

Valdez! The spoken magic word tied everything together for Vivaldi. His temples pounded furiously. *There was no mistake!* This was his daughter! The flower of his seed! *Blood of his blood! The embodiment of his love for Victoria Valdez!*

Matteus, overwhelmed at the denouement, left the room lest he too be compelled to question her. The sight of Darius's fury signaled trouble to him. It would be impossible for Darius not to sense that the girl's presence meant something special to Vivaldi.

He was right. Darius, livid and bewildered at the blatant intrusion upon Valentina's past—even he hadn't known the details of her birth—strode past her. Outside, beyond the terrace, he called to his men sipping wine under the pergola. "Pascal, come. Requisition these items from the citadel at once." He quickly scribbled on a notepad.

Pascal approached wiping his lips, retrieved the outthrust list, scanned the contents dubiously. "Is it wise to leave you here? These will take at least a half hour to scrounge up, perhaps more."

"Two of you go. One remains. Prepare to leave for St. Flo-

rent within the hour. Urgent business, Pascal,'' he added the
instant doubt registered in the other's eyes.

"St. Florent! Djebel, are you *cafard*? Enemy strongholds at
all sides—to the north, south, east, and west. The Axis hospital
is located there.''

"Precisely. It's our destination.'' The words and annoyance
in Darius's eyes stopped further negation.

"*Oui*. I go at once, Djebel.''

He watched the two men retreat beyond the terraces, his outrage at Vivaldi's rude persistence in questioning Valentina still
fermenting. He reentered the house, strode through the butter
room, and scaling the narrow back staircase, went in search of
his mother. *Damnation*. Why hadn't Barbone sent a proper
courier? Why Valentina? And what the bloody blazes was she
doing here in Corsica to begin with?

Dariana's bedroom was empty. So was Sophia's room. He
heard muffled sounds coming from the third floor. *What the
devil?* Taking the steps two at a time to the third landing, he
moved along the corridor, opening and closing doors.

Inside a storage room, Dariana stood staring at the uncovered
oil portrait of Victoria Valdez. Approaching footsteps, Darius's voice calling, startled her. She hastily re-covered the oil,
and was one step out the door when he spotted her. "Mother,
we must leave. Did you find suitable clothing for our guest?''

Dariana fell into his arms, hugging him, lavishing maternal
kisses on him. She searched his face. "Thank God you are
alive. I cannot believe my eyes. How you've grown. Listen to
me chatter like a cuckoo bird. Come, we'll find the clothing
you need.''

Holding hands, they descended the steps to the second floor
and Sophia's room, talking as they went. "What can you tell
me of Sophia's disappearance, Mother? Who were her friends?
Who saw her last and where?''

Dariana gathered several of Sophia's garments, her voice
soft, confidential. "If I impart what I know, will you promise
not to tell your father?'' She placed a finger over her lips,
scurried to the door, glanced over the balcony at the trio below
them. She quickly returned. Before Darius negated or confirmed her conditional response, she began an emotional outpouring. She told him of Sophia's experience with the Italian

Major at the cathedral on Christmas Eve day. "Then a week ago he came here looking for you."

"Mother, you make no sense. If you know Sophia's whereabouts, it is your duty to inform Father." Darius stiffened. "*Who* came here looking for me?"

"No! I'll tell your father nothing!" Her hand flew to her forehead as if she were suddenly disoriented. "Who came for you? I told you. The Major. Major Victor Zeller. He was here asking for you by name. I cannot tell your father. I must not. Why is he looking for you? What does it mean?"

Darius lied adroitly. "I have no idea. What did you tell him?"

"The truth—as I knew it. You were dead! You disappeared four years ago. Dead—a victim of Corsican vendetta. Darius, why did you send no word?" Her voice contained traces of bitterness. She searched his face, traced the minute scars with her fingertips.

Darius grabbed her hand, kissed it. He had no desire to engage this fierce warrior in verbal contest over the inexplicable drives and warped emotions that had led him away from home. He used expert diplomacy to steer her off track.

"Mother, I strongly urge you to reflect on the matter of Sophia's disappearance and reconsider telling Father."

"I tell you, no! I can't! I won't! I don't dare!" She began to mutter absently, dissembling before his eyes. "Call it woman's intuition. I've nothing factual to go on. I don't remember everything."

"When you come to your senses and remember what you refuse to tell your husband, send Matteus with word that you need to see me. My code name is Djebel. Let the name Darius remain buried with the past. If the Italian Major or anyone should return here, keep in mind your first response. Darius is dead. Believe it, and when the war ends I shall return to fill you in on the past four years."

"Djebel. But he knows your code name too. He knows your purpose in Corsica. He asked that you surrender to him, not to the Germans. He promised to be merciful, to help you." Dariana turned from him.

Darius sensed the reasons for her hesitancy. "You—you got the distinct impression—" He held her shoulders, turned her face toward him. "You think Sophia may be with him—this Major Zeller?"

"Against her better judgment. I am certain!"

"Zeller! Victor Zeller!" The officer mentioned at Malta! The possible defector! The officer he and Pluto had encountered near St. Francis Convent. *"When?* Tell me when he came here looking for me."

Dariana knew the date, the hour, the very minute of Victor's visit. Every detail of that encounter was indelibly etched in her mind. Darius listened to every word. When she finished, he made no comment. He glanced at his watch. "Come, Mother. The Lieutenant's presence here poses complexities and dangers I have no wish to combat on this day. We must leave here to bring no trouble to Terra Bonifacio."

"Mother!" He paused on the stairs to see Dariana reeling dizzily. He grabbed hold of her, steadying her. "Are you all right? This is serious. What are you holding back?"

"You see through me." She caught her breath, steadied herself.

Darius kissed her brow. "Don't fret. You'll tell me in good time. Now, help our guest into these clothes while I rummage about for some disguise. I'll need time to speak with your husband."

Alone with a somber-faced Vivaldi, Darius spoke first. "I know that Daniel and Robert are fighting with the Resistance near Calvi. Do they still hate me?"

"They never hated you!"

"How would you know? You had no time for them."

"You have changed, my son."

"None of us remains the same forever."

"Are you romantically involved with the American?"

"She came here risking her life to deliver an urgent official business memorandum. If the Italians or Germans had got hold of her— Get word to Barbone. He should not have revealed my whereabouts. Now, please, we have little time. Explain your connections to Chamois Barbone."

Matteus entered carrying suitable clothing for Darius. He laid the items out on a chair. Darius began at once to disrobe and don the black trousers.

Vivaldi was visibly exasperated. "Must I explain myself to you now?"

"Only when I ask you to." Darius pulled on a black cotton shirt.

"You have changed."

"And you are becoming repetitious." He tucked in his shirttails.

"It must have been important," Vivaldi said, "or else Barbone lost his head in sending the American here. He is not a careless man. Unthinking at times but never careless."

"It is extremely serious," he snapped. "Robert is at St. Florent, near death."

"*What?* Robert is what?"

Matteus sprang forward like a protective tiger. Vivaldi paled. "How? When? Is this the message she brought? Why didn't he radio the citadel?"

"You ask questions I've asked myself since her arrival. I shall learn the answers or Chamois will taste the fury of my wrath. Believe that. The Lieutenant and I leave the moment my men return from the citadel."

"No! You must not go! It may be a trip. The Lieutenant may be the bait. You stay. I shall go," Vivaldi insisted. "I beg you say nothing to your mother until it is verified." He ran nervous fingers through his hair. "How bad is he?"

"I told you. Near death. He refuses to see anyone but me." He jerked a ratty sweater over his head. "You, Matteus, will accompany me. Is it compatible with your plans?"

"You need ask?" The Moor poured three thimble-sized glasses of Manzanilla. "Here, drink. It's like a tonic. We all need it. The work of Moloch is unending in its loathsome content."

Vivaldi sank dismally into his chair, the news a bitter pill to swallow. Darius pressed, "Now perhaps you'll tell me what it is that fascinates you about our guest. You questioned her as a barrister might at a trial."

Vivaldi, startled by the terse tone, sighed. "She's in love with you. Is it wrong for a father to question the woman his son might marry?" One more lie didn't matter.

"Unfortunately, there's no time to pursue the falseness of your words," Darius retorted, donning a pair of peasant's boots. "When this dirty business of war finishes, you'll be honest with me." He shoved a black beaked cap on his head and stalked out of the study.

Outside, in the light of a lemon-yellow sunset, Darius helped Valentina into the waiting lorry. She was dressed in a black cotton shift and wore a matching shawl to cover her hair. Her turquoise eyes glistened like azure sapphires against the dark vegetable stain Dariana had applied to her skin. Darius huddled with Pascal for several moments, then kissed Dariana in parting. "Remember, if anyone comes snooping about, Mother, you have not seen me."

"Yes, yes, I understand. I shall repeat what I told the Italian Major when he came looking for you." She stopped, her faux pas evident. In spite of the blush tinging her cheeks, she maintained her poise.

"Italian Major? What Italian?" Vivaldi demanded. Dariana faltered. "You mentioned this before, then denied it. Why?"

"I forgot. You were seldom home. It slipped my mind." No one believed her. The others' lack of confidence in her heightened her anxiety. "Be careful. You'll come back, my son. You'll come back."

Matteus swung into the lorry as it started up and settled down near the rear, laying a rifle across his lap as the vehicle moved down the hill.

Dariana's inscrutability and the strange encounter with Darius's father had unnerved Valentina. How could anyone miss the shock of recognition that registered in his eyes the moment he saw her. Disturbed by an eerie, pervasive feeling, she wondered if they had met before.

Déjà vu, Val? Leave it alone.

Silence. Ten uncomfortable miles of silence while they jolted and jostled unmercifully over crude rutted roads. Soon her discomfort changed to awe and fascination at the primitive regions they traversed. Uphill, downhill, over roads that were not roads but trails, around the sheerest of pinnacles, the travel northward became an exercise in sheer nerve. The breathtaking panorama, braying dogs, shrieking wild pigs, goats, sheep grazing through chestnut groves and larch forests, all inspired Valentina's reaction.

"It's like being in every corner of the globe at once," she told Darius. "You described Corsica's strange enchantment, but I never imagined this. You too are everything all at once, like Corsica. Your parents are—"

"Different. Is that what you mean? I told you—worlds apart."

"I didn't mean to imply—"

"Worlds apart and never the twain shall meet."

"Why do you do this? Why is your antagonism toward me so—"

"Tell me about Robert." His words were like saber swipes. "Then tell me what in damnation brought you to Corsica."

St. Florent Hospital, confiscated by the Axis to patch up and heal their own soldiers, was strictly off limits to civilians and resembled a cell block housing Marquis de Sade victims. Intimidating German and Italian soldiers posted as sentinels in every corridor stood at attention, eyes piercing every visitor. Visiting hours were hectic; it was a perfect time for laxity. The visitors queued up, brandishing red, white and green cards stamped permissively with Axis headquarters seals, and were passed on through the front desk with little or no contest.

Sterile, antiseptic smells overwhelmed the trio as they rushed inside the crowded, open-walled ward housing hundreds. The stench and sight of horrible suffering and death bounced off the walls and ceilings and hung over the enormous room. A frocked nun took their cards, directed them to the west wall. Darius, beaked cap in hand, kissed the nun's hand and muttered a felicitation in French. They moved along the aisle counting the beds crammed together along the designated wall, stopping at bed 272. The visitors, senses reeling, steeled themselves, eyes riveted to the pathetic creature on the bed.

Robert was unrecognizable. The discolored face was a mass of angry sutures, a facial contour map patched together by ugly, disconnecting lines. Where the nose should be, there was an open black-and-blue hole, a half-cone-shaped splint taped over it protectively.

The frocked nun moving in behind Darius and held his arm. "*Monsieur,* one arm is gone, only half the other remains. Both legs were removed above the knee. It would serve no purpose to mention it to him. He does not know."

Darius, sickened by the sight, did not turn from his brother. He moved in closer to the bed. Valentina, suddenly nauseous, gripped the white iron railing to keep from fainting. Matteus, prayer beads in hand, stood like a carved mahogany statue as two-decade-old images rushed past him, memories of a bloodied massacre, of his brother Pablo, his eyes shot out from his head.

Darius knelt over his brother, whispered to him, "Robert . . . it's Darius. . . . Can you hear me? I'm here, next to you. Are you awake?" He saw movement under swollen eyelids. The lips quivered, struggled to form words. The heavily bandaged head moved a fraction.

"Robert, it's Darius. Yes, yes, your brother." He wanted to touch Robert, hold his hands comfortingly, but Robert had no hands.

The aperture of each eye widened a hair, closed again, pained by sensitivity to light. As Darius cooed his words, the sounds stirred Robert inwardly. Collecting every vestige of strength, he forced the lids to open wider, bit by bit. Inner panic was reflected in the dark eyes swimming in blood-clotted whites. Robert's focus wavered.

Internally Robert resisted Darius; he denied the truth. What confirmed it was the shadowy form of the bull moose at the foot of the bed. His lips moved, excitement propelled an inner energy and he muttered, "Matteus." Tears of recognition trailed into an audible gasp, an agonized cry, damning the Deity for forcing him to be viewed as he was, a basket case. His body shook uncontrollably, his desperation heightened by the trauma. "D-Darius . . . is it y-you? N-Not a-an a-apparition?"

Darius commanded his brain: *Be cheerful. Minimize the shock of encounter. React only to what you remember of Robert—not what you see.* "Yes, yes, it's me, Darius."

"D-Don't t-tell M-Mother. . . ." The agonized words floated up at Darius, barely audible. He leaned in closer. "Promise m-me!" Robert's pleading eyes leaped from Darius to the Moor. He blinked at the presence of the woman. "S-Sophia, g-go a-away."

"Our mother will want to know, Robert. What happened?"

"N-No!" he wailed, bansheelike. Heads turned toward them. Darius hushed him. "T-Tell h-her I d-died." He fought gallantly to choke back the realization. "Th-There i-is n-no l-life for m-me as a m-m-man. *C-Comprenez-vous?*"

"How did this happen? Can you tell me?"

"B-Betrayal," Robert hissed, tears streaming down his scarred face.

"Betrayal? I don't understand? Who?"

"*D-Danseur esprit! F-Fantôme.*"

Darius, barely able to make out the words, felt a strong hand on his arm. He looked up into the Moor's eyes. Footsteps approaching along the wooden floor caught his attention. "Come, we must depart. One of Barbone's men approaches. Military rounds will commence in a short while. We must be gone. If the Germans learn of Robert's identity, that he participated in the ambush at Furiani, they will finish him off. Go! You must be protected at all costs. I'll remain behind to watch over Robert."

Darius leaned over Robert. "Whoever is responsible will pay. I promise I shall return for you. The score will be settled."

"*F-Fantôme . . . D-Danseur esprit!*" He mouthed the words, turning from Darius. "God, let me die now."

"Matteus, he mentioned betrayal. Try to learn what happened at Furiani, who was involved."

"Go," the Moor urged. "Take the woman and go quickly."

Darius and Valentina, led by Barbone's sentinel, departed. Matteus scanned the hospital chart at the foot of the bed. He read: "Mario Antonio Dante, Corporal, victim of mine explosion. Condition: critical. Prognosis: unfavorable. Injuries: terminal." He glanced at his watch and remembered he'd seen water flasks lined in a row on a cart near the door. He walked the full length of the overcrowded ward to the carts. Hospital charts on a medication cart nearby solidified the prognosis for the patient in bed 272, Mario Dante. The morphine prescribed for him would incapacitate an elephant.

"May I be of assistance, *monsieur*?" the ubiquitous French Mother Superior inquired of the Moor. Accompanying her on her rounds was a bland-faced German soldier. He glanced at the Moor apathetically.

Matteus held up a water flask. "My nephew in bed 272 requested water. It was not my intention to disturb you, good Mother."

The woman in white starched ecclesiastical garb shook her head balefully. "Ah, *monsieur, monsieur,* you have my deepest sympathy." She gestured to the soldier to move along, then muttered dolorously about the Dante case, the lack of qualified surgeons in critical war times. She ranted melodramatically to deaf ears.

At Robert's bedside, Matteus soaked a cotton wad with water

and dripped it economically, drop by drop, between Robert's cracked lips. Recognition flickering in his eyes, Robert muttered broken words and phrases to the Moor. Listening intently, Matteus nodded. "Is the pain so great, dear Robert?" Robert nodded.

They spoke again. Matteus listened, the prayer beads skimming through his fingers. He questioned Robert; he had to be certain.

He was. When the talk ended, Matteus muttered an Islamic prayer.

"Forgive me, Christian God, for presuming myself to a position of a winged messenger from your heavenly abode. I supplicate to you to send your angels of death to embrace your son Robert Bonifacio. His soul will better serve thee if it is free of his ruined earthly temple. If he is left here as he is, people will scorn and pity him. I implore you to relieve him of so horrible a burden. Can he be of use to you here as he is? If by my supplication, my act displeases or upsets the balance or order in your domain, condemn me before my God, Allah. I shall accept whatever punishment is meted me when I travel my final journey to eternity."

Silent and unmoving, Matteus listened to the buzzing of incoherent monologues and heartrending laments of the other patients. His mind was firm, resolute; he would not be deterred.

Moments later he emerged from the ward unnoticed just as the white-frocked nurses began their rounds of medication.

Four hours later, he returned to Terra Bonifacio, the bearer of bad tidings. He confronted Vivaldi. "Robert is dead, Vivaldi. Tell your wife. It is better she mourn him for one year than the rest of her life."

And when Vivaldi questioned the riddle, the Moor explained himself, imploring Allah to have mercy upon his soul. Tears streamed down his craggy cheeks. Vivaldi reached out his arms, embraced the Moor.

"You did the right thing. Only God shall know the measure of your bravery this day."

Matteus wiped his eyes, cleared his thick throat, and when the convulsions shaking him subsided, he said quietly, "When you finish with your wife, return to the vendetta room. I shall tell you of the betrayal and why Robert and his fighters were sacrificed. We must get the information to Darius."

* * *

Matteus's perfectly timed departure from St. Florent had
thwarted the aims of Sturmbannführer Hans Hesse and his adjutant, Fritz Schmidt, both recently recovered from their near-
fatal accident at Île-Rousse.

The cadence of leather boots striking the wooden floors
echoed throughout the hospital and descended on the ward
where Mario Dante lay in repose. The starched Mother Superior in her enormous headgear approached the German officers.

"Take us to bed 272!" snapped Lieutenant Fritz Schmidt.

Hesse, leaning heavily on a cane for support and glowering
darkly, swept past the Mother Superior, eyes behind dark
glasses scanning the infirm with hauteur. He loathed hospitals.
His sole purpose in coming back to this primitive medical facility was to clear up the damnable muck-up at Bastia headquarters.

The body of a dead Italian soldier, stripped of clothing and
all identity, had posed an enigma at the compound for better
than a week. A unique snake-and-dagger tattoo identified him
as a former member of one of Il Duce's youth groups. A comrade had recognized the tattoo, had insisted the dead body was
Corporal Mario Dante. Then who, wondered the inquisitive
Fritz Schmidt when he reviewed the St. Florent infirm list, was
the patient at St. Florent occupying bed 272, who was also
listed as Corporal Mario Dante? Schmidt had quickly confronted Major Hesse.

Now here they were at St. Florent. They stopped before bed
272. Schmidt, a wicked gleam in his eye moved in swiftly
alongside the patient and jerked back the sheet, half expecting
to find an identical tattoo. The Germans stared stonily. The patient had no legs!

"Gottverdammen!" muttered Hesse. "Transfer this patient
to the prison facility at the garrison in Bastia. Prepare him for
interrogation!"

The Mother Superior recoiled at the brash, arrogant demand.
"This patient's condition is critical, Major. He cannot be
moved."

"Do as I say, woman. There is a cloud as to his identity. He
is a prisoner. He's not entitled to the privileges and treatment
reserved for our men!" Hesse snapped.

The solemn-faced woman bent over the patient, slipped a

thermometer between Robert's lips. She placed expert fingers on the aorta in his neck. Mother Marie-Teresa suppressed her gloating. "Too late, Major. The patient has expired." She pulled the sheet over his face.

Schmidt jerked hard at the sheet, unveiling the body. He moved in at bedside, pried upon the eyelids, searched the staring eyes, and let them fall back into position. He gave the Mother Superior a scathing look. "This insolence and lack of proper procedure in patient admissions shall not go unpunished."

An outpouring of wrath, spoken in regional French, spilled from the Mother Superior's lips. "Don't start with me, Major! You and your warriors explode guns, use vile weapons, blow up men, return human wreckage to us. Patch them up, you say! Hah! To my meager staff they no longer resemble God's creations. To us they are strangers, including you, Major Hesse, whom we patched together not long ago following your recent mishap." She was not to be intimidated by conquerors.

Hesse, flushing crimson, bridled angrily. About to leave, he stopped abruptly, his demeanor suddenly gentle. He spoke accented French. "Mother, has bed two seventy-two received visitors? It is essential we notify the family."

"*Oui.* An uncle, brother, and sister came only today."

"An uncle? Brother and sister?" His eyes darted to Schmidt's and locked. "From Italy? *They came from Italy?* Now, don't you find that interesting, Schmidt? Can you describe them, good Mother? What were their names?"

"Names? You ask their names? Perhaps you can check the passes authorized by your soldiers?" She tossed her hands into the air in helpless resignation. "Describe them? I see so many. But one moment, I remember the uncle. He was a large man, a Goliath, skin of umber and bearded." One vision conjured up another. She paused reflectively, taken by her own words. "The patient's brother was handsome, tall, erect, proud. He spoke French like a Corsican and moved like a soldier."

Hesse, enormously excited, blurted out, "Spoke French like a Corsican, Mother! The dead man is Italian! Surely your suspicions were aroused."

"Major, I am not the Gestapo! I am telling you only what I recall. I personally did not ask their names, since they identified themselves as kin of Corporal Mario Dante. It didn't occur to me they might be impostors. It is not my business. It's yours." Turning to leave, she was restrained by a firm hand on her arm. A syrupy voice prodded.

"One more question, good mother, and I shall not bother you again. The girl, the sister, can you describe her?"

"Dark, dirty, dressed modestly like a peasant. They had traveled a distance. I remember their boots were covered with ocher dust."

"That's all? Nothing else?"

"It is important to you, Major?"

"It is quite important, good Mother."

"Worth enough to requisition some of that miracle drug, sulfa powder, from your stores at Bastia?" she negotiated cannily.

"That much."

"It's a bargain?"

"It depends upon the information."

"The woman had eyes of azure tinged with the viridian of the sea. As outstanding as those of her brother. His were the color of a stormy green sea. How much sulfa powder will you send us?"

"You've told me nothing to support your demands."

"He wore a pagan medallion around his neck. A death's-head amulet," she said tentatively.

A death's-head amulet! Hesse closed his stormy eyes. He gripped his cane tightly.

"You'll get your sulfa, Mother." Hesse knew it! *A death's-head amulet!* The legionnaire Darius Bonifacio, code name Djebel, was here! His eyes darted to the remains of Robert. "If only we knew *his* real identity, Schmidt. We'd know where to find our enemy." They turned to leave the premises.

"Can you, for additional information, conjure up a qualified surgeon from Paris, Major Hesse?"

Hesse stopped, his eyes fixed on the crafty woman. "You are a shrewd negotiator, good mother. I can only try. Surgeons are in high demand presently. But if your information serves our purpose—"

The Mother Superior beckoned them closer. She whispered in Hesse's ear. His eyes widened in astonishment. He quickly glanced in the direction she designated, stared at the patient in bed 274 and the box camera resting on the bedside stand. The scent of victory intoxicated Hesse's senses.

Two hours later, Hesse and Schmidt stood over the developed photographs of an unsuspecting trio taken by a camera buff who had chronicled his involvement in the war by photos and a religiously kept diary. Promised the negatives and a set of enlarged photos for his cooperation, the Italian soldier did not refuse Major Hesse's request.

Hesse was stunned. Schmidt's jaw dropped in astonishment. *Pythia!* There was no mistaking her. Azure eyes, dark hair, slender, upturned nose! The spy Pythia! Here in Corsica! With Darius Bonifacio!

Hesse and Schmidt left the infrared developing chambers and returned to his office at the garrison. Hesse sat in his chair, turned it around, and gazed down at the courtyard contemplatively.

"These are hectic, complicated times, Schmidt. In my mind there brew more questions than there are answers. But one thing is certain: Operation White Coral is a diversion. Something else is happening here. Why else would Pythia be here with Darius Bonifacio? Why would the OSS agents and SOE's Lieutenant Ivar Morely be here? The man is SIS! Britain's top man in secret intelligence!"

Schmidt could offer no answer.

Pythia had disappeared from Paris as if she had never existed. Hesse didn't like the idea of her possibly conspiring with ragtag Resistance fighters. *Who the devil is she really?*

"Schmidt. I want you to arrange to bring me all of Major Zeller's files. I mean all of them. I don't care how you do it, but I want every single file stored in his secret vault."

The protest forming on Schmidt's lips disintegrated. The impossible order loomed enticingly in his mental landscape. "You think Major Zeller is holding out?"

"Schmidt, don't think. Just move! Move, and we shall win this *Gottverdammen* scuffle on this worthless island. Then back to Paris, *jawohl?*"

Chapter Eleven

The modest hostelry possessed redeeming graces. Its windows opened onto a flower-filled balcony and walls of cascading bougainvillea overlooking the sea. What luck, thought Valentina, bathing, scrubbing the root stain from her skin. The concierge, a sucker for lovers and money, had readily supplied black market vintage wine, fresh lobster, and total seclusion. Valentina stepped out on the balcony, towel drying her freshly shampooed hair while Darius bathed. How easily they fell into a pattern of domesticity, she thought.

Darius came out onto the balcony and found Valentina wrapped in a towel, droplets of water on her body reflecting the moonlight. She reached for him at the sound of his footfall. They clung together tightly in a silent embrace. Darius had been locked in silent torment for the past two hours; the unrelenting memory of Robert lying helpless, near death, seared his guts, rendered him numb, mute. Forced back to the moment, the stony sensation he had endured was dissolving in Valentina's love. Time. Oh, Christ! There never seemed to be enough of it. He tipped her head back, stroked the fiery curls that never ceased to fascinate him.

For a wild moment he projected his thoughts to another life, a world filled with impossible dreams, promises impossible to keep. He kissed her lightly, then with increased ferocity. He stopped abruptly, almost savagely held her from him, then tearing his eyes from her, heaved a sigh of desperation as he stared noncommittally at the waves crashing on the shore. "You're far away from me," she whispered. "You left me before you left North Africa, and you *didn't* come to Corsica for me. That should tell me something," she said quietly.

"Wherever I go, you exist in my heart, forever a part of me," he replied. "In London, North Africa, here, as usual I am compelled to push thoughts of you deeper in my mind. Believe me, beloved, thoughts of you keep me alive and manacled despotically to you. But—"

"Until this war ends . . . I know. I *know!*"

"It's for your protection that a wedge of estrangement exists between us."

"Why? Why are you so driven to protect me?" She plucked petals from a rose, held them to her cheeks, drawing each across her lips before tossing it to the winds to sail to its own destiny. "I've managed fairly well without you, haven't I? It's been a year since we saw each other."

"The longest year of my life—one month and three weeks exactly."

She fell into his arms, ecstatic. "You play it so tough, don't you?" She touched his gold watch.

"Kiss me once and kiss me twice and kiss me once again . . . it's been a long, long time."

Clinging to each other, they went back inside, prepared to retreat from the world for as long as the world ignored them.

"Val, don't read more into this than there is. I have no right to make commitments, not until after the war, if at all."

She closed her ears to the words, her eyes to the strain and fatigue evident in his handsome features. Soul-stirring music piped through a battery-powered radio played havoc with their emotions. They made love feverishly, frenetically. And through it all Val refused to admit what her senses relayed to her. *This might be their last time together!* Darius's passion vaulted at a feverish pitch, his desire overriding thoughts of the past or future. Only this moment counted. Valentina abandoned herself to him, subordinating all thought to the experience. They were two lovers engaged in a conspiracy against time.

They exploded in orgasm.

"I'll take you any way I can," she said breathlessly, picking up on his last remark. "I love you. I shall always love you. For whatever it means, I've not been with another man since Dover."

"So where is my wild, worldly, madcap butterfly?"

"You singed her wings, grounded her, and tuned her in to your frequency for life."

Darius smiled wanly. He lit a cigarette, lay back against the pillow, and let Val feed him chunks of fresh lobster between sips of wine. "You'll spoil me, Val," he whispered with sudden sobriety.

"My intentions from the first." She sipped her wine and slid down over his body, taking in every inch of his lean, hard nakedness. Her cool face against his thigh sent shivers through him. She was like an intoxicant, her hot tongue and soft lips devouring him.

Suddenly struck by an unknown terror, Darius gathered her into his arms. "This is torture for us both. Understand what I am saying. You must leave Corsica at once." He stopped abruptly, frowning. "How the devil did you get here? You never explained."

"Sorry. I can't tell you. Top secret and all that."

"I must know, Val. It's a matter of security."

She plucked a morsel from a lobster claw. "You suggest I'm a shill for the Axis?" She drew back from him with exaggerated mortification.

"In my position I can't overlook the most minute detail."

"You're serious." Her eyes flared, aghast at the implication.

"Fucking right!" He sipped more wine.

Valentina sighed. "Monsieur Creneau," she said quietly.

Darius cut her a sharp, protracted glance, his thoughts convoluted. "I suppose the Miles Carter heiress can buy her way any place."

She recoiled. "I don't deserve that, *mon cher*." She grew hesitant at the rebuke. "How do you know about me? I never told you my history." Her voice was cutting. "I purposely refrained from discussing my patrimony. Dammit, Darius, is *that* why you cut me off so unfairly in London? You didn't answer my calls." She was hurt, angry, humiliated. "When I think of the frustration, the red tape you put me through to locate that

bloody airfield, and the plane ready for takeoff barely giving us
time to say good-bye, and those two years in between, those
fucking, empty years walking the battlefields and deserts of the
living dead, frightened that I might find you among them and
kicking myself because I lacked the maturity to hang on to
you!'' On her feet, she paced the floor in a rage. ''Goddamn
you, Darius! Goddamn you! You win! You hear? You win! I
won't fight for you anymore.'' She glanced at her watch,
strapped it securely around her wrist. ''Soon I need to rendezvous with my escort back to Malta.'' She was fumbling with
her belt. ''General Furstenberg sends you his warmest greetings and this. . . .'' Feeling along an inner lining, she reached
for her knife, moved the belt closer to the candle glow, inserted
the blade's tip into a minuscule slit, separating the leather. Out
popped a thin microfilm container. She tossed it in the air to
Darius.

Daarius snatched at it, both furious and relieved. He twisted
open the heel of his boot, dropped the dime-thin disk into the
depression, and clicked it shut. He suddenly unleashed upon
her the extent of his fury at Furstenberg for entrusting risky
business to a neophyte. He raged, cursed, assailed the damnable war and its ambitious officers who'd stop at nothing to gain
their ends! ''Goddamn them all!'' he said in a husky voice, a
whisper that belied the acrimony and contempt in which he held
those responsible for sending Valentina to Corsica.

''Go home, Val! Home! Back to America! This accursed war
will get worse before it ends. Espionage is a damned risky business! My God! How dare they send you? You aren't even
trained for it!''

Valentina, mixed feelings shuddering through her, thought,
He loves me! He must love me deeply to care so much. She
wanted to justify herself to him. *Pythia, without training, had
delivered! Pythia was terrific! Hadn't he heard?* But she didn't,
except to say, ''Risky? You dare use that word to a Croix de
Guerre recipient? After the horrors of war we both endured in
North Africa?'' Valentina paced the floor, temper rising. ''Go
to hell, Darius! Just you go to hell! You make no damned
sense. If General Furstenberg trusted me . . . Dammit! Just go
straight to hell! I could have given the film to the Resistance,
but did I? Oh, no, I was dying to see you. I begged for the assignment. Isn't that a kick in the ass? Valentina Varga longed for

you, ate her heart out over you, and gearing for the worst, risked her life just to see you again. You're a fool, *dammit!* A fool!"

"God, what a woman! When your temper flares . . ." He grinned, then sobering quickly, asked, "Where do you rendezvous with your contact?"

Valentina shrugged a haughty shoulder, pursed her lips defiantly.

"I *have* offended you. I *know* I flaunted my stupidity. See how it is? I'm no good for a woman like you. How can I nurture your love with so many treacheries underfoot? Can't you see through my flimsy bravado? My God, I fear for your life. It's precious to me. Now tell me, where do you rendezvous?"

She was intractable. He bridled. "Whether it pleases you or not, I intend to escort you to your point of rendezvous. If anything ever happened to you—" He moved off the bed and began to dress. "How much time have we?"

"Forty-five minutes."

"How far must we travel?"

"Five, perhaps ten minutes from here." She wrapped herself in a towel. A knock at the door startled them. Concerned glances were exchanged. Service pistol in hand, Darius edged closer to the door. "Who is it?" he asked in French.

"Pascal."

Darius quickly unlocked the door, cautiously eased it open, gun at the ready. A woman, partially hidden in the shadows, breezed past Pascal into the room. She embraced Darius, kissed him with solicitous murmurings. Valentina, coolly taking umbrage at the demonstrable affection, moved toward Pascal. "Did you bring my uniform? I'm very late." She snatched the parcel from his hands, snapping the strings.

"Val, I want you to meet—" Darius was cut off.

"No thank you!" She swung her body around, grabbed the champagne bottle, and entered the small bathroom, slamming the door behind her. She fought to control the rising anger, the mortification. Whipping off the towel, she slipped into her tailored skirt and was donning her jacket when Darius entered. Quickly she grabbed the champagne bottle, waved it before her, and guzzled from it. "Best way to forget until you find something worth remembering, *chéri!*" He took the bottle from her hands.

"You're being childish, Valentina. This is time for love, honor, passion, and above all, sacrifice."

"Don't you *dare* tell me what I am or am not! Don't you dare." She shoved his hand aside angrily. "Don't touch me."

He smiled at her, but she refused to be placated. "Would it help to tell you your assessment of the situation is wrong?"

She clamped her hands over her ears. "Don't! Don't give me lame excuses. I'm sick and tired of running after you. You aren't worth the effort. I'll simply collect my memories, stow them in my duffel bag, and perhaps pull them out in fifty years in order to laugh at my stupidity."

Her heated diatribe ceased at the sound of loud voices in the next room speaking in rapid French. Most was gibberish to Val, but a portion came out loud and clear.

"Take a message to Monsieur Creneau, *oui?* You are to tell him Zahara arrived safely in Corsica. We shall begin the offensive at once."

Valentina froze. She thawed quickly. "She is Zahara?"

"Who?" Darius's expression was bland.

"Oh shit!" Valentina said, exasperated.

The cove, hidden by high palisades and plagued by rough crosscurrents, was perfect, Darius thought, watching Valentina disappear into the British submarine that surfaced in the distance. He caught sight of the long boat returning to shore. Behind it the submarine crash-dived, carrying Valentina out of his life. Was he crazy to think her transportation safe? Memories of the HMS *Hyperion* and the wolf-pack U-boat attack scuttled his bravado.

Driving back along the blacked-out shore roads, skillfully swerving in and around German checkpoints, the locked emotions held in check during his respite with Valentina were now unleashed. *Sophia!* God, where would he begin to search for her? And Robert! Poor, pitiful, beloved, and most gentle of hearts! Unaware of Matteus's act of mercy, he wondered how he would fare in so uncertain and demonic a future. And Dariana! Surely that strong wall of iron determination would collapse after the heartbreak of the past four years.

In the darkness, Darius saw the signal from Pascal's hand torch. Pascal and Zahara, awaiting his return, piled into the covered lorry. Lucien pushed his way in behind the driver's wheel, edging Darius to one side. "I know the area better. It's best you and our guest speak on matters of a vital personal nature."

Darius, annoyed, scowled darkly. He had no time for this. Zahara especially should know this. "What is it, this matter of personal importance? Our involvements are grave, our risks increasingly dangerous. Surely, Zahara, we're professional enough to set aside personal matters."

"You were rough on the American."

"She doesn't belong here. It isn't her war!"

"In war we take all the help we can get."

"She isn't equipped to handle the rigors of war. She can easily be killed."

"And you too. And what of me? Are we both immune to bullet fire, exempt from bombs or devastating eighty-eights?"

Darius let loose a string of curses in Farsi and French. "She hasn't the savvy or the training to be plunked down in a war of no concern to her."

"Wrong, *mon ami*. As usual, men in love have myopic vision, view the object of their love in a somewhat biased way."

"*Merde!* Zahara, I need no craziness spun on my thinking today."

"Your current behavior and mannish stupidity distort the fine image I've always had of you. Demand to see the Pythia file! Furstenberg cannot—*will not* deny you. It is essential you know."

"*Know what? For Christ's sake, who the hell is Pythia?*"

"*Sacre bleu!* Just like a man. *C'est incroyable!* You want only to know what pleases you for the moment. The rest is *merde!*"

"Zahara! Either make yourself clear or cancel the subject until a more opportune moment. The Resistance leaders await us. The OSS and SOE with their countless black-hearted intrigues are breaking my back. My family is in dire jeopardy and I carry stunning information that must be decoded and transmitted to Malta! It's a waste of time to discuss matters over which I lack control. A cancer without remedy eats at my heart, and you insist on aggravating the affliction."

The utility careened sharply, turned off the sandy stretch of beach, and wound up the craggy incline, down-shifting as they scaled steeper roads. Shouting over the groaning engines, constant shifting, wheels skidding over rocks and sand, Zahara muttered broken words, curses, and demonstrated an impatience seldom displayed to Darius. She shouted louder. "The American Lieutenant is Pythia! You fool! Pythia helped save the precious asses of your Mozarabe and you here in Corsica. If not for Pythia's effort to help avert the German machine . . . You had best bone up, *cher*!"

"Pythia? Pythia who? Dammit, Zahara, tell me! Now! Pascal, stop the utility!"

The truck came to a skidding halt, kicking up pebbles, sand, and a screen of dust. "Get out. We talk now, Zahara. Now."

Darius led St. Germaine back over the rocks to a remote spot away from Lucien Pascal. He lit two cigarettes, gave her one, and sat down upon the rocks. She explained Pythia's role. Darius, tight-lipped, silent, brooding throughout, listened intently, fanning the fires of ambivalence searing his conscience. Flashes of Valentina intruded upon him, shaking his composure, flooding him with anguish. For so long his mind had been controlled by codes, ciphers, surveillance, deception, betrayal, lies, distortions. In the presence of death, he had choked back his emotional response for too long.

St. Germaine fished through her shoulder case. She removed a ship's manifest. "For you, *mon ami*, from Monsieur Creneau. It came by diplomatic pouch before my departure. The log, officers, and crew of the HMS *Hyperion*. Examine it carefully. Locate the name you seek. It's there. Monsieur Creneau is certain you will know it on sight."

"I didn't see his face!" he lied. "Now I will know the name on sight? Ask me to direct a camel through the eye of a needle, *chère*. The task set before me is impossible."

"For you nothing is impossible. You'll sort it out. *Je t'aime, mon ami*." She embraced Darius, kissed him affectionately. "Just be kind to yourself. Remember, not everyone who searches finds, and not everyone who escapes flees. The American loves you desperately."

"Youseff is mad for you," he replied, "yet you elude him. What drives you in separate directions?"

"Madness. Sheer insanity! A promise made to a ghost I've never seen. *Un fantôme—un esprit*."

"It's time to lay all ghosts to rest, *chère*."

"At war's end. *Allez*, I must make haste to rendezvous soon.

See how mad we are, you and I? Overhead a gigantic moon winks down at lovers, and where are we? Apart from those we love. Madness infects us, Darius. Pure unadulterated madness.''

''Who the hell ever said war is sane?''

They drove back along the deserted road to the camp south of Calvi. Zahara was deposited safely with the Resistance forces at Barbone's crude but ample headquarters. Fifteen minutes later, after coffee and refueling, Pascal wheeled the lorry south, headed for the citadel. Darius turned, glanced back at the dimmed lights of the port of Calvi under blackout restrictions. *Here's where it all began for you nearly four years ago. Or was it five years ago?*

Across the sea to the north, Europe was in chaos. Here in Corsica he must prepare for the turning point. His thoughts drifted back to what Zahara had told him of Valentina, and the shocking denouement of her dangerous role as Pythia took a stranglehold on him. Was she some crazy fool risking her life? The next time they met . . .

He couldn't stop thinking of Robert. Oh God, poor, sweet Robert! What was he chanting so frantically? A betrayal had occurred. How? Why? *Un danseur fantôme!*

Un danseur fantôme! Oh Christ, Ghost-Dancer!

Was that what Robert was trying to say? *Betrayed by a man called Ghost-Dancer?*

''Pascal! Stop the car! *Now!*''

He slammed the brakes hard, the lorry lurched and careened dangerously over the narrow road, coming to a stop so precariously close to the edge that a gentle breeze would push them over the precipice.

''Are you crazy, Djebel? *Mon Dieu!* Do not move. Do not speak a word or we are dead men! Let me inspect our chances against the devil.''

Darius barely saw Pascal ease himself out from behind the steering wheel and move on the balls of his feet around the chassis to assess the dangers. ''*Sacre bleu!*'' he heard Pascal whisper. The front wheels of the lorry were suspended over a cliff. Below them was a sheer drop to the sea. Up ahead some six or seven hundred yards 'was a Genoan watchtower near Ponte Rossa. An Axis stronghold! He moved back along the rear of the lorry to the driver's seat. ''Can you move back over the seat to the rear of the lorry, Djebel?'' he said, explaining the dilemma.

Darius came out of his brooding and scanned the moonlit area. He opened the door, looked down at the whitecapped waves crashing on the shore a thousand feet below them. A sickening sensation wormed through his stomach. Easing himself gently out of the seat, he stepped back, inching along the truck until he was on safe ground. He caught Pascal's distraught expression, one of absolute terror. Pascal, paralyzed by fear, had wet his trousers.

Both men broke into uncontrollable laughter.

They had faced death in countless skirmishes and Pascal ashamedly admitted this was the first time he'd wet his pants.

Tension was relieved. It was time for positive action. Darius removed a thick coil of rope from the rear of the lorry, tied one end to the rear axle, and together they unloosed the line bit by bit, held it firmly in their hands until they had anchored it several times around the thick trunk of a tree some fifty feet away. ''Here's what you do,'' Darius began. ''Get behind the wheel, start the engine, shove the gears into neutral, and release the hand brake. Return here and we'll both pull the truck back onto the road. We can't afford to lose the vehicle.''

It was as far as Darius got. A blinding explosion rocked the earth. Enormous flashes of fire spit upward. They dove for cover just as the lorry exploded, spewing red flames and black smoke.

The next ten minutes were madness. There were more explosions as they lay in protected positions, hands covering their heads. Fragments of the lorry soared overhead and came down toward them like fiery comets. Potholes exploded at all sides of them. A fusillade of gunfire dusted the road. Darius and Pascal unholstered their guns, crawled out of the line of fire.

What the devil? Coming at them from the Genoan tower were two squads of Axis soldiers. Orders were shouted. Darius yanked on his belt. He bit the pin from a smoke grenade, hurled it overhead. It landed at the rear of the lorry, in the path of the approaching soldiers.

''Pascal! Come! We've got to run for it. Across the road into the *maquis*!'' Under cover of thick black smoke and a totally disorganized offensive, the two legionnaires moved with the speed of cheetahs, crossed the road, scrambled up the incline to the goat track above. Breathless, panting hard, they stopped some fifty yards above the skirmish below them, eyes scanning the scrambling soldiers sorting out the pieces of the wreckage.

"Plastic explosives timed to go off at—" Darius glanced at his watch. It was eight-fifteen. "Eight o'clock." He accidentally tripped the mechanism on his watch. The tune "Lili Marlene" began to play. Mumbling a string of curses under his breath, he stabbed furiously at the watch, jammed his thumb hard against the mechanism, ending the song abruptly. A whisper in the night was carried swiftly on the wind in this area.

"Djebel!" whispered Pascal. "You realize if you hadn't ordered me to stop the car—" He removed his pith helmet, wiped the sweat on his brow, and whistled low. "What made you make me stop?"

"As assassin. An *assassin* saved our lives this time. Next time we may not be so lucky. At Camp Calvi, did you leave the lorry when I deposited Zahara with the Resistance leaders?"

"Only in the time it took to get jerricans of gasoline and a thermos of black coffee."

"The explosives were fixed into place during those—how many minutes?"

"Does it matter? Five, ten, twelve, fifteen?"

"It matters. Only very specially trained experts can accomplish the job in a matter of moments."

"SOE?"

"Or OSS."

"Even Mozarabe?"

Darius glanced at him sharply. "Even Mozarabe," he said quietly.

"Pascal, the fate of our country is at stake. What happens here in Corsica determines its fate, *our* fate, the fate of your family, the fate of mine. We must insure the success of White Coral. Tell me, do you believe the Allied effort can drive the Axis soldiers into full retreat?"

"Is the moon a paper balloon, Djebel?"

"That's what I admire most about you, Pascal. You are an optimist," Darius said wryly. "Come. If we're careful, we can make it to the citadel before midnight."

"An assassin, eh?" Pascal muttered over and over again, caught with the idea and the phrase. "Perhaps one day soon you will explain the enigma so this hard head of mine grasps the meaning of your words.''

There was no need to answer . . .

Chapter Twelve

"He is an inefficient, traitorous, lisping queer, and I don't want him near me," Himmler said rancorously of the notorious Ghost-Dancer.

"Odd," the Führer said quietly, out of character, "I find him an extraordinarily intelligent man. A bit unscrupulous, yes, but we must consider his past. He was left an orphan early in life, but the family was respectable, wealthy, and trained in the finest Bavarian traditions. Unquestionably he is a devout German. His dossier, allegiance to the Third Reich is unimpeachable, don't you agree, General Kaltenbruner?" Hitler addressed himself to the third man present this day in his study at Berchtesgaden.

"He may be a devout German, *mein Führer,* this British agent under our control, but we believe he conspires against you," Himmler insisted.

The Führer turned vacant eyes upon the head of the SS. Then he lowered them to the open dossier on his desk. "That hasn't been sufficiently proven to me. Until all the facts are in—"

"*Mein Führer,* is it not more prudent to check him out thoroughly before we entrust him with more secret missions? His position with us and with the British is precarious."

"As you said earlier, he is a British agent under *our* control. He makes no moves unless we know beforehand precisely what he is entrusted to accomplish, *ja?* Where is the jeopardy?"

"He could turn around. *Mein Führer,* the man is an assassin, a born killer, the best in the business."

"At age eighteen? That doesn't say much for the tried and truly experienced agents provocateurs, does it? Let us not forget he has served the Fatherland well."

"What is his price, Führer?" Himmler demanded. "What does he ask?"

"We all have our price, *nein,* Heinrich?" They stopped talking as a servant entered, wheeling a service cart. He placed hot chocolate before the Führer, and from a bowl surrounded by crushed ice, he spooned a large island of whipped cream onto the oversized cup. He served the others coffee at their request and left the room.

"It is a period of great uncertainty, high tensions in world affairs. You both ask at this time that Ghost-Dancer who, may I remind you, has performed incredible feats for the Fatherland, be snuffed out?" He studied the steam rising from his cup as the whipped cream's pinnacle broadened at its base and overran the cup. He spooned a small amount of the cream. "We are not yet finished with his services." Hitler sipped the chocolate and taking it in hand, moved out to the open balcony to gaze at the magnificent landscape he had come to love.

It was a perfect May day; the view was stunning. Spruce trees, a brilliant viridian, seemed dipped in the bright lacquer of sunlight. The mountaintops with their jagged peaks sharply outlined against the backdrop of an azure sky, stood out boldly. It was a morning of sharp contrasts and bold, fiery colors.

The Führer, standing erect in his immaculate, understated uniform, inhaled deeply. He scanned the countryside, picked up a pair of high-powered binoculars, and sweeping the panorama, picked out one spot nestled along the side of a hill. St. Bartolemò. How long ago was it? Seven, no, eight years ago when he'd made a bargain with two ten-year-old youths, both *orphans* who'd been swindled out of a fortune, an estate worth more than twenty million Swiss francs. He had no actual figures, but the estimate, a conservative one, had staggered his imagination.

His staff, those closest to him, failed to understand his devotion to the highly specialized assassin. Ghost-Dancer and his enigmatic brother were very special to Adolf Hitler; so special he refused to discuss them, both personally and professionally. In a professional vein, Ghost-Dancer's talents and scope of capabilities were beyond measure. And personally . . . Hitler sipped the hot chocolate with gusto, a rare smile curling his lips. Ghost-Dancer's existence and that of his brother Anton, now studying at Cambridge under an alias, could still all the vicious rumors as to his masculinity or lack of it. Alas, he could never point to Eugen or Anton Schuller as the legitimate issue of his loins, not even to dispel the rumors. He knew this and it didn't matter to him. What mattered to Hitler was the consummation of his master plan, that the Third Reich live to prove his theories. He had thoroughly convinced both lads, Eugen and Anton, of the vital importance their silence meant to Germany, to history.

Ghost-Dancer would do it! Ghost-Dancer would succeed. He must!

When was it, four months ago? Eugen, a.k.a. Ghost-Dancer, had arrived in a secret rendezvous with the Führer at Berchtesgaden in the shroud of a winter night. Wearing an SS uniform and dark glasses and carrying high cover credentials, he had passed through the several levels of guards, entered via a secret rear entrance, and climbed three flights of hidden stairs to Hitler's private study. They embraced, and after talking for nearly an hour, Hitler had spoken as if endowed with prescience.

"Do not fail me, Eugen. When it's over, no matter which way the cards fall, the King's men will come to your aid. You will carry on our plans with their aid. There are friends among friends. Remember this always. It could happen that I might not be there to share in the joy of victory."

"Oh *mein Führer,* do not speak this way."

"We must be realistic. You've discovered one major conspiracy. How many more will set out to slay me? You think our enemies will let it end here or in Berlin? My blood shall be in high demand. I will be blamed for more war crimes than there are names. But it matters not. Arrangements have been made even now, before anyone knows the outcome. There shall be numerous attempts to kill me, but all who try will be thwarted. What I require from you today is reassurance, your word that you will carry on, using the blueprints we've discussed in the past.''

"And if I do not survive, *mein Führer?* My work is exceedingly risky. There is no assurance I will survive the war to—''

"You will! You must! I demand you survive! They don't call you Ghost-Dancer the Magician for nothing. You have a way of making people and things disappear as if they never existed! You must live to join your alter ego, Anton, to carry out our plans.''

"How can you trust Anton? We are not one and the same.''

"I trust you with my life, Eugen. If he proves traitorous and refuses to join in our scheme of things, *exterminate* him. Assume his identity and take over from there. It is a safer plan overall.''

"But we are no longer identical twins. The operation on his left foot did not remove all traces of the natal deformity, while mine was completely successful.''

"Since when do disguises or duplicitous challenges deter you from your ultimate mission?''

Ghost-Dancer, squirming uneasily, stared at the Führer, who was building temples with his fingers.

"The moment Operation Overlord commences, I will need you in London.''

"I see. It's best you know I failed with the Corsican.'' He waited for the worst to come. To his astonishment, Hitler treated the matter as inconsequential.

"It doesn't matter. *He* doesn't matter.''

"What of Amadeo Zeller? The man who robbed me of my inheritance should not get away with his black-hearted deeds.'' Ghost-Dancer, alias Eugen Schuller, nephew to the dead cleric Heinrich Schuller, was the son of Bertha Schuller. "As my father, you cannot deny me that much.''

"You know I personally cannot legitimize your birth, neither yours nor Anton's. *Never!* For your protection your mother gave you the family name Schuller—for legal reasons and to facilitate the retrieval of your fortune.''

"Why can't I simply kill Zeller?''

"He has made himself too important. He's availed himself of numerous corporate entities. The man must be stopped. Anton cannot do it. He becomes more British each passing day. Therefore he must be exterminated at the proper time.''

"A fratricide. You would condone it?"

Hitler ignored the scornful tone and pounced on Zeller. "Amadeo Zeller, with the aid of his international money belts, has already engineered three attempts on my life. One you already discovered. He buys and sells fascist and Nazi generals with the skill and ease of a plenipotentiary born to power. I don't like it. I know that behind it all is a grim determination to break Mussolini. The man is possessed with *Entschlossen*; he perceives what needs to be done and has the courage to do it decisively. You too must be possessed with resolute determination to take a firm stand. You read the files, detected the bitter venom between Mussolini and Zeller at once. One day he will succeed, and I dislike being used as a pawn between madmen. The man is dangerous. I am beginning to detect Zeller's ulterior motive bit by bit. It isn't clear yet, but believe me, Eugen, I shall outwit them all." He balled his fist, slapping it in the palm of his other hand repeatedly. "My friends in England stay in close touch with me. They will help you at the proper time. Now listen carefully. There is a daughter named Clarisse. I am told she is a carbon copy of her father. She might be a perfect pawn. One to be cultivated."

Ghost-Dancer's eyes lit up with an unnatural glow as his mentor spoke.

Chapter Thirteen

Truth is so obscure in these times, and falsehood so es-
tablished that unless we love the truth we cannot know it.

—Pascal

Sophia Bonifacio had no idea that her arrival at Bastia headquarters would coincide with an irreconcilable clash of personalities between two volatile enemies, Majors Victor Zeller and
Hans Hesse. How could she know the deviltry brewing in Victor's mind, that he entertained no intention of handing over his
highly coveted files or the keys to the Italian command to the
Germans? She didn't know him at all.

Moments before her arrival at the post command headquarters where she'd traveled from Ajaccio to learn more about Darius, Victor Zeller was packing his files, planning to flee back
to Rome. The German, Hans Hesse, had failed to inspire his
confidence. Besides, what assurance had he, once the official
changeover took place, that Major Hesse wouldn't arrest him
on some fraudulent charges, imprison him, even kill him?

Leaving nothing to chance despite the assurance from Rome
about his safe return passage, he had covertly arranged other
means of debarkation. He was quickly packing highly classified files the day fate willed Sophia to seek him out at Italian
headquarters.

Her presence instantly sent into motion a host of daring, volatile thoughts. Several perils communicated themselves at

once. If Major Hesse learned that Victor knew the whereabouts of Darius Bonifacio's family—that he'd failed to make a full and complete report of the incident at Terra Bonifacio—and *why* he didn't still baffled him—he'd be torn into shreds and used as dog meat.

In the whirlwind activity of his covert departure and Sophia's unexpected appearance on the scene, Victor's mind gave birth to a crazy scenario. His dramatic powers of persuasion coupled with the perfect timing—Victor both welcomed her and conveyed such fears for her safety and that of her family—convinced her it was best for all concerned that she accompany him to Rome until it was safe for her to return.

They both sped out of Bastia, northward to Brando, boarded the waiting Italian Savoia-Marchetto, took off under cloud cover, and landed several hours later in a remote airstrip outside of Rome.

Sophia understood neither the complications of espionage nor the untenable position Victor found himself in with the Germans. They were allies, weren't they? Then why had Victor fled Corsica like a thief in the night? Victor tried to explain, but Sophia's innocent, uncluttered mind failed to grasp the nature of clandestine intelligence and its darker political implications. Victor's putative knowledge of Hesse's games, the black side of his hatred for Darius Bonifacio and the Mozarabe, and his concern for Sophia, made his position more difficult.

None of what Victor said made sense to her. She'd only wanted to learn of Darius's whereabouts. Instead, Victor had convinced her she must leave Corsica, if only to protect her brother and family. A more willing victim than Sophia could not have been found; she would have gone to hell and back to save Darius.

Now here she was in Rome in a suite at the exclusive Hotel Excelsior. The *contessa* and her daughter, Clarisse, Victor told her, had traveled south to a safer location.

Where in southern Italy could anyone be safe? German soldiers proliferated in every major port. Today, like every other day in this strange environment, Sophia rued the day she'd left Ajaccio and gone in search of her beloved Darius.

Assailed by mental anguish, she wandered about the room, gazing at the spendid wardrobe filled with beautiful clothing Victor had provided her. Through the black market he had pur-

chased garments of silk and satin, stunning suits and shoes
made by craftsmen in ramshackle basements. Black market
prices, Victor insisted, had forced him to pay dearly, but Sophia was unimpressed. She was homesick, lonely, confused,
and alienated.

What had she done, coming to Rome with an absolute
stranger? Was she mad? She must be deluded or naive beyond
redemption.

Sophia moved to the balcony, flung open the doors on the
late spring day, and gazed out at the rooftops of Rome. She
leaned over the balustrade, looked into the streets, at the people, seeing nothing. Her thoughts turned inward to Darius. His
four-year absence from Corsica had nearly killed her spirit. For
four years his memory had plagued her constantly. She found
him in the *maquis* or while daydreaming at the citadel or in a
stranger's laughter or in a song or a scent. He was everywhere
in memories of her childhood. She'd written him long letters
every day, filed them in a box in her room, waiting to learn
where he'd gone so she could hastily post them. She couldn't
believe he was still alive and had found no way to tell her. In
time she believed he was dead. That Christmas Eve day at the
cathedral in Ajaccio when she first set eyes on Victor Zeller,
she felt a sort of kinship with him, as if they were not finished
with each other. Victor's arrival at Terra Bonifacio with the
stunning news of Darius's presence in Corsica had brought her
to life again. *Darius alive!* She had lived each day praying and
believing Darius would come through the doors at any moment.

He had not. Morning, noon, and night, each day she had
waited and still no Darius. Her thoughts wandered back to Victor Zeller. Had it been a trap, or had the dashing Italian arrived
at Terra Bonifacio purposely seeking her out? That day, Dariana's disclosure of the close ties between herself and the
contessa had shocked them both. The earlier hostility of their
first encounter had dissolved. Later, her recollection of her
mother's exuberance and warmth had instilled in her a growing
need, an inclination to seek out Victor to learn the real truth
concerning Darius.

In Bastia, greeted by a stunned but quick-thinking Victor
moved by a blaze of last-minute decisions, she found herself
bending amenably to his suggestions, the image of her mother
cordially embracing Victor fresh in her mind. *Silly girl! What*

can go wrong while you are in the hands of the son of your mother's most precious friend? Victor had assured her he'd take her directly to the *palazzo*, to stay with Contessa Marie Clotilde.

And he would have, but in Rome it was altogether another story. The *contessa* was gone. Victor had apologized, secured a suite at the Excelsior, showered her with new clothing, perfume, and jewels and treated her like a princess. He submitted daily bulletins, but the *contessa* remained absent from the *palazzo*. At once caught up in the excitement of Rome—it seemed a stunning fairy tale city untouched by war—its history and antiquity fascinated Sophia. She naively failed to note Victor's rising passion, or if she did she minimized it.

Victor proposed marriage the third week. She refused. He suggested they take up residence in the *palazzo*. She refused. He described the dangers of living at the hotel with forged papers, especially with the Germans' strict checking of documents and the obviously shaky dictatorship. The Duce was ailing, he told her. His position was weakening in the face of all the subversives undermining him and his command. Besides, Victor might have to leave for Zürich at a moment's notice. He failed to impart the full extent of the dangers to him while in Rome, but he patiently painted a clear picture of the lies, subversion, treachery and deceit. He finally persuaded her that it was necessary for their safety to move into the *palazzo*.

In the great villa, it became impossible to assuage her loneliness. She missed her mother, Corsica, the *maquis*, her friend Arrigo.

Victor persisted in courting her.

It happened one night. He appeared, toting champagne and a culinary feast; in his pocket, a diamond bracelet. He begged her to marry him. She refused. He insisted. She desisted, grew sullen and suspicious of his motives. "Have I been duped from the beginning? I feel awkward, terribly lost in Rome. Perhaps you had better provide me proper escort back to Corsica!" she demanded hotly.

What knowledge has this Corsican waif of international warring boundaries? That at this moment Italy itself was besieged with a thousand enemies all vying for control? That Operation White Coral and a dozen other covert Allied operations were about to bombard all of Italy? That General Patton's army was about to land in Gela, Sicily, and General Montgomery was about to lay odds against who got to Palermo first?

Victor brought her none of the news propaganda, but Sophia, listening in secret to the radio she found gathering cobwebs in the servants' quarters, began to feel stranded. Victor's ulterior motives were growing apparent. Empty, desolate, and without hope, abandoned to her fate, Sophia fell prey to his seduction. She let him into her bed.

Why hadn't she protected herself against Victor as she might have in Corsica, as she had trained herself to do following the traumatic rape done her? She might have fared better had she put up a severe defense—but she hadn't. Instead, she reaped a vituperative outpouring of rancorous remarks.

"You're not a virgin!" he spat at her furiously. "You've no doubt consorted with brigands, Corsican peasants!" He comported himself as if he felt contaminated, his tone insulting, disparaging.

Sophia's temper came alive. Reaching for a sharp knife, pointing it at Victor's heart, she warned him never to darken her path again. And Victor, furiously incited, his manhood shattered by the revelation, cursed at her. "You'll never see me again, you bitch. I'll give you a week to pack your bags and leave my house."

The next week turned into a nightmare. Terrified, lonely, the political news in Italy frightening, Sophia remained in the *palazzo,* uncertain where to go. The Allies had landed in Sicily. All Italy was gearing for invasion. Before the week ended, gardens of flowers began arriving with gifts, perfume. Victor sent dozens of apologetic notes, asking forgiveness for his crass, unspeakable behavior. A true test of his love was to still desire her despite her previous despoiling. Sophia let the gifts pile up on a corner of the desk, unopened. Listless, she only lived to hear the news.

Never anything about Corsica!

Her moods varied from elation to despair, depending solely on the news. The sooner the Third Reich and Italy were felled, she believed, the better for her.

"The Allies have landed on the mainland!" came the squawky-voiced narrator in a moment of panic. "They've come to kill us all!" An hour later Sophia, dressed in a conservative suit and suitable walking shoes, opened the door to the cherry-blossom *palazzo*, ready to leave it forever. She stood arrested, rooted to the spot as one of the most beautiful women she'd ever seen entered the darkened foyer, more startled to see Sophia than Sophia was to see her.

"Buon giorno, signorina," said the apprehensive but stately woman. "I am Countess Zeller. May I be of some assistance to you?"

Sophia flung herself into the woman's arms and poured out her soul. Three days later, Sophia was shuttled north to a convent near Verona, carrying Victor's child.

In Corsica, Operation White Coral had begun. Darius and the Mozarabe grew testy, weary of the world of espionage, ambushes, battlement raids, and death. Their time was absorbed taking sightings, calculating tables of expediency, and encountering nothing but delays, delays, more delays. All they wanted was to get the damnable war over with. It left them no time to be human. If the war ended tomorrow . . . But it wouldn't. Tomorrow was light-years away.

By mid-June the colorfully garbed Moroccan *Trailleurs* arrived. Disciplined front-line soldiers were desperately needed to support the operational groups and guerrilla forces. The only chance of combating the Wehrmacht soldiers was to draw them out into unfamiliar territory. It was North Africa all over again.

It was the infighting between the British and OSS that exasperated Darius. The British were making attempts to control the OSS in all key theaters of war. What made it even more unpalatable was that the ubiquitous General Donovan had at least fifty sorties going at once all over Europe, taking Brad Lincoln and Jim Greer temporarily off OWC.

Darius, seated alone in his cell-like office, made a war-journal entry.

AUGUST 1, 1943

Il Duce has fallen from grace. What next? The OSS takes umbrage at my strategies and battle tactics. Their personal dislike of me and Corsicans in general is a stumbling block. They merely tolerate us. This morning they joined with British MI-6 suggesting a change of our operational base to a more central location south of Corte, near

Vizzavona. I rejected their plan outright, pointing out the perils. Central location without adequate cover facilities would be open to aerial detection and bombing. It would be out and out insanity. Axis tracking devices would locate our transmitters. Messerschmitts crossing the sea from Marseilles would deliver bellyloads of bombs and *finis* Corsica. Both British and American intelligence feed us substantially with information that keeps our units intact and spirited. Both Lincoln and Greer are substantial men who belong to a phantom world, one so different and alien to ours that we possess no way of measuring their needs against ours. Captain Lincoln's alienation since his return from London gets in the way of his work. He's an excellent man in his field, but his mind is tricky, duplicitous, and works in ways that at times become unfathomable, at times fatiguing. Pray God he sticks to his line of expertise and refrains from advancing strategy to my commando units. The Americans are all for getting the show on the road and over with, regardless of the consequences. Unfortunately, my concern with the consequences is dire. Not for any altruistic reason but one far more practical: I as a Corsican will be here to clean up the litter and rubble of dead men long after the Americans and British depart. I must answer for the bloody carnage and mass destruction, come victory or defeat.

AUGUST 28, 1943

Darius stood atop the battlement of the ancient Genoan watchtower, a fort a short distance from Cargese, a seaport on the west coast of the island. Nearby, German soldiers at an Axis arsenal and food warehouse were fighting off a surprise commando raid. Darius heard the distant rumbling of gunfire, bombings. Commandos and Mozarabe leaders, burp guns in hand, blasted away at the enemy, taking careful measure not to explode the arsenals—not yet. Machine gun bursts toppled four of the advancing soldiers into a bloody, spurting heap. The wild, impractical firing with shells falling short of their targets turned into an exercise in futility. Then, suddenly Darius heard booming sounds where no sounds should be. The booming sounds of .88's! He wondered if his exhaustion was playing tricks on him.

No! No tricks at all! The sounds were unmistakable—he'd heard them often enough. German guns! He recoiled from the unexpected shock. Before his eyes, the antiquated fort collapsed like a papier mâché reproduction. Darius called to his assembled men, plowed through the smoke to assess the damage. The towers were gone, the wall breached. Bombs were falling at all sides of them.

He studied the enemy's vantage point. Dutch O'Reilly and Tamir Mandel appeared, wading through the dense debris of falling rocks and stones. "We'd best retreat. Those .88's will knock the shit outa us, Djebel! Shall I give the word, suh?" Dutch thought him mad to be standing like a golden statue in the midst of the fusillade.

"Not yet!" It was crazy, thought Darius, observing the skirmish. Why the protective aircraft support? Unless it was a pure fluke. . . . He'd memorized the terrain. A stone mountain upon which the old watchtower was built separated them from the waterfront warehouse. Darius peered through the embrasures, binoculars to his eyes in the setting sun. He spotted Limey Whitehall sprinting toward him, walkie-talkie in hand.

"Major! Major! German motorcycle recon approaching on the double! North to south on the coast road. Headquarters reports them sighted north of Cargese—south of Point Orchino!"

"Damn! Can the men head them off at Point Omignia?"

"I'll get back to you, Major!" Before Whitehall could contact radio point of origin, there was a deafening crash. Several mortar shells exploded on all sides of him. He contacted Darius. "Too late! Too late! They have passed Point Omignia! Over and out!"

Darius turned to his men. "We've only one chance. To take advantage of the eighty-eight blasts, the enemy would have to climb the hill, cross the rubble, take us at bayonet point, hand-to-hand. They can risk it. They have enough men."

Darius was correct.

Time worked against the Germans. The air cover *was* only a fluke. Some hotshot Condor pilot had seen a skirmish, dropped a few bombs to dust the inland perimeters, and taken off. The damage that had seemed devastating at the outset proved minimal. A few buildings, lesser arsenals had taken some direct hits. Walls were blown out but miraculously, a sizable number of weapons remained intact. The treetops had collapsed on the buildings in shapeless splendor and there were fires, fires on the lee side of the coast blowing out to sea.

A German officer in charge of defending the redoubt measured their disadvantages with calculating good sense. His hesitation in taking action gave Darius a distinct advantage. The road was blocked, and while the Germans removed the obstruction, Darius's familiarity with the terrain produced quick diversionary tactics.

Observing the coup from a nearby cover position were Captain Brad Lincoln and Lieutenant Greer.

While a few men kept the Germans busy with machine gun fire, most of the commandos, including Darius, scaled the seawall of the old fort, dropping foot by foot to the ramparts. They slid down the steep, pebbly incline and circled in behind the Axis breastwork, crept forward silently without warning, and snuffed out the lives of twenty soldiers.

Quickly his men donned the helmets and jackets of the German soldiers. By the time the motorcycle reconnaissance squadron came rumbling down the road to the Gulf of Sagone, they saw nothing unusual. Four German helmeted men patrolled the fortification as usual. The two guards at the gate were talking languidly.

Twelve German and Italian cyclists roared toward the gate. The leader of the group saluted with a "*Heil* Hitler!" The salute was returned. Machine gun fire opened up from the ramparts and cut the twelve men in two. "Two coups for the price of one and not a scratch," boasted Brad Lincoln. "Well done, Djebel! Well done!"

Darius said nothing. He left some men in charge, unloading this duty on the British. "Man the fortifications! Teach the Resistance how to handle the eighty-eights!" Darius spun around, tight-lipped and glowering inwardly. In spite of all the activity, his mind wasn't on the fighting. Too many unanswered questions assailed him.

God, make it easier on me! Point out the real enemy! I implore you. Let Ghost-Dancer come alive! Let me come face to face with him, so I can ferret out the betrayers!

* * *

Darius stared at the names on the report: Sturmbannführer Hans Hesse and Oberleutnant Fritz Schmidt! In Corsica! They were the power now. Months ago, according to the report, the Italian intelligence officers had pulled out. The Germans were charged with the destruction of Operation White Coral! Darius handed the communiqué to Pascal. He read it, black eyes sparkling.

"We must get word to Zahara," Darius said dully. "If they find her, make the connection . . ." His voice cracked.

Pascal drew an imaginary line across his neck and rolled his eyes. Darius nodded. "The trick is to get into Bastia without detection."

Later Darius addressed the Allied force leaders. "We begin by accelerating the OWC thrust." He described Hesse and Schmidt, their infiltration of the Legion at Sidi bel Abbes, his grave concern over Zahara's safety. Marie-Pierre Marnay nodded and told an interesting story to Darius.

"It was Major Hans Hesse who discovered the manner in which we finessed our injured to the hospital. Every serious injury is fine-combed before admittance. The Mother Superior watches every moment. Guards are doubled at St. Florent. You see, Mario Dante died only moments before they discovered the deception." He chose his words carefully, his eyes on Darius as the information was digested.

Robert! Robert! You are dead! Dead! DEAD! May God have mercy on your sweet soul!

Darius turned from the others, his soul heavy, his heart like ice.

AUGUST 30, 1943

The Axis stronghold in the port of Girolata on the west coast between Calvi and Porto contained the largest stores of weapons and ammunition outside their main headquarters at Bastia. To minimize the importance of this vital redoubt, the Germans manned it sparsely to give the Corsicans a false impression. The garrison didn't lend itself to commando raids. It was isolated on a peninsula jutting over the Bay of Girolata. It took special tactics.

Sabotage! Internal sabotage.

Aided by Resistance agents dressed as maintenance men, the four guards at the arsenal entrance—two at the gate and two in the tower—were given a special potion in their wine after dinner.

On this moonless night, the commandos crept into the main arsenal while the guards drifted into a twilight sleep to commence the tedious process of emptying the ammo crates into large rollaway carts. The crates were replaced, neatly restacked as before. The men worked laboriously through the night, leaving moments before dawn. The guards, coming to shortly thereafter, thought they had fallen asleep. A cursory scan of the warehouse bore no signs of the deviltry done them this night.

Darius and his men chuckled for days. When the time came for their enemies to depend on the weapons stores, they'd be in for a stunning surprise.

BOOK TWO

I have a rendezvous with Death
When spring brings back blue days and fair
It may be he shall take my hand and lead me
Into his dark land and close my eyes and quench my
  breath
It may be I shall pass him still
I have a rendezvous with death.

—Alan Seeger (1888–1916)

Chapter Fourteen

The long-awaited, meticulously planned offensive finally began.

Beginning at Fort Bonifacio at the southernmost point of Corsica, the Mozarabe-trained Resistance and operational groups attacked and overpowered all Axis garrisons, decimating the German and Italian redoubts. They then worked their way up both sides of the east and west coasts toward the capital city of Bastia. Once finished at each garrison, they left skeletal crews of ablebodied soldiers to guard fortifications and man communication centers. The radio depots proved invaluable, confirming the movements of four separate divisions working in perfect synchronization.

The Resistance knew how it felt to be losers against the Germans. *It would not happen again!* If they lost, the dead bodies of Frenchmen would be lined up one street and down the next from one end of Paris to the other. Prisons would overflow; the hostage ratio would swell to a hundred dead Frenchmen for every German killed. *No!* It would never happen again. This

277

thought, paramount in the minds of the Resistance fighters, became the driving force behind their zeal.

The difficult campaign, fraught with dangers, was never one general matching wits against another. The enemy had no faces, yet wore everyman's face. German and Italian uniforms were the enemy. Anyone caught wearing one was instantly shot. They took no prisoners. Progress came bit by bit, battle by battle. The fighting forces along the east coast made rapid strides, since it was nearly a vertical drive from north to south. Due to its complex morphological design, numerous sweeping baylines, inlets, and hidden coves, the west coast mileage was nearly double that on the east, and progress along it became a series of closely fought altercations.

The battles took shape as commando raids, successful ambushes, attacks against fortifications and garrisons or against anything marked with a swastika or flying red, white, and green banners. German and Italian regulars, unfamiliar with rugged mountain fighting, were euchred into mountain regions and ancient citadel ruins where their soldiering became impotent against the guerrillas. Often the Axis soldiers would spend agonizing hours in pursuit of the enemy, making their way to the tops of the ruins to find them empty. Disgusted, annoyed, embittered by the ragtag charades, their guards down as they left the ruins, they were usually ensnared and machine-gunned.

Each village became a battlefield, a land of ambush and enfilade where vigilant drivers of donkey carts and alert wandering shepherds were members of the vast silent army of the Resistance. Redoubts were toppled, confiscated. Food stores were blown up by the enemy to spite their attackers. The spirit of the Resistance inflamed Corsican hearts. The legends of centuries came alive, and for the first time in modern history Corsicans inclined themselves to collaborative efforts against a common enemy.

The island, a spectral giant from a distance, also came alive, glowing with fire and black smoke, throbbing under the booming sounds of artillery fire. She spewed flame and smoke like an angry, pulsating volcano.

At Axis headquarters in Bastia, no one had an inkling of what was happening beyond the environs of their city. Resistance fighters manned communications centers at each garrison, intercepting any and all warnings bound for the capital city.

SEPTEMBER 10, 1943

A blow was struck at Darius's emotions. His brother, Daniel, was killed in a skirmish at Brando on Cape Corse. An hour later news of Sophia arrived. An agent had spotted her in Rome in the company of the Italian Major Victor Zeller. *In Rome! With Victor Zeller!* Darius sent word that he wanted more proof. A day later a photograph arrived. It was Sophia and Zeller!

SEPTEMBER 12
PIETRANERA, CORSICA

The current objective of Operation White Coral was to overcome enemy fortifications and weapons arsenals. Darius approached this tactic as he might have approached a personal gunfight. Excited by the prospect, aroused beyond any possibility of restraint, he wanted to meet his enemy head-on and crush him swiftly, but he could not. He advanced a wooly scheme to his men. They reacted as if he were *cafard*. By midnight on this night, they'd know if he was crazy.

Darius understood the dangers he ran by splitting his forces to engage in the planned charade, but it was vital to instill in the enemy a false sense of security. The men for this assignment were handpicked; the fiercest, fastest, canniest of his desert marauders and commandos, those cronies who had fought off the Arabs at El Bayadh.

At the outskirts of the sleepy seaport village, a short distance from the largest weapons arsenal the Axis maintained on the island, Darius confronted his men. "From here on we play games with the Germans and Italians. We will be silent, tricky, on the alert. Here you make a noise, there you creep. You look but hide from being seen. Make the enemy edgy, alert. Key them up, make them jumpy, agitated. Any trained soldier worth his salt will sense you instinctively. But you will remain hidden until the explosives planted in the smaller, subsidiary arsenal and fuel depot are detonated. You will demonstrate no skills, understand? No matter how it hurts, retreat, draw their fire into the hills and scatter."

A tired, haunted Brad Lincoln and gaunt-faced Jim Greer, never far from Darius, listened and observed him critically. Lincoln, unable to restrain himself, remonstrated, "You're taking a hell of a chance risking your best men, Corsican."

"Precisely why I am using my best men. They know exactly what I expect of them."

And they did. Before midnight, they had implemented Darius's scheme. By prowling about at night, they had the advantage of withdrawing in the dark. Attention brought to one area, when they were at an opposite location, drew wild firing from the Axis soldiers. Monkeys and cats, they were all over and nowhere at all. By the time the Germans and Italians mounted pursuit lorries, those remaining behind were busy trying to put out the fires. Up in the hills, squads of *Trailleurs* covered the commandos until they scattered. The pursuit lorries found themselves chasing phantoms.

Darius permitted one telephone call, one radio dispatch to reach Bastia Axis headquarters. Grinning broadly in an underground radio depot, earphones to his head, he listened. The relayed message inflated Darius's twenty men to legions with a blown-up verbal picture painted of their attack, pursuit, and victory.

Within days the situation changed with dramatic suddenness. Weapons supplies were short. Food was scarce. Displaying touches of larceny and black-marketeering, the men left behind to man the garrisons had absconded by boat, loaded with guns, food stores, ammunition. To be robbed of victory at the last moment was anathema to Darius's nature.

A change in tactics and strategy was in order.

Brad Lincoln needed a swift boat. If he could get to Sicily, make contacts with AMGOT (Allied Military Government of Occupied Territories), he felt certain he could requisition enough supplies. There was no time. No time to find a boat, no time to waste transmitting signals for help and running the risk of an enemy intercept. Darius huddled with Marie-Pierre Marnay and Claude Montreaux. They listened, their low spirits suddenly infused with galvanic energy. Darius was not finished with them. "I am not averse to making a pact with the devil to defeat the Axis. Understand?"

No matter the recent past, no matter their differences, no matter the recent intelligence reports on Montreaux and Marnay, this was not the time for judgments. The war must be won in Corsica at all costs. And Darius meant to deliver on the dotted line.

SEPTEMBER 15
BASTIA, CORSICA

A lemon-yellow dawn burst above the horizon on this special day. Special because it marked that momentous pause between the preparation and execution of a battle. Solid ground forces formed an impenetrable line of defense closing all southern roads. Shepherds, hillsmen, and soldiers were united in this last decisive thrust. On Cape Corse, beginning south of Brando to the outskirts of Pietranera, a phalanx of additional ground forces stood preventing escape to the north. For the Axis soldiers, only one escape existed—the sea.

Darius, sensing the cynicism of the British, the French, and the OSS agents, was the first to admit he expected the impossible. The odds were against him in this final plan. Resistance fighters, ill equipped to fight the sophisticated, technically trained Axis soldiers, were the dirty-tricks specialists, cloak-and-dagger experts, purveyors of misinformation. Commandos were hit-and-run artists, excellers in ambush, superior in hand-to-hand tactics. For this reason Darius had sent for the Moroccan *Trailleurs* to balance the need for technicians. But the combination of these forces was of no use without weapons. They might last a week—no more. Darius could not chance catastrophe. They needed a miracle.

A miracle! The miracle proved to be Lomay St. Germaine. Zahara!

SEPTEMBER 20
MAYOR'S VILLA, BASTIA, CORSICA

The splendid villa, despite the blackout curtains, was ablaze with brilliant light, laughter, music, and a banquet fit for kings. Fresh seafood delicacies, meats sautéed in fragrant sauces, fresh fruits and vegetables were served in dazzling china, wines in magnificent crystal. "Nothing is too good for the Axis soldiers," said the rotund collaborating Mayor as he toasted his guests.

Fresh bouquets of wild flowers formed centerpieces between sterling silver candelabra. German and Italian flags on sterling bases crossed at the stems were woven in and out of the decor along the tables. Musicians played a potpourri of sentimental Italian and German tunes. Periodically a German grew misty-eyed, an Italian melancholy, but the emotion would pass in the laughter of the next joke or imperial boast. Plainclothed and uniformed SS and SD officers mingled with the guests, eyes alert for any possible euchering.

Dressed in a spanking new uniform and bright brass, Sturmbannführer Hans Hesse arrived at the Mayor's villa with his aide, Fritz Schmidt, determined to forget his archenemies this night. On the ride from headquarters to the Mayor's villa, he'd been deluged with the insufferable Voice of Freedom. Zahara's infuriating voice laced with boasting and purposeful propaganda had blasted away at him. In the distance a detonation or two reminded him of the proximity of the dangers facing them. What he didn't understand was the failure of the mainland to give them air cover. But then, nothing had made any sense in days. Radio dispatches to Marseilles had been scrambled, distorted beyond coding. He'd sent a trio of couriers working in tandem to Marseilles by boat, unaware they'd been captured and were held incommunicado. Sardinia was falling. Would Corsica be next? Not if it were up to Hans Hesse! In Sardinia, there were three hundred thousand soldiers still loyal to Il Duce, despite his fall from power in July. In addition, portions of the Herman Göring Division were still there. How could they succumb?

No matter, he was here this night to forget Zahara and the Resistance and to erase from his mind that both were put here on earth by Satan to bedevil him, drive him mad. Hesse was not a joiner. He considered himself several notches above the usual Wehrmacht officer. Bureau VI of the RSHA were the elite. Tonight he needed the company of real men. The gala, the gesture on the part of Corsican collaborators to fete him and the Italians had been accepted. Bracing himself, he moved past the greeting politicians and took his place as guest of honor.

Instantly the room went dark. Algerian musicians took their places on a small bandstand in an alcove in the large baronial salon. Waiters poured vintage spirits and French champagne.

Intermittent spotlights swept the room, holding, then slowly expanding until a half dozen sensuous belly dancers appeared in the swelling lightbeams, swaying their bodies rhythmically in erotic gestures, finger cymbals clinking in a tintinnabulation in time to the music. The look-but-don't-touch expression flashing in their dark eyes just visible above the silken yashmaks caused temperatures to rise, temples to throb, mouths to gape. Full, wispy, golden silk skirts whirled wildly like delicate ostrich feathers until the music stepped up in pace to a crescendo and the dancing grew frenetic. A clash of cymbals sent spine-tingling expectations soaring. The dancers were blacked out and another spotlight formed at center stage, bringing attention to an indefinable object. As the spotlight widened, a shroud of black spun silk spattered with shining gold objects became the curly jet-black hair of a woman. In her raven hair were fastened shimmering butterflies. The coppery skin and black onyx eyes glowed under the light as the voluptuous, oiled body came into full view.

Gasps of delight escaped from the audience, such was the star's electricity. Dinner guests craned their necks to see over their neighbors' heads. Amazed, anticipatory expressions crept into their features. Seven sheer pastel silk veils hung from a jeweled girdle hugging the dancer's gyrating pelvis. Her torso was nude under the veils. The lights went up, revealing the other dancers around her.

Zahara, the star attraction, knew her own magnetic powers and moved with full command of her artistry. Her body moved ten beats faster than the other dancers, as if she were gathering into herself the energy of the others who, one by one, moved off the stage like liquid shadows, leaving her to perform as she had never before performed in her life.

The legendary Dance of the Seven Veils, made famous by Salome, was performed as only the inimitable Lomay St. Germaine could perform it. The music modulated, the tempo seemed to express her inner libidinal pulsations. She was Delilah, Jezebel, Sheba, Messalina, a combination of every meretricious, attractive, seductive whore in history. Mysterious were the libidinous communications she succeeded in arousing in each man. She made love to her body with each veil, transferring her personal erotica to each guest as if he were the personal recipient of her passion. Voluptuousness personified, her dark eyes held promise of anything her body failed to communicate. The movements were animal, disciplined, stimulating; she shimmied, she swayed, she undulated her wares until her audience felt their throats parch with desire.

They reached for wineglasses filled with sherry and champagne, anything to relieve the heightening signs of passion. A few massaged their crotches with lingering gestures.

In the background, members of the Mozarabe dressed as waiters stood in the shadows, watching, waiting, marking time. Fritz Schmidt tensed at the sight of the dancer. He nudged his superior. "There is the *Nachtisch ich brauche*!" He laughed suggestively. "That black-haired beauty with the gold *papillon* in her hair." He stopped at once.

Hesse wiped his lips daintily on a *serviette,* glanced over his shoulder at the spectacle mesmerizing the other guests. He groped for his glass case on the table, lifted the glasses from it, and with his one good hand adjusted them into place over his nose.

Gold *papillon*?

Zahara!

Successive detonations burst inside his brain. He stiffened, eyes fixed on her. Images flew past him: flashing white teeth, sinewy voluptuousness, undulating movements—his enemy!

"St. Germaine!" his voice, in a hushed whisper, cracked. "Fritz, you see who it is? We've found her!"

The dancing grew more frenzied, the music and drums ascending to an unbearable tempo, difficult for her to match. Such velocity of movement pitched the revelry of the guests to a higher plateau of sensuality. Her dark eyes fixed on Hesse subtly, quick to sense his recognition.

Music drowned out every strange noise and utterance in their midst. It struck Hesse in an instant. "Wherever Zahara is, the Resistance is nearby, Fritz!" he muttered incautiously, then, "*Dammit! Dammit! Hör auf damit!* Stop it, I tell you! Stop the music! Schmidt! Make them stop!" He turned in his chair just as the adjutant's head fell forward to the table with a loud thud. He was gagging, his hands grasping his throat, bulging eyes staring helplessly, the fingers of one hand clutching at the air. Hesse, tensing, glanced at either side of him in the candlelit room. He heard a series of dull thuds.

The music had stopped. The dancing had ended. The players on stage as the lights came up were not the former players; they were soldiers, guns at ready, standing in a dull, eerie glow of unreality.

The venom had begun its paralyzing journey, spreading through tissue, nerves, blood, and bones until the strychnine burst into their brains. The victims valiantly tried to effect an exodus, darting in all directions, tearing at their flesh with their fingernails, vomiting their dinner, squirting a bloody flux.

Hesse, no more nor less godly than the others in the final throes of death, tried to push back his chair. He made a silent appeal to all the Frenchmen coming toward them from the alcoves to observe the mass death. Hesse, on his hands and knees now, fighting for life, caught sight of Darius Bonifacio. He could not talk. His swollen, shredded tongue hung from his mouth like that of a panting dog, blood spurting on his chin and chest. He looked up into Darius's cold, set features, then at the other fearless, unforgiving faces who had survived his brutality in the prison of Abu Hammid. The men of the Legion stared at Hesse, remembering every brutality meted out to them: third-degree burns that left them scarred; the honey on their bodies, the insects swarming over them; the rock piles, the beatings. And they showed him no mercy. Each man, Delon, Whitehall, Longinotti, O'Reilly, Pascal, and the others of Delilah's Dream who remembered Hesse, Schmidt, and von Luden, spat at the obscenity at their feet.

A freshly slain sheep's head came flying through the air, landing with its glazed, staring eyes fixed on Hesse's body. Behind them a cheer arose. The Corsicans ran forward to pick clean the clothing of the slain officers. Engaged in a boisterous rodomontade, they shouted an ancient Corsican cry of victory, "An island atrocity is settled by a Corsican!"

By October 4, 1943, Corsica was liberated. The Italians and Germans had retreated, and in a last-minute effort raced to the Italian transports anchored in the waters surrounding Corsica.

Now to prepare for the liberation of France!

Smoke spiraled up from the burned rubble, rising up through the shafts of early morning sunlight. Darius and the Mozarabe had rounded up the Corsican collaborators in the public square near the government buildings in Bastia. Darius read from a prepared text.

"You are convicted of collaborating with the enemy, of profiteering, of abusing the people in your jurisdiction, denouncing the poor, innocent citizens, handing them over to the Germans.

Because of you, they were executed. Because of you, many young Corsicans are dead. What say you to these charges?"

"Convicted?" the Mayor exploded in a burst of curses. "By what authority. What legal right have you to presume judgment of me? I am the duly constituted authority until—"

"Did you or did you not deliver into the hands of the Nazis two thousand Corsican men and women to work in German factories?"

"I was under orders by the Vichy government—"

"And I, Signor Mayor, take orders from the Free French!" Darius nodded grimly. The firing squad stood at attention and took aim on his signal and fired. Darius stared at the carnage, muttered softly, "That, Sophia, Robert, and Daniel, was for you, wherever you are."

Brad Lincoln, Jim Greer, and the English glanced at the dead men, then at Darius's cool composure, unable to read the man.

"The OSS has captured its first large enemy territory, Sardinia, an important outpost of Fortress Europe. Now we have Corsica." Brad Lincoln raised his glass of wine in toast to the gathering of Allied officers at the newly confiscated military post. The Resistance and Mozarabe leaders were all there, edging closer, clustering about, talking, drinking, smoking rich Havanas, nibbling at the lush buffet.

"Corsica," continued Brad, "and Sardinia are as important to us as Sicily is to the invasion and conquest of Italy. Both are vital to the Allied effort. With ports and airfields on all the islands, we can gravely embarrass the rear areas of the German armies in Italy and France. Corsica especially is within hit-and-run distance of what is now part of the front line of Fortress Europe, the coast between Nice and Leghorn, which is extremely vital to us."

"The battle of Toulon has commenced. For us, it's on to Marseilles."

Darius listened, knowing he had things to wrap up in Bastia first. Suddenly, the men all heard the dreaded, terrible sounds. They cocked their heads to listen. Had they heard it or imagined bombings? Wailing sirens brought the men back to their senses. It was nothing imagined—it was real! The familiar sounds were appalling but made them intensely curious. They scurried to the windows in the large, spartan room adjoining the communications center at the former Axis headquarters, scanning the sky.

"*Jesus H. Christ!*" Lincoln shouted. "I see it but don't believe it. Bombs falling from the bellies of American B-17's."

Buildings exploded, crumbled to pieces. Human beings in the streets went wild, running for cover. Shock, disbelief, and fear registered in their panic-stricken eyes as they paused to stare, mouths agape, at the enormous birds overhead.

Americans? What the hell is wrong with them?

Corsica had been liberated. The Axis soldiers, those who could, had escaped by boat and air to Italy. Corsica was Allied territory. Why then, were the Americans bombing them? No one was as shocked as Lincoln and Greer as they exchanged murderous glances.

Terrifying explosions hit, split the earth, forming deep craters in what had all the earmarks of an intensified bombing mission set to destroy Corsica. Flushed with fury and displeasure, Brad ran into the radio room. "Get those *fucking* fly-boy eagles on the horn!" he shouted to the operators. "Don't they fucking know the difference between Marseilles and Corsica?" he screamed at Greer.

Six communications experts manned the radios, desperate in their attempts to intercept the B-17s' radio frequency. "Bastia, Corsica, to bombardiers. Identify yourselves! Do you read, fly-boys? You are bombing Bastia, Corsica. Answer, *goddammit*, do you read?"

A hollow voice shrouded in static came through in the distinctive Texas drawl of a Southerner. "Come in, Bastia . . . over. We read you."

"What the *fuck's* going on up there, cowboy? This is Captain Bradford Lincoln, OSS, Special Forces detail. Why the fuck are you striking Corsica, you sons of bitches?"

"Your rank and squadron leader!" Lincoln demanded, shouting into the microphone. "You'll hang for this, fly-boys!" He cursed aloud, using words and phrases alien to the listeners. However, there was no mistaking the intent behind his words.

Moments passed. Static, squawking interference, shrill, ear-splitting sounds shuddered through the building before a meek voice came over the loudspeaker. "Sorry Captain, sir. Miscalculation. . . . Glad you caught the error."

"Error? *Error!* You fucking greenhorn! I'll have your stripes for this. Who's your navigator, you crazy bastards?" He was livid.

Delon signaled to Lincoln, pointing to the radar blips. "The bombers are passing out of range, *mon capitaine.*" Lincoln flung the microphone and headgear hard against the wall. He clenched his fists, shook them skyward. "I'll get those sons of bitches. I'll break them in two. We could've gotten killed!"

They could hear the aircraft climbing as the strike was curtailed, but the bellyload of bombs dropped on Bastia was still doing its damage.

Darius, in his attempt to assess the damage and round up emergency salvage squads among the panic-stricken men, bolted outside, zigzagging through the disemboweled alleyways of the Bastia redoubt, avoiding explosions and spreading fires. The narrow cobbled streets were filled with panic-stricken people and dead, bloodied bodies. Struck by an exploding incendiary device, Darius was lifted into the air and propelled backward by the impact. He fell to the ground and reached for his head. Blood streaked down his face into his eyes. Pain stunned his senses, fire burst in his brain, disorienting him. His gun fell from his hand; he was unaware of the struggle between life and death gripping him. A dark, sinister circle closed in on him, long sinewy fingers of blackness beckoned to him. He lost consciousness.

"It's a miracle. Exploding shrapnel . . . through his temporal lobe. . . . He still lives." Elliptical, strained voices, curt, clinical, and devoid of emotion, came to Darius in bits and pieces. Behind burning eyelids death's-heads paraded, flinty specks of fire sparking from empty eye sockets. Focus, when it came, arrived in pathetically slow spurts of blinding light. The pain seared his eyes. He tried to avert his head; he could not.

Darius regained full consciousness at St. Florent Hospital a month later. Everyone told him it was a miracle that he lived. The shrapnel had barely missed vital gray matter. Life for Darius had meant flight and pursuit, struggle, endless desperation. It had meant wanting, needing, hurting, being hurt; it meant long days, endless nights filled with specters of the past, visions of a future. Death would have meant letting go, the end of everything he knew. The end to the hopelessness of existence.

The end of feeling and knowing. But somehow life had prevailed.

Darius, on the mend, arrived while a battle raged within a storm-beleaguered Marseilles. A fierce and tireless contingent of warriors—five thousand in all—trotted in knee-deep mud beside heavily laden mules through the hills rimming the city. The Gourmiers, Berber tribesmen from the Moroccan Atlas Mountains, together with the Mozarabe, provoked official concern about their violent instincts. The French General de Lattre spoke brazenly to Captain Brad Lincoln as they observed the plodding men doggedly pursuing their goals in the raging storm.

"I vehemently protest their participation in the battle of Marseilles, Captain. I have no intention of allowing our troops to be contaminated by these men."

Brad Lincoln turned to Darius as he entered the coterie of brass-buttoned officers. "You hear, Djebel? It seems the new C.O. cannot agree with our motives. I don't think he likes us."

Darius, recalling the words of General de Gaulle, *"All France must rise to insurrection to get rid of the enemy,"* leveled the "Corsican eye" on the General. It was deadly and described perfectly what Darius thought of de Lattre or any French officer who dared denigrate the Mozarabe of the North African fighting forces.

Lincoln, Greer, and their British counterparts fumed. Darius calmed their outrage quietly. "No matter who enters the warring arena at this stage of the game, hear my words and hear them well. Should any of you men leading squadrons have the opportunity to . . . You saw how we operated in Corsica. Repeat the victory, *dammit*!"

Three weeks later the OSS, the Resistance forces, and the Mozarabe peeled off from the original attack force and followed a French tank force column in the dismal rain through massive German roadblocks into Marseilles. Under a bombing run the men took cover. The skies exploded. Flashes of white lightning against thunderous black skies multiplied the ominous German air strikes. People were running everywhere. Potholes erupted along the muddy road in the strafing and tanks burst into fire and flame and black smoke. Visibility was nil. The

column, taking cover where they could, moved forward to their
rendezvous.

Darius, pale and gaunt, calmly observed the activity from a
cover position. ''Defenses are anchored on redoubts in the port
area to the north and on the heights of Notre Dame de la Garde
to the south. On the whole, Captain Lincoln, the defense system
seems impressive, but actually it is riddled with gaps. What
say we exploit it?''

Brad's eyes lit up. ''Now you're talking, Djebel.''

He and the British split up, taking squadrons through the narrow
back alleyways of Marseilles. They would rendezvous at
the intersection of a crossroads to Martigues at the edge of Marseilles.

That day at three P.M. it seemed like midnight. The aerial
strafing and dive-bombing had ceased. Decoy squads of commandos
had lured the enemy in directions away from the rendezvous
with short bursts of gunfire. Brad Lincoln glanced at
his watch.

*Sons of bitches! Where the hell are the Resistance leaders
flown from Paris hours ago?*

An abandoned building stood less than fifty yards away.
Brad and his squadron waited, watched, then on signal crept
forward, encumbered by rain gear and heavy artillery. They
made it to the building, crept along musty, rat-infested corridors.
Brad shivered.

A shaft of dim light pierced obliquely through an open door.
He crept forward cautiously, service pistol in hand. Later, he
remembered only that he had leaned against the wall, kicked at
the door, and crouched in the open doorway when a woman
came at him, knife in hand, her face bloodless, expressionless
in the dim shadows. It was a woman of the Resistance in a sexual
interlude with Marie-Pierre Marnay, the Resistance leader
who should have rendezvoused with them earlier. Brad remembered
the gleaming metal of the upthrust bloodied knife in her
hand and the blade coming at him, a blood-drenched man on
the bed. He hesitated a moment too long. The skillful thrust
plunged straight into him. A whirlwind force coming from behind
him forced the thrust to be averted, missing his heart. The
impact staggered him, knocked him unconscious.

He knew nothing else, remembered nothing. Two weeks

later, he was told the name of his rescuer—Djebel, the Corsican.

Darius had sent a coded message to General de Gaulle: *"Today, D plus 13, in Army B Sector there is no German not dead or captive."*

Chapter Fifteen

ROME
SPRING 1943

The Zeller *palazzo* was deserted, the windows, French doors boarded up, a padlock on thick linked chains entwined through the spiked iron fence at the front entrance. Inside was the eerie atmosphere of specters of a bygone past. Most of the furniture had been stored; the pieces remaining were dust covered.

Hidden in the attic, accessible only through a series of secret, labyrinthine passageways known only to the Contessa Zeller, were two refugee families. They were on the verge of collapse and desperately needed medical attention. Deborah, wife of Ugo de Portola, was ailing. Foodstuffs, stockpiled survival stores that had been more than ample four months ago were dwindling. The de Portolas and Gallezzianos, the Jews, draft dodgers, and military officers could not continue without help.

Marie Clotilde dispatched an urgent message to her personal physician, a man she trusted without qualification. Dr. Rinaldo Corsi arrived at the appointed rendezvous in the gray-misted drizzle of a rainy evening.

Clotilde, gaunt, emaciated, and weary, waited downstairs at

the villa's rear entrance. She saw the physician alight from a taxi a block away. He opened his umbrella, padded along the bleak, uninviting *strada,* clutching his collar to him with one hand, the other holding umbrella and bag.

Clotilde reached out of the shadows, pulled him into the dark corridor, holding an oil lamp to his face. Relieved, she fell against him, giving thanks to God for his safe arrival. Corsi's expert eyes detected lines of stress and slight degeneration in the otherwise beautiful face. "Don't fuss over me, Rinaldo. There are a dozen others who urgently need your attention." She blindfolded him apologetically, led him through the myriad passageways, unburdening her soul at the dilemma of the poor, wretched, defenseless souls in her care.

An hour later Dr. Corsi counseled his patients sternly. It was a warning: they must leave the cold dampness of Rome for warmer climates. "Consumption is inevitable if you remain. Inactivity, immobility in the dampness of a stone building creates a private hell for the elderly among you." He forced a tonic on Clotilde. "If you fail to make your own health a priority, how can you assist anyone in need of your help?"

She thanked him, blindfolded him again, walked him back through the darkness to the alley entrance. The rain was swirling in the wind, lashing at everything in sight. "Go with God, Renaldo, *tante grazie.*" Briefly she watched as he opened his *paracqua* to shelter himself and fight his way in the torrent along the *strada* to the square. Clotilde lifted her face to the rain, let it beat against her skin, invigorated by the fresh smell. She returned to the dismal, huddled refugees, forcing a cheerful countenance, words of hope.

The next morning slightly before noon, Clotilde and the twelve refugees tensed at the alien sounds. For the past four months, their ears had been attuned to indigenous sounds. The slightest irregular noise was cause for alarm. On their feet at once, the wretched souls huddled together in the damp attic, eyes widening in fright and concern. The plip-plopping of rainwater leaking through unrepaired tiles on the roof sounded like kettle drums in the silence. *Dio mio! What is happening?*

Marie Clotilde, her finger to her lips gesturing for silence, discerned the sounds of workmen hammering, sawing, tearing down walls. Curious, she moved stealthily through secret corridors between the walls, peering through several peepholes aghast. *What the devil?* Clutching at her breast as if to still her wildly beating heart, she moved farther along the darkened corridor, pausing at a vantage point where she could see into the larger salon.

Crews of workmen? Renovating the palazzo*? By whose orders?*

This was not to be believed! She stared at the men laying drop cloths on the floor as other men set up ladders and prepared to paint the interior. Draperies were down, jalousies removed from the windows. A conservatively dressed man wearing dark glasses strutted imperiously about like a landlord, snapping orders. Periodically he referred to the blueprints held in his hands as he explained his plans to various artisans.

Wherever the stranger moved, to whichever room he gravitated, Clotilde followed through inner corridors, her anger on the upswing! Just who did he suppose he was? Giving orders in her domicile! The flamboyant, fraudulent landlord ambled through high-ceilinged rooms, spurred by more than a decorator's fancy. Her curiosity heightened, Clotilde suddenly stiffened. Her hand flew to her mouth to stifle her shock. *It can't be!* God help her, it was Michael Bertelli!

Michael! Dear God, it's Michael! How many years has it been?

She suppressed the rising urge to clear her arid throat.

As Miguel exited the larger salon, she anticipated his moves, ran along the dim inner corridors washed periodically in a ray of light by some minuscule opening or crack in the wall. She peered at him from various peepholes, and as he ascended two at a time the spiraling marble steps to the second floor, Clotilde scaled the hidden steps and secret passageways, determined to learn why he had endangered his life to come here.

Michael nonchalantly entered the upstairs study. He sent two of the workmen downstairs, closed the door behind him, and padded across the room to the fireplace wall. He glanced sharply at the walls, then choosing the east wall, began to tap it lightly. He called her name softly, knocked again, paused, listened, and repeated the process. His voice became imperative, demanding. "*Clotilde!* Clotilde, answer me!"

Both panic-stricken and relieved, reluctant to inculpate him in her felony, yet desperate for help, Clotilde's heart pounded savagely. She took a step, tremblingly opened a wall panel. "Michael," she called to him in a hushed whisper.

He spun around and, locating the open panel, stepped inside the cramped quarters, searching her face. "Clotilde?" His voice was tentative, alarmed at her appearance. "Thank God I found you!"

Clotilde's features were ashen. She seemed absorbed in thoughts that were not to be intruded upon. Then, "Were you followed?"

Bertelli, gravely disturbed at the dark hollows under her eyes, understood Rinaldo Corsi's concern. Her eyes glowed maniacally, a sign of physical neglect, and near starvation. Taking instant command of the situation, Michael instructed her, "Prepare to leave at midnight with your people. A lorry will come."

"We are too many. Save them—"

"Don't argue. Do as you're told. Rinaldo spoke of an alley entrance. Is it next to the tailor?"

She nodded. "Between *numero quatro* and *cinque* there is a door. Knock five times, pause, then repeat it."

"Very well. Midnight sharp." Michael heard footsteps. "Go, we will talk later." Quickly he reentered the study, rolled out blueprints, and greeted the returning workers and a foreman.

At midnight, Clotilde and the refugees boarded a camouflaged Italian army lorry and drove south out of Rome buried under mattresses and boxes of produce. Stopped at several checkpoints, the driver's credentials inspected, they were waved on through toward Naples. High above the sleepy fishing village of Positano, the lorry turned south, entered the guarded gates leading to the Bertelli villa, and stopped in a stable. Behind guarded walls, the refugees alighted from their cramped quarters and entered the villa.

For the next week they ate, slept, and bathed luxuriously, sunned themselves, dreamed of hope and a better future away from enemy eyes.

Michael Bertelli arrived the following Friday. He found Clotilde on the balcony. They stared at each other in a molten silence. He resisted the desire to draw her close to him, while Clotilde wanted nothing more than to yield to him, fall into the comfort of his strong arms. Could they resurrect the love once shared? Twenty years—an eternity—had passed.

"You look the same, Michael. You haven't changed." She groped for words.

"Where is your husband?" The words were brash, brittle.

"Switzerland, I suppose. Once again you come to my rescue?"

"You left me for him!" She heard the despair, contempt, acrimony dripping from his words. "I pray you are sublimely happy."

"Will it help you to know the truth? I am miserable."

"Don't. It was cruel of me. Don't talk about the past. I can exist only if I deny that time between us ever existed."

"You cannot deny our *son's* existence—not Darius!" She turned from him, gazing out at the calm beach, the sea beyond, the shadowy island of Sicily in the distance where she'd learned an army was garnering strength to oppose the Axis. "He's a year older than Victor. I wonder where he is. Did Dariana ever tell him the truth?"

"Clotilde, stop! We have enough problems. Ours—yours—your friends'. We must provide sanctuary—"

"It's true? The rumor. You joined the *partigiani* in Trieste?" The look in his eyes was answer enough. "*Why*? In God's name, *why*?"

"You ask *why*? You've lived in terror these past many months—"

"How do you know?"

"Oh, Clotilde. There is nothing I don't know about you."

"Are things so bad you joined the *partigiani*?"

"I don't believe you ask such naive questions. Are you immune to what is happening in Italy? Il Duce betrayed us. Our factories, retooled, now produce warring weapons and vehicles at an alarming rate. And without our permission! The industrialists were not consulted. The *fascisti* confiscated everything. We, all of us, have been sucked up into Hitler's dreams of conquest—no matter the cost. Worse, *cara mia*," he added scoffingly, "your *protector*, Il Duce, seems not in possession of his mind. Some say it's drugs. Most rumored of all causes is paresis."

"Then it's true? Someone plots Il Duce's demise?"

"Daily, my dear Clotilde. Daily his enemies multiply."

Michael moved closer to her until they stood inches apart.

"You left me for him," he repeated, crestfallen.

"I did what I had to do." Here in paradise, on the same balcony where once passionate love flowed between them and white bursts of gunfire nearly ended their lives, nightmarish ghosts, never laid to rest, still haunted both.

"Despite your cruelty to me, you still leave me breathless," he said softly, stroking her face, committing the new Clotilde to memory. He brushed a strand of hair from her face. Michael's features relaxed, the lines of fatigue melting into tenderness, heartfelt concern. "Clotilde, you must listen very carefully to what I tell you. You are in grave danger. By harboring the Jews, you imperiled your life. You are on Colonel Dollman's list of potential troublemakers—an enemy of the Axis powers. They have not forgotten you are married to Zeller. Il Duce is losing his grip. His protection means nothing."

"You tell me nothing I haven't known for the past six months, Michael."

He placed his fingers over her lips. "Shh. Listen. By now, you and I, all of us, do what we must. I cannot dissuade you from doing what you feel is the humane thing to do. But you must think of your son, Victor, and of Clarisse. If you will steer your refugee friends to safety, be aware of the pitfalls and innate dangers to those you love dearly. Take caution. Trust no one, understand? My men will guard you here. In the storehouse—the cellar reserves contain a six-month supply of food. Ration it wisely. I have provided, through my man Guido, new identity papers for you and your refugees. The Jews are rumored to be aiding and abetting the antifascists. Retaliation came four days ago. Their temple in Rome was desecrated. Kappler's men wrecked everything, including the sacred Torahs. Jews are being press-ganged everywhere. You must exercise caution and sagacity. Since the Nazis occupy Italy, the Jews are no longer considered Italians, but Jews, enemies of the state. And you, by harboring them, become an enemy of Italy and Germany!"

Clotilde studied him, only half believing his words. Her world, the world she'd known, was crumbling all around her. What insanity was this? "I will go to your uncle Cardinal Bertelli."

"Oh, my dear sweet Clotilde. You don't understand. The pa-

pacy lives in fear too! There is a man, Monsignor O'Flaherty—
but he is being watched. I shall think of something.''

Clotilde watched him toss his seaman's jacket on a cane-
backed chair. He affixed a shoulder holster to his body,
checked the gun. The metallic blue sheen of the gun jarred her
to reality, forcing her to reconcile the past with the present
strife. She seemed unable to catch her breath.

"Should it become dangerous for you to remain here, I will
get word to you. Oh, my beloved,'' he murmured, inescapably
drawn to her, gathering her in his arms. "Take care of yourself
and your daughter. It's war and death out there, not life, galas,
and endless whirlwind parties. There will be an Allied invasion
soon. And when it comes, Italy will be a shambles. I couldn't
bear it if you became a part of it.'' They embraced, they kissed,
and time dissolved. It was yesterday again, two decades ago,
and they were rapturously in love, the nightmares dissolving in
a kiss. "I must go, *carissima*. Remember all I've told you and
try to understand: what must be done, must be done. Trust no
one save my man Guido.''

She watched the man she'd loved for two decades, the father
of their son, Darius, leave the balcony, descend the steep rocky
incline to the whitecapped waters below where he boarded his
waiting motorboat. Her heart turned over.

Neither Clotilde nor Michael had sensed the curious, inscrutable eyes observing their every move, ears listening to their
most intimate words. "Who was that man?'' Clarisse, seven-
teen, wide-eyed, precocious to a fault, approached her mother,
her manner aloof, frigid. Clotilde, unguarded, flushed rapturously, her eyes on the scene below.

Clotilde held out her arms to embrace her daughter, but the
girl resisted, noting the flush of crimson on her mother's
cheeks. "He is a kind, wonderful man, a very precious friend.
Our host and benefactor. Oh, Clarisse, he is the quintessential
man,'' she added in a voice rosy with love.

"Have you no shame, Mama? What would Papa say to find
you in this stranger's arms?''

Clotilde turned sharply to her daughter, then quickly glanced
back at the bay, saw the motorboat approach the *Golden Medusa*. Her mind burst open like a lush pomegranate with a hundred magnificent memories buried in each bleeding seed, and

in those split seconds, she relived every moment of her past with Michael, forgetting her daughter.

"You act as if my father is dead!" Clarisse snarled, running to the balcony to see what it was that made her mother teem with life.

"Perhaps he is dead. He *did* abandon us, didn't he, darling?"

Clarisse clamped her hands over her ears. "I won't listen. He'll come for us, you'll see!"

Clotilde turned to her daughter. "The *signore* risked his life for us—all of us. Have you no gratitude, Rissi?"

"None. I loathe him. I wish Papa were here." She ran from the patio in a burst of temper.

Clarisse was not easy to know. An annoyingly private person, she brooded, seldom ventilated her thoughts. Her intelligence was never reflected in her handsome features, and if she possessed any innocence, this was equally subdued. Finishing school had failed to produce Clotilde's expectations. It merely escalated Clarisse's contempt of woman's role in the world. Clotilde, studying her daughter at length, felt certain Amadeo's darker nature germinated in her, and the thought drove her crazy. She'd walked too many floors at night, unable to sleep thinking of the demons flying about in her daughter's future.

Clotilde and the refugees had just finished dinner when Guido, thirtyish, sandy-haired, dark-skinned, with eyes like glazed black olives, appeared on the balcony off the open-air dining salon. He was beckoning to the *contessa*, a note in his outthrust burly hand.

"*Con permesso, contessa,* I was instructed to deliver this personally into your hands."

Struck with foreboding, Clotilde approached him, accepted the sealed note, broke open the seal, and holding the letter under a dimly lit light fixture, scanned the contents swiftly. She blinked hard. "Is this authentic, *signore*? I mean, did it come from our host?"

"*Signora la contessa,* what do I know of authentication, eh? I do only what I am instructed to do."

"Did Signore Bertelli know of this communiqué before he departed?"

"But of course. It was he who gave it to me."

"Why didn't he tell me himself?"

"For such an answer you must question the *signore.*"

Clotilde swallowed hard. Assuming a regal bearing, she inhaled deeply, resolute in manner. "Very well, I shall tell the others. We shall be ready in two hours."

He shook his head. "*Con permesso, contessa,* there is no time. You must be prepared to leave within the hour. A half would be better."

She bit back the protest forming on her lips. "As you say."

A half hour later Clotilde, Clarisse, and twelve frightened humans safely boarded a lorry and were driven to a private airstrip and taken aboard a private plane.

Kloten Airport, Zürich! Marie Clotilde saw the signs; she didn't believe her eyes! *Michael had sent her here! To Zeller! Why?* Amadeo Zeller failed to greet his wife or her guests, but she knew he wasn't far away. Clotilde and her brood of refugees were whisked away to a hideaway inn outside of Zürich, and two days later were driven in buses out of the city to the Zeller château.

Greeted by a staff of servants, the wide-eyed, bewildered refugees, housed in the guest quarters of the great manor, were awed by the ostentatious surroundings high atop icy peaks overlooking Zürichsee, wondering at their uncertain future.

Clarisse, at once at home amid the splendid surroundings, did not wait for her father to appear. She went in search of him, found him at his desk in the library. Ecstatic, she dashed across the room, raining kisses on him, hugging him dearly.

Marie Clotilde stood in the shadows nearby, observing the touching scene through the slightly open doorway, unconvinced at Amadeo's forced, solicitous manner. She withdrew in silence, keeping well hidden. Amadeo's attempts to fulfill familial duties reeked of deceit—she knew him too well.

In the silence growing between the lord and mistress of the manor, Clotilde barely saw or spoke to Amadeo for a fortnight. He pretended to a constant, overburdened schedule. What free time he had, he spent doting on Clarisse. The closest thing to love and affection Amadeo demonstrated was patient tolerance. For Clarisse, who mistook it for parental adulation, it sufficed. She poured adolescent love on her father, and although he seemed to dote on her, Clarisse felt the undercurrent of fierce competition for his attention with an unseen force. Her youth afforded her little insight into his complex nature. She sensed that his interest, however convoluted, was centered on her mother. And Clarisse never took kindly to competition.

I hate my mother! Clarisse decided one day not to hide the feelings she had harbored for so long. *I wish she were dead!* She knew her father was the power in the family, believed her mother to be a weak woman without backbone. She had no real knowledge of the poisoned relations between her parents, yet aware that something ominous tainted the relationship, Clarisse took sides and decided to rid her father of the unpleasant situation as best she could and as soon as possible. She began by avoiding Clotilde, remaining in her own apartment more than usual, dreaming up plots. All sorts of diabolical ideas journeyed through her strangely afflicted mind. There was a naked delight in her eyes as she conjured up all sorts of remedies for the scenario being enacted between her estranged parents.

One evening following dinner, after Clarisse had retired for the night, Amadeo entered Clotilde's quarters, a luxurious suite on the second floor of the château opposite the spacious *galleria* and his personal study. The utterly feminine boudoir, a replica of the one in the Rome *palazzo,* had been decorated by Amadeo with the intent of disarming Clotilde, to make her feel comfort amid the otherwise hostile surroundings.

He knocked on the door, entered carrying a crystal-and-silver decanter of sherry and two glasses, inviting Clotilde to drink with him.

Seated opposite her in a high-backed, winged, brocaded chair before an inviting fire, Amadeo was polite, stilted, yet silky in his approach to her. He inquired after her activities following his departure from Rome. Clotilde described the turmoil and the subsequent assurance from Il Duce, who promised his protection to her and the children.

"It cost a small fortune to get you and Rissi out of Naples," he said with a touch of gloating. "The *partigiani* would sell their souls for gold."

She blanched for an instant. *Has Michael sewn together some conspiracy with Zeller? Oh, God, no!*

"Questions put to willing ears plus the lure of gold—"

"That's how you found me?"

"That's part of it. My spies kept the *palazzo* under surveillance, my dear Clotilde. How noble of you to help my people."

"Stop it! Don't pretend with me. I'm onto your sham."

"For enough gold the *partigiani* would—"

"They fight for a cause. What's your excuse?" Clotilde grasped his insufferable inference, but held her calm. *Michael wouldn't sell her out for gold—would he? No, I shan't believe it.* Clotilde sipped her wine, her features implacable. Internally she blazed with trepidation. *Hadn't she given up Michael for something considerably more precious than gold?* Their son, Darius? *Oh, God!*

Amadeo, observing her, contemplated their earlier years. "Once I thought you were entirely frivolous and without womanly merit. You have matured considerably, evolved into a tower of strength." He sipped his drink. For too long he had lived in the shadow of Bertelli's love. His departure from the fascist Rome scene and his daily loathing had added fuel to the rage burning inside him, spurred reminders of the cuckold he'd been—a laughingstock to those snide *fascisti*! He'd never forgive her, *never*! Always guarded, seldom spontaneous, yet given to capricious spasms of affection before his daughter Clarisse, he had never permitted her to view his fits of temper or violence. At the opportune moment he'd let the world know exactly how devoted a husband and father he'd been, the epitome of a doting father whose interest in his children must reflect extraordinary martyrdom and selflessness. Only he and Clotilde knew it was all an act. And he knew Clotilde wondered when the final curtain would fall on this incomparable performance of perpetual deception.

A look of benign congeniality came over Amadeo's face as he said softly, "You are breathtakingly stunning this evening, my dear. I admire your new coiffure. I think it admirable how you care for yourself, not permitting age to touch your spirit."

"Since compliments do not become you and are a rarity, what shall I credit them with? The Swiss air? You approve of my looks, is that it? Well, you've said what you came to, I hope. Now, if you don't mind, I have a headache."

"I came to ask of Victor. Have you heard from him?"

"How long have I been here? Now you ask about your son?" She sighed impatiently. "He is in Corsica."

"*Corsica!* The ironies of war always stagger me! My son is

fighting so my enemies will win. Il Duce's annexation of Corsica in his hope to build an empire will be his downfall.''

"Be thankful Victor is the Duce's favorite, especially chosen to head the Corsican assignment. Since your departure from the gladiators' arena, the Duce needs friends. He is ailing. He isn't the same—''

"He will live two more years," Zeller cut in with trenchant hauteur.

She cut him a sharp, reproving glance.

"Actually," he continued, "his demise is scheduled for April of 1945. Two more years is all he has. He and the Führer will walk in the valley of the shadow of death. The Allies have landed in North Africa,'' he mused. "Yes, by spring of 'forty-five it will be *finis* for your Duce and the German wolf.''

"I suppose some prophet has foretold the future to you?'' She watched Amadeo pour more wine into her glass.

"My dear Clotilde. *I am that prophet.* I move the wheels of destiny, set war machinery into operation. Haven't you guessed by now at the power clenched in these two hands?''

The silent threat unmistakably couched in his words shook her.

"You see, the *contessa* does not believe me. Yet she would believe *Signor* Bertelli,'' he said snidely as if addressing another person.

Clotilde drew herself up imperiously. "If you intend to rehash tired and stale business. . . . Nearly two decades ago you were proven wrong. You still remain unconvinced?''

"I was never convinced of your innocence. Recently someone described Bertelli's love life. It seems he was in love with a *contessa*—''

"For the love of God! You know how many *contessas* reside in Italy? My dear, they gestate like rabbits.''

"—a *contessa* married to someone high up in the *fascista* ministry. A *contessa* who bore his bastard. A *contessa* who made a cuckold of her husband.''

Clotilde felt the icy chill of death permeate her body. *Now, the moment is now! Give him nothing to chew on—nothing!* "You finished your wine.'' She crossed the room, held open the door. She carried herself grandly in a detached manner that maddened him.

"Your worst, most viable enemy, Amadeo, has been your

overactive imagination. I cherish no inclination to fathom your black-hearted thoughts. My God, you are tedious. I'd appreciate it if you'd rein those wild imaginings. I don't want Clarisse exposed to them.''

"Madame! You think more of *his* bastard than you do our legitimate issues. Don't deny it. I know that your trust was slickly converted into assets for *him*.''

"For whom, Amadeo?'' Her tone was frigid.

"Have it your way, *contessa*. The final accounting is due soon enough. Then we'll see who gloats best. You put your life at risk to save Bertelli's bastard!'' Contempt dripped from his lips.

"Is—uh—that what I'm doing?'' She raised her smoldering eyes to his. "Risking my life?''

"By God, madame, you shall see. Slowly the circle of death closes in on my enemies. My dear,'' he paused, back in control, "you look fatigued. I had hoped the rest here at the château would help erase the pale, gaunt, haunted expression.''

"Earlier you said I looked breathtakingly stunning. Have you amended that opinion? I suggest you do not concern yourself with *my* health. Rather look to yours.''

"Will you not permit me to be the concerned, solicitous husband I really am?''

"What you *really* are is tedious and revolting. My health is perfect. I detest maladies and refuse to coddle myself. Certainly I need nothing from you. What I don't understand is why you had me transported here despite the dangers in Italy. Now if you don't mind, leave me. I am tired.''

"Certainly, madame. Shall I first ring the servants to bring you a comforting glass of warm milk?'' A fraudulent mask of tenderness covered the deception admirably.

"Bother the devil! Leave my room at once!''

Amadeo bowed deferentially. He picked up the decanter and two empty glasses. "I shall take my bottled friendliness elsewhere.''

Clotilde slammed the large door behind him, fell against the carved wooden panels in near collapse. At her last glimpse of him, the obscene glimmer of triumph in his colorless eyes, she grew unduly panicked. She seemed unable to control the muscles twitching in her face. Her mind whirled with thousands of possibilities. He knew something! What in God's name had he learned? *Twenty years had passed.* Why couldn't he forget it? *A contessa married to someone highly placed in the* fascista *ministry! What does he know? What?*

Clarisse moved in the shadows and observed her father leave her mother's suite of rooms. She mulled over the conversation between her parents, her face screwed into puzzlement. She'd always sensed the loathing between her parents. Now any doubts she'd had were dispelled. Pure poison hung in the air between them!

In the next several days, Clotilde noted the changes in her daughter. Clarisse belonged in school, she thought, away from her father. She must separate them, she must. Amadeo's influence was corrupting the girl. *Then think, Clotilde, think!* School was again the only answer. Her last school had been a disaster. Clarisse had managed to convince Amadeo she'd fare better with tutors here at the château. *Over my dead body,* thought Clotilde.

It was winter. Morbid clouds of gray mist enveloped the château like prison walls obstructing the view of the panoramic Zürichsee. Switzerland's similarity to Austria had provided Clotilde some emotional comfort, but she still searched for an answer to her dilemma with Clarisse.

Clotilde sat in her room, daubing in oils before an easel. There was a knock on the door. "Enter," she called, adding a few brush strokes to the still-life canvas. She smiled at the sight of the dark-haired, bright-eyed Jewess Deborah Portola. "Come in, come in, Deborah dear. Why haven't I seen more of you and the others?"

Deborah came in hesitantly, then with bravado. "We were told you were ill and were ordered not to disturb you. But you look well, *contessa*. Is it anything we've done to offend you?"

Clotilde frowned. "No, no, my dear, not at all. I've been slightly ill, but not enough to keep me from your company." She didn't tell the girl she'd been forbidden to trespass the guests' quarters, instead said something about a quarantine imposed on them by two house physicians.

"We have felt so deprived of your company, *contessa*. Since we leave tomorrow for Palestine—"

"Palestine. Tomorrow?"

"—we wanted to see you before we departed. You didn't know?"

"No. I did not. This is the first I heard."

"It is not sudden. We have been preparing for two weeks."

"*Two weeks!* No one bothered to tell me. *Why?*"

Deborah, a slim wide-eyed beauty, shrugged with exaggerated innocence. "I thought you knew. It didn't occur to me—to any of us—that you would not know. Herr Zeller told us you were ailing—" She scrutinized Clotilde's pale face. "It's true; we were a drain on you, exhausted your reserves."

"Nonsense. I am fine. Tell me about yourself and the others. Are you happy to be leaving? You want to go, don't you?"

"What right have we to object? We must go or else we get no protection. But I am afraid. Word is that most who journey there die en route or are killed. Which fate is worse, *contessa?*"

Clotilde drew the girl into her arms, hugged her reassuringly. "None of us knows what's best in these frightening times. I am dismayed by the indifferent tone humanity takes against humanity. But you must have hope. Without hope there is nothing. Now brush aside the tears. You must help to inspire hope in the others, the older ones."

"Why—because the elders have no reserves of hope left?"

"Deborah, don't go. You are safe here. Why not remain?"

"But we cannot. Herr Zeller tells us we must go to Palestine. There is danger here, he tells us. Any day the Germans can march on Switzerland as they did on Austria."

"The Swiss are neutral! The Germans cannot—will not—"

"But they invaded France, all the other nations. They are powerful enough to do what they wish. Didn't Dollman succeed in Rome?"

Clotilde could not refute history. "You will write to me. Inform me of your progress. Do you need anything?" She moved across the room to a money chest, opened it and scooped out a handful of Swiss francs. She pressed them on Deborah. "Use it however you can, for whatever you need." She hugged the girl again, tears welling in her eyes. "I am so sorry, Deborah. The world is insane!"

The next day she stood in the atrium, watching the dozen refugees depart the mountaintop aerie in two lorries. Emotionally distraught, she clutched at the shawl around her shoulders. Of late she was ailing again. She felt icy, frigid, as if her blood were turning to an icy mass. *Dr. Corsi—I need you, wherever you are!*

Spring arrived before Clotilde realized she was a prisoner at the château. Restrictions imposed upon her and Clarisse tightened, and when each complaint brought a rash of new restrictions, she ceased complaining. Internally she held counsel with herself as plans formulated in her mind.

The world, no matter how dismal and bleak in the winter, always took on a virginal splendor in the spring. It was the first of May when the sun broke through the clouds of Clotilde's mind. She spotted a familiar face among the armed guards at the château.

Guido! The partisan! Michael's man!

Her unrestrained surge of joy was instantly arrested and masked at the silent warning in his eyes. At once impersonal, she moved past him, barely nodding.

Ten minutes later, ruminating over all the possibilities, Clotilde paced the thick-carpeted floors of her suite, at war with herself and her emotions. She needed assurance that all was well with Michael. How would she approach Guido? What must she do? What *could* she do? Her eyes, trailing to the letter on her desk, widened perceptibly. The school! She had corralled a school to accept Clarisse at midterm! Ah! That's it! The thought struck her just as a fickle triumvirate of imperious felines mosied in through the open door, three matched Siamese cats with azure eyes—Pandora, Pegasus, and Penelope. "You've brought me luck, my beauties," Clotilde murmured, picking up her favorite, Pandora, and stroking its sleek head. "Clarisse simply cannot attend school without proper clothing, now can she?"

Clotilde let the pampered cat spring from her arms to join her capricious co-conspirators in foraging about for whimsical playthings.

Clotilde sat at her escritoire planning the shopping spree as meticulously as she'd plot a coup d'etat. She must learn from Guido what was transpiring.

The next day proved tedious and boring and Clarisse turned out to be an absolute witch. Finding no opportunity to chat with

Guido, her sullen daughter commanded her full attention. Clarisse grew resentful, militant, and outrageously rude to her mother.

Was it ever not thus? Clotilde solemnly resigned herself to the chore like an iron-handed matriarch, a role she loathed. With Clarisse, there was no in between. Clotilde was forced into wielding the matriarchal scepter and received no reprieve from the role. It was nearly five in the afternoon when they exited the last shop in Zürich and boarded the Zeller Mercedes with several clerks at their heels, toting tilting towers of parcels.

Guido stepped in, took the parcels, and placed them in the car's bonnet under the watchful eyes of two plain-dressed, well-armed guards. Clotilde entered the sedan and sat down, exasperated and fatigued beyond endurance. Clarisse, a holy terror, was neither pleased nor placated by the shopping, the luncheon, or the prospect of having to go to school. She complained about her mother's inclination to rid herself of her daughter's presence, understood less her father's willingness to cart her off to school. In a morose, imperious snit, she had thundered about the château, raising hell with the servants, finding fault with them, ordering them about like chattel until even Amadeo had sanctioned her matriculation in school.

Growing pains were one thing, but Clarisse's black moods wrenched the heart and soul from Clotilde. At times she wondered if the girl had sprung from her own womb.

Luckily for Clotilde, she possessed a mysterious ability of blanking from mind the most painful things in life. She employed that tactic momentarily, dismissing Clarisse from mind, concentrating on Guido. How could she get him to carry the parcels to her apartment?

It took a mere order from her lips to achieve the deed. "Take the parcels to my suite, Guido," she snapped curtly.

Inside the suite, she managed to slip him a letter addressed to Dariana Bonifacio in Ajaccio between two Swiss bank notes, a smile on her face as she whispered, "Tell your *padrone* I am in grave danger here. Go with God."

Wordlessly Guido stuffed the money and letter into his tunic, tipped his visored cap, bowed deferentially, and left her quarters.

Three days later, Guido's body was fished from the Zürichsee. That night at dinner, Amadeo broke the information casually. "What a shame about the accident, my dear *contessa*. That new chap, the Italian we placed on staff in a position of trust, turned out to be a dealer in contrabrand. As the authorities tell it, he was making some deal in Zürich, was chased onto the high corniche by bullet fire. They say he lost control of the auto and went plunging into the Zürichsee to his death." Zeller's eyes remained fixed on Clotilde over the wineglass rim. Instantly she knew the truth. Her amplified fears mellowed only in the knowledge that her letter to Dariana contained nothing incriminating; it was written in a code only the two women could understand.

In the next several days, Clotilde rankled over the total absence of news. She knew little of what went on in the outside world save what Amadeo permitted at the château. Radio reception was censored; the periodicals received were at least six months to a year old. She wondered about the war, Italy, how her son Victor was faring. She never stopped thinking about Darius, not since Dariana's man had come to her—when was it, four, five years ago?—to ask if she'd heard any word about Darius. The mails in Rome trailed for several months; here in Zürich she had received none at all. How long had she been here? Months, years? Lately she seemed incapable of holding a thought. Always crystal clear in the past, of late they grew muddied and at times an old speech affliction returned to trouble her. And Clarisse . . .

Clarisse was of no comfort or consolation to her mother. Unwillingly preparing to leave for school, Clarisse thundered about the château amid a maelstrom of curses and brooding, poisonous looks, spouting unholy maledictions at the forces at work in her life conspiring against her. The day before her departure, Clotilde gathered her daughter lovingly in her arms, assuring her she'd be back in two months on vacation.

Clarisse, estranged from the *contessa,* did not believe her. And Clotilde's heart felt heavy over the girl's profound misery. She had no idea what went on in Clarisse's mind, that Clotilde herself, for as long as she lived, would be an impediment to the love the girl felt for her father. Clarisse had patiently vowed to mark time waiting for vacation to end this nightmare threatening her life. In two months, she would plot Clotilde's demise with an expert cleverness her father would laud. This time Electra—not Orestes—would slay their mother.

"Good-bye, Mother," she said in a docile, duplicitous tone. "I shall truly miss you. War is such a bother. Everything's so dreary. I know I've been an absolute horror. It's the war, really."

"Don't worry, darling, nothing will happen to you. Father won't let the war touch you. You'll be just fine."

Clarisse smiled. *That's more assurance than I can give you, Mother dear.*

In the next two weeks, Clotilde wondered if she was wrong about Clarisse. She missed having late afternoon tea with her daughter, even though Clarisse always spoke to her in a condescending manner. The guilt she felt concerning Guido's death was reflected in her attitude and comportment. She asked none of the servants for news, certain they would report her queries to Amadeo. Oddly enough, her health improved in Clarisse's absence. Zeller, thank God, was away from the château more often of late. She had heard him mention something about a trip to the Middle East. She wondered about Deborah and her family. She'd heard nothing, absolutely nothing in all this time. Was Amadeo going to the Middle East on similar business dealings? Oh, God, she supplicated nightly, would that he'd leave forever.

In his presence, her uxorial performances were commendable. She behaved with dignified respect, made a show of listening when Zeller launched into long, convoluted monologues concerning global affairs and the Luciferian dimensions of Adolf Hitler and Mussolini. At times Clotilde was appalled at the intensity of his loathing. He was like a beast feeding upon the beasts. But all this was fine for Clotilde. Let him rave on and on about anything save Michael Bertelli and the bastard son he'd sired that Zeller would one day annihilate. *Anything but that.*

One day during one of Zeller's frequent absences, Clotilde, in a bout of restlessness, cleaned out drawers in the bathroom searching for a bottle of calmative powder. She accidentally spilled the bottle, sending it crashing to the tiled floor, the powdery substance settling in piles like tiny snow drifts. She summoned a servant, Gerta, a middle-aged scullery maid from the lower chambers, and ordered her to clean the mess.

In need of a calmative and aspirin to ease the near-blinding headache, she ambled along the upper *galleria* toward Amadeo's suite of rooms, moving under the grace of wood-beamed ceilings, past the art collection, over the *galleria* bridge to his section of the château. The silence struck her midway. She paused, glanced below the arched bridge into the enormous sunlit, gold-tessellated foyer. No guards? The large clock below struck the hour. *Noon!* Perhaps they were at lunch? It was just as well. The area was *verboten* to her. All she needed was aspirin and a calmative. Surely Amadeo wouldn't begrudge her?

Inside the massive, elegantly furbished suite of rooms, she hurried on through to the large tiled and mirrored bathroom, opened a chest over the commode, found what she needed. Anxious to depart, she headed back immediately, retracing her steps to the double-doored entry. She paused, caught sight of a thick, leather-bound, gold-engraved tome on the desk.

Clotilde, seldom prone to prying—it was uncharacteristic of her to care an iota what Zeller did—was compelled toward the desk by something stronger than her own will. She turned on the Tiffany lamp, wondering at her own curiosity, when she gave a start. Something swished past her legs. She clutched at her heart, her breathing accelerated. It was Pandora, one of the Siamese cats. She had come prancing in the open door, rubbed against her, then capriciously pranced back and out of the room to whatever business she was about before. "You'll be the death of me, Pandora!"

Expelling a relieved sigh, Clotilde shuffled through the book, glancing at the accumulated news clippings. Most were about Amadeo's feats in the Fascist Party . . . speeches given at fascist social affairs. She flipped through them, picking up the pages from the back of the book. She was just about to close it and leave the room when she caught the date on one article; it was approximately the time of Zeller's exodus from Rome. She flipped on past, then suddenly flipped the pages back as an afterimage struck her. *Come on, where was it? Keep turning. Ah, here it is!* Her eyes danced over the article concerning the mysterious death of Amadora Bertelli Donatelli. *Amadora Donatelli!* Her mind skirted back to the unsolved tragedy that had shocked Rome society. *Why would Zeller be interested in such a news item? Why?* She flipped forward, caught sight of several follow-up notices, then—nothing more on the subject.

Clotilde stood there, myriad thoughts parading through her mind as she remembered cryptic words Zeller could have only known from someone who knew of the affair personally. In that moment it all dovetailed. She knew Amadeo was somehow involved in the woman's death. *Michael's sister's death!* She didn't know *how* she knew; she had nothing logical to fall back on. Nothing spelled it out, but she knew Amadeo was diabolically involved!

Her heart pounded furiously, sweat poured from her brow, and her stomach felt queasy. She fell against the desk, bracing herself.

Suddenly a scream pierced the dense silence, snapping her out of the momentary reverie. She slammed the book shut, pocketed the calmative and aspirin in her robe pocket, and rushed out the door in the direction of the scream. From her quarters? *What the devil?* She entered her apartment just as Gerta came screaming hysterically out of the bathroom.

"Look, look here, Countess!" She pointed inside the bathroom, a wealth of tears spilling from her eyes. "I had nothing to do with it. It is not my fault, Countess. *Es tut mir leid.*" The poor woman frantically pointed to the floor.

"What on earth is the matter, Gerta—" Clotilde stopped abruptly, her eyes on Pandora, the cat, cavorting about in the throes of death. Foaming at the mouth, she spit, arched her back, leaped about, came down stiff legged, and lay prone on the floor, her muscles taut. Finally her jaws opened and blood spurted from her mouth.

Gerta described the seizure in provincial German. "I was cleaning. In comes the cat. It licked up the powder off the floor. I tried to shoo her away, but she would not be shooed away."

"Get a box," Clotilde ordered sharply. "And keep the other cats away from here." Gerta left to do her bidding. Clotilde stared at the crimson streams spurting from the cat's jaws.

Clotilde refused to believe the alarming messages her brain signaled. She bent over several times before Gerta returned to clean up the mess. She touched the powder to her lips, grimacing at the taste.

Poison! She could supplicate to God all she wanted to make it not be true, but it was and she had to face the reality that someone wanted her dead. *Two guesses who, Clotilde!*

Surprised at her own Herculean strength for not succumbing to the iron jaws of fear, she took time for earnest reflection and evaluation of the situation. Thunderstruck at the thought of being victimized, slowly killed by the application of the calmative, she reflected on the methodology. She was flabbergasted. Amadeo wasn't ready to dispose of her yet. Clotilde had figured that would come *after* the war. She continued to pace the floor, sipping sherry, and when her mind unfolded the plot, she refused to believe it.

Clarisse! No! . . . No, it couldn't be! *My daughter? The infant I have birthed, suckled at my breasts, my own flesh and blood raised with love has turned against me? Tried to kill me?*

Since Clarisse's departure for school, Clotilde's health *had* improved, hadn't it?

For the next few hours Clotilde punished herself unmercifully as she thought about each of the principal players in this sordid scenario, trying to learn the motive.

Does Clarisse loathe me enough to plan my death? Why? Perhaps it wasn't her, but Amadeo. Yes, yes, it must be Amadeo! Only he had sufficient reason to detest me and want me dead!

But wait, it was Clarisse who purchased the calmative from the Zürich apothecary! Don't jump to conclusions. Amadeo could easily have slipped the poison into the bottle without Clarisse's knowledge. No! No, not Amadeo. Not yet. She was still his connection to a fortune, and Zeller had not asked for her signature on any legal documents—not that he needed it—but he had attained a modicum of stature, and since it was easy to do things the right way, why jeopardize loss of a fortune for a miscalculation of intelligence?

Yes . . . no! Could be . . . couldn't be. What is it to be? Who?

She didn't know, but was determined to find out.

She fled her apartment, scurried down the hall to Clarisse's quarters, flung open the doors, and stood on the threshold, peering at the numerous photographs of Amadeo gracing the tables and walls. His eyes, those colorless, detestable eyes peering down at her from every corner of the room, imprisoned her, annihilated her with their unwavering stare.

Clotilde began what ended up being the most painful episode in her life, other than the closeted love affair with Bertelli. She had no idea what it was she searched for, but she began at the desk, opening drawer after drawer, shuffling through papers. She felt a traitor. A surge of guilt spread through her like a hot iron.

She found nothing. Leaning against the desk to catch her breath, Clotilde's fingers clutched at the edge as she peered about the room. Her fingers encountered an obstacle. Quickly peering under the desk top, she found a key affixed to it.

A key! Admirable, Clotilde. A key to what? It could be anything!

She held it in the palm of her hand, wondering, moving about the room, in and out of wardrobes, searching for a lock to the key. Her thoughts raced over the recent past, at the information she had received from Mademe le Luce from the École Konstanz-Heiden, the school Clarisse had last attended. Clarisse had returned to Rome disgruntled, at odds with everyone there in authority.

Those letters from Madame le Luce! What else did they say? Strange, damnable letters concerning Clarisse's comportment at school! Clotilde vaguely recollected a superficial perusal of the letters: A list of grievances—none too serious—most bore the earmarks of usual childish pranks and adolescent behavior.

But had they been pranks?

Why hadn't she been more circumspect, examined them more judiciously? What had she done with the letters? *They are at the* palazzo *in Rome with the other nightmarish ghosts of the recent past, fool! Where else? What were Madame le Luce's words?*

Clarisse is strange. She does not mix well with the girls. Xenophobic to a fault, she makes no effort to relate to her classmates. She is mature beyond her years, espouses with prodigious understanding subjects relating to womanly things: thieving servants, women who flout the sacrament of marriage, philandering husbands whose peccadilloes she magnifies beyond credibility. She constantly provokes arguments, calls her classmates hypocrites blinded to the truth. *Madame la contessa,* your daughter is abnormally jealous of her classmates. She demonstrates a vile, unac-

ceptable behavior and temper. She is arrogant, refutes crit-
icism from any source. She is highly intelligent and of
course wealthy enough to buy École Konstanz-Heiden outright, as she has threatened to on numerous occasions. But
surely she is too young, too affluent, and from too excellent a background to permit green-eyed monsters to run
amuck inside her. Perhaps you should seek medical advice?

And on and on it went, thought Clotilde, rummaging in chest
drawers, one after another, searching for the elusive lock. She
found nothing! She peered about the room, lifting carpet corners, examining every piece of furniture, turning some upside
down, nearly inside out. If only she knew for what it was she
searched! She searched under the bed, between mattresses, in
pillowcases, behind the brass headboard, even tried to unscrew
the balls and spindles of the design. Nothing! Momentarily
flustered, Clotilde paused. The floodgates of her mind were
now open, and she was unable to dam the barrage of negative
indictments hurled against Clarisse. Memories waltzed past her
inner eyes. Unpleasantnesses, too harsh to be dealt with, dismissed at the time, now appeared like horned demons jeering at
her. She moved about the room, at a loss, sinking fatigued on
the chaise longue, staring at the key in her hand.
What does this fit? A box? Trunk? Diary? What?
She closed her eyes. Memories, thoughts floated past her and
with them, the contents of Madame le Luce's letters:

My Dear Madame la Contessa: It displeases me to write
you as always on an unpleasant note. The situation with Clarisse grows progressively worse. Perhaps if you confide in
your husband, a father upon whom Clarisse dotes, he might
find a solution to the promiscuity breeding inside her. Last
week she was absent without leave from school. We found
her in the village in a shabby room with several cadets from
the nearby military school. Need I be more explicit, *Madame*? Surely you can read between the lines.

My Dear Madame la Contessa: Our responsibilities in
assuming care of our students here at École Konstanz-
Heiden are enormous. We pride ourselves on instilling a

rigid discipline, stressing high morality. In the matter of your daughter, Clarisse, we admit to absolute failure. Unless you contact us within five days, we shall be forced to send her home to Rome. A refund of the semester tuition will be forthcoming.

So many letters! Accusations! Counteraccusations! Reprimands! Nothing had helped. Clarisse returned to Rome armed with a thousand excuses for what she cleverly alluded to as discrimination. She was loathed due to her family's wealth, her father's political posturing, the *fascisti,* anything but her own personality problems.

At times, watching the crocodile tears spring from Clarisse's eyes, the tightening tension of her heaving body with each excuse, you'd have thought the poor child had really received the shafting end of every stick. At one point, a sudden anxiety filled Clarisse. She knew that having gone this far, she must manufacture more lies, eventually spoiling the magnificently constructed edifice of deceit she'd designed. Cold and hostile, she condemned her mother for siding with the witch le Luce. Then, instinctively nagged at by some built-in warning monitor, she realized if she trespassed the line of credibility, she'd be in deeper trouble. She stopped to reconnoiter and let up a bit. Clotilde, intimidated by the endless procession of wild ravings, histrionics, and outward lies, put up defenses like the vanguard of an army. She knew if she looked deep into Clarisse's soul she would encounter the loathing and violent passion of a transgressor.

Clotilde recalled the time vividly now. The Nazis had been vigorously asserting their coercive legerdemain in Rome and she had no stomach to view the image of her husband in her daughter. Besides, her friends, the Portola family and their relatives, were in dire need of safe refuge. Clarisse's problems, kept in check, were quickly relegated to the dustbins of Clotilde's priorities. What occupied her every waking moment was the survival of the twelve refugees, herself, and her daughter.

Clotilde lay back on the chaise, eyes trailing languidly about the room, ceiling, ornamental trims, and wainscoting. Her eyes fell on the gracefully carved étagère across the room. She studied the molding on each door, the curved domes above the doors at either side of the center, and sighing with magnified vexation, glanced away. Just as quickly, her eyes darted back, her curiosity heightened. Her eyes fixed on a hatbox. She sat very still, staring . . . staring.

Slowly she arose, dragged a chair into place before the large enclosed shelving, and stepping on it, retrieved the hatbox. She stepped off the chair, blew off the dust, and placed the box on the bed. She untied the ribbons, shoved aside the white tissue, removed two hats.

Voilà! A small box. Her heart was pounding when it opened with the key. For a moment she hesitated. Had she unearthed a Pandora's box? Well, no matter. She carried the box to the escritoire, lifted from it a small brown leather diary tooled in gold with the name Clarisse inscribed upon it.

For an hour Clotilde read and reread the indictment in her daughter's handwriting, her earlier suspicions looming vividly in her mind. She sat for a time, staring at nothing, activating memories she had buried long ago. Then, undaunted, she closed the diary, wiped it, and replaced it in the box, placing everything in neat order. She moved out of the room imperiously, every inch a woman of regal bearing.

A shudder swept through Clotilde, a sense of premonition which activated inner tremors and heightened fears. It wasn't easy for her to face the facts she earlier suspected, that her daughter was a murderess and she was the victim.

In her quarters, behind locked doors, she sat before the fire, sipping tea. Gerta had removed all traces of the dead cat, Pandora, and the lethal drug. No wonder she had felt better in Clarisse's absence! She had stopped taking the calmative. Prior to her departure for school, what solicitous concern she had extended, persuading her to take the calmative twice, even three times a day! *God, Clarisse! Are you truly infected with Amadeo's hideousness?*

Oh, Christ, Clarisse! How many doses before the fatal blow?

She sat in the darkness, refusing dinner, watching Gerta light the kindling in the fireplace, thinking she must flee Zürich. She must return to Rome—to Positano—even Corsica! Anyplace but Zürich! She was alone now as never before, without allies. What must she do to remain alive? She must talk with Victor unless Amadeo had hardened his heart against her! God knew where to find Michael in this brutal war.

Darius! Oh, Darius, my beloved son, where are you? I am in trouble and I need you desperately.

Then she remembered Cardinal Bertelli in Rome!

And Monsignor O'Flaherty!

One or the other, preferably Cardinal Bertelli, would send an appropriate message to Michael Bertelli to explain her plight, wouldn't they?

The thought struck her. Amadeo wouldn't deny her religious participation. She needed the trusted services of a Catholic priest somewhere in Zürich. *The confessional!* Through the sacred tenets of the confessional she could get a message to the Cardinal.

It was the perfect time. Zeller, preoccupied with an all-consuming project in the Middle East had thankfully kept his distance. There were many nefarious comings and goings at the château, and along with the increased renovations under way, a constant influx of workmen appeared daily on the scene. After Guido's luckless fate, Clotilde kept her distance, barely looked at them. Servants had let it be known Zeller was preparing to leave Zürich for an extended stay in the Middle East. Servants had a way of knowing everything she'd been unable to learn. Although they were all in Amadeo's pay, surely one or two detested him.

They did. And Clotilde made her plans. The moment Amadeo left for the Middle East . . .

Eugen Schuller, a.k.a. Ghost-Dancer and a dozen other aliases he'd assumed in his young years, walked out of an alcove in the cloister at Kappel, awaiting the arrival of Contessa Zeller.

"Zürich is a predominantly Protestant city, my dear," Zeller had told his wife in one of the rare truths to spill from his lips. "I have therefore arranged for one of the priests who visit the cloister regularly to hear the confession of the Carmelite nuns to sit with you and accommodate you in your religious pursuits. Kappel is a mere fourteen miles distant. You shall be helicoptered there and back."

"How thoughtful of you, Amadeo," Clotilde had replied, unable to reconcile this unusually grand and noble gesture with her monstrous husband. If she had only given it consideration . . .

Zeller had relayed the story to Ghost-Dancer, who presently

wore the ecclesiastical garb of a priest. He was not bald, but wore his naturally curly light brown hair cropped close to his head. A shaven circle of hair had been carefully sculpted for his priestly role. Thick, steel-rimmed glasses were set into place over his nose. How perfectly this artist at disguises changed his appearance to accommodate his roles. He had to, or it was curtains for him. So far luck had been on his side in all skirmishes, except for the one involving the Corsican. Ghost-Dancer thought about this as he ambled along the pebbly path between parterres, alongside the open loggias in the stunning floral garden of pearly goldenrod, joe-pye weed, hydrangea, globe thistle, blue salvia, and Silver King artemisia.

The Contessa Zeller would be a snap. First he must cultivate her trust, he had been instructed, and only then, after her confession, would he exterminate her. She was an important requisite only in raising his worth in Zeller's eyes. In a brief period of time, he'd learned how formidable an enemy Zeller could be, just as the Führer had emphatically cautioned. Eugen's fascination for this satanic man and his inestimable plans was something to be revered *and* used. He saw an association with the financier as a means of advancing his own ambitions. Power was his god, the common ground upon which the greatest minds in the world focused and met in brotherhood.

Now as he moved along, reading from a Catholic missal, neither Zeller nor the Führer nor Marie Clotilde was on his mind. His thoughts centered on Anton Schuller. Anton . . . dear Brother Anton who was presently ensconced at Cambridge in England, being tutored in political science and affairs of state under the cover of "Anthony Harding," was another matter. Planning and engineering Anton's death so he could assume his brother's identity would present several obstacles. The bastard had made too many friends, friends who could detect the slightest nuances of change between them. No doubt existed in Ghost-Dancer's mind that he could assume Anton's identity without the slightest resistance, but complications did arise from time to time to jam the most sophisticated machinery.

The false cleric turned the pages, glanced up at a covey of black-garbed nuns moving in a body toward the chapel. He glanced at his watch, scanned the sky. The chopper was late. His eyes scanned the epistle, barely reading the words.

For the past six months, and until Zeller summoned him,

he'd been at Cambridge living with Anton. He had studied his brother like a germ on a slide, memorizing his habits, friends, the subjects he was studying. He had scrupulously searched his brother's mind until he felt secure in the knowledge he'd amassed. The moment had to be perfect for the death and disappearance of Ghost-Dancer.

It couldn't come until after he had plenty on Zeller, after the *contessa* was exterminated *and* after he traveled to St. Bartolemo, met his brother on the pretext of imparting vital information concerning their inheritance and their vendetta against Amadeo Zeller, their sworn enemy. And then—instant eternity for Anton. He, Eugen Schuller, would disappear and let it be known that Eugen was dead. Word would spread that Ghost-Dancer had met his demise. Then which of his old enemies would trouble themselves to search for him?

He would assume the Anthony Harding role in England, then on to America where he intended to play havoc on the political and foreign-policy system of the nation. Anton had written several important papers concerning espionage and the affairs of state in the changing world. His papers on Russia were sterling. Eugen had memorized them all.

The faint *putt-putting* of that new contraption the helicopter drew his gaze up. It was coming in for a perfect three-point landing.

"Now, *madame la contessa,* I am ready for you."

As the helicopter prepared to land, Clotilde thought back to her encounter with Sophia that day nearly nine months ago.

It had happened shortly after Victor's arrival in Rome before she and Clarisse had decided to become Deborah's benefactors and save the two families, before the *palazzo* had turned into a mausoleum.

She had left Clarisse in Capri, returned to the turmoil of Rome, took funds from her personal safe, and was ready to depart when in walked Sophia. She had stared transfixed at the young beauty, aware of her remarkable resemblance to someone from her own past.

Sophia, standing in a shaft of sunlight, had stared at the regal *contessa,* searched the azure eyes, took in the blond honey-colored hair tinged with gray, and knew the woman at once. "I am Sophia—"

"Sophia, the woman who has captured Victor's heart," she had interrupted. "My son is so in love with you," Clotilde said, taking her hands and leading her to the sofa in the sitting room in her suite. "Yet how tormented he is. He tells me you will not marry him."

Sophia sat primly next to the *contessa,* clear-eyed, honest, and open. "I cannot marry him, *signora.* How many times I've attempted to explain the unexplainable. We are worlds apart. The Corsican mentality, my upbringing . . . He will not listen."

"You must be homesick, child. How old are you?"

"Very homesick. I am nineteen."

Clotilde gasped. "Victor plucked you from your home at so tender an age? Were you not betrothed to another? What must your mother and father think? Have you at least written them? Perhaps you wish me to do it for you. I shall explain that you are safe, that my son is infatuated with you and wishes to marry you. If they know you are under my protection in these precarious times—"

"No! Please do not concern yourself. They would not understand. Let them . . . It's best they think me a victim of the war—that I am dead."

Clotilde studied the seraphic face, the splendid bone structure, the natural beauty of the young woman. "Sophia, it's very strange. You remind me of someone. The feeling refuses to abate." She agitated the air about her with a straw fan, thinking as she did about the girl and friends, dear friends, she could contact in Ajaccio. "I have friends in Corsica who will speak for me."

"I am Sophia Bonifacio, *contessa,*" she said, stressing the last name.

"Bonifacio! Dariana's daughter?"

"*Sì, signora.* I wish to bring no misfortune to your house. Corsica is a land of vendetta. My family would bring vengeance upon your house for Victor's actions. He has been good to me. If I were not Corsican, raised to think, feel, and believe as a Corsican, it might have been different between us."

"You *sound* like Dariana. The resemblance is uncanny!" Clotilde summoned a servant, ordered tea for them. "Thank God one or two stayed here to watch over the premises," she said quietly. "Now, suppose you tell me all about it. Surely I can help to mend the broken fences."

"If any still exist. Oh, *contessa,* there are too many. You are not a magician."

A quarter hour later, after tea, after an outpouring of her soul, Sophia dried her eyes. "Promise me you will never tell Victor about the baby. *Never!*"

"Then you do love Victor? When is the baby due?"

"I do not hate him. It is simply that I cannot love him. My heart belongs to another. Oh, I am so ashamed. To talk about it brings a feeling of degradation I cannot handle, yet deep in my heart I am unconsolable. I am in love with a man I cannot love, yet I carry another man's child. Don't you see?"

"No, child, I'm afraid you lost me. *You are in love with a man you cannot love?* Who, for pity sake?"

"My brother. My brother Darius. It is forbidden to love one's brother as one would cherish a husband. All my life it's been Darius. Oh, *signora,* I am so miserable! What have I done to earn God's vengeance in my young life?"

Clotilde opened her arms, and Sophia fell into them, her head against the other's heaving breasts, sobbing her heart out.

Clotilde sat there frozen, her features stark, anguished. The collapse of her own world was imminent. The Germans were running Rome. Il Duce, her benefactor, was being subjected to coup after coup and had fled the city for a time. The Jews, no longer under her protection, had fled. She thought of Monsignor Hugh O'Flaherty, of Cardinal Bertelli and the new refugees hidden in the convents beyond Rome. In one convent, Notre Dame, her friend Deborah was hidden. It would be the only place for Sophia now. The only place she could keep Victor from learning of her whereabouts would be Notre Dame Convent. But should she keep Sophia from Victor? *Oh, God, if only I could right the wrongs of the past.* Her one sin, the sin of infidelity, was the most grievous sin of all and had already ruined two lives, hers and Michael's. Now it threatened the second generation: Darius and the innocent Sophia, who were in love and rightly so, since they were not blood related. How could she tell Sophia the truth without shaking the foundations of her own trembling world, without bringing immediate destruction and death to her and to other innocents? She could not. The burden grew cumbersome, unbearable. She rocked Sophia in her arms. "Your brother, this Darius you speak of, is he much older than you?"

"By two years. Is it such a sin to love one's brother? As a child, Darius took me for long walks, talked to me about many things, of faraway kingdoms, the stars. I have loved him from infancy. I say it unashamedly."

"Does he look like you, child? Whom does he favor—your mother or father?

"No one, *signora*. He is tall, with powerful muscles, eyes of verdant seas, hair the color of golden chestnuts. But I have not seen him in a long while. He disappeared one day. Oh, *signora*. I cannot talk about it. Victor appeared one day at our house, seeking him, insisting he was an enemy of the Axis nations. He called him Major Darius Bonifacio." She recounted the story, explained how she had traveled to Bastia to learn more about Darius.

Clotilde wanted to tell her the truth that day, to send her back to Corsica, but she could not. Too many lives hung in the balance. Instead, she helped Sophia disappear into the cloister at Notre Dame. Later when it grew too dangerous for Deborah and the two families to remain, Sophia was sent to Verona, ironically the city of the Shakespearian lovers Romeo and Juliet. Clotilde had supplied her with enough lire to keep her for a few years after the baby was born. "Then, Sophia, follow these instructions. Take the child, return to your family in Ajaccio. You have merely to say that your husband was a war casualty." She outlined the rest of the plan. "I will provide you with the name of an Italian soldier who died in action. Give that child his name. Perhaps after the war, when things return to normal— and God willing they will—the people you love will find it in their hearts to forgive you."

The helicopter was coming in for a perfect three-point landing now. Just prior to leaving today, Clotilde had received a note reading: "Bernadette was born three days ago." Clotilde smiled a sad, reflective smile, thinking of Victor's flare-up upon his return to the *palazzo* to find Sophia gone. He had blamed Clotilde.

"Sophia's disappearance is unacceptable, Mother. I entrusted her to your care and you betrayed my trust!" He had left Clotilde's suite that day and returned to Sophia's rooms, searching every inch for his beloved. The loss had left him shaken, frantic, dolorous, unable to cope. She'd taken no clothing except what she wore. Jewelry, furs, perfumes, exquisite lingerie, all of it remained neatly stacked in drawers in the elegant dressing rooms adjoining the boudoir. The articles remained there for the next ten years until he finally had the flat refurbished. Collecting all her things, he saved them as icons. For nearly two years after Sophia's disappearance, Victor had detectives search for her. He abandoned the search when the investigators inclined to believe Sophia had met with foul play. Their curiosity had increased. Nothing of value was missing? Who disappeared without taking something? What else could it have been? Foul play must have descended upon the hapless victim.

Clotilde stepped from the helicopter, hugging her warm sable coat around her in the icy cold wind as she walked forward toward the young priest warding off blasts of wind, his cape flapping behind him like the wings of a giant bird of prey.

Thank God! A kaleidoscope of thoughts worked intricate designs in Clotilde's mind. For too long she had carried the burden. Now the life-saving release of confession would ease her pain and dissolve the tangled, unrelated clumps of memories that haunted her and left her agitated. Surely in taking her confession, the priest would transmit a swift message to Monsignor O'Flaherty or Cardinal Bertelli, wouldn't he?

She had so much to confess. How frightening that she must trust one man, one person, to so many things. But she had to, hadn't she? Anyway, speaking to a priest was like speaking to God.

"Father?" she called above the sounds of whirring rotors, "I've so looked forward to this meeting with you."

"No more than I, *madame la contessa*," said the fraudulent priest. His eyes sparkled triumphantly.

Chapter Sixteen

The nightmare of the Paris liberation and incessant political wheelings and dealings are over. World War II has ended, but problems for Corsica escalate. Starvation is upon the land and inflation. Black-marketeering and all sorts of nefarious goings-on have come home to roost. War is an abomination. I loathe it. Anathema to me are the politicians. The manipulations of the common man by those who have declared themselves the paternalistic protectors of mankind are reprehensible.

Military strategy no longer intrigues me. Is it due to my close encounters with death? I am not certain. Perhaps it is due to the expression on the faces of all the soldiers I've met: the staring eyes, slack lips, sleepwalker's stance, hard, set features. These men are like machines, not human; they have seen it all, journeying to hell and back in the battles fought. No wonder soldiers learn to live for the moment. Worse than could be imagined is the anonymity of servitude, the unnamed, faceless men wearing identical uniforms, their faces hidden under identical helmets, forced to accept the inevitability of dying in a foreign land, thrown into a pine box like a stinking mass of putrefaction.

The Mozarabe and I have walked the perimeters of the vast cemeteries of France and England, understanding less and less the reasons for wars. And now, just as the current war ends, a new enemy looms on the horizon—communism!

Communism, the new threat to world peace, struck before Paris was liberated and VE-day culminated. Our reports to General de Gaulle intimated the growing presence of Reds among the French Resistance before he could establish himself as the unquestionable leader of France. It was vital that de Gaulle and his Free French Army became acknowledged as liberators of Paris. By August, 1944, Allied troops swept eastward across France. Teams of Gaullist supporters, administrators, police, supply officers, even a traveling court-martial board followed at their heels, taking control of local governments in the name of the French Committee of National Liberation and Charles de Gaulle. These auxiliaries were under stern and specific orders to gain control of the newly liberated French cities and towns.

At this transitional stage of the war, the French communists presented as fearsome a menace as had the Germans. The OSS were vexed. "How many communists do you believe have infiltrated the French Resistance?" Captain Lincoln had asked me in one of our expedient five-minute meetings. "Twenty-five thousand, give or take a few," I told him, adding, "the communists will launch their insurrection if it means destroying the most beautiful city in the world," to which the American retorted glumly, "Why do I have a stinking suspicion you are right, as usual?" His voice was absent of the usual rancor.

It was becoming evident that the French Resistance fighters under communist sway did not want de Gaulle to march into Paris at the head of a conquering army and find the city gratefully prostrate at his feet. They had different intentions! God, it was frustrating.

While the Gaullists and Allies were scouting possibilities of a march into Paris, a stirring battle cry that had echoed throughout Paris's revolution-filled past—*aux bar-*

ricades—stirred the Paris populace. Four hundred barricades! The people of Paris rallied to the effort. They tore up paving stones, felled trees, ripped up railings, overturned cars and trucks, then piled the debris into boulevards and alleyways to hamper German movement. In St.- Germain-des-Prés at the corner of rue St.-Jacques, battered pictures of Hitler and other Nazi leaders were hung on barricades in exposed positions. Hour by hour, methodically the barricades closed in around the Germans like a trap. Patiently, cunningly, with the vast fury of insurgent Paris, the spiderweb was woven. Street fighting flared. The Resistance made steady gains. Dozens of key buildings fell into their hands. A tricolor hung from the facade of the Bank of France while Resistance fighters divvied up a treasure stored inside worth more than money in luxury-starved Paris—four hundred thousand bottles of cognac, three million cigars, and 235 tons of sugar. There were cease-fires, shattered cease-fires, debated cease-fires, and restored cease-fires decided by a violent conclave of factional leaders.

General Chaban-Delmas, the Gaullist General, denounced the truce with the German General Choltitz: ''We don't make gentlemen's agreements with murderers!'' Roger Villon, the communist political leader, accused Chaban-Delmas of wanting to massacre 150,000 people for nothing. Alexandre Parodi, the Gaullist political chief, succumbed. ''My God, they're going to destroy Paris now. Our beautiful Notre Dame will be bombed to ruins.'' Villon, unmoved, retorted, ''Better Paris be destroyed like Warsaw than she live through another 1940.''

In the end a German, General Choltitz, saved Paris by choosing to ignore Hitler's order to immolate the city. So Paris was saved by the enemy without, not the enemy within.

It seems incredible that three men—Roosevelt, Churchill, and Stalin—could control the destinies of millions upon millions of men.

I returned to Corsica late in March, 1945. The death of FDR on April 12, followed by Mussolini's brutal assassination with his mistress, Petraci, and the liberation of northern Italy marked the war's decline. On April 30, Hitler's death was reported to the world. On May 8 the world celebrated V-day, and I clumsily stepped upon a mine. Fortunately, the injuries were minimal.

In August the atom bomb exploded over Hiroshima and Nagasaki.

The entire world filled with dread.

I no longer entertain the urge to die, but to live, if only to destroy that horrible testimony to mankind—the atom bomb.

Following the Paris liberation, the Mozarabe returned to Corsica and camped out at the citadel, awaiting some word from Darius, some sign to assure them he would recuperate from the injuries. Forty-five men, his most loyal supporters, continued their vigil and refused to leave.

Eyeing them daily, observing the men train religiously, Vivaldi and Matteus revived the tenets of the Garduna Parchments and began to see in perspective the first viable signs of personal victory. Darius and these men, if properly inducted into the precepts of the Garduna Parchments, could form the nucleus of strength, the force to bring their plans for Amadeo Zeller's downfall to fruition.

At last! It would happen soon! Very soon!

Darius was still numb, too numb from war to do anything but wander about Terra Bonifacio like a lost soul.

The changes in Dariana at the loss of her sons and Sophia's disappearance grew marked. She adored Darius and cherished his presence, but she understood his need for solitude to recuperate both mentally and physically from the war and to mourn privately for his brothers and Sophia. His introversion grew more noticeable daily. At times when Vivaldi sought to engage him in conversation, he merely left the room without a word.

It was October. A north wind came early and cut sharply through Terra Bonifacio. Darius, dressed warmly in a heavy sweater, corduroy trousers, and leather boots, trudged wearily, like a lost soul, through the rear terrace filled with brambles and partially denuded trees. He was en route to the citadel to talk with his friends.

Dariana turned from the window, faced Vivaldi quietly.

"Let him go," she said. "Let him be free of your inherited vengeance."

"What are you saying, woman?"

"If you don't release him from this self-imposed purgatory, I shall. Are you blind to the love he feels for Sophia? He has always loved her. He ran away to North Africa to shed the guilt he felt for loving his sister. Have you no compassion?" She hurled a maelstrom of curses upon him, hoping to relieve her anger.

"You wouldn't dare."

"Try me," she said.

"You're crazy! What's got into you?"

"You ask that of a woman who has lost her children in a senseless war? One that's left us worse off than we were before the pestilence? Our money, *your* money is nearly worthless. Inflation is prohibitive. Still you persevere. Daniel, Robert are dead. God knows when we'll see Sophia again. From the beginning, my husband, I knew what was in that vile mind of yours and refused to admit it. Even now, the mention of Amadeo Zeller turns you into a beast." Tears welled in her eyes. "I had no chance with Darius. From the moment you cradled him in your arms as you walked these lands, whispering to him, instilling in him a fraudulent heritage, I had no chance at all. Whatever I have done, you have made me do. That which keeps you occupied in this—this *vendetta* room is evil." She glanced at the thick sheaf of papers spread out on his desk and, hugging her sweater closer to her shivering body, moved toward the fireplace. "I recall the first time I entered this room. The sign of the marten on your shield should have sent me fleeing, but I remained. That day I told you you were no Corsican, but I was wrong. If a man, by wearing the Corsican mantle over his brain, can become Corsican, you have achieved your goal. You are more Corsican than any man born to its soil. You have absorbed only the evil interred in its soul. Blood vengeance is imprinted in your mind."

"You don't understand," Vivaldi said slowly. "You never understood what drives me. I tried to tell you. You refused to listen. 'The man I married is Vivaldi Fornaro Bonifacio,' you told me. 'I know no Francisco de la Varga.' Well, it's time you knew the real me. Do you hear me, woman? I have endured the agony of hell when your questioning, doubting looks condemned me before I was tried. If I failed to confide in you, it was because I wanted to spare your feelings, cause you no momentary distress. It was a burden, a stone around my neck which had nothing whatsoever to do with you. Agreed, it took its toll on us. I am committed, Dariana. Nothing I can do will wash away the nightmares of my past until those things which must be reconciled in my life come to fruition. If I, as the last of the de la Vargas, am to hold up my head and restore to my family those things that are theirs by birthright, I must finish this thing between Zeller and myself. Your sons and daughter were not mere Corsicans. They have Spanish blood in them and in their own right are millionaires, landowners.

"*In their own right? My God, where are they? Dead!* They didn't return from the war, so they've either run away or are dead! You speak of them in the present. Tell me, Vivaldi, are you failing to reveal the truth because you wish to spare my feelings?"

"No dammit, woman! They *are* dead. Robert was killed first, then Daniel!" He exploded in wrath, his face engorged with blood. His hands were balled into fists and he shook as he endured the frozen expression of horror on his wife's face. Vivaldi expected a veil of tears, an outburst of grief, an emotional outpouring of hatred, sorrow, a dolorous despondency. Instead he felt, along with the sudden peace of unburdening his soul, her vile contempt.

Dariana's heart bled, but she maintained her composure. "I never dreamed our love would fall upon such evil days. What is this martyrdom you inflict upon me? This torture of the damned. Why couldn't you have told me straight out instead of letting me go on hoping? For this I find you a growing anathema to me, Vivaldi. Now I ask you very carefully, and be careful how you answer me, for I too can exact a vengeance upon you. What of Darius? Is he part of the de la Varga legacy you bear?"

"He is no kin. No blood of ours runs through his veins."

"Ah, you finally admit it?" She jerked her head around, dark eyes blazing. "He is more *our* son than those who carry the blood of our blood."

"No!"

"So you intend to sacrifice him? Darius is the sacrificial lamb to be laid open at the altar of Amadeo Zeller!"

"That is a cruel judgment."

"It is a cruel act. If you are determined to destroy Darius, better I tell him and destroy us." She averted her eyes as her fingers slowly peeled the rustic tiles from the wall, dismantling a large section before she was aware of the destruction. She quickly tried to replace the tiles.

"Stop that. Stop this nonsense, Dariana." Vivaldi turned from his wife, opened one of the doors, and stared off at the windblown landscape as the rising wind whistled through the tall trees.

The sounds of crackling fire attracted his attention. Turning, he caught sight of Dariana burning the Garduna Parchments. He panicked, ran toward her, shoved her away from the fire, grabbing at the shredded remains. He shrieked, screamed at her, "What have you done? The work of a lifetime! Treasure of centuries! Gone up in smoke." He spoke elliptically, unable to make sense of her actions and his own anguish, the violent anger and wrath coiling deep inside him. He wanted to strike at her, but he tried instead to salvage what he could. Then remembering as his anger abated a notch or two, he said, "You have only destroyed the copies. The originals are locked up tight in my safe where you can't get at them."

"Then I'll end it now. Let you live with guilt as you've lived with another guilt all these years."

He barely glanced at her as he retrieved what he could from the hearth. Suddenly, as the afterimage of Dariana imprinted itself upon his mind, he realized what she was doing. He sprang forward, dropping the papers, and rushed to her side. He grasped her right wrist in a viselike hold until her fingers relinquished their grasp on a small vial containing a pale green liquid. The stopper popped open, spilling a few drops on the bowl of freshly cut green roses. Before Vivaldi's eyes the green petals dropped, turned brown, and withered.

Dariana stared at the dying blooms. "You've condemned me to die, just as my *roses-Noël* will die," she said quietly. "You can do nothing to circumvent my death. I've lost all will to live. There are a number of such vials around the house, placed carefully during my recurring depression, where you'll never find them. If I mean anything to you, if anything remains between us, spare Darius. Release him from the poison well in which he drowns daily."

Vivaldi flung the vial to the floor, crushing it savagely under the heel of his boot as if he were killing a lethal serpent. He turned to her in violent outrage, studied her pale, hollowed face, a face as yet unlined with age, yet etched with the suffering of the death of her loved ones.

"It's too late. Far too late. Fighting is in his blood. If I were to cut him off now, he would continue in his own direction and find nothing but grief and trouble awaiting him. At least I can guide him. I have the power. Don't you see? Darius is very special. Most unique. He is the real power." Vivaldi addressed her between gasps and long-drawn breaths.

"How long has it been? You and Matteus have masterminded, cleverly organized this wickedness. You are playing with human lives. The future is not predictable because the human factor is unpredictable. Emotions cannot be relied upon."

Vivaldi turned on her. "What do you know. Your father and mother and sister were not slaughtered by a madman! Your birthright wasn't snatched from you by a lying, conniving, godless man who continues to destroy mankind wherever he alights like some maneating vulture taking, *taking,* from anyone who stands in his way. The man is utterly without morals! Without decency! Why should he be permitted to devour whatever pleases his fancy?"

For the next half hour Vivaldi continued the tirade. He resurrected old pains and memories that tore at him, broke open the casks of venom fermenting inside him since his arrival in Corsica. "You cannot take away any chance I have at righting this grievous wrong, Dariana. You, a Corsican, above all! It was you who educated me in the ways of the Corsicans, and now you turn from your heritage and traditions as if they were a pox."

Vivaldi's words increased her apprehensions, gave her insight into his closely guarded plans. She saw two men before her, the stranger who lived a life alien to hers before he met her, and the man she thought she knew intimately since her marriage. Both frightened her. She recognized in each the dedication of a fanatic. The knowledge heightened her angst. Threats were no longer effective, she reasoned. Her death would do no good. Alive she might be of use. The odds were in her favor.

Dariana's dark eyes flashed with renewed hope. She *knew* Sophia was alive. She had received a letter long ago from her dear friend Clotilde informing her of Sophia's fate. She knew where Sophia was living. She decided to gracefully tell Darius the truth after thinking it all out carefully.

She left a depleted Vivaldi and ran into Sophia's room, dug in a bottom drawer in her chest, and removed several letters written to Darius by Valentina Varga. They had arrived in Darius's absence well over a year ago. She had forgotten them until this moment. She stared at them. She had never trespassed before upon the privacy of her children, but she sensed that these letters bore ill tidings. Darius could take no more adversity in his young life. She crossed herself and gently opened the envelopes.

Meanwhile, Vivaldi paced the floor of the vendetta room. He told himself that Dariana didn't understand. They had faced famine and severe hardships. Their monies in Italy had been confiscated. Those in the banks in Marseilles were worthless since the economy had bottomed out. Black market goods were being sold at precious prices. How long could they exist? Shipping to Corsica from the continent had ceased. They existed on what was available from North Africa—very little. Fortunately Dariana had put up preserves, stores of them in the cellar. But with Darius's friends at the citadel, those stores would dwindle soon.

The time had come. He and Matteus must convince Darius of the gravity of the situation.

Dariana left the storage room on the third floor. Downstairs in Vivaldi's study, she peered through the window, caught sight of Vivaldi and Matteus heading toward the citadel. Quickly she locked the study door, opened the door to the walk-in safe, and worked the combination, determined to begin a systematic declaration of truth to Darius. Click . . . click . . . click. The safe door swung open. She hesitated, momentarily guilt-ridden. She had never encroached upon her husband's privacy. Traitorous feelings surged through her. Taking a deep breath, she determined nothing would stop her. She glanced about the closetlike room. Her eyes fell to the enormous scrapbook Vivaldi had collected over the years. Its contents dated back to 1919. Dariana heaved the heavy tome back to the desk, opened it, and commenced to read the newspaper clippings and the compilation of investigative reports.

Amadeo Zeller was a monster. She knew that before she perused Vivaldi's scrapbook. But the extent of his monstrosity was unknown to her until now. Certainly Clotilde was not safe in this man's presence. She understood Vivaldi's dedication now as she had never understood it in the past. Now more than ever, Darius deserved to know the truth. But how? How, without destroying her husband's faith and trust in her? She replaced the scrapbook carefully. Over the next three months, Dariana returned to the safe to continue her education in the life of Amadeo Zeller.

It was late December, 1945. The holidays were upon them. The Mozarabe, renamed "Corsican Coral," were still ensconced in the citadel. Dariana replaced the scrapbook in the safe. It was then that she noticed the black velvet case for the first time. She reached for it hesitantly, unprepared for its weight. Removing the black velvet sheath, the beauty and magnitude of the jeweled Sword of Damocles staggered her imagination. After so many years, she had nearly forgotten. . . . She recovered it, placed it back in its original position. She closed the safe, went upstairs to Sophia's room where she had secreted the strongbox under a chest of drawers. She should have placed it in the safe. She unlocked the chest and stared at the gold coins accumulated over the years for Darius, money sent by Clotilde that Vivaldi knew nothing about. Clotilde's father had conspired with her to transfer to Darius the monthly allotments from his trust fund. At the beginning of 1940, a letter came to Dariana from the Banque Suisse Royale advising her of the termination of the trust. After reading Vivaldi's notebooks, she saw Zeller's hand in the dirty business. *The wolf preys upon the lamb in the dark of night but the bloodstains remain by day as evidence of his handiwork.*

Dariana's health was in a steady decline. Her aging father, Angelo the apothecary, medicated her with digitalis. She refused medical attention, insisting old age was creeping up on her. The shock of Daniel's and Robert's deaths had done little to ameliorate the damage done to her heart. Sophia's absence compounded the depression. For the next four years she took to her room, staring fixedly at the ceiling, coming alive only when a past nightmare recurred to strike terror in her heart. Then one day following a near-fatal coronary occlusion, she summoned Darius to her bedside.

The day abounded with stillness. Only the muted sounds of her beloved hills and the chattering of her precious cuckoo birds wafted in through the open balcony door. Darius scaled the stone steps to her bedroom two at a time. She was sitting up in bed, a white shawl around her shoulders. Dariana trembled inwardly at the sight of her tall, handsome Darius. Her eyes leveled upon him until he sat alongside her and gathered her into his powerful arms.

"I'm cold," she whispered. "I no longer feel anything."

"It's the morphine, Mother, to kill the pain. Please, lie still. Do not exert yourself. The doctor said if only you took better care—"

"Darius, listen to me. I can endure this secret burden no longer. I haven't much time. But know this: you are my loving son as *if* I had borne you. You are as much a part of me as were Daniel, Robert, and Sophia." She grasped his hand tightly, squeezed it desperately. Her voice turned feverish, eyes glazed unnaturally. "My milk nourished you. I raised you, fed you, nurtured you to manhood. I patched you up when you fell or hurt yourself. And it was I who listened when you ran to me with childish woes, and it was I who made the terrors pass. Does not that make you as much mine as the woman who carried you in her womb?"

"Mother!" His anguished voice turned abrasive. "Are you delirious? What are you saying? You make no sense at all. Because I of all the children am the only survivor, do you find it necessary to punish me? You think I haven't wondered why of all my brothers and Sophia I am the only survivor?"

She raised her hand to him, shook her head sadly, afraid she'd be misunderstood. Her hand was on his face, one finger over his lips. Darius grasped the frail hand, kissed it, searching her eyes for an explanation. It came in agonized bits and pieces. The moment of truth approached.

"It's true. You are my life, my every breath, Darius, yet you are *not* of my flesh and blood. Your real mother is Contessa Marie Clotilde de Bernadorf—" she added the last name in anguish, "—Zeller. Your real father is Miguel Bertelli—the automobile designer and builder. It's all in here," she added, pulling a diary from under the bed covers. "You were born—"

"*A bastard!* Is that what you're saying? I don't believe you. None of this is true! You *are* my mother. Vivaldi *is* my father! Tell me I am not wrong. Tell me!"

Tears spilled down her faded cheeks. "Sweet Jesus of Mary, would I could have carried the lie to my grave. I cannot. You are entitled to know your true heritage, the royal blood inside you." She continued the story, bringing him up to date as best she could. She bade him pick up the chest she had placed under her bed.

"Open it," she told him. "I insist. You must know everything."

Darius's internal disintegration had commenced. Not even the sight of the Sword of Damocles or the gold could assuage the terror he experienced in finding himself a sudden stranger in a world he'd known intimately.

"It was to educate you formally, to prepare you for a future world where every advantage would be readily available to you. Vivaldi had different ideas. You must learn for what he prepared you. And choose for yourself the life you want."

It was happening too swiftly. The wild disorder of his life whirled about his head. He could find no words to express his emotions. War raged within him. Surfacing in his mind was the terrible guilt he had felt in loving Sophia! *Oh God! She was not a blood relative!* The implications of this one revelation infused him with a newfound energy. Almost without conscious volition, he uttered her name. "Sophia! Sophia. All these years of denial for nothing!"

Dariana, observing him, grew weaker. She reached under her pillow for two frayed, badly crumpled tear-stained letters. "You must give me your word never to show this to Vivaldi." Her voice strained, her frail hands clutched the letters tightly.

Darius frowned. "Why is deceit necessary in this final moment of truth, Mother?"

Dariana could not answer except to say she wanted things to be less ponderous for him. "Vivaldi is bound to fume and snort like a raging bull and demand instant justice with righteous indignation. God only knows what he'd do!"

Darius, still trembling inwardly, looked at the first letter. It was from Rome, dated February, 1945. It was from someone who called himself "Kanguru"! He was the courier from Rome, or was it Trieste? The mysterious courier who had identified Sophia in the company of an Italian officer! The letter was written in Italian. Darius read:

February 8, 1945.

My dear, compassionate Dariana: A partisan was killed in an effort to smuggle this letter out of Zürich. I will not elaborate further on this except to indicate the grave risks she took to forward this information. Once you read the letter, you know where to reach me. As usual, employ the code you employed with her. No doubt exists in my mind that you know to whom I refer. Your devoted servant, *Kanguru*.

Darius glanced at his mother. Her eyes were closed. He opened the enclosed letter without a postmark and commenced reading:

July, 1944.

My dearly beloved Sister: You *are* more than a sister. Because of your tremendous sacrifice on my behalf, I must end your suffering. My loyalties are torn in two. I only recently met the young woman my son Victor has lived with for a year because he indicated he wanted to marry her. He was summoned to Zürich by his father a few days ago and brought her to the *palazzo* for safekeeping under my protection until he returned. I received her, comforted the strange child, who appeared shy, introverted, and totally at a loss with her surroundings. In Victor's absence, we became friendly and I told her how much my son loved her. I asked her why she persisted in refusing to marry him. Victor had expressed his anguish to me over this. The young woman confided to me that it was not in her to hate Victor, but that she loved another. She also expressed dismay in having left her home in a hurry. From the moment he laid eyes on her in Ajaccio, Victor became totally obsessed by her. When he left Corsica, he coerced her into accompanying him against her will.

I suggested that she write her family immediately to relieve any worry on their part. Did she wish that I perform the act for her? I would have been happy to mend the rift if one existed. Perhaps if I spoke on my son's behalf, they would take to the idea without ire. She protested. She insisted it would be best if her family considered her dead. As I studied her, my dearest friend, noted the angelic face, stunning bone structure, I couldn't help feeling I was in the company of someone I knew intimately. Yet I was certain we had never met. To assuage her fears, I mentioned I had friends in Ajaccio who could intervene with her parents, to bring calm to an otherwise erratic and emotional involvement.

She proceeded to tell me about Corsicans, the way they think, feel, and experience life and family unity. Oh, my dearest beloved sister, it was as if I were listening to you all over again, bridging the gap of time between us. It was at that moment that I mentioned she was the image of my dearest friend, Dariana. And she said she knew! She had known since the day you explained but had hesitated in confronting me.

Darius crumpled the letter in his hand. He had read enough. *Victor Zeller!* The Italian Major had abducted Sophia. She was alive! *"Loved another"*! Was it possible she had saved herself for him? He turned back to Dariana, his face suddenly blanching. She was watching him, waiting. "Mother—are you suggesting that Victor Zeller and I are half-brothers?"

"Did you finish reading it?"

"I've read enough."

"Finish it," she said sternly, pulling herself upright. "You must learn the entire truth."

Darius reluctantly smoothed out the letter, his eyes scanning its full contents. He read it twice to make certain. "Oh, Christ! You can't be that cruel! She's had a child. Victor Zeller's child! Are you really trying to kill me, Mother?" He glanced at the bed. It was empty. He spun around. "Mother! What in God's name are you doing out of bed? Get back!" She stood near the French windows, weaving unsteadily on her feet and yanking at a linen coverlet on an object against the wall.

Darius stared. Unsheathed was an oil painting of Valentina Varga!

"But this is madness! Where did you get this oil painting of Valentina Varga? When did it arrive?"

"Look again, Darius, study the date. It is not that girl, that

American lieutenant, but her mother. That girl Valentina is the daughter of Francisco de la Varga, the man you know as Vivaldi Fornari Bonifacio.''

Darius could feel the outer skin of his being peel away as a reptile might shed its skin. His inner stability was dissolving. He fell heavily into a nearby chair. He couldn't remove his eyes from the portrait. It *was* Valentina! And this was all some hideous joke. His eyes trailed across the room to the lace-covered drum table laden with photos of Sophia, Robert, Daniel, and himself as children and young adults. At this moment, the overwhelming memory of Sophia produced a longing in him, and he felt powerful waves of hatred for Victor Zeller. Shafts of pearl-gray light shone obliquely through the shutters as he stared out the window, suddenly drained of all emotion, as if some powerful force prevented him from feeling the welled-up hurt, shock, turmoil, and confusion he knew must be rumbling about inside his head. His mind was going blank. He felt like a stone, immovable, dead! *Oh, Christ! Why present me with a new list of insurmountable obstacles? Why?*

Dariana clung to the furniture as she made her way with surprising strength to the étagère. She opened a box and handed him a small pile of letters. ''I don't know what these letters contain. They appear official, bearing some strange coat of arms. Perhaps you will find them less offensive than the bad tidings I've already presented to you, beloved Darius.''

Darius was silent, still. He was in another dimension of time and thought. Dariana brushed at her tear-drenched cheeks and placed the neatly wrapped packet in his lap. She fell to her knees, her head lying on his lap, murmuring, ''Forgive me, Darius. Forgive me. My only sin in not confiding in you sooner was to spare you the hurt I knew was inevitable.'' She begged him, implored him to forgive her and not be too harsh in his judgment of her. ''*Kanguru* is your father, Miguel Bertelli. Yes, you are half brother to Victor—''

''I forgive you, Mother, for everything except for Sophia. Had you confided in me that day shortly after her disappearance, I might have found her and returned her to you and Terra Bonifacio and she'd be here in my arms where she belongs. I denied myself, endured the tortures of hell for so many years because of my unrequited love for Sophia and

the guilt I experienced for what I believed were incestual
cravings. How I punished myself! Now must I fight a
brother for her love?''

Dariana sighed heavily, disconsolate with grief. She drew
herself to her feet slowly and padded across the room with
barely enough strength left in her to fall into bed. She turned
from Darius and sobbed into her pillow.

At this moment Darius caught sight of the embossed golden
seal on one letter.

From Youseff Ben-Kassir!

The letter was dated six months before. He broke open the
wax seal, opened the envelope, and read:

> Djebel, My Beloved Brother: It is with a sick heart that I
> write to you from Marboro Hall. I have not as yet returned
> to Algiers because my beloved Lomay has been missing
> since the end of the war. I have moved mountains, carved
> through stone in my attempts to locate her. Word was she
> was captured by the Germans after the liberation, smug-
> gled through American lines back to Berlin. After VE-day
> in May of '45 I lost all traces of her. I fear she might have
> been captured by the Russians. No one is saying. An
> agent, a British agent, brought me information. There's a
> good chance she might be in Moscow. Why have you not
> contacted me? Monsieur Creneau asks about you each
> time we meet. He is not happy with the present politics.
> You must know the problems he is having in Paris. Incred-
> ible! After all he's done for Free France. Write to me. Call
> me. Come to London. I miss you. I refuse to believe the
> information I received concerning your injuries. The Brit-
> ish and OSS believe you to be deceased. I don't. *I won't!* I
> shall write you weekly until I know for certain. Please be
> alive, *mon cher ami.* [signed] Youseff

Lomay St. Germaine missing? In Russia?

Darius hurriedly opened the other letters. They were similar.
No mention of St. Germaine's whereabouts. Certainly British
MI-6 had the clout to find her. The last letter stirred memories
in Darius. Memories of hatred. The lines that incurred his rancor read:

The agent Ghost-Dancer—perhaps you've heard of him by reputation—has word that the Russians have Lomay for certain. He is unable to learn anything else. Our Russian allies, who may not be allies for much longer, are aching to cause dissension. They've never forgiven us for opening a second front through Sicily to Italy, denying them much needed supplies during Operation Barbarossa. So much for wounded pride and the brutal realities of a god-awful war. Please contact me somehow. Global events are being orchestrated by alien forces that bear watching. It's imperative that we meet. There is a coterie of financiers in Zürich and Geneva that must be crucially observed if we don't want another Hitler. Their plottings are older than my years on earth. A lifetime of secrecy, camouflaged by the cunning of generations, support their legerdemain. Surely this will titillate your sleuthing prowess, restore my Darius of old. You cannot be hibernating, my brother. Not now, when the world needs you even more than it did during the war. [signed] Youseff

Darius let the letter fly to the floor. Youseff hadn't forgotten him, after all. He was tired, so tired and deeply wounded. He glanced at the bed, at Dariana. She was asleep. Her erratic breathing became long, even breaths.

He thought back to another time, one of uncertainty, frustration, indecision—the one-week interim that had changed his life drastically. It began with Tamir Mandel. Darius couldn't forget.

"Djebel." Tamir had begun that day on a formal note. Dressed in a dark business suit and carrying a small valise, he stood in Vivaldi's study, loath to impart a farewell. "I am leaving. My people are forming a new nation. After the devastation under Hitler, the leaders of Ersatz-Israel are calling for all Jews and friends to come to Palestine to work collectively toward the formation of a political state for my people."

Darius, jolted from the ennui at war's end, had stared at him in wonder. "You would leave us, Tamir? Your brothers? To join strangers?"

"They are my people, Djebel." His eyes darted furtively in all directions. "May I call you Darius, now?"

"You can call me Darius whenever you desire. Come. Before you go—certainly you won't depart this moment—we must talk seriously. I had plans for you, Tamir. It may take a week to explain it properly.''

"My mind is set; you cannot change it.''

"At least let us talk.''

"Yes. We should talk. We shall break bread, sip coffee, enjoy a little schnapps, but I warn you, *you will not* change my mind.''

"I have no intention of changing your mind, but to make you broaden your vistas. Have you any arguments to pose against broadening your vistas?''

"None.''

That's how it began. At war's end Vivaldi's and Matteus's words concerning implementation of a force necessary to stabilize Corsica had failed to make an impact on Darius. When Tamir announced his departure, Darius's first instinct was to round up the Mozarabe and travel to Ersatz-Israel to join the legions of freedom fighters. It was Vivaldi who wisely stayed him, assuring him he should mend the fences in his own backyard before he departed again to mend the fences in other nations.

Darius agreed. He said his farewells to the lonely Jew who had become a valiant Mozarabe. Before he left, Tamir had played his flute with great talent, then in a melancholy voice sang them a song he had composed. "It is a gift for you, Darius,'' he said.

The light of Israel burns bright, from borders to the sea
A blazing star to brave each night, claiming Jewish hearts are free.
The light of Israel burns bright within each heart of man
From worlds apart they'll come to fight, making Israel— homeland.
A life-long battle bravely won, for Jewish hearts all beat as one.
Faith filled each heart of man with love, and their guidance came from above.
God's beacon stands for all to see, a nation fraught with might.
Man must be free eternally so, the light of Israel burns bright. . . .

Darius observed the misty-eyed men as they listened, knowing each possessed a hunger, a thirst to share Tamir's passion. But they demurred from joining him. Their ambivalence lay in what they saw as duty and honor to Darius Bonifacio.

As Darius listened to the song, Prince Ben-Kassir's parting words at the Alexandria airport rang clearly in his mind. "You, Darius, do not belong to the past. The future is yours. *What will you do with it?*" Darius wondered how he could concern himself with a future he didn't recognize. The present was his reality, the past long gone. Why had everyone seen in him a future he was unable to discern for himself? It was Vivaldi's constant hammering that finally got him off his duff, willing to do something in the present.

Vivaldi, disconcerted and rankling at his frustrated efforts, told Darius straightaway that day in the vendetta room, "During the war the Italians and Germans monitored our every move. They proscribed our prayers and our songs. They violated our wives, daughters, loved ones, and you have the gall to stand there refusing to gather unto you a fraternity where all men unite against the oppressor to avenge the darkest deeds done to them?"

"Right or wrong are convertible terms," he had replied.

"A lie repeated a hundred times may not deform truth, but that same lie repeated thousands of times is accepted as truth. When this happens, the adversary is hypnotized, rendered incapable of defending himself with his reasoning powers or instinctive good sense."

"Don't preach politics to me. Altruism, courage, and idealism have been lavished in perfect good faith upon the most abominable of outrages. I know what you're thinking, Father. Those men, the Mozarabe, are trained faultlessly. They have to be or it's curtains for them in any project. Their ears are attuned like those of blind men, their eyes like those of the deaf, their senses honed a dozen times sharper than the psychic's third eye, making them capable of delivering results split seconds before altercations occur."

"Precisely." Vivaldi's green eyes lit up; he hoped to inject the same enthusiasm in Darius's being. "The raw material has become perfectly synchronized in a body. They are ready, Darius. Grasp the moment. I have waited a lifetime for this moment."

"The intention of untutored minds, raw material for secret societies," began Darius, musing to himself, "may be admirable, but the effects can often be disastrous."

"Not when the power is directed. In the hands of satanic self-seekers like Zeller, power becomes an apocalyptic beast deliberately trained for universal threats and mass slaughter," Vivaldi said quietly, glancing at the Moor. "Why must I sell you the idea? Can't you see that poverty has been extended and magnified by such men? Their apparant successes have imposed long periods of unrest, confusion, untold corruption, intolerance, national bankruptcy—almost as disastrous as winning a war. My God, aren't they all labeling your patriotic hero de Gaulle a traitor? A man who should be France's leader is being shunned and damn near persecuted."

Darius's head jerked up, his attention frozen. He hadn't thought about General de Gaulle during his convalescence, and thoughts of Youseff and General Furstenberg had often assailed him. Politicians and their canny machinations had long since violated Darius's sense of justice and fair play. He had severed all ties, except with the Mozarabe.

"Understand, Darius," Vivaldi told his adopted son, "the power of which I speak can create governments, topple them, or influence them anywhere in the free world."

Darius drew his brows together in a fierce scowl and said nothing.

"You think British SIS or the American OSS are different from what is proposed in the tenets of the Garduna Parchments? Study the differences well, Darius. They derive their vast intragovernmental power through their relationships with private industry, mutual funds, investment and publishing houses, and universities. My son, they are enhanced further by the power of the gun."

There were times when Vivaldi seemed positively brilliant, while other times his emotions reduced him to a mere child. Darius thought of this en route to the citadel to mull things over in his mind. Delon, O'Reilly, Pascal, and Longinotti approached him, their expressions glum.

"A threat continues to disrupt our lives. Communism," Delon said quietly. Darius stared at him in silence, anticipating the next remark.

"General de Gaulle is appalled at the treatment he receives from the insurgents," said Pascal, reading from a frayed newspaper.

"What do you expect, mates?" O'Reilly muttered, swilling wine from a bottle. "The left promises the reversal of all the rotten politics tha' forced the masses to undergo the dregs of misery during the war."

Darius, still silent, felt their itch, their desire to return to combat, excitement—something! Anything rather than vegetate at the citadel, living on what they could forage from the very few wealthy Frenchmen living to the north of the island.

"It's worse," moaned Lucien Pascal, "since the communists have infiltrated. Total chaos exists, Djebel. The men wish to leave for Marseilles. Countless Corsicans are flocking to the lucrative port city. Corsica is too poor to support us. Marseilles's enormous waterfront is an international oasis for adventurers, the homeless, the woebegone, and criminals."

"You aren't criminals!" Darius stormed.

"Criminals whom the sea has washed to shore," Pascal continued. "We are soldiers of fortune, temporarily without portfolio. What is left for us? We fought in a war, sacrificed our lives, and for what? None of us has received amnesty for our previous crimes before we joined the Legion. What do we do now except revert to our professions? The Marseilles waterfront is a criminal's hideaway."

"A smuggler's paradise," volunteered Longinotti. "A revolving marketplace for contraband where a man can buy, sell, or trade any item, large or small, stolen or smuggled from any part of the world. We could get rich and never have to worry a day in our lives."

"As a great seaport," began Delon, caught up in the fever, "Marseilles's heart is commerce. The tentacles of its criminal octopus reach far beyond the borders of the city itself."

"As I see it," Pascal insisted tightly, "domination over these various lucrative crimes and rackets must be won eventually through wits and guns by a single group of men—Corsicans, us! We are the most qualified."

"And if I can produce an alternate means of making money, existing with pride and allowing you to be counted as citizens?"

"With full amnesty for our previous crimes?" O'Reilly pressed.

"With full amnesty. . . ." Darius's voice trailed off, his inner mind working full speed. He remembered the words of Vivaldi.

> *The Seven Garduna Parchments contain secrets of inestimable power. Our forefathers, in 1822, put them to rest when leaders of the Garduna-Zaragoza Brotherhood, preparing to hang in the marketplace for deeds of violence, were rescued by their blood brothers. By producing the contents of an inflammatory ledger, recordings of clandestine involvements with high-ranking men of government and ecclesiastical princes of shady repute, the Garduna-Martens could have bargained for and received immunity for their crimes! . . . received immunity for their crimes!*

The words replayed in Darius's mind. Immunity! Immunity! It was a starting point, wasn't it?

The men were sorting through de Gaulle's skillful attempts at political legerdemain when he returned to the moment.

"Word has it the General seeks you out, Djebel," Delon said quietly. "I think he's in trouble."

"He's in trouble!" Darius snapped unexpectedly. "What of us here in Corsica? The war has proved no godsend to Corsica. True, we are weakened by the eruptions of political volcanoes in Paris. During the retreat, villages were burned, railroads, bridges, and power plants decimated by the retreating Germans. Inflation soars and starvation permeates our land worse than during the occupation."

"It is the same everywhere," Delon said quietly.

"Well, I say charity begins at home. First our people here, then we'll concern ourselves with France." But in his momentary anger, Darius had made his decision. He would begin to gather unto him a force more powerful than the Garduna-Zaragoza combine. He would begin with the Mozarabe, who for reasons of camouflage chose the name "Corsican Coral." Corsican Coral! There would be no other group like them under the sun—none at all!

According to feudal laws, in the absence of government anyone who could seize power had the right to govern and make laws to meet the situation at hand without concern for permanency. Feudal laws didn't restrict the ruler's right to judge or interpret law. Those subject to his laws must obey regardless of other circumstances.

It was the only way to prevent a communist insurrection!

Darius was determined no strangers would ever mar Corsica's shoreline again. He would enforce his own laws on the island to prevent his people from starvation and despair until an effective government could be established.

In the next few weeks, Darius came to know himself intimately. He found himself in constant revolt with mankind. Most men were pitiable, ridiculous, and grotesque. In Darius's mind ideas were forming, ideas that would connect him and his men to a world from which they too eagerly attempted to divorce themselves.

From the moment Dariana had revealed his true heritage, he couldn't help but compare himself in the faintest of images to his illustrious ancestor. Imagine, his mother was a direct descendant of Napoleon! For a time he regarded his religious schooling and wondered if he might be the reincarnation of the great Emperor himself.

Darius sometimes felt like the frustrated and forlorn hero Ulysses, wandering through a deserted labyrinthine temple seeking a holy place of refuge, cursing, vilifying the mother who bore him as a whore, contemptuous of the father who hadn't the courage to claim him as a son. Like a hero lost in a crowd, a man rejected and despised, he felt unreal. And when he considered everything realistically, he stopped cursing the fates, the circumstances that brought him to Corsica to be raised as the son of the Bonifacio family. Wasn't it ironic that the man he was programmed to destroy might have been his own father?

What will I do with them? Darius thought about his men at camp. *They have stuck with me as if I were a magnet, refusing to be shaken off.*

He asked himself this at the end of week one, and at the end of week two, he still had doubts. These were the seasoned soldiers, the professionals, the very special men who had done their country an honorable service. They could not be cast off like barnacles at war's end. He would not permit it. Amnesty must come first, then some sort of reparation. Darius saw his men in an honorable light, for they had shown courage, immutable bravery. They could fight forever; victory or defeat meant very little. It was all in how you got the job done.

The third week he remembered. He searched frantically through his war mementos for Pluto's memo, written on foolscap, what Darius had deemed to be a recitation from memory. *Voilà!* He found it and perused it carefully. The words lit up his mind. "Clandestine whisperings . . . scholars who create blueprints for a society to suit our technology. . . . Many are stifled to suit those in higher echelons of government. . . . Another power . . . *another power!* A third class of individuals apart from political leaders must exist, as an arm, an extension to be put to the task of thwarting mistakes, diagnosing areas of potential world disequilibrium and eradicating potential disturbances. . . . A body of formidable men capable of distilling the grape before it turns into vinegar, or put more succinctly, capable of killing any group recognized as a potential danger against the state."

Darius read on. "Men trained in covert offenses . . . act ruthlessly, without fear . . . sober-minded men without personal ambition . . . men competent to the needs of world society . . . take necessary steps to prevent this society from permanent collapse. . . . No room for error . . .''

Darius stopped. A chill coursed through him as it had when he had first read these cryptic, volatile words that fairly leaped off the foolscap at him. *"Third class of individuals."*

He had the tools to create a new global entity of such scope, magnitude, and power! Taking from antiquity the tenets of the Garduna Parchments and adding to them the formidable knowledge of the French NAIS, American OSS, and British SIS and SOE, how could they fail? How?

He thought of Pluto, their long talks of the present and future. He also thought of how black market profiteering ran rampant and those who dipped into the till profited enormously. He had seen American and European racketeers hobnobbing with top army brass on foreign soil, served generous helpings of the enormous pie of wealth gleaned from their nefarious activities. The sheer magnitude of graft and corruption promoted by American politicians whom the Americans had naively elected to office galled him; the fact that these men could dip their hands into the pockets of the people to legitimately steal what a poor beggar would spend ten years of his life in prison for opened Darius's eyes wider to political life.

Ghosts walked the land, thought Darius, the ghosts of old traditions, of shattered human rights, of deadly enmities that flocked from every corner of Europe. Some of these ghosts were returning to Corsica. Had he seen the American Jim Greer at the citadel only yesterday? He hadn't acknowledged the man yet. Pascal would tell him what Greer wanted.

On this day Darius climbed higher into the mountains. He tugged on his jacket collar to keep out the sharp, cold wind as he straggled through patches of snow. The icy peaks this high seldom melted, even if spring was nigh. The thought struck him that nothing changed. Another season would only bring more poverty, famine, and higher inflationary spirals. France, stuck in her own political quagmire, could do nothing for her Directory; she was too busy attempting to mend the giant rips in government.

Darius sat on a rock taking in the majestic panorama; sea to the east, west, south, and north of him. Still rejecting Dariana's revelation concerning his heritage, he could not help but think about Bonaparte and the zenith of splendor to which he had brought his empire by the time he was forty. Bonaparte knew that the governing powers of Europe thought him to be a common adventurer, a liar, thief, a low-class upstart. He was not a sovereign and didn't belong to their class. A flashing comet sweeping across the sky, they attested, always passes quickly out of sight. Then the sky becomes the same as ever.

How would Darius reign supreme? How could *he* manage to create a dynasty greater than that of his illustrious forefather? He was twenty-five, but felt as if he'd lived for centuries. In a sense he felt invigorated, at ease with himself as he often did just before an inner revelation inspired him.

He trekked down the mountain, leaning heavily on his cane, thinking hard on his decision. By the time he reached the jeep parked at the fork in the wooded path, he was convinced that no man should become slave to illusions he knew to be untrue. He must tear down the false front that masks itself as dignity and enter into an existence where he can accept his aloneness and the possibility of sudden death to find the potential for freedom and authentic identity.

He started up the army surplus jeep and took the south-western road back from Blood Mountain. It was still early. Bright morning light shot across the windshield, creating a celluloid reflection of tall trees and boulders in a glittering of odd shapes. Darius took a sharp hairpin turn and shoved the gears into low on the descent. His head ached. The pain in his temporal lobe since the Bastia bombing had abated but returned with annoying frequency when he was forced to ponder heavy subjects. He still limped slightly, necessitating the use of a cane. He had stepped on a mine and it was a miracle he had escaped with only a few broken bones, severe sprains, torn ligaments, and multiple bruises and abrasions. He was lucky to be alive to reflect on his battle-scarred body; others had not been as fortunate.

He glanced at his watch. Another half hour and he'd be back at the citadel. These past weeks he'd sojourned at Blood Mountain, at the very spot where once as a youth he had encountered the *moufflon*. Blood Mountain is where it all began for Darius, where he was forced to choose one life for another. Someday, he thought, Blood Mountain is where it would end, neatly tied up in a bright red bow.

As he viewed the portents of chaos and destruction everywhere, the barbed wire fencing, the battle-scarred hills beyond where only recently men had killed and been killed, he grew aware that his fate and survival had less to do with his own actions than with the assents and dissents of power figures too fear-stricken to make firm decisions. The past had lost its relevance, the future receded farther from his control. Only the present held possibilities of meaningful participation. He could always possess the moment.

Terra Bonifacio was in his sights. *Yes, Darius. Live in the present! Cut yourself off from those visions of yourself as a hero of history.* Suddenly Darius stopped the jeep. He pulled himself up on the back of the seat and felt a stone weight lifted from his shoulders. Long-term goals suddenly lost their relevance. Even marriage, made and perpetuated in order to provide for family continuity, became form without substance in this age where tomorrow's horizon had been darkened by a mushroom cloud. Work, with its myriad reward in status and well-being, became time spent in thrall.

His credo would become simple and direct on this earth careening to its doom. He would meet reality as he found it in all moments, whether this brought him agony or joy.

Chapter Seventeen

Major Brad Lincoln stood next to Jim Greer at the cargo area of the airport in Paris. Several army officers milled about. Soldiers stood guard near hangar doors. Not far away an American transport was loading cargo and passengers. "I don't understand why you don't come along to Berlin, now," Lincoln said. "Why must you return to Corsica? I thought you were sick to death of the shifting political factions and fickle loyalties within the Resistance."

"I am all that and more. Their nonsensical bickering and wasted time created procrastination we Americans aren't used to, Brad. Certainly they frustrated our efforts and made us feel alienated from OWC. But I must go back. There are a few loose ends that have to be tied up. I've worked closely with the British, and they believe something untoward is about to happen in Corsica. I want to check it out."

"We didn't make too many friends there—" Brad said somberly. His voice contained an edge of caution. "My actions especially were a pose; everything I did, said, and deliberately articulated was done in the broadest brushstrokes designed to bring out the Corsican's rancor. Dammit, the man was a brick.

But my actions were the sort of attention I needed to win friends and influence the Resistance.''

"Hah! Now most have turned commie. Sons of bitches! Christ! Cutthroats, sharpshooters, former felons, the motliest goddamn group I've ever worked with, and fuckin' good on top of it.''

"They make the best killers. Look, Jim, we've dealt many hands in this poker-game existence and never chose the players. Most of the Resistance are the scum of Europe's back streets. Bear it in mind every minute and trust no one. Christ, I don't recognize myself. I am by my own definition a goddamned con man, but during the war I was legal. Don't you think I knew Djebel sensed this and fortified himself against me? I had to present myself as an abrasive personality, one that inspired little confidence among the Allies.''

"But see how they flocked around Djebel? As if he were a god.''

Brad winced. "All right. It's over now.''

"Is it?''

"Christ, Greer, do you have something I don't have?''

"Your orders are to go on to Berlin and clean up after Paris. Mine are to watch the Corsican. You forget how close he is to de Gaulle. And the Reds just don't want de Gaulle to come in and carve up the pie. Our guess is he'll use the Mozarabe to do his dirty work. There's still the matter of Superman's three-day disappearance from Corsica.''

"What's your educated guess?''

"Not a guess. Facts from British SOE.''

"*Facts?* From British SOE? Why wasn't I told? Kept apprised? What damned facts?''

"Djebel was in Malta with de Gaulle, Furstenberg, and the Algerian Prince. Pluto, the wire specialist who had wired Paris for the SOE, was also there. En route Djebel was nearly killed by a German agent named Ghost-Dancer. And then Montreaux and Marnay disappeared for three days shortly after Djebel returned with Pluto and the wire men. Men came and left without explanation to us. I didn't like it. The British didn't like it, and while you were with General Donovan, the SOE did some rapid inquiries.''

"And you didn't tell me?'' Brad fulminated. A giant B-17 was coming in for a landing, the motors drowning out their voices. The men held their visored caps in place, tugged up on their fur-collared jackets, and turned their backs to the tunneling winds. "Who the hell is Ghost-Dancer? Anyone I should know about, Mr. Photographic Memory?"

"A killer, Brad. The best in the business. A cloud of mystery hangs over him. Conflicting reports. Even SOE is close-mouthed and restrained in discussing him. It's as if they are uncertain of him."

"Uncertain of him? C'mon, this is Brad you're trying to con."

"I swear it's no con." Greer recounted the dossier information almost verbatim. Listening to him over the roar of huge engines, Brad Lincoln's face was unreadable. Internally he was puzzled, frustrated, worried. He resented the slights from the British and the superficial politeness he'd received from the French allies. "But they sure turn to the good ole U.S.A. when they need us, don't they? Now listen, Jim, I don't know why your orders got snafued. You are or were under my command. If you don't cotton to the SOE, just give me a call in Berlin. I'll sure as hell need you there."

A soldier was wagging his arms at Brad, urging him to board. "All right! All right, I'm coming. You listening to me, Jim? I don't know what's itching your ass, but if you need me, I'm there." The look he leveled on Greer was disbelieving. It was a look he had in untenable situations or when he took little stock in spoken words. They shook hands. Brad, bucking strong head winds, fought to board the transport. He did not rest easy all the way to Berlin.

Chapter Eighteen

When man is prey to his own emotions, he is not his own master but lies at the mercy of fortune: so much so that he is often compelled, while seeing that which is better for him, to follow that which is worse.

—Spinoza, circa 1660

At first, to save his people, Darius and Corsican Coral smuggled everything from American cigarettes, razor blades, automobiles, and foodstuffs into France. The black market in consumer goods flourished beyond control in Corsica and France. It became a way of life and branched out into other avenues of revenue: diamonds, rare artifacts, priceless paintings reconfiscated from the Germans. Anyone who could smuggled, but Corsican Coral operated on the scale of an industry—a big industry.

The group flourished for two years under the quasi aegis of the provisional Premier-President of France beginning in November, 1945. Two months later, when de Gaulle resigned from office, Corsican Coral enjoyed freedom along the Marseilles waterfront.

On occasion, contraband shipments were confiscated when certain government officials didn't know the importance of Corsican Coral's participation, but not once could a case be made against Darius Bonifacio, for he was slowly becoming a

355

nonentity. Whenever and wherever the police or French Sûreté attempted an investigation, they were cut off at the source, ordered to drop all actions against this nonexistent person. Corsican Coral was the best-kept secret in France.

In May 1958, France was confronted with a threat of civil war over the question of Algerian independence. Charles de Gaulle was called out of retirement to serve as Premier. The National Assembly granted him power to rule by decree for six months and approved his plan to supervise the drafting of a new constitution. No one but those in the know knew of Corsican Coral's participation in laying the groundwork for de Gaulle's return to office. Enemies were gotten rid of, dissenting communists disappeared mysteriously, and by the time the French people cast their votes in September, 1958, de Gaulle was overwhelmingly elected President of his newly created Fifth Republic of France. He held this office until his resignation in April, 1968, following thirteen attempts on his life.

In Corsica in the year of de Gaulle's resignation, Dariana's health was failing rapidly. She hadn't seen Darius in months and refused to die until she delivered into his hands a packet of letters from Valentina Varga. She hadn't opened them, dared not, but as she grew weaker in her confinement, she could no longer bear the suspense. One day she opened one of the letters.

It left her in a breathless state of exhaustion.

Valentina had given birth to Darius's daughter, named Valerie, on February 8, 1954! In August, 1953, she had married Commander Hartford Lansing to give her child a father. Dariana reread the letter. The exact words were:

When last we were together in Corsica in 1944, before I left for Malta, you gave me no indication we might share a future. When we met again in 1953 in Paris and spent a heavenly week together and you lavished such affection on me, I had dared hope. . . . But at week's end, you were the same man you were in Corsica nine years before. I have never forgotten you; I never shall. I can love no other the way I love you. But I am tired of commanding my sensations and my thoughts to do what you will them to. You have occupied the whole field of my attention, Darius. You are a unique, singular, remarkable person, but now I must expunge you from mind and hasten to dispel all thoughts of you. The dawn is entering my room through the shutters in oblique shafts of muted pearl-gray light, and I now realize that my love for you will never be finished. But I must be done with dreaming impossible dreams that include the two of us. I will not seek the memory of you in my husband, for I would suffer greatly at not finding you.

If it's of any interest, Valerie looks like me, with my coloring. I had hoped for a miniature Darius. When I learned of my pregnancy and was forced to make a decision, God forgive me I let Hartford believe she was his child. I couldn't let her grow up without a father as I did and be cheated out of a vital relationship. Forgive me, beloved. I still love you desperately. Perhaps that was our problem. If I loved you less, you might have been mad about me. Always yours, Valentina.

Dariana wept bitterly. She folded the letter, replaced it among the others, took them to Darius's room, placed them neatly in a desk drawer. In due time. . . .

"Matteus! Matteus, where are you?" Vivaldi called to the Moor. "Come at once."

The Moor came scurrying through the great house into Vivaldi's study. On the desk were strewn photos and newspaper clippings.

"What is it?" His dark eyes fixed on a news clipping outthrust at him. The photo was of a newlywed couple cutting a wedding cake.

"Do you see what I see? Tell me my eyes are not lying!"

Matteus studied the photo; his eyes scanned the clipping, reading the caption first, "Wedding pictures of Anthony Harding, U.S. Ambassador to Great Britian, and his bride Clarisse Zeller—" He stopped. "Amadeo Zeller's daughter?"

"Look! Look! Don't you see it? The diamond necklace, the earrings! For the love of God, tell me I'm wrong!"

Matteus's eyes narrowed, he studied the jewelry. Magnifying glass in hand, he scrutinized the jewelry. "It's difficult to tell in a newspaper clipping—" he began.

"Then by all means study the reporters' photographs my ferrets dug up." He handed him glossy eight-by-tens. The Moor glanced at the first photo and gasped. His mind rolled back to three decades ago. "The Isabella necklace and earrings!" he exclaimed, shocked by the audacious public flaunting at what he construed to be a black deed.

"Yes. The Isabella necklace. My heirlooms. But that's not all," Vivaldi said tightly between clenched teeth. He was blazing. The years had not ameliorated the anguish or hatred, the desire for vengeance. All this seemed to fire his purpose. "He has the gall to flaunt his felony publicly."

"He doesn't know Francisco de la Varga is alive. Why wouldn't he give it to his daughter after the untimely death of his wife?" Matteus said, scanning the newspaper report of Clotilde's accidental death in a helicopter crash as she flew to Zürich from Kappel. Even the newspaper had made a big thing of taking a helicopter to travel the distance of fourteen miles. Why not a car? What had been so urgent that the travel demanded a helicopter? Everyone was baffled. Then, as usual, with time the story was swallowed up by more current news, relegated to past history.

"Look at this one, Matteus." Vivaldi thrust another photo into the Moor's hand. Seated across the desk from him, Matteus's eyes fell to the photograph. The Harding couple was aboard ship. Harding, the clipping stated, was returning to America to assume an important role, serving as foreign policy adviser to the President. Clarisse Harding was wearing a tailored suit. A vaguely familiar cross hung around her neck.

"A platinum cross? If it were opened, my old friend, would its cavity contain diamonds, ruby roses, and emerald-green leaves?" Vivaldi stared hard at the duplicate photo in his hand as Matteus fixed on the memory of that day in Don Diego's study when the *hacendado* had taken time and patience to demonstrate the precious contents of the platinum cross. "So he gives it to his daughter rather than saving it for his firstborn wife. That tells us something, doesn't it."

"You have me at a distinct disadvantage," Vivaldi said, exasperated.

"If he did not give it to his firstborn to keep it in the Zeller family, then animosity must exist between father and son."

Vivaldi studied Matteus, rolled his words over in his mind. But his mind was working in other directions. "Is there some way of recovering those articles and returning them to their rightful owners?''

''You ask that such a simple task be undertaken while Corsican Coral is at our disposal.''

"Corsican Jade now, Matteus. Corsican Coral has gone by the wayside as Jade must do shortly. Darius has chosen the word ''Moufflon'' as his code name.''

Matteus nodded. ''We are getting closer every day.

And so Moufflon was born. Darius gave himself passionately to the cause of peace. In the beginning he resolved that peace must be extended to all peoples in all nations globally. They must be offered new ideals and hopes, not revolutions and armies. He was no mere dreamer, this Moufflon. Already a mighty new plan, greater by far than all the plans of war, was germinating in his mind. France would lead the world in peace; not a peace of the handshake, not a truce on her frontiers and coast, but an all-embracing peace of the heart, peace of the soul, and a safe world in which mankind could thrive and share communal secrets for its betterment. His eyes overflowing with this vision, Darius accepted Vivaldi's hypothesis and took the Garduna Parchments under critical scrutiny.

It was déjà vu for Darius. He felt he'd traveled this road before. At every word, every sentence, paragraph, chapter, and verse, the words he read became echoes of other words imbedded in his brain. As if the test had been memorized like a Shakespearian quatrain, he could recite each written word leaping at him from the translations that Matteus had painstakingly prepared.

He studied the organizational processes. Hadn't he employed these same tenets in the careful selection of Delilah's Dream, the SAS commandos, the Mozarabe? How had he known, subconsciously or instinctively, what to do?

Considerable changes had occurred in Darius and his closely knit coterie of former Mozarabe. Six of his most trusted men had taken up residence in various world capitals where they maintained low profiles, became respected, law-abiding citizens, and existed under aliases known only to Moufflon. Together they operated a worldwide anti-terrorist, anti-criminal network that reached endlessly into every global conspiracy.

Moufflon had learned to trust no man. There would be no Judas to his Christ, no Brutus to his Caesar. The priceless jeweled Sword of Damocles, the gift from his father, Michael Bertelli, had been sold for funds to finance his operation.

Moufflon was now one of the richest, most powerful men on earth and the most anonymous. He was known as a man at the epicenter of indescribable power, who had become the master choreographer of impenetrable, clandestine forces that dismantled the covert operations of countless greedy nations bent on conspiracy, bloodshed, and powerful government takeovers.

The construction of his hilltop aerie began.

Personally for Darius, there were still ends to be tied. Ghost-Dancer, the assassin, had eluded him. Whenever he'd sent feelers out, no one—even if they knew his true identity—divulged an iota of information. The war was over. Ghosts deserved to fade into oblivion just as all spies who had served their nations and done their jobs deserved to muster out of the service if they chose.

Late in the autumn of 1960, Darius sat in the screening room in his new quarters atop Blood Mountain, studying an accumulation of newsreels and tapings. The image of one man among a group of world dignitaries attending a conference in Leopoldville in the Belgian Congo caught his attention.

"Stop the film, André!" he called to the camera operator in the adjoining room. "Go back, roll the film back several frames." The pictures on the giant screen whirled backward, froze momentarily, then came forward.

"Slow down the frames," Darius coached, speaking into an intercom. "Zoom in on the man in the middle, on Anthony Harding. . . . Freeze the frame." His instructions were obeyed. "That's it. Now come forward, slowly . . . slowly . . ." Darius intensified his scrutiny. "Repeat the process," he said quietly. "Back up . . . freeze . . . come forward slowly. Zoom in closer, magnify."

Darius studied Harding's movement, the cane in his hand, the way he walked, moved, held himself. "Youseff! What do you make of that?" he asked the Algerian Prince, who had returned to Corsica with him.

"I don't follow your interest in Anthony Harding. Why not Lumumba? He's far more interesting game. Don't you agree?"

"You don't see it? The limp? The use of his cane? Dammit,

the movement is affected! He's faking the limp. Now, why would Anthony Harding be faking his lameness?''

"Unless he isn't lame? I give up," Youseff said patronizingly.

"Precisely. I used a cane long enough to know how to use one. His moves out of synch with his game leg." Darius moved to the wall, pressed a lever. The wall slid open, revealing vast metal files along every wall. "Anthony Harding," he said aloud, going directly to the file containing the H's. He pulled it from the metal drawer, returned to his seat, and opened the file. He scanned the highly classified dossier lifted from British SIS years ago when he had received a note from Pluto. The name on the file was Anthony Harding. No more, no less. However, coming from Pluto, who still dealt in clandestine comings and goings, it was enough to alert Darius. Anthony Harding must mean something to Pluto. Later when Darius discovered Harding had married Amadeo Zeller's daughter, Clarisse, Darius's half sister, he took note of the man and studied the interesting dossier. Instinctively, he *knew* the dossier had been manufactured, so he had his ferrets go back in time. The man with no beginning couldn't have descended upon the world fully grown as a manufactured commodity, could he?

"André," Darius spoke into the intercom, "Do you have the other film on Harding?" He waited several moments while Andre scanned an electronically controlled file.

"Harding and his wife at a White House dinner reception."

"Roll it. And keep the first film at hand. I may want you to reschedule it."

Within moments the screen filled with the merriment of a White House gala. The celebrities and guests were panned by the camera alongside President Kennedy and the First Lady. Darius shouted, "There they are. Anthony and Clarisse Harding. See? The cane in his left hand. André, freeze the frame, then come forward slowly. Keep your eyes on him, Youseff. See how he moves."

"I fail to see what your eyes reveal."

"Go ahead, keep rolling," Darius instructed. Scene after scene changed. Some contained Harding, others didn't. "Go back to the first film in Leopoldville." While André reloaded his projector, Darius picked up a paper tablet and began sketching a facsimile of Harding. Then on another sheet he drew the same form without hair, with steel-rimmed spectacles instead of the elegant tortoiseshell glasses Harding wore. Finished, he propped up the two drawings, stood up, backed away, and drew Youseff into his circle of thought. "Is it possible, Youseff? Now look closely—these two sketches could be of the same man. Don't answer immediately. Study the sketches and consider I am not Raphael but a layman with a good memory."

"If I really stretch it?" Youseff smiled mischievously, then sobered at Darius's serious posture. For several moments he studied the sketches, shook his head dubiously. "The shapes of their heads are alike, the jaw structure, the eyes. You even captured the man's arrogance, but . . ."

"But what? Tell me."

"I don't know."

"Let me pose a hypothesis. Suppose there are twin brothers. One is a spy, an assassin, an international murderer. Let me put it more succinctly. One is a British spy once under German control who may be under Russian control today. His brother is a scholar, serious, studious, brilliant, a think-tank genius. Now, if an altercation existed between two brothers and enmity sprang between them, which of the two would be most likely to survive?"

"Without contest the assassin would be more adept. What are you saying?"

"By my guest, Youseff." Darius tossed him the file on Ghost-Dancer, a.k.a. Eugen Schuller. "It should interest you enormously, since he was the German spy who—"

"You said, *British* spy before."

"—under German control in the war betrayed Zahara, shipped her back to Germany where the Russians got hold of her. She's behind the Iron Curtain."

Youseff, at once anguished, said in disbelief, "You knew this and never discussed it?"

"The facts became clear only moments ago. I had assumed, as the dossier indicates, that Eugen Schuller, incredibly expert in the art of disguises, code name Ghost-Dancer, died shortly after Nuremberg."

"And now? What makes you so adamant in your convictions?"

"That man on the screen, Anthony Harding, is Eugen Schuller, not Anton Schuller. He's faking the limp or he's extremely careless in a disguise that has been accepted globally.''

"If as you say—and I find it a complex maze to follow—that man on the screen is Ghost-Dancer, an incredible expert in the art of disguises, how is it possible he fouled up in what must be the ne plus ultra disguise of his career?" Youseff scanned the file.

"Only an expert eye would detect the sham. It's the way he handles the cane, Youseff.'' Darius, nodding assuredly, observed the action on the screen. "He's faking the limp. I'd stake my life on it.''

"According to the dossier," Youseff said solemnly, "Eugen Schuller and all his aliases were accidentally killed in a mountain-climbing incident at Les Diablerets in the Swiss Alps.''

"Precisely where Amadeo Zeller's special scientists fell to their deaths. Coincidental?''

" 'The brother, Anton Schuller, is using the cover of Anthony Harding with accompanying credentials put together by a cartel of powerful men and has entered into a global political conspiracy,' '' Youseff read, scanning the impressive list of credentials ascribed to the Anton Schuller persona.

"See, Youseff? Look there on the screen. He uses his right foot simultaneous to the forward thrust of the cane. Watch—it never varies. André, repeat the action several times," he said into the intercom. "Anton was born with a clubfoot and used a cane properly. Forward thrust of the cane and the left leg, placing his weight on the good leg—the right one. Even the cleverest of men are sometimes foiled by the most ridiculous errors. He's gotten away with it—how many years?''

"He sprang up in the fifties, a star on the horizon of global politics, and has gathered unto himself tremendous stature and power. There's talk he'll be the Secretary of State soon. The second most powerful man in America. No! Actually the first, since he advises the Chief Executive, *oui?*''

Youseff stared in fascination. "I would never have caught it. *Never!* How did you—''

"He made two mistakes. First, he didn't die. Second, he didn't study anatomy. I've carried the man's image—the image of my would-be assassin—in my brain ever since we rendez-voused at Malta with the General. It's been reinforced periodically by the fact that he was the only failure in my life to date. His is a far more clever mind than mine. More like the mind of—'' He stopped, tapped his forehead in sudden illumination. ''Of course. He married Zeller's daughter. Zeller, the very foundation of his strength and clout. With Anton's credentials and Zeller's guidance he'd be every bit the genius his brother promised. What I don't understand is the Zeller tie-in and how it came about.''

''Suppose we dig further. I am certain British SIS must have more answers.''

''Buried in the literature of the Ghost-Dancer dossier are provocative hints, sometimes surfacing only in cryptic footnotes,'' Darius said quietly. ''André, turn off the projector,'' he said to the man in the next room. Instantly the screen went dark.

Darius poured cognac for Youseff and himself. They clinked glasses. ''Here's to the uncovering of every shadowed ambiguity that points to certain unsettling and unexpected interpretations.''

BOOK THREE

AUGUST 1984

Beneath the broad tide of human history there flow the stealthy undercurrents of the Secret Societies which frequently determine in the depths the changes taking place upon the surface.

—Arthur Edward Waite

Chapter Nineteen

In Moscow, Premier Vladechenko leaned back wearily in his leather chair. At seventy-four he was tired, desperately tired of the infernal pace he had maintained this past year following a massive coronary. This power mogul, living by sheer will-power, dedication to Mother Russia, and a well-practiced self-discipline, sat back now to reflect on his formidable career. In his youth his methods had been rough, his nature intractable, grating. He'd corrected anarchistic tendencies in others, but had permitted his own to guide him on occasion. It could be said of Nikolai Vladechenko that his courage, integrity, intelligence, and concern for his fellow man had superseded all else.

His eyelids drooped closed, then snapped open in recollection. He leaned forward, opened a drawer in the hand-carved ebony desk, a Ming Dynasty treasure given to him by the Chinese when their nations were on more sociable terms. He removed four voluminous, frayed, finger-marked files submitted to him months ago when Moufflon appeared before the world peace conference in Maui. The files, laboriously compiled by his First Field Directorate Chief Andreivich Malenekov, had undergone his repeated critical analysis. Now he shuffled through them, perusing them diligently, searching . . . searching. *Ah! Here it is.*

The Zeller File! Amadeo Zeller. The man had to be stopped.

Assaulted by excruciating pain on the heels of a seizure, the Premier reached for the only relief available. Shoving aside a monstrous tray of ineffective vials, he unlocked a drawer in his desk, removed his jacket from one arm, and rolled up his shirtsleeve, grimacing in pain. He bound his upper arm with rubber tubing and yanked it tightly with his teeth, securing it. He dispassionately plunged a hypodermic syringe filled with morphine into his arm, watched the fluid drain, and snapped off the tubing. In moments his stertorous breathing eased. He withdrew the needle, awaiting the relief that would come to ease the torturous pain. He rubbed the needle mark with a cotton swab, bent his elbow, and leaned back in his chair, reflective.

Vladechenko had spent his entire life dedicated to serving Mother Russia. Why couldn't she let him die in dignity? He was once a slender, handsome young man, an energetic and staunch Party member with a keen eye for politics. He'd earned the respect and admiration of the Communist Party. Today, in these troubled times, he'd become the Party's security blanket, a strong, formidable Gibraltar. And they refused to let him die! Fang-toothed political tigers prowled restlessly within the Politburo, thirsting for his death, prepared in a second to take over, destroy what he'd labored long and hard to build. He knew too much, far too much, and of late grew fearful for Russia and the world.

In the past three years, four assassination attempts on his life had made no headlines. The Kremlin frowned on adverse publicity. The attempts spurred the Premier to think seriously about his successor. No one in Russia could best Uri Mikhail Gregorevich! Handsome, brilliantly educated at home and abroad, the remarkable young Russian had one black mark against him—his age. He was only thirty-nine. Youth in Russia was a word to be spat upon by diehard Party men.

At the pinnacle of the Communist Party was the Central Committee, an antiquated lot of the most powerful men in Russia, the youngest among them sixty-eight years old. Invested in the Central Committee was the power to select the Secretary General of the Communist Party, the most powerful position in the U.S.S.R. The authority of Vladechenko's office, his caution to make no enemies within the Politburo or Central Committee, his discreet use of power and reliance on a coterie of loyal allies had enabled him to prevail for two decades without a hint of scandal. Recent political winds in the Kremlin created divisions, divisions that influenced friends, the staunchest of diehards, toward a man he detested. Political power in the U.S.S.R. lay in the cradle of a self-protecting, self-selecting bureaucracy effectively controlled by a cautious elite of fourteen men. And the Premier, one of those fourteen elite, wanted Uri Mikhail to be his successor.

But shaking the rafters, making himself heard in the Supreme Soviet Parliament, came the ambitious voice of Gorky Sakharov, a loyal Russian with proper Party credentials, yes, and with surprising clout. He had raised and debated issues at each of the two meetings permitted Parliament yearly, to publicly take issue with Vladechenko's leadership. Oh, what an ambitious voice!

"The Premier fails to ameliorate Russia's problems! We are stifled by excessive centralized economic planning, stagnated by a proliferation of bureaucratic spirals and political patronage that reward sycophancy and caution while discouraging innovation! I accuse Premier Vladechenko of total inefficiency, inflexibility institutionalized in the flagging economy and the very political system itself! The voice of Russia cries! The voices of its people complain of food shortages. Our virtual zero population growth and the high birth rates among the non-Slavic regions in Russia threaten our citizenry. By the year 2000—if we live so long—we shall be a minority. A demographic time bomb ticks away inside the Soviet economy and Premier Vladechenko does nothing!"

And I, Comrade Sakharov, accuse you of the four assassination attempts upon my life and of collusion with foreign nations to bring Russia to its knees!

The Premier permitted the opiate to overwhelm his senses, dissolving the beast of pain that wracked him. *A curse on Sakharov!* he grunted despairingly. *A curse on those invisibles who keep me out of the Middle East! What do any of these old, dying codgers know of demographics? Of projections concerning the future?*

In their halcyon days, most of the stouthearted septuagenarian-octogenarian vodka-drinking studs would have populated ten nations. Now they vegetated at home, addicted to vodka, amenable to outside voices, yet unable to produce sperm to respectfully populate a decent household. And Comrade Sakharov's addiction to little boys produced nothing at all, not even in his image, thank God!

Gorky Sakharov blamed *him* for the afflictions of Russia. The man, three years Nikolai's junior, waited greedily at the perimeters of death to ease himself into the Premier's chair. No, no, no! If the Premier endured, he would not permit Gorky to occupy his seat. Gorky was unworthy, a dictatorial despot who would plunge the world into eternal darkness and damnation rather than subordinate himself to a position of equal or lesser rank than any man on earth.

The thought struck the Premier as humorous. He laughed in a sudden rare burst of mirth. How could that be? One man already considered himself the highest of any man—no less than a god. And Comrade Sakharov wanted to match wits with Zeller? One Zeller was more than the world could endure. Two? Never!

Uri Mikhail must become Russia's new leader. He must! For this reason, Vladechenko refused to die. For this reason he had outwitted assassins' bullets and vials of poison!

Caught up in a coughing spasm, the Premier pounded his chest, sipped water, grimaced, and reached for forbidden vodka. He poured a glassful, gulped it defiantly. The world needed levelheaded, incorruptible men to iron out mankind's difficulties. More desperately needed was a body of power able to weed out the psychopaths who with fanatical demagoguery scaled the rungs of leadership ladders, seduced the uneducated masses. The Premier grimaced, then cocking his head, listened wistfully to the refrains of a Russian melody played on a balalaika somewhere inside the Kremlin. Chafing at the thought of death's harbingers lurking close by, licking greedy lips in anticipation of his demise, he thumbed his nose at the specters.

"You will wait, you vicious bloodsucking pallbearers. Yes, yes, you will wait for Uri Mikhail to become Premier of Russia before I go!"

Irritable, listless, impatient, yet determined to have his way, he picked up a file from his desk, read the title: "Zeller Foundation, Zürich." Amadeo Zeller! Hah! At last! This persona non grata human was in his grasp. Nikolai knew the truth about this man but not quite all. He had waited half a lifetime to capture the cowering jackal.

He opened the file, set his glasses into place, and read.

There was a knock on the door. The Premier pressed a button on a desk panel. The door swung open. It was Andreivich Malenekov.

"Mr. Premier, we must speak. I have come on urgent business."

"Yes, yes, Comrade Andreivich. What has the KGB chief to sell me from his bag of tricks? Come, come, I can read your face like a road map. It bodes dark, stormy seas."

"Worse, Comrade Vladechenko, much worse. There is no way to tell you except straightaway."

"Then pray let it be straightaway before I die of suspense instead of old age."

"Comrade Premier, our Uri Mikhail is missing. The Moufflon Lodestar returned to Paris, but the Scorpion and principal task force did not. I have withheld informing you of this calamitous information until we—the KGB—received official information."

Vladechenko turned ashen. He gulped for air, clutched at his chest in the area of his heart. He cleared his throat. "That information is unacceptable. I demand you produce proof. I want no official reports, but proof. I will not believe it. No, never!" The Premier stared dully at Malenekov, his brows rising, falling softly into place. "Something else stirs you. I know you too well, Comrade Andreivich. Well, out with it."

"You studied the roster, Mr. Premier. You know the enemies aboard the Scorpion. The man Velden Zryden will not permit Uri Mikhail to live. He may, in fact, be the reason the Scorpion is missing."

"Velden Zryden," the Premier said flatly. "You mean Victor Zeller? The monster his father masterfully created in his own image when brilliant scientists performed the cranial microchip implant? Yes, yes, he is the man to whom you point as most dangerous. And he is. The man himself, plus the knowledge stored in his father's brain, can easily turn into a devastating weapon, Andreivich. Why didn't we see it before? Why subject Uri Mikhail Gregorevich to such a diabolical fiend? Were we under the sway of demon vodka, comrade?"

"One Zeller is far more than the world can endure," said Andreivich, echoing the Premier's earlier thoughts.

"That a father perpetuated his own greed for power in his son was insanity. Why hadn't we recognized it as such and put an end to it when our agents spotted him in Paris? Before he joined the task force," the Premier lamented.

"Truly, neither of us believed in the possibility, let alone the probability of such an occurrence, Mr. Premier."

"The mysterious deaths of the six scientists performing the experiment was proof enough of the perfidy!" The Premier banged his desk with a fist, upsetting the contents. He poured two glasses of vodka, pushed one toward Andreivich. "Drink, comrade."

About to protest, the KGB Chief remained silent, disobeying orders to keep vodka away from Vladechenko.

"All this fooling with science, courting human disaster was predicated to achieve control and manipulate the world of men. Someone has to rule," the Premier said ironically. "Who are better qualified than men of high intellect, strength, money, and unemotional judgment?"

"Perhaps the belief had validity at one time, Comrade Nikolai, before an entire planet could be destroyed with the touch of a button. But ever since the limited nuclear war in the Middle East last July, the entire globe appears to be dancing softly through the intricacies of complex, highly volatile politics. Each nation holds its breath, fearing total annihilation."

"Still, the Western world deploys its missiles! *Da?*"

"I had actually believed, after studying Victor Zeller's dossier, that the son was a far different species than his father, Amadeo. But after the Munich events when Victor's cohorts actually murdered an innocent family and Victor assumed the dead Zryden's persona in the French Embassy in West Germany—" Andreivich stopped. The subject was mind-boggling, too incredible a story to believe. Yet he knew the truth. Victor Zeller, posturing about as Velden Zryden, had infiltrated high corridors and gotten himself assigned to the Moufflon Task Force amid other scientists who had planned to fly over the Middle Eastern pyres to learn that they could about the nuclear devastation."

"That he is with Uri at this moment fills me with dread and

ominous foreboding, Comrade Andreivich. Such a man will do anything to have his way. *Anything!*''

Andreivich gulped down his vodka and braced himself for the next distasteful unveiling of news. ''Mr. Premier, the American President has just demanded the resignation of his Secretary of State.''

''But he was only recently appointed!''

''Yesterday, on the last day of the month, the resignation was demanded.''

The Premier's eyes fell to the Zeller file. He heaved a despondent sigh. ''So we have failed. Yes, it is so. We have failed both in dissuading the Americans to rid Europe of its recent missile deployment and in making Anthony Harding more palatable to them. Do they know something about Harding we don't know? Do you, Comrade Andreivich, know something you aren't telling me?''

''His detractors fueled the fire.''

''His *personal morals* fired the pyres. I am not enchanted with Harding, comrade. He merely was the best we had and as deeply as we probed, his loyalty and deeds in clandestine service since World War II has been impeccable. But I have never fooled myself. I know the man to be an impresario at orchestrating a subterranean information war, portraying the powers that be as doing the bidding of some clandestine organized spy ring when it is he himself who waves the baton. Yes, yes, his morals and his ethics are what I find appalling. This predatory assassin is no better than the lowliest of animals.'' The Premier clutched at his heart. His eyes bulged grotesquely.

''What is it, Nikolai, comrade, sir? What is happening? What can I do to help?'' Malenekov rushed around behind the desk. ''You must tell me, Nikolai! What must I do?'' He pivoted on one foot, pushed all the buttons on his intercom. ''Hurry, hurry, you jackasses. Come quickly! Something is happening to the Premier. Quick, summon emergency hospital staff, his physician! Someone. Anyone! Come quickly.'' He was pounding on the buttons, pushing, pulling levers excitedly, trying to give the Premier some solace. ''They are coming, Nikolai. They are coming to help. Hang on. Hold off the messengers of death. You cannot die. You must not die. Not now!''

But before help came, Premier Nikolai Vladechenko died in the KGB chief's arms.

* * *

The lights were on late at Party offices and the KGB headquarters at Dzerzhinsky Square. Strains of Chopin and Schubert
could be heard echoing through the deserted streets. Moscovites trudged to work through a raging rainstorm, an unexpected rarity in this season. At midafternoon, newscasters
wearing black suits appeared on Moscow television. The message was plain. A funeral cortege would wend its way through
Red Square. Workers were ordered to fly all flags at half-mast
for Premier Nikolai Vladechenko.

"Whistles will blow for three minutes. Factories and farms
will stop production for five. Vladechenko's body will be
placed with the venerated dead behind Lenin's Mausoleum. . . ." The newscasters unfurled the agenda.

In the neo-Renaissance office of KGB chief Andreivich Malenekov, Uri Mikhail's staunchest supporter was stunned,
stupefied as the Committee stood before him with the news.
"Comrade Malenekov, the Politburo has named you General
Secretary of the Politburo," the spokesman said quietly and
with great dignity.

Andreivich's first reaction was to want to ask, *"Why me?"*
Of course he restrained himself. He shook hands with the bear-
ers of enormous tidings and responsibilities. He carefully chose
his words, tears rolled down his cheeks.

"You understand my grief. The Premier was a father to all of
us." He collected himself with the consummate skill of a diplomat. Suddenly his thoughts lingered on Uri Mikhail. It was he
who should be the leader of the Party, not Andreivich Malenekov. Uri was born to the position, trained to political rhetoric,
protocol, and decorum.

"You have been chosen by the Central Committee to succeed Premier Vladechenko. Until the position fits you, merely
stress old alliances. Signal new approaches to any political issue with a judicious handshake, perfunctory nod, and quietly
invite our European and American friends to future talks concerning vital issues until we regroup. You were the first to
know what the world suspects. The Kremlin will make the official announcement in a day or two."

"I understand," said Malenekov. "Comrades, you will prepare for the state funeral. And please note, I am only General
Secretary of the Politburo, not the President of the Presidium."

He spoke almost apologetically, knowing how Uri Mikhail thirsted for the position.

Malenekov, following the customary vodka, politely sent the entourage on its way. "You understand, comrades, I've so many things to do."

Malenekov stood at the iron-grilled window, staring down at Dzerzhinsky Square. Barely a mile away was the Kremlin. He shook his head at the rapid changes.

Imagine, he, Andreivich Malenekov, General Secretary of the Politburo, was a whisper away from being named President of the Presidium. Given the KGB's awesome power and reputation for ruthlessness and brutality, it had long been assumed that the men who rule the Soviet Union would never allow a secret-police chief to hold the nation's highest post. Today, that obstacle had been surmounted.

"Oh, Uri Mikhail Gregorevich, where are you now that I need you most? You cannot be dead. If you were dead you would have found some way to communicate with me, if only through your ghost."

Ghost! Damnable Anthony Harding! He had never trusted the man. Never! What merit had Nikolai Vladechenko seen in him? Not even Uri Mikhail knew the absurdity of his involvements. That Harding was the Big Mole was whispered about throughout British and CIA intelligence communities. In the absence of the definitive discovery of the Big Mole or proof that his existence was a sophisticated Soviet disinformation plot, the allegations mounted, festered in the files, poisoning the perceptual apparatus of the Western nations, paralyzing an entire espionage establishment. And at the heart of all this doubt and ambiguity was the mysterious relationship between Amadeo Zeller and master KGB mole Anthony Harding. To make matters hideously complex, there was Harding's incongruously intimate marriage to Zeller's daughter, a deadly embrace.

A KGB agent using the cover of Sir Alexander York was with Uri, watching over him. Accidents can and did happen, but it seemed inconceivable that both men would be lost. It simply could not happen. The entire Moufflon Task Force lost? No! Never! He wouldn't believe it!

Andreivich Malenekov needed the company of a woman tonight, although he knew he should no longer be led by his passions. He was the General Secretary of the Politburo! *Un-*

derstand, comrade Andreivich? You must mend your ways. It is unacceptable for the General Secretary to lust after pleasures of the flesh. You must be discreet. Most discreet.

He poured a tumbler of vodka, guzzled it down, and opened a highly classified file titled: "For The Eyes Only of Premier Nikolai Vladechenko: Anton Schuller, a.k.a. Eugen Schuller, a.k.a. Ghost-Dancer.

Malenekov was not an erudite scholar of Vladechenko's class. Instinct guided his every move—instinct and a nose for sleuthing. He was a master propagandist and recognized the masters in every land by their proficiency at the game. Vladechenko, a hard-driving, hard-drinking exuberant man until illness slowed him down, was the quintessential Russian, a mixture of caution and opportunism, a genial knee slapper who never hesitated to crush his opponents.

Malenekov downed the vodka, poured another tumblerful, wondering how he would succeed in filling Vladechenko's shoes. A mystery man to the West and a cloud to his own people too, Malenekov must do his job well whether or not he proved to be merely a transitional leader.

Chapter Twenty

An unmarked government sedan rumbled through the gates of the Central Intelligence Agency complex in McLean, Virginia, and headed through the mists of a gray dawn to Washington. A half hour later it arrived at the west entrance of the White House.

Today there was something very special to mark this briefing, evident from the urgency in the eyes of the briefing officer, Lieutenant Colonel John Clay, a usually reserved, snow-white-haired man in his sixties who'd served the CIA since its creation following World War II. Today his briefcases contained sheaves of high-altitude photographs taken by satellite and overhead reconnaissance systems.

Yes, today would be different! Today John Clay would be marked as a hero. Not because he took the photos, for he hadn't. Photo lenses peering down from a variety of orbiting satellites whizzing about the earth were the real heroes. John Clay merely read the photos with uncanny talent. It had taken him the better part of forty-eight hours to spot the incongruities. A call was then made to the Chief Executive. And in moments John Clay would tell President MacGregor the most astounding news. The Scorpion helicopter carrying the Moufflon Task

Force was not missing. It had been found! And John Clay carried the proof in his briefcase.

President John MacGregor was made both ebullient and solemnly introverted by the news. After John Clay left the Oval Office, the President sighed with relief. His first impulse was to summon his aides, Bill Miller and Tom Kagen, but the President hesitated.

The sun, shimmering toward its zenith, glistened beyond the blue-green-tinted, bulletproof glass windows of the Oval Office, mottling the walls with pale and irregular shapes and adding a colorless dimension to the room. It was in this room that the President had signed the order giving birth to the highly clandestine Moufflon Task Force. In this room he had signed the pressing request from Valentina Lansing to permit her daughter, Valerie, a Georgetown lawyer, to accompany the task force. And it would be from this room that he would make his call to Valentina to assure her of her daughter's safety.

MacGregor made his clandestine call to Senator Lansing's wife. At the other end of the line, he heard several gasps, a tremulous voice muttering, "Thank God! Thank you, John, for letting me know to ease the pain I've suffered. I should have known Moufflon had some secret plan for directing the Scorpion toward its destiny. Before this is over, he will obtain the information we desperately need to learn who orchestrated the Middle East devastation. The Scorpion's sting will be felt worldwide. Project Moonscape will succeed, John. Be proud that you authorized the expedition!'' she said ecstatically. *Valerie was alive! Darius too!*

And when they returned from Project Moonscape, what marvels would unfurl? Valentina hung up the phone, reeling under the marvelous news. Once over the initial impact, she considered her daughter, Valerie. Truthfully, she was the daughter of Darius Bonifacio in every sense of the word, including her bravery and bulldog determination to settle the Zeller score for the death of her grandmother, Victoria Valdez Varga, and the plundering of the de la Varga and Valdez fortunes.

President MacGregor reexamined the aerial photos, the definite outline, even the name and I.D. numbers on the Scorpion. What would the ignominious truth be?

The President scanned the names on the task force roster. There was, of course, Darius Bonifacio, Moufflon himself, and

General Brad Lincoln, Lieutenant Colonel Jim Greer, and Valerie Lansing representing the U.S. Uri Mikhail Gregorevich represented the U.S.S.R., Prince Ben-Kassir, an international figure, represented France, Dr. Sen Yen Lu was from the Far East, Colonel Kusububu Katanga was from Nigeria, and Sir Alexander York from Britain. Matteus Montenegro and Gabriel Gadi were personally recommended by Moufflon himself, and no dossiers accompanied their briefs. There was also one addition, Velden Zryden, whose dossier, MacGregor had been told, was manufactured by the shrewdest, most imaginative experts in the business. The President's advisers had rejected Zryden, Katanga, and Sir Alexander York, but Moufflon, whose word was engraved in jade, insisted that these men, whatever dangers they posed, were necessary to the overall Moonscape plan. Moufflon knew that the answers he sought were somehow tied up with the operation of a secret space colony settlement in Mongolia. He was on his way there now with his task force, unbeknownst to the rest of the world, including President MacGregor.

"It's your show, Moufflon," the President mumbled aloud. "Now that I know you're alive, I wish I could transport myself to your destination, if only as an observer."

He turned his attention back to the recent imbroglio that threatened to explode into a political scandal—the dismissal of Anthony Harding as Secretary of State.

Chapter Twenty-one

A young, lean desert Mongol emerged from a crudely constructed lean-to, a shacklike structure well-camouflaged on a barren expanse of sand. Dressed in swathing robes and goatskins, the rawboned, bronzed desert warrior strode stealthily through the filthy canvas flaps of the makeshift door, his fierce black eyes searching the swiftly darkening ebony skies.

It was hot. A blazing sun beat down on the molten surface of sand and rock like a torch ready to set the world on fire. But now as he scanned the darkening plumes in the distance, the Mongol knew reprieve from the suffocating heat would soon be upon him. He pulled his robes about him, for despite the fierce heat, the wind, when it came, could drop temperatures to freezing.

The horizon, an unbearable pulsing crimson, was bitten into by miles of black, teethlike hills. To the east the heavens were a dim, spectral pink. The western sky gave no light to the earth. The Mongol, a British agent, was used to the Gobi. The land was always there, infinite, intractable, and would be here long after his own time on earth. He pulled his *ghutra* across his face, shielding his eyes from the glasslike grains of sand whipped to a fury by the increasing onslaught of winds tunneling at him. He'd been all over the world, but nowhere were the elements as devastating, as destructive, as abhorrent as in this desert.

The Mongol reached into his robe, probing his windswept garment for a compact communications relay unit. He tugged at the pencil antenna. Winds ballooned his robes and he looked as if he'd lift off the ground on his own power. His eyes scanned the immutable, approaching storm. Speaking in a clipped British accent, he made his first attempt at contact. "Artana to Z-12. . . . Come in, Z-12. . . . Come in. Artana, here. Do you read me?"

A filtered voice, cracked, exceedingly faint, popped from the hand-held CD unit. "Storm's on our tail. We can barely make you out. Are all the flights in?"

"No sign, sir. The winds are showing ugly eyes here. If contact breaks down, my orders are to proceed to an alternate plan."

"*Hold on, Artana.* . . . Message coming through. . . . What rot! Looks like you've got an hour to sunbathe in luxury, old chap. They've been sighted passing the midpoint to target. Shall we settle at 2400 hours, Artana?"

"You *are* optimistic, Z-12." He shoved the antenna into place, immobilizing the relay unit, and headed back toward the shack. The wind rose to the roar of thunder, assaulting the shack, causing it to swell and shake. The tentlike flap covering the entrance sunk in and out in frantic agitation, like a banner orchestrated by hidden demons. Artana had lived most of his young life in the Gobi Desert in Outer Mongolia, save for four years during his hitch in Nepal with British intelligence forces, but he'd never seen the likes of these infernal winds. He scanned the frightful, raging isolation of the sky. Dark, pulsating clouds bore ominous tidings on the horizon.

It's best the plane is delayed, Artana told himself. Clutching the goatskins tightly to his body, he turned his back on the ravaged earth and walked backwards, bucking headwinds. He made his way to the shack and disappeared inside.

Having arrived under cover of the storm, clusters of robed figures crawled forward on their bellies, inching their way toward the shack. Their dark eyes were ferocious with dedicated intent as they rushed the shack, broke in on Artana, and expertly slit his throat. In quick metamorphosis, two guerrillas slipped out of their robes and manned the communication devices.

One man, bearing an uncanny resemblance to the dead Artana, glanced at the apparent leader of the coterie of Chinese guerrillas who was awaiting a signal. "Turn on the playback feed. Shall we listen to the last few communiqués?" the lean Oriental asked in Mandarin dialect.

Artana's replacement nodded. He turned on the playback apparatus, listened to the last few recordings, cocking his head. The guerrilla leader cautioned the fraudulent Artana as the latter mouthed the words he heard and mimicked Artana's voice with extraordinary precision.

"You will listen, Chang Chou. Please exercise extreme caution. Sleep on straw with your shield as a pillow. You will report to your superior officer the moment you reach Ulan Bator and join the Moufflon Task Force. Is this understood? You know the passwords?"

"A lame man treads on the tail of the tiger."

"I say well done to the newly incarnated Artana. And the reply?" the Guerrilla leader asked.

"As above, so below; as below, so above."

"Well done, Artana. May the great spirit guide you."

The winds howled at hurricane decibel. The Moufflon Task Force alit from the Scorpion helicopter and moved in a body through the tunneling winds, clinging to one another for support. They headed for the Quonset hut, entered a large, cavernous area that resembled a deserted hangar for a dozen 747's. It was a drab, uninviting, rectangular-shaped interior that had withstood the abrasive elements and ravages of time. Here and there were scattered several portable screens on wheels, blackboards, and displayed weather bulletins. Supply and equipment requisitions were tacked to walls consisting of planks nailed together. A few makeshift desks and chairs were clustered together in groups about the room.

The new arrivals stared in silence, wondering, unable to reconcile their expedition and its relationship to this barren hinterland. *The Paris seminars had prepared them for this?*

"Where the devil are we?" Valerie Lansing asked Uri Mikhail.

"I'm afraid to venture any form of speculation. I'll say one thing for your Moufflon. He does what he believes in and always what best suits his purpose."

"Now, what the hell is that supposed to mean?" she asked.

Before Uri replied, they were ushered through the next room. Several men and women manned an electronic nightmare of wheels, turbines, and scale models of a wide variety of craft. It all resembled a gigantic motion-picture set for an extraterrestrial movie. Each man and woman was preoccupied with his or her project and was barely aware of the newcomers.

"What the bloody devil?" Alexander York moved closer to Jim Greer. "Do you know where we are?"

"Beats the hell out of me, sir," Greer replied, eyes widening in astonishment.

Valerie stared at the various models, at the beehive activity, and knew they were witnessing something so highly classified it had not been discussed at the briefing in Paris. She saw laser antimissile systems and something resembling an outer-space wheel with orbiting spacecraft models buzzing in and out of its atmosphere.

"Shades of Walt Disney!" she muttered to Brad Lincoln. "Where are we, General," she asked in a hushed voice. "Certainly you'd know."

"I'm as surprised as you are," he confessed.

Valerie and the others walked in dislocated circles, forward, backward, eyes roving in all directions. Awestruck at this mammoth mock-up of a space colony, they found the labyrinthine setup captivating. A thousand questions formed in their beleaguered minds.

"A full-scale space settlement here on Earth?" Most gasped at the awesome sight, unable to reconcile their mission with their presence here—wherever they were.

So mesmerized were they by this other world, they hardly noticed that Moufflon, Prince Ben-Kassir, and Matteus, the latter always a hairbreadth away from Darius, had led General Brad Lincoln toward two men who were stepping out of spacesuits on a ramp six feet above the ground.

Commander George Robbins and Dr. Bill Malay signaled an acknowledgment and began to descend the iron steps to the platform where the task force members gazed out into the complex spacecraft mock-up. Robbins, a tall, muscular man in his early fifties, was silver-haired and had an easy smile. Malay was an impatient Eurasian, small framed with dark inscrutable eyes. Both men possessed an unmistakable geniality.

"Welcome to Z-12 Andromeda," said Commander Robbins. "We laughingly call it 'Narcissus' due to that gigantic mirror you see in the mock-up. It's actually about a mile in diameter and floats weightlessly above the ring of the settlement and reflects constant sunlight on to smaller mirrors which direct it into the ring through shutters fixing the length of each day. Without this giant mirror, Narcissus would cease to exist."

Both men had shed their spacesuits and moved about easily in casual khaki uniforms. Robbins waved the group closer to the guardrails. "For the moment you are viewing the marvels of space technology. Soon you will walk along the boulevards, enter the houses, swim in the swimming pool. Tomorrow we shall convene formally. However, it is necessary to leave you with a vital fact to ponder. What you see stretched before you to near infinity—the main settlement—is actually inside an enormous tube. We have endeavored to simulate space down to the reproduction of a force that feels like gravity. The settlement is a gigantic wheel inside a tube some four hundred feet in diameter, surrounded by spokes stationed inside the ring a mile across. Once every minute, the wheel spins gently. Now here's the provocative point. This leisurely rotation differs infinitely from the lunar modules that first transported man to nonterrestrial soil. Do any of you care to hazard a guess as to why?"

Dr. Sen Yen Lu nodded. "What you said earlier. The spin produces a force that feels like gravity."

"Correct, Dr. Lu. The human body needs gravity to prevent deterioration, and gravity also makes normal activities for us earthlings practicable. Imagine flipping a pancake only to see it drift weightlessly around." He smiled, but the others barely reacted. "The artificial gravity inside the tube of the main settlement makes the hubward direction equivalent to 'up.' The ground is inside the tube, farthest from the hub. The need for gravity commits us to building space colonies instead of sending settlers to an existing location—the moon or the planets. The moon, however romantic it is for lovers, is irretrievably inhospitable. Its gravity is minute. Imagine fourteen days of sunlight followed by fourteen days of night. Agriculture would be nil, solar energy an impossible dream. So my friends, attendants will show you to your quarters. Unfortunately you will not be permitted inside the tube until you've been thoroughly briefed."

"Is it within the realm of possibility to know where we are? And how long has this, uh, space-colony settlement been on the drawing board?"

Valerie Lansing posed the questions burning in the minds of the new arrivals.

"We are somewhere in the upper Gobi between Ulan Bator and Lung. The answer to your second question is that we're long past the drawing-board stage and are into actualizing the plan. We've been here for approximately fifteen years."

His reply drew astonished reactions. "You find that difficult to believe? Consider it a well-kept secret. Concealed from the general public until we researched the possibilities of actualization, it's no longer a dream. You will go to your quarters, freshen up or rest, and we shall meet again in the mess hall at 1800." Commander Robbins stepped from behind the podium, turned off the microphone, and edging in closer to Darius and Prince Ben-Kassir, was about to speak when he caught sight of a flashing white light on a panel on the podium counter. Robbins frowned. "Excuse me, gentlemen." He moved back and, holding an earphone to his ear, listened. He lifted his eyes, scanned the faces of the task force. "Yes, I'll take care of it."

He returned to Darius's side. "Major, which among the task force members is Uri Mikhail Gregorevich?"

Youseff tensed. Darius, without being obvious, asked, "Can you tell me the problem?"

"His nation's leader has died. We think he might want to know."

"Premier Vladechenko is dead?" Darius reacted to the news.

"Youseff." He turned to the Prince. "Do you wish to tell him?" He looked directly into Youseff's eyes.

Youseff's dubious look was answer enough. "It's best the official communiqué come from Soviet command headquarters," he instructed Commander Robbins, who agreed.

"Something else," added Robbins. "Did you pass over Substation Z-10 en route to Z-12?"

"We maintained momentary radio contact," said Darius, "but a desert storm shot us off course. I switched to radar and the Grim Reaper, our on-board computer, maintained our course. Why?"

"Something we hadn't counted on. A muck-up somewhere. Three days ago we changed our codes and ciphers. Z-10 didn't give the corresponding ciphers."

"Meaning what? Give him the benefit of the doubt. Perhaps he forgot. The desert can do strange things to a man's mind."

"We did. The cipher was coded twice. When it wasn't properly coded back, our technicians fed his voice through the detection machine."

"And?"

"Bingo." Robbins scratched his chin thoughtfully. "The agent manning the Z-10 substation *isn't* our man. Worse, he's coming in by chopper in a day or two. We're to send his replacement."

"Why is he coming in?"

"Routine, end of a three-week hitch. You're right. The desert can fry a man's brain. He's in for a week and out for three."

"Then you'll be able to spot him and act accordingly. What's the problem, Commander?"

"A thousand francs to one says he'll be a clone."

"A clone? You mean a reproduction?" Darius's astonishment communicated itself to Youseff Ben-Kassir, commanding the Prince's rapt attention.

"I've seen some astonishing things here at Z-12. Among the most baffling to me is the rate at which spies infiltrate the area. How they get past our Fort Knox security is baffling. It's clipped our wings, become an embarrassment we've been unable to circumvent."

"This business concerning cloning—surely you jest?" said Youseff.

"It took sharp eyes and experts to tell the difference. Our men were being replaced with doubles. Actually we used our technology to ferret out the impostors. We proved our suspicions to be correct in two instances. Before that? . . . Well, which one is Uri Mikhail Gregorevich?" Robbins asked, anxious to be finished with his business.

Darius indicated the man standing close to Valerie Lansing. The Commander addressed himself to the task force. "Before you adjourn to your quarters, will Uri Mikhail Gregorevich come with me to the communications center?''

"Uri, you're wanted. Communications center? Does that mean we have contact with the rest of the world?" Valerie sighed in relief as Uri, at once displaying the decorum of his nation and office, nodded and moved forward, excusing himself to her.

The two men moved off the platform steps and headed toward a glass-enclosed room containing wall-to-wall electronic communication devices. Valerie peered after them, then sighting Velden Zryden's interest, blinked, turning toward Brad Lincoln. "I'd give anything for a cup of coffee."

"Music to my ears," Brad said. "You'll want yours, of course, with chocolate."

"You are discerning, General."

Uri Mikhail collapsed in the chair. His breathing came rapidly, erratically; he was left breathless by the astounding news. His first reaction was stupefaction, then hurt and emotional stress. The Premier had been like a second father to him; the loss was great. Then remembering Uncle Nikolai's age, his recent infirmity, he grew less aggrieved. He brought his face forward into his hands, needing to shield his tear-stung eyes.

"Of course I must return to Russia," he said, drawing himself erect. "Commander, it is imperative that I return."

"Negative. Negative. The best I can offer you is satellite transmission to the Premier's interim successor, General Secretary of the Politburo Andreivich Malenekov."

"Andreivich? *Andreivich Malenekov!*" Of course. Why not? Uri, at once deflated, understood party politics, the need for immediate command. "You suggest you can patch me through to Moscow."

"On an open line. You understand, any satellite can pick up the transmission. So, Mr. Gregorevich, if you plan to speak of private matters, I would advise against it. I suggest you speak only in the most general terms unless you are familiar with ciphers. Unfortunately, there's no transportation out of Z-12 until the Major flies you out in the Scorpion. You'll rendezvous with the—" Robbins stopped. "You understand. Security, you know."

"I understand. How long will it take to get me through to Moscow to the General Secretary."

"It depends. Since the Middle East fiasco. . . . I'll give you a quarter hour's preparation. Is that enough? Then we'll try for transmission. We're nearly two thousand miles from Moscow in a remote area man has only seen recently through the marvels of satellite photography."

"Chanda!" Darius called to the tall, bronze-skinned officer. "What the devil are you doing here at Z-12?"

Dai Chanda, once Major Chanda of the Fourth Indian Brigade in the North African campaign during World War II, turned, struck by the voice. Recognizing at once the former SAS commando, he walked forward and shook his hand.

"This is a most welcome surprise, Major Bonifacio. I am here with Z-12 for ten years," he said in his precisely clipped King's English. As he explained his involvement and interest in survival in space as a possible remedy to overpopulation and worldwide food shortages, Darius recollected the valuable service the turbaned Sikhs of Britain's Fourth Indian Regiment performed in World War II. The sappers, best in the world, were most unique in their ability to perceive the vast numbers of hidden mines that had eluded metal detectors. Darius had sought Chanda's company. Dinner followed. Chanda delighted to be sought after and interrogated concerning the Sikhs' special talents, had explained the philosophy of his people, the practice of meditation to bring about inner peace. Darius had asked him, "Why do you, a man of peace, fight in the military?" Chanda had replied, "In India, we follow the dictates of the Crown. Military service is required, and one must adapt to the society in which he lives. In his spare time, he can be what his heart whispers to him, that which he sees clearly with his third eye."

"Is there a way in which this third eye can be developed?" Darius had asked. His questions overwhelmed Chanda. How many years does such development take? Would Major Chanda impart this valued information to Darius? Could this capability be used to defuse war in the minds of tyrants?

Major Chanda had explained the merits of transcendental meditation. He explained that the powers were not his to disseminate, but he could instruct Darius on proper techniques.

"The powers must only be used for doing good in the world, or the law of recompense will hurl itself back upon you in godawful force."

Now he asked Chanda to dine with them.

"I want you to tell me the wonders you've perfected here at Z-12 Andromeda."

"I will talk with you, Major, but my conversation is limited. Security, you know. We are under tight wraps. The recent Middle East fiasco taught the world nothing. Many surviving nations covet this information. Global 2000, the Malthusian concept of systematic euthanasia and the destruction of certain nations by the year 2000, faces the peoples of this earth, and still the nations scramble for power. Total annihilation is what they'll reap if they are not careful."

"What exactly are you trying to say?" queried Darius.

Chanda glanced about at the cluster of people nearby and drew Darius off to the edge of the room, away from the television scanner. Darius noted his disquiet at once. Chanda removed a gold pin from his jacket pocket and inserted the pin close to the top of a tiny crystal ball on a chain around his neck. "Shall I walk you to your quarters? Perhaps later we shall talk. Total insanity permeates Andromeda," he said quietly, escorting Darius through the narrow, dark corridor into an adjoining complex.

"Here at Andromeda there is no privacy. Paranoids man the controls."

"Commander Robbins?" Darius stared at the crystal amulet.

"No. His superior, the scientist Jonathan Marl, is the real commander. You'll meet him. Be careful, Major. The man is eaten by hatred, greed, avarice, and revenge."

"Then it's no different here at all. Mankind has learned few lessons." His eyes were riveted fiercely on the amulet. Questions surfaced.

"None, Major. I shall get word to you where we can meet to talk without fear of being videotaped and recorded."

"That bad, eh? Chanda, what the devil is that thing around your neck?" he blurted finally, unable to check his curiosity.

"A communicating device. It works on the principle of holographic photography, and also contains electronic transistors. Plunging the gold pin into it disengages it. Otherwise it is activated by sound. The mere sound of my voice or yours . . . So

if anyone asks anything concerning your interest in me, I'd say
that you asked me to show you your assigned quarters. It's best
you keep your distance from me from now on. Here we are,
Major. I believe you've been assigned separate quarters with,
uh, Prince Ben-Kassir and Gadi and Montenegro. The task
force is assigned to adjoining quarters. Now, good day, suh.''
Chanda saluted and, turning spiffily, pivoting on one foot with
a British officer's panache, and walked briskly away. He
stopped, retraced his steps to Darius. ''Major, suh?''

Darius, pondering the man's words, had not budged a step.
''Yes, Chanda.''

''Should you meet other old friends, may I suggest you exercise extreme caution?''

''I had thought here at Andromeda things would be different.''

''Where human nature is concerned, nothing will be different
until there is an international raising of consciousness. Where
there is money, you'll always find greed for its acquisition.
Where ambition breeds, jealousy and hatred lurk around the
corner. You need no philosophic romancing, Major, suh.'' He
turned abruptly and left Darius again. Darius stared after him,
saw him pause en route to the enormous Quonset hut. Darius
was unable to see, but he was certain Chanda had removed the
gold pin from the crystal and slipped it into his pocket. Why his
hush-hush attitude? And who the devil would he be encountering among his old friends? Why must he employ extreme
caution? He'd gone over every inch of this project back in Corsica for the past five years. In the past five months he had pored
over the plans for Z-12 Andromeda. He was certain the project
of manning space colonies was as viable as the beam-weapons
program.

Darius entered his quarters. They were modest, military issue with bare walls, two rooms, an adjoining portable shower.
Two bunk beds in the first room, a desk, and wall pegs for
clothing. The second room was similar and would house Matteus and the second bodyguard, Gabriel Gadi. Darius opened
his briefcase, removed the Jonathan Marl dossier, sat at the
desk, and began to read.

Youseff entered in moments, his face drawn, deep concern
etched on his face. ''You were right. I should have spoken to
my son. If I didn't feel like an intruder on his sorrow, I would

have. How ambivalent I must seem. I, Youseff Ben-Kassir, warrior of the Great Atlas, am hesitant to face my own son. It makes no sense. I make no sense. Darius, what's wrong? You look as if you've seen a ghost.''

"I have, and I may be about to encounter another. I'd say your choice of words is most curious; you elected to say 'a ghost.' '' He lifted his eyes from the dossier. "Youseff, if I declared the world had gone mad, would you think me daft?''

"The consequences of thermonuclear war are dancing on our tail and you ask such a question?''

"We came to Andromeda to learn, among many things, who might be responsible for exploding the nuclear warheads in the Middle East.''

"Yes, yes, it's our goal, our quest, your obsession. What else? You've stumbled on something noteworthy?''

"Why don't you remove your boots, get out of your spacesuit, don your khakis, and relax. How much time before mess?''

"Two hours, perhaps less.''

"It'll take more than that to unravel this can of worms. We both agree there's only one condition that would prompt a superpower to launch a thermonuclear salvo against the adversary's homeland, right?'' Darius, suddenly remembering Chanda's neck crystal, glanced about the room at the electronic equipment. He'd seen the stationary scanner lens on entering. The lens had been activated. Housed in a corner recess, the wide-angle lens had only to sweep slightly to comb the room. That slight movement did not escape him. "I'm tired, we'll talk later,'' he said, muttering in a Farsi dialect. "Talk is limited. The room is bugged. We'll talk later. Meanwhile, read this.'' He tossed Youseff the highly confidential Jonathan Marl dossier.

Valerie Lansing was ushered into her quarters. Privacy at last! It was a compact room containing a bunk bed, desk, video monitor, intercom. There was even video recording equipment to play video cassettes, a means of enlightening the task force on the merits of Z-12 Andromeda. On the bed were a pair of khaki camouflage fatigues. She turned on the VCR. Instantly a man appeared on the screen, narrating a warm welcome to members of the task force.

''It's a pleasure to receive you, my friends. Hopefully, you will find your accommodations suitable following your harrowing journey. Clothing—not designer labels, but appropriate nonetheless—is provided for you. You have communication devices on your wristbands which will not work on our frequency. Please leave them with Captain Joseph Carlini and wear the ones you find on your desk. They have the same capabilities as the ones you'll temporarily discard. Inter communication is permitted with task-force members. We ask only that you do not wear devices into the settlement. Its frequency bands are antagonistic to the frequency levels inside the space colony. Upon your departure from Andromeda, you will leave these behind with the orderly, who will return yours. Now, as you make yourselves comfortable, we shall briefly pan over the space colony to familiarize you with the marvels of space science, to prepare your inquiring minds for any questions you might have during briefing tomorrow.''

Valerie instinctively felt the camera scanner sensors activate. She spotted the lens, feigned nonchalance, and with a trained eagle eye measured its capabilities. She located a stall shower in an adjoining niche. Realizing she actually had very little privacy, she placed fresh clothing on a chair propped next to the stall shower, got inside, and began to undress. *Big Brother be damned. Here in Outer Mongolia yet! Incredible.*

In less than eight minutes, she had showered and dressed in the khaki camouflage fatigues and stepped out from behind the louvered shower doors. Scooping flight suit and accessories up, she hung them on hangers on the wall pegs. She glanced slowly about the room, her eyes stopping abruptly at the desk. Something was different! Something had been placed on the desk while she showered. A small box and a card. She turned behind her, studied the door. Why hadn't she locked it? There was a bolt she could have used. Slowly, somewhat dazed at her carelessness, she moved to the desk. She opened the card, read its contents: ''Miss Lansing: A small gift to welcome you aboard. The Andromeda staff.'' Relieved for a moment, she sank into the chair. *Easy, Val, you're too far away from home to be gripped by paranoia. So open your gift. Don't be so dumb. What can happen to you here?*

She opened the box. It was a crystal ball on a silver chain—or was it platinum? She smiled, lifted it from the box, wrapped the chain around her fingers, and dangled the ball before her eyes, swinging it back and forth in small circular sweeps. A voice from seemingly nowhere came at her. The damned crystal fogged up, held her captive as a scene formed within it.

C'mon, girl, watch what's happening. Don't be moved by tricks!

A hologram! That's it; it must be a hologram! The mist layered and circled about inside. Bright lights bounced off the crystal. The voice became clearer. "Valerie Lansing, place the amulet around your neck. It will protect you while you are at Andromeda. You are in dire need of protection. The amulet of protection shall serve you well. Go ahead. Around your neck."

Valerie, startled, peered about the room. She'd heard something, someone. *What?* Her eyes fell on the amulet. Slowly the voice repeated the message. It was a voice within a voice, and it seemed to come from inside her. Somnambulistically, she did the voice's bidding.

She was like a woman in a trance, aware of her mental suspension but unable to circumvent her actions. Once the amulet was around her neck, Valerie felt a surge of electric power, indefinable energy, totally indescribable. She braced herself against the desk and gulped long, deep breaths.

"You realize we are quite isolated here," Youseff said, tossing the Jonathan Marl dossier back to him. "If anything should happen . . ." On his feet, Youseff peered about the windowless room. "Do the Moor and the Israeli bodyguard have alternate plans in case things sour here?" Once again they spoke in Farsi dialect.

"You ask a needless question. Why?"

"The Scorpion is hangared in a sealed compartment, and guarded."

"Those are the accommodations I demanded at the outset of our negotiations. I wouldn't want any neophyte near the Scorpion to sabotage it. I intend to get my task force home to safety. That is my commitment. That is my promise. And my word shall not be despoiled."

"If we live to leave," Youseff admonished. "That dossier indicated Marl possesses an unstable mind. Why did you not have doubts before Andromeda? And if they are doubts, tell me what you suspect. My concerns are superficial, but I am sure, knowing you, that you see far more into the dossier than I.''

"It is said, and wisely so, by master sleuths that a criminal using an alias is usually caught because he clings to something from his past. The slightest little thing, like smoking the same brand of cigarettes, can be a tip-off. Or employing his real initials with a different name. Even an infirmity, some little birthmark, unless it is excised by surgery, can be a giveaway, as can any habit, likes, dislikes. It takes the cleverness of a real psychopath to plot deviousness for years, with the idea of vengeance. Crippled, isolated personalities who only live for the day of magnificent redemption. And schizoid personalities, Youseff, whose lives are made up of these things. They nurse injustices with bitterness, sorrow, and hatred that fester over the years.''

"What are you saying?"

Darius stopped abruptly. Once again remembering Chanda's crystal ball, he glanced at the scanner and quickly turned so his lips were impossible to read, lowered his voice, spoke in a regional Farsi, suggested they not discuss anything of importance.

Youseff understood.

Dr. Jonathan Marl sat in his makeshift office in the Quonset hut compound, observing a video screen. Valerie Lansing onscreen was placing the crystal amulet around her neck. Marl, in his sixties, was of medium build, barrel-chested, with a shock of curly white hair. He wore thick tortoiseshell glasses, a beard, and a mustache.

With him, seated around the desk, observing the action on the screen, were Commander Robbins and the Eurasian scientist, Dr. Bill Malay.

"Did you decode the Russian's message to Moscow?" Dr. Marl asked George Robbins.

"Cipher experts are on it, sir. The sources were the KGB. For a period of time we were out of contact. The nuclear explosions in the Middle East may be cause for interference. The Caspian Sea became a virtual cauldron of boiling water. Fallout continues in the Caucasus. When will it end, sir?"

"When I decide it will end."

Commander Robbins, a military man through and through,

merely nodded. He'd learned not to incur Jonathan Marl's rancor or fire his wrath. Beyond the obsessive-compulsive lunatic fringe of immoral global politicians, whom he'd gladly boil in oil and fricassee, marched a controlled lunacy of men and women who had laid their innocence upon sacrificial altars before their god science. Robbins loathed them and their xenophobia and their complicated mathematical equations designed to confuse mankind. Centered in a realm of ideas and equations comprehensible only to their elite minds, these mathematical geniuses with *Star Wars* mentalities created tools of global annihilation, mathematically precise war games designed to wipe out not only their enemy but mankind in general. These revered men of science actually dreamed up doomsday machines to annihilate the two-fisted, tough battleground soldiers who actually fought the wars. Now they all became cannon fodder for the space technology. And all of it was camouflaged by this fifteen-year involvement with space colonies, a dream of the future. Who was kidding whom? Would it ever work? If Robbins brooded over his inner thoughts, he learned not to dwell on them, for that S.O.B. Marl could damn near read— Did he say damn near? The man was a clairvoyant. Not only did Robbins check his words, but he'd programmed himself never to think unless Marl was fully concentrated on another subject.

Dr. Marl snapped off the television monitor, a triumphant leer settled on his face. He glanced at the wall clock. "We have time for a game of chess, George." He pulled the black-and-white board, with its geometrically shaped chess pieces, toward him.

He tossed the crutch lying at his elbow to the floor. "Russia, America, or us? Who will win out?" His laughter filled the room.

Dr. Malay, an imperceptible scowl on his face, turned around at his desk across the room and quickly absorbed himself in a stack of files.

"Wouldn't you be surprised if the final outcome proves in their favor?" George Robbins asked his host as he placed a chair next to the desk. His eyes silently challenged Marl. In a precise but gentle movement, Robbins lifted the chessboard and the chessmen toppled to the floor. "It really doesn't take much effort to upset the entire game play, does it?"

"Must I remind you I am in charge here? If you don't like it, Robbins, why do you stay?"

"Good question. Give me the dossier compiled on me and I'll leave at once."

"No! You're too valuable. Men of your loyalty and caliber are not easy to come by."

Bill Malay pushed his glasses over his inscrutable eyes. "Really, gentlemen, we've come too far for this type of behavior."

"Yes, we have," snapped George Robbins, picking up the pieces. "Now," he addressed Marl, "for some insane reason, one quite beyond our comprehension, you find it necessary to play God."

Marl blinked, his serenity thoroughly punctured by this time.

"Play God?" Marl posed the question in mockery. "I wonder," he added. "Would you, could you ever understand?"

"You could try me," Robbins said, dumping the chessmen onto the board. He paused to light his pipe, eyeing Marl over the smoke rings.

Bill Malay moved in, reassembling the chessmen. The sooner they commenced the game, the less volatile Marl would become. "Isn't it enough we've come this far," Malay reasoned, "actually writing our own ticket? If we are patient, gentlemen, we can sell our services to the highest bidder and retire like pashas. This animosity breeds hatred, and hatred paves the way for errors and irrational judgments."

"How would you know how I was treated?" said Marl. "But you're right. I am filled with hatred. But I'll make no errors this time. My fervent dedication to my adopted nation gave me no protection. They permitted me to be murdered. Yes, I said murdered! Their complicity spelled my doom and all because I was too honest to play their sneaky games. I was murdered. My real dossier, under my real identity, claims me a victim to a mountain-climbing accident. They came to me, those men of the cartel, and in confidence asked me to be part of a global conspiracy. In all conscience, I could not, I told them. Think on it, they said. They romanced me for six months. My continued refusal rankled them. I am a man of science. I have made a commitment to the world, I told them. God, how naive I was. No one listened. So they found their godless man. Their assassin, the man who with skillful expertise could take my role in life—my brother! He moved in with me for six months, learned all my idiosyncrasies. We were twins, you see. The assignment wasn't too difficult. He took me to Bavaria on the pretext of business. What easy prey I was for him. An accident while mountain climbing. I can still see his face leering at me while he removed my spikes and jerked the rope, my safety net. I went hurtling past him, down . . . down . . . into caverns. But I didn't die. The snow itself became my savior. I was hurt, badly injured. My left leg was and is badly mangled. But I survived. From a hospital bed I learned that *I* didn't die at all. That *my brother* had fallen to his death. Actually, for nearly a year I believed the story. I believed that I, not Eugen, was the survivor, that my eyes had been playing tricks. That my brother hadn't intended to kill me at all. Then one day I read about the strides *I* was making in England at Cambridge. Naturally I wanted to get out of the hospital, but I remained there two years, barely able to talk from the shock and multiple operations done to save my leg."

"Why have you never told us this before?" Robbins asked quietly.

"I have my reasons."

"We've been your family for fifteen years. You could have confided in us. We share far more horrendous secrets, Jonathan."

"It's a private matter. I want vengeance."

"So you play God and destroy the world because you're angry at your brother?"

"Angry? *Angry?* I would kill the bastard if he were here this minute. What gives them—and the politicians—the right to deal nuclear trump cards to the unsuspecting masses? *Play God,* you say? Where does the chain of command begin? With us, the scientists! Not with those politicians oozing with saprogenicity. Those puffed-up men, swollen with their own self-importance, are locked into a time warp we control. The fruits of their labor will be death."

"Whatever forces are at work inside you, I suggest you thrust the hatred from mind."

"Is there no limit to their perfidy?" Marl snapped, running his fingers through his shock of white hair. "See, the trauma, shock of my murder turned my hair white. For a year, I struggled to learn how to speak, only to keep silent about my accident. I became a madman, yes, possessed night and day by vengeance, the need to be avenged. Two years later, when I was well enough to leave the hospital, I did. I took a lowly clerical job in a library and began to accumulate news clippings about my illustrious brother who took over my identity. Oh, he had changed his name, metamorphosed into a spectacular political-science genius, but I'd know him anyplace. Then I read about the space program, and I knew the future rested in space. I went to my former home in St. Bartolemo, a home that along with an inheritance had been stolen from me. I broke into the house and stole every valuable art object I could lay my hands on. Then I sold the goods for a substantial sum, enough to buy me new papers, a name, and a profession so I could join the remote brotherhood of scientists then working with lasers.''

Marl was sweating. He leaned in, opened a desk drawer, and removed several vials and a syringe. He removed his bush jacket, rolled up his sleeve, bound his arm with rubber tubing, and injected himself.

"Let me do that," Robbins said, moving forward.

"No. I can do it myself. Not a pretty sight, is it, my two devoted friends." He removed the syringe, broke the needle, and tossed the empty into a waste receptacle. For a moment he leaned back in his chair, his pained eyes rolling upward until the rush produced the expected euphoria. Then he pulled up his trouser leg, baring the grotesquely malformed leg in a brace from the knee down.

"Look at this leg. Tell me, reassure me that this monstrosity is not real. Is it a figment of my imagination? Tell me the pain I still feel after fifteen years is not real. Tell me I am not helplessly and hopelessly addicted for all time to heroin to ameliorate the assaulting pain. Tell me I have but to snap my fingers to escape this state of the walking dead.''

"I had thought you a superman," said Robbins. "That despite this infirmity, you had devoted your life to science. You're alive, Jonathan. Look what you and your staff have accomplished. Look out at the settlement, and think how year after year of laborious, painstaking, precision work and brilliant brainpower, you created the answer to mankind's dilemma—survival. You've suffered anguish and pain. You've suffered unthinkable horror. In all fairness, I beg you bear this in mind. If our country hadn't helped you—the equipment, the manpower, whatever you needed, they sent. Now you're ready to sell them down the river.''

"Helped me? Oh, yes, they *helped*, didn't they? When they saw what I had dedicated a lifetime to—fifteen long, arduous years of my life in constant pain. Yes, they aided and abetted me, requisitioned all our needs. They want me beholden to them. They want to announce to the world, "We made it possible for Jonathan Marl to perfect his theories. That will be the echo, mind you. 'We did it'—not 'he did it.' ''

Marl leaned in toward the intercom, snapped it on, and barked, "Joseph, where the hell are you? Bring some coffee.''

"Yes, sir, I'll be there in a moment," the filtered voice came back.

Marl reached for a cigarette, lit it himself, ignoring the outstretched hands with lighters. He waved them off. "Too late to teach an old dog. I'm used to doing for myself." He puffed on the smoke, inhaling deeply. "Play God, you say, Robbins?" He shook his head. "If by playing God you mean that I am entitled to decide who reaps the benefits from my fifteen years of dedicated work, then yes, I play God. I am entitled. It's only fair.''

"To kill off one-third of the world? You call that fair?"

"Both Russia and the free world are thoroughly educated in the lessons of foul play, and you expect me to be fair.''

"The odds are stacked against the free world, and you know it!''

"Ah. That's when the game becomes interesting. As soon as the odds increase against one or the other—''

"It's a shame you should remain so bitter and feel nothing but self-pity." He stopped as Marl's aide entered wheeling a tray with freshly brewed coffee on it.

"I didn't bring sweets. You dine at 1800, Dr. Marl," Joseph Carlini said quietly, placing coffee on the desk for the three men. Carlini, a bantamweight wearing thick-lensed glasses, was in his fifties. He was on the staff of scientists who worked closely with Jonathan Marl. Carlini had elected to make himself indispensable to the Chief of Staff. Sensing he had stepped into a hornet's nest, he quickly retreated, shutting the door behind him. In the next room, Carlini retired to his office, turned on a recording device and an intercom. He locked the door behind him, secured earphones over his head, and listened to the conversation in Jonathan Marl's office.

"Whether or not you like it, you'll hear me out," Robbins continued. "For years I've considered it an honor and privilege to work with the revered Dr. Jonathan Marl. Recently, when I discovered the despicable game you played, I tried to understand the motivation behind your loathing. As a participant in the integral teamwork of the last fifteen years, the surmounting of uncountable obstacles, hardships, I've seen miracles performed. Yet what you did, what you are about to do, is a flagrant crime of unspeakable horror. It is inexcusable—"

"I don't have to listen to you."

"But you will. Consider this, Jonathan. Consider this carefully. Because of what happened to you—the obstacles, deprivations, even *your own murder*—what you consider to be handicaps are possibly the very tools that jarred you out of your state of self-satisfaction."

Malay retreated into the shadows as the electricity mounted between the men.

"Are you quite through?" Marl said caustically.

"Are you—with self-pity?"

Marl smashed his cigarette stub in an ashtray, his face suffused with anger, but Robbins refused to let up on him.

"No ordinary man delights in the prospect of facing life as a cripple and drug addict. But you, sir, are no ordinary man. Whatever power rules the universe chose you. Only a man who has endured what you've endured could have brought fifteen barren years into fruition—precious, unendurable years that made you a giant among men. Just think, Jonathan. If you hadn't been *murdered*, if you hadn't overcome all those obstacles, you might have been a nobody back home, a comfortable, stodgy nobody with an atrophied brain instead of an atrophied leg."

Marl reached for his crutch, raised it in the air, and brought it crashing down on the chess set. Turning the crutch around to the armrest, he swung broadly and finished the job. The chess pieces went flying every which way. Then rising on one foot, pulling himself up painfully, he slipped his arm in the crutch bracelet, leaning on it for support. His body slumped over, his chest heaved. He waved the two men out of the room belligerently and fell into his seat when the door closed after them. Muffled sobs racked his body uncontrollably.

General Brad Lincoln, Jim Greer, and the others entered their quarters. Seven cots occupied one wall, a foot locker at each. The showers were at the end of the bare windowless room. The task force moved slowly into the barracks and selected cots randomly, each staking his own claim. Most of the men, dazed from what they'd seen, fell immediately onto the cots, introverted, barely noticing their companions.

"Interesting, isn't it, Greer," said Brad, observing the others nonchalantly. "In Paris, aboard the Lodestar and Scorpion, I got the distinct feeling that the men possessed some demonic loathing for one another."

"It's what we saw over the Middle East. What we've been privvy to here, something rather spectacular. Did you know about Z-12? Were you briefed? What are the chances of outside communication? Why did Robbins single out the Russian? What the devil is going on?"

"Did I know about Z-12? No. Was I briefed? No. In answer to the rest of your queries, I don't know."

Joseph Carlini entered the barracks, stood at the entrance, introduced himself. "Gentlemen, I will pass among you to distribute orientation summaries." He turned the lever on a complicated wall console containing a large video screen and telephone intercoms. The screen lit up. He inserted a video cassette. In moments briefing officer Bill Malay appeared on the screen.

"Before I turn up the volume to activate the cassette, let me explain. The video is a form of briefing we employ here at Z-12. You are not required to watch and listen, but what you learn from Lieutenant Commander Malay will answer many questions forming in your minds and shorten the actual briefing when we visit the settlement tomorrow. Please remove your communication wristbands. I will give you replacements attuned to our frequency bands. They are much like the devices you employ."

Carlini moved among them, making the exchange. "Remember, chow is at 1800," he said before departing. He raised the volume on the video recorder as he left.

All eyes, all ears were on the screen, listening.

"It isn't the George V, is it?" hissed Alexander York to Dr. Sen Yen Lu. The Oriental's eyes left the screen momentarily, glanced at York, and turned back to the screen without comment.

"I'd like to mosey around a bit," Greer said, barely glancing at the screen.

"At your own peril, of course," Brad said, eyes riveted to Bill Malay on the screen as he moved into the space-colony settlement. "Be careful, Jim, their security is tighter than a plug in an electric socket. I'd suggest you remain and get oriented to your surroundings."

"I hadda ask," Greer said tightly. He returned to his cot, eyes on the screen.

The men, while watching the video cassette, began to remove their spacesuits and change into khaki fatigues. An impenetrable silence permeated the room. Brad Lincoln peered about casually, noting the men who clustered about the screen in a semicircle, seated in chairs. Behind them, resting on the cots, Alexander York, Jim Greer, and Velden Zryden listened, but avoided watching the screen.

Colonel Katanga, the least likely among them to show interest in the project, was glued to the set. Periodically he scribbled in a notebook.

Velden Zryden, a.k.a. Victor Zeller, lay back on the cot, his eyes and ears tuned inwardly. Where the hell was the Russian, Gregorevich? Why had he been singled out for a little tete-à-tete with Commander Robbins? And where was that bitch Valerie Lansing? He had a score to settle with her. Passing herself off as Veronique Lindley, indeed! On board the Lodestar all his attempts to communicate with her had fallen short. He needed to ask her questions. *Victor* needed to. *Oh God, why must I give up the love of my life? Damn the cranial implant! Damn my father!*

Briefly, as Uri Mikhail entered the barracks, eyes glanced at him, then returned to the screen. Uri peered about, found the one empty cot, tossed his flight bag on it, and began to change his clothing. Silent, chewing his underlip thoughtfully, he ignored the others, glanced cursorily at the screen, then went back to completing his dress. It was nearly 1700. One hour to dinner. The message had been sent to Andreivich Malenekov, despite the bad transmission. The words exchanged had been minimal. The mood was formal, the words clipped, the message filled with grief for the Premier's death. But Andreivich was trying to tell him something. *What?* Something about "a lame man treading on the tail of the tiger." It had made no sense, none at all. He didn't understand why Malenekov could not have sent a plane from Moscow to pick him up. Then he recalled the rocky pinnacles surrounding Z-12 Andromeda, the inability of a powerful jet to land anywhere nearby. But an army helicopter could be flown in from some main airport, couldn't it? Unless they were *not* near Ulan Bator as they had been told. Uri frowned. Why would anyone deceive them? What would be the purpose?

Suddenly he remembered Valerie. He glanced around, somehow expecting her to be here with the others. Seated at one of the desks, he scribbled on a notepad, then tore off the sheet, folded it, and tucked it in his bush-jacket pocket. He pulled up a chair close to Brad Lincoln, and passed the note to him along with a pencil.

Brad accepted it and read: "Where is Valerie Lansing?" He scribbled back: "In her quarters." He handed both the pencil and paper to Uri. Uri read the reply, tore the sheet to bits, and excused himself.

"Uri." Valerie glanced up from the busy video screen where Commander Robbins was explaining the intricacies of the space wheel:

"Long-distance travel—to the other side of the ring—will be novel. There are six hollow spokes to the wheel with lift shafts to the center. To reach a distant part of the ring, you'll take a lift to the hub and continue to the other side."

Valerie lowered the volume, rose to greet him. "What is it? Why did they want you? Is something wrong? You look drained."

Uri explained, "It was expected, but as usual, shock follows the incredibility of the loss."

"Please accept my condolences. I know the extent of your loss. I've read of the deep affection between you and the late Premier. God, Uri, I am so sorry." She moved toward him. In the single moment of her outpouring, Uri was so engulfed with emotion he reached for her, drew her toward him, and kissed her, hesitant at first, then after the surprise registered between

them, lingeringly. They parted, Valerie gasping for breath, Uri
fired by desire.

"You kept me waiting so long, Valeruska," he said huskily.

"I'm a fool," she replied, falling against him for another
soul-searing kiss. They parted again.

"My sensations, my thoughts, all of my being have been
yours since I first saw you, Valeruska, at the home of your parents in Virginia. Look how much time we've lost."

She sighed against him, trying to feel with every fiber of her
being. "I too felt a bond with you the moment I met you, so I
deliberately kept my distance. I had things to do, places to go,
people to deal with."

"I know. I know."

"It hasn't been easy, believe me. I've endured a living hell."

"I know. I know." He nuzzled her.

"What do you know?" At once alert, she stepped away from
him, searched his eyes as if they would relay the truth to her.

"Everything, Valeruska. I know everything about you."

Her amazement turned to irritation. *"What do you know?"*
she asked evenly, afraid of his answer.

"Everything except your true motivation. Why you'd risk
your life to venture into the lair of man-eating tigers in Zürich."

For an instant she was furious. Then as the picture in her
mind adjusted and she reconciled his position with the Junior
Politburo and his close ties with the late Soviet Premier, she accepted his revelation in the proper context. "I should have
known you'd know everything about a person in whom you
showed any interest. It's the way things work." She glanced at
her watch. "We don't have much time. I'm not certain Z-12 is
the place to discuss my motives and overall goals, Uri. I'm not
even certain I should confide in you. There is nothing between
us that commands my obedience."

"You love me. I love you, Valeruska."

"That's as absolute a statement as I've ever heard." Then,
softly, "I love you the way you roll my name off your lips
. . . . Valeruska."

"Valeruska . . . Valeruska," he said, claiming her lips
again.

Valerie kissed him back, then drew away as he hardened
against her. "Uri—not here. Not now. God, you don't know

who is listening, watching!'' She pointed to the electronic equipment, the scanner.

''Let them all see. Let them all hear. I don't care.''

''I don't believe this.'' She giggled like a silly schoolgirl, pulling him out of scanner range. ''I cannot permit your love—''

''*Our* love. You feel it. I know.''

''Very well, our love, to eclipse the work of a lifetime.'' Her voice dropped a few decibels. She peered around the room. ''Perhaps after dinner we can go for a walk. We'll talk then.''

''You are a world unto yourself, Valeruska. You are a firmament moving at a different pace from anyone I have ever met. I have loved you for too long to let you slip out of my arms. Now, Valeruska, I want to make love to you, be a part of you, make you feel me deep inside of you.''

''Oh, Uri,'' she moaned softly, falling against him. ''There's no time. We must wait,'' Valerie said, feeling an orgasmic rush. ''Eyes must be focused on us,'' she whispered into his ear.

At once Uri stiffened. He stepped back, searched her eyes. Then peripherally he saw the extent of the electronic communications wall center. ''Of course. I understand. Forgive me. I lost my head,'' he said, at once formal, aloof. With his back to the scanner, he winked at her in understanding. ''My mind has recently become a battlefield for Mother Russia and you, Valeruska. You are constantly face to face, disputing the territory within me. Between the two of you, I am torn limb from limb. It seems I exist only to house that conflict.''

''It is a conflict of which I knew nothing.''

''Now you do. As you say, this moment is inappropriate to disseminate our personal feelings. Will you accompany me to the mess hall? Valeruska—Valerie—what's wrong?'' Uri detected a change on her face. He held his breath, uncertain of what was causing the sudden alienation. She was groping behind her on the desk as if under a strange compulsion, her eyes glassy, her breath uneven.

''Valerie!'' The movement was swift, a bit amateurish, but nevertheless she aimed a razor-sharp knife at his heart. Uri parried the thrust, broke her hold on the knife. It clattered to the wooden floorboards dully and came to a spinning stop. ''Valerie!'' Uri grabbed her shoulders, shook her until the trancelike expression broke and she blinked back to the moment.

''Valerie!'' He held her shoulders, pinning her arms to her sides. ''What the devil possessed you? Does sweet-talking love turn you vicious?''

''Uri?'' She glanced at him, dazed. Her head ached, and she shook it as if to loosen the cobwebs. ''What happened? What's wrong? Did something terrible happen? Why does my head ache? The strangest feeling came over me—''

Uri, one eye on her, the other on the knife, retrieved it. ''This is what happened, dear Valerie. You tried to sink this into my heart.''

Aghast, disbelieving at first, she shook her head in denial. The thunder inside her head wouldn't abate. Throbbing temples, palpitations shook her. ''You lie! Why would I want to kill the man I love?''

''Ask a black-widow spider the same thing.''

''Uri, I'm not a black-widow spider. Why would I do such a thing?'' She lurched unsteadily. Quickly Uri grabbed hold of her. ''It's best you lie down. There is still time before dinner.''

''Yes. I'll lie down. Fifteen minutes only. Promise. I'll feel better by then. I need two aspirins. They are in my flight bag,'' she said meekly, turning her face from him. She was trembling. What had come over her? Had she tried to kill Uri? No! It wasn't possible. Oh, Christ! What next?

Uri gave her the aspirins, followed by a tumbler of water from a carafe on the desk. He sniffed it first, tasted it, then gave it to her. ''Fifteen minutes, then. You're sure you're all right?''

She nodded.

They sat around a circular table in a modest office. Jonathan Marl, Lama Dalei Dei, and another holy man named Krishnam. Krishnam, a tall, muscular man in his fifties, was dressed in army camouflage fatigues and boots. The man looked thirty, not a day older. He wore his hair longer than army personnel, below the ear, banded around his forehead with a scarf. His eyes were calm, magnetic, and he appeared to be totally in control of himself, as did the Lama. Dalei Dei, a Tibetan-trained priest garbed in flowing robes, sat erect in his chair. His eyes, slightly slanted, were at times verdant, other times hazel under shaggy brows. The three men had observed the vignette enacted by Uri and Valerie moments ago. And when the startled couple moved a fraction out of camera range, their conversation continued to be recorded through sophisticated video equipment.

Each of the trio was profoundly absorbed in the goings-on, for each had a singular purpose to accomplish—the destruction of the Zeller-Harding power cartel. This was as good a power base as any. Each had combined forces to spring a trap to ensnare their prey. Decisions made long ago were coming to fruition. The Omicron power cartel would be destroyed; it must be if the world was to survive. These three men, better than any, save Moufflon, knew the sordid truth concerning the Zeller-Harding cartel, and they had plotted, connived, schemed, and planned to exterminate the powerful financial titan and his protégé of nearly three decades, Anthony Harding.

The three men came from diverse backgrounds and various parts of Europe, and each had begun his peregrination to the land of the Dalai Lama seeking solace. Meeting in Tibet, journeying on to Outer Mongolia, Krishnam and Dalei Dei had found their way to Z-12 Andromeda where fate had decreed they would meet to seek inner strength and peace. A comparison of stories amazed each man, for each believed he had been guided by an incalculable force, to amass the strength to one day strike a blow against the seemingly indestructible Omicron cartel and its subsidiaries.

Jonathan Marl, a brilliant nuclear physicist, had been plotted against and left for dead. Jonathan Marl was Anton Schuller.

Krishnam, a.k.a. Mario Morosconi, son of Major Morosconi, code name Pluto, had arrived at home one day from the University of Milan to find his mother and four sisters dead, murdered. His father had disappeared without a trace and Mario assumed he was dead. Quickly hidden by friends, Mario learned that the family estate had undergone a systemic embezzlement through Italian banking affiliates dictated by Zürich. The brutalizing of his family had destroyed Mario for a time. When the enemy learned one Morosconi family member had survived, they began to track him. Mario fled to a country in which he could get lost—India. From Calcutta he ventured north to Tibet, entered a Tibetan monastery and joined the priesthood. He changed his name to Krishnam, became a learned yoga, teaching neophytes the art of transcendental meditation.

Dalei Dei's background was similar. It was laden with a hatred and irony that had not transcended to another plane, but still burned within him from the moment his father was caught and tortured by Zeller's henchmen and later put to death in a most ghastly way. Hatred had remained alive in Dalei Dei's memory. Had he not witnessed the atrocity as a young man and the systematic destruction of his father Michael Bertelli's industrial empire, he might have been less affected. If he had not witnessed the mental deterioration of his American-born mother, whom his father had wedded following his estrangement from Marie Clotilde, and her subsequent death, and if he had not been forced out of his rightful inheritance, his vengeance might have abated over the years. But he'd seen his father tortured, then slain; his mother go mad. How does one erase such incidents from memory? Hidden at the estate, afraid to show himself for fear of death, he'd read his father's most secret files concerning his dealings with Amadeo Zeller. Dalei Dei knew the true identity of the enigmatic Moufflon. They were half brothers. He kept this in mind when he covertly made inquiries of the man Darius Bonifacio. Everything belonging to Michael Bertelli had been cleverly manipulated by the Zeller cartel. He mailed the diaries to his cover name at general delivery, New Delhi, India, and booked passage to flee Italy. From New Delhi he made his way along the River Ganges to Rishikish where the wandering wayfarer in search of a new identity paused to study Yoga among the masters. His peregrination took him to Tibet where he spent time among the lamas, studying transcendental meditation and the esoteric philosophies of these unusual holy men possessed with remarkable powers.

In the late 1960s when news of Z-12 Andromeda began to filter into the lamasery, Dalei Dei's curiosity peaked. In his pilgrimage he'd met Krishnam, and over the many miles of journeying to Ulan Bator near Lung, both men had found a rapport. Coincidentally, they discovered both had similar pursuits. Their studies had taught them that men are united, brought together from what appeared diverse interests by dominant thoughts, that the law of attraction is the most forceful of all physical laws. Their arrival at Z-12 marked their encounter with Jonathan Marl. The hatred in the man transcended all else. Both Krishnam and Dalei Dei believed they had met life's true challenge in Marl; the conversion of Dr. Marl from loathing animal to caring human commenced. But they hadn't counted on the degree of his loathing. Since time did not exist for these newborn ascetics, time was not of the essence. Jonathan Marl's ordeal as Anton Schuller had revived bitter memories in the other two men. They would dedicate their lives to breaking Amadeo Zeller's and Anthony Harding's power structures—all of them.

There was strength in numbers, they thought.

"Our meeting will be short. The purpose is to again ask you, Jonathan, to change course. You must resist dealing further with the Mongolian factions. The nuclear fiasco in the Middle East changes nothing. The nuclear arms race among superpowers continues as usual even if it terrorizes virtually every person who dares think of it," Dalei Dei said quietly.

"You ask the impossible," said Marl. "I can do nothing except to proceed with—my orders. You saw how they decimated Artana at Z-10."

"It's never too late," Krishnam suggested. "It is fast becoming a world in which the survivors will envy the dead. What is too horrifying to conceive we suppress in our imaginations. The situation has grown beyond us and our petty grievances."

"What has become of our united plan against Zürich?"

"It melted in the countdown of the nuclear explosions in the Middle East. I can't put it more succinctly."

"The men with whom I dealt will not be pacified with less than the promise to which I affixed my signature. The Mongolians and I are working together towards Global 2000. I can't back out of the deal now. You've never encountered them. They work a thousand tricks up their sleeves, every minute. Can't you see I don't want to go through with it. I thought I could. The hatred possessing me took over my soul. Earlier when Robbins held a mirror up to me, I detested what I saw."

"Jonathan, in the many years of our friendship, have you ever known us to improperly direct you?"

Marl shook his head.

"In due time you will be correctly guided."

"Meanwhile, how do I avoid the dangers to us—all of us?"

"Fifteen years have passed, Jonathan. We came as strangers, now we are brothers. We have come to know you. Odd that you haven't come to know us."

Jonathan blinked hard, the truth relaxing his features.

"Troubles," said Krishnam, "are ephemeral. Prepare to meet a problem and it will vanish into nothingness. This man Moufflon is a true ally. We were correct in our assessment of him."

"And what of the Chinese? The Russians?"

"We bide our time. At times passivity is power."

Chapter Twenty-two

"Uri," Darius called to him on the way to the mess hall. "May I offer my condolences. The world lost a most remarkable man in Nikolai Vladechenko. Perhaps after dinner we will talk, time permitting." What a stately bearing, thought Darius. Youseff must be very proud of Uri.

"Will you accept my earnest sympathies," Youseff said, wanting desperately to initiate a dialogue with his son, yet uncertain how to begin. Coping with the tension of waiting for the right moment was causing Youseff pain, actual physical pain.

Uri paused. His dark eyes swept over Youseff, eyeing him critically. "Thank you, Highness," he said with overt politeness.

With distinguished ease, Uri moved forward, catching up with Valerie. Together they entered the large room filled with fragrant aromas. "At least it won't be K rations," Valerie said, glancing about the busy room. "Uri, you haven't told anyone what—" He shook his head and walked inside.

The Prince placed a slender hand on Darius's arm. "It's very difficult, old friend, to mend so many bridges left in disrepair so many years."

"It's not too difficult. Just open your mouth and say to him, 'Uri, I am your father.' "

"And you, Darius? What of you? Is it not time that the young woman who is the image of her mother know of your relationship?"

Darius moved forward, ushering them to their seats. "We have both conquered mountains. This is the most difficult climb of all."

"Not too difficult. Just open your mouth and tell her, 'Valerie, I am your father,' " Youseff mocked politely. Darius scowled.

"Youseff, sit down with the others. I left my cigarettes in our quarters. I'll be right back." Darius exited the mess hall and returned to his room. Matteus signaled to the Israeli, Gadi, to follow him. Gadi fell in a few paces behind Darius, his piercing blue eyes looking in all directions at once.

Inside, Darius located the cigarettes, then heard something dripping. Instantly he removed a gun from his boot, crouched, ears attuned to every noise. Gadi entered. Catching sight of Darius's posture, he retrieved his knife from his boot, aware of impending dangers. Commander Robbins's voice on the videotape still described the ever-increasing wonders of Andromeda. Gabriel turned off the cassette, crouched, knife at the ready, and crept forward toward the disturbance. He signaled Darius to back away from the sounds.

"Dripping water," Darius hissed, pointing to the showers and latrine.

Gadi moved in closer . . . closer . . . his fingers to his lips. In a sudden thrust, he slammed the louvered shower open with a loud crash. Gadi's eyes registered shock. Darius moved in behind him. The sight of Chanda, the dead Indian sapper, stunned him. For a moment he was unable to catch his breath. The garrote around his neck was done SAS-commando style—or Mozarabe? Or was it Corsican Coral or Corsican Jade? All were similar with a few additions. Who here at Andromeda knew the skillful techniques of the Mozarabe or the rest of the subsidiary branches of the main tree? The thoughts running through his mind chilled him. Someone had seen them, or heard his conversation with Chanda; a former Mozarabe had used a characteristic means of death to telegraph his message.

"There is more, Djebel," said Gabriel Gadi, the son of Tamir Mandel, who had been sent by his father before the nuclear holocaust in the Middle East to apprentice for a time with Corsican Jade. "It need not be what we both are thinking—that an old Mozarabe performed this deed." He removed a note from the pocket of the man hung on the overhead water pipes who had, in addition to the garroting, been painted. His forehead contained a cyclopean eye drawn in red lipstick.

Gabriel had taken an Israeli name meaning "God is my strength, God is my fortune" during his formative years. The stories told by his father portraying Darius as a young god had piqued his interest. When he finished law school and had insisted on taking a sabbatical to train with Moufflon, Tamir had approved.

Gabriel cut down the body. "What will I do with it?"

"It must not be found with the task force members. Wait here."

Darius stepped back into the barracks, located the scanner. Pulling a chair along one wall out of scanner range, he stood on it, quickly draped a towel over it, stepped down, and in moments with Gadi's help, inched past an unsuspecting guard. "Gadi, dispose of the body. It must not be found until departure, understand? Use whatever resources you can." To Chanda's mutilated body, his words turned apologetic. "If it's any consolation, old friend, I shall mete out to your killer what was meted you. Your death shall not go unavenged."

Finished, they returned to quarters, removed the towel, replaced the chair. Standing in the doorway, Darius read the note:

A warning to you, Moufflon. Return to your home base, else one or more may be killed. You may be next. Perhaps your daughter.

A cyclopean eye! What the devil had a cyclopean eye to do with him?

Then it wasn't the best-kept secret! Who knew of his relationship to Valerie Lansing? Had he arrived in a purgatory on earth where man must answer for all life's transgressions? The wrath of many enemies had willingly or unwillingly fallen upon his shoulders in war. They couldn't stall any longer.

"Come, Gabriel, we must return to join the others before we are missed."

* * *

The mess-hall lights were dim. Commander Robbins's image reflected from a giant video screen. Darius and Gabriel took their places, eyes on the screen. They listened to the narration, their faces stone masks.

"No doubt before the task force members leave Andromeda, they will tire greatly of seeing my face, listening to my voice. In the essence of expediency, we must double the orientation period. I shall make every effort to avoid redundancy. In Paris you were introduced to theoretical and conceptual analysis, brainwashing techniques, even the Delphi technique. Now I ask you to set aside most of what you absorbed and trust that after nearly two decades of in depth involvement in the space colony settlement, we have proven and reproven all theories to where they are no longer theories but actualizations. I suggest, before you retire, that you prepare from the orientation summary, briefs listing all your questions concerning our floating outer-space city. Now enjoy your dinner and feel free to discuss among your colleagues all the questions that plague you."

The video cassette ended and the screen went black.

"It's a delightful way to learn," Valerie confided in Uri.

"Are you all right? Has the headache passed?" She nodded thoughtfully.

Commander Robbins tapped the glass before him at the head table and stood up. "Forgive me, I failed to inform you that on your arrival you all passed through invisible metal detectors. Your weapons—if they are for self-protection—will not be needed here at Z-12. We respectfully ask all of you who carry such weapons to please turn them in to Captain Joseph Carlini after chow. Before departure to the settlement, you will be subjected to further detection tests. All are voluntary, of course, and those who refuse to submit to search shall be refused entry into the Andromeda superstructure and shall be confined to quarters. The settlement is off limits to anyone carrying firearms. Due to the sensitivity of the simulated extraterrestrial atmosphere, one we've spent years perfecting, we cannot permit any disruptive forces on what is essentially a scientific research outpost. Another precaution: if any of you are wearing pacemakers or other devices implanted in your bodies to help sustain your life, we must ask that you be eliminated from the expedition or permit us to re-implant devices that are more acceptable.''

Valerie jerked her head around. Her eyes in mild alarm met Velden Zryden's eyes. *She knows! She bloody knows!* Velden recollected those moments back in Paris when he had suspected her thoughts. Now no doubt existed. Quickly his mind rolled back to Commander Robbins's words. *Implants!* How the devil would he overcome this obstacle? How would he know if he'd escaped detection through invisible metal detectors when he hadn't known at what point the detectors were employed?

They were sipping coffee and cognac when Commander Robbins spoke to them through a microphone piped into their earphones.

"It is now my honor to introduce Dr. Jonathan Marl, the modest scientist whose two-decade dream and dedication made Z-12 Andromeda a reality.'' He proceeded to describe the pitfalls, the obstacles that would have deterred the average man, and how he had garnered unto himself the most brilliant scientists of the world whose burning dedication matched his. "Short of funds, long on hope, knowledge, and brainpower, they set about in this remote desert outpost to create hope for mankind—and survival! Perhaps the only answer to nuclear warfare. Your presence here today and for as long as you remain is based on hope too. Hope that each of you shall return to your nations and begin to disseminate the truth! The truth of what is possible, what we've done to ameliorate the fears of an actual Global 2000. Systematized euthanasia is not the answer to world hunger and survival. What you'll witness here at Andromeda is our only attempt to foil the planned Global 2000 genocide! Not the proposed military policies the world is spurred into actuating.''

A burst of applause followed.

"Dr. Marl,'' said Robbins without further preamble. Another burst of applause rang out. The task force members gave him a standing ovation. Jonathan Marl rose unsteadily to his feet, leaning on the podium. He wore khaki fatigues and a leather jacket with a fur collar to shake off the icy chill forever permeating his body. He wagged his hand at the greetings, affected a rare modesty. As he collected himself, preparing the short talk, Darius turned to the Prince, at once transported back in years. "Youseff, tocsins are ringing at the very bottom of my being. Am I suddenly confronted with a presence from my past? I know of no Jonathan Marl except as I encountered the man in my briefings and the man enclosed in my dossier.''

''According to the dossier, he was nowhere near our theaters of action. I never met him in the forty-year interim since the war. As I understood it, he's been a recluse since the late fifties, studied intently throughout the sixties, got accepted into the Kennedy space program, and relocated shortly thereafter with his own grant through efforts with NASA here in the upper Gobi.''

''Why then does my flesh quiver, Youseff? My mind is winding up tight; tension grips me. Flashes of my past are rotating on a reel at a hundred frames per second. Corsica. France. Malta. The Hyperion. Pluto. Marseilles and the Paris Liberation! This man is somehow important to my existence. It's the reason I am here. Three times in the past, since I first heard of Andromeda in the late 1960s, I made trips here to observe its progress, believing, actually believing it is mankind's only answer to survival. Each time I failed to meet the enigmatic Dr. Marl. There was no need. Commander Robbins and Lieutenant Commander Malay had meticulously briefed me and I, in turn, influenced the funding of Andromeda from private resources.''

''I know. I know. You tapped me considerably.'' Youseff smiled. ''Never—*never* was I permitted the opportunity to meet Marl. He was always on some inland expedition with the holy men seated at either side of him—or I was told that for expediency.''

''Now you believe . . .''

''I believe he is more than a central issue to this project, that something most unusual has happened, or is about to happen.'' He dropped his voice to a monotone. ''Look around you. Do you not detect a change in the men?'' Darius didn't wait for Youseff's reply.

''From the moment we left the Scorpion and confronted the miracles of the space colony, four assassins were with us, according to the reports. I no longer envision any of them as assassins. When the attempt comes on my life, it will not be through Colonel Katanga's efforts, or those of Sir Alexander

York. Not from Dr. Sen Yen Lu—not even Velden Zryden, who is actually my half brother, Victor Zeller.''

''What gives you so audacious a certainty? As a matter of fact, I was outraged, disgusted that you failed to deny their participation in so clandestine and dangerous a mission. Why increase the odds against your success?'' He nudged Darius, his eyes on Jonathan Marl. Darius turned, his X-ray eyes riveted on that face, that shock of white hair, the tortoise-rimmed spectacles.

A chill shot through him. Jonathan Marl was a man in his sixties, the blue, piercing eyes of a fanatic, and the hoarse, clipped voice of a man possessed. His movements were slow and fluid; he was at once theatrical and ominous. Darius found him too poised, as if his cultivated appearance had been thought out carefully and refined in the corridors of his neurosis. When Darius saw the one-armed crutch leaning against the podium, he listened with all senses attuned to the man, his words, his comportment.

Marl had transcended the welcome and was well into the body of the text by the time Darius concentrated upon him.

''The bitter lessons of twentieth century wars have not, will not be learned unless mankind itself undergoes a total regeneration of values, morals, ethics. Man will always prey upon his fellow man unless new, viable values are integrated into the mental landscapes of the very young. A revolution must come about to change the mentalities of the political and financial leaders of our day who set themselves up as plenipotentiaries. . . .''

Darius, seated opposite Valerie Lansing, noted her rapt absorption in Marl. Suddenly his eyes riveted on her, on the crystal at her neck. *Like Chanda's crystal! Damnation! Christ! What does it mean?*

Instantly he removed a notebook from his bush-jacket pocket, scribbled a note, and slipped it across the table until she saw him. Glancing around then, directing her steadfast gaze into his eyes, the electricity of excitement sprang through her. She took the note, read it: ''After dinner, please join me for a walk through the compound.''

Valerie, having stolen secret looks at him throughout dinner, faltered, flustered by his attention. She wrote: "What do I call you? Moufflon, Major, Commander, or simply Darius?"

Darius was all for simplifying it to plain *father*. He wrote: "Darius will do. I know you well enough to forgo formalities."

Valerie's heart was pounding. Was Uri correct? He had told her that Darius Bonifacio was her father. She nodded, tore the note into bits, stuffed an ashtray with portions of it, and placed the remaining shreds in her pocket.

"Why," confided Prince Ben-Kassir to Matteus after dinner, watching Darius wait a respectable moment or two before following Valerie out of the compound, "why do I get the feeling of impending doom here in this godforsaken place? I've traveled a long journey with Darius these past forty years. Still my bones shake at his daring."

"And I who have journeyed longer than you ask that you not abdicate Allah at this juncture. As usual he works a potent *baraka* on Darius."

"It was I, not you, Matteus, who opened the windows of vulnerability, exposing him to this project. If not for me he would have remained invisible. Since the disastrous Maui conference last February, he is hounded by assassins."

"Long ago, Highness, I ceded to Allah all my worries over Darius."

"Would that I possessed your faith. Tell me, how do I disregard the dangers? Look at them! Global assassins scramble for laurel wreaths and the incredible monetary sums offered for our Corsican's fine, noble head."

Matteus changed the subject. "What a fine son you sired."

Youseff's eyes shifted, settling on Uri's profile. He wiped his sweaty hands on a *serviette,* shook his head at the internal changes. "I should have confided the truth to him long ago. He might have held sway over that aggregation of birdbrained fools dominating the Maui conference. I shall never forgive myself, Matteus. Those imperceptive cretins posturing about as world leaders deserve castration. As long as they live—if any possess a shred of decency—the infamy of the Middle East will weigh heavily upon their souls."

"Does your son speak for all Soviets?"

The Prince swiveled in his chair, his face piqued. "All Soviets?'' he whispered. "Pray tell who speaks for *all* Soviets? Perhaps the new General Secretary? The interim Premier—'' Youseff stopped. Suddenly all Uri had worked for all his life was at stake. "I have no right to deny him what he's worked toward all his life. You realize he can one day become Premier of the U.S.S.R.?''

"With Premier Vladechenko dead, the winds will shift.''

Chapter Twenty-three

"Are you ready for this? Bed at 8:30 P.M.?" Uri said to Valerie following dinner.

"When in Gobi, do as—"

"I know. I know."

"Uri, go ahead. I want to walk about alone."

"You think it's wise?" He peered about in the darkness. The sky was overcast. The silent aftermath of the storm deafening. "You're not venturing beyond the compound?" he asked, concerned.

"No. I promise. Please, I need time to think." She pulled up the collar of her jacket. "Chilly."

"Valeruska," he said softly, "talk with me. Perhaps I can help you sort things out and—"

"And what?"

"Nothing. No, it is not the truth. I am curious about that bauble you wear. I haven't seen it before, not in Paris, not aboard the Lodestar nor the Scorpion."

"Of course not, silly. It's a bauble from the Andromeda staff, welcoming me to Z-12."

Uri moved in closer, picked the crystal ball up in his hands, stared at it, turning it over in his fingers. A shaft of light coming from the mess-hall entrance shone on it. "Hmm," he said. "It appears a strange gift here in Mongolia. Why not flowers, or a bottle of wine, even candy? Why a bauble such as this? What does it represent?"

"The globe, dear Uri. I assumed so at the outset. It takes a man so much ruminating before he wades through the whys and wherefores of so innocent a gesture."

"It will be 2100 in a half hour. I'll expect you back by then. The temperature is dropping and those gray clouds darkening the sky are ominous. Shouldn't you wear a heavier jacket? In the desert temperatures can drop to subzero in a twinkling, Valeruska."

"I'll be fine. I promise. See you at 2100."

Uri watched Valerie move along the shadowy, dimly lit buildings in the compound. Behind him the task force members mingled with the Z-12 crew, asking questions. Uri peered about, lit a cigarette, and backed himself into a better vantage point where he could see nearly every man.

"Gregorevich," said Youseff Ben-Kassir, approaching him.

Uri turned to him, stiffened, in a near-military stance. "Highness."

"It would be to my liking if you could manage a few minutes. It is essential that we talk."

Beyond him, Uri saw Dr. Jonathan Marl exit the mess hall, hobbling on one crutch, dragging his left leg with each step, sandwiched in between Commander Robbins and Dr. Malay. The deliberate pace he maintained, the man's build, the shock of white hair disturbed Uri's mental repose. "Highness, do you suppose we could postpone the talk—" His eyes on Marl caught Youseff's attention. He turned and stared after the man. "Except for the crippled leg and white hair, I would swear—" Uri said, and stopped.

"What is it about that man that causes me to be upstaged?" Youseff said jocularly. "Earlier, our host was practically mesmerized." Youseff had considered it as good an opening as any. He wasn't certain how to finesse the delicate situation. Now, he was determined to come straight out with it. "Uri Mikhail, there really isn't much time. There's no other way to put it. It isn't easy, and I hope you're strong enough to bear it, but the time has come to tell you—"

"I know. I know. *You're my father!* I've waited nearly forty

years. Can it not wait a few moments longer? You will excuse
me, sir.''

Uri bolted into the shadows, trying his best to remain hidden,
but he was onto something very extraordinary. It was hanging
in his memory by a fine thread and could evaporate into nothingness if he didn't stay with it.

Youseff, stunned, coping with the paralytic words immobilizing him, stared after him. *''I know. I know. You're my father!''* rang in his ears. Then he broke into a radiant smile,
followed by a lighthearted laughter. He ran his fingers through
his hair, stroked his beard, still chuckling. And he had compared the denouement to fighting lions of the desert! The ice
was broken! That's all that mattered. What the devil was Uri up
to? he thought as normality filtered back into his consciousness. What mirage was he chasing? Something struck him and
he meant to ferret it out. *What?* He went in search of Darius.
What the devil was wrong with Darius? Earlier when he had entered the mess hall with Gadi, Youseff had read the expression
in his features. *Something had happened.* He headed for their
quarters.

For Uri the moment passed; it was of course possible that Dr.
Marl had crossed his path in any number of situations worldwide. They could have met in a thousand scientific laboratories
in the Soviet Union, in the satellite nations, in a university,
anyplace. Yes, it was entirely possible but highly improbable
that Uri would have forgotten both the leg and that unruly shock
of white hair. Both stood out like semaphores, and his mind
tried desperately to connect them to something else. Should he
go straightaway to Dr. Marl's office, introduce himself, and
pay his respects—those of nations and his own personal dictates? Would it be considered proper decorum?

*If you meet him and scrutinize him from a closer vantage
point— Yet don't be too pushy. It may be nothing. Bide your
time, Uri.*

Uri hung back, meditatively trying to piece the puzzle together. What the devil did Andreivich Malenekov mean? If
only transmission hadn't confused the message. What was it?

''A lame man treads on the tail of the tiger.''

A lame man? Marl! Yes, yes, it must be Marl! Something to
do with Marl. Damn! A string of Russian curses escaped his

lips. He must try for transmission to Moscow again. Surely the KGB was aware of the incomplete transmission. *Enough to get you killed, Uri, but not enough to save you.* The tail of the tiger . . . the tail of the tiger. . . . Damnation! Then he remembered Youseff. By the time he walked around the buildings of the complex, Youseff was gone.

Valerie ambled along the path past night workers busily rolling carts toward the Andromeda space-colony wheel through an electronic gate. Pausing momentarily to observe them in the wash of floodlights, she barely escaped the jabbing elbow and warning calls, "Coming through, Miss," of other workers. She quickly moved out of their path and, sighting an open, unguarded gate, slipped through unnoticed.

She shuffled thoughtfully beside the stunted, deformed vegetation smoking a cigarette, absorbed in agitating and conflicting thoughts. The porphyritic boulders were barely visible in the cloud cover of night. Valerie unwittingly approached the edge of a cliff. She crept forward, inching slowly, taking another step, then suddenly as the loose ground underfoot began to crumble and fall away, she flung herself backward, spun around, and clung desperately to a projectile of brush. She slipped. The brush gave way, and Valerie clung for dear life to a jagged promontory of rock, suspended desperately in midair, in the blackness of night unable to make out shapes and forms. She tensed, held her breath, swung forward, kicking out her boots before her, feeling ground. *That's it, grab a momentary foothold.*

Oh, Christ! She wanted to scream, yell up a storm, but she'd had enough discrimination in Paris. She could just hear them say, "Isn't that just like a woman!" *No, damn it! I'll get out of this mess myself!* She cleared her throat. Even if she had wanted to scream, she couldn't; fear had paralyzed her vocal cords. *Damn, damn, damn!* What the devil had driven her this far from Z-12? She must have walked at least ten minutes. Now she hung here, clinging to the precarious promontory, her shoulders aching from the strain. How much longer could she last? *God help me!*

If I stay here . . . Stay here? Hanging by my hands? Better jump than stay put. Uri will miss me. He said 2100. A half hour.

Valerie, holding her breath, let go. She fell several feet, landing on a steep, craggy rock. She was badly cut up, her fingers bleeding.

She wiggled each of her extremities, sighing thankfully. *Nothing broken. Stay calm. Sit here. Someone will miss you and begin the search.*

Her chest heaved in spasms as she fought for control. Visibility was nil. For all she knew she had landed in a nest of anacondas. *Oh, God, not snakes!* A feeling of suffocation came upon her. The minutes dragged by. It dawned on her to use her wrist radio. Yes, yes, that's it! Use the damn thing. Robbins said it worked on the same principle, only the frequency was different. Valerie moved slightly, and a rumble of loose rocks avalanched under her. "Oh Christ!" she called aloud. "Don't let me die, not now. I've too much to do." Mindless panic held sway. Lying on her back, she brought her left wrist close to her eyes. The dial was luminous. Oh God, thank you. She'd been gone a quarter hour. In another, Uri would come looking for her. Dare she move? *Move one leg—that's it. Feel around with your foot. Good. Now the other. Very good. The ground under your body is firm. Better yet.*

Suddenly the moon appeared from behind the clouds and Valerie, staring straight up, saw the silhouette of a man standing very close to the edge of the cliff where she had foolishly stumbled.

"Hello up there. Hello! Can you hear me?"

Darius looked down, fell to his knees just as a bright streak of light shot at him. A laser! A damned laser! In the brilliant flash of light, he saw Valerie some six feet below him on a promontory and jumped below, landing next to her.

"Be still!" he commanded, crouched alongside her, shielding her. Another streak of light blasted away at the top of the cliff, then moved to either side and evaporated.

"You may not know it, but you just saved my life," Darius said huskily. "How the devil did you get here?"

"The same as you. I fell. I came here to do a little soul searching and—" Valerie's words were cut off by Darius's hand clasped over her lips.

"Look there!"

Various rays of light began to converge and spread fanlike around them. The rays took on an aura of color, each ray illuminating the section of land until they both realized they hadn't fallen into a deep pit, but a huge pothole. They had only to move a few feet either way to fall into its depths. Darius and Valerie, captivated by the extravagant sight of colored lights blending into the others, made no move to stand up. "Look there, Darius," she whispered, pointing to an enormous boulder. Scenes formed before their eyes. In a quick montage, they saw prehistoric scenes, Egyptian-era tableaux, Caesar, Cleopatra, Moses on Mount Sinai with the stone tablets. This was followed by the crucifixion of Christ, King Richard and the Crusaders, Columbus discovering the new land, Washington at Valley Forge, Lincoln at Gettysburg, scenes from World Wars I and II, Kennedy's Inaugural Address, man's first trip to the moon.

"If this is a lesson in history—" She stopped abruptly and cocked her head as if listening to an inner voice.

"Valerie . . . listen carefully . . . you have but to push him a bit to the right or left and your enemy will no longer threaten you. Obey my command. Get to your feet then shove him, hard."

"Valerie! Valerie! What's wrong? Tell me." Darius shook her. She struggled against him, fought him, shoved, but was no match against his muscular strength. She fell against him, disheveled.

She sat there, imperturbable, her lips slightly parted, trembling, a frown creasing her brow. She clutched at her head, holding the throbbing weight. Darius, catching sight of the crystal ball at her neck, reached out, grabbed it, and yanked it off. The ball turned red and felt hot to the touch. He released it, dropping it nearby. They both stared at it. Valerie fainted in his arms.

She regained consciousness moments later, awakening to the filtered sounds of a two-way transmitter.

"Identify yourself."

"Moufflon, here. There's been a slight accident. My companion and I are approximately ten minutes north of the west gate of the compound. Please hurry, bring a medic. Miss Lansing has been injured. Over and out."

"Miss Lansing has not been injured," she said weakly. "What in damnation happened?"

"You could answer that better than I."

"Suddenly I had the overwhelming urge to send you reeling over the edge of this cliff."

"*What?*"

"It's a good thing you stopped me. Earlier I tried to kill Uri Mikhail. What is happening to me?"

Darius was peering at the crystal ball on the ground. He leaned over, picked it up. The chain hung free. He held only the crystal globe between thumb and forefinger, rotating it.

"Are you my father?" she asked in a sudden straightforward manner, momentarily throwing Darius off keel.

"Yes," he replied as quickly. "When did you suspect?"

"I never did. Uri Mikhail let the cat out of the bag. He suggested I received special task force favors and told me why."

"And?"

"Because I am your daughter. I might add that it was a bit of a shocker."

"I'm glad you know, although I hadn't this sort of a reception in mind for the unveiling of facts."

"Nothing cleans out the psychological system like shock." Then: "What the devil were all those scenes?"

"Holographic photography. Why it was directed here, at us, at this moment is—" Darius stopped. "You said you had an overwhelming urge to toss me over the cliff. Was it a command or an instinctive urge?" He searched her face carefully from every angle.

"It's nothing I'd do on my own. I'm not homicidal," Valerie snapped a bit caustically. "You *really* are my father?" Her voice filled with awe. "Where do we go from here?"

"It's a good question. One I cannot answer for the moment. Pray someone comes for us."

"I think someone's coming. I hear the jeeps, the engines. Shall I acknowledge you as my father, here at Z-12?" she asked, concerned. Now they could clearly hear the series of loud crashes, vehicles approaching, running feet, shouting, concerned voices.

An indescribable feeling quivered through Darius, awakening every nerve center in his body. She was Valentina all over again. Except for the hair. He couldn't help but ask, "Why, why in God's name did you change the color of your hair, Valerie?"

"If I told you, you wouldn't believe me."

"Try me."

"I'm not certain we have the time here. Perhaps later. It has to do with Velden Zryden," she said hastily as a spotlight shone down on them.

"Hold on, Major, we've sent for rope ladders," shouted Dr. Malay when they spotted the couple. "It'll take five minutes, ten at the most."

"You mean Victor Zeller?" Darius whispered.

"You know? You know what's happened to him? The cranial implant by his Father? He has become a multiple personality. He vacillates between—"

"There's little I don't know. The Zeller château gets a periodic bugging. Besides, some of Moufflon's best-trained men are known to be employed there, undercover of course."

"I'm talking about the brain implant, Darius. Surely you understand the ramifications of so revolutionary an implant? In Paris—"

"Shh. We've transcended Paris for the moment. We are in danger here."

"You didn't answer my earlier question. Do I acknowledge you as my father here at Z-12?"

The rope ladder was being lowered. Darius held her arms tightly.

"Valerie, listen to me. The answer is no. Especially not here at Z-12. If anyone suspects, your life might be in danger. Already there's been one death, a man I once knew in the war. We were seen chatting together. Now Chanda is dead. I can't risk such a fate for you. We won't have much time to talk. I have one question. You've been on the Washington political scene. Does Dr. Jonathan Marl resemble anyone you've ever known or come into contact with? Don't reply now. You have to examine the man carefully, study every characteristic, every nuance. If you come up with anything tangible, get word to me through Uri. Remember, keep your distance from me."

"If I'm suddenly homicidal, shouldn't I keep my distance from everyone?"

"Whatever you did is connected to this crystal ball in my pocket. Trust me. I'll learn its properties and contact you at the right time. Meanwhile, stay alert, be very cautious."

"We could leave, return home."

"And never learn the answers we seek? Someone was responsible for the Middle East holocaust. We must learn who, why, and all the reasons such insanity proliferates."

Giant searchlights shone down on the couple. Voices called to them. Rope ladders were being lowered. They were safe. The screaming Valerie had earlier suppressed now came out in joyous exultation.

She fell into Uri's arms, bleeding hands and all. Neither cared, knowing she was safe. The questions and condemnations came later when medics cleaned her abrasions and medicated her.

Murder was not the sort of greeting Valerie had in mind when confronting Darius, her father, face to face for the first time. The moment, fraught with terror and fear, had upset her decorum. What had come over her? What had possessed her to try to push him over the edge, kill him? That she'd nearly become an instrument for his and Uri Mikhail's death appalled her and filled her with angst. Her father's words of caution and his request to think back in time had intrigued and disturbed her: "Think of Jonathan Marl. Think, if you can, of a prominent man who resembles Marl. Take away the limp, the snow-white hair, a man who might adopt several guises. Perhaps someone highly placed in government, unostentatious, but powerful."

Outside the Quonset hut, a few steps from Valerie's quarters, she said good night to Uri Mikhail. "I'm fatigued. The fall, the trauma of thinking I would die, has exhausted me. You will forgive me if I say good night? We shall see each other in the morning at the Andromeda briefing."

"No. I shall stay in your quarters tonight. I've ordered a cot brought into your room, an extra chair. I intend to stay awake to make certain nothing happens to you."

"It isn't necessary—"

"It is. Don't argue with me."

"All right. All right, I won't argue. First, before we go in—" She stopped, glanced at her wrist-radio device. "How do we know our conversations are not being taped?" She unbuckled the device, placed it in her pocket, and indicated he should do the same. Uri accepted her judgment.

Uri Mikhail did not argue the point. "What makes you so paranoid?"

"Have you told anyone else your suspicions?"

"Suspicions? Concerning what?"

"That Moufflon—Darius—is my father."

"He is? Then I was right."

"Please, Uri, I beg you to keep it confidential. No one here at Andromeda must know. None of the task force members, at least, are to suspect the truth."

"We both have something to celebrate, something we must keep well secreted," he said sotto voce.

"What does that mean?"

"I too am unable to speak of it. But there is something we can talk about, providing Big Brother isn't eavesdropping on us."

"We may be safe out here," she began. "You've been in and out of the Washington political scene long enough to ponder this riddle." She reiterated Darius's words concerning Jonathan Marl's lookalike. "He can be an official in government, perhaps a consultant, not necessarily an aggressive man, but bearing a strong resemblance to the brilliant scientist. Take away the white hair, the badly crippled left leg, and—"

"You saw it too? The resemblance struck me at once. Just as quickly I dismissed it. Dr. Marl cannot be taking his place. He's been on the Andromeda space project for fifteen years. It is documented. I have received reports of Z-12 for nearly all that time. I was briefed thoroughly over twelve years ago when we first considered the alternatives to the beam-weapons program advanced by world scientists as a deterrent to thermonuclear war."

"You—meaning the Russians—considered alternatives to thermonuclear war that long ago?"

"Longer, perhaps. Ever since Hiroshima and Nagasaki. And most especially since the Cuban Missile Crisis in 1962 when the likelihood of intercontinental thermonuclear war became a frightening reality."

"Uri, back to the posed hypothesis: you spoke of a resemblance. To whom? Whose place did you think Marl was taking?"

"I didn't. The man has had a separate career running concurrently. It is physically impossible for one person to occupy two different professions at the same time." He stopped.

"Unless— No. No, I'd be foolish for advancing so lame a theory."

"Unless there *are* two separate persons. Is that it? That's what you're trying to say? What would you say if I told you that one of these two men—Marl or his double—was a German assassin during World War II."

Uri moved in close and kissed Valerie, a long, hard kiss. At first she struggled, then fell limp against him, the medication melting her resolve. His words, in a near hiss, shook her.

"Don't think about it. Don't suggest it. Not the merest hint! Understand me. Oh, Christ! Damn Moufflon for subjecting you to all this." He was trembling against her, shaking profoundly. "What concern is it of yours? Stay out of it, Valeruska. Meddle if you want in outer space, play with the space-colony settlements, but stay out of politics. God, I want you alive!"

"You—you really love me," she said, stepping back from him, searching his eyes in the floodlit illumination.

"What in God's name do you think I've been trying to tell you since we met in Virginia? Do you think I've been whistling Dixie?"

"What's so terrible about Anthony Hard—"

His lips covered hers again. Then: "You silly fool, shut up. Don't mention that name. Don't ask me why, but don't you dare mention that name again. Not here—not in Andromeda. If anyone guesses you entertain the slightest hint—"

"Bull's-eye! Just tell me. They are not one and the same, so they must be brothers. All right, all right!" She held up a hand to ward off his fury. "Just one more question. Is my assumption correct?"

"No! One was murdered. Now go inside, get into bed, and I'll join you as soon as my cot arrives. And remember, Valeruska, this conversation never took place. We discussed nothing except our scintillating romance, which I hope has not been nipped in the bud."

"Silly you." Valerie went inside, her head buzzing with a thousand questions. Anthony Harding, Secretary of State, was Jonathan Marl's brother? Harding was her father, Senator Lansing's devoted friend and adviser, and was involved in some intrigue. *Which one had been murdered?* Oh, shit! She was back at square one.

Valerie remembered. A few lines in a newspaper had brought Anthony Harding prominence. Granted a few lines in a newspaper do not make a man famous, but it was a beginning.

Chapter Twenty-four

"It's a recording device, a relay unit, a trigger for hypnotic suggestion," Darius told Youseff, Matteus, and Gabriel Gadi as they stood about in a circle out of scanner range, a towel over the lens for good measure. On the desk in the glare of a flashlight in the blacked-out room, Darius had crushed the crystal ball, located the minute transistors, and confided his concern to his men.

"What exactly does Chanda's death mean?" Youseff asked. "Miss Lansing's attempt on your life? And you say Uri's also?"

"Someone up here doesn't like us," Gabriel Gadi said in jest.

"Attempts on my life rarely succeed. Chanda, however, didn't deserve to die. And if Miss Lansing was deployed as a means to kill Uri and me, the efforts were foiled. What say we get a good night's rest before the Andromeda briefing in the morning?"

In Washington, D.C., President John MacGregor stared at Anthony Harding's resignation lying on his desk. Ending all ties had been a necessity. Repercussions had not yet commenced.

Give it time . . . give it time. *That colossally audacious strong-armed henchman tried to blackmail me, the President of the United States! I'll show the bastard who wields the biggest stick!*

In Zürich, at the French château of Amadeo Zeller, a limousine pulled up through the guarded gates. Anthony Harding and his wife, Clarisse, alighted from the sleek silver sedan and stepped along the bricked walkway inside through the aviary. They boarded the elevators and headed for Amadeo's study in silence.

"Are you concerned, Anthony? This time I believe you have incurred father's displeasure."

Anthony Harding said nothing. Words between them had always been scarce in this marriage of convenience. Both had their modicum of private freedom, but in the political limelight, their lives were open books, projected by clever P.R. work that depicted them as a devoted, loving couple, free from flaws. As long as they were discreet in their personal lives and neither embarrassed the other, they could embark on their own secret trysts. On their wedding night, when Clarisse had asked, "Will I ever turn out to be what you really want? Can I?" he had answered simply, "I doubt it. Just don't smother me. Don't try to smother me and you'll have things your way. Besides, you have your papa's blessings. I should think that will keep you happy."

"It should," she had retorted enigmatically.

Anthony Harding had kept his doubts about Clarisse in prudent reserve.

On three occasions in the first year of their marriage, beginning with their first night together, he had attempted pathetically to make love to her. It hadn't worked. Clarisse then admonished him not to darken her boudoir again. He had not. Clarisse had her own lovers, men she loathed. Men for whom she had no respect. Was it possible she was as queer as her eccentric husband? Were her standards for men too high? Was she frigid? A thousand questions were answered by her physician, who sent her to a psychiatrist. *The Electra complex.* She suffered from excessively high expectations. Because every man she met was her father's inferior, she lacked respect for them and consequently rejected them physically. The shrink had suggested that she lower her standards. Lower her standards, indeed. She'd been privileged to be sired by the most brilliant man in the world. Why should she reject the notion? Encountering a man of Amadeo's equal could mean bringing exquisite delight to her drab life.

Husband and wife stood for a moment in total silence as they deboarded the lift and walked across the *galleria* to Zeller's study.

"Are you certain you don't wish to freshen up?" Harding asked, daubing at the perspiration beading on his high round forehead.

"First I'll see Father. Then I can take time to freshen up," she said snidely, contemptuous of his obvious squeamishness.

"Very well then. This may not be the proper time to say this, but I almost wish we could have begun anew, fresh, as lovers, without any of the past to circumvent. I remember seeing you for the first time. You were beautiful, mysterious, proud, arrogant, conscious of admiring eyes. And when our eyes met, a certain shyness entered—just the right amount of modesty. Seeing you was a stunning shock, an aesthetic experience. Having seen you, who could doubt that any but a god had created you?"

"You're right, Anthony. This is not the proper time," she snapped icily and opened the door.

"You fool! You needed to hang in there another month, perhaps less, and it would have all been ours. The Vice President will become enmeshed in the Central American quagmire. The President, involved in political scandal, will be forced to resign. The reins of government would have rested in your hands—a four-decade dream come true. Instead you've destroyed everything." Amadeo Zeller's thin voice croaked on like a bleating ram the moment Clarisse exited.

"You seem unable to transcend your gutter morality," Amadeo continued. "You've carried it forward into the career I carved for you from the pyres of your black-hearted deeds. I carved a formidable empire for you and Clarisse. I positioned you carefully in the precisely constructed edifices of my power. I made you the keystone, Anthony. With the keystone removed—"

"With the keystone removed, all my contacts will shift,

force the President, whoever it might be after this coming election, to accept us—our clout. My gutter morality, as you quaintly put it, will be a savior for the Zeller empire. I have enough on all those key men, those Senators and congressmen you frequently and flamboyantly boast are tucked tightly in your hip pocket, to carry forward the Zeller-Harding influence into future generations of power.''

"Mistakes were made. Serious errors in judgment on your part.''

"On all sides, admittedly. But with mistakes came learning and the promise of future reparations. Rapprochement is possible, nothing is ended, merely the office I held.''

"We are a vast entity without limitations," said Zeller. "We need no promises of reparation, we dictate our own. As for rapprochement, my men are busily at work trying to mend the fences you destroyed. You based your power on misrepresented facts and exaggerated associations. Mine is based on facts I created and held fast to.''

"You assume I am accepting this forced resignation lying down? At once I began leaking to the proper press outlets—our allies—false reasons for my dismissal. I am not without resources. The American President shall witness frightening wonders of what is really possible from Z-12 Andromeda.''

"Victor is there.''

"Our agents also. Very talented men.''

"I don't want Victor destroyed," said Zeller.

"You can't have it both ways. Which is it to be?''

"Damn you, you presume too much.''

"The master taught me things he didn't teach his son. Face it, Amadeo. We are both devious men. I truly reflect what should have been born of your seed.''

"Never! Filth! Animal! Butcher! Assassin!" he screeched.

Harding laughed contemptuously. "I have all the qualifications you possess in a capsule. Without them I'd have never caught your fancy.''

Zeller's eyes, those colorless orbs, galvanized the other. His rasping, croaking voice triggered memories in Harding. Memories of promises he'd made to another man, the great man whose death had been an abomination to the Fatherland. He recalled how he and Anton as children had shivered behind that study door at Berchtesgaden as they awaited audience with the

Führer. After he became infamously known among certain elite circles as Ghost-Dancer, he had learned the full extent of his relationship to the German leader. After Anton's death at Les Diablerets and *after* he'd assumed Anton's persona and perused the vastly informative secret files in Anton's house in England, he'd understood at last the nature and extent of his dedicated mission. His determination to succeed in a plot to exterminate the enemies of his father and Fatherland were superseded only by his unique talent and fierce dedication. "You killed my father," he said quietly. "Oh, you didn't know he was my father, but you and your diabolical double-dealing cronies betrayed him to the enemy—"

"What?" Zeller croaked.

"—just as you executed my uncle and stole from my brother and me our rightful inheritance, our legacy."

"That's a lie! You're crazy! What's come over you, Anthony?" Zeller fumbled under his desk for a secret lever that would summon Mosha Bauer.

"I wouldn't do that, Amadeo." Harding whipped out a gun, aimed it menacingly at the financial mogul. "I haven't forgotten my talents. I've kept them rapier sharp following the numerous attempts on my life by clumsy assassins. Seven in all, that I was made aware of, never saw headlines of their deeds. I hushed them all up to keep away the lunatic fringe. When the first apparently failed to make headlines, those who followed lost interest in my liquidation or were bought off. Were any operating on your orders? Perhaps you learned my true identity after all. You have the means." Harding sat on the arm of the chair opposite Zeller. "Tell me—" he leaned in toward Zeller, "—do you recall Brother Heinrich Schuller?"

"Heinrich Schuller. No! Why would I? What is he to me?"

"Liar! You would forget a man who started your depredatory wealth? Think back fifty, perhaps sixty years ago. You were a young man then, not a crotchety old man who grows more dilapidated daily."

Zeller leaned back in his chair, his face a death's-head mask as he searched his memory. *Schuller . . . Schuller!* The cleric at Admont Monastery. A mass of raw nerves had been exposed. Zeller, sitting perfectly still, said quietly, "You *know* it's true. Why would I deny it? It was before your time. His death suited my immediate purpose. You, above all," he said at length, "should understand my reasoning."

"I understand that two very young, homeless men were deprived of their inheritances. We were forced to endure squalor until I sharpened my wits and met adversity head-on. Once I asserted myself, the way became clear for me to become an agent for British MI-6."

"Under German control," Zeller added hastily, his eyes dead under the subdued lighting. "Loyal to Kaltenbruner—to Hitler himself." Zeller stopped, winced under the assault of truth. Then he treaded softly. "If the Western world were suddenly to receive a recorded avalanche of your sordid past—"

"For every file you've amassed on me, I have more sophisticated, verifiable files on you and your cronies, those whose loyalties you solicited through blackmail, bribery, and all the devilish tools you've employed during your tenure on earth. Do we understand one another?"

Harding paused and remained motionless, waiting for Zeller to put it all together. If he did, the octogenarian gave no sign of it, but he fumbled with a golden globe paperweight etched on four sides with the U.S. eagle, the British lion, the Russian bear, and a Nazi swastika. He kept turning it slowly in the palm of his hand, his eyes on Harding. "I'm going to confess something to you, Anthony. If I appear awkward, it's because I very seldom flatter a man. I have never really given you the credit you deserve. You have always impressed me in everything you did. So why the need for this animosity between us? We are family, *ja?* You are spouse to my Clarisse. Why quarrel when we are nearing our goal? In less than twenty-four hours Z-12 Andromeda will cease to exist. And with it go all my enemies, including my most bitter enemy, Moufflon, the only failed assassination attempt of your lifetime. Even so, you boast a spectacular record of achievements. Many Moufflon associates await my word that his demise is secure. They are only too willing to come over to the winning side. They are tired of his altruism."

"Z-12? Andromeda? Then it's true? I wasn't spinning daydreams. You intend to decimate the laborious efforts and futuristic marvels of two decades? Christ! Your own son is there! Moments ago you led me to believe you didn't want him hurt. Now in this denouement, I learn the truth. You are the quintessential villain of all who went before you. Lucifer himself. *Gottverdammen! The flesh of your flesh!* If you would do this to Victor what have you in store for me?'' His finger tightened on the trigger. ''I've performed ghastly deeds in my lifetime in the name of expediency, but to exterminate your own son?''

''There is always Clarisse to follow in my stead. Think, Anthony, think. Last spring . . . following the Maui conference, Clarisse spent six months here with me at the château. When I first saw signs of dissension in Victor, I knew my duty.''

Harding struggled to remain calm. He removed his tortoise-shell glasses with his free hand, his eyes never wavering from Zeller. He was suddenly aghast as the meaning clarified in his mind.

''*The brain implant!* My God—you didn't!'' He set the glasses back into place, his eyes blazing. ''You turned her into a zombie like Victor?''

''I did. With her full consent. Actually it was her wish. Her fervent desire and perfect logic inspired me. Then there was the matter of Victor always needling me, demanding explanations for my driving ambitions. One gets tired of a lack of appreciation, don't you agree, Anthony? Victor rebuked me at every turn. I tell you the destruction of Z-12 Andromeda is an expedient vital to our plans. Clarisse is a virgin in politics; no dirty files defile her past. She'd make a perfect Prime Minister or Premier. Her powers of persuasion, as you may have noticed, are formidable. Besides, time, sister to opportunity, is on our side.

''Black propaganda colors the Chinese scene. Clandestine radio stations start rumors in an attempt to discredit leaders. It has been reported that guerrillas opposed to China's leaders are fighting in the southern Chinese provinces. Angry troops have looted state granaries in east China to get food to the masses. Factory workers, coal miners in northern provinces have gone on strike for higher pay and better working conditions, and soldiers called out to suppress them have instead rebelled, shot their officers and Communist Party officials.''

''None of that's true!'' Harding exclaimed heatedly.

''Of course it isn't. People believe what is reported in the paper even if it is all misinformation. Misinformation serves our purpose. Rumors to encourage unrest and plant seeds of doubt in the minds of the masses are as vital to us as our lifeblood. As long as it erodes support for the government, we can blame the total annihilation of Z-12 Andromeda upon the Chinese guerrillas.''

''That rumor of sixty thousand alleged executions—''

''Incorrect. False. All manufactured to serve our final purpose in Z-12.''

''Z-12 complied with your orders by triggering the nuclear holocaust in the Middle East, and this is their payoff—annihilation? The destruction of their life's work?''

''Can you think of a better way to achieve our goals? A single spark can start a prairie fire. Should any man survive, and I doubt any will, he will immediately be flung into China's *gulag*—political prison camps. Actually, Anthony, I am doing this for you.''

''For me? I am touched.''

''For you and Clarisse, and of course for the perpetuation of the Zeller dynasty.''

''How can a dynasty be perpetuated when my wife refuses to bed with me?''

''It's up to you to find a way. Back to Z-12. The communist guerrillas are moving in closer daily.''

''*Communist guerrillas?*''

''Very well—mine. Our own men. Their coded passwords are apropos, Anthony. '*A lame man treads on the tail of the tiger.*' ''

''What, pray tell, is the significance of those esoteric words? Am I supposed to know?''

''Think, Anthony, do you know—have you ever known a lame man who might ostensibly tread on the tiger's tail?''

''I haven't the foggiest notion.'' For a split second Harding took on the inert expression of a lizard. ''To borrow a phrase from Hamlet, 'Suit the action to the word, the word to the action,' '' he said. ''I have known many lame men, metaphorically speaking.'' He tensed, preparing himself internally. ''Whatever my transgressions, Amadeo, have we not gone beyond the guessing-game stage? Say it and be done with it.''

''Anton. Anton Schuller did not die at Les Diablerets. Anton Schuller, a.k.a. Jonathan Marl, head of Z-12 Andromeda, prepares for your destruction.''

''Liar! I s<u>aw</u> him fall to his death. No one could survive that drop to an icy grave. You'll have to do better than that if you think to intimidate me."

"Apparently survival runs in the family. Anton survived, I tell you. Why would I lie? He was a scientist, not a soldier of fortune or an assassin. He put all his efforts into Project Andromeda. A scientist's logic guided him while developing the most brilliant mind in the field."

"How long have you known this?"

"The better part of a decade."

"You kept it from me to use as a cudgel at the opportune time." Anthony Harding, a.k.a. Eugen Schuller, a.k.a. Ghost-Dancer, lunged to his feet and in a quick, nimble movement dropped the gun and thrust a sharp stiletto through Zeller's heart. He yanked it out savagely and plunged it in again. "Liar!" he hissed. "Viper! You should have known you'd never get the best of Ghost-Dancer!"

"Fool! You—impossible—fool. Why d-do you think Z-12 will be d-destroyed?" Zeller's breathing grew labored. Blood dripped from his lips, trickling from the corners. His eyes rolled upward. "T-To—protect—y-you." He grinned demonically. "F-For this r-relief—much thanks."

Harding moved around to Zeller's side of the desk. In moments he prepared a false death scene, arranged Zeller's body to simulate a suicide, a self-inflicted fatality. The expert assassin knew precisely what to do.

He had overlooked one thing. The golden globe paperweight clutched tightly in Zeller's left hand, the swastika side pointing toward his heart.

It was the first thing Clarisse saw when he summoned her. And she knew her father's murderer.

"He's done it. What he's threatened to do of late. He was despondent, Clarisse. Before I could move to his side to dissuade him, he plunged a knife into his heart, not once but twice. If it's any consolation, it took courage to do what your father did." He spoke slowly, with just the proper amount of anxiety and sadness required after observing a great man's suicide.

Clarisse stared vacant-eyed, but she missed nothing. She studied her father's skeletal remains, scanned the bloodied shirt front, the crimson blood pooling on the desk. Her eyes riveted on the golden globe, the swastika on the gold sphere pointed toward him. And she knew. It was precisely what Amadeo had predicted.

The Nazi swastika was the dead giveaway. Harding had murdered her father.

Before she conveyed either tears, accusations, or sorrow, she addressed Harding. "Summon Mosha Bauer. He'll know what to do. Well, what is it? Are you wondering at my comportment? No tears. No wringing of hands. No sorrowful supplications. None of those things, Anthony, become the daughter of Amadeo Zeller. I am that, if nothing else. I am my father's daughter."

Moments later Clarisse was in her quarters, locked in, observing a videotape reenactment of the earlier scene between Harding and her father. She heard everything, saw everything, knew what must be done. For Amadeo Zeller had already explained the scenario to her, knowing that by her recent cranial implant surgery he'd left a carbon copy of himself behind. Victor had failed him. Long live Clarisse.

In Moscow at his office at KGB Headquarters, Andreivich Malenekov was stewing over the fouled up transmission. Millions of dollars spent. Millions? *Billions* had been poured into modern technology. At these prices, should transmission between Ulan Bator and Moscow suffer? Uri had had no time to hear the second phase of the password. Pray he understood. Suddenly irked at the sound of his intercom, he pounded on the lever. "Before you bend my ears with your troublesome news, prepare for me another transmission to Z-12 Andromeda. Do you understand, young Commissar Petroff?"

"*Da! Da!* Permit me to enter, Comrade Malenekov. I bear strange tidings." Andreivich released the enter button. Young Petroff, his face a blustery red, burst forth with the utmost respect. "Comrade. Word from Zürich. Amadeo Zeller has passed on. He is dead, in a shroud of mystery. Our agent Gouseev denies the mystery. Zeller was murdered."

"Yes, yes, tell me more, you idiot. You know more, I see it in your face. Well, well, why do you wait? You stand there like a wooden stick. Speak up, young Commissar Petroff. Speak up."

"A knifing, clean and through the heart, performed by Eugen Schuller, a.k.a. Anthony Harding."

"There were witnesses? Well, speak up."

"Not the usual witnesses. A videotape recording in his wife's possession."

Malenekov gave out a low sigh. "Aha. So it has come to this? Word must reach Z-12 Andromeda without fail. If I know Schuller, and I know him well, Ghost-Dancer is about to put in an appearance at Z-12. We must get word to Uri Mikhail Gregorevich. Well done. Well done, young Commissar Petroff. Be gone and come back when you have Z-12 on satellite transmission."

Chapter Twenty-five

Commander Robbins's image filled the screen; his voice permeated the task force's barracks:

"For two decades we've imposed a wall of silence around our work, provided a smokescreen around the project. I'm talking dropping acoustic sensors into trees and brush to pick up the sounds of motors, human voices, any noise out of the ordinary. Seismic sensors designed with spiked noses are jabbed into the ground around the perimeters of Z-12. Positioned all around us are well-camouflaged ground-to-air missiles able to destroy aggressive enemy aircraft in midair in seconds.

"We plotted, schemed, dreamed what two decades ago was considered an unrealistic future. But the longer we persisted and reconnoitered under Dr. Marl's guidance, marshaling all our inner resources and strengths, we were forced into constructing barriers isolating Z-12 Andromeda from any experiment of its kind.

"There were moments when we looked at one another and declared ourselves mad. At times the agony of living superseded the ecstasy of death. Times when the pain of failure, hurt, and unacceptance could not compete with the sweet silence of death.

"But we overcame those feelings and persevered. And now there is an alternative to life and survival. An alternative lifestyle, one to which we must adapt or the planet Earth as we know it shall be extinct.

"The solemn pride which must be yours for daring to venture here to us at Z-12 is commendable. But enough philosophy. Let us segue to science, the brilliant realization of the space-colony settlement."

Commander Robbins's image disappeared as the camera panned over the space-colony settlement. The giant space wheel was orbiting. Every task force member's eyes were glued to the screen.

Joseph Carlini entered Moufflon's quarters. He peered in at Darius.

"Major, sir, you are wanted in Commander Robbins's quarters. It's urgent." His nose, sharp as a bird's beak, stood out in sharp profile. Matteus, staring at him, nodded to Gabriel Gadi. Gadi sprang to his feet, prepared to accompany Darius. "Alone, sir. The Commander requests only the presence of your company."

"Sorry, Carlini, Gadi goes where I go."

"Have it your way, sir."

The trio departed.

"Good of you to come, Major," Robbins said, extending his hand. "Come in, please. I don't think it's necessary to have your man with you. All weapons have been collected. A squadron of our men passed among the task force, and they willingly relinquished all arms."

Darius nodded to Gadi. "It's all right. You can wait or return to quarters. The briefing is more important." Gadi hesitated, then reluctantly took his leave.

"Forgive the hush-hush attitude, Major, but Dr. Marl and his two guests, Krishnam and Dalei Dai, feel it urgent to confer with you before tomorrow's briefing and the arrival of our men from substations Z-5 and Z-10."

"Of course."

A few moments later Jonathan Marl greeted Darius far more warmly than he had on his arrival. This time, he put Darius at ease. "Please join us for tea."

They sat at the round table in the confines of Marl's inner office. Dalei Dei, the apparent spokesman, extended their hospitality. "Since you were here last we hope you feel the developments at Z-12 constitute verifiable and authentic progress."

Darius nodded. He watched Krishnam reset his bifocals on his nose and pour the steamy tea. "I can label it nothing else but astute and unquestionable progress." Darius looked into their eyes, which for reasons he attached to their religious philosophy, they kept averted.

"We feel we've known you forever," Dalei Dei said quietly. "Actually it's difficult to know where to begin."

"The beginning is usually best." Darius observed the tea ritual, wondering why they requested his presence. On his previous visits to Z-12, this trio had kept themselves aloof.

"There are three beginnings, one for each of us. Which would you prefer first?"

"I shall leave that to your impeccable discretion, Dalei Dei."

"Perhaps there is no beginning. You were here before any of us in a history already waiting for us. By the way," Dalei Dei assured him, "no intrusion upon your privacy is intended. Words spoken in this room will not travel beyond these walls."

"Electronic marvels transcend walls of stone," Darius said, his eyes sweeping the communications wall display.

"Dr. Marl has astutely dismantled any alien and unwanted recording devices within these walls. This is our private room for consultation. It does not compare with others, but in the Gobi it suffices. We assure you no eavesdropping is possible."

"Then you won't mind my cynicism." Darius removed a pen-sized electronic detector and padded about the room, holding it above his head, then below, waving it around him. The needle failed to move from point zero. Not the slightest wavering was visible. He nodded in appreciation and resumed his previous position at the table.

"See?" Krishnam said in a voice as monochromatic as his bland garb. "The walls are solid sheets of specially treated nonconducting metal placed between stone. Transmission of any sort is nil. Our only contact is through the closed-circuit video monitor and VCR, to be used at Dr. Marl's direction and discretion."

"Perhaps I'll commence," Dalei Dei began. "You entered my life long before I was born. We are, you and I, brothers in the strictest sense."

What the devil? He studied the holy man intently.

"Your father and my father are one and the same—Michael-Miguel Bertelli."

He continued the disquieting tale: "We have different mothers."

By now Darius's stomach muscles had tensed in an effort to conceal his abject astonishment. He broke into a cold sweat, stared hard at the high cheekbones and almond-shaped eyes of the half-Oriental, half-Tibetan holy man. "I don't understand."

"Let me explain. We are not here to cause you disquiet, Moufflon, only to announce our camaraderie with you. We are not enemies, understand. We are on your side. We too long to break the Zeller-Harding cartel of global power."

"And you," said Krishnam, "came into my life by way of my illustrious father, a former war comrade of yours, Major Morosconi, who was massacred with my mother and sisters while I was attending classes at Milan University. Perhaps you'll remember him better by the code name Pluto."

"*Pluto?* Oh, my God, Pluto! Dead? At whose hand, as if I need ask. Better, why?"

"By the man who could identify him from the war. A man with a deep past. A man who for several years following World War II was in the confidence and pay of the British, Russian, and American intelligence communities. A man who became so ambiguous he didn't exist," said Krishnam with a sardonic tinge. "We had countless tips from our friends in the Mossad and in the Sûreté, even British SIS, but the British ran us up dry creeks because of their involvement in the man's beginnings."

"It was *my* murder, *my* death, the obliteration of *my* persona," interjected Jonathan Marl, "that led me to Ambiguity, as he was becoming known among the underground moles of international intelligence communities."

"*Your* murder? *Your* death?" Darius sipped his tea, totally absorbed in the fascinating narrative.

"I alone knew Ambiguity, although in essence I hadn't known him at all. It was my brother, Eugen Schuller, alias Ghost-Dancer, who condemned me to death once the unholy alliance was made with Zeller and Omicron International. They plotted, schemed a black scenario of inestimable power, stole Lord John York's plans to reshape and redesign the borders of the Middle East. The game was deep, dark, hatched in the minds of Zeller and Harding. Their only chance to convert a mortifying failure during the Lebanon-Israeli war into a clandestine success fell flat; they hadn't counted on the refusal of the Israelis to put their land, their people at grave risk. Anthony Harding, then Eugen Schuller, had played this entire game out of his hip pocket, and in a moment-by-moment scenario, beginning with the knowledge that my death would catapult him farther into areas of trust, he staged the clever scenario of my death in the icy tombs of Les Diablerets.

"He watched me hurled to my icy grave, satisfied that my death was imminent. He returned to Cambridge, assumed my persona—he'd already cultivated me to the fullest. He took six months to prepare for the role. Upon news of Eugen Schuller's death—he had carefully planted his identity and passport in my backpack—he was accepted as Anton Schuller at face value. He involved himself in my activities while I languished in a hospital bed under an alias, recuperating from my fatality—yes, my death, for I did die that day, internally, and again when I learned how Eugen had carefully and with premeditation planned to do me in."

Marl raised his hand and yanked off the unruly white wig. "You see me as I am. The shock, trauma, fright, and God knows what else that was done to my body and mind left me irrevocably crippled and completely bald." He left the wig off, slid his tortoiseshell glasses onto his nose. With steel-rimmed glasses I could pass for—"

"*Ghost-Dancer!*" Darius hissed. "Years older, but I haven't forgotten that face, those eyes, that countenance since I encountered it aboard the HMS *Hyperion*." The implications boggled Darius's mind.

"No—not Ghost-Dancer, his brother, Anton," said Krishnam. "Ghost-Dancer, the assassin you and my father knew intimately, took over Anton's identity, amalgamated himself with Zeller, and became an American phenomenon, Anthony Harding. You see, it happened when a breakdown in KGB ciphers lifted some of the ambiguity from Anton Schuller and put the Cambridge spy ring out of business. A new identity was provided him by Zeller's Omicron, a deal was struck. He was a free man to wheel and deal under the Zeller umbrella in any way he chose. Now the consensus is that Harding runs Zeller.

Not the other way around. I am certain you have followed the brilliant and varied Harding career to its latest developments.''

"Resignation forced upon him by the American President."

"Which makes very little sense, since MacGregor's most influential advice has come from the duplicitous Anthony Harding."

"Perhaps the President has entertained a change of heart?"

The phone on Dr. Marl's desk rang shrilly. He glanced at the others in annoyance, then picked it up. "Yes, yes, Joseph, what is it?" He listened. "But we are not finished here." He listened again. "Very well, I shall tell him." He replaced the phone. Darius leaned over, placed a paperweight on the phone lever to depress the button and unscrewed the mouthpiece. He removed a dime-thin sensor.

"Bugproof, eh? The simplest, oldest ploy in covert operations."

Marl's head reddened to a bright crimson. He quickly and deftly set the wig into place. "It's for you, Moufflon. The Russian, Gregorevich, insists upon speaking with you on a matter of urgency. If you desire you can step outside, then return," Marl said, turning the dime-thin microphone sensor over in his hand. "How could we have overlooked this?" he asked his companions as the implication of the bug struck home. Each of them paled. All their efforts—cloaking their past in innuendo, using provocative generalities when asked about their lives prior to coming to Ulan Bator—had been for naught.

Someone knew their identities!

It was an unforgivable oversight. *A telephone bug!* Anonymity was their defensive weapon until their plan orbited into place. "Three of Z-12's most astute minds have overlooked the obvious."

"But for how long?" Krishnam asked suddenly, with renewed hope, as they awaited Darius's return. "I looked in that same intercom phone only a month ago and found nothing."

"A month?" Marl's agitation abated. "A month ago, you say. Then perhaps less harm was done than we imagined."

Marl flipped through the pages of his monthly agenda. "A month, Krishnam? To the day?" He touched his fingertips to his wet lips, then shuffled pages forward, backward, stopping at a three-day interval. "Satellite transmission via closed channels had announced the Moufflon Task Force takeoff from

Paris a month ago. No one from the outside world knew or should have known the flight schedule, the Scorpion's destination.''

"Someone here at Z-12 did know. Damn! Commander Robbins, Dr. Malay, the three of us, and perhaps a dispatcher or two."

"Then someone here at Z-12 is an enemy. Someone among that list," Darius said, reentering the room, his solemn face tightly drawn.

"Not necessarily. Someone could have cut into your radio frequency from the Scorpion. Did you employ all electronic countermeasures, Moufflon?"

"Everything was programmed through the Grim Reaper."

"Could anyone tap into the computer?" Mark asked. His clear eyes behind the horn-rimmed glasses shone with intelligence and profound scrutiny.

"Anything is possible," Darius said, crestfallen.

Dalei Dei sighed. "Do you know how many spies Commander Robbins has caught in the past six months? Just before your arrival, Artana, the agent at Z-10 was contacted and failed to respond with the proper ciphers. Artana was here during that three-day interval you speak of, Jonathan. He left for Z-10 for his usual three-week hitch in the desert immediately after and is due for a week's relief.'

Darius's eyes narrowed and turned a murky, trouble-filled green, his chaotic thoughts brooding.

"The cleverness of someone's duplicitous achievements is about to descend upon Z-12," Krishnam said. "Pray we prepare for any possible skulduggery."

"Gentlemen," Darius said at last, "Uri Mikhail Gregorevich has just learned through his superiors at the Kremlin that Amadeo Zeller is dead."

The three men stared in disbelief.

"Which means—" Marl began.

"Which means the son stands next in the power structure," Dalei Dei muttered, snapping a pencil in two and tossing it on the tabletop.

"*Nein, Nein!*" Marl snarled, reverting to his native German. "Last night, upon his own instructions, Velden Zryden—Victor Zeller—turned himself over to our medical facility for the removal of a cranial implant."

"Victor Zeller?" Darius exploded. "Why wasn't I informed?"

"The patient requested total anonymity. Permission to enter the space colony was denied to any wearing pacemakers—"

"Then who will head Zeller's Omicron?" Krishnam's surgically slanted eyes narrowed.

"Don't rule out the son," Marl stated flatly.

"I wouldn't do that yet," insisted Pluto's son. "It all boils down to what was really transacted between Zeller and Harding these past two decades."

"Who is the logical corporate successor?"

"Harding," Dalei Dei said venomously.

"Harding," Marl said with perceptive simplicity. "If my intuitive faculties are working as usual, I'll wager that Harding, whatever alias or disguise he assumes, is about to pay Z-12 Andromeda a visit."

Darius, stunned at the unexpected order of things, sat back in his chair, deflated. "Do you have something stronger than tea, Jonathan?"

The Chief of Staff of Z-12 placed a decanter and four brandy glasses on the table. He filled each and placed them before the men.

"Merci beaucoup," Darius said, tilting his glass, downing the contents in two gulps.

"Pas de quoi."

"Your mortal enemy," said Darius, "your brother will not permit you to live, Jonathan. You represent everything in this world he fears most—a conduit to his exposure. We must assume that Zeller or someone got word to him that you're alive and in charge of Z-12," Darius mused. "I won't know for sure until I return to Corsica and review the clandestine tapes tapping into his inner sanctum."

"You have Zeller's château bugged?" Each man arched his brow.

"The marvels of modern-day science shouldn't surprise any of you. So assume Harding went to Zürich after his forced resignation as Secretary of State and got slapped on the wrist by Zeller. Perhaps it was more than a slap on the wrist. Zeller was furious. Removal of a key man after twenty years of setting him in place wouldn't sit right with him. So he excoriated the pompous oaf, rubbing in the most humiliating defeat of all, his failure to kill his brother. It's logical, it plays. So Harding kills Zeller and moves a step closer to the power throne. But one last obstacle remains. Anton Schuller is alive under the cover of Jonathan Marl, a brilliant scientist in charge of Z-12, the most coveted secret project outside of NASA. Worse, Anton Schuller, a.k.a. Jonathan Marl, is the only man alive who can betray Anthony Harding to the world. What would you do if you wore Harding's shoes?''

"Kill Jonathan Marl. Or provide an accident of sorts. In any event, death is the only option open to Harding. An absolute.''

"Precisely, Krishnam. We must prepare for adversity from any front. Last night, Miss Lansing nearly finished me off. She caught me unawares. She wore a crystal ball around her neck—a gift, she said, from the Andromeda staff. Are you—any of you—familiar with the device?'' he asked straight out.

"I took it apart. Very clever properties. A suggestionary device, like a posthypnotic trance,'' he said in a deliberate voice.

The troubled trio exchanged concerned glances. Reluctant to speak, they shuffled uncomfortably in their chairs. Krishnam poured more tea and rose to his feet to set a kettle to boiling on the Franklin stove in the corner of the spartan room.

"I destroyed the crystal ball after learning its properties. Whatever hold it had on Miss Lansing is finished. I leave you to your thoughts and consciences. Oh, yes, the Scorpion must be ready to depart in forty-eight hours in order to rendezvous with the Lodestar. Before I depart, I leave you with a thought. Think on it. There are men who will resist change whenever change is threatened, preferring personal aggrandizement and the security of their wickedness. Pray, do not tarry too long before certain safeguards are employed. My men and I will do our best to protect you from outside dangers. You who command the military here at the base—'' He stopped, interrupted by a burst of static from Dr. Marl's intercom. Joseph Carlini's voice erupted from it.

"Dr. Marl! Apache helicopter coming in at three o'clock. A Titan escort hovering close by. We've had no prior communication heralding their arrival, no prior flight log discernible. They are not communicating distress signals but request landing permission.''

"They're ours, aren't they?'' Marl snapped in annoyance.

"They came in on different channels, sir.''

"Permit them to land. Restrict them to security-cleared channels and make certain they are interrogated by Commander Robbins. And Carlini—"

"Yes, sir."

"Instruct Commander Robbins to place Z-12 on security alert. Man all stations of defense for a twenty-four-hour watch. Keep all communications channels open."

"Yes, sir. Over and out."

Marl turned off the intercom key. "What do you make of that?" he asked the others.

"We'll learn soon enough," Darius said, exiting quickly.

In his absence, Marl exclaimed, *"The crystal ball!"*

"The Chinese communists! How the devil did they infiltrate Z-12 and gain access to Miss Lansing? And why her? Why not Zryden, York, or Katanga?" Dalei Dei ran nervous fingers through his long hair.

"What of the fourth man?" Marl flushed with indignation.

"We don't know who he is, do we?" Krishnam muttered. "Do we, Jonathan?" he repeated.

"He's a killer! A bastard! Don't forget it!" The words rang shrilly in their ears. "And he takes orders from Anthony Harding. He may be one of us! Or one of Moufflon's task force. Did you give Moufflon the dossiers on all Z-12 personnel as requested?"

Krishnam nodded. "Carlini had them prepared the moment they were assigned quarters. Moufflan has perused them religiously."

"Including ours?"

"Especially ours. I wonder what he thinks now that he knows they were manufactured dossiers."

"We'll know, won't we, before the Scorpion chopper leaves Z-12."

"What we must bear in mind," Marl said judiciously, is that Zeller and Harding were equals, two brilliant men who shared a more intimate and knowing view of the hidden reality of world affairs than any other two world figures.

"But both with ulterior motives," said Krishnam succinctly.

"Precisely." Marl nodded in agreement.

Chapter Twenty-six

Outside, the early sun simmered to a full boil. At five-thirty A.M. following a sleepless night, Valerie sat at her desk, writing in her notepad:

This space-colony settlement must encompass several hundred acres. It is a gigantic, wheellike structure, a tube more than four hundred feet in diameter bent into a ring just over a mile across. We learned on our arrival that the wheel spins gently once a minute. This rotation makes the settlement different from the U.S. Shuttle or Russian Salyut because it produces a gravitylike force. Our orientation papers explain that on the space settlement there can be farming, factories, houses, meeting places, and nothing is designed by guesswork.

Floating farms will be arranged terrace-style with fish ponds and rice paddies in transparent tanks on a top layer, wheat fields below, vegetables and soybeans and corn below that. There are even minipastures for space-age cattle and sheep. Absent are the glass towers and underground caverns science fiction writers have projected in fable. Save for a few unusual geometrical shapes and forms,

Z-12 Andromeda looks very much like a modern-day rural community with condominiumlike homes.

It seems ideal, but I question the need at all. The work must commence with the reshaping of man's mind. Without a change in man's consciousness, we can try to conquer every planet in the solar system to no avail. The irony of it all is that alongside this peaceful, most serene community where ten thousand settlers have been living for nearly two decades, there is an arsenal of weapons.

I call it the *"dark side of the force."* Commander Robbins promises to explain its necessity while still selling us on the need for space-colony settlements in the year 2000.

There was a knock at her door. Valerie shut the notebook, tucked it into her flight bag. "Who is it?"

"Uri. May I come in?"

She had reached the door before he opened it. She glanced at her watch. "Now, that's what I call record time. Fifteen minutes to shower and change, but you didn't shave?"

"Valeruska, I have news. Amadeo Zeller died sometime yesterday or the day before. I am uncertain about the time. I know only that he is dead."

She blinked hard. "Victor! Does he know?"

"Victor? Victor Zeller?"

"Yes, Velden Zryden is Victor Zeller. Oh, God, he'll be the next threat! The next head of the Zeller cartel." Her anxiety shifted gears. "It isn't fair! I didn't have time to confront him. I couldn't make amends."

"Valeruska! What's come over you? What is this all about?"

"I can tell you nothing. You are a Russian! A communist. I am American. Don't you see? Our political differences will never permit our love to move beyond a quick flame."

"What are you saying?"

"The truth, Uri. Face it."

"I thought we were in love."

"Are in love, Uri, but it's no good. It won't work."

"I see. Capitalistic thoughts parade through your head. Victor Zeller will now wield the scepter of his father's power. You intend to gravitate to him."

Valerie stopped her tirade, humiliated and downcast. "You

believe that? I love you, Uri. But I'm no fool. It wouldn't last. You will be Premier of Russia—''

"And you will be Victor Zeller's bride."

"No. You don't understand."

"You lived together for nearly a year. You loved him! Don't deny it. Why else would you endanger your life?"

Valerie placed her fingers over Uri's lips. "There is something very wrong with Victor Zeller. Something drastically wrong. I thought, in Paris, when I asked so many questions concerning cranial implants, you'd catch on to my inference. And when aboard the Lodestar, I tried to discourage you whenever Velden Zryden tuned in his wristband to our frequency."

Uri removed her fingers from his lips. "Late yesterday afternoon, Velden Zryden had the cranial implant removed. He—"

"*What?* What are you saying?"

"It's true. His desire to traverse the space-colony settlement was so fervent, he requested the surgery when he was denied admittance."

Valerie sat down heavily in the chair. "Two shocks before the sun's at its zenith. How many more before this day is up?"

"If I had a brandy flask I'd be happy to offer you a stiff bracer," Uri said in a soft voice.

"That bad?" She sighed. Behind the labyrinthine corridors of Valerie's disquiet lay several contributing factors. But none equal to Uri's next words.

"Valeruska, I tell you in the deepest of confidence. The KGB has reason to suspect murder in Zeller's case. Yes, yes, murder," he insisted at the disbelief creeping into her expression. "At times such things offend our sensibilities, but surely you have no reason to be offended."

"Murder is always offensive. Do they have proof positive? The man is protected. My God, Zeller's château is an arsenal of expert marksmen, skilled, professional assassins. How could anyone gain entrance. Was he alone? Who was there? Surely—"

"Valerie Lansing, always the lawyer. All your reservations concerning Zeller are correct. The place is a fortress. At times the cleverest among us becomes unguarded. He was with Anthony Harding. Harding claims Zeller took his own life. He spoke of a despondency at the shape of world politics, the fear that the marvelous work done by Moufflon had ended in a plane crash."

"*What?* That's preposterous! Zeller loathed Moufflon!'' Ex-

pressions of disbelief and unadulterated anger alternated on
Valerie's face. Springing from her chair, she paced the confined space, slapping her hands together, wringing them,
pausing periodically, too furious to articulate her thoughts.

"Does my father, uh, Moufflon, know?"

"I told him straightaway."

"And? . . ."

"His shock was total, but as usual he tried to be casual. He
attached far more importance to Harding's company. He knows
more than he's telling me."

"And that leaves you where, Uri? Back at the Kremlin with
your Soviet cronies."

"Valeruska. Sit down, please." He glanced at his watch,
then pivoting, he swung around, his eyes on the electronic communications center. In a few swift movements, he yanked the
scanner from its niche, pulled the video screen from its shelf,
yanking on the wires. "What I intend to say to you is for your
ears only.

"Now sit down. We have a half hour before space-colony-
settlement briefing. SCS can wait."

He poured coffee from a thermos into two tin cups. "There
was once an Algerian Prince and a modern-day Mata Hari who
were terribly in love. But their duty to their respective countries
stood in the way of their marriage. We are speaking of circa
1940. Now, this Prince adored the woman Zahara. . . ."

The morning sky was oddly divided—a ceiling of darkness
ahead, a curtain of moonlight and the dimmest outline of a fading full moon behind. The jeep bounced over the dusty desert
road to space-wheel Andromeda. Valerie was silent, Uri unburdened.

"You realize your life is in jeopardy if anyone learns of your
ancestry. My God, Uri, you cannot be Premier of Russia!" she
exclaimed half-joyously, half-timorously. "I feel as if we're
both airborne and spiraling forward in a tailspin. My stomach is
doing cartwheels and my heart, loop-the-loops. Does my father
know?"

"Moufflon?" The jeep bounced and swayed precariously.

"Yes, yes, yes. Moufflon—" She stopped suddenly, panicked. "Oh, God! My other father, Senator Lansing, is well

connected to Anthony Harding. You don't suppose they conspired together?''

"Anything is possible."

"Your driving is frightening me. How much farther do we have to go?'' she asked breathlessly, watching him cut corners between buildings, turning, lurching, jamming on the brakes.

"I've never driven before," he said. "I've always had a driver."

"Oh, Christ! You'd better let me take the wheel. Stop!"

"How does one stop this crazy machine?"

"You don't know how to— Hell!'' Valerie leaned over, turned off the ignition key. "Now just brake it easily. That's it. Good. By Jove, you did it. Now scoot over." She jumped out of the jeep, ran to the other side, climbed aboard, and glanced at the plastic card indicating the location of every building at Z-12. "Let's see. I go along Broadway to Manhattan, turn right at L Street behind the fuel dump, then make a sharp left to the entrance of SCS Andromeda."

"Valeruska."

"Yes, Uri?" She turned the key in the ignition.

"Listen to me when I speak to you. Will you become my bride?''

"Oh, Uri, the calculated effects of the truth upon your people are frightening. You know too much. You realize you'll be imprisoned for life. Sent off to some *gulag*. Right now, I am scared silly! Yes, me, the bright, levelheaded, confident, unpredictable courtroom barracuda, is scared silly over what can happen to you. The KGB won't permit you to marry me and live an idyllic life in America. They'll kill you first! You'll have no opportunity to defect. Why did you have to shoot for the moon? Why couldn't you have been an ordinary Russian citizen?''

"Would we have ever met then?"

"No."

"Well, then. I must think things out clearly. I must ponder our situation. You could always come to Russia to live with me."

"As a prisoner in Siberia?" She started the engine with a thrust of finality, ending the impossible daydream.

Uri bridled at the ring of truth to her words. No one knew. No one in Russia knew of his illegitimacy. Vladechenko had died, the truth locked inside him, if he had known at all. *What am I doing? I want it both ways, and that is impossible. I want the premiership and I want Valerie.* His shock was total, his bewilderment masked by an exaggerated air of condescension. In disputing the internal contradictions, Uri found he was emotionally tearing himself apart.

Before they alighted from the jeep at SCS Andromeda, Uri took hold of her. "I won't press you. We both have to think on the matter. I have only one thing to say. Pray neither of us permits history to repeat itself as it did between your parents and my own."

"Oh, Uri." Tears welled in her eyes. "*Damn* you! My memory will always hoard images of you."

They stood in a body on a platform, peering through the labyrinthine, bullet-shaped hub of the space-colony settlement, their eyes darting every which way. Ten thousand settlers had manned this settlement, adjusting, readjusting, always trying to improve living conditions within the colony.

"It looks like a modern community along a green-lawned, tree-lined boulevard in America. Look there—the buses, the autos along the streets. That giant structure resembling the Arc de Triomphe is actually an office building with elevators and special windows," Valerie told Brad Lincoln as he eased himself alongside her.

"Have you heard the news?" he whispered, turning off his wristband radio.

"Which news?" she asked casually.

"All of it. Vladechenko's and Zeller's deaths within days of each other. Look, how well do you know the Hardings?"

"General, I thought you knew my business better than I."

"Let's talk at dinner. I want to know what happened last night out there with Moufflon."

Valerie lowered her voice. "I suggest you ask him. Is it true about Velden Zryden? The implant? He's not here. Is he all right?"

"He'll join us later. Something about miracle drugs and ointments that heal with the speed of lightning."

"Does he know about his father?"

Brad Lincoln, bending over the ramp, pointed to the swimmers clustered around the pool. "Look at the acrobatics possible in the low-gravity environment. Eavesdroppers are all around. Exercise caution." He moved along, limping toward Dr. Sen Yen Lu.

"Members of the Moufflon Task Force," said Commander Robbins, standing at the podium "may I have your attention? In the Paris laboratories, you were briefed, prepared for your virgin flight over the nuclear wasteland of the Middle East. Paris failed to divulge, for security reasons, the Scorpion's final destination.

"In the short term of your visit here, it isn't feasible to instill in you what should be a two-decade learning process. Consider this a crash course." Commander Robbins, a narrow-faced, thin-bodied man of medium build, was a stickler for formality of speech, manner, and uniform, and he knew his business. He was thorough and precise and gave exact answers to all queries.

"On your briefing forms, we anticipated and answered a number of questions. But if any of you have inquiries beyond those covered in the briefs, do not hesitate to speak up. What you see is spacecraft traveling through the spokes of the wheel. For the people in the settlement, it's much like taking a Sunday jaunt in an automobile. Many of these craft spin off from supply ships and carry vital parts to our settlement, parts for machines or replacements we are unable to manufacture in the settlement itself.

"We will enter one of the spokes and take the elevator to the hub where the actual settlement is located. I am here to emphasize that you are only seeing the tip of the iceberg from this vantage point.

"Before we embark on that leg of the journey—"

"Commander Robbins," Valerie said, "our briefing material speaks about the 'dark side of the Force.' Can you tell us about that?"

"Excellent question, since what you are about to see will boggle your mind. Look yonder, at the portion midway up on the Arc de Triomphe–shaped edifice. Direct your attention to the enormous turbine at that point, at the concave area that resembles a giant screen. Through the scientific marvels of holographic photography, we shall simulate a typical morning on Mars. What happens on Mars every morning is what permitted our work to evolve to the space-colony settlement, which our scientists, with NASA's inducement, believe will be ready within two decades.

"Now, look to the screen, please. In the fleecy coral flush of daybreak, a laser dawns on Mars. It flares forty miles above frigid deserts of red stone and dust. Here on Earth our eyes cannot detect the marvels, but I assure you from sunrise to sunset the red planet bathes in dazzling laser-shine. Think back to your Buck Rogers days. Before that to H. G. Wells's *War of the Worlds* when the Earth was scourged by Martian invaders holding laserlike death-ray guns in their hands.

"Those intermittent beams of light blasted brick-fired streets, pierced iron as if it were paper, decimated concrete walls as if they were blackboards."

The helicopter carrying Artana and a companion was bucking head winds as it came in for a landing. The chopper was rotating savagely, but both men's eyes were on the video screen, observing Commander Robbins's seminar with the task force.

The chopper landed. The two Mongols were ushered quickly inside their quarters as the engineers wagged the chopper off the helipad into a hangar. Outside, the sudden desert squall was erupting in all its fury. Desert squalls were sudden and when they came, the Z-12 crew had learned to be prepared to avert disaster.

A closed-circuit video camera panned over the two deplaning Mongols to the staff's barracks. Inside, another scanner picked them up.

"Which one is Artana?" Darius asked, his eyes fixed on the second man, wearing a fur-lined goatskin coat and a hat tugged well over his brows.

"The thinner man," Krishnam said. "The other is—"

"Chanda!" Darius muttered, aghast.

"You know Chanda, the Sikh?"

Darius's eyes darted to Gabriel Gadi's, then locked with Youseff's. He said quietly, "I know Chanda, the Sikh." His heart iced. Internal screams threatened to tear open his throat. Chanda was dead! But he was not!

Oh Christ! What the devil was going on?

Darius drew on all his reserves to remain calm. His eyes telegraphed danger to his coterie of friends. He said nothing to

Krishnam about his suspicions. "I suppose I'm to meet them later at chow. I think I'll join the task force," he said, excusing himself.

Dr. Jonathan Marl was strangely aloof this day. He sat at his desk, his eyes on the task force as Commander Robbins initiated them through the vast space-colony settlement. The briefing was being videotaped, every question and answer recorded for posterity. If at some moment he felt like participating in the affair, he need only flip on a microphone switch to patch into the group via two-way transmission.

Over the years, he'd disciplined himself like an ascetic. He had spent years without laughter or amusement, had developed a will of steel. Marl was not popular among the men of his command; he was too feverishly dedicated to his chosen role in life. He had no weaknesses save for the physical deformity, his dependence on drugs, and the ongoing hatred increasing daily in his mind. The hatred was confined within justifiable bounds, but too often he knew he spilled his venom on those closest to him. He loathed promiscuity, laziness, blasphemy, coarseness, and vulgarity. He was sensible enough to realize his hatreds and his prejudices were personal judgments and tried not to inflict these judgments on others. Only in the company of Dalei Dei or Krishnam did he ever deign to drop the restraints and show his true self. He worked steadily without pause save for those moments of euphoria produced by the massive doses of drugs he took. He was a humorless, highly opinionated man with scrutinizing eyes and a constant frown. Now that Zeller was dead, he considered his brother, Anthony Harding, to be possibly the most dangerous man in the world, for Harding knew precisely what and who had detonated the nuclear blasts in the Middle East.

Dr. Marl observed the satellite transmission from Paris sedately announcing the death of the world financier. "Amadeo Zeller of Zürich, financier extraordinaire for the past six decades, is dead. He is survived by a son, Victor, and a daughter, Clarisse Zeller Harding," said the newscaster, his image fading in and out on the screen ". . . wife of the American statesman Anthony Harding . . . resigned from office. . . . comments from world luminaries . . . sketchy . . ." The transmission broke off as the desert storm whipped across the Gobi.

Jonathan Marl turned off the outside screen, zoomed in on the SCS transmission and observed the question-and-answer seminar between Commander Robbins, Dr. Malay, and the Moufflon Task Force. He depressed the intercom lever. "Joseph, where the devil are you?" Irked by the lack of response, Marl picked up his crutch, slipped it on, and limped heavily out of the room.

He returned moments later, took his chair, placed his crutch nearby, and dug into the pile of paperwork on the desk before him.

The cleanly shaven, bald Mongol seen earlier on the closed-circuit television monitor moved stealthily toward Marl's office door, unseen by Gabriel Gadi, portraying the role of an aide. In quick, silent movements Gadi was garroted, felled, his motionless body pulled into a closet. The expressionless Mongol locked the closet door behind him. He opened the office door quietly, stood poised for a second, observing Marl at work.

"Turn off the electronics, Marl."

Marl glanced up casually, then flipping a few switches on the elaborate console on his desk, did the other's bidding. The screens went blank.

"A lame man treads upon the tail of a tiger," he said.

"As above, so below; as below, so above," replied Marl, setting his glasses up on his nose. Raising his eyes slightly above the blinding lenses, he riveted them on the intruder, rolling the years back to 1943 aboard the *Hyperion*. The Mongol placed steel-rimmed glasses into place above his nose.

"Are all the recording devices disengaged?"

Marl nodded.

"So, Anton, you didn't die." The Mongol then began to mutter garbled words in German. Suddenly the words became insane expletives, deranged references to times and places of the past, of moments in which two frightened brothers had shared a horrifying childhood. But the words stopped, and the Mongol brandished a knife. He leaped over the desk, his outthrust hand shoved hard. The blade sliced through, lodged to the hilt in the leather-upholstered chair. The man in the chair lurched away from the desk, leaped over his assailant, and in a powerful thrust sent him crashing into the wall, dislodging the steel-rimmed glasses from his nose.

Darius raised his hand, yanked off his wig, and shouted. "Who are you? You are neither Chanda nor Ghost-Dancer! Who the devil are you? Identify yourself or you'll taste the brand of my death."

"Artana! I am Artana, British agent from Z-10! MI-6."

"*Merde!* You are neither Chanda nor Artana! Now, why did you want to kill Dr. Marl?"

"I tell you I am Artana. British SIS. I swear. Look, I'll prove it to you." He removed a fingernail fitted over another, turned it inside out, with numbers etched into it. "I know you. You're Moufflon with the task force. My orders were to liaise with you, but the Chinese Reds beat us to it. The man they killed in my place was a decoy, set up by SIS when the plans became known."

"Where's Chanda?" Darius handed back the plastic nail.

"He reported to his quarters. Said he'd meet me in a half hour. He has flight papers to fill out."

Darius studied the man who claimed to be Artana. He pointed to the almond-shaped eyes. "How did that happen?"

"A quarter hour in a plastic surgeon's office back in London. Back teeth removed to heighten the cheekbones. The Gobi sun turned my skin dark enough."

"Why exterminate Marl?"

"He's a clone. The real Marl is in Manchuria."

"I don't believe you." Darius moved in behind him, knife at the man's throat, his back arched into a bow, ready to snap. He touched a few pressure points. "Liar. I've seen men like you all my life and I know treachery. I can smell it a mile away."

"I swear the real Jonathan Marl is miles away in the Great Khingan Range in the *gulag* at Pokotu."

"Liar! I'll need more proof than a plastic fingernail with numbers inscribed on it." Darius's thumb depressed a pressure point. The man screamed, twisted, tried to wrench free. "Bloody bastard, I'll get ye for this!" The obvious Cockney accent didn't move Darius. He bent the man's back an inch closer to the breaking point.

"Give me names, places, or this knife will steer clear to your guts and twist full revolutions for good measure. Name your control."

"And get me bloody head chopped off?"

"Either that or it's your balls, blood, and guts!"

"All right. All right. Loosen up and I'll give you bloody what you want, guv'nor."

Darius relaxed his hold. The man broke loose and spun around. Shoving Darius hard against the wall, he whipped out a gun, held it to Darius's neck.

A gunshot crashed through a minute crack in the door. The door was kicked open. Matteus and Gabriel Gadi, fiercely yanking off a garrote collar, sprang forward. A bullet went through the stranger's head and lodged in Darius's arm. Icy pain spread through his arm, shoulder, down to his numb hand. The clever Mongol spy looked up at Darius with glazed dark eyes, his broad sardonic grin dissipating as death shuddered through him.

"Dammit. Get him out of here! I've got to reset the scene. I'm certain the man posing as Chanda is Harding."

Joseph Carlini and Krishnam entered the study, followed by the imposing figure of Dalei Dei, who peered at the dead man at Darius's feet. He stood motionless, staring at Darius's bleeding arm.

"Carlini, get my bag," Dalei Dei said quietly. "Sit down, Major."

"There's no time. Chanda is on his way over here."

"Chanda is a man of God. He is not a violent man."

"Chanda is dead," Darius said testily. His eyes signaled Gabriel Gadi to remain alert. "Why didn't you tell me about Marl?"

"What about Jonathan?"

"That he was being held prisoner in Manchuria, Pokotu in the Great Khingan Range to be exact."

"You believed this man?"

"He was convincing."

"He nearly blew your brains out."

"He was convincing. He was about to name his source when—"

"You lost your advantage, and he turned around to kill you. Your men foiled his attempt. Now please sit while I attend to your arm."

"Is all this worth anything? Space-colony settlements? Survival of mankind. They are all base. The work must begin on man's mind.''

''I do not disagree, Moufflon. To do that, civilization must commence again, incorporating what we know now. Or else it's doomsday for us all.''

Joseph Carlini entered with Dalei Dai's medicine bag.

''I didn't know you were a physician as well as a mind healer,'' Darius said. ''Just patch me up so I can greet Chanda. He and I have a great deal to talk about.''

''Why is that?''

''Stick around, Dalei Dei. You'll see.''

Dalei Dei removed two vials from his bag. They were marked EWH1000 and IAS1000: respectively external wound-healing substances and internal antishock stabilizers. ''The bullet deflected bone and exited through your arm. You're lucky. I'll clean both perforations and by tomorrow you'll be good as new.''

''Tomorrow?'' asked Darius, and Dalei Dei explained the miracle drug.

Darius listened intently, fingering the death's-head amulet around his neck. Could anything cure the sudden ghastly death that shaped strychnine poisoning? Darius requested that the others leave him alone with Dalei Dei. ''Now we're alone. Tell me about Artana. Chanda, told me some of the men are cloned. Well, to be more exact, surgery is performed on them to share likenesses with others.''

''Chanda told you that?'' Dalei Dei seemed disturbed.

''Is that what you and Krishnam had done to keep you from being singled out as Caucasians?'' Darius asked.

''Yes. It was done for that purpose. It's kept us safe for decades. We had hoped it would protect us until vengeance was ours.''

''Now Zeller is dead.''

''Harding still lives.''

''And he's here.'' Darius's skin prickled.

''The assassin is about to be trapped.''

''Ghost-Dancer has danced his last waltz,'' Darius said tightly. ''How long was Marl at Pokotu in Manchuria?''

''Never. He was never there. Krishnam was there. They wanted Pluto's plans for the beam-weapons program he and a team of scientists developed long before the idea was fancied as a deterrent for thermonuclear war.''

"Pluto? Responsible for perfecting the system? They thought his son had the plans. Harding *knew* about the beam-weapons system?"

"He knew. He sold the idea to the free world, on a cost-profit sharing basis. He also knew Major Morosconi in the war. Your friend Pluto, a man with his head in the planets, spoke innocently of such marvels. After the war, he was given a grant to perfect such a system by the Zeller-Harding cartel. He had no idea strings were attached. They betrayed him. Sold him out to the Chinese. They too secretly covet the plans."

Darius observed as Joseph Carlini packed Dalei Dei's bag. A perceptive awareness shook him. He studied the frail man and was struck by an indefinable foreboding, an instinctive feeling he couldn't shake. Carlini padded softly out of the room. Darius glanced at his watch. "I think the curtain is soon to go up. If you'll excuse me."

Dalei Dei placed his hands together, bowed, and backed out of the room. "I pray your intuition is working on all burners, Moufflon."

"Perhaps when this is over we can meet on fraternal grounds. We do have the same father, no?"

How many more versions of a story would he be subjected to? Which could he believe? *Oh Christ, I need be Solomon in all his wisdom to get through the mountain of fables.*

Darius, settled again in the Dr. Marl disguise, picked up the receiver, tapped his palm impatiently, and replaced it. He turned on the SCS monitor, observing his men moving through the settlement in wide-eyed wonderment. Darius tried counting. Moving as they did among the real settlers, he was unable to get a fix on the task force.

It was the longest wait Darius could remember. He attempted to reconstruct the scene that had just occurred to see if he could understand it. The scenario was an original, with too many unpredictable twists and turns. A complex scenarist would find it mind-boggling, an assassin his cup of tea.

Commander Robbins was explaining the dark side of the force again for Valerie Lansing's benefit. Darius smiled, actually beamed, at his daughter's intelligence, her ability to grasp the complicated scientific terminology. She had guts. But he was dismayed at the love she felt for Uri. It was a no-win situation. Uri was born and raised with a Russian's mentality. He was meant to be Premier. He was a fine diplomat. Youseff was right. How could he begin to wean him away from the Soviet role of Premier?

Darius shrugged his shoulders, placed Marl's thick glasses over the bridge of his nose, tugged the wig into place for good measure, and began the wait.

The task force settled inside a screening room. He listened to Commander Robbins's voice:

"You've witnessed the positive side of the force—the settlement, the modern medical wonders with lasers, the industrial benefits. Now for the darker side. Through the marvels of holographic photography, once again we simulate a battleground. Observe the scenario, my friends. Aggressor tanks sweep across from the east of your screen and laser beams sweep across the plains to greet them."

"War games again," Valerie said. "Always present, never absent, always prominent and foreboding."

"It helps even the odds, Miss Lansing. We cannot hope to build enough tanks to meet the Eastern bloc threat," Dr. Malay told the group. "But we can use our technology to reduce the effectiveness of the formidable tank."

Brad Lincon spoke up. "Small lasers can guide weapons with unprecedented accuracy, beaming across long distances to pinpoint vulnerable targets as was done in the Lebanon-Israeli skirmish as well as in the Falklands."

The door to Marl's office opened. "Dr. Marl? Chanda here," said the man entering. Incredible, thought Darius. The voice, the modulation, the British accent were perfect, flaws barely detectable. Darius glanced up from the screen. He was hunched over, his head resting in his left hand as he leaned on his elbow.

"Joseph asked me to bring your tea, sir. I hope you are not displeased."

"Harumph." Darius cleared his throat and moved the crutch at his side. He studied the demeanor and carriage of the fraudulent Indian Sikh. Darius watched the false Chanda pour hot water into the pot of Ceylon tea, and cover it with a cozy. And

Chanda, in turn, scrutinized the scientist. A strange anxiety marked his comportment. He glanced at the screen.

"Commander Robbins is most persuasive, is he not, Dr. Marl?"

"Harumph," Darius said, wiping his lips with a *serviette*. Behind the thick linen square, he mumbled, "Yes, yes, convincing. Quite convincing." Darius recognized the degree of his own fury. The bastard was good. He'd had a lifetime of practice. In World War II he'd been the best. Now his disguise was superb. The makeup was impeccable, his stance, carriage, accent all meticulously refined. If he didn't know better . . . But he did. This was not Chanda. It could not be Chanda. Chanda was dead, hidden somewhere at Z-12. Darius pressed a knee lever, activating a recorder.

"You heard of the tragedy, Dr. Marl. The financial world has lost its most benevolent benefactor, one of your most generous contributors."

"Vladechenko?" Darius muttered hoarsely, about to chomp on a tea cake.

"No. The financier Amadeo Zeller, sir, passed away."

The impostor was watching Darius closely, *too* closely. Darius's survival antennas moved into place. The *tea cakes*! Damn things were probably poisoned. It wasn't Ghost-Dancer's style. But here at Z-12 style was negligible. Expediency was the order of the day. Get in, do the job, and get the hell away from here before anyone knew what happened. Placing the *serviette* to his lips, he spat out the bitter cake.

"What's wrong, Dr. Marl. Does it not please your palate? Shall I send for more?"

Darius shook his head, faked a coughing spell, and drank from his decanter of brandy. Casually he fingered the death's-head amulet under his fatigues. It was easy to read the assassin's next step. It happened quicker than expected. Harding stood before the desk, obstructing Darius's view, certain the scientist would object to the blatant interruption.

Darius shoved the thick-lensed glasses up on his nose, his eyes magnified to enormous size. He cocked his head questioningly.

"Anton, how long will you continue the charade? Don't you recognize me?" Harding gloated. "Tell me how it is you didn't die at Les Diablerets. How did you survive? I saw you fall. I arranged it; it should have happened. Instead, Zeller told me you were alive. I tell you no man could have survived that plunge to an icy tomb. Zeller could have fooled me. He described you to the letter. Now, as one expert to another, tell me how you survived?''

"My good man, just who are you? What is it you are saying? Chanda, are you daft? Has the desert finally begun to play tricks on you?'' Darius raised himself to his full height and looked down at the sickening countenance of the yellow-skinned assassin before him.

"Anton! It's Eugen! But . . . but you are *not* Anton!'' he screeched, comparing their height. "Who are you?''

"Dear Chanda, you are such a bore. Who else would I be but Jonathan Marl? You've known me for how many years and you still play such childish games with me?''

Anthony Harding, a.k.a. Chanda, Ghost-Dancer, Anton Schuller, and every other imposter he'd played in his life, waffled outright. "You are not Anton! Anton is dead. He's been dead all the time. Zeller tricked me! Yes, yes, he tricked me and I played into his hands. Even in death he has bested me!'' He swore a string of German curses. His eyes grew maniacal, bulging in their sockets.

In a sudden blur of activity, bodies went flying. The dynamic muscularity of Joseph Carlini burst into the room and came at Harding, a Magnum in hand, the trigger depressing repeatedly. One bullet struck Harding's shoulder, another his hip, still another penetrated the fleshy part of his leg. The recoil sent him spinning.

"No!'' Darius shouted. "No! Not yet! I don't want him dead until he knows the avenging body behind his downfall. I want him paraded before the world, disgraced, robbed of power, jailed without a shred of clout, stripped of his manipulatory powers.''

Darius removed the wig, glasses, the outer jacket belonging to Jonathan Marl.

"You!'' Harding hissed, staring at the metamorphosis. "Moufflon!'' Impaled against the wall, cowering, riddled by a fusillade of bullets that should have killed him, he sank to the floor, eyes filled with shock and disbelief.

Darius moved over to Carlini, removed his rigid grip on the Magnum. "You always were a lousy shot, Pluto, old friend.''

Carlini's eyes sharply darted to Darius's, questioning. "Y-You knew?" He cleared his throat, dabbed at the welling tears. "You knew from the first?"

"Almost at once. In reality your boots gave you away. But only after I studied your comportment and saw the resemblance between you and Krishnam, old friend."

"You won't tell him, Djebel. Promise you won't tell him. He thinks I'm dead. It must remain so until we unscramble the riddle of Z-10 and Z-5. The Manchurian communist guerrillas want Z-12 Andromeda. Harding was about to hand it to them on a silver platter."

Commander Robbins's voice filtered in over the VCR:

"The objective of each superpower is to develop field-dependable, portable lasers, powerful enough to disable the optic lenses of an opponent's gun sights, range finders, viewing ports, and lasers. At the middle right part of the screen, you'll find an overlay of a gun sight. . . ."

"Get Harding to the infirmary. Post a guard around him, chain him to the bed, anything, but remove the bullets and get him on the mend. Meanwhile, Pluto old friend, get your most skillful interrogators on him, use drugs, anything necessary to break the code. We must know how the communists intend to take over Z-12."

"Djebel—"

"Darius. Call me Darius. The war ended forty years ago."

"For you perhaps; it never ended for me. I know half the magic formula. I picked it up on the transmission from the Russians to Gregorevich. There's no cipher invented that Pluto couldn't break."

"And?"

" '*A lame man treads on the tail of the tiger.*' The corresponding code: '*As above, so below; as below, so above.*' "

Darius repeated the phrase.

A gunshot, then another, exploded nearby. "Get Harding to the infirmary, Pluto. Give me your gun. I'll need another clip or two." He grabbed the gun clips and ran out of the room along the dim corridor. He pulled up short, just before the entrance to the next building; two men were grappling, fighting over a gun.

A bleeding, dazed Brad Lincoln was locked in a lethal stranglehold with Jim Greer. Lincoln fought, scratched, used every tiger hold he knew, but Greer, holding the advantage, was slowly siphoning out Brad's life.

Darius sprang forward into the melee and forcibly grabbed Greer, pulling the two men apart. He lurched over a fallen chair as his hands gripped Greer's gun, twisted it upward, away from Lincoln's temple.

It fired. Darius lunged forward, crashing his body into Greer's, shoving him hard against the wall. Greer's neck arched backward as a bullet tore through the side of his throat. Blood spurted from Greer's neck onto Darius's hand. Greer turned, furious, moving in blind obedience to something sinister commanding his brain. He fired at Lincoln, missed as Brad scurried for cover.

Kusububu Katanga, snarling, moving in split-second timing, had fired his Magnum with a silencer attached. He fell to a crouch, his bestial eyes bloodshot, bulging.

"No!" Darius yelled. "No, Katanga! Stop!" Darius leaped over the bodies and chopped the Nigerian's wrist, breaking his viselike hold on the deadly Magnum. Too late! Brad Lincoln, struck in the chest, had flown backward from the bullet's close-range impact, the air expelled from his lungs, fighting for breath. Jim Greer, holding the gaping wound at his throat, flung himself against the opposite wall, his chest and shoulders tunneling rivers of blood.

Katanga, snorting like a vicious predatory beast, lunged at Darius, wielding a knife. Darius backed away from the knife thrust, circled behind the black man, secured a foothold, and broke the knife from his grasp. Bullet fire rang out once . . . twice . . . three times in rapid order. Jim Greer shot savagely at the black man. He shot again. Click . . . click . . . click. The bullet chamber of the Magnum was empty! In a savage thrust accompanied by an animal grunt, Greer struck at Katanga with his gun. Still the bull moose failed to stop. He went after Greer like a charging warthog ready for the kill.

Darius froze. A heavy hand clamped on his shoulder and pulled him back from the fray. "Nothing will stop him, Darius," Matteus said. Darius shrugged it off, eyes blazing. "Something will stop him; it must." In a sudden movement he tore off the death's-head amulet, moved in swiftly, and drew it across Katanga's face.

"No!" cried Matteus. "Not him! The other."

Too late. It took but seconds before the black man fell limp, his ebony, psychotic eyes rolling upward into his head. Blood boiling inside him from the poison gurgled out from between his lips.

Moving out from his cover position where he awaited the outcome of the shootout, Alexander York fell forward, the victim of several wild shots. He was signaling to Darius, to Matteus.

Matteus moved in swiftly, leaned over as the man's lips moved. By the time Darius reached him, York was dead. The Moor spoke quietly to Darius for several moments before chaos and bedlam erupted at all sides of them. Everything turned to pandemonium as orderlies and soldiers rushed through the corridors.

Darius paled, sickened by the unholy slaughter. Sun peering through the corrugated window slats mottled the walls with alternating light and shadow, lending an eerie dimension to the room.

Behind them, Anthony Harding was being wheeled on a gurney along the corridor toward the infirmary. A medic rushed forward, binding Greer's throat.

"No!" Gabriel Gadi screamed, running forward from behind Matteus where together they had witnessed the death of Katanga. Brad Lincoln lay hovering between life and death. Greer remained frozen against the wall as the medic worked on him, injecting him with morphine.

"Harding is mine, Darius!" Gadi shouted. "He betrayed my father! Israel! The entire Middle East! He's mine. He must be killed. His tentacles are too far-reaching!"

"No!" Darius cried, his voice like barbed wire cutting through the Israeli's fervor. "He has more than one crime to answer for before an international court of justice."

"Kill Harding! The beast snorts fire and shits lightning bolts, not bouquets of peace. Kill the bastard! Kill him, Gadi!" Greer snarled hoarsely, holding the binding at his throat firmly with his hands.

Gadi's gun went wild as Pluto ran the gurney through the corridor. Matteus moved in and broke the Israeli's hold on the gun. "Moufflon says no! Listen to him!"

"The butcher will never snort, *'Pax vobiscum!'*" Youseff said, moving forward into the melee.

"Christ!" Jim Greer shouted feebly. "Can't you see the truth? No court in the land will let Harding stand trial. Omicron owns them all!" He moved reluctantly, prodded by the medic, toward the infirmary.

"Truth?" Youseff shouted angrily. "Truth? What truth, Greer? Tell me where among the lies in which our lives are steeped daily does the truth lie?"

"Get Lincoln to the infirmary!" Darius shouted, leaning over him, listening for his heartbeat. "He's still alive! We must save him."

A crowd of curious people from the space-colony settlement began to rush to the scene, drawn by the gunshots, screams, and unusual activity. Dr. Marl hobbled in closer to Krishnam and Dalei Dei as medics prepared a litter to transport Lincoln to the infirmary. Their faces betrayed bewilderment, inner panic, and finally resignation.

"Greer," shouted Darius. "Get that throat cared for. We'll talk later. Get the dead man into the morgue," he commanded the outpost orderlies. "Matteus, instruct the task force to pack up and prepare for departure at 1900 hours. I'll address them at 1800 hours in the orientation room."

"Get yourself into the infirmary and get those injuries tended to," Marl instructed Darius.

"What the devil is wrong with you, Darius?" Youseff attacked him unmercifully. "Why didn't you let Gadi tear Harding apart? If I hadn't learned to become civilized these past many years, I'd avenge Zahara. He must answer to me for Lomay St. Germaine. He stole her from me, smuggled her out of Corsica, and led her into German Abwehr hands. Then the Russians—"

Darius observed the infirmary medic patch up the knife slices about his wrists and arms. "This Harding business isn't finished," he said confidentially to the Prince once the medic moved out of hearing distance. "Harding's crimes are immense, but his death will not serve us or the world. There is still the matter of knowing how far-reaching the Zeller-Harding tentacles are. The infamous criminal network must be unveiled. Harding's falsity has been exquisitely calibrated, and we still must learn why Harding killed Zeller. I have to wonder who was running whom in Zeller's last few years. Was Zeller running Harding or was Harding running Zeller and for what sinister purposes?''

Youseff's eyes lit up in speculation. ''Always a new hitch to overcome, *oui?*''

''Jonathan, we must talk,'' Darius said as he entered Marl's office. He found Marl alone, studying the infirmary activity on a closed-circuit television screen. He took the chair opposite Marl, accepted the proffered brandy. ''You told me about your early life, the seduction done on your brother, Eugen, to kill you and take your place under an alias. But you neglected to tell me enough. There are holes in your story that fail to compute logically.''

''Yes, I know.''

''You know?''

''To divulge the entire story would wreck my career here at Z-12, cause the entire project to go up in smoke. If the slightest iota of truth escapes, it would be blown up out of proportion.''

''Your secret remains a secret with me, providing I can patch together a proper conspiracy, one that doesn't reek of half-truths and misinformation.''

''The name you know us by is Schuller. Anton and Eugen Schuller. It was my mother's name. We were born out of wedlock. Our father was—'' Jonathan hesitated. He poured more brandy, sipped it, swallowing with difficulty. ''It's very difficult to speak of it,'' he said, turning off all the electronic devices. He flipped on a switch. A flashing red light came on. ''It's safe now. We can talk.

''Some called him a genius. Others called him a beast. History will become the best judge, if the propagandists will permit it.''

Marl told Darius the truth, that Adolf Hitler was his father. The name evoked a hundred images of the Nazi Party leader. Marl was right. Of the hundred images, which reflected the real man? Psychiatrists since the war had found him an enigma.

''My uncle, Heinrich Schuller, was murdered by Zeller, his worldly goods and heritage plundered by the banker in his early days. So Eugen and I determined at an early age we'd find a way of settling the score with Zeller. We lived for vengeance. Our father helped educate us. He sent me to England to live and study among friends. Eugen chose to stay in Germany and become a double agent. I am not certain when or why I suddenly became a liability in both my father's mind and Eugen's. Perhaps I had become too British. Perhaps my pacific ways and deep interest in science necessitated my death. You know the rest. I was approached to get into the diplomatic service, change identities, and travel to America to infiltrate the highest posts in government and spread the Zeller gospel. I refused. The man, in certain respects, was a genius for funneling money to the right people. He bought his way to the top, gaining absolute control. In any event I refused, and by my refusal signed my death warrant."

"You've told me enough," Darius said. "I shall be discreet. You have my word, Jonathan, that the truth ends here."

"Be careful that the truth doesn't end your life."

"That's a cryptic statement."

"It's not a threat. But others who may know the truth might begin to eliminate all those who do know it."

On his way to his quarters, Darius passed the infirmary. Jim Greer was hoarsely arguing his case with Krishnam and Pluto. "No matter what you do to Harding, you'll never get him to talk. You should kill him. Killing is too good for the bastard."

Darius moved into the fray. "Sophisticated drugs can perform miracles, Greer. I think you're out of order in this case. You're under my command here at Z-12. I suggest you prepare for departure along with the rest of the task force," he said, terminating the chat.

Valerie and Uri Mikhail rushed into the infirmary. "We came as soon as we heard the commotion," Valerie exclaimed excitedly.

"What happened? Are you safe?" Uri asked, concerned at the sight of Greer's injury, his sullen, blustery exit from the infirmary. "What we heard," Uri said firmly, "are rumors. Were several men killed? Was Secretary of State Harding here? Is he here?"

"Former Secretary of State," interjected Valerie tightly.

Commander Robbins's voice and face in a tight close-up on the video screen begged for attention:

"I ask you to keep your eyes above the field. See them flying overhead? A deadly flock of remotely piloted vehicles called RPV's are known as Aquilas—eagles. From miles behind the lines, pilots man the controls of consoles to guide the smaller, propeller-driven drones through maneuvers designed to disorient and incapacitate an on-board pilot. . . .''

Darius's attention caught and held on the screen. He blinked at the images forming in his mind, then moved away from the others. He pulled Pluto to one side and spoke in hushed tones out of the others' range of hearing. "What in God's name is happening? I just saw General Lincoln on the video screen with Commander Robbins."

"The lecture ended over an hour ago. You are observing a video cassette. You've heard of video cassettes, Djebel," he said wryly.

"Back there at the altercation between Greer and Brad Lincoln, it was the Commander I saw. I was certain it was Commander Robbins who remained in the shadows, but with the ferocity of the altercation I couldn't be certain."

"Too much was happening too fast. I failed to see him."

"If you should learn Robbins's whereabouts in these moments, I'd appreciate knowing, old friend."

The old friend arched his brows prodigiously. "Djebel—"

"Darius."

"Very well, Darius. It's hard to break a forty-year-old habit. I recall in Corsica the closeness between Brad Lincoln and Jim Greer. What do you suppose prompted the altercation between them?"

"That, old friend, poses complications and implications I dare not contemplate at this moment. I had no recourse but to stop it. If one dies, how will I ever learn the truth?"

"I shall order the guard around Lincoln doubled. He is responding to treatment. Tread carefully, Djebel old friend. Remember all your Corsican tricks and keep them at hand every moment. It is a most confusing situation."

Pluto was gone before Darius could question him further.

Darius made his way along the metal ramp suspended over the lower walkways that adjoined the barracks building past the infirmary. Across the compound he caught sight of the hangars. He thought about Marl's conversation, his words with Pluto. What was it Pluto had said? *It's a most confusing situation?* He didn't know the half of it.

Darius swung off the walkway and, hugging the building against the endless tunneling winds, peered around as he made his way toward the secured Scorpion. He hadn't stopped to count how many people were gunning for Harding. Not that it surprised him.

He was aware of the pronounced hostilities, implied threats, erratic behavior, and flagrant loathing emanating from each man with a score to settle; their screams of protest, desperation, anger, and violent reactions to the man had given Darius pause to ponder the situation in depth.

Methinks they all protested too vehemently.

And that rancor and lethal hostility between Brad Lincoln and Jim Greer? What had set off the combat between them? Matteus had shouted something concerning Katanga. What? So much had happened without warning, it was difficult to grasp the entire scenario. None of it made sense, especially the Lincoln-Greer animosity, unless . . . *Which of them has something vile to hide? Which was suddenly forced into burning his bridges?*

The death of Anthony Harding would let a number of men breathe more freely, wouldn't it?

Oh, Christ! What a conundrum!

Sometimes it paid to wait and do nothing. Let nature take its course. Darius stopped midway to the hangar, retraced his steps to his quarters.

Inside he opened his briefcase, removed the dossier on Commander Robbins. He read it several times. Damnation! The thing reeked of misinformation. It was a manufactured dossier. It was too pat. Why hadn't he caught it at the outset? *You had no reason to question him then.* He's a NASA scientist. What he needed to do was board the Scorpion and put the Grim Reaper to work.

He took his briefcase with him, glanced at his watch, and quickened his pace. He slipped into a jacket, brooding thoughts assaulting him.

You can't save the world, Darius. Let it alone. Let the key men at Z-12 do it their way. Bring back to civilization what you got here at Z-12. Let the world dig its own grave. If they haven't learned lessons from the Middle East fiasco, they never will. You can't be responsible for the entire world. You brought a task force here. Return them, let them tell the world what they observed, the possibilities of new horizons to conquer. . . .

Oh Christ! What's the purpose in it?

* * *

"We must talk, Darius," Pluto said, entering his quarters. "If Harding is taken before an international court of justice, our work here at Z-12 will be gravely discredited. The combined efforts of gifted scientists, technologists, incredibly knowledgeable men and women dealing with aerospace and computer technology who have made miraculous strides here at Z-12 may be forced to abandon their work."

"How do you figure that? How would Harding's standing before a court of justice influence the world to stop work on so valuable a project?"

"By twisting the truth. I've seen him work. I've heard his rhetoric. He is a case-hardened counterintelligence officer who knows all the angles."

Darius sighed. "If mankind united as a whole, devoid of petty jealousies, hatreds, and prejudices created by ambitious politicians—"

"Clever politicians like Anthony Harding and his mentor, Zeller, make it impossible. Their network of duplicitous, parroting ferrets—actually a vast army of men and women spreading vicious low-level conspiracies—are never ending."

"They could survive if they shook themselves loose of the tentacles spread by the deadly men of finance," Darius said somberly.

"It is difficult to estimate the damage done to the people by the Zeller-Harding cartel and their army of mesmerized sheep. They grind out massive doses of propaganda, divide and weaken the people by a welter of brainwashing. They intimidate by creating climates of hatred, distrust, exigency, and enmity. Provide Harding with a platform and he'll convince the working classes they are unbearably oppressed, incite them to envy and lust, divide labor from management, and plow fertile ground in preparation for wars, exploitation, despotism, and a pacific slavery under a benign, seemingly innocent elite."

"You've just recited a four-decade-old odyssey."

"Precisely. Worse, Harding will convince the world to believe in his innocence. Public opinion will bow in his favor. He'll be acquitted."

"How can you make the enemy believe false information is true?" Darius mused. "You put it in the mouths of false defectors you've turned to work for you. A simple disinformation operation begins with the propagandists, the communication centers—''

''Omicron has already mounted a complex diversion operation to protect their clandestine activities. Darius, you cannot, you must not, allow Harding to face a court of justice when there is no justice. Have you ever wondered why Justice is blindfolded? Because under that blindfold you'll find Justice has no eyes—she is blind.''

''Nevertheless, if I didn't bring him back, we'd lose an inside track on curtailing the power and forces Harding has garnered unto himself. We must know how far those tentacles reach. China, perhaps?''

Pluto said nothing. He trailed out the door after Darius, watching as he headed across the compound toward the hangars.

Darius spent an hour inside the Scorpion. The Grim Reaper had provided him with a fund of information. Finished, Darius digested the readouts, turned off the controls. Suddenly there was a loud crash. The hangar doors slid open, alarms went off, the sound of running feet approached, and into the hangar poured a squadron of armed soldiers escorting the bewildered, questioning task force to the helicopter. Amorphous figures huddled against the onslaught of a chilling wind.

What next? What in damnation? An armed, hostile squadron herding his people toward the helicopter? Then he saw Pluto speeding ahead in a jeep. It stopped suddenly, braking swiftly, the tires screeching as they burned rubber.

''Darius! Darius!'' Pluto called as Darius emerged from the cockpit. ''We must talk.''

''What is it? What's happened?''

''Commander Robbins has just declared Z-12 off limits to all visiting personnel. While you were here, he ordered your task force, at gunpoint, to prepare for departure. I brought your things. Right now your fuel tanks are being filled.''

Darius peered out at the hive of activity. ''Rather sudden, isn't it, Pluto?''

''Call me Morosconi. The war's over.''

''Very well, Morosconi. Please explain the sudden hostilities.''

''Harding and Greer have disappeared.''

"*What?* Impossible! Harding needed medical attention!"

"He got it, posthaste. Recall the marvels of miracle drugs."

"And we learned nothing from him. Initiate a search."

"Darius, Z-12 is under strict security wraps. Your work here has been terminated. For your sake, for that of the task force, follow orders—for once in your life. You've all become persona non grata. Go. Leave Z-12! The faster the better for all concerned. Leave Harding and Greer to their own fates."

"I can't do that. I must take them back to Paris."

"Greer was Harding's man."

"I know."

"You know? And you've done nothing?"

"For nearly three decades, I've known he had infiltrated my domain. Later when he left Jade, he hibernated in Switzerland. Berna, one of the most trusted members of my group, filled me in on all his dealings and of course my men in the field. I gave him rein to see where it led."

"Then go. Leave now while you can. Do not meddle in business that concerns you less than others."

"I can't leave Harding," Darius insisted. "There is much I don't know."

"Whatever you wish to know, Darius," said Victor Zeller, approaching the Scorpion's hatch door, "I will provide. May I come aboard?" he said quietly. "I am very tired and filled with sorrow over Berna's fate. Had I known—" Tears welled in his eyes. Victor had only recently learned that he'd been responsible for the death of his own daughter, born to Sophia so many years ago without his knowledge.

Darius stepped to one side. "Come aboard. Take the same seat, Victor, as the one you were in on our approach to Z-12."

"You have two empty seats. Take Dalei Dei—your brother—with you. Krishnam will remain behind with me for a week. We shall rendezvous in Paris in a week, my friend," Pluto said. "*Bonne chance.*"

"I have no choice?"

"None."

Commander Robbins, seated in a jeep, pulled to the head of the squadron; he issued sharp orders. The soldiers broke rank, stood abreast, guns at the ready. Through a raucous bullhorn, he commanded the task force.

"Climb aboard the chopper one at a time. It's been our pleasure to host you. Now the party's over. Go. Leave Z-12 with our prayers.''

He gave instructions to his driver, and the jeep sped out of the hangar at breakneck speed. The glum, uneasy task force began to board and take their respective seats.

''I regret it must end on so low a note, Morosconi. Since I have no choice but to obey the Commander's dictates, give my regards to Dr. Marl. Commend him on the job well done at Z-12. Shall we say the George V in Paris in a week?''

''The George V it is.'' Pluto saluted Darius.

Fully dressed in his protective fatigues, Darius swung to the opposite side of the Scorpion, opened the cockpit door, and sat behind the controls, buckled in properly. The fuel trucks sped off. Darius turned on the motor, taxied out the hangar, and engaged the rotors. Revving up at one end of the open field was an AH-64 Apache attack-and-escort helicopter. As the Scorpion lifted off, the Apache did likewise. Every dip, every banking motion the Scorpion engaged in, the Apache imitated. They were airborne hours before Darius's planned departure. It was all so premature. Why?

The sun was setting. Everything glowed with icy incandescence. Darius gazed at the west; the sky was a dark, luminous silver. Along its higher edges ran the flaming fires of sunset. The mountains and desert for as far as he could see to the east, north, and south seemed formed in petrified flame. A gigantic tangerine moon, anxious to make its debut, literally seemed to shove the sun off the horizon. And through the fiery landscape, Pluto's words crashed through his mind like live thunderbolts.

Leave now. Do not meddle in business that concerns you less than others!

The leaping conflagration of the fireballing moon and sun caused his senses to tingle. He saw the scene below him vividly, in clear perspective, and banking at once, circled overhead and came in lower.

''Darius,'' Youseff's filtered voice warned through the earphones. ''What are you doing? An Apache is on our tail. Do you want us blown out of the sky?''

Darius turned off the intercom. Pondering the scene below him, his thoughts rode herd with ferocity. He turned on the video cameras, all the photographic equipment. He circled again, came in lower . . . lower. . . . *Come on, cameras; do your work. Don't fail me!*

"Scorpion . . . can you read? This is Apache Warrior. You're off limits! . . . Answer, Scorpion, dammit! What the hell's wrong with your radio? I'm firing a warning shot! Get your tail out of here!"

Darius saw the nose-turret lasers aim. The Apache fell back, behind him. A barrage of gunfire spurted from its guns, dusting the Scorpion's tail. Darius switched on radio contact. "Dammit, Apache Warrior! You're supposed to escort us out of here, not dig our graves. What in damnation's wrong?"

"Apache Warrior to Scorpion. Get your tail out of Z-12 perimeters. I *read* you, but apparently you don't read *me,* so I'll fire-dust your tail until you get the message. Get the hell going and on your way out! Over and out." Another barrage of gunfire at either side of the Scorpion shook it savagely. Darius engaged his antitorquing devices, steadied the aircraft. By then he'd gotten what he was after. Soaring higher, Darius lowered the rotors, leveled off and flew eastward toward the darkening horizon.

The Apache tilted, circled beneath the Scorpion, and fired a round of farewell shells as it soared back to home base.

Darius engaged the video cams, and with the Grim Reaper's help replayed the scene. *Oh Christ!* What had he gotten? He engaged the radar and took a moment to view the screen. He heard the loud gasps of the task force coming through the earphones. What he saw was horrendous. What they witnessed was stupefying!

Two wooden crosses arose from mounts on a hill. Two men had been crucified. Their arms spread-eagled and nailed to the wooden beams, their feet crossed and pounded through with one large iron nail. Around the crosses, flames licked up angrily at the men.

"Harding!" Valerie Lansing gasped aloud.

"Greer!" Brad Lincoln, sedated, came awake in stupefaction.

The flames rode up higher on the naked men, licking at their bodies. The powerful roar of the Scorpion's engines drowned out any possible sounds the pipe microphone parabolics might have picked up. The endless wind whirled the fire into frenzied whips lashing out at the tortured men on the crosses. Their faces twisted in agony; their silent screams filled the Scorpion's cabin.

Darius disengaged the video; the screen went dark. The task force's features turned grim, immutable, struck by the horror of the vision.

Amadeo Zeller was dead.

Anthony Harding too.

The third man, Jim Greer, the traitor, the agent skilled in the double and triple cross, the man who'd done Harding's mule work, the very man who'd killed the infamous Grunelda in her surveillance whorehouse at Café Lili Marlene, had received his just desserts by the dead Grunelda's brother, Commander George Robbins.

Darius had learned plenty from the Grim Reaper when he re-evaluated Commander Robbins's dossier and learned his true origins in life. Grunelda had secreted her only brother out of Germany prior to World War II, and he was adopted and raised by an American family, and after college was hired by NASA. Z-12 Andromeda came later and with it fulfillment of his plan to kill Greer once he learned who had murdered his sister.

The Scorpion soared higher toward its rendezvous with the Lodestar. Imprinted upon Darius's mind were the faces of the men standing at the base of the crosses as they stared at the conflagration, the arabesques of dancing flames reaching higher and higher, devouring each man.

Commander Robbins, Jonathan Marl, Krishnam, and his old friend Pluto had been avenged.

"How is General Lincoln's condition?" Darius asked Youseff.

"Falling. They did everything possible for him at Andromeda, but if we reach Paris and he's alive, it will be another miracle."

"We must try, Youseff. Pray to your God Allah that he is saved. We need his expertise in the days to come."

"He turned over his briefcase to me and revealed some vital information. We'll discuss all this when we reach our destination. Meanwhile, I shall pray to all gods to be merciful and save him."

All gods were not merciful. General Brad Lincoln, subjected to more trauma and injuries than any ten men in a lifetime, a true servant of his country, never saw Paris again.

In his final moments, exhausted by the pain of the numerous gunshot wounds, Brad Lincoln leaned against Youseff's body in the narrow confines of the Scorpion. Scenes from the past flashed before him. "Get Greer," he whispered with effort. "Greer shot me. Greer . . . I'll see you in hell!" He heaved forward, was held in place by the restricting seat belts.

"Too late," said Youseff. "Too late."

Epilogue

Corsica at Christmastime was at its most beautiful. The view from Moufflon's mountaintop aerie was devastingly stunning, its panorama of cerulean seashores and windswept landscapes breathtaking.

Darius Bonifacio, playing host to the welcome group of travelers who had arrived over the past few days, was enjoying the rest, relaxation, and getting-acquainted period. Victor Zeller and Michael Bertelli II had been with him a week. Valerie Lansing had arrived two days ago and now stood near the helipad where Prince Ben-Kassir and Uri Mikhail Gregorevich were momentarily expected.

Victor Zeller stood in Darius's den before the fireplace, studying the magnificent portrait of Sophia Bonifacio. For days he had lingered around the portrait, recalling the bittersweet memories and the unusual bits and pieces of her mysterious disappearance and subsequent death at the abbey in north Italy. Worse, the burden of knowing he personally had ordered the death of his own daughter, Berna, tore at him, ate at the core of his being. How could he have known of the blood ties of the courier who had arrived at the Geneva bank to collect payment on the Zeller debt to Moufflon? On a nearby wall, Berna's handsome features stared down at him from an oil painting. Oddly enough the artist had captured something of Victor's own brooding looks in Berna's eyes.

Victor couldn't bear to look at her bewitching, mischievous smile without feeling pangs of guilt and remorse.

He had lost considerable weight after the removal of the diabolical cranial implant. His thin hands clenched the back of a chair before the fireplace as he became consumed with the first real hatred in his life—for his father, Amadeo Zeller. The havoc wreaked upon his life by this man stirred fires of hatred in him, never felt so strongly as in this moment. The knowledge that he was dead failed to ameliorate his loathing. He understood now why some men would kill, feeling he would have killed his father in this moment if he were still alive.

"The past is gone forever," Darius said, standing in the archway, observing Victor's internal agony. "You must learn to part with it." He moved to the serving cart to pour coffee.

"It's difficult when it becomes too much a part of you. These past several days while I've been laying before you the vast Zeller network, memories have sparked brooding fires, and some have ignited." Victor turned to him, accepted the hot coffee, and sat down in a high-backed wing chair opposite Darius. "Have I left out anything. Since the cranial implant was removed, I may have overlooked mentioning some of the preprogrammed material contained on the microchip implantation."

"You've given me enough. I can fill in the loopholes with my own material." Darius sipped his coffee and stared out the glass doors beyond the snow-covered terrace at the *moufflons* grazing nearby.

"When we succeed in removing my father's former sentinels from the estate in Zürich, namely Mosha Bauer and the brothers Kosevo, we shall fly to the château together. I promise you shall marvel at the complex embroidery of the disinformation theory used by the Zeller network."

"There are all types of deceptions, Victor. The most fascinating lie in distorting the interpretation or meaning of the pattern of data, rather than the observable data itself. It is mind bending."

"How did Uri Mikhail manage to defect without international fanfare?" Victor asked as he walked to the liquor cabinet, opened a bottle of brandy, and filled a tumbler. "I need this more than coffee," he said with an apologetic air.

Darius waved the words aside. "How did Uri exit his former role gracefully without making headlines?" He smiled enigmatically. "We were discussing forms of deception, disinformation that emanates from the highest levels in government, *oui*. Let us call it secret strategy, the motives of those in command. In Uri's case, I, through a compromised channel of communication in the Moufflon network, leaked information to the KGB. Our conduits performed superbly. Once Uri's mind was made up, they relayed information that Uri Mikhail Gregorevich was accidentally killed at Z-12 Andromeda. Since Z-12 Andromeda is a highly classified covert operation, the Soviets could not leak the news. Besides, it served Andreivich Malenekov's ambitions to become Premier. As for Uri—a little surgery, a nip and tuck here and there and *voilà!* he assumed his rightful heritage as Youseff Ben-Kassir II. The Prince is ecstatic to have claimed his rightful loving heir. Married to Valerie Lansing, my daughter, they have both settled down to domesticity. Uri, in his new role, has accepted a professorship at Harvard—and Valerie? She may or may not practice law. But be aware, Victor, she is intent on demanding retribution for what your father stole from the Valdez Argentine millions."

A smile trailed over Victor's lips, then faded as tense memories of pain and survival welled up inside him. Images of Valerie and the love they'd shared in Paris and Zürich paraded through his mind. He remembered the lengths to which she'd gone to meet him that day in the Paris art gallery, and the intensity of their sexual interludes. A hot erection caused him to squirm, his face flushed. "I am still in love with Valerie. No matter how I try telling myself it's a bit like lusting after my own niece."

Darius remained silent as Victor unburdened his soul. He measured the differences in their temperaments, marveling over the fact that they had the same mother, Contessa Marie Clotilde. God, he wished he'd at least gotten to meet her and Michael Bertelli in his lifetime. His thoughts were cut off as Victor's question captured him.

"Tell me, how will you, one man alone, hope to transcend the frozen attitudes of the world to preach peace? Others have failed."

"Once the Zürich power cartel is eliminated, the frozen attitudes of the world, no longer controlled by them, will thaw. I promise. And Victor, don't change the subject. The de la Varga holdings in Spain must have accrued millions and millions over the past sixty years. Those sums must be restored to their rightful owners, including titles to all lands."

"You drive a hard bargain, but a just one. Consider it done. But those predatory properties my father stole over the years of which no traces exist—what am I to do about them?"

"When the time comes, a sizable donation to the cause of peace might be in order."

Victor rose. He flipped on the remote switch to an enormous television screen. "Do you mind, Darius? The American President is supposed to make a stunning announcement this evening via satellite transmission. He won the election in a landslide victory. Can you believe it? The worse he does, the more the people love him and rally behind him."

Darius agreed. He rose, went to the liquor cabinet, poured two Napoleon brandies. "Shall we drink a toast to our illustrious ancestor?" he said, smiling playfully. "To Bonaparte."

The American President's image filled the screen. He began to speak.

"My fellow Americans, it is with great pleasure and pride that I name my new Secretary of State, Clarisse Zeller Harding.

A loud roar of applause was heard by a coalition of women voters seated in the Rose Garden at the White House.

Clarisse stepped to the podium.

Victor, stunned, looked at Darius, whose face was suffused with rage.

"He's done it, Darius. He's come back from the grave to haunt us. We'll never be done with him—never."